Wife Number Three

Rose Horobin

MAPLE
PUBLISHERS

Wife Number Three

Author: Rose Horobin

Copyright © Rose Horobin (2024)

The right of Rose Horobin to be identified as author of this work has been asserted by the author in accordance with section 77 and 78 of the Copyright, Designs and Patents Act 1988.

First Published in 2024

ISBN 978-1-915996-44-2 (Paperback)
     978-1-915996-45-9 (eBook)

Book layout by:
    White Magic Studios
    www.whitemagicstudios.co.uk

Published by:
    Maple Publishers
    Fairbourne Drive, Atterbury,
    Milton Keynes,
    MK10 9RG, UK
    www.maplepublishers.com

A CIP catalogue record for this title is available from the British Library.

All rights reserved. No part of this book may be reproduced or translated by any form or by any means, electronic or mechanical, including photocopying, recording or by any information storage and retrieval system without written permission from the author.

This novel is entirely a work of fiction. The names, characters, and incidents portrayed in it are the work of the author's imagination. Any resemblance to actual persons, living or dead, events or localities is entirely incidental.

The views expressed in this novel by the fictional characters do not necessarily reflect the views of the author.

CHAPTER ONE

March 2019

Gary concentrated on swiping right on the dating site to add to the pool of potential candidates that he was considering, to find the next woman to take forward his plan, The Plan, that he had embarked upon in his early twenties. The Plan had already delivered some of the dividends he was hoping for and now was time to consolidate and broaden his financial security and property portfolio.

He wasn't one of those guys who swiped right on every woman so that it increased their chances of being matched with someone, anyone with a pulse. The losers. But he did consider each profile carefully, to try to detect the specific requirements he was looking for.

Now, at the age of thirty-five he was ready to locate, form a relationship with, and then marry the lucky lady who would become Wife Number Three. After Number Two he had taken a break, let his hair down, and had a good time with plenty of available lovelies for casual fun, nothing serious. The marriage bit was hard going, due to having to execute the plan which could not be rushed, though at times he had wanted to end things a lot earlier than he had anticipated. The failings, and personality traits of the wives, often made it difficult to endure them over the long term but Gary was nothing, if not tenacious. Still, in both cases, he had endured and he had benefitted from his endurance and reaped the rewards. The time out after Number Two had been needed to re-charge his batteries, hook-up with sexy women and enjoy a taste of the high life. But Gary was careful. He had not come this far to squander the money on expensive holidays, bucket loads of champagne, or gambling, though he had indulged in these pleasures for a short time. No, he needed to build on the solid foundation he had made, by expanding his business enterprises and property holdings.

He had started the search six months ago and had been chatting to, and dating a number of women, all over thirty, as he had no time for younger ones, who would not have the assets he was seeking. Once back on track with The Plan, Gary did not want to lose focus or waste time. Dating younger women was obviously pleasurable but he saved those pleasures for other times.

He was now at a critical stage, trying to get down to two or three likely candidates, before he selected, and committed to, his final choice. Gary knew that women found him attractive, as he was good-looking, tall, physically fit with dark brown hair and brown eyes. The two women he was currently dating were both keen to see him again, and he kept a strict rota, to ensure that he saw each one in turn, and for similar amounts of time, so he could be sure in his evaluation of their suitability.

First in his circle of interest was Elizabeth, 46 years old. Potentially in the lead over the other contender, at the moment. A medium woman. Medium height, mousy brown hair to her shoulders, medium eyesight assisted by varifocals for distance and reading. The first date had been at a National Trust property for a walk around the grounds and a coffee and cake in the excellent café. Gary had dressed casually, for the early spring day, in black jeans, light grey jumper, black jacket and blue/grey striped scarf. They had arranged to meet at the ticket sales area, where she flashed her annual membership card and he paid the daily rate. He was five minutes early and waiting patiently as he spotted the woman, who liked to be called 'Lizzie', as she approached with her Jack Russell terrier, Charlie. With a 'hi, you must be Lizzie' he hugged her gently before greeting Charlie with a generous pat to the head, as the little dog jumped up his legs. The low-level growling did not deter Gary from commenting what a lovely little chap he was.

Walking together on one of the dog-walking routes, on a day with a clear blue sky, and the touch of the heat from the sun, was pleasant, though Charlie would get excitable when seeing other dogs, so Lizzie was propelled in their direction on a number of occasions. For a small dog he seemed to have a lot of strength and determination. As they walked side by side, Gary was more confident to ask more probing questions than if Lizzie were facing him. He was interested in her job as a librarian, at a small branch library, and she enthused about her favourite authors, Bronte, obviously, George Eliot, but she had real taste for crime and horror genres. In her personal life, she lived with, and cared for, her elderly father, and had always lived with her parents. She and her father were still grieving the loss of her mother two years ago. Dad was in poor health, with multiple ailments including heart problems which had resulted in stents being fitted, type two diabetes and was recovering from a broken arm from a recent fall. Sadly, Lizzie was an only child so all the responsibility of caring for her father fell to her. But dad retained all his mental faculties and loved wild life programmes, a frequent supply of books on war, military weapons and strategies, and completing the Daily Telegraph's cryptic crossword.

Sitting in the café after their walk, Lizzie ordered tea, scone, butter and jam and Gary ordered a large Cappuccino, no food. As she sat opposite him at the table, he registered her features close to; pale blue eyes made larger by the varifocals, straight nose, thin lips, a straightforward face. She frequently looked away as his eyes settled on her face and he was sure that she was not used to being alone in the company of a man, as a shy blush touched her cheeks.

In terms of relationships, Lizzie divulged that she had not really had any long term relationships, one in her early twenties with a Museum Curator had fizzled out after nine months. A second relationship in her mid-thirties with an Accountant, she met at a Writers' group, had been promising but her care responsibilities for her frail mother, and ageing father, and his duties in caring for his father, meant that meeting frequently was problematic. They attempted a walking holiday in the Lake District but had been called home early due to her mother's trip on a wonky mat resulting in a broken hip. Lizzie was now venturing out into the world of dating at dad's instruction as he did not want her to waste her life looking after him. In contrast to Lizzie's openness in sharing her life, work, and responsibilities with him, Gary shared very little. On this date, he was the good listener, the attentive companion and the giver of one or two compliments to boost a lonely woman. Nothing creepy. At one stage, he commented on her floral perfume, the smell of fresh flowers, which captured the essence of spring. The beam of a smile that formed on her lips was worth it, it was as if had told her she had the face of Scarlett Johansson and the body of Kim Kardashian.

Back home, with time to evaluate the date, there was a lot going in her favour. She was lonely, a woman caring for an ageing father, with no siblings, and not many friends, from what she had said. Her job as a Librarian paid a reasonable salary of over thirty thousand per annum but she had access to finances on the death of her father. She would be sole heir to his property, a Victorian detached house in Warwick, and wealth he had accumulated from his professional life as a university lecturer with associated savings and pensions. Father had a number of health problems, with heart issues the most pertinent, and Gary guessed, from what she let slip, that dad was stubborn and so would not forego his pleasures of red meats and whisky to improve his chances of a longer life. With any luck dad would not be on Planet Earth for too long.

Looks-wise, she was just his type. Plain, but slim, with an unimpressive figure that had no curve to it for a man to become excited about. On the date, she had come across as shy, almost timid, and it was clear that she was not comfortable in the company of an attractive man. She said that she was surprised that he had wanted to go on a date with her, as she could not possibly be his usual type. Gary explained that he liked to be with quiet, thoughtful, educated women and not the strident, opinionated types that a lot of men went for.

If The Plan were to succeed, he would be in it for the long haul of a few years, and he would have to come to terms with what he would deem to be her short comings.

Number one on the list would be the bloody dog. Gary did not consider himself to be an animal lover. He hated cats and all their stuck-up ways. He could tolerate dogs, but little Charlie had got on his nerves immediately with his jumping up, pulling on the lead in charge of his mistress, his intolerance of other dogs, and his major interest in food as he tried to scamper onto the table at the café for any tasty morsel. If any male was going to be in charge of Lizzie, it would be Gary, so Charlie would have to go.

Number two was the father. Gary acknowledged that the father's health problems could deliver him to the Pearly Gates any time soon but things may not prove to be that straightforward. There's an expression that 'a creaking gate hangs the longest' so daddy could stumble on for another twenty years with no inheritance coming to his dear daughter. Also, the father was an intelligent man, but would he be the kind of brainbox who floats on lofty clouds unconcerned with the troubles of those around him or was he an astute individual who would quickly recognise Gary's intentions to his daughter?

Number three was that she was timid. He had endured stupid with Wife Number One. He had put up with neediness and weakness with Wife Number Two. Would timid prove too boring and would he tire of her easily and then The Plan would have to be abandoned?

Would his next date with the second contender replace Lizzie as the favourite?

CHAPTER TWO

March 2019

Gary decided that watching a rugby union game on a damp Saturday in March was not his idea of fun. His date, Angela, had suggested it as a different way of getting acquainted rather than the usual of drinks in a pub or coffee in a café. Gary was surprised at this choice of venue as having met Angela on a previous date she did not strike him as being the kind of woman who would take any interest in team sports. If he had to guess Angela's favourite pastimes, he would opt for eating cakes, drinking soft drinks and watching films. Anything unrelated to sports, exercise and exertion. Their first date had been at a town centre coffee house where she indulged in two classic hot chocolate drinks and a chocolate muffin, total kcal approximately 900. Gary's one caffe latte was 180 kcal. As Angela pointed out, in a jovial way, she was quite capable of eating her own body weight in chocolate, her favourite guilty pleasure. She added that as she didn't drink alcohol, smoke, or take drugs that she was allowed one little vice, chocolate, or honestly, food in general. And it showed, as she could be classed as overweight, bordering obese, but this didn't deter her from being a funny, confident person.

They both sat, gloved fingers clutching their disposable coffee cups, this time filled with low calorie, scalding hot, reasonably flavoured coffees, while they waited for the game to commence. Angela's interest in the game was not sport-related but family-related as she had come to watch her stepson, Aiden, play for his local town. She had been with Aiden's father for ten years so had known the boy from primary school up to the present, where he was a second-year engineering student at Coventry University.

Angela informed Gary that she was 46 years old, and twice divorced, and was getting used to being upgraded by the current husband for a younger model every ten years. She was definitely now an old banger (her words) with plenty of miles on the clock. This tendency of hers to make jokes about old cars had started when she discovered that Gary owned two used car dealerships. She added that it was lucky that Gary knew a thing or two about old wrecks. The jokes were now wearing thin, and as Gary had pointed out, his cars were quality vehicles, so no old bangers allowed.

Gary had enjoyed some team sports at school but he now preferred to keep his fitness levels up by running and attending a local gym with emphasis on cardio exercises, including the treadmill, bikes and rowing machines. When Gary had pressed Angela on her knowledge of rugby union she was a bit thin on the details. She knew that there were fifteen players to a team, Aiden was a 'winger' and she understood what a try, a conversion, and a scrum were. She had only watched a game on a few occasions when she could be guaranteed that Aiden's father, Gerry, and his new girlfriend, the floozy, would not be in attendance. Gary surmised from this that the new girlfriend was younger, prettier and slimmer than step mum, Ang.

Having survived two divorces, Angela had come out of them, financially secure. She and Gerry had sold their detached 1920's property in south Warwickshire for a tidy sum each and she was able to purchase a new build, semi-detached property in Rugby, near to her place of work as a Practice Manager, for a GP surgery. She lived alone, and sadly, according to Angela she had not been blessed with children from either union. The first husband had a low sperm count and the second had a high sperm count but liked to share it around with a number of willing women, Angela informed Gary, who felt slightly nauseous at learning this information.

As they watched the match, Angela generally only got excited when Aiden, a winger, six feet tall, and fourteen stone of solid human, was in charge of the ball and scored three tries to add to the final score of 27 to 26, to Aiden's team. Angela advised Gary that Aiden sometimes felt like her own child and her only real sadness at the end of her marriage to Gerry was that she would see less of the boy. Angela knew that the 'floozy' was unlikely to be a motherly type who baked him cakes, washed his kit and tended to his cuts and bruises from the games.

Gary assessed that in her personal life, having been cut adrift from the philandering Gerry, she had no immediate family in the Midlands, as her mother, father and younger brother, all lived on the south coast of Devon. Her full-time job at a GP's surgery kept her busy but she had a small circle of close friends she had made from previous jobs, and her current role. Her hobbies included baking and she had a yearning to go on the 'Great British Bake Off'. She was a member of a local amdram group but was only fully committed when they were putting on musicals and upbeat dramas. She gave special mention to her role as nun in the 'Sound of Music' and Rosie in 'Mamma Mia'.

Their post-match venue was a quiet, cosy pub in south Rugby, where Angela opted for a soda and lime, and Gary for a bottled lager. Angela tried to extract details of his personal life, and dating history, but he was quicker at swerving a question than a rugby winger at accessing the ball. Like Lizzie, Angela had been curious as to why a good-looking man like Gary would be interested in her, a middle-aged, overweight woman, when men in general, always went for younger, slender women. Gary advised her that he found younger women very disappointing. They were either too vain, too self-absorbed, and lacking any knowledge about subjects such as news, politics, science, art and literature or they were too strident in their views and basically knew everything. Both types were totally exhausting. Gary stated that he wanted a witty, confident, sociable woman who had a spark, a vital interest in the world. Plus, he didn't want to spend time with women obsessed with their bodies, picked at food and droned on about calories and exercise. Angela had glowed when he had expounded on the type of woman he was seeking as she did seem to fit his criteria, as she was funny, got on well with people, had travelled extensively and loved her food. When he commented that he did not like a Skinny Minnie, he thought she would explode with joy.

Later, at the post-date evaluation stage, there were some things going in her favour. She was a divorcee with no blood relatives in the Midlands area, as her family lived miles away at the coast. He had searched salaries for Practice Managers and guessed she was on around 40k per annum. She owned her recently acquired semi-detached property, which was mortgage free, and would likely have other savings from years of working.

Looks-wise she was just his type. Fairly pretty in an unkempt sort of way but she was too overweight for his taste, so he would never be overwhelmed by her attractiveness. All the better for keeping emotions out of any sort of relationship. She was also jokey, and sociable, which could be advantageous at the early stages, as he had to have stamina to stick with The Plan, get married, and then work to the usual resolution of ridding himself on any hurdles and extracting the financial assets. Again, as with Lizzie, Gary would have to come to terms with what he viewed as Angela's potential problems.

Firstly, was the stepson, Aiden, who had come over to speak to them at the end of the rugby union match. He had greeted Angela with a big bear hug, which she loved, and was genuinely pleased to see her. He was the same height as Gary but filled the area with his physical presence. Gary feared that his right hand may be broken after being gripped in Aiden's giant paw. Gary strongly felt that Aiden wasn't overly thrilled at meeting him, as if the young man had looked into his soul and seen its blackness. Gary shivered slightly as the man's eyes locked onto his to deliver a warning not to hurt his step mum. He described her as the best stepmum anyone could wish for and he would not tolerate users and fakes who may take advantage of her kind nature. Gary could almost feel the huge hands tightening around his neck. This stepson might be young but he had the presence of an older, wiser man who understood how the world worked.

The second problem was the friends. Angela may not have a family close by, clutching her to its bosom, but the friends she described, seemed to be caring, loyal and constant. It was sometimes easier to ward off the fickle family members than the interfering friends.

Thirdly, was her jokey, sociable nature. As he had admitted, this could be an advantage at the beginning as he would need a sense of humour to spend hours of time with her. He suspected that she could be the type to treat everything in a light-hearted manner and hopefully miss the malign nature of his plan, as he strove to isolate and brow beat her. Gary was an enigma in terms of personality, some people viewed him as reserved and cold, while others discovered the friendly, chatty Gary. Friendly Gary would be present here, at first, but he did not have the stamina for long term jollity as the colder side of his personality generally took over.

Yes, these two women, Lizzie and Angela, were still being strongly considered. But there was a third who had just presented herself. Eva. She was late to the party. He was yet to meet her on a first date but that had now been arranged in two days' time.

CHAPTER THREE

April 2019

This mid-April day had been unusually warm, and so Gary was hoping for a pleasant evening, with no sudden drop in temperature, so that he could meet with his date at an outside table of the pub, located next to the Grand Union Canal. It was a popular venue, and as it was a Friday night, from past experience he knew that all the tables in the water side beer garden would fill up quickly, so he had arrived early and had managed to bag a table adjacent to the canal.

He was eagerly anticipating the arrival of his date, Eva, who was thirty-two years old, and a primary school teacher. He had been entranced by her dating profile and photos, a pretty woman with shoulder-length hair, mid-brown with auburn highlights, and a natural wave. It had gone against all the protocols involving The Plan to choose her but something about her drew him in. He argued that he could adapt The Plan, if necessary, as long as certain established criteria were in place.

As he sat at a table half way along the line of tables, he noted a lone female standing nervously between the two lines of tables and guessed that could be her.

He sent a text. 'Hi. I'm here and I've got a table near to the water's edge.'

He watched the woman as she read the text, pleased that it was in fact her. He'd had a moments worry as another woman had followed her into the garden area, with auburn hair, but smaller and rounder, and Gary crossed his fingers that she wasn't Eva.

'Great. I've just arrived and in the garden,' Eva texted back.

'Walk between the two lines of tables and I'll shout you,' he replied.

His eyes followed her as she moved cautiously on the grass area between the tables, glancing along the line of tables nearest to the canal, and she discounted any table with more than one person. As she reached the half way point of the line of tables, he shouted 'Eva' and smiled as she came to a halt next to his table. He had dressed casually in black jeans, a light grey, crew neck, cotton jumper and navy quilted bomber jacket. He got up from the bench seat and came to greet her with a gentle hug. 'When I saw you down there, I was hoping you were Eva. Great to meet you in person, at last.'

He noted that she was dressed in slim fit blue jeans and a light green blouse with a floral print in golds and blues. She carried a pale blue puffer jacket in anticipation that the temperature would cool as the evening went on. Instantly, he was pleased that he had decided to meet her. She had a lovely face, with dark blue eyes, and, for Gary, she was wearing the right amount of makeup which accentuated her eye colour, and a subtle red lipstick to enhance her lips. She was perfectly dressed for the date, as the blouse suited her colouring, its delicacy hinting at the curve of her breasts, and two front buttons were undone, leading his eyes down to a glimpse of cleavage. Her whole look was natural, fresh, and when he had moved in for the hug, he appreciated the delicate undertones of her floral perfume.

He hovered by the table, as she sat down, and she looked away as she felt the intensity of his gaze on her face. 'If you like, I'll go and get the drinks, while you sit here. What would you like?'

'A half of dry cider would be great. Thanks.'

'Won't be long, I hope.'

As he waited at the bar to get served, he was already thinking that if in the end he favoured Lizzie or Angela to keep The Plan on track, he would have to arrange to see Eva again. Normally, when The Plan had been executed, and he was progressing in his quest to consolidate his relationship, to the goal of marriage to Wife Number Three, there would always be a second woman he could call on to satisfy his needs, when the wife was unexciting. Could that be Eva?

After ten long minutes to purchase half a cider, and a bottled lager, he made his way outside, placed the drinks on the table and sat down with a sigh of relief. 'Phew. This pub is a great location but it's really too popular on a Friday evening. Anyway, cheers.' He clinked his bottle next to her glass.

In some ways it was distracting that she was so attractive, and it surprised him that he was finding it difficult to make conversation, something that confident Gary never struggled with. It was back to his first date, at age fifteen, with his school crush, Maisie, who he took to the local cinema. He had been grateful for the dim lighting and the loud sound track, so he didn't have to speak and could concentrate on trying to fondle her breasts.

Starting the conversation was awkward, so Gary opted for a topic which would get her talking. 'You're a teacher, and therefore, I think you are very brave as I could never teach a class of children. How do you keep them all in line?'

Eva sipped the cider, then put the glass down. 'It's easy when you get used to it. I generally do the junior school ages, and on the whole, they are delightful children.'

'Well, they are lucky to have you as a teacher. I remember some of my female teachers from school and they made Miss Trunchbull seem warm and cuddly. They certainly weren't as pretty as you. If they were, I might have tried harder.'

Eva looked a little shocked by this personal comment and Gary now regretted making it so early in the date. Being over familiar with attractive women could come across as cringy, and he normally controlled his lecherous side, so as not to put them off. 'I've always wondered how you keep them in the classroom and persuade them not to leg it out of the door.'

'We try to make lessons as interesting as possible, so that learning is fun.'

'Lessons were never that interesting when I was at school. Just one long slog of maths, spelling tests and writing stories of what you did in the holiday,' Gary groaned, recalling the sheer tedium of his school days. 'I confess to playing truant at secondary school and my mum and dad would go mad when the school phoned to report my absence.'

Eva laughed nervously. 'You were a bit naughty then. Though we try not to describe children as naughty these days as it can be a label they carry with them all through school.'

Oh yes, the dilemmas faced by modern parents and teachers, Gary thought. 'Call me old-fashioned, but how do you make a child see the difference between good and bad behaviour, if no one is ever naughty.'

'Overall, we encourage positive behaviour and discourage negative labels. If a child does something that is not acceptable, we would explain that they have done something they shouldn't, and give a reason why. It's the difference between that was a naughty thing to do and you are naughty. I think it is a more effective way of guiding children.'

Gary pulled a face, as he was finding it difficult to agree with this approach. It was the same thinking that gave all runners in the egg and spoon race a prize just for taking part, thus undermining the achievement of the winner. He now joked. 'It's a good job that I'm not in charge or I would call bad behaviour out for what it is 'naughty.' He didn't add, if it were up to him, he'd bring back the cane.

Eva nodded, in some agreement with him. 'Yes, it can be hard at times, particularly as a parent, as they can be very frustrating when they are toddlers and throwing a tantrum, as then there is no reasoning with them. Luckily, my son is older now and can be cajoled, or bribed, to behave appropriately.'

He ascertained from his questioning that she was a widow, whose husband had died fourteen months ago and she lived with their son, Alfie, aged nine. She owned a house, and from a snippet she said about insurance money when her husband died; he guessed it was mortgage free. Gary never ceased to be amazed by how women frequently gave details of their personal lives to people they had just met. Details that could immediately leave them vulnerable to those with malign intent who were checking out their wealth or their living arrangements. Eva had freely disclosed that she had financial assets and lived alone with a young child. A welcome sign for those with nefarious motives of robbery or worse. Arrange date number two, discreetly follow her home, and boom.

He discovered she had a close family, including parents, brother, and deceased husband's parents, who all lived nearby and helped out with childcare. There seemed to be a number of friends around as well, who popped in regularly to offer support and help.

As the evening progressed, and turned cooler, they continued to sit outside as there was still enough warmth in the air to keep it the right side of chilly. It was pleasant to sit by the water's edge, as darkness fell, as outside lights illuminated the water, and they could still hear the quack and flap of ducks as they splashed on the canal. Gary had ventured back inside the pub to buy a further drink each and had been insistent that he would not take the cash she offered to cover the price. 'Call me old-fashioned but I'm happy to pay for a few drinks. I hope I don't upset your feminist sensibilities.'

After two and a half hours, they strolled to the car park and he walked her to her car. For a moment, he did think about kissing her, but he sensed she was nervous, so leaned in to give her a brief hug, and advised her to 'drive carefully.' To ensure her safety, he remained nearby as she opened the car door, sat in the car and then closed the door. She started the car engine, put on the car headlights and pulled away, as he walked towards his car.

Back home, relaxing on the sofa, with a de-caffeinated coffee, Gary did his usual post-date evaluation. There was not a lot going in her favour. Firstly, she was not his type in terms of The Plan. Too damn pretty. He liked to keep things clear and she would only blur the lines. He could not get away from the fact that he found her very attractive. A lovely face with deep blue eyes, delicate nose and such a kissable mouth that he had to keep looking away from her or she may have become uncomfortable under his unremitting gaze. He also found it hard to stop his eyes falling to the area where her blouse was open, revealing the hint of rounded breasts. She was also intelligent, and quick-witted, though there had been stilted moments in their conversation, as he kept losing focus whilst admiring her face and body, and at times she seemed a little shy.

Secondly, there was the presence in her life of her nine-year-old son. Gary generally hated kids, and with a kid in tow, it would make any sort of relationship that much harder. He really wasn't known for his fun-loving personality, or his patience, so having to tolerate the constant demands of a young boy could be a major difficulty. If he were to enter her life, then both her and the kid would be subjected to his authority whilst The Plan was executed. On the plus side, there was no divorced dad to step in if Gary's handling of the kid got on the heavy side.

Thirdly, there were the family and friends, a whole gang of them that seemed to be constantly checking on her well-being since the death of her husband. From all accounts, even the neighbours were frequent visitors, or she was at their houses for cups of tea, and cake, and sympathy. It all felt a little Ramsey Street. Oh yes, and to add icing to the flipping cake, the immediate next-door neighbour got special mention, Andy or Pandy, or something, who was a police detective inspector on a Major Crimes Investigation team. Oh joy.

Going in her favour, she was a widow, with property, and probably other assets. But if anything were to happen to her then all this would be inherited by her son, so another obstacle to be overcome.

Yes, in terms of the plan, she was number three on the list, behind both Lizzie and Angela. But choosing Eva as Wife Number Three would make the next few years so much more bearable. He imagined being in bed with her, having sex with her, which would be no hardship given he was becoming aroused thinking of possessing her delectable mouth with his lips, and kneading her perfect breasts with his fingers. There was no twitch of arousal in his groin when he thought about Lizzie and Angela. He yawned slightly, deciding on going to bed. He had only been on one date with Eva but on two dates each with the other two. Tomorrow he would have to make a decision on the best way forward but the one important factor was to stick clearly to The Plan.

CHAPTER FOUR

April 2019

It didn't take long on Saturday lunchtime for Tania to appear at Eva's door. Eva had enjoyed a lie-in, followed by a leisurely bath, as Alfie was spending the weekend with her parents and was expecting to be taken to Warwick Castle for a full day of historical adventure and fun. He boasted that he was particularly looking forward to the tour of the Castle Dungeon, and learning about the 'torturer' with his special implements, and a cook with 'special ingredients'. For all this bravado, Eva hoped he would be ok as it was an interactive experience with live actors and special effects, and it had all the potential to be terrifying. She and Niall had been a few years ago, with Niall's parents, and the four of them had walked through the experience all holding hands in a line, and jumping out of their skin at what seemed to be the living dead shrieking at them.

Tania hurried into the kitchen, sat down at the table and placed a brown paper bag down in front of her. 'Right girl, I've brought goodies, an apple cinnamon pastry for you, and a chocolate covered doughnut for me. Put the kettle on for a coffee and then tell me all about it. Every minute detail.' Tania was Eva's friend from secondary school, so they had known each other for two thirds of their life, and were there for each other during the highlights and dark times. Eva's life had more significant moments, including meeting and falling in love with Niall, getting married, having a child, Niall becoming ill and then dying. Tania's life had kept on an even keel, no exhilarating highs but then no earth-shattering lows in terms of relationships.

Tania was petite, with long, straight dark brown hair, and green eyes, beauty gifts from her mixed heritage of Welsh mother and Indian father. She was small in stature but made up for this in terms of personality which was confident, talkative bordering on loud. If Tania was in the room, you never failed to notice her. She was able to attract a selection box of men of different types, short or tall, slim or cuddly, young or middle-aged, fitness addicts or video game nuts, comedian funny guys or cerebral dullards, and she had tasted many samples but was yet to find a constant favourite. Tania's love life had kept Eva entertained over the years, as it was such a contrast to her married with kid domesticity, and sometimes she envied Tania's freedom and fun as a single woman. Tania desired Eva's great love affair with a handsome husband and insisted that this was her ultimate goal, as she searched amongst the stream of grey, dull gravel for a nugget of gold.

The kettle boiled, Eva took two mugs out of a top cupboard, spooned in the instant coffee and poured on the water. 'Are you having milk this week or not? If you are, it's the stuff from cows, and not from oats, almonds or whatever.'

'The dairy one will be fine, thanks.'

Eva retrieved the semi-skinned milk from the fridge, poured a splodge in each mug and placed the mugs of coffee on the table. She sat down, with a slight touch of nerves, as if she were to be interrogated by a skilled operator, to divulge national secrets. Tania was an expert in extracting information from people, and Andy, her police detective neighbour always commented that she would be an asset to the police service. This comment was made after the first time she had met him and quizzed him on his relationship status, future ambitions in terms of marriage and children, and his preferences in terms of women. Afterwards, Andy told Eva that he had been tempted to answer that he was thinking of becoming a Trappist monk so his relationship status would be single. Had no intention of marrying again or having more children and he was going to enjoy the single life.

Ripping open the brown bag, Tania took out the doughnut, broke it half and bit into with much pleasure, savouring its chocolate sweetness. Eva helped herself to the cinnamon pastry and shredded off small pieces to eat, and ate it slowly.

'Ok, let's have the gory details. Firstly, does he look as fit as in his photos or had he posted someone else's and he's a short, fifty-year-old with a spare tyre that would fit a tractor?'

Eva hesitated, as she wasn't as impressed by good looks as Tania, so to concentrate on his looks as their first talking point seemed rather shallow. 'Yes, he was 'fit' in terms of your criteria, as he was attractive, tall, and was definitely not carrying any extra weight on his body. I guessed that he would be the type to exercise regularly, which is great, as long as he's not too single-minded about it all.'

Tania licked her lips slightly and Eva wasn't sure it was just to remove doughnut crumbs. 'Sounding good already. Facially then, what was it like being gazed at by those deep-set brown eyes, as per the photos?'

Eva sipped at her now cooling coffee as she recollected her impression of him. 'You are right about his eyes, he does sort of fix you with those brown eyes, and it's hard to escape his stare, as if he can look into your mind and read your thoughts. He is good-looking, no denying it, but as I always say, it's not about the looks.'

'Well, so far he's ticking quite a few of the boxes. You're not giving much away, what did he tell you about himself?'

'That's the weird thing. He'd didn't say very much about himself at all. We talked a lot about my job, and I don't think he likes children much, and he hasn't got any kids of his own. I told him a bit about my life, you know, Niall, Alfie, my family and friends but I didn't learn a lot about his life, past or present. Two things of significance were that he's a widower, and has been married twice, his first wife died in an accident. He was vague about the second wife and I'm not sure if she died or they divorced. We do have some common ground in that we both have been widowed. Job-wise, he owns two car dealerships, selling used cars in Warwickshire. We won't have much in common on that score, as you know I have no real interest in cars except to get you from A to B.'

'Maybe so, but he could be useful if you want to trade in your car for a newer model and get you a good deal.'

'Perhaps. But I've always trusted dad to help with that, even when Niall was alive, and dad has always considered used car salespeople to be pushy, slick and dishonest, you know, that they're all dodgy Del Boys.'

Tania shook her finger at her friend. 'Now, now, we shouldn't be stereotyping people. There will be some bad apples but they can't all be dodgy. Did he seem like that?'

'No, not at all.'

'There you are then. And he ticks another box which is that he is a business man and having two dealerships implies that he is competent at what he does.'

'I suppose, but I can't comment on his business capabilities, as he might be up to his eyes in debt and looking for a rich widow to bail him out.'

'Well, that counts you out. Does he know how much teachers get paid? I digress. From what you have said, he does have potential, so would you want to see him again?' Tania asked.

Eva sighed heavily. She spent most of last night thinking about the date and whether she would want to see him again. They had left it very open, and he had said he would text her, but she wasn't overly convinced that he would. 'I don't know. I'm not sure we would agree on a lot of issues, as I think that he has more strident views on things than I do. For example, with children, I think he favours the 'children should be seen and not heard' approach and I have to be careful about going into a relationship with someone who isn't keen on kids, as I must put Alfie's welfare first.'

Tania, being Alfie's godmother, was very protective of her godson. 'Absolutely. We must protect Alfie at all costs. But you could meet this guy again, see how it goes, and then if you want to give it a go, take it slow. No need for him to meet Alfie for ages.'

Eva got up from her chair and picked up the two coffee mugs. 'Want another?' Just at that moment, there was a knock at the front door, so Eva went to investigate who it was. Two minutes later she was back in the kitchen, followed by Andy, her next door neighbour. Tania immediately sat up straight in her seat, smoothed her hair, and pushed the brown paper bag which had contained the doughnut away from her, so he wouldn't know she had eaten a sugar-laden treat. Tania gave him the benefit of her most radiant smile. 'Hi Andy.' Tania, who was normally poised and confident around attractive men seemed to morph into a shy, tongue-tied teenager in Andy's company. And to use the language of a teenager, Tania considered Andy to be 'beyond gorgeous.'

Eva could concede that Andy was definitely handsome, in a physical way, with height of six feet three inches, sapphire blue eyes, mid-brown hair short at the sides and longer at the top, which he swept up and gelled to the side. He had the body of a man who kept fit, by running, as Eva had often spotted him in running gear heading for the nearby country lanes and she suspected he did some weight training as his body was well-toned but not overly muscular. Tania had taken to calling at Eva's more often than strictly necessary, even for a caring friend and godmother, and it was with the intention of catching a glimpse of Andy. She would then sit day-dreaming about situations where she might be thrown into his company. The option of committing a murder, and thus being arrested, to be interviewed by him, was quickly discarded as a non-starter.

Eva recognised that Andy was an attractive man but she liked him more as a kind friend and neighbour, who she had started to get to know when he moved in next door, with his daughter, Hannah, one year ago.

Andy sat down on a chair next to Tania who grinned at him, a wistful expression on her face.

'Have you got time for a coffee, Andy?' Eva asked, knowing that he was very busy with work and taking care of his daughter.

'Yes, please.' He picked up the brown paper bag which had contained the pastries. 'I see I'm too late for whatever was in here.'

Tania nodded her head. 'Yes, too late. Once Eva sets her eyes on a chocolate doughnut there's no holding her back.'

The sound of the kettle boiling covered Eva's cry of surprise at this comment. 'Tania, you are such a liar. You've just eaten the doughnut, with great relish, I might add.'

Tania gazed at Andy, her lovely green eyes, focused on him. 'So, Mr Detective. Who do you believe? Who ate the chocolate doughnut? Me, with my lovely slender figure who never touches sugary snacks, or Eva, who can't resist anything sweet and chewy, and it shows with her spotty face and flabby middle.'

Eva, who continued to make the coffee, shook her head at hearing Tania's comment. Tania was always outrageous and very competitive, particularly if there was a man she fancied. Luckily, Eva knew Andy had no romantic interest in either of them as he had a girlfriend, so her friend's teasing was said in the spirit of good fun.

Placing the coffee mug in front of him, Eva sat down at the table. 'Ok, Andy, who ate the doughnut?'

Andy drank his coffee carefully and grimaced slightly and Eva was not sure if this was because the coffee was too hot or he was not wanting to play the 'doughnut' game. 'Right, first things first,' he said, looking fondly at Eva. 'If Eva is a secret doughnut eater it doesn't show as she has lovely skin and there is no sign of a flabby middle. Now, using my very honed detective skills, and after assessing the situation carefully, I am confident that Tania ate the doughnut, as there is chocolate icing at the corner of her lip.'

'Damn,' Tania responded, before rubbing her finger at the corner of her mouth to get rid of the evidence.

Andy laughed. 'Enough of that. I'm here to find out how the date went?'

Eva blushed slightly as he focused on her. 'Ok. We got on quite well. There were no really awkward moments, but I think we might have different viewpoints on the world, and I'm not sure he likes children, so that would be a major issue.'

Tania chipped in immediately. 'Don't listen to her. He's got a lot going for him as he is good-looking, physically fit, a widower with no kids, and has his own business. Take it from me, and my dismal dating experience, he is not to be dismissed too easily. As you know, I have dated a long line of losers, and not many of them have such good credentials. Think balding, paunchy, never bother the dentist types, whose idea of a good time is four cans of lager and a chicken tikka watching the footie. Other end of the spectrum is the great hair, six-pack types, with teeth so white you need to wear sunglasses and they are only bothering with you till Margot Robbie comes along.'

Andy sighed, wanting to refocus on Eva's first experience of dating for many years. 'Thanks, Tania, but if we get into your dating history we could be here until Prince William is King. The most important thing is whether Eva wants to go on date number two.

Her two friends now eagerly awaited her answer with Tania nodding her head to offer her encouragement to give it a go. Eva hesitated. 'I'm really not sure. I doubt if he'll contact me again as I thought I came across as a bit dull and there wasn't a lot of laughing going on. Yes, physically he is attractive, but I felt I really didn't get to know him at all. If I had to use a word to sum him up, I would use 'intense' and if he isn't going to get on with Alfie then there's no point to it at all.'

CHAPTER FIVE

June 2019

Gary had now been dating Eva for two months, in order to progress The Plan to secure Wife Number Three. He had been surprised how he had talked himself into picking her over the other two, more suitable, candidates Lizzie and Angela. It was the fact that he was physically attracted to Eva which was causing the problem, as normally, in order to execute The Plan smoothly, he would have to be emotionally disconnected from wifey-to-be. It made the inevitable parting so much easier. On the evening, at the end of the first date with Eva in April, he had one hundred percent decided not to see her again, and to focus on L and A, with the objective of making the final choice within the next week.

After his first date with Eva, on the Friday in April, he had arranged to see Lizzie on the following Sunday. They had decided on a five-mile walk starting at the National Trust property of Packwood House, following a trail that included the junction of the Stratford and Grand Union Canals, along the Grand Union Canal, and the other nearby NT property of Baddesley Clinton. The weather was warm, and Lizzie wore a maxi length blue dress and brown leather boots, which was over dressed on a day that other women were in shorts, skimpy tops or sundresses. Overall, the walk had been a long, tedious trudge. Lizzie's shyness meant that he quickly became strident in his views, as she did not know how to rein him in and at one point he almost told her to shut up, as she told him about staffing issues at the library where she worked. Library Assistants turning up for work in ripped jeans and with tattoos, who would have thought it? Then, she had to bring the bloody dog, who pulled on the lead the whole way, barked at every single duck on the canal, and tried to nip Gary's legs if he tried to take over the lead and teach the dog to walk to heel.

The whole of the walk, Gary's mind drifted to being with Eva. Eva who would be pretty in suitable clothing, jeans and a T-shirt, or summer dress, giving him glimpses of tanned legs and arms. With Eva, he would have stopped for a drink at a pub along the route, in order that he could enjoy his time with her, and gaze at her lovely eyes and sensual mouth. He would have made a tentative move to either hold her hand, or risk a kiss on her cheek at the end of the date, to fulfil his longing of having her body close to his. There wasn't much chance of hand holding or a kiss with Lizzie, as Charlie the dog called the shots, and dragged his mistress wherever he wanted to go. Gary, felt less inclined to hold or kiss Lizzie, than he would to hold and kiss a scarecrow, but if she were to be the next wife, he would have to persist with the physical stuff if the relationship were to appear real.

The next date, the following weekend, had been with Angela. All sports interest now put aside, they indulged in Angela's favourite pastime, eating, and went for an afternoon tea at an upmarket garden centre. Whilst, Angela ate a selection of sandwiches, scones with cream and jam, and fancy cakes, with several cups of tea, Gary drank coffee and ate two tuna and cucumber sandwiches. As she chomped down on the food, Gary could not help but think of the 80's computer game 'Pac- Man' as her mouth devoured all the food within her sights. After the cream tea, they went for a walk around a local park, and Angela talked about doctors, patients, and various unusual ailments that seemed to afflict the good people of Warwickshire. Gary was relieved that she was only the Practice Manager, and not an actual GP, as Angela gave vivid descriptions of plagues and pestilences that beset folk, including pus-filled boils, swollen big toes and brittle ingrown toenails.

If The Plan were to be propelled forward with Angela, then he must start on the physical contact that would convince her of his intent to have a genuine relationship. A hug, a kiss or holding hands would be appropriate at this stage but he had all the enthusiasm for touching her that a dog has for a visit to the vet. It all felt like time wasted when he could be concentrating on the lovely Eva.

All in all, after these dates with L and A, he decided to put them on hold in terms of meeting up, but he would keep them dangling by sending texts and holding out the promise of the next date. Instead, and against his better judgement, he decided to forsake all others and concentrate on Eva. They had since gone out on a few more dates, one for a meal, one to the cinema and one for a country walk and he had ensured that he was relaxed, jokey and teasing with her, to put her at her ease. At the meal, she had looked heavenly in a blue satin dress that enhanced her eye colour, and accentuated the auburn in her hair. At the cinema, he had revelled in her closeness, as they watched a psychological thriller that at times had spooked her so much that she grabbed hold of his hand. A walk in the country, at the beginning of May 2019, was a seven-mile route around Kenilworth Castle and she glowed with beauty as the sun's rays highlighted the red in her hair and a breeze blew her hair around gently, to frame the prettiness of her face. When she occasionally walked ahead of him on more narrow pavements and pathways, Gary really had to control his urge to caress her shapely bottom, encased in tight-fitting blue jeans. This was now their fourth date, and there had been no physical contact between them, mainly, as all the dates were in public places. He was trying desperately to take it slow, to not scare her off, as he sensed that she was still finding it hard to get used to the idea of being with another man after all those years of married life.

Occasionally, when Gary was not concentrating on The Plan, he would treat himself with a date from a dating app, that was purely for the purpose of having sex. He'd pick an attractive girl, decide that they were both up for it, and meet at his place or hers. No time wasting, no small talk, no niceties, just straightforward shagging.

As they completed the walk, and returned to their cars, Gary suggested to Eva that they ordered a takeaway and went back to hers. The kid was with the grandparents. This could be the evening when he finally got to have her. She had been hesitant at first, fully realising what may be about to happen, but then she had smiled to confirm that she liked that suggestion. At her house, they ordered pizza, drank white wine, and he sat close to her on the sofa, with a little of the nervousness of inexperienced teenage boys, as they struggle to kiss or cuddle their girlfriend. After two hours of watching a series on Netflix, Gary could stand it no longer and lay Eva down on the sofa. He lay next to her, carefully studying her face, and trying to gauge what was going on in her blue eyes, with a blueness equivalent to the depth of the sea. Kissing her possessively, to fully encompass her delicious mouth, he concentrated on watching her face and her reactions, as she gave herself up to the kiss. After the sexual repression of the earlier weeks, he was now unleashed, and this could not be stopped. He moved his hands and mouth down the nape of her neck, to the deep, enticing darkness of her cleavage, and on to exposing her breasts and nipples to the erotic roughness of his touch. As he became fully aroused, he explored downwards to free her body of the tight blue jeans to reveal white panties that he pulled down over lightly tanned thighs and legs. As the passion soared in him, and he touched her intimately, for a moment, he thought that her hand was holding onto his with the intention of making him stop. He pushed her hand away, and continued to caress her, until she was moaning softly. This was the point of no return, no time for regrets on her part, as he swiftly entered her, and continued with a rhythmical forceful pace until his climax was achieved. He had no idea at this moment if she had experienced sexual satisfaction but he knew that this was a gift worth having, one which he had sacrificed the principles of The Plan to acquire. The days of stoking the boilers of his previous wives, Claire and Jess, and future potential labours in lighting a spark in Lizzie or Angela, were all forgotten in this moment of physical bliss.

CHAPTER SIX

Four weeks later, Gary had concentrated all his energies on Eva, and it was paying off. She seemed happy and relaxed around him, and he progressed carefully, making her laugh, buying inexpensive little gifts; a small chocolate teddy bear, a summer bouquet of white gardenias, blue freesias and creamy white roses, and a selection of herbs to grown in pots when she expressed an interest in gardening. It was easy and fun, just the two of them being together without other people around. Their dates did all have to fit with her childcare arrangements for her son, Alfie, who seemed to have a busy life seeing friends, having sleepovers, playing football and staying with grandparents. Gary had not met the kid yet and was putting off the moment when that would inevitably happen.

The problem was that Eva was a sociable person and was keen for Gary to meet some of her friends. Again, he had been resisting this idea but then accepted her suggestion for meeting two of her closest friends, and their partners, at her house and she would cook.

Her best friend, Tania, was present, a petite brunette, who talked a lot and listened less. Gary reasoned feminists would refer to her as 'feisty' but Gary considered her to be a female who had to prove how intelligent she was by constantly giving her opinions on everything and never shut up. The price to be paid for female equality was male earache, in his opinion. She had dragged along with her a quiet boyfriend, Edwin, who had yet to speak except to say yes to a beer.

Andy, Eva's friend and next-door neighbour was also present, much to Gary's disgust. When Eva had mentioned that her neighbour was a detective with the police, he made a mental note to avoid meeting this man, as any dealings with the police always caused him anxiety. When Eva informed him that the police officer would be attending, Gary figured that not all detectives were of the calibre of Poirot and Morse. Some had got to be more Inspector Clouseau in the old 'Pink Panther' movies. As Andy entered the room, Gary knew from his bearing and presence that he was a competent and capable police officer, who was on the young side to be a detective inspector, the leader of a team of detectives. He greeted Gary pleasantly with a friendly smile and firm handshake but Gary was struck by his physicality, the type of man who could overpower a criminal, and place him in handcuffs, without breaking sweat. A man not to be underestimated.

Andy's girlfriend, Natasha, was a blonde beauty, all immaculate makeup, glossy hair, manicured nails and perfect body in a tight fitting, blue mini dress.

As she entered the room, she gave Gary one of her dazzling white smiles, as she sought to add him to her list of admirers, bewitched by her charms. Gary did not react to the smile and ignored her as he did not want to play her games. She was the type of woman he despised, the wicked queen, who seeks to destroy those she sees as rivals to what she wants in life.

As they sat to eat the meal of lasagne, green salad, coleslaw and garlic bread Eva had prepared, they were all served portions of the lasagne by the nervous cook.

'I hope this is ok. It's a long time since I've done any entertaining, since ..Niall…' she paused, as this dinner party was one more step on the road out of the life with him and her exploration into new territories.

Eva handed a plate to Natasha who eyed it with a level of suspicion normally seen on the faces of contestants in 'I'm a Celebrity…Get Me Out of Here' when given a plate of Witchetty grubs or crocodile penis. 'That's too much for me, I'm not a Sumo wrestler, you'd better give that to Andy.'

'Sorry, Natasha, I'm only used to serving up for growing boys with hearty appetites. Will half of that be, ok?'

'Yes. I can't afford to get fat or Andy will go off me.' She placed a hand on Andy's upper arm and stroked it seductively, making him wince slightly at this over-the-top possessive gesture.

Eva was now asking everyone exactly how much lasagne they wanted so as not to cause further embarrassment. Tania, not to be out done by Natasha, ensured that her portion was just a tad smaller than Natasha's so as not to be side-lined in the quest for a slimming club award rosette. Edwin muttered that he would accept whatever he was given and smiled shyly at Eva as he accepted the plate of food.

Eva was by now drinking more white wine than sensible in order to calm her nerves, Gary noticed. He was musing on some of his own techniques he would apply later to reduce her stress levels when she succumbed to his soothing hands. While he was satisfied by their love making, he sensed that she was still feeling shy with him, after years of being with only one man, and so some alcoholic sedation could relax her inhibitions.

Andy tucked into the lasagne hungrily. 'This is great, Eva, you could make an Italian nonna proud with this. It's very good.'

Tania chewed slowly on each piece of the lasagne and frequently eyed the remainder in the dish. Gary smiled to himself, as he knew Tania would be enjoying a late-night snack when she got home. To fill the gap left empty by lack of food, she was now swigging mouthfuls of wine quickly, on the way to getting drunk. 'Right, folks. These dinner parties can get boring as we don't all know each other. I suggest an ice-breaker game of telling the truth. We will start with an easy one, what's your biggest fear? I'll start, and it's easy to answer, it would be going into a room full of snakes. Edwin's next and then he nominates the next person, and so on?'

Edwin shrunk slightly in his chair as all eyes focused on him. 'Er, er, being in a room of strangers and they're all watching me.' Everyone laughed at this, the first thing he had said. 'Actually, mine's simple, I don't like heights. Eva next.'

Eva thought for a moment. 'We are all interpreting this as phobias. But my biggest fear is the death of people you love the most. And on that gloomy note, I'll pass to Natasha.'

Natasha yawned, as if this was all too childish for her. 'Nothing really. I stand up to my fears. But I suppose I must play the game. I do fear running out of fake tan.' Everyone laughed, as she nominated Andy.

As Andy concentrated before answering, Tania stared at him longingly, whilst finishing the last dregs of wine in her glass. She picked up the nearest bottle which was empty, stood up, and headed for the wine cooler. 'I'll help myself Eva, is that ok?'

Andy sighed as the group waited for his response. 'Ok, I think it's a fear of illnesses that rob you of your mental faculties, like dementia. And in a couple of years I believe I will develop a fear of adolescents, as Hannah reaches her teenage years. It's bad enough now when three or four of her girlfriends come round and giggle and shriek, unceasingly. There is an actual name for this fear…I will google it.' He picked up his phone and tapped quickly. 'Oh yes, Ephebiphobia. Ok, Gary's turn.'

Gary's eyes searched the group, to hold their attention on him. 'Mine's easy. A fear of being broke, so all my life decisions are built around ensuring that I am financially secure. I had enough of poverty as a kid and I'm never going back to that again.'

Tania tapped her glass with a spoon. 'Ok, that all got a bit gloomy and not what I was looking for so let's try another. Has anyone ever broken the law?'

Andy looked nervous at this suggestion. 'Tania, you do remember I am a cop so please be careful if any of you are going to admit to being a serial killer or a burglar.' He laughed but his facial expression was a mix of trepidation and anxiety. 'Ok, I'll nominate that Eva goes first as I'm sure we have nothing to worry about with her.'

Natasha nodded in agreement. 'Yeah, no worries there with her. She's probably never even got a parking fine.'

Eva looked peeved at Natasha and scowled openly at her. 'How do you know I'm not a high-class jewellery thief and I am planning to raid the Tower of London and walk off with the Crown Jewels.'

Andy laughed loudly. 'Please let me know when this is going to happen as I could get an immediate promotion and a salary increase or I could help you with the raid and we could spend the loot together.'

Eva smiled at him. 'Don't go ordering a Lamborghini yet. I have no crimes to own up to really. As a teenager a group of us broke some flower pots in a garden whilst playing rat-a-tat ginger. Natasha next.'

Natasha sighed. 'See I told you it would be boring. I'll admit to using coke at parties but before Andy gets cross with me, it was years ago. Over to you, Tania.'

Tania avoided Andy's gaze as she confessed. 'I did steal a lipstick from Boots when I was thirteen. What's the punishment for that crime, Andy?' She slightly licked her lips as she now looked at him. 'Will you be putting me in handcuffs and roughing me up?'

Natasha didn't look too happy with this obvious flirting. Andy smiled wickedly at her. 'I'd bring back some old-fashion methods of punishment. Put you in the stocks and throw rotten fruit and veg at you.'

Tania frowned. 'Spoilsport. I was looking for something a little more personal. Ok, Edwin?'

Embarrassed by Tania's flirting with Andy, he quickly said, 'smoking a bit of weed, that's all. Andy next.'

Andy shook his head and surveyed the group. 'Nothing really, as you'd expect. Some anti-social behaviour as a kid as I always seemed to like getting into fights. And I too did smoke some weed in my teens, so don't tell my boss. Gary.'

As all eyes alighted on him, Gary could feel the cop's eye's boring into him with with the intensity of a drill fracturing his brain. 'I did get done for driving over the limit some years ago which is not great for making my living as a car salesman but I got through it.'

As everyone had finished eating, Eva got up to gather together the dirty plates and dishes, and Tania and Andy volunteered to give her a hand. Edwin advised he was going for a smoke in the garden. 'Andy, it's not weed, I promise.' He smiled sheepishly at Andy, feeling slightly vulnerable speaking about drugs to this imposing police officer.

Andy gave him a 'I've got my eye on you' look which made Edwin blush as he exited the kitchen area to go into the garden.

Gary replenished his glass of red wine from a nearby bottle. 'Do you want some?' he asked Natasha. She held her glass for him to top up her drink. He then got up from the table, and walked out to the patio, to sit at the patio table. The June evening still retained some of the heat from a warm day. Natasha followed him, and sat down, sipped her wine and concentrated on messaging on her phone. Gary focused his piercing gaze on Natasha, who looked up from her phone, aware of his eyes on her. 'You think you're something else don't you darling, with all your blonde hair and fake smiles.'

Natasha glared back at him, large brown eyes radiating animosity. 'What's that supposed to mean?'

'That you think that all men will fall down at your pretty feet and worship you, but some of us can see what lies inside, your brittle and cruel heart.'

'Oh my God, are you for real? And yes, I usually eat men like you for breakfast and then spit you out?'

'I don't think so darling. And don't think that you're much prettier and sexier than Eva who you keep making snide digs at. I've only met your cop boyfriend today, but I can tell you he cares for Eva, and you'd be very unwise to keep taking aim at her, as he won't necessarily be on your side.'

Natasha's face was now flushed with anger but she did appear shocked at what he had just said. 'He'd never look at her when he's got me.'

Gary's cold dark eyes swept over Eva. 'Don't be too sure, darling. How do I know. You and me are very alike, cold, hard, uncaring and prepared to sacrifice everyone who stands in our way. You are driven by the need for power and money, so Andy is only a pleasant diversion, on the road to riches. Eva, now, she's warm and sexy. Men like Andy go for women like her and it won't be long before he tires of you.'

CHAPTER SEVEN

July/August 2019

After the dinner party at Eva's, meeting her best friend, Tania, and neighbour and friend, detective Andy (emphasis on 'detective'), Gary decided to call a halt to his fledgling relationship with Eva. He had hoped he could progress The Plan, with Eva, a widowed young woman with her own home, but in reality, there were too many obstacles in the way for it to work. It had been a pleasure to have Eva in his sights as potential Wife Number Three. She had a lovely face and an exciting body, which thrilled him, and for the moment, satisfied his sexual urges, which was a major bonus compared to the other two incompetents who he had chosen as wife material. Normally, the lack of sexual input from the wives was not an issue, as he could seek gratification elsewhere, quite easily, but as Eva was so delicious it was going to be difficult to give her up. It wasn't really a question of sexual acrobatics or technique, as he had known a lot of women who were experts at the art of intimacy, more so than Eva. It was something else, something more, an underlying sense that she satisfied him more deeply, physically and emotionally. It was a certain vulnerability to her that caught his attention, tapped into his masculinity, so that he wanted to possess her, and protect her, but it brought out an inclination to want to dominate her as well. It was all so bloody confusing, and, in reality, annoying, as he normally executed The Plan with single-minded efficiency, and in a cold-blooded manner, that was not complicated by feelings and emotions. This could be good news for Eva, because if she had become his wife, he would not just be viewing her as a commodity, a means to add to his property portfolio, so the short period of their life after marriage could be a more pleasant experience for her, than it was for the first two wives. Alternately, it could be worse for Eva, as this connection to her, aggravated an itch at the core of his being, an irritation that was only soothed by roughness, by scratching to cause pain. The need to destroy those with whom he made an emotional connection had started with Lisa. Until Lisa, the turbulent maelstrom of feelings of hate and anger, that had swirled in him from a young age, had only been relieved in minor ways, self-harm, inflicting pain on younger, weaker kids or seeking out pain for himself by goading more powerful people. With Lisa, for the first time, there had been the sublime bliss of eradicating for a short time, the traumatic emotions he could not escape. He would normally expunge his inner rage by dealing harshly with employees, or intimidating those he felt were inferior to him, or unnerving women he had sex with, but these things only scratched the surface of his inner bomb waiting to explode. With Lisa, he had harnessed the rage, and used his physical might and divine power, to experience the ultimate in human potency by ending a life. By letting go of all inhibitions, he had allowed the inner bomb to detonate, glorying in the intensity of the explosion before finding perfect peace and calm.

Having weighed up the pros and cons of continuing with Eva, he decided with a heavy heart that he would have to stop seeing her. Her son, Alfie, was a major part in this decision. He had not yet met the boy, and Eva had not suggested any meetings, as she told Gary that she would not introduce her son to any man until she was confident that the relationship had a chance of longevity. Gary had fully supported her thinking on this as he was anxious to avoid meeting the boy for as long as possible. Alfie, was nine-years-old, and from Eva's description was a clever, kind, loving and a well-behaved child who was loved by family and friends. Gary did not know if he would be able to act with consistent patience and friendliness around the boy, as he could not be sure of keeping his temper in check if the boy annoyed him. Eva spoke very caringly about her son who she stressed was her number one priority. Alfie's life and happiness would not be upset by any third party entering their lives, she declared, ensuring that Gary understood that Alfie came first. This did not necessarily suit Gary, who did not want to be second fiddle in the orchestra, he wanted to be the first violin and Eva would dance to his tune, not her son's.

Yes, the dinner party had been the decider for Gary. He had not taken to Tania, Eva's best friend, who he found to be over-confident and familiar, not afraid to quiz him about his past relationships and intentions towards Eva. At times, he thought that she was flirting with him, as she liked to be noticed, trying out her feminine wiles to entice a man. Tania was the type of woman who always came across as desperate, to men. Tania had a lot of favourable attributes, including prettiness, sociability, sense of humour and self-assurance. Gary assessed that she wanted to be viewed as a modern woman, career-orientated, financially independent and not actively seeking a man in her life. In actuality, Tania's insecurities radiated from her, waves of neediness, loneliness, and males could smell the scent of desperation on her. She would attract men but not hold on to them. If Gary were to stay with Eva, he didn't see Tania as a major obstacle who could thwart his plan. If she were to become a nuisance, he would have easily persuaded Eva to evict her from her life, so she was no more than a gnat at dusk who needed to be swatted out of the way.

It was Andy that Gary had major concerns about. His position as a Detective Inspector in the police service, at a youngish age, meant the man was highly competent in his job. He was friendly with Gary, trying to get to know him for Eva's sake. However, Gary could not shake the feeling that Andy was instinctively wary and cautious with him, which made Gary uneasy as his past would not stand up to scrutiny if a trained investigator dug too deeply. He also recalled what he said to the bitch, Natasha. He had observed Andy closely whilst they played the stupid game devised by Tania. His eyes lingered on Eva a lot, and they were kind eyes, looking out for her welfare. Andy was not pleased with Natasha when she made the fuss over the portion of lasagne she had been given. Later, Natasha made a snide remark to Tania about Eva's nails not being well-manicured to salon standards. Andy chipped in to comment that not everyone had time to be obsessed with beauty regimes when they had a full-time job, a child to care for, and a house to maintain. Gary recognised in Andy a true advisory, a sharp, police-trained, physically fit combatant who would not want to see Eva and Alfie harmed.

At the beginning of July, Gary ceased all contact with Eva. No explanatory phone call to end it politely, no short, sharp text to say finito. No point twiddling his thumbs, kicking his heels or chewing the cud. There was a plan to implement, a third wife to acquire and money to be made. His work regarding Lizzie and Angela had been put on hold but it was now time to consolidate and move forward.

Two days later, a Saturday, Lizzie was sitting in Gary's apartment, nervously perched on his sofa, glass of red wine in her hand. She had been delighted when he had contacted her, offering a million apologies for not being in touch. An elderly aunt had been gravely ill, and sadly died, and he had to take care of the funeral arrangements and putting other matters in order, as the executor of her will.

Lizzie smiled at him shyly, as she sat on the sofa, legs drawn in tightly together, a tension visible in her body as her back was straight and he could spot a rigidity in her neck and jawline. She was dressed in a midi dress, a green material with a busy pattern of red, yellow and blue, with full pleats and long sleeves. The only body part he could see, and speak favourably of, was her slim ankles. Sensing her anxiety of being alone with him in his flat, Gary deliberately made himself comfortable by stretching out his long legs, with his feet on the coffee table. He was wearing skinny black jeans and a tight-fitting, short-sleeved, grey T-shirt which emphasised his chest muscles and toned arms. When he had handed her the wine glass, she shrunk back into the sofa, possibly hoping that it had some kind of hidden compartment where she could flee into a magical, safer world. Gary chided himself on this little game he was playing, using his masculine presence to unsettle her, and boost his feeling of dominance over her. But what the heck, it was fun. For a woman in her forties, she was timid, and fearful around men, and he had met eighteen-year-olds who could teach her a lot about being with a man. He suspected that the two brief relationships she had mentioned may not have been consummated. If they had, she had not been with experienced types, more likely fumblers and clumsy clowns. This could be fun as he helped to overcome her hang-ups but he would move cautiously as he did not want to be accused of assault.

Gary sat next to Lizzie on the sofa and leaned over to pick up the wine bottle off the coffee table. 'Drink up, there's more of this, if you want it. It will help you to relax as you seem very tense at the moment. Don't worry, I don't bite.' He said this with all the reassurance of the wolf giving comfort to Little Red Riding Hood, as a big smile revealed its canine teeth, a mouth drooling with saliva, and the need to kill apparent in its murderous eyes. Lizzie quietly obeyed his order, and gulped down a few mouthfuls of the wine, to relieve her anxiety.

Gary glanced over at her. 'Yeah, I think I should apologise to you again for not making contact. It was most rude of me but I was a bit overwhelmed by the death of my beloved aunt, Aggie. She became very ill, very quickly, and it sort of stopped me in my tracks,' he paused, his voice quavering slightly. 'After she passed on, there was all the responsibility of arranging the funeral according to her wishes and starting to sort out the house contents and so on. There's still quite a bit to do in terms of the will.'

He could see that the pain and sincerity in his voice had now hooked her in. She turned to look at him, and her right hand briefly extended towards him, before being retracted, as if she wanted to pat his hand in acknowledgement of his grief.

Her pale blue eyes, made bigger by the varifocal lenses, reflected the sadness that he would be feeling. 'I take it you were very close to Aunt Aggie?'

He drew in a deep breath before answering, giving depth to his Oscar winning performance. 'Yes, she was my dear dad's youngest sister and she always spoiled me, you know. Lots of sweets, chocolates, a five-pound note here and there, you know what these doting aunties are like. She was not really that old either, only in her late sixties but it was decreed by a higher power that her time was up.' Gary did now allow his voice to crack as if on the point of tears.

Lizzie now bravely did extend her right hand to pat his and he held onto her hand before she could pull back. He put down his wine glass, moved closer to her and held her chin with his right hand. Gently bringing his mouth down onto hers, the kiss was gentle and exploratory but the pressure of his hand on her chin meant that she could not break away. At first, she did not respond, and he detected a tremor in her body, a vibration of fear, and he guessed that she was not used to physical contact with a man. He found that kissing her was bearable, and as he progressed the kiss, he could feel the tension in her body easing, though he did not follow through with any other moves. Breaking off the embrace, he whispered softly. 'That's just what I needed, to soothe the stress of the last few weeks.'

They remained close to each other, and she drank more of the wine, quickly, and he refilled her glass. Again, she glugged down a few more mouthfuls and her cheeks were becoming reddened as the alcohol flushed through her system.

Gary now placed an arm around her shoulder to draw her against him. She removed her spectacles but tried to avoid his eyes, as he stared down at her. 'Lizzie, I realised whilst going through the trauma of my aunt's death that it would have been wonderful to have someone by my side, helping me through it. I imagined who that person could be and often my thoughts did turn to you. And now you're here and we are making a proper connection. What do you think, are we connecting?' His laser-like gaze focused on her eyes, and she quickly looked away, not sure how to answer.

She whispered, hesitantly. 'I think so, but I'm not really used to this. It's been a long time.'

He kissed her again and she was ready for it this time and kissed him back. Though the kissing was now boring him, he stretched it out so that she relaxed and would not panic if things went further. As her eyes met his, he noted the anxiety present, and in all honesty, it did send a little shiver of excitement through him.

As he pulled her down on to the sofa and lay beside her, he gently caressed her body through the many folds of material of her dress. 'Don't worry, Lizzie, I am a great teacher.' As his hands explored under the layers of her clothing, and she gazed at him with anxious eyes, he closed his own eyes, and concentrated on more kissing and fondling. In his head, the woman was not Lizzie, but a smaller, sexier one, with wavy auburn-brown hair, deep blue eyes, a truly luscious mouth and curvier body. That was the woman he was now making love to. Eva.

Through July and August, he saw Lizzie at least twice a week, and they would go out for walks, or for drinks at country pubs before returning to his apartment. She had started to stay over on occasional nights at the weekend when she wasn't at work the next day. Her father declared he was quite able to look after himself for a few hours and told her, jokingly, that he did value the time he spent on his own. Gary enquired frequently about dad's health, in a kind and curious way, which Lizzie appreciated. His cardiologist had declared that the stent had been a success and his medication was controlling symptoms of angina. He was now trying to eat a healthier diet with Lizzie's encouragement. His broken arm had healed well and full mobility had been restored. Gary cursed, as rumours of dad's imminent demise had been greatly exaggerated. Lizzie declared happily, that dad was fully intent on reaching his hundredth birthday, and receiving a letter from King Charles.

As the two months had gone by, Gary was finding that spending time with Lizzie was becoming more and more boring. Her life was insular involving caring for daddy, undertaking library duties, walking at National Trust properties, and reading profusely. She had a good knowledge of current affairs and politics but she had limited interested in films, television programmes, sports, and modern issues so they did lack common ground on which to base conversations. Her politics was left leaning, and a lot of her views were irritating to him, as she had great sympathy for scroungers, addicts, prisoners and other wastes of space. Gary's more forthright views on dealing with wrong doers, did shock her at times, but he often said outrageous things to wind her up and get a reaction out of her. Her overall timidity was becoming downright unattractive.

Hypothetically, he had been hoping to hurry the relationship along so that they would become established as a couple and he could move in to dad's house. He had not yet met the old bloke but as long as the house was reasonably clean and tidy, then he could help dad along his way to life in the next world. Once that goal had been achieved, then a year or so with Lizzie tops, would see her neutralised as well.

A Saturday evening, in late August, and Gary and Lizzie were at his place and he insisted that they watch a horror film together, an experience that he knew would upset her. He was in one of his dark moods, ready to inflict pain on a suitable candidate, but not necessarily physical pain, just yet. As he sat on a second sofa whilst drinking bottled lager, he realised that he could no longer continue to see her to progress The Plan. Too many things were niggling him now.

Firstly, and importantly, her shyness made her dull. He found he was getting more controversial in his comments, and views, just to try to get a reaction out of her but it didn't work as she seemed to go more and more into a shell, a little turtle frightened by the shark. Frequently, Gary enjoyed being around timid women as he could easily make them scared of him, and he would gain some perverse pleasure from this, but he could never be with them for the long haul. No, he actually, did like a spark in a woman, a friction, a resistance so that he could enjoy crushing them. Wife Number One, Claire, had been an ocean-going bore in the end, no sense of humour, no intelligent conversation, no sexual excitement and when the end came for her he had truly welcomed it. If only to keep his own sanity. Wife Number Two, Jess, had been more challenging. An older woman, who lived life, never hesitated to offer an opinion on everything and made Gary work harder to achieve his goal of acquiring her property and wealth. After the wedding, he did successfully start on a process of attrition, to wear down her self-esteem, intensify her insecurities and anxieties, a full-on gaslighting experience. Jess did become a faint shadow of the feisty, confident woman he had met on the first date but Gary had found raging the war intoxicating and the final battle had been exhilarating.

Secondly, with Lizzie, he did not think he could stand having an on-going sex life with this woman. She was another Claire in bed, immobile, nervous and leaving him to do all the work, as he laboured to excite her body.

He eyed her as she sat on the second sofa, opposite him. He sensed her shakiness, still in part, due to the zombie blood fest they had just watched. 'I'm going to have some whisky, do you want some or more wine?'

'Wine, please. I can't drink whisky it makes me ill.'

In the kitchen, Gary took a bottle of scotch and a glass tumbler out of the cupboard. He half-filled the glass and drank it quickly, in a couple of gulps. Carrying the bottle and glass through to the lounge, he sat next to Lizzie, poured more whisky in the glass and drank a few more swigs. The alcohol would soon do its job and any inhibitions he had would disappear. Whisky was the drink that brought out his colder, nastier side. 'Ok, then Liz.' He lay down on the sofa, his head propped up on the sofa's arm, gazing intensely at her. He placed his feet in her lap, which caused her to look startled at this unexpected contact. He had the whisky tumbler in his hand, and he now sipped at the whisky, a smirk of a smile on his lips. 'Lizzie, Lizzie, we have had sex a number of times now, and, frankly, it has been disappointing as you do not make any effort to participate. We'll give it another go, shall we? But I'm not going to be too happy, if you don't up your game. Now, come here.'

This time, he took no account of her inexperience in dictating the pace of the encounter, the positioning of her body, and his hammering into her, without any concessions given for her satisfaction. As he collapsed at the end of his exertion and she lay still, she rolled over to look at him, her large eyes glued onto his, a grateful smile on her lips. A small voice, said 'wow' and he recognised, for the first time, that there was passion within her which had finally been ignited, burned, and exploded. Too little, too late, as this was the end of it for him.

She continued to look at him, shyly now. 'I've never……'

Gary laughed, amazed by the way she was now viewing him, as if she were an infatuated teenage suddenly meeting her pop star idol. 'You enjoyed it then. Let that be my parting gift to you.'

Lizzie's smile disappeared off her face as quickly as the sun was blocked out by a cloud. 'What do mean?'

'That this is the end. We are over. It wouldn't work long-term as you are not really my type, as I really do like prettier, sexier women. Let's just leave it at that.'

CHAPTER EIGHT

September 2019

Gary didn't wait long to contact Eva. He made initial contact by text in a 'remember me' kind of way to find out how she would respond. She replied 'not dead then' which surprised him as she didn't come across as overly sarcastic. Two days later he had been invited around to her house for a drink, and a catch up, and she made it clear, it would be nothing more. Gary could be the obedient, conciliatory boyfriend if she wanted him to be.

He arrived at the door with the largest bouquet of white roses, green chrysanthemum, blue sea holly and eucalyptus. She invited him in, but there was no welcoming peck on the cheek or radiant smile, just an 'hello'. She thanked him for the flowers as he gave them to her and he followed her into the kitchen. As it was early evening, she offered him tea or coffee, so Gary surmised that he was going to have to work hard to win her over after the way he had ghosted her. Auntie Aggie was going to have to play a blinder.

He hovered by her, near to the sink, so she indicated he should take a seat at the dining table. He sat down on a chair, so he could watch her as she filled the kettle and switched it on. She was wearing the tight-fitting blue jeans he loved her in that highlighted her curvy buttocks, as she reached up to take two mugs out of a kitchen cupboard. The sight of her bottom, her slim waist, and glossy auburn-brown hair, today straightened, caused a physical ache in his groin as he remembered their love making. With the jeans, she wore a floaty, V-necked, long-sleeved, pink blouse with tiny blue flowers, which fitted at her waist. It was achingly feminine on her, and it brought back the images he always had of her as fragrant and fresh, a spring garden. Lizzie, in her acres of floral materials was more overgrown garden, by comparison. Having decided he wanted a coffee; she made the two drinks and placed them on the table and sat on the chair next to him.

She picked up the coffee mug, blowing lightly on it to cool it down, as she glanced at him, and Gary knew he now had to earn his right to be here and present the case for his two-month absence. He smiled awkwardly, feeling an actual shyness which was something that he never normally experienced around women he fancied. 'I know I have some explaining to do, as I did rather rudely stop contacting you. Firstly, let me say, you look absolutely beautiful, and I'm not saying this to win you over but I really can't take my eyes off you, at this moment.'

She pursed her lips and failed to smile at this compliment. His attempts at flattery were not going to work. 'Look, Gary, I don't want to hear any lame excuses and I'm not impressed with the way you just stopped contacting me. I don't expect you to go out with someone you don't want but please have the courtesy to end things in a grown-up way and speak to me about it. I did text you a couple of times but they weren't answered. I felt well and truly ghosted.'

Gary had the decency to look reprimanded and drank his coffee before replying. 'I know I have been stupid as I let a wonderful woman slip away from me.'

'Cut the bullshit. I need an explanation, or you can go out of that door now. It had better be good; volunteering in Africa, working in orphanages in India, pilgrimage to Lourdes, that sort of thing.' Eva stared directly at him, a glacial coldness in her blue eyes, a strict teacher addressing the pupil who had failed to give in his homework by the designated deadline and not willing to listen to pathetic excuses of aliens taking it, or dogs eating it.

Gary stuttered slightly, as he spoke. 'Well, after our last date, the dinner party, I was informed that a beloved aunt had died suddenly. I had responsibility for the funeral arrangements, and sorting her affairs, as the executor of her will.'

Eva sighed and did not look particularly empathetic at hearing of his loss. He had evoked a lot more compassion in Lizzie. It was not going to be so easy to win Eva round, as he had thought. 'I'm sorry for your loss, Gary. But I still find it hard to understand why you couldn't text or phone. I note that you have a full set of fingers and thumbs thus you didn't have some sort of freak accident that left you unable to use a mobile phone.'

'I know I should have made contact with you, but in the end, I think I left it too long and thought you wouldn't want to know.' Gary gave her a beguiling smile.

'Yet, here you are now, with a gift of flowers. And when you contacted me, I thought I would give you a chance to find out what had happened. What exactly do you want now?'

Gary leaned in towards her, wanting to touch her hand, but knew that she would probably bat him away if he did. 'I want, sorry, I would like you to consider if I could start seeing you again. I really enjoyed the times we shared together and think that you are a beautiful, intelligent, caring woman which any man would be proud to have in his life. I know that if I leave it too long you will meet someone else, who is worthy of you, and I shall regret that I didn't try to contact you.'

'I don't know, Gary. I can't have a man in my life who thinks he can dip in and out when he likes. I need a man who is consistent, honest and trustworthy. If you are not these things then it will never work. As I have told you, my priority is Alfie, and he will always come first. If I started seeing you again, then you must accept that. And, if I introduced you into his life, I don't want him getting to know you, and then you disappear in a puff of smoke.'

Gary rubbed his head, as if alleviating a headache. 'Ok, ok, cards on the table. When I stopped contacting you it was around the time my aunt died. But I think I also panicked as I felt we were getting closer, and at some point, I would have to meet Alfie. I've never been around kids and I'm not sure how I'd be with him.' For all his unaccustomed honesty, Gary was not feeling friendly waves of forgiveness washing over him from Eva. He could actually do with a strong drink right now, a large whisky.

Eva sat rigidly, still assessing his responses, and finding them lacking. 'I think that when I invited you round, I was open to considering (this word was emphasised strongly) whether we could start to see each other again. I am still extremely annoyed that you stopped all contact in the way you did. It showed an immaturity and callousness in your personality. The fact that you are also uncertain about Alfie really means that this can go no further.'

The darker side of Gary's nature, the devil in his brain, was tempted to cut and run, as he did not want a character assassination by a woman, and he was a proud man. But as he now sat tantalisingly close to Eva, he was enraptured by the intensity of his need to possess her body again. It took all his self-control not to reach out and pull her to him, for his mouth to consume her moist, red lips, and his fingers sensually explore every inch of her pale golden skin. Gary recognised that for once in his life, if he wanted to reconnect with Eva, he would have to put ego aside and grovel. 'Eva, I know that I have a lot of bridge building to do, but I am prepared to make it up to you, if you will give me a chance. As far as Alfie is concerned, I am uncertain, as I have no experience of nephews, or nieces, or friends with children, so I am a complete novice. And kids do scare me a little, as they are so open and honest, and you feel that they are assessing you, then finding you wanting. It's like dogs, they have a very good instinct for people, and can sniff out the bad ones.'

Eva laughed. 'Better not put you in a kennel full of dogs, then Gary.'

Gary laughed too, but it was a nervous cackle, as the dogs would definitely smell the rottenness inside of him. He was encouraged that she had finally laughed, so perhaps a tiny speck of progress had been made in melting the iciness that had greeted him. 'I take it that Alfie is with his grandparents at the moment. As you are currently child free would you allow me to take you out for a drink.

I will have a chance to beg you to forgive me for my sins, of not honouring you as you deserve, and for treating you badly. If I was the monk, Silas, in the book 'The Da Vinci Code', I would use a whip to self-flagellate, to inflict pain on my body, in penance for my sins.'

'Be my guest.' Eva commented abruptly but she did smile nervously at him. 'But I would like to go for that drink. It's just a drink, for now. It does not mean that I have forgiven you or that I want there to be any further contact after today. Let's take it one day at a time.'

CHAPTER NINE

October 2019

Six weeks later, in mid-October, Gary felt that he had grovelled so much to Eva that he had worn out the knees on his trousers. It had worked, as his persistence in winning her over was yielding results. Two weeks ago, she had allowed him to stay at her house, whilst Alfie was away, and they renewed their sexual relationship, though she was back to being self-conscious and cautious with him at first. He had slowed everything down, dampened his own searing lust, to ensure that he carried her along with him to reach a mutually exquisite pleasure. Afterwards, as she lay in his arms asleep, her glossy dark-auburn hair spread over the white pillowcase, her eyes flickering slightly as she dreamed, he gazed at her beauty and innocence and felt a purity within him, a unique experience in a life of hate and death. His decision to reconnect with her had been the right one. The Plan was now back on track. He put aside all thoughts of how The Plan should be concluded, as for now, he wanted to savour this moment of tranquillity.

It was now the half-term holidays and so Eva and Alfie were both out of school and away from their usual routine of lessons and homework. Eva suggested to Gary that perhaps the time was right for him to meet Alfie. It was decided that Gary would collect them both in his car, then they would go ten-pin bowling. It was Eva's suggestion as focusing on the bowling would perhaps dispel any awkward moments between Alfie and Gary.

As Gary entered Eva's house, she advised that Alfie was playing computer games in his bedroom and she would call him down in a moment. They had booked a game in two hours' time and would have to leave the house in about one hour. Eva offered coffee and Gary accepted. He sat at the table in her kitchen/dining area, feeling nervous, which was not something Gary experienced very often. His dealings with people, either in or out of work, were undertaken with confidence bordering on arrogance. Gary never saw himself as equal to other people but superior to them. He was puzzled why he should be fearful of a ten-year-old kid.

Suddenly, the kitchen door flew open, and a mini whirlwind blew into the room and came to a halt in front of Gary. The boy was slender, with blondish-red hair and fair skin, and facially he resembled his mother but with paler blue eyes. The eyes now scrutinised Gary's who felt he was being watched by an inquisitive puppy hoping for a treat. The boy was a little cautious of approaching but he extended his hand. 'Hi, I'm Alfie.' Alfie, a sociable and likeable boy, was confident around people as it sort of went with his approach of 'if you like them, they'll like you'

Gary shook the small hand, whilst Eva looked on, as he greeted her son. 'Yes, hi, I'm Gary, nice to meet you, Alfie.'

'Do you like computer games, we could play them together?'

'A bit but you'll have to show me what to do as I'm an old person.' Gary hoped his jokey response would win the kid over.

'No probs. I've just got Splatoon 2 which is really good. And Granddad Frank got the hang of it quite quickly and he's a bit older than you.'

Gary smiled, tentatively. 'Thanks, I think.' Guessing that Granddad Frank was probably at least sixty, Gary was cautiously confident that he could get the hang of this game, even with his old brain cells. 'We'll have to have a game next time I see you.'

Alfie hopped about from one foot to the other, one of those kids who seemed to have boundless energy, and never kept still. Gary knew that this would irritate him right from the start. 'Yes, cool. I really want to play Fortnite but mum says I'm too young which is really unfair as lots of boys in my class play it.' He had now stopped hopping and was now jumping up and down near to Gary, with an acute danger of toppling over.

Eva, who was leaning against a kitchen worktop, shook her head. 'I've told you Alfie that you are too young to play it, at the moment, so don't keep asking. And please stop that jumping by Gary and go and get ready to go to the bowling alley. Go and brush your teeth, put your shoes on, and your coat. Scoot.'

'Ok.' Alfie stared at Gary. 'Are you good at ten-pin bowling? I scored a strike last time I went.'

'I can see that I am going to have to be very good to beat you.'

'Alfie, go and get ready now or we will be late.' Eva reminded her son.

As Alfie left the room, Gary glanced over at Eva, smiling nervously. 'He's very energetic. He's worn me out just watching him.'

She laughed. 'He does have a lot of energy like a lot of boys his age. I think he's very excited at the moment because of meeting you. He'll calm down when we get in the car and get to the bowling. Relax, as you look a bit anxious.'

Once in the car, Alfie was seated on his booster cushion, with a seat belt strapping him in place, so his 'Tigger' impersonation had ceased. As he drove the car to the bowling alley, Gary soon realised his first rookie mistake. Do not put the child behind you, if you are driving, as you will receive the odd kick to the back of the driver's seat, a second source of irritation in a very short time.

At the bowling alley, Gary's competitive nature took over, as Alfie insisted that he was really good at this game. Alfie started disappointingly, with only two or three pins toppling over, and then the bowl was ending up in the gutter on a number of occasions.

Alfie looked to start to cry at this stage. 'Not fair, I can't do it. I am seriously going to lose now.'

Eva lightly hugged her son. 'It's too late now to change things. That was only your first try and you'll get better as we get more into the game.'

In actuality, his game was very erratic, up and down, with a lot of low scores and few eights or nines. Gary felt his hackles rise if Alfie started to whine when things weren't going his way. At the end of the game Alfie's score was 58. It turns out the 'strike' was scored on the previous game when he was aided by the buffers and this time he was bowling without. Gary found that he was good at bowling for someone who had not been to a bowling alley for about fifteen years. His score was a total of 145. Eva was average, happy with a couple of strikes, and an overall score of 114. Gary was chuffed that he done well and did experience a moment's pleasure that he had beaten the kid. If he and Alfie were to play games together in the future, there would be none of this nonsense that some parents indulged in, of 'letting him win'. Under Gary's tutelage he would discover that the world was a harsh place and not everyone could be a winner.

Back at Eva's after the bowling, she agreed with Alfie that there could be takeaway pizza as a further treat, and then they would all watch a movie together. The adults shared one large Capricciosa with ham, artichoke, mushroom and olives and one small Margherita for Alfie. Bowling certainly gave Alfie an appetite. He easily ate his four slices of pizza before greedily eyeing the three leftover slices on the larger one. Gary was thrilled that Alfie's movie choice was 'Incredibles 2', and yawned, wondering where his life had gone so wrong; extremely irritating ten-year-old boys, bowling alleys and children's movies. Perhaps Lizzie had been the right choice after all.

At nine p.m. after what seemed to Gary as the longest day of his life, Alfie went off to bed. Gary was doubly pleased to have the kid out of the way and Eva all to himself. Apart from the kid being a vast irritant, a biting insect one wanted to swat, he also took Eva's attention and time. Gary liked to have Eva to himself, to slyly fondle and kiss, and he could do none of that under the boy's watchful gaze.

They now relaxed on the sofa, Eva with a white wine, and Gary with a bottled lager. She asked him how he had enjoyed his first outing with Alfie. Inwardly, Gary was thinking it was something he never wanted to repeat but if he did want Eva, he would have to persist with Alfie. And he did want Eva.

Gary breathed in deeply. 'Yes, it was ok but it is quite exhausting, keeping kids entertained. And expensive, when you add in the cost of the bowling and the pizzas. That boy has got quite an appetite. I'm sure he ate more than me.'

Eva laughed. 'Yes, he really can eat but luckily he seems to stay quite skinny, so that's ok, for now.'

Gary, now fed up of thinking and speaking of ten-year-old boys, leaned in to kiss Eva, in a long and lingering way. 'This is my type of activity which I have been looking forward to all day. I have earned a little reward for being on my best behaviour.'

As the kissing intensified, and he started to explore her buttocks with eager hands, Eva reacted nervously. 'I'm not sure we can do this at the moment, as Alfie might walk in and catch us.'

Gary was not going to be deterred from what he wanted and he had been longing to have her all day. He pulled the throw down from over the sofa and placed it over them. 'If he comes down now he won't need to attend those sex education lessons, so a win-win.'

By November, Gary was regularly dropping round at Eva's when Alfie was there but Eva was insisting that there could be no sex unless Alfie was out of the house. Gary believed he was friendly with the boy but honestly couldn't say that he was taking to him, though he acted as if he was, when he was in the child's company. On a Saturday evening, after watching another children's movie, Alfie had pestered for the three of them to play a board game together, '5 Second Rule Jr.'

As they progressed slowly along the board, various squabbles broke out as Gary disputed Alfie's answers on a few occasions.

Gary read the card. 'Reasons to have a party'

Alfie. 'Birthday. Er….Halloween. Er er…..sleepover.'

Gary. 'No, not sleepover. Sorry, but that can't count.'

Alfie. 'Mum, what do you think?'

Gary. 'I've just said you can't have that. End of.'

Alfie now stuck out his bottom lip and scowled at Gary. 'But the rules say it must be a decision by all the other players, not just you. Doesn't it, mum?'

Eva sighed but had to agree with Gary. 'I don't think we can count sleepover.'

The game continued.

Eva read Alfie his next card. 'Name three things which go with chips.

Alfie. 'Fish fingers. Fish. Mayo.'

Gary chuckled. 'We can't accept mayo. That's daft. What do you think, Eva?'

Eva hesitated. 'I disagree with you, Gary. I think chips and mayo go together. It counts.' Gary was not happy that he had been outvoted but had to concede. At the end of the game, Alfie was the winner. Being on a winning streak seemed to make him hyper-active. He started jumping up and down on the sofa until Eva told him to stop and go and get ready for bed. 'Pyjamas on and teeth brushed and I'll be up in a minute to tuck you in.'

Ensuring that Gary had a lager, Eva disappeared upstairs to settle her son, and agreed that he could read quietly for half an hour before going to sleep. When she re-appeared, Gary pulled her up close on the sofa but it was made very clear that there could be no sexual activity except for some kissing and cuddling. Gary's mood was not helped by this information. Spending time with Alfie did not improve his temper and he needed something to de-stress him after having to force a smile on his face for quite a number of hours, making his jaw ache. He kissed Eva lightly but resisted the urge to take things forward and they decided on a film on Netflix.

After half an hour, Alfie was in the room, complaining that he had seen a giant spider in his bedroom and he couldn't get to sleep. Eva advised, 'I doubt it, Alfie, as they only come into houses in September and October, generally. I think you were dreaming.'

Alfie sat firmly on the sofa, next to Gary, refusing to budge. 'I know what I saw. Can you check or I can't go to sleep.'

Gary was now glaring at Eva, hoping she wasn't going to get into this wild goose chase, or to be more accurate, this hairy, spider chase. 'Look, Alfie, your mother is right, there are no spiders around now. So just go to bed.'

Alfie folded his arms with a determination not to move. 'I'm not going until you look. Please. Also, can I have a glass of milk when you come back?'

Eva got up from the sofa knowing that there would be no peace until a full spider sweep had been undertaken. 'Ok, ok, I'll go and check for the spider. But you are pushing your luck at wanting milk. You'll have to brush your teeth again.'

Sighing heavily, she left the room.

Gary immediately turned to look at Alfie, still sitting arms crossed, in blue pyjamas with various coloured dinosaurs. Gary pointed at the T-rex on the pyjamas. 'Do you see that dinosaur, the T-rex, what do you know about him, Alfie?'

Alfie looked down at the pyjamas. 'That he's the biggest, strongest dinosaur with massive teeth.'

Gary nodded. 'Correct, he is. If he's in a fight with another dinosaur, who normally wins?'

Alfie laughed. 'He does because of his fierce teeth which rips the flesh out of the others.'

'Yes, that's right, Alfie. He wins every time. And, Alfie, look at me.' Gary poked a finger at Alfie's chest to get his full attention. 'You don't know me well, yet, Alfie, but let me tell you I am like a T-rex, fierce, and can get very angry. You don't want to mess with me. In the two short months we have known each other, I am finding that you don't seem to be able to do what your mother tells you to do. We will all have a good time together if you do as you are told, the first time, and do not keep arguing. Do you get what I am saying?'

Alfie looked down at the finger which was still prodding his chest. 'Yes, I think so.'

The prodding stopped, but Gary's deep, menacing eyes held the boy's eyes, which were now fearful as the message sunk in. 'This little chat is just between me and you, to get things straight, so we will get on in the future. But remember, I am a T-rex and you don't want to see me angry. Understand?'

Alfie hiccupped, as if stifling a sob. 'Yes. I understand.'

'Good.'

Eva returned with a glass of milk which she gave to Alfie. She sensed an atmosphere between Alfie and Gary. 'Everything ok? I've searched all round and I cannot find any spiders. You can go back to bed now.'

Alfie sipped at the milk which left white liquid on his upper lip. 'Are you sure, as I won't be able to sleep?'

Gary now stared directly at Alfie, and spoke in a low, but determined voice. 'There are no spiders. Now go.'

Without another word, Alfie got slowly up off the sofa, careful not to spill the milk and muttered 'night' as he exited the room.

Eva looked at Gary. 'Gosh, you were pretty firm just then. He would normally try another few attempts at trying to stay down here.'

Gary pulled Eva back down next to him on the sofa. 'I am not used to being with kids, as you know, but all this negotiating nonsense only makes matter worse. A firm instruction seems to work best.'

CHAPTER TEN

July 2021

Memories of birthday celebrations when Niall was alive filled Eva's head with images of her husband, his blue-grey eyes that sparkled with happiness as he tended to the BBQ, wearing the personalised black apron she had bought him, with 'Hot Stuff' written in white. He truly was hot stuff, her Niall. Six feet two in height, medium build, curly brown hair that all added up to a handsome, physically fit man who she had been attracted to when they met, she aged twenty and he aged thirty. One of his favourite things was to do BBQs for family and friends. He had to be in charge of lighting up the BBQ, marinating the chicken, providing tasty vegetable options and cooking all foods to golden brown perfection. He would boast that his secret recipe for chicken marinade of dried chili, smoked paprika, Dijon mustard, runny honey and tomato ketchup had been passed down through the generations of males in the Brennan family. Considering that Niall's father did not know how to use a tin opener or how to boil an egg, the family used to smile when Niall referred to the cooking abilities of Brennan males. Niall's grandfather famously existed on a diet of sandwiches, ready meals and tinned products after his wife died, as he could not figure out how to turn on the oven.

Eva sat at a table, sipping white wine, and was enjoying a quiet moment alone after mingling with all her friends and family. The BBQ was arranged to celebrate her dad, Frank's, sixtieth birthday, so his brother and his best mate and their wives had been invited. She had also made it an excuse to invite her friends, including a few teaching colleagues and neighbours she got on well with.

She was happy to scan the garden and see people back together, laughing and drinking, after the long days of lockdown. There were no longer any legal restrictions on social contact and how many people could meet. She had invited about thirty guests, in an outdoor setting, which felt comfortable, especially for those still nervous about social interactions. The weather for July was quite disappointing with below average temperatures. At least today was mostly sunny though the temperature barely reached the high teens.

A gazebo had been erected in the garden, just in case of an unexpected rain shower. It was decorated with a mix of mid-blue and silver balloons for the birthday boy, denoting his sixty years on Planet Earth. Blue and silver bunting was hung around the gazebo, with tiny silver triangles noting 'Happy Birthday 60'. A large banner with 'Happy Birthday Frank' was secured to the table where the food had been placed, and which had now been eaten except for some bread rolls, the last spoonful's of salads in bowls, and a few crudities of celery and carrot sticks. Dirty paper plates, serviettes, and paper cups littered the table.

Watching her partner Gary, standing at the BBQ, tongs in hand, laughing and joking with their guests as he doled out cooked food did cause a physical ache to her gut as she missed Niall so much. She had previously mentioned to Gary about Niall's love of barbequing and he had since developed a zest for preparing and cooking the best food anyone had ever tasted. She had heard him asking some of the guests what they thought of the grilled steak, the marinaded chicken and the veggie kebabs and he beamed when the responses were favourable. She had been shocked to overhear him ask a couple of the men if the food tasted better than when Niall used to do it. She had noticed this thing with Gary lately, if Niall had done something well, Gary had to do it better. Niall liked to play seven-a-side football once a week with a group of friends. When she first met Gary, he had been dismissive of team sports, as he admitted to not being a team player. But now he had taken up football and started playing with Niall's team mates. To Eva, it was getting a bit creepy, as if Gary was trying to morph into Niall, and then trying to outperform him in everything he did. As she looked at Gary, as he charmed and entertained their guests, she wanted to wrestle the BBQ tongs out of his hands and tell him that he would never be as competent a cook as Niall. The fact that he was wearing Niall's 'Hot Stuff' apron wrenched at her heart, as he had no right to put that on, and after today she would wash it and hide it away.

The other issue, clouding Eva's mind, and slightly souring her enjoyment of the day, was that something had happened earlier between Alfie and Gary. She had entered the lounge area after hearing raised voices, mainly Gary's, but she had heard Alfie shout back at him. On asking what had been going on, she was initially met with a wall of silence. Gary was angry and Alfie's cheeks were red and he was in tears. Eva demanded to know from Gary why Alfie was crying. Gary explained that he had ordered Alfie to tidy up in the lounge, as the sofa was covered with crisp packets, biscuit wrappers and crisp crumbs, with dirty glasses left on the coffee table. According to Gary, when Alfie had not obeyed his instruction immediately, he had shouted at Alfie which made him cry. Eva was torn. She knew Alfie was a typical kid who tended to do things in his own time and Gary believed that children should do as they were told immediately. After what she now deemed to be the 'honeymoon period' of their life together as a family, Gary was now asserting his authority over Alfie. And Eva was starting to feel uncomfortable with this approach.

Eva had invited Gary to move in with her about a year ago, during the first lockdown, mainly as she felt lonely. Alfie was her precious boy, but ten-year-old boys were not known for their conversational skills. She missed the presence of an adult in the house with whom she could have stimulating chats. At first Alfie was delighted that Gary had moved in, they got on well, and spent some of their spare time playing computer games, leaving her time to read and unwind. The three of them spent family time together, playing board games, going for walks and watching films. Alfie seemed happier than at any time since his father died and Eva liked the idea of him having a stepfather. Mostly, the relationship between her partner and her son had progressed well but Eva was starting to notice tensions between them, and Gary's increasing lack of patience with Alfie.

'Hi, darling. You're looking a bit sad at your dad's party.' Tania sat down at the table next to her. 'What's up?' You have many reasons to be happy. It's the end of the lockdown restrictions, the start of the school holidays, and it's summer but somebody should tell the weather that. Love your dress but you do look a bit cold.'

Eva was wearing a sleeveless, blue dress with floral print, which fitted at the waist then flared to her knees, highlighting the curves on her slim figure. Her shoulder length, dark brown hair with auburn highlights, waved naturally around her face, accentuating the blueness of her eyes. 'Yes, I am a bit cold. I might pop inside and grab a white cardie. I was trying to stick it out and pretend that summer was really here.'

'I'd say it's bloody cold,' Tania commented. 'Can't wait to get on a plane and go somewhere warm with sandy beaches and hot men.'

Eva laughed. Her friend was always on the lookout for men, hot or otherwise. Whoever coined the phrase 'unlucky in love' must have had Tania in mind, as all her romantic encounters seemed to end quickly after a few months, with none really hitting a milestone of one year. Tania was outwardly confident and did have a good deal of success when attracting potential boyfriends. She was petite, slim, but she did have some hang-ups about her figure. She referred to it as a triangle, as she had small breasts and slightly wider hips, and she yearned for an hourglass shape. A savings fund was currently gaining pounds as she saved up for a 'boob' job. Tania insisted that this breast enhancement would be subtle and not an eye-popping, silicone balloon job last seen twenty years ago on reality TV programmes. The fund stood at approximately two thousand five hundred pounds and needed to be doubled to finance the operation. As Tania was hopeless at saving money, breast implants may finally be achieved on her fiftieth birthday.

Tania was more suitably dressed for the cool summer day, in skin tight blue jeans, white T-shirt and navy jacket with silver buttons and white sneakers kept her feet warm. 'I see your other half is playing to the gallery again, doing a full-on celebrity chef impression. I swear I heard him speaking in Italian just now as he piled your dad's plate with steak and sausage. Stupido idiota, as they say in Italy.'

Tania made no secret of the fact that she could not stand Gary and made it clear that Eva had lost her marbles when she asked him to move in with her. In March 2019, the two women had joined a well-known dating site and they had both received lots of male interest, though Eva did attract the lion's share. They had both, separately, liked Gary's profile of a good-looking, dark-haired man, and had both swiped right, and Eva ended up on a date. For three months, it was dates, dinners, walks, gifts, as Eva and Gary got on well, had good chemistry and he had showered her with affection. Then, it stopped. No texts, no calls, nada. Tania reckoned that she had been love-bombed, he'd gained her affection, slept with her, achieved his goal and was off. According to Tania, Eva had a lucky escape from someone who was a player and she was better off without him. But he returned to Eva, with a tale that a beloved aunt had died, and due to grief, and being the executor of his aunt's will, he didn't have time to stay in contact with Eva. Tania had found this all hard to believe and declared it was all a 'pile of shit'. Eva took him back and the relationship developed from that point onwards. Tania made it very clear to Eva that she did not trust him.

Eva finished the rest of the wine in her glass. 'I'll go and get us a bottle for a refill then I must go and mingle but I will admit feeling a little flat today. Not really in the party mood.'

As she got up to get the wine, Tania hissed. 'Oh my God, Andy has just arrived. Do I look ok? Is my makeup ok? I wish I had worn a dress now so he could get a glimpse of my legs. They are one of my best features.'

'Tania, do shut up,' Eva advised. Andy has got a girlfriend, as you well know, so is not going to be interested in you.'

'I know but if I'm clever I could arrange for her to be kidnapped and sent to Outer Mongolia which leaves the coast clear for me. Oh no, he's coming over to talk to you. I always say the wrong thing when he's near me. He must think I am a complete idiot.'

Eva grinned as her friend did seem to go all jelly-like and quivery whenever Andy was around. Her brain seemed to stop functioning so that gibberish came out of her mouth. 'Hm, last time you spoke to him you caught the tail end of a conversation and piped in without listening first, too eager to impress, me thinks.'

Tania pulled a face on recalling this encounter. 'You were talking about a principle of law, or something, and I chipped in and started wittering about my old college principal, Mr Sagebody, and his tendency to pass wind. At which point, Andy's lovely face looked completely bemused before he started to laugh uncontrollably. I have never been so embarrassed in my life.'

Eva shook her head, trying hard not to laugh at her friend's misfortune regarding Andy. Tania had declared undying love for Andy from the first moment she set eyes on him but her attempts at behaving as a sophisticated woman in front of him rarely happened. She was usually more Victoria Wood than Audrey Hepburn. 'Don't beat yourself up about it as he has got a great sense of humour. But I stress again, you know he has a girlfriend. You have seen Natasha on a number of occasions and she is absolutely stunning so no other female stands a chance with him.'

Tania sighed heavily. 'Yes, reluctantly, I will admit she is beautiful but I cannot get on with her as she is so up herself. I really do not know what he sees in her when he could have me.'

Eva laughed. 'Yes, Tania, you are lovely. But Natasha looks like a supermodel and I feel very frumpy when I am in her orbit.'

Tania nodded. 'I agree, as I feel the same but she is so unsociable and haughty. An iceberg. Anyway, it pains me to say this but I have always thought that he has a thing for you. Natasha can be quite mean to you at times and he always takes your side.

At this moment, Andy arrived at their table, 'Hi, Eva, Tania. Thanks, Eva, for inviting me. I'm glad I could make it and it's great to be back to a bit of normality after months on not seeing anyone except work colleagues. I've brought a red and white wine and have left them in the kitchen. I helped myself to a beer, I hope that's ok?'

'Really glad that you could come, Andy, and thanks for the wine,' Eva stated. 'If you want any food you had better be quick as its running out fast. There are still some burgers and sausages and that's all.'

Tania was now staring at Andy, mouth open, and not making any sound. She was making a good impersonation of a fish out of water, gasping for air.

Andy was looking handsome in dark blue slim fit jeans and mid-blue, short sleeved shirt which accentuated his toned arms. Eva recognised that he was a good-looking man but she liked him more as a kind friend and neighbour who had moved in next door to her in April 2018. They had hit it off straightaway, and would go around to each other's houses for tea and coffee, when their work schedules allowed. Eva asked, 'will Natasha be joining us?'

Natasha, the beautiful blonde who Andy had been dating for well over two years, and who had moved in with him at the start of last year's lockdown. Eva often wondered how many relationships were moved forward, in terms of co-habitation, as a result of Covid restrictions.

Tania tensed, and sat straighter in her seat, awaiting his answer. She crossed her fingers behind her back in the hope that the girlfriend would not be arriving. Natasha was not the easiest woman to get along with. She seemed to view herself as the most beautiful in all the land, so other women were dismissed as inferior, and not worth the effort of getting to know. It was obvious what Andy saw in her in terms of her looks but she did not have endearing personality traits. There was little to detect in terms of a sense of humour or caring nature towards fellow humans.

Andy confirmed that Natasha was on her way but had been delayed due to her job as an estate agent and a viewing that was running late. They had met, initially, as she was the agent involved in selling him his current house but they had only started dating after bumping into each other at a supermarket. 'Yeah, she'll be here soon. Hannah's on a sleepover at a friend's so we'll have the house to ourselves later.'

Eva smiled as she noticed Tania's facial expression as he mentioned having his house to himself without his teenage daughter cramping his style. Tania was probably fantasising about being alone with Andy and was almost swooning like a heroine in a nineteenth century novel. Pass the smelling salts.

Andy addressed Eva, 'where's Alfie? I hoped Hannah would want to come to the BBQ. But no, she had a better offer to try on clothes, makeup, and lust over Timothee Chalamet, who I've never heard of. I feel so old and I'm only thirty-six.' He groaned softly and pulled at his hair. 'I'm expecting grey hairs anytime soon.'

'Alfie's upstairs playing computer games with one of his school friends, Jai. They've been down for food so I doubt we'll see them again today. I'm just going inside to get a cardie or jacket as it isn't very warm out here. Be back in a minute.' This would give Tania a unique opportunity to speak to Andy as long as she did not remain tongue-tied or fail to engage her brain and come out with some ridiculous comment. No mention of college principal, Mr Sagebody, and his unfortunate wind problem.

As Eva entered the kitchen, Gary was looking in the fridge for the last of the food to be barbequed. Eva went over to see if she could assist him. 'Hi, Gary, how's it going? Have you nearly finished the grilling now?'

'Hi, darling, yes I have. I'll just cook these sausages and then that's it. Your father has such a capacity for sausages that we will have to stop calling him Frank and re-name him Frankfurter. I see a cholesterol-related heart attack happening in the near future,' Gary suggested.

Eva registered shock on her face as he said this as she could not bear the thought of something happening to her beloved dad. 'Oh, don't say that. He does try to cut down but does find it really difficult. He does like his food.'

Gary walked towards her carrying the last pack of sausages. He placed them on a kitchen unit and placed his arms around her. 'Well, I like you just the way you are, slim but not skinny, and with curves in the right places.' He ran his hand down her bottom to indicate his approval of its shapeliness before giving it a tiny nip. 'If you end up with a paunch like your dads, I will leave you instantly.'

She felt slightly hurt by this comment as most people gained and lost some weight throughout a relationship. Gary was very body focused in terms of women, and they were only rated as fit, if he decreed it. There were a couple of her friends that he could barely speak to, as they were overweight, and so held in contempt by Gary. It made Eva inwardly fume. Gary was reasonably good-looking but he was no Ryan Reynolds. His short brown hair was closely shaved at the sides but slightly receding at the front. His deep-set brown eyes and well-defined eyebrows gave him a permanent intense look which some people found intimidating without ever speaking to him. People did approach Gary with caution, so often they were surprised when he charmed them and made them laugh, if he was in a good mood. Gary in a bad mood was not so charming and overall the bad moods seemed to out number the good.

Eva eased out of Gary's grip. 'I'm just going upstairs to grab a cardigan as its not very warm out there.'

At this, Gary pulled a face and held tightly onto her wrist. 'Well, don't come down in something my grandmother would wear as I want you to look sexy and all mine.' He leaned in and kissed her lightly on the lips. 'Off you go, see you in a minute and you can do your share of the clearing up, as I've done all the cooking.'

Eva moved towards the door, out of the kitchen, doubly annoyed with Gary. His comments on her clothes, and what and what not to wear, were now getting a little tedious. He harped on about how she should look feminine but not dowdy. She should be subtly sexy but not obvious and sleazy. But all this was for his benefit only and if a man complimented her then she was at fault for encouraging it and Gary quickly showed his displeasure. Also, Gary's comment about the clearing up was a little grating as she had done most of the prep work for the BBQ including preparing the green salads, the coleslaw, the Greek salad, the carrots, celery and cucumber for the dips, the vegetables for the kebabs, and the breads.

She had put the meats ready on plates so that he merely had to put them on the BBQ.

Also, the earlier disagreement between Gary and Alfie was still troubling her. What had actually gone on? She would ask Alfie for his version of events when she went upstairs to get her cardie. Eva was now finding this relationship with Gary, which she felt had started out as equals, was now drifting towards him wanting to have the upper hand in all matters. His 'rules' were creeping in, as he was very keen on orderliness and routine, and tensions within the family were starting to exist. Initially, Eva went into this relationship as she wanted to re-create the warmth, love and security she had with Niall. She had missed having a loving partnership and the closeness of a sexual relationship. Naively, she had imagined that all men would be kind and caring like Niall who had never shouted at his son. If Alfie was acting up, Niall would address the issue in a calm manner and then praise positive behaviour. Recently, Gary decided that cajoling Alfie into doing things was too soft an approach and didn't work. His favoured tactic was to shout at Alfie and expect the boy to do as he was told immediately. If Eva stuck up for Alfie, she was shouted at too. Eva sighed loudly, as overall, life with Gary was beginning to grind her down.

CHAPTER ELEVEN

Aware of Gary's instruction not to wear a 'granny' cardigan, Eva put on a semi-fitted, white one that complemented her dress and would protect from the cool summer weather. She stood by the window for a few minutes before going back downstairs. She could hear the laughter of her family and friends as they mingled in the garden. She was pleased her to see her mum, Julia, talking to Niall's mum, Norah, and laughing together over some shared joke. Eva had loved Niall's parents from the time she first met them and they accepted their son's young, pregnant girlfriend, into the family.

Her dad was drinking his bitter ale from a glass, never a bottle, and speaking to Niall's dad Michael, and two of her male neighbours. The male voices carried up to the open window but she could not get the gist of the conversation. Knowing her dad, it would be a political or topical subject, where his firmly held views on Covid regulations, lockdowns, vaccines and post-Brexit issues were put to his current audience. She hoped that no arguments ensued. Her father's right of centre, intransigent views could rile some of her left-leaning friends but he got away with it as they all recognised that he was a well-meaning, friendly person. That did not stop her father frequently stating that he should be running the country in place of the current Prime Minister, and he would not waste public money re-decorating the Downing Street premises. Mum, Julia, would have to put up with the last incumbent's taste in wallpaper and carpeting.

Watching her parents, and Niall's parents all mixing together, enjoying the BBQ, it did puzzle her why she had never met Gary's family. From the little he had said about them, she discerned that his mother and sister lived down south and for reasons that were unclear, he had nothing to do with them. He had mentioned that his father had died a few years ago but he did not seem upset at his loss. When she pushed him for a little more information, he either clammed up or got annoyed, so now she tried to avoid raising the subject.

At that moment, Gary was talking to his friend from work, Simon, a man that Eva had met a few times but could not warm too. He was tall, skinny, balding, with penetrating eyes that seemed to follow you around but who rarely spoke to her, if she was in his company. Frankly, he gave her the creeps and she avoided him as much as possible.

Eva shook her head to clear her thoughts and reminded herself that she had guests that she should be attending to, however, she did want a quick word with Alfie before going downstairs. As she approached her son's bedroom, she could hear shouts, laughter and loud bangs as they played a computer game. She opened the door, and Alfie ignored her as he concentrated on driving a high-performance red car in a race against his best friend.

'Alfie, can I have a quick word?'

Go away, mum, or I'm going to lose this race.'

It won't take long, so please do as I ask.' Eva insisted. Reluctantly, Alfie put down the controller, and followed his mum into her bedroom, and she closed the door. 'Alfie, I just want to know what happened with Gary earlier, when you got upset.'

Alfie stood by the door, moving from one foot to the other, and avoiding eye contact with his mother. There was still a redness to his face, particularly on his left cheek, which Eva assumed was from the crying. Alfie stuttered, 'don't know. It was the usual thing of him shouting at me for nothing.'

Eva was annoyed at her son's reply. 'I don't think it was for nothing. He asked you to clear away your mess which was reasonable. I do think that you do take too long to do things, when asked. Try to do things when you are told to and then there would be no arguments.'

Alfie scowled; his lips pursed out in disapproval. 'But he's not my dad, so he's not the boss of me.'

Eva felt sorrowful as she looked at her son's angry, boyish face. 'No, he isn't your father and no one can replace him. But Gary lives here now, and life for all of us would be easier if you just tried a bit harder to tidy up after yourself, without having to be reminded more than once, ok.'

Alfie nodded, and as he was eager to return to his game, he conceded, 'ok, I'll try a bit harder, if I have to.'

Good. We all need to get on together when living in the same house. Off you go.'

Alfie turned quickly, and bounded out of the door, happy to escape the conversation.

At the dressing table, Eva re-applied her lipstick, ran a brush through her hair and sprayed on her perfume. She hurried out of the bedroom, down the stairs and back into the kitchen/dining area. Andy was there, helping himself to a second bottle of beer. 'Hi, hope you don't mind me getting this as the hostess seems to have disappeared.' He laughed as she said 'sorry'.

Yes, honestly, please help yourself. I will admit to being the world's worst host, today. I really can't get into the party vibe.'

As a hint of sorrow entered her eyes, Andy noted that she was looking sad and downbeat. 'Right, you sit down there on that stool and I will get you a glass of wine to perk you up. Then, you can tell me what's the matter.'

They had been friends for a while now and could each pick up on the other's mood. Andy had moved into the house next door, two months after Niall's death and had been a friend from when they first met. When at times the rawness of her grief was too much, and she had sat in her car crying, so not to upset Alfie, Andy had got her to go to his house, made her hot tea, offered a large, ongoing supply of tissues and allowed her to cry.

Eva sat down on a kitchen stool, as Andy filled a glass with dry white wine and brought it to her. He sat down on the stool, next to her, sipping from his bottled beer. 'What's making you so sad today? This should be a good day. It is summer, the end of lockdown and restrictions and you're having a party.'

Yes, I know and Tania said a similar thing. It has really got to me that Niall is not here doing the BBQ which was one of the things he loved. Gary has taken over the role of BBQ King and he's trying to gain support that his cooking is better than Niall's. He's even found Niall's 'Hot Stuff' apron and so that has really upset me. Plus, Gary and Alfie are not getting along too well. They seemed to get on ok last year during the first lockdown, with only a few flare ups, though I really do think that Gary does struggle having Alfie around. Now, Gary is slowly morphing into the stepdad role and calling Alfie out on things he is doing wrong, or not doing. Their relationship is starting to fracture and I'm stuck in the middle.'

Andy sighed heavily, wanting to be clear with Eva on his opinion of Gary. 'Well, as you know I am not Gary's biggest fan but I respect that you have chosen to be with him. I will say, though, that I do wonder about Gary's past as he is very evasive if you try and have a conversation about his family, past relationships, previous jobs and all that. You know me, as a cop I can't help but ask questions. Maybe I say that as an excuse because perhaps I am just nosy.' He grinned at her sheepishly, as she often commented that he asked questions of people, as if they were being interviewed by police under caution.

Eva laughed, a genuinely warm sound. 'Yes, you do have a tendency to put the spotlight on everyone, in a Columbo kind of way, so I'm always waiting for the killer question.'

He raised an eyebrow at this suggestion. 'So, you see me as some sort of shuffling detective in a crumpled, beige coat, do you? I am mortally offended. I rather see myself as one of The Sweeney, Jack Regan, and yearn for the old days when coppers could give the deserving pondlife who kill women and children a good thumping before extracting a full confession. Alas, today, it is the softly,

softly approach, and you have to listen politely to all the lies and excuses when you know they are guilty as sin.'

Well, Gary is certainly wary of you. He once commented that you do treat him bit like a suspect being interviewed for a crime. He said he expects to be fitted up for any unsolved murders in the area, if it were left to you.'

Andy laughed but then became more serious as he addressed Eva's worries regarding her son and her partner. 'Gary is probably just finding his feet within the relationship. I don't think it's easy to live with other people's children and he isn't a parent himself. Alfie is eleven, growing up fast, and he is moving towards the teenage years when they tend to be lazy and monosyllabic which can try the patience of a saint. See how it goes.'

Eva nodded. 'Yes, you're right. Everyone has to adjust when a new person moves in with an established family. There will be teething troubles. Perhaps I was a bit naïve to believe that it would go smoothly. I just sense that Alfie's not happy and it is my priority to protect my son.'

'Just remember, you are not alone. Hannah has adopted the role of argumentative teenager with unqualified zeal and she's not thirteen till November. To her, I am some crusty old codger who doesn't understand the modern world. I did think that being a young dad would make the teenage years easier but how wrong was I?'

Eva looked at him in a kindly way. 'I feel your pain. Teenage boys may be lazy, and don't talk much, but teenage girls seem to acquire a worldly knowledge, way beyond their years and are not afraid to let their views be known.'

Andy groaned. 'Kill me now, as she is twelve going on thirty. Also, her and Natasha do not get along. I am constantly trying to placate one or the other over some issue such as Hannah using Natasha's expensive makeup, perfume or clothes.'

'I suppose we should remember what we were like as teenagers. I did give my mum and dad some grief as I liked to do my own thing regardless of time. I could never grasp the concept of getting home at the designated time, so I did receive a few watches as gifts for birthdays and Christmas. What were you like?'

A broad, mischievous smiled flashed on his handsome face. 'Me, a perfect little soldier. Never caused my parents a moments worry. Homework done straightaway, cleared up after dinner, school bag packed for next day so no searching for missing books and off to bed early for plenty of sleep.'

Eva shook her head in disbelief. 'I'm sure I remember your lovely mother telling me you were a right pain in the bum when you were younger. Smoking, drinking, fighting and that was at Primary School.'

They both laughed loudly as the kitchen door opened, and Natasha, Andy's girlfriend, entered the room. She was dressed smartly in her work clothes of blue trouser suit and white blouse. Her silky, blonde hair was tied in a ponytail, and she walked towards them a vision of perfection, carefully applied makeup accentuating her deep brown eyes, sharp cheekbones, and a mouth enhanced by a coral lipstick. She seemed to approach in a haze of perfume, sweet floral scents dampened down by a hint of musk. Her eyes focused on Andy as she moved in to kiss him, placing herself between him and Eva. 'Hi, darling, sorry I'm late but the viewing took ages. It's a million-pound property just outside of Solihull and the prospective buyer had so many questions that I thought I'd be there forever. Still, that's it for the day now. Me and you can go and chill over a bottle of white wine. We must take full advantage of Hannah being away for the evening.'

Natasha was now sitting on Andy's lap, as she moved in to kiss him more possessively. Eva noted that Andy did not appear comfortable with this overt display of affection and he quickly ended the kiss.

Andy smiled at Eva to alleviate the awkwardness of the situation, as she was being ignored, and blocked by Natasha. He got off the stool, forcing Natasha to stand up. 'I haven't been here too long. I'll get you a glass of wine and we can go and mingle with Eva's guests. And I might grab a sausage in a bread roll before they all disappear.'

Natasha scowled at him as if being put to death by lethal injection would be a more favoured option. 'God, Andy, you must be joking. I've just been talking to really rich people about buying a million-pound, second home, and you want me to relax by mixing with a lot of provincial nobodies.'

Eva's eyes widened as she heard the brutal assessment of all the people she held dear to her. 'How rude. That's my family, friends and our neighbours that you've just disparaged. I would point out that you are only selling those properties not buying one. If we are not good enough for you then you had better go.'

Andy looked from one woman to the other, openly mortified by the hostile atmosphere between them.

Natasha now focused her eyes, laser-like on Eva. 'Well, you certainly fit right in here, in this neighbourhood. Boring little schoolteacher with your weird boyfriend, always trying to garner sympathy because your husband died.'

Andy shouted loudly at Natasha. 'That's enough. Eva does not deserve any of that and she has had an extremely tough time since losing her husband.'

This now riled Natasha further. 'Typical of you to take her side. You are my boyfriend and are supposed to stick up for me.'

'Not when you are behaving like a spoilt brat. Eva did not start this argument, you did.'

Natasha moved away from him and picked up her bag from the kitchen island. 'I don't know why I came. That millionaire guy wanted to take me for a drink, I wish I had gone.'

Andy nodded his head. 'I think we all wish you had. Just go home, I'll be there shortly.'

Natasha had been convinced that Andy would leave with her. She was now irritated that he was not intending to dance to her tune and follow her out the door. Without a further word, she flounced out of the kitchen.

This confrontation with Natasha had left Eva shocked and slightly shaky. 'That was really hostile, I am stunned.'

Andy noted the hurt in Eva's eyes and that she was closes to tears. 'I'm really sorry about that. I know that she can be difficult but that was totally out of order.'

'Yes, it was, but it wasn't you saying it. You had better go, as your loyalty is to her, not me. Thanks for coming and bringing the wine.'

'Ok. I'll speak to you soon.'

As Eva watched him depart, she was deeply regretting this BBQ, even if it was a celebration for her dear father.

CHAPTER TWELVE

Gary stood behind the BBQ, finalising the grilling of the remaining sausages on the two separate grills. All cooks must adhere to the rules of not mixing meats and vegetables on the same grills, so as not to offend those people who were vegetarian or vegan. What was it with sausages on BBQ's that made them really popular? Gary believed that he could bring out an endless supply of them and there would always be someone who could eat just one more. The coals still had enough heat to finish off this last batch of twelve, to fill the remaining bread rolls, and then that would be it.

As he started the cooking earlier, he had glanced around at the gathered group of Eva's family, friends and neighbours. Since moving in with Eva during lockdown last year, he had not really had chance to get to know people well. He thought he got on with Eva's father, Frank, who was friendly, but he did get tedious when started spouting on with his opinions on everything as if he were the font of all wisdom. Gary couldn't summon the energy for too much political debate as generally all politicians, in his opinion, were useless wankers. Eva's mother, Julia, was ok, but was quiet compared to her husband, so was as exciting to talk to as a potted plant. Eva's brother, Liam, and wife, Steph, were not interesting, with Steph trying too hard to be the perfect mother to her two over-indulged offspring, Marigold and Orion. Gary vowed that if he ever had a kid of his own, he would be in charge of it, and not it in charge of him, as many parents seemed to let happen these days.

It also narked Gary, that Eva's previous husband's parents, Michael and Norah, were always involved in any family gathering and so a physical reminder of their perfect son, Niall. Or Saint Niall, as Gary liked to call him. Niall, by all accounts, had been proficient at everything throughout his life. Top marks throughout school, A grade 'A' levels, University of Warwick, PGCE, Deputy Head at thirty, head at thirty-five. Niall had also been good-looking, physically fit, a loving husband, great dad, sociable with a wide group of friends, funny, kind to grannies and all round perfect human being. So perfect that the angels were missing him in heaven and he had been called back to join them at the age of thirty-eight. Gary noted that when Niall's parents and Eva's parents were together earlier, they swapped shared stories of Niall's successes and funny stories. As Gary doled out the perfectly cooked steaks, sausages and burgers on to their plates, he got a brief thank you, but it could have been anyone serving, so he felt like a cook at a burger bar.

As he attended to the sausages and burgers, to the observation of the gathered guests, he had been diligent in keeping the meat versions and vegetarian versions separate on different grills, and using different tongs. Both types of sausages looked identical, fat and golden when cooked, though the vegetarian ones lacked the sizzle of the pork ones. So, his little joke, had paid off as he handed veggie ones to the older carnivores, Frank, Eva's dad, and Michael, Niall's dad.

Frank, placed his sausage in a finger roll, smothered it with ketchup, and took a bite. 'Great, sausages, Gary. I think only Niall could cook them better than this.'

Michael agreed as he dipped his sausage into a smear of mustard on his plate. 'Yes, Frank, our Niall was the Master Chef, but these could pass muster, or in this case, pass mustard. Get it?'

Frank chuckled, 'I do get it, Michael. Good joke.'

Gary was now silently seething as he did all the work without the recognition. 'Bloody perfect Niall, isn't here to cook is he, as he's up in the sky, playing his harp, so bloody fucking useless,' he wanted to say. Nevertheless, the two older men did declare the sausages a hit as they returned for seconds, and in Frank's case, thirds. In a fit of pique, he served meat ones to Eva's sister-in-law, Steph, purely for being an annoying, save the polar bear zealot, who should be toughening up her wimpy son and brain box daughter, to save them from a life time of bullying. Flapping around the BBQ, asking a million questions about what was in each food, before her delicate offspring ate anything, did not help Gary's state of annoyance at the shortcomings of Eva's idiot family.

Where exactly was Eva? Gary noticed her earlier talking to their neighbour Andy, and felt his temper rise, hot and furious, as she laughed and joked with this man, and Eva's friend, Tania. Andy was strikingly good-looking, was physically fit, had a good sense of humour, was sociable and pleasant to everyone, and got on really well with Eva. All reasons why Gary loathed him. Gary, also, had reasons to be wary of Andy, a serving police officer, and detective inspector. Gary did not have an unblemished personal history, and he often felt nervous around Andy, as if the man was reading his mind to find out where the bodies were buried. Anytime spent in Andy's company made Gary feel as if he were being interviewed by MI5 for a breach of national security, as he felt Andy's blue eyes boring into his own, shifty brown ones.

The last sausage was given to Steph's weedy son, Orion, another veggie, but he was now chomping down on the best non-veggie sausage he had probably ever tasted. Gary smirked then picked up a stack of dirty dishes to take to the kitchen.

As Gary walked in, Andy was leaving and said a brief goodbye to him. 'Hi, Gary. Got to go, but thanks for the invite. Sorry I missed out on the food, it looked good.'

Gary placed the pile of assorted plates, bowls and dishes, next to the sink. He walked over to where Eva was seated on a kitchen stool. 'Where have you been, people keep saying that they haven't seen you?'

'I went to get my cardie, then I got talking to Andy, and just now I've had a sort of argument with Natasha. Apparently, I'm a boring little schoolteacher.' Eva decided not to enlighten him on Natasha's other comments particularly the one where she had referred to Gary as weird.

Gary assessed that Eva looked upset. 'Don't take any notice of her. She's a stuck-up princess who thinks she's better than the rest of us. I can't think why as her mother only lives in a terraced property in Coventry. Mixing with rich buyers is giving her ideas above her station. What did Andy make of it all?'

'I think he was really embarrassed and really shouted at her.'

'Natasha is a beautiful woman, but so are you, and I don't think she likes that you get on so well with her boyfriend. Having said that, nor do I.' Gary stood next to Eva and pulled her against his chest in a gesture of comfort.

Eva pushed back against him and glared up at him. 'I've told you before, Gary, Andy and I are just friends, that's all. I wish you'd stop reading more into it.'

'I note that you were laughing with him earlier, with Tania, and you always seem relaxed around him. I don't like it,' Gary stated.

Eva laughed, to try to disperse the tension she felt at this comment. 'Get over yourself, Gary, you are being ridiculous. I am really sick of jealous people, today.'

Anger now crossed Gary's face, his deep brown eyes locking on to hers. She felt his hand grab her hair, forcing her to look at him, as his mouth hovered near to hers. 'Are you mocking me, madam, because if you are you will soon regret it.' He yanked on her hair which hurt her scalp, then he clamped his mouth down on hers, in a possessive, brutal kiss.

Eva's felt stifled and unable to breathe, as she pushed him off her. 'Gary, please stop, you are hurting me,' she muttered as he pulled away. 'What's got into you?'

He moved away from her but the rage on his face still contorted his features. 'I'll tell you what's wrong with me. I've been out there, cooking for all your moronic family and friends, whilst listening to their memories of perfect fucking

Niall. You had gone missing so leaving me with all the work and then I find that you are in here talking to the cop. Well, I'm going for a rest, so you can go talk to the guests, and do all the clearing up.' With that he went out of the room.

****

Eva remained in shock, seated on a kitchen stool. Her head felt sore from the way he had tugged on her hair and her lips tingled from the harshness of the assault from his lips. What had just happened?

At that moment her mother and Norah walked in carrying more dirty plates and glasses. 'We've come to give you a hand with the clearing up, love. Haven't seen much of you, are you ok?'

Her mother went over to where she was seated and noted that her daughter looked upset. Her mother's arm went around Eva's shoulder when she saw the tears in her daughter's eyes.

Eva relaxed against her mum, happy to have the closeness from a person who truly loved her. Since Niall had died, and she and Alfie were left alone, she had felt adrift in the world, sailing a mighty ocean in a yacht, without the weight and security of her anchor, Niall. She loved Alfie with all her heart, and she had to be there to be his anchor in their new tempestuous world, but she frequently felt alone and lost.

She believed that she loved Gary but she had to recognise there was not the depth of feeling in her love for him as she had for Niall. She and Niall were always a united team, sharing their domestic responsibilities, agreeing how to raise their son and respecting each other's views in terms of how they saw the world. They did not always agree but did not let differences of opinion or arguments fester for too long. They weren't though, those type of couples that did everything together, so, each went out with different friends and pursued different interests. Eva was never going to take up seven-a-side football. Mostly, she missed their physical closeness. Not just the sex, though that had been hot and wanton at times, or slow and sensuous, but completely satisfying. That depth of passion was definitely missing with Gary. He was always keen to initiate sex and knew how to arouse her in a mechanical, follow the guidebook instructions sort of a way, but her body and soul felt empty afterwards. Gary always declared that she was the best lover he'd had so presumably she was putting in the effort for his satisfaction. He was now starting to take her down a new route of sexual adventure, in terms of the bedroom activities, and using handcuffs and blindfolds were his current focus. If she were honest, these shared experiences were not exactly pleasurable for her. To place yourself in someone else's control had to start from a place of trust and confidence in your partner. The use of restraints to secure her body was not enjoyable, as Gary relished the sense of control this gave him, and on a couple of occasions she felt fear not pleasure. She now wanted this type of activity to cease but telling Gary was not going to be easy.

But if Eva were to be completely honest with herself, she was starting to find living with Gary was becoming uncomfortable. At first, on moving in, he had been jokey, happy, undemanding and eager to share the chores and sensitively navigate his way into a new life with Eva and her son. Gary had no children of his own from two previous marriages, so having a child in the house was a new experience, and he respected Eva's style of parenting Alfie. This tentative approach by Gary paid off, and for the first year, they established a new family unit and all three seemed content with how things were progressing.

Six months ago, things began to change. Gary went from being patient with Alfie who was for ever misplacing items such as school books, shoes, phone, keys, and, then needed them as everyone was trying to leave the house for work or school. His bedroom had turned from a clean, tidy space to a junkyard for the collection of dirty plates, cups, pizza boxes, discarded clothes, sweet wrappers and empty cans. Eva did firmly tell her son to clear up the mess which he did after much reminding. She invoked penalties such as stopping computer game playing, or meeting friends, if he persistently failed to do as he was told. Gary now, more secure in his role of stepfather, had decided to adopt the shouting approach which only made Alfie more determined not to co-operate, so tensions within the household were common. When Alfie failed to comply with Gary's instructions, then Eva was also shouted at for being 'too soft' and 'too indulgent' as a mother. Eva would shout back to defend herself, and her son, but this was not really her style, and this had rarely happened with Niall.

Eva was starting to detect a nasty side to Gary that was slowly emerging like a butterfly emerging from its chrysalis but there was nothing beautiful here. Alfie was the main focus of his verbal attacks but Eva was starting to be on the receiving end of vocal put downs and censure. Today, his sharp pull on her hair, causing pain, and that jarring kiss, were something new, a physical correction to seemingly bring her into line. Eva was not naïve; she knew that this was inappropriate behaviour by Gary but she decided to see if it was a one-off episode. She hoped for the return of the happier, kinder Gary she had become fond of over last year.

****

Alfie lay in bed, pleased that the BBQ was over and that everyone had gone home, including his friend, Jai. He wanted a quiet time, away from family and friends, to think about what had gone on with Gary today. Alfie was getting used to Gary shouting at him, on almost a daily basis, if he made a mess, did not immediately comply with Gary's orders or if he argued back. Alfie generally got on well with all the adults in his life, his mother, grandparents and teachers. He knew that adults could get annoyed at their children from time to time and would shout occasionally if they thought a child was misbehaving. His mum, and dad, had rarely shouted at him and usually made him do the right thing by explaining clearly what was expected of him. Then they showed their disappointment if he failed to co-operate. Alfie didn't like to disappoint his mother so he did try his best to be good.

In terms of the adults in his life, Gary was a whole different ballgame. Alfie reckoned that shouting was Gary's default setting when it came to him. Gary never wasted time gently coaxing Alfie to do something or giving reasons why something should be done. Gary gave an instruction, or an order, and expected it to be obeyed immediately, and without question. Alfie thought this approach was all well and good if you were a sergeant major in the Army, addressing the lowest ranks, but Alfie knew he had no intention of joining the Army when he was older. Alfie hated being shouted at, it upset his tummy, made his cheeks blush, and caused tears to form in his eyes. It also made him angry and so he would deliberately ignore Gary until it became clear that he would have to do as he was told. Gary seemed to have different levels of anger; starting with the firm, louder voice, then the redness developing on his face, the hardness in his cold eyes, before the final low growl of fury when Alfie knew he must obey. Alfie felt like he was playing with a wolf, he could taunt it only so far until he was in danger of being eaten. At times, Alfie wanted to push Gary further, to prod the wolf with the stick until the low growl intensified, and white, snarling teeth were bared. Today, he had poked the stick in the wolf just that little bit too far. After repeatedly ignoring Gary's shouted order to tidy up the lounge, Alfie had shouted back at him.

Immediately, Alfie was tugged forward by the front of his shirt so that he was standing up close to Gary but prevented from moving away. Gary pulled Alfie upwards so that he was forced to stand on tiptoe. 'Right, you,' Gary snarled, white teeth showing and eyes blazing. 'I've had enough of your not listening to me. If I ask you to do something, you will do it, understand?'

Alfie's head was forced backwards, and he felt choked as the pressure of Gary's fingers on his shirt constricted his throat, and he could not find his voice. This lack of a response only inflamed Gary further. 'Understand?'

Alfie tried to nod, but could not, so he whispered, 'y-y-yesss.'

Gary responded by starting to release his grip on the boy's shirt. Alfie sighed with relief that this telling off was over but suddenly a slap landed on his left cheek. 'That's just a little incentive to help you remember to co-operate in the future, are we clear?'

Alfie immediately replied, 'yes, Gary.'

'Get on with the clearing up then,' Gary ordered, and stepped away as Alfie moved to pick up the food wrappings and glasses. 'And I don't want your mother finding out about this little chat, ok. It stays between us.'

Hours later, Alfie was pondering what had happened. The slap was not hard, but it had shocked him, as this was now an indication of what Gary was capable of. Alfie realised that life with Gary was not going to be easy.

CHAPTER THIRTEEN

September 2004

Gary Dawson watched as the two young women walked towards him. He drew in smoke from his cigarette, enjoying the sensation as it filled his lungs, making smoking one of his two greatest pleasures in life. His other pleasure, in human form, was walking towards him now. Long, dark hair, bouncing around her shoulders, laughter on her sweet red lips, a sparkle in the violet eyes as she knew he was focusing on her rounded breasts, in the soft white, T-shirt, as they bobbed enticingly, trying to free the confinement of her bra. A short denim mini skirt, emphasised her slim, golden legs, made more slender by the high heels she always wore. God, she was beautiful and Gary physically ached to caress her body and claim her fully, recollecting those clandestine encounters when he rammed into her.

As the girls stopped next to him, as he sat in the seating area outside the factory, he extinguished his cigarette before picking up his coffee mug. 'Hi, Claire, darling, hi, Lisa, lunchtime already, how the time flies when we're having fun.'

Claire bent down, and placed a shy kiss on his cheek, before taking a seat at his table. Lisa, also sat down, slyly smiling at Gary as she saw him ogling her legs.

Claire was Gary's wife of four months. She was uninteresting to look at and could blend into a crowd as easily as 'Where's Wally'. She was of medium height, with no shape to a straight up and down figure, and her facial features were small; soft blue eyes, button nose and petite mouth. Her greatest asset, and reason for Gary's interest, was that she worked in the Finance Section of RQ Car Screws and Bolts Ltd, and her father, Robert Quall, was the wealthy owner.

The girls unwrapped the sandwiches they had bought from the canteen and started to eat. Claire munched heartily on her cheese and pickle, hungry after four hours of number crunching. With long, red fingernails, Lisa picked at her tuna salad sandwich, discarding all the crust and most of the bread.

Gary regarded his wife with a scathing look as she devoured her sandwich. 'Claire, what have I told you about making healthy food choices. Eating all that cheese will make you fat. Why can't you pick healthier options, such as tuna, but without the mayonnaise.'

Claire sighed heavily. 'Sorry, Gary but I was really starving and this is my favourite.'

'Well, then don't blame me when I go off you and seek a divorce when you get as big as a whale. I suppose I should be hopeful that some of the fat went to your boobs, and made them bigger, but it all settles around your middle.'

Lisa laughed. 'Gary, stop being so unkind to your wife. She's not overweight.'

'Well, I wish she'd got your figure and I could squeeze it in bed every night.'

'Never going to happen, Gary, as you're not my type and you're married to my best friend.'

Gary smirked at Lisa's comment to his wife, her friend and work colleague. He didn't need to imagine the feel and taste of Lisa's body, as he was familiar with all its curves and erogenous zones, as he had screwed her in his car on many occasions, before and after meeting Claire. It was the only consolation for having to make love to the leaden lump who was his wife.

Poor Claire. Gary believed that Claire hoped that being married to him would make her happy as he was a handsome young man who was ambitious. She could not believe her luck when he asked her out, eighteen months ago. He made no secret of fancying Lisa, who didn't, but it was Claire he had asked to the works Christmas dance, where their relationship had started. They had now been married since May and were living in the house her father had helped them to buy. The very generous deposit meant they only had a small mortgage and Gary was already talking about buying a bigger property next year.

When he had started at the factory, in his role of Procurement Assistant, he spotted the boss's daughter and decided on a plan to further his ambition to acquire wealth quickly, without the tedium of working his way via the professional route of years of toil and night school. The Quall family were the owners of a profitable business of producing screws, nuts, bolts etc to the automotive industry and Gary conceived a way to fast-track his career development. It was already working as Daddy Quall was already considering him for the role of Procurement Manager when the current post holder retired, in a year's time.

A few hours later, Gary and Claire were home from work. Claire was preparing dinner as Gary lounged on the sofa, smoking and reading the newspaper. He could hear her banging pans and plates about in the kitchen but he was not hopeful of any culinary delights being presented for his dinner. The Quall's employed a housekeeper, so subsequently, Claire had little idea where the kitchen was in her parents' house and what went on inside.

Their open plan dining/living room area was pleasantly decorated with cream walls, and carpet, a mid-green sofa and two matching chairs, at one end of the room. A mixed green/cream chenille-style rug was in front of a fireplace with electric fire. An oblong, oak dining table and four chairs were at the other end of the room. Gary glanced up from his paper as Claire placed two plates on the table.

'Dinners here, Gary,' Claire informed him.

Gary got up from the sofa and walked to the table, adorned with green raffia placemats, to discover that tonight's dinner was fish fingers, mashed potato and garden peas. 'Another gastronomic feast, I see. Can't you actually cook anything that hasn't come out of a packet?'

Claire looked down at her plate, afraid to meet his eye. 'I peeled the potatoes, boiled them, and mashed them. I put butter in too.'

Sarcasm dripped off Gary's tongue, as honey off a comb. 'Wow. All them famous television chefs better watch out as you'll be stealing their crown. Trouble is you've been spoilt all your life and never had to learn the essentials of looking after a home. Well, you had better start to learn as I want to see an improvement on this. We will never be able to invite anyone over for dinner if you can't cook.'

Claire started to eat her meal, scooping mashed potato on to her fork. 'I believe, Gary, that as many women and men now both work full-time, there are plenty of men who do the vast majority of the cooking.'

'I am not one of them. Why buy a dog and bark yourself?' He cut into a fish finger and lifted it to his mouth with little enthusiasm. 'This married life with you is going to be a struggle for me. I've yet to discover something you can actually do, as you can't cook, you're abysmal at cleaning, washing and ironing. You are not great company, in that you lack a sense of humour, and really have no grasp on what goes on in the world. You've lived in your family bubble too long and you've never had to strive for anything as it was all done for you.'

Claire continued to eat her meal, her eyes focused on her plate, and away from the gaze of her husband. 'I'm sorry, Gary, I am trying to learn but it is all a bit new to me. I was thinking I might ask Janet over to give me some pointers on what to do.'

Gary's hand slammed down hard on the table, making Claire jump. 'Don't you dare bloody show me up by asking your parent's housekeeper to come and help out. I expect you to figure it all out.' He took hold of left hand, and pinched the skin on top of her hand, making her cry out. 'You had better start to learn fast. I want to build up a new list of potential suppliers to impress your old man and a way to do that is through holding dinner parties. Dinner parties where the little wifey provides the food.'

Claire felt tears well in her eyes as she concentrated on finishing her meal. 'I will try to learn, I promise.'

Gary's Nokia phone rang and he got up from the chair, went to the sofa, and picked up the phone. 'Hello, yes.' Pause. 'Ok, I'll see you in the pub in fifteen minutes.' He turned to look at Claire. 'Right, that was Simon, he wants to meet for a pint in the Crown, so I'm off. Tidy up here and then iron my shirts for the rest of the week.'

Clare did not respond as he walked towards the door and Gary ignored her, pleased to be spending time out of the house.

....

Thirty minutes later, Gary's black VW Golf was parked up a country lane three miles from his home. The windows of the car were steamed up on the inside, as Gary and Lisa's hot, steamy breath from their exertions clouded the car's windows. Gary eased himself out of her, as she lay beneath him, soft breasts released from the captivity of a T-shirt and a bra, and were now moist from the touch of his mouth. The back seat was always cramped but he always managed a prolonged, pounding of her body as she moaned in ecstasy and quivered in her orgasm. Now, he leaned on his elbow, to take in the details of her face, as her breathing steadied, and her luscious mouth remained open, awaiting further attention from his lips. There was a full moon this night which illuminated the dark sky, and as he gazed into her violet eyes, they were as two deep, dark caverns, drawing him down into a black hole of depravity and sin. He could remain here for the rest of his life with this woman and know the rapture of sexual bliss.

His mind briefly drifted to Claire. He was her first lover and she had no idea how to move and respond in a sexual way. His attempts at trying to arouse her were futile as she did not seem to like any physical contact and brushed his hands away when she could. He did persist in consummating the marriage. He did not want any excuse for it to be annulled, in the future, if things didn't work out. But things were certainly going to work out. The Plan was simple, court Claire, the boss's plain daughter, marry her, produce a child and tie himself to the Quall family, and their money until boring Claire was helped to disappear from his life, forever.

Lisa now started to move to sit up in the car but before he allowed her to, his lips claimed hers, before his mouth travelled downwards to devour her nipples. Lisa moaned but pushed him off. 'No, Gary, not again, as I must get home. I told mum I wouldn't be long. She's starting to get suspicious as to what I'm doing.

I have told her I am seeing a bloke called Jamie but mum's puzzled as to why I don't stay out very long. We are going to have to go on some proper dates soon, you know, for at least three hours, before we come here to shag. Make it all seem more legit. I think she suspects I'm seeing you and she will not approve.'

As she sat up on the back seat of the car and pulled her skirt down, Gary tickled his fingers along her thighs. 'What's this Jamie like, then? Handsome? Good in bed?'

'No, I said he's some tosser I met in the Crown and likes to fuck in the back of his dirty old van. Really bad at it he is. Can't keep up an erection and wheezes like a steam train.'

Gary laughed loudly. 'If you've told your mother that load of garbage, she'll think your new lover is ninety years old with asthma, in need of Viagra.' He pinched her thigh playfully. 'I don't need Viagra when I'm with you, sweetheart. You're all I need to make me as hard as rock. Anyway, we had better go. The missus will be waiting and we are trying for a baby, so I will need to perform, again.'

Lisa scowled, as she did not like to think of him with her friend. 'Honestly, Gary I wished you'd never thought of this plan to marry her and have a kid. It's all going to take too long before you are back with me properly. I'm not jealous, as I know you don't fancy her, but this making out in the car is not exactly luxurious.'

'Don't worry, it will all work out. Trust me. You are lucky, you don't have to go back there and try to raise some enthusiasm for shagging her. She has all the vitality of a dead body.' Gary sighed, acknowledging that his choice of Clare for a wife was starting to prove profitable in terms of career development and acquiring personal wealth but having her as a wife was testing his endurance to the maximum. Unattractive, un-sexy, dim-witted and lazy were at the top of the list of her many faults and the Quall family owed Gary for taking her on. Owed him big time.

CHAPTER FOURTEEN

August 2021

As the plane landed in Menorca, Eva felt elated that they were able to resume foreign travel after the last eighteen months of frequent lockdowns and restrictions. Gary, Alfie and herself had visited Dorset, and stayed in a superior caravan in Lyme Regis, during mid-August 2020, and the weather had been generally mild, with temperatures in the high teens and one day of rain. UK holidays are nothing without a rain shower to remind us all of where we are. Alfie had loved the caravan, which was ultra-modern, and spacious, and she was grateful to get away as millions couldn't, but it still didn't feel like a holiday. No wall-to-wall sunshine guaranteed, no turquoise seas, no outside restaurants serving fresh fish and dry white wine, no warm evenings eating tapas at a restaurant in a plaza of a small Spanish town. On the plus side, no mosquitos or sunburn. Eva, and Alfie, had to be careful in the strong Mediterranean sun, as with their fair skins they burnt easily, and a lobster-red face and limbs were not a good look.

In Menorca, they opted for a two-bedroom apartment, in a modern complex, in the resort of Santo Tomas. The apartment had a kitchen/lounge area, two bedrooms, a modern bathroom with power shower, and balcony with sea view. It was decorated pleasantly, with cream walls, and blue the dominant colour in the furnishings, sofas, rugs, and paintings, with cushions in patterned creams and blues. The apartment was on a complex with others, and as breakfast was included, Eva stuck to her policy on holiday of not preparing any meals, so lunch and dinner was eaten in local restaurants. Alfie loved to be in the swimming pool as much as possible, smothered in factor 50 sun cream, and a lot of time was spent around the pool area. By day two, a routine was in place. Get up for a buffet breakfast, morning spent at the pool, a light lunch at the pool bar, an afternoon of activities if anyone was inclined, relaxing dinner at a local restaurant and a last drink at the bar before retiring to their room. Today, Eva was relaxing on a sunbed, under a parasol, trying to read a novel about a lottery syndicate of close friends who hit the jackpot, and won millions, and how the win shattered their group. Alfie was in the pool, having made friends with a boy of a similar age from another family, and Gary had disappeared for a walk into the local town. Eva was wearing a flattering light green, swimming costume, with V-neck to accentuate her breasts and which gave definition to her legs which were a pleasing shade of light gold, and not scorching red, as she had been careful not to stay too long in the hot sun. The upside of being a school teacher was that she had six weeks holiday in July and August. The downside was that holidays abroad were often spent in the hottest parts of Europe that did not favour her fair complexion. Her hair, which could easily turn to frizz, from a combination of sun and chlorinated pool water, was currently lightly waved and glossy, having been tamed by the purchase of expensive hair masks and conditioners in the UK.

While keeping an eye on Alfie, Eva sipped on a Mocktail Mojito which was a refreshing combination of lime, mint, sparkling water and plenty of ice. She finished the drink and placed the glass on the small side table next to her sunbed. She resumed reading her book and was feeling perfectly content, without Gary's presence.

'Hola, senorita, would you like another drink?'

Eva blinked slightly as she looked up from the book, to find an extremely handsome man leaning over her. He was tall, with well-cut thick black hair, brown eyes and neatly trimmed beard. Feeling the intensity of his gaze on her face, she blushed slightly. 'Yes, ok, I will have another mojito, a real one this time.' She had not intended to have an alcoholic drink until the evening but what the heck, she was on holiday, after all.'

'No problem, senorita, I will be right back.' As he picked up the empty glass from the table, she swore that he winked at her.

At this moment, Eva wished that her friend Tania were here so they could have a giggle about dishy Spanish waiters and reminisce about holidays in their late teens, when men like that, were the sole purpose for going on holiday. Having married Niall so young, and having Alfie, stopped her young, free and single days in their tracks at an early age, and a small part of her did hanker after those carefree days of love and lust in the sun.

'Here you are, bella dama, a special mojito just for you.' He placed the drink on the table. 'Are you enjoying your holiday in Menorca?' He lingered by her sunbed, his eyes concentrating on her face.

'Yes, thanks, we got here two days ago. It's lovely to be able to go abroad again after all the lockdown restrictions.'

'We are happy to have you Brits back after all the problems last year. It's good to try to return to a normal life.'

'We are happy to be able to come for the sun and the sea. English summers can be very changeable.'

He nodded in agreement. 'Yes, I came to your country, in August, a few years ago and it was very cold, so I got, how do you say, frost bite.'

Eva laughed, noticing the sparkle in his deep brown eyes. 'You came for one of our good summers. We don't build sandcastles on the beach in England, in summer, we build igloos.'

'Anyway, I love your beautiful country but I will suggest that your weather can be terrible. Enjoy your drink and let me know if you want another.'

As he departed, Alfie ran up and picked up his towel to dry himself with. 'Mum, can I go and play pool with Joseph?' He rubbed himself with the towel and Eva helped him to pat his back dry. She examined him for signs of sunburn, as he had been in the swimming pool, for thirty minutes. 'Yes, it a good idea to come out of the swimming pool now and put on your shorts and T-shirt. I'll stay here, so find me after a couple of games, ok? And, you will need to re-apply sun cream before you go back in the swimming pool.'

As he started to put on his shorts, Gary came to join them and sat on the adjacent sunbed. 'Where's he off to?'

'He's going to play pool with a boy he's made friends with.' Eva leaned over to pick up her bag, retrieved her purse and gave Alfie some Euro coins. 'This should be enough, for now.'

Alfie quickly put on his flip flops and took the money from his mother. 'Thanks, Mum. Gary, she's gone off you as I saw one of the waiters chatting her up, he was talking to her for ages.' Alfie left, unaware that his comment was a hand grenade thrown into a market place, as Gary's face turned to anger.

'What's going on with the waiter?'

'Nothing, we were just discussing the English weather in summer, that's all. A topic that is a constant source of amusement to anyone from hot countries. He was just being friendly.'

'Well, I don't like you talking to men, especially not the waiters. They are all flashing brown eyes, and dazzling white teeth, smiling at the women.'

'Don't worry about it, Gary, this one had wonky eyes and crooked teeth, so you have nothing to worry about with your handsome looks.' Now, ignoring him she picked up her book, and dived back into the story of friendship and betrayal.

Gary eyed Eva suspiciously, as he was unsure that she was joking or not.

Later that evening, they had a dinner of paella for Eva, Spanish style pork chops for Gary, pizza for Alfie, at a beautiful beach front restaurant. They strolled back to apartment block, where Alfie found his friend Joseph, and the two boys went off to the games area to play air-hockey. As Eva and Gary sat at table, by the pool, the waiter from earlier came to take their order.

His eyes focused solely on Eva. 'Hola, senorita, nice to see you again. Another mojito?'

The black, sleeveless dress with floral design of orange and cream, suited Eva to perfection, and flattered her honey-toned skin and emphasised the auburn highlights in her brown hair. The dress fitted at the waist and finished just above the knee, and, as she was seated, smooth thigh was revealed and noted by the handsome waiter. 'No cocktails, this time. I'll have a large glass of dry white wine, thanks.'

Reluctantly, the waiter turned his gaze on an unsmiling Gary. 'I'll have a beer.' It was said brusquely, with no please or thank you. Eva presumed that the waiter would slip away quickly to avoid Gary's scowling expression but he seemed to linger to give Eva one last smile.

As he went to get the drinks, Gary was fuming, a kettle full of steam about to erupt from his ears. But though his anger had initially erupted at the cocky waiter, it was now a hot, scalding liquid hosing down on Eva. 'So, that's the waiter from earlier, is it? The one with the wonky eyes and the crooked teeth. His teeth are so straight and white he could appear in a toothpaste commercial. And, the eyes aren't so wonky when they're looking up your skirt.'

The waiter returned with the drinks and placed them on the table. Eva said thank you whilst Gary remained silent.

The waiter gave Eva a lingering smile. 'No problem, bella dama.' But now sensing Gary's animosity, he quickly departed to collect glasses at the nearby table.

Gary picked up his bottled beer and clasped the bottle rim between his teeth as if he were going to bite it off. 'Drink that up and we'll go and get Alfie. I'm not sitting here being disrespected by my girlfriend who is flirting with one of the waiting staff.'

Shrugging her shoulders, Eva sighed, 'I'm not drinking this quickly as I will get drunk. Relax, enjoy your beer and the lovely warm evening.'

The annoyance on his face was now apparent, as his eyebrows dipped inwards and his brow furrowed. He slammed the bottle down onto the table and got up from his seat. 'I'm going back to the room. You can bring Alfie.' At that he was gone.

Eva picked up her wine and sipped the cool drink, determined not to do as Gary was expecting, that is, immediately follow him. They had only just started this holiday and it was beginning to get increasingly difficult to read Gary's changing moods. Yesterday, on day one, he was happy and friendly, making Alfie laugh as they splashed about in the pool and telling her she was amazing as they shared a late evening glass of wine on the balcony before bed. Today, he must have got out of bed on the 'wrong side' as his mood switched between uncommunicative and narky. His jealousy of other men, which she could be aware of at home, particularly over Andy, was more noticeable here if any male looked her way. Gary, on the other hand, was free to ogle, salivate and pass comment on any pretty, young girl that caught his eye.

'Senorita, you are alone again, this should not be,' the waiter commented.

Eva was aware of the man's intense gaze upon her and she sipped nervously at her drink, to try to deflect him from staring at her.

'I am Antonio and I am finishing work in about ten minutes. Would you like to come with me for a drink at a local bar. It is quite lively, with a guitarist playing, and we could have some fun. You always look quite sad, I think.'

This offer of drinks and fun with this gorgeous man was a very tempting proposition, as Gary's erratic moods were starting to get her down, not just on this holiday but at home as well. As Eva looked at Antonio, her younger self would have considered that she had been extremely lucky to meet such a man and she would have had no doubts about accepting his offer. Her older, sensible self, whispered in her ear not to do it. 'Thanks, Antonio, for your invitation, but I am on holiday with my boyfriend and son, so it is not possible.'

'I am sorry that you cannot join me. Goodnight, senorita.'

As he said this, Alfie rushed up, halting any further discussion. 'Mum, mum, can I have some more money for the air-hockey?'

'No, Alfie, it's time to go back to our room now. Say goodnight to Joseph.'

'Night, Joseph. See you tomorrow.' Alfie waved at his new friend before he wandered off with his parents. 'Does that waiter fancy you, mum? He keeps coming over to talking to you.'

'No, Alfie, he doesn't. He is just being friendly and doing his job. Don't say anything about him to Gary as it makes him annoyed.'

Alfie's face looked concerned. 'I won't mum. I don't like Gary when he gets angry as he can be quite scary.'

As they entered the apartment, Eva and Alfie, found Gary lying on the sofa, watching TV, drinking a whisky, and he ignored them as they walked in. Alfie rushed through to go to his room shouting, 'night' to Gary. Eva reminded him to brush his teeth.

She then went over to the fridge to remove a bottle of water, took a glass from a cupboard, and filled it with the chilled liquid. 'Is there anything I can get you, Gary?' she asked.

'Yeah, an apology for being a bitch,' he replied. 'But you won't find it in the fridge. Come over here.'

Eva drank from the glass as she went to sit on the sofa next to Gary. He sat up so that she could sit down. He took the glass out of her hand and placed it on a coffee table. He, then, cupped his hand under her chin, forcing her to look at his face. 'You are a pretty woman, Eva, and men find you attractive but I think we need to be clear on what I expect now that we are a couple.' He paused to survey her face, a mixture of anxiety and puzzlement registering in her blue eyes. 'I expect that if a man speaks to you, and chats you up, then you will firmly make it clear that you are not available. I do not like to be disrespected and made to look like the loser who is with a woman that puts out for any man.'

Uncomfortable with Gary's fingers digging into her chin, Eva tried to pull away from him but he restricted her movement. 'Gary, there is nothing going on between me and the waiter. I have not encouraged him but I am not going to be rude to people just to please you.'

'Well, I am not happy. You have made a fool of me and I am now going to make sure that it doesn't happen again in the future.'

A defiance now apparent in her eyes, she jerked her head out of his grasp. He placed his left arm around her shoulder, pulling her into him, strong fingers digging into the top of her left arm. He then pushed her roughly down onto the sofa and was leaning over her, his weight anchoring her body so she could not move. For a few seconds he stared into her eyes, not speaking, but indicating the presence of his anger by the coldness in his brown, almost soulless eyes. Eva trembled, not liking the feeling of being restricted and scrutinised, as if she were about to be supper for a boa constrictor. In the next moment, Gary brought his right hand down hard on Eva's left cheek. The shock of the attack caused her to cry out, which she instantly regretted, as she didn't want Alfie to hear.

Gary then yanked on her hair, to re-focus her eyes on his face. Anger still distorted his facial features and his mouth hovered near hers, as his whisky breath assailed her nostrils and his spittle spotted her lips. 'That should teach you not to make a fool of me with Spanish waiters. Understand?'

Tears formed in her eyes but she was too traumatised to answer. Her failure to speak was now inflaming him more and a second slap from his right hand slammed into her face. 'Understand?'

As shudders racked through her body, she started to sob, but she did manage to respond with shaking breath. 'Y-y-es, Gary.'

'Good, I'm glad that's clear. We can now enjoy our holiday with you behaving appropriately. Now go to our room and I'll be in shortly.'

He took his weight off her so that she could move and Eva slowly got off the sofa, still too much in shock to co-ordinate her body. Her legs felt heavy and leaden as she tried to stand on them. She struggled forward, desperate to leave the area he was in, but the trauma was paralysing her body and mind. The only sensation she could feel was the stinging of her cheek where he had battered her face.

Getting into the bedroom, she collapsed face down on the bed. The horror of what had just occurred stunned her. Gary, the man who apparently loved her, and the man she had grown to love, had assaulted her. She allowed hot, scalding tears to fall but cried into her pillow to muffle the noise of her sobbing in case Alfie was listening. She felt utterly alone, without family and friends, with a child to protect, in a foreign country with a language she could not speak. Alone, with a man who did not love her, as this attack was a strong indication that he did not do love, only control.

CHAPTER FIFTEEN

Next morning, Eva woke early after a long night where she did not sleep, except for a few fitful episodes of light dozing. She mostly lay awake, not daring to move, and listening to Gary as he breathed evenly in blissful sleep, except for the odd period of snoring. Often, when he snored, she would gently dig him in his side with her elbow, which would cause him to grunt and then stop. This night she did not nudge him, or touch him, as she clung to the edge of the bed as far away from him as possible.

As dawn broke, she eased out of bed, and went into the kitchen area to make a coffee, a hot, caffeinated drink to rouse her body and brain as she tried to make sense of what happened. Sitting out on the balcony, she looked out at the pale blue sea, as the bright sun, a yellow globe emerging from the water, created a vivid orange and purple glow in the sky. It was a sight of sheer beauty which would normally make her heart sing but today her heart was flat and worn, a pump barely able to keep the blood flowing in her injured body.

As she grasped the coffee mug, allowing the steam of the drink to heat her cold hands, she thought about all the repercussions of what Gary had done. In that instant, Gary had changed from a man she thought she knew, who was generally, kind, caring and funny, into a man she did not know. If she were honest with herself, she had begun to notice some behaviours towards her she did not like in recent months. He was definitely more prone to anger and keener to take control of the household. He was becoming more demanding of Alfie and muttering more about the importance of discipline with children. The incident at the BBQ, when he had sharply pulled her hair, had been the first time he had been physically hurtful to her, and this had now escalated to what he had done last night.

She knew that not all her family and friends had taken to Gary. Her dad thought he was ok and could be relied upon for a bit of political jousting over favoured topics including Covid, Brexit, the EU and any topical issue at the time. Her mother, who only saw good in everyone, felt sorry for him, as she recognised that he had a hard act to follow, as they all fondly remembered Niall. Tania made it known to Eva that she did not like Gary but she did try to tone down her dislike of him when other people were around. As Eva frequently joked, Andy viewed Gary as a person of interest in a crime, yet to be decided, but approached him as a police officer, keeping an open mind, but proceeding cautiously as the investigation was on-going. Other friends and family who had met Gary, only briefly, because of lockdown restrictions, were not going to be starting up a fan club for him any time soon. Her brother, Liam, summed it up about Gary, 'creepy', in a Norman Bates way, 'and has anyone seen his mother?'

So, what should she do? Eva was an educated woman, a school teacher, and had been aware of issues of domestic violence with reference to some of her pupils, in the past. Like most people, she found it hard to imagine how any woman would stay with a man who verbally or physically abused her. But rationally, she knew that it was never as simple as it seemed to end this type of relationship. To end it with Gary would be relatively easy in some ways, as they were not married, she owned the house she lived in, and they had no children. But she guessed that ending things with Gary would not be straightforward. He was a man who liked things on his terms, to be in control, call the shots, and definitely would not want to be humiliated by a woman. For now, all she could do was see out the remaining days of the holiday and make a decision once she got home.

Mid-afternoon, Eva was once again reclining on a sunbed, under an umbrella, trying to continue reading her novel. The area of her face where Gary had slapped her remained red, with a shading of red/purple bruising under the corner of her left eye, where his finger had caught her. She had plastered concealer and foundation over the area, and wore sunglasses the whole time, except when reading the book. Alfie had gotten annoyed with her earlier as she had refused to get in the swimming pool with him but she couldn't risk other people noticing the markings on her face, once the makeup had been washed away by the pool water. Luckily, Joseph had appeared and they were now playing happily, floating around on inflatable lilos, splashing and trying to dunk each other. Gary was once again off on a walk to the next town of Son Bou, an hour and a half walking distance away. He had continued to act moodily with her this morning, at the breakfast buffet, where he had insisted on a full breakfast of cereal, scrambled eggs, toast, fruit and yoghurt. Eva had approached the buffet cautiously, only taking items when there was no one next to her, so had hurriedly gathered fresh bread, butter and honey, and a coffee, before rushing back to her seat. She then sat with her back to the room, at a table facing out to sea. She could not wear sunglasses inside as it was deemed pretentious, an affectation, only just about carried off by A list actors and rock stars.

Alfie, munching on his crunchy nut cereal, did notice that there was a puffiness and redness to her eye, despite the concealer. 'Mum, what have you done to your eye, it looks a bit red?'

Eva smiled at him, eager to down play it, so as not to alarm him. 'Yes, I was opening a cupboard door in the kitchen and caught the corner on my face. Clumsy really.' She sighed, doing the thing that abused women had done for centuries, covering up the cause of their injury. Was it to protect themselves, the man, or the shame of the situation? She knew she was lying to protect Alfie as she didn't want to upset or frighten him. He had been through too much in his young life.

Gary did look a little embarrassed listening to this conversation. 'Yes, she is a bit clumsy, as I always tell her. Cut her finger on the tin opener last week when making tuna sandwiches, so it was a good job I'm around with my First Aider training and supply of plasters.'

Alfie nodded in agreement. 'Dad always used to say she could damage herself in a padded room. What's a padded room?'

Eva stated, 'a room where the walls and floor are covered in soft materials to stop someone hurting themselves perhaps in a hospital for patients with mental health issues.' Explaining this to Alfie was getting awkward so she hoped there would be no more questions. The mention of his dad, Niall, felt like a physical shock to Eva, as she remembered her loving husband. The ache in her stomach of missing him, was as an actual physical blow, a swinging wrecking ball shattering her insides.

As Eva now sat by the pool, she was finding it difficult to focus on the book, as her mind kept drifting back to what occurred last night. She lightly touched her cheek and it felt delicate and sore to the touch. She found it hard to understand how anyone could inflict pain on another human being, especially on those they professed to love. That was the key question, did Gary actually love her?

'Buenas tardes, senorita. How are you today?' Antonio, the waiter was now standing beside her sun lounger, his lovely brown eyes smiling down at her, delicate creases forming at the sides of his eyes. 'Can I get you a mojito, a mocktail or the real deal?'

Eva tried her best not to catch his eye, so she focused her eyes away from him and looked down at her book. 'It's, ok, thanks. I'm just drinking water today and I have a bottle here. She pointed at the bottle of water on the side table in case he needed proof of her temporary sobriety.

'Too many wines last night, eh?' he teased, 'but I can get the bartender to make you his special hangover cure cocktail, if you wish?'

She looked directly at him, to give a reproachful stare so that he would not make assumptions about a non-existent hangover. 'I will point out that I am not hungover, just not wanting to drink alcohol too early.'

He suddenly looked around the pool area and then, to her utter surprise, he sat down on the edge of her sun lounger. 'I do not wish to be nosy but what happened to your face?'

Eva went to pick up the sunglasses but realised that it was too late to hide the mark on her face. 'Oh, nothing. I just caught it on the corner of a door in the kitchen.'

He carefully considered what she had said. 'Yes, these doors are very dangerous, you must watch out for them.' He then lightly touched her hand. 'I do not always work as a waiter, as I am studying to be a el abogado, a solicitor. We do a total of five years study at university and I have just finished my Master's degree in access to Legal Practice. I have studied domestic abuse as part of a degree module, and know that here in Spain, eighty percent of victims do not complain. It will be roughly the same in the UK.'

'Honestly, I did knock my face with the kitchen cupboard door.' Eva blushed slightly while saying this, she was not good at lying. 'I was a little clumsy, that's all. It looks worse than it is.'

'I will believe you, Senorita, if that is what you want me to do. I do not know how many times you have had such an accident,' he hesitated here to emphasis that accident may not be the right word to describe what had occurred, 'but once a line has been crossed; these things do not stop.'

Eva felt the intensity of his gaze on her and admitted defeat. 'I know what you are saying and you are right. I will be re-evaluating things when I get home and decide what to do. I have got the safety and welfare of my son to consider.'

He stood up off the sun lounger to resume his duties. 'You must also protect yourself. Anyway, if I get to be a judge, men who commit acts of violence against women will get the most severe sentences.'

Later that evening, Eva was pleased that Gary had stayed out of her way for most of the day. For their evening meal, they went to an Italian restaurant and Gary spent his time teasing Alfie, and making him laugh. He avoided looking at Eva as much as possible but was attentive over small things; ensuring her glass was topped up with wine, insisted that she had the sea view at the restaurant table and hassled the waiter to light the T-light candle on the table as darkness fell.

As they walked back to their apartment, he tried to hold her hand but she pulled away. The air was warm, there was the smell of night-scented jasmine and the sound of cicadas, all adding to the exotic beauty of their surroundings.

Gary now walked with Alfie, as Eva lagged behind them. 'Do you hear those clicking noises, Alfie?'

'Yes, it is some sort of insect, isn't it? I think they sound really cool.'

'They are called cicadas and they are the world's largest insects.' He took out his phone and started to search for information on cicadas, 'it says that the male cicadas have sound boxes in their abdomens which expand and contract a membrane called a tymbal, to make the clicking noises, when they are ready to mate with the females.'

Alfie looked disgusted by this information. 'Oh, gross. But I do love the clicking sound. I wonder if I can find one.'

'They are very difficult to find but if you are lucky, you might find one on the bark of a tree.'

As Alfie came level with a tree, he stopped to exam its bark and any low branches, before deciding that there were no cicadas present and running off to the next one.

Gary now walked level with Eva. 'It's a beautiful evening, isn't it? Did you enjoy your meal?'

'Yes, it was lovely but I wasn't too hungry. But we must go there again. It was a really friendly place and Alfie loved his ice cream chocolate sundae.'

They were soon back at the apartment complex and Gary suggested that they buy a bottle of wine at the shop and drink it on their balcony. Eva had mixed feelings about this as she was anxious about being alone with Gary. But if they remained for a drink at the bar area, she didn't want to bump into Antonio, after their chat today.

Alfie immediately found Joseph and he begged to be allowed to go to the games room for a while, with euros in his pocket, to play pool or air-hockey. It was agreed that he could go with Joseph as his parents were having a quiet drink by the pool. They would ensure he was returned to his apartment in about an hour.

Gary bought a bottle of Sauvignon Blanc and they strolled back to the apartment. He told her to sit down while he collected glasses and poured the wine. The view from the balcony was of a deep turquoise sea and a deep blue skyline, only interrupted, by the lights of a nearby town, falling as orange stalactites into the water.

'You are looking beautiful tonight, sweetheart,' he commented, as he raised his glass and tipped it against hers. 'Cheers to my lovely girlfriend.'

Eva was wearing a yellow, floral, above-the-knee, sundress with short sleeves which defined her figure and gave her a fresh, summery look. Her hair was softly waved around her face and gold, hooped earrings adorned her ears. She used concealer and foundation on her face to cover the red marking on her cheek, and the now purple bruising at the corner of her left eye, though the earlier puffiness had now faded. Darker brown eye shadow, black eyeliner and mascara was used to emphasise her eyes and draw attention away from the bruised area on her face.

'I have bought you something to say a heartfelt sorry for last night.' He turned his chair so that he was facing her and placed a tentative finger on the left side of her face. 'I swear that I will never hurt you again. I really do love you; you know.'

From his pocket, he took out a small, white paper bag and placed it in front of her. 'Sorry about the bag, the little gift shop in Son Bou didn't have any jewellery boxes. Go on, open it.'

Eva picked up the bag, and withdrew the gift, a crystal, tennis bracelet in rose gold. 'It's lovely, thanks.' She placed it on her right wrist and fastened the catch. It was a very pretty gift but she couldn't get too enthusiastic for something which was meant to offset his guilt for the harm he had caused.

He now drew her off her chair and onto his lap. He clasped his arms around her, firmly but not constricting, as he examined her face and eyes. He lightly touched the area of the bruising on her cheek and she flinched slightly, in anticipation, that he may cause more pain. 'What have I done? Please forgive me, as you are the most precious person in the world to me and I do not deserve you.'

Eva hesitated, not really knowing what to say, but to not address the issue now would be wrong. 'Then how can you hurt someone you profess to love?'

His facial expression was a mixture of guilt and contrition. 'I don't know. I was jealous of you and that waiter, he obviously fancies you, and you were egging him on.'

Eva would have laughed if she hadn't been so close to Gary and still not sure of what his reaction would be. Being next to him, at this proximity, constrained in his grip was making her nervous. It felt as if she were trapped in a cage with a sleeping tiger and any wrong move could provoke an attack. She could feel herself tense as he held her and now the conversation was heading down a path of confrontation as he was accusing her of being the cause of why he lashed out. 'I did not egg him on, I was being polite, that's all.' She wanted to add 'and to compensate for your rudeness.'

'OK, ok, we will call a truce as this conversation could inflame matters all over again and I don't want that.' At this, he drew her face towards him and started to kiss her, gently at first, and then more possessively. He continued to hold her firmly as his fingers started to trail down her neck and onto her breasts. He was drawing in deep, shuddering breaths as his mouth devoured hers.

Eva pulled away from the kiss, noting the extreme annoyance in his eyes as she did so. 'Gary, we can't do this here and now, as Alfie is due to return any minute. We need to wait until he is in bed.'

Reluctantly, Gary released her, and she retook her seat and drank the now tepid white wine.

He rubbed his forehead, as if he were developing a severe headache. 'Bloody kid, always getting in the way.' He refilled his wine glass and drank a few large mouthfuls, as if he were drinking water.

There was a gentle tapping at the door and Eva went to let Alfie in. She asked if he'd had a good time. He nodded before scooting off into his room, to play a computer game. 'Only half an hour,' Eva reminded him.

Eva resumed her seat, on the balcony, looking out at the sea, the sea and sky now both deep blue with only a faint trickle of white cloud visible. She sat silently, sipping her wine, as Gary's mood had gone from pleasant to brooding and sullen. She quaked slightly, partly due to the declining temperature after the hot day, as the cooling air touched her skin but also due to anxiety which jangled her nerves. Living with Gary was becoming harder, draining her energy, and tiring her out. He could change rapidly from loving to angry, in a matter of minutes, if he didn't get what he wanted. She was learning to approach him with extreme caution for fear of being hurt.

CHAPTER SIXTEEN

Andy Leyton physically relaxed his shoulders as he drove onto his driveway and parked his car. He was ready for a few days off after a long ten days of working on the murder case of a male in his twenties, which was now concluded, but there were always ongoing cases to keep under review, in his role as detective inspector in a Major Crime Investigation Team.

As he exited his car, he noted that Eva was taking shopping bags from her car. He waved, and then, called out, 'hi Eva, wait a minute, glad I caught you.'

Eva waved back at him, unloaded the bags, and closed the car boot. 'Hi, Andy.'

Andy strolled onto her driveway and noted the bags in her hand. 'Spending all your hard-earned cash, I see.'

'Just a few new clothing items for work and T-shirts for Alfie. I can't keep up with these growth spurts he's having, he seems to be all long legs and arms, and wobbles around like a new-born foal.'

'Well, I suggest we do a swap for the next seven years. You have Hannah and I'll look after Alfie. The world of girls is a complete mystery to me, they are aliens from another planet. I listen to Hannah when she speaks and sometimes I really don't know what she saying. Then I get the eye-rolling when I don't understand immediately.'

Eva laughed. 'I feel your pain.'

'Thanks. I get very little sympathy from Natasha who thinks it's all my own fault for being stupid enough to have a child in the first place.' As he stood next to her on the driveway, in his fitted white shirt, sleeves folded over his lower arms, blue trousers, blue and grey striped tie askew, Eva thought of Tania, and how she would like to be here right now, as there was no denying, he was a very attractive man. His designer stubble, normally neatly trimmed, was developing into a beard, and he seemed tired around the eyes, his under-eye area slightly grey and puffy.

Eva shared with him that secret smile that only members of the parent club understood. 'I don't know which is going to be worse. The baby and toddler years of intermittent sleep, colic, nappies, different contagious viruses or the unchartered waters of the teen years ahead. I sort of feel like I am about to embark on a voyage of sailing single-handed around the world, don't know what to expect, and will lurch around giddily for many years.'

Andy groaned loudly. 'Yes, we should join up, and go off together, and land on a sun-kissed beach in the Caribbean for the foreseeable future. At least we will have each other for support. The baby years were bad, all that unbroken sleep, but I fear that this is going to be worse. All parents of teenagers all look slightly wide-eyed and desperate to me. Anyway, I digress, as I wanted to know if you and Gary would like to come over to my house on Saturday, for a take-away, or I could cook. Believe it or not, I am quite good.'

'Thanks, Andy, that would be great but I'll have to check to see if Gary has any plans. Can I get back to you?'

'Yes, no problem. How was the holiday, by the way? You are displaying a nice shade of golden tan so I assume the weather was good.'

She was dressed in blue denim shorts and white T-shirt, which did show off her foreign holiday acquired tan. 'Yes, overall, it was good. The weather was very hot, so I did spend quite a lot of time in the shade, as I burn quite easily, but somehow, I did manage to get a light tan without the sunburn. Alfie had a great time and made a new best friend, Joseph, so we didn't have to keep him occupied the whole time.'

'Nice for you and Gary to have some time together as a couple, then.' This was made as a comment but ended up feeling more like a question, an enquiry by a police officer.

Suddenly Eva looked uncomfortable, avoiding Andy's eyes, as she responded, 'yes, I suppose we did have a bit more time to spend together. But we do both like some time to ourselves. I tended to sit by the pool, under a sun umbrella, reading a book and watching Alfie. Gary likes to walk around the nearby resorts which is a bit too hot for me in the scorching Mediterranean sun.'

'Great that you could get away. Natasha and I are hoping to get away somewhere in September, Covid restrictions allowing. Hannah is annoyed as she will be at her mums, and going to school, so I expect the week before we go there will be lots of sulking and tantrums. And that's only Natasha.' He gave a sheepish grin as he said this. 'Don't tell her I said that or my team will be investigating my murder.' Andy as a detective inspector, with a Midlands police service, was frequently called Inspector Morse, by Eva.

'Right, better go. Hopefully see you on Saturday, at say, 7 p.m. Hannah should be home unless she has any plans to go for a sleepover with one of her friends. So, her and Alfie can spend some time together.' Andy and Eva were often surprised that Hannah and Alfie genuinely seemed to like each other, as twelve-year old girls weren't overly tolerant of younger boys.

'Bye.' Andy walked over to his driveway as Eva went into her house. He had known Eva for over three years now, as he got to know the newly bereaved Eva who was grieving for her husband, when he moved into the house next door. Andy had to admit that he was very fond of her, as a neighbour, and as a friend. He always hoped that he had offered some comfort to her, when at times she had cried when speaking about Niall, in those early days when her grief was still so raw. There was a vulnerability to Eva, and at times Andy had wanted to take hold of her to offer comfort and support, but realistically this wasn't an option.

Andy had been surprised when she started on-line dating but reckoned that she was making a positive statement to move on with her life. Andy's biggest disappointment had been that she had met Gary. Andy could not take to the man and put it down to his well-honed police instinct at recognising a 'wrong un'. The man was definitely evasive about his past life, relationships, family and jobs, so that he only gave a sketchy impression of the previous thirty-eight years of his life. Also, Andy sensed that his relationship with Eva, and Alfie, was evolving. When he first started to date Eva, she sang his praises, how he prepared her favourite meals, bought her flowers, took her on picnics and dreamt up small surprises to make her feel special, including leaving her love notes in her bag. This impressed Eva but to Andy it all seemed to be trying a bit too hard. Gary also made great efforts to get along with Alfie, and they forged a strong, early friendship, as Gary was a book full of jokes, an expert on difficult maths and science homework, and a video games' enthusiast. Recently though, Andy began to notice a change in the dynamics of the family. Gary was exerting more control with the things he wanted including Eva having less contact with family and friends. Eva parroting Gary's opinions on topics when he knew she would not normally agree with some of the things she was saying. Gary was starting to make small, snide comments about Alfie's behaviour and undermine Eva's parenting skills, when Andy knew she was a loving and competent mother. Slowly, Eva and Alfie were becoming quieter, and more anxious. Andy sensed that there had been an issue on holiday, as she was unhappy talking about it, and, usually, on returning from a holiday one was re-vitalised and glowing.

****

Saturday, and Eva, Gary, Natasha and Andy were seated on Andy's patio enjoying pre-dinner drinks of Mojitos, red or white wines, or Corona beers. Andy, as chef-in-chief, was surprisingly relaxed as he drank his bottled beer whilst the Mexican dishes he had prepared were cooking perfectly. Eva reflected that if this was her dinner party, she would now be in a state of panic, red-faced and sweaty, as the nerves kicked in. That actually was not strictly true. It wasn't the nerves that could decide if the dinner was undercooked or burnt, it was her tendency to have one or two glasses of wine, getting into interesting conversations, and then forgetting that she was in charge of the cooking. Tonight, she could totally chill out and enjoy the Mexican experience. The food smelled lovely as spicy, garlicky aromas wafted out of the kitchen.

On the patio table there were a selection of dips, including guacamole, sour cream and chive, and spicy tomato salsa served with tortilla crisps, celery, carrot, red and yellow peppers and cucumber sticks. Alfie and Hannah had just selected a plateful of dips, crisps and crudities and Alfie was sternly reminded by Gary not to re-dip his crisps after taking a bite. 'We don't want your slobber and germs in them, thanks.' The two children then disappeared into the house to watch TikTok videos on YouTube.

Andy slipped out of his chair to go and check on the food. Natasha had been designated the task of ensuring that everyone had drinks but was neglectful of her duties, as she seemed pre-occupied with her phone every time a message pinged for her. Eva had drunk her first glass of the Mojito cocktail, which had been refreshing with its tastes of mint and lime. Gary had finished his bottled beer, and was ready for a second, so decided to go inside the kitchen to search for a second.

Natasha was dressed in a fitted, above the knee, off the shoulder pale blue dress that flattered her honeyed skin and silky blonde hair. Her makeup was expertly applied to runway model standard, with well-defined eyebrows, long, thick black eyelashes and eyeliner and coral red lipstick on her soft lips. Manicured nails were highlighted in a glossy, scarlet red. Eva, knowing that she usually looked like the dowdy friend next to the dazzling Natasha, had worked hard to dress in an enticing way. Her red dress with pink polka dots, was sleeveless, above the knee, with ruffle hem and showed off her light holiday tan. Her hair fell gently to her shoulders, the auburn highlights adding depth and richness to its glossy waves. Her makeup was striking, brown eye shadow, and black mascara, emphasised her deep blue eyes and a matted deep pink lipstick plumped her lips. Natasha continued to ignore Eva, and concentrated on her phone, as the constant pings were signals that she was receiving and sending messages.

'You're very popular tonight, Natasha?' Eva commented, trying to initiate a conversation and take the woman off her phone.

Natasha looked up, remembering that Eva was present. 'Yeah, I am. The trouble with my job is that I meet a lot of men with plenty of money to buy expensive houses and they want me to come as part of the package. They all seem to want to ask me out and I spend a lot of time trying to convince them that I am not available. Today, I met an Arab guy who has properties in London and he wants to buy in Warwickshire. I gave him my private number just in case he had any urgent questions and the only question he's got is will I go to bed with him. Andy would be livid if he found out.'

'Well, you are really lucky to have Andy as he is an exceptionally nice person. Don't go hurting him,' Eva stated, knowing that this comment was likely to provoke Natasha.

Natasha ceased the relentless typing on her phone and scowled at Eva, her perfect eyebrows dipped inwards and the red lips thinned in anger. 'Don't tell me what to do. I know that Andy is 'nice' (she did an air quotes sign with her fingers) and he is also super-hot and sexy. If I were to have a little dalliance with the Arab it would not have anything to do with you, or him, as long as he didn't find out. The man is certainly loaded, with properties all around the world, a range of high performance cars and access to his father's millions, so I like to keep my options open. Sadly, he is quite short, and uninspiring looks wise, but it might be worth going with him to get a taste of the lifestyle he could offer me.'

Eva was shocked to hear Natasha's cynical statement of 'keeping her options open.' She made herself sound like a high-class hooker who was always on the look out for someone better to come along. 'Andy cares about you and money is not everything.'

'I know,' Natasha spat this out at Eva, who felt that she was about to add 'dumb bitch' to emphasise the point. 'But I can get any man I want, and right now Andy will do. Anyway, if we do split up don't think he would be interested in you.'

Eva was completely flabbergasted as to where this conversation was heading and Natasha's nasty tone with her. She felt as if she were a target, in front of a crossbow being fired by Natasha, and every arrow was about to land in her heart. 'Why do you say that? Andy and I have only ever been friends. There has never been anything romantic between us.'

Natasha smiled, a gesture that was sly and mean, taking the beauty from her face. 'I know he would never fancy you. Firstly, he is only attracted to tall blondes so, you hardly fit that description. Secondly, he specifically told me that though you are not plain, and some men would find you pretty, he said he couldn't see what the attraction was.'

This final arrow from Natasha's crossbow seared through Eva's heart. It was a vicious comment but Eva found it hard to believe that Andy would actually say such a thing. Still, this remark did upset Eva, as she believed that Andy was a genuine friend to her, and didn't think him capable of that type of comment. If he did say it then she didn't know him as well as she thought she did. Also, Eva knew, from having seen photos of Hannah's mother, that Andy's first wife was not a tall blonde but a pretty, petite brunette.

Andy re-appeared from the kitchen and sensed there was an atmosphere between Natasha and Eva. The plan for this evening was for them to get to know each other better, so that a friendship developed between the two couples. At the moment he would need a NATO negotiator to dispel the frosty atmosphere between the two women, despite it being a warm evening. He noticed that Natasha was concentrating on her phone and neglecting her one task, to keep their guests provided with drinks. Natasha could take the art of laziness to a whole new level. Teenagers were criticised frequently for not pulling their weight regarding household chores but he constantly bickered with Natasha over her reluctance to do any kind of work in the house. Prior to her divorce from a wealthy banker, she had employed a cleaner to service the house, used a laundry service to do the washing, and a gardener maintained the garden area.

'Ok, girls, dinner is ready. Natasha, you were supposed to serve the drinks but I suspect all you've done is send messages on your phone. You are worse than Hannah. I've put some wine on the table so there is really nothing for you to do, for now.'

They entered the kitchen area and Gary and Alfie were already seated at the dining table. The room was light and airy, with high ceilings and Velux windows, and on this mid-August evening the patio doors were open to admit the outside warm air. The kitchen area was ultra-modern, with a functional vibe, with handle-less doors, for a simple style and easy clean. The units were in a pale grey, finished with grey/white pebble laminate worktops and the flooring was a mid-grey laminate in a chevron pattern.

Hannah was lighting four T-light candles in speckled red votive candleholders, on a table with red napkins in silver napkin rings. Hannah took a seat between Natasha and Alfie. Eva and Gary sat adjacent to one another, furthest from the kitchen island and cooked items. Andy had placed a green salad, guacamole, lime crema, a fresh sour cream and lime dip, tortilla crisps, and grated cheese on the table. He now brought over the two main dishes, chicken and bean enchiladas and taco shells with minced beef. Each person was given a warmed plate and Natasha, quite firmly, was asked to pour the wine and provide soft drinks for the children. Andy then asked each person in turn, starting with Eva, what they would like and dished out portions of the hot dishes as requested.

The food was delicious. The enchiladas had just the right amount of chipotle paste, garlic and peppers to be spicy but not overwhelmingly hot. Flavours of garlic, oregano, ground chilli, cumin and paprika could be detected in the minced beef and the taco shells were crisp and tasty. Additions of guacamole, lime crema and grated cheese, all added new levels of flavour to the taco dish.

'This is amazing, Andy. You are a really good cook and Natasha is very lucky to have you.' Eva commented between mouthfuls of spicy food.

This now seemed to inflame Natasha's hostility towards her some more. 'He is the one lucky to have me, as I could have my pick of a number of millionaires, as I keep telling him. There are a lot more important skills than being good at cooking. I am very good at those skills, as Andy will tell you.'

Alfie paused from stuffing an almost whole taco into his mouth to ask. 'What's more important than cooking. If no one cooked, we would all starve. What other skills are you talking about?'

All the adults smiled at Alfie's question but no one seemed keen to enlighten him. Andy smiled at Alfie. 'Natasha has some very well-developed skills,' he paused and all the adults waited nervously for him to continue, especially Eva, 'she's very good at blowing her own trumpet, which means boasting about herself, while putting down other people. Alfie these are not skills we admire but being able to cook is one very important life skill for everyone to learn. Do you like cooking?'

As the group looked at Natasha for her reaction to Andy's censure, Alfie chomped on a crunchy taco and replied, 'it's ok. Mum and I did some cooking during the lockdowns, cakes, biscuits, rice crispy cakes and crumble pudding.

Gary commented, sarcastically, 'yes, as you can see, Eva is fond of promoting healthy eating when teaching her son to cook. No vegetables and fruit involved.'

Alfie clarified, 'there was fruit, it was apple crumble.'

Eva blushed slightly, while adding, 'we did other dishes including meat balls, spaghetti bolognese, stir fry and salads.'

'It sounds as if Eva is doing well in teaching Alfie to cook,' Andy said, smiling at Eva. 'Life would be very dull without cake. Ok, right, does anyone want another drink, or any more of the enchilada dish, there's still some left? Eva? I can see that Alfie's eyeing up the last bit so I'll offer it to the adults first, as he has had two helpings already.'

'I'll have a very small piece, if that's ok,' Eva said. 'It's so delicious.' Andy gave her another spoonful, and smiled, 'glad you like my cooking.'

'Gary?

'No thanks, and two helpings is enough for him.'

'Natasha?'

'No, I have got to keep my figure in shape. As a high-end estate agent, appearance is important if you are selling to wealthy clients. These type of clients expect us to be beautiful, well-groomed and slender. In other jobs, you can get away with being overweight,' Natasha commented, as she glanced at Eva.

'Hannah?'

'No, thanks, dad. I'm with Natasha, got to keep thin.'

A small portion of the chicken and bean enchilada dish remained and Alfie eyed it longingly. 'Can I have that last piece, Andy?'

At that moment, Gary banged his knife down on the table, making Eva and Hannah jump. 'I've just bloody told you, you have had enough, so listen to me when I give you an order.'

Alfie's face flushed brightly and tears were detected in his pale-blue eyes. He looked at his mother, wanting to rush over to her, but resisted the urge as it would appear babyish, at his age of almost twelve in one month's time.

Andy, extremely annoyed with Gary, told Hannah to take Alfie and watch TV. He advised them that there would be some ice cream on offer, shortly. As the youngsters exited the room, Andy addressed Gary. 'You're a bit too hard on him, he's only a kid.'

Gary glared at Andy, as his temper flared, and a cold anger was present in his dark eyes. 'Don't you fucking tell me how to parent that kid. I'm the one that works to buy the food he eats. Just because you are a cop, it doesn't mean you are in charge of me.'

Andy now spoke in an authoritative manner and there was a hardness to his features as he continued to address Gary's behaviour. 'You should remember that children don't always respond well to orders issued in anger. A calm but firm approach works better.'

Gary's level of temper was now rising to off the scale. 'You are such a superior bastard. I don't want any lessons on parenting from you.'

Eva, sat between the two men could feel red hot waves of hostility oscillating between them, so hot that she felt she would burn and be reduced to ash. 'Gary, please, that's enough. Let's have a drink, let the kids have ice cream, and just all of us get on.'

Gary did suddenly lose the anger, as it deflated and dispersed, like a popped balloon, luckily without the bang. 'Ok, let's forget it. He can eat as much as he wants, get sick or fat, or both, see if I care.'

CHAPTER SEVENTEEN

As they entered the house, Gary marched into the kitchen, opened a cupboard door, removed a whisky tumbler then filled it with whisky from a bottle in an adjacent cupboard. Alfie strolled in, cautious of not going too close to Gary, as he sensed that he had not been forgiven for their blow-up earlier.

Eva came into the kitchen, placed her bag and keys on a worktop, and took a glass out of a cupboard to fill with tap water. Drinking the Mojito cocktail and several glasses of white wine had made her thirsty.

Alfie hovered close to his mother and asked, 'mum, could I have a can of coke as I only had one at Hannah's.'

Eva was about to refuse this request as caffeine just before bed time would only keep him awake. 'It's not really a good idea to have one now, Alfie. You had one at Andy's and anymore caffeine now will keep you awake.'

'Oh, go on mum, just one more can. I promise I'll go to sleep.'

Gary was now standing, leaning against the kitchen worktop, watching this interaction between mother and son. 'Right,' he said, in a loud, harsh tone, which scared Alfie slightly. 'You have just been told no. No more coke tonight. You're too bloody greedy and I won't forget that you showed me up next door.'

Eva glared at Gary. 'He didn't show you up, you over reacted.'

Gary now ignored Eva and moved closer to Alfie, glowering down on him. At nearly twelve-years-old, Alfie was amongst the tallest of his peer group, at just over five feet tall but he was very slender, no defined muscles on gangly arms and legs. Gary's height of six feet, and gym-toned arm muscles and six-pack abs, now imposed a physical barrier to the young boy, a tall mature oak bearing down on a young sapling. Gary poked his finger into Alfie's chest. 'Look at me. Learn to listen to what you are told and learn to listen for the word 'no'. If you are told no, it is not an opening for extensive negotiations, as we are not the United Nations here. No means no, from me, or your mother. There will be consequences if we have to have this conversation again. Do you understand?'

Alfie looked down at his chest where Gary's finger had poked him, quite hard. He stared, with frightened eyes, into Gary's unsmiling face. 'Er, yes, I think, I do.'

Gary relaxed his lips into a half smile. 'Good, I think we are making progress. Now, if you are thirsty go and have a drink of water, and then off you go to bed.'

Moving quickly away from Gary's proximity, Alfie rushed out of the room before Gary could speak again.

Gary then turned his attention on Eva. 'Sit down and we can have a little chat about tonight and the way forward with regards to Alfie.' He picked up the whisky bottle and tumbler, carried them over to the oak dining table and sat down on one of the chairs. He poured whisky into the glass, half filling it, before taking a long swig.

Eva sat on a chair adjacent to Gary, anxious eyes watching, as he consumed the whisky. Gary was not pleasant when drunk and whisky was the worst drink for making him nasty. 'What do you mean about the way forward with Alfie?'

'I mean, that as I live here now and have taken on a stepfather role, I will have more of a say in what goes on with him on a day-to-day basis. Until recently, I have held back, as I respect that he is your son and it is up to you to direct and guide him. But I think it's time that I stepped in, particularly as he is going towards the teenage years, when boys are in need of a firm hand. And you are too soft with him.'

Eva shook her head, not willing to agree with Gary, but concerned as the stern expression on his face suggested that what he was going to say would not be up for debate, but more of an instruction for her to follow. 'Niall and I were always firm but fair with Alfie, and when we said no, we liked to back it up with a reason and not just say no for the sake of it. So, with the coke, I said no, but told him why it was not a good idea to have one just before bed.'

Gary's laughed in a sneering way. 'Oh yes, that worked really well, as he thought the whole thing was up for debate and would probably have won you over after five more minutes of exhausting discussion. As I said earlier, he will learn that no means no, end of, no further discussion. If he starts the arguing after that there will be consequences, as I suggested.'

Eva swallowed a mouthful of water in order to calm the queasy feeling in her stomach. 'What do you mean by consequences? It all sounds really menacing and I will not stand for you touching my son. I will remind you that I am his mother and you are not his father.'

Gary now pulled his chair closer to Eva so that he was facing her directly, his knees touching hers. 'For now, the consequences will be suspension of pocket money, no playing of computer games or not seeing friends. You do not see any of his faults, but I am telling you he is lazy, greedy, selfish and argumentative and all these behaviours need nipping in the bud before we have a mouthy, pot-smoking adolescent to deal with.'

Anger was now flaring in Eva. 'Alfie will never be like that. He's is a lovely boy and no better or worse than any boy his age. Life is harder for him, as he lost his father not so long ago, and he doesn't want to live in some sort of military boot camp.'

Gary, seeing that he may have gone too far, lightly touched her knee to disperse her anger, and lighten the mood. 'Look, it'll all be ok if he does as he's told. I think I made myself clear and we will see how things go from now on. Now, enough of him, as I am looking at a really sexy woman in a beautiful red dress who I want to concentrate on.' He pulled her onto his lap, and kissed her, a long embrace that washed away the lingering traces of her earlier anger. She chided herself for this weakness but couldn't help but respond to the depth of passion that the kiss aroused. He pushed the material of her dress upwards, touching her smooth thighs with his fingers. His fingers continued to explore until he found the inviting area at the top of her thighs, concealed by white, lacy briefs. Despite her rational brain still being annoyed with him about Alfie, her traitor body reacted as he caressed her further, so that she moaned softly.

Gary broke off the kiss, his voice low and gravelly in her ear. 'You are looking super gorgeous tonight, and we should continue this upstairs but you are not going to be excited so quickly. I want you to be patient as I tease you mercilessly. To rein in your passion, I shall have to restrain you, and then torment you until you beg me for mercy. Miss Brennan, I will be the teacher, not you, and you will be the willing learner. Come on.' He tumbled her off his lap and onto her feet. He swigged the remaining whisky in the tumbler quickly and took hold of her hand to guide her up the stairs.

CHAPTER EIGHTEEN

The final week of August was rushing Eva and Alfie back to school, Eva to work and Alfie to start his first year at secondary school. Eva hated the last week of the school holidays before the return to the full-on pressure of the start of a new term. A class of thirty, Year 4's, would be awaiting her and the first few weeks seemed to be an endless stream of putting faces to names, assessing each pupil's standards, particularly in terms of the core subjects such as English, mathematics and science, as well as starting on the 'foundation' subjects including geography, history, art and design, computing, design and technology, PE and so on. This week was a chance to finalise any outstanding jobs so that she was 'school ready'.

They had been to a nearby retail park to buy Alfie a new pair of shoes for the new school year. He had argued with her about the type of shoes to buy, wanting a trainer style, when the school guidelines were very strict on the style of shoe which must not resemble a trainer. Eva was pleased that Gary was not present for the discussion that ensued, as it would give further ammunition to Gary's insistence that Alfie never listened to the word no.

Driving back from the shoe shop, Eva had started to feel a bit queasy and hot. She turned the air conditioning up to the top setting so cold air was flowing around her face, as she was sweating, and her skin was clammy. Trying not to go over the speed limit, she was desperate to get home, as she felt that she was about to faint. Pulling into the driveway, and bringing the car to a halt, she bent forward holding onto the steering wheel as a wave of dizziness prevented her from getting out of the car.

Alfie undid his seat belt and was opening the car door when he noticed that his mother's head was now resting on the steering wheel. 'Mum, we're home. Are you ok?' As she did not answer, he poked a finger into her left arm. 'Mum, don't go to sleep here, let's go into the house.' She still did not respond and now Alfie was worried. He got out of the passenger seat, and rushed around to the driver's side, only to see that his mother was still not moving.

Starting to panic now, he looked across at the neighbour's house and was pleased to see Andy getting out of his car, a laptop and pile of papers in his hands. Running now at top speed, Alfie rushed onto Andy's driveway and shouted, 'Andy, Andy, there's something wrong with mum. She's fallen asleep at the steering wheel and I can't wake her up.'

Andy assessed the terrified face of the young boy, a face so pale that all blood seemed to have drained out of him. 'What's up, mate?'

'Mum's fallen asleep and I can't wake her up.'

Andy now ran towards Eva's car, to the driver's side, opened the car door to find Eva slumped over the steering wheel, though she did now seem as if she were starting to come to. Alfie stood next to him, fear apparent on his face, and tears in his eyes.

Andy gently touched Eva's face to lift her head up and try to assess what was going on. 'Eva, its Andy. Lift your head up for me. What's happened?'

She slowly started to pull her head up, but looked at him blankly, and did not seem to know where she was and what was happening. He touched his hand to her forehead which felt cold and clammy and there were beads of sweat on her upper lip.

Andy shoved the laptop and papers he was carrying at Alfie. 'I think she's fainted and she should be ok in a minute but I need to get her in the house.' Andy took the car key out of the ignition, saw that the house key was with the car key, and gave it to Alfie. 'You go ahead and open the door, quickly.'

Andy now started to gently pull Eva out of the car, with his left arm supporting her back and his right arm under her legs. He lifted her up and carried her towards the door. She was slumped in his arms, her head fallen back, with her brown hair spilling away from her face. Her left arm dangled lifelessly downward. He strode purposefully through the door, into the hallway, and then into the lounge and placed Eva gently down on a three-seater sofa. He laid her flat on her back, but with her legs raised, so that her feet rested on the side edge of the sofa. Andy stood close by, watching her, and waiting for her to come round, which she was doing. Her eyes blinked open and she looked around. 'What's happened?' She gawped in surprise to see Andy standing near to her, a very concerned look on his face as he gazed down at her.

He gently placed his hand on her shoulder. 'You fainted in the car, and Alfie alerted me, so I brought you in here. Now, try to get up slowly, and if you feel faint again, lie down.'

She started to pull herself up to a sitting position but did immediately go dizzy again and so she lay back down.

Alfie was now in the room, very worried that his mother did not seem to be recovering. 'Is she going to be ok? Do we need to call an ambulance?' he asked Andy.

Andy placed his hand on the boy's shoulder as a gesture of reassurance. 'No, Alfie, she should be alright in a moment. Don't worry.'

Eva slowly came round this second time and Andy assisted her to a sitting position on the sofa. He stated, 'just sit still and don't move for now. At least you look a bit better and there's a bit more colour in your face. How are you feeling?'

'Ok, I think. I did feel dizzy a moment ago but that seems to have passed. I should be ok now.' She now leant back on the sofa. She was wearing a pink T- shirt and pale blue, mid-thigh, denim shorts which highlighted her tanned, slender legs and she felt self-conscious as he continued to scrutinise her in case she fainted again. Alfie hovered, not sure of what was going on.

'Alfie, go and get your mum a glass of tap water that's not too cold.'

As Alfie went out of the room, Andy took a seat on the two-seater sofa opposite Eva. 'Do you know why you fainted?'

Eva sighed heavily, before glancing over at him. 'Maybe. I donated blood this morning and afterwards I had a cup of tea and a biscuit. But since then, Alfie and I have been shopping, and I haven't had anything to eat or drink. Alfie had a burger, fries and coke earlier but I didn't feel like anything. I should've have known better, as this has happened before, if my blood sugar levels go down after giving blood.'

Alfie came back in with the glass of water and handed it to his mother.

'Right, sip it slowly, don't gulp it down,' Andy advised.

'Thanks, Alfie.' She sipped slowly on the water as instructed, all the time feeling better, though she still felt a little bit cold and shivery. She pulled the fake faux, light beige throw off the back of the sofa and wrapped it around her bare legs.

'I think I'm ok, now.' Looking at Alfie's still troubled face, she said, 'Alfie, I'm fine now, you can go to your room if you like.' She then glanced at Andy. 'Thanks for your help, Andy. I'm sorry to have troubled you.'

'It was no trouble, as I would always help out a friend in need. Right, I am going to make some tea and find some biscuits.'

'You don't need to do that, Andy, the water is fine.'

Andy laughed. 'It's not for you, it's for me, as I have had a shock finding you like that. So where are the biscuits?'

'They are in one of the top cupboards, in a tin, if we've got any. Gary's not keen on having biscuits in the house as he's all for healthy eating.'

Andy got up from the sofa to go and make the tea. 'I'm a good detective, I'm sure I will find where you have hidden them.' He pretended to twirl an imaginary moustache in the manner of Belgian detective, Hercule Poirot. Eva chuckled, making her hand shake enough to spill some of the water.

Ten minutes later he was back with two mugs of hot tea and a packet of chocolate digestive biscuits. He put the mugs of tea on place mats, on the side table, between the two sofas. He sat down on the other sofa opposite Eva. 'I know you don't normally have sugar in tea but do you want some now?'

'No, thanks.' She moved across the sofa, dragging the throw with her, to keep it over her legs, and she put down the glass of water. She picked up the mug of tea, holding it with her two hands, enjoying the heat from the steam, before she took a tentative sip. "This is good, thanks.'

Andy continued to concentrate his gaze on her face. 'You look a lot better. And I am not leaving here until you eat a biscuit.'

'You have suddenly got very bossy, Inspector Leyton. I expect you are used to issuing orders to your team at work. Are they scared of you?'

He gave her a mock smile. 'Of course, they are, or the lazy buggers wouldn't do any work. But I save my really scary persona for the criminals when I am arresting them. I love the bit where I get to shout at them if they are resisting arrest. Talking of arresting people, I did have a moment's worry when I saw you slumped in that car that perhaps you'd been drinking, and I'd have to arrest you for being over the limit.'

Eva realised that he was deadly serious as he said this. 'Yes, I suppose I would expect you to. Lucky for me it was you that helped me and not one of your colleagues.' She leaned over and picked up the packet of biscuits, took one out of the packet, and nibbled on it half-heartedly. 'Please help yourself,' she said to Andy as she placed the packet back down on the table.

'What time will Gary be home?'

'He won't tonight. He's gone down south to check on one of the houses he owns. There's a problem with the boiler and he needs to organise a replacement. He'll be away for two nights.'

'How many houses has he actually got?'

'Two, I think, one from each of his previous marriages. I don't know too much about these properties or where they exactly are. I think one is in Berkshire but I'm not sure about the other one, just that its somewhere around Stratford. He rents them out, and does employ an agent to oversee them, but occasionally he will go and sort out a major problem. He also has an apartment where he lived before he moved in here which is in the Kenilworth area. His friend Simon lives there at the moment.'

'He seems to have fallen on his feet financially, as an outcome of these two marriages, if he has acquired both of the marital homes,' Andy suggested.

'Yes, he does seem to have come out of tragic circumstances fairly well off.'

'What do you mean by tragic circumstances.' Andy could not help himself in asking more questions about Gary's mysterious previous life. His inbuilt antennae, for honing in on some people who he sensed had hidden agendas, was now twitching.

'From what he has said, his first young wife died from an accident, some sort of fall, and the second one died due to a drug overdose, accidental, I think. She was quite a bit older than Gary, I think. That's all I know.'

'Not exactly the most open of people, is he?'

'If I ask about his wives, he clams up, and I think he just gets upset. I know what it's like as I don't always want to talk about Niall. Anyway, I must thank you for the other night, I had a good time. Who knew you were such a great cook?'

Andy nodded his head to accept her thanks. 'Yes, I am truly amazing in the kitchen. I will be bringing out my own range of cookbooks any time soon. Andy's Handy Cooking recipes.'

'Good idea. You could be on the front cover for the book. You, with just an apron on, nothing more, and I'm sure it would sell very well,' Eva suggested, then blushed slightly at what she had said.

Andy raised his eyebrows, faking a look of horror. 'Ms Brennan, are you suggesting that I sexualise myself to sell cookbooks? And you a primary school teacher. Tut, tut,' he laughed, mischievously. 'It's a whole new concept of the Naked Chef.'

'Forget I said anything.'

He noticed that her face had reddened but he did enjoy teasing her and found her fun to be with. Having fun with a woman was something he had forgotten how to do recently. Natasha was starting to be hard work, always on her phone, droning on about the 'millionaires' and lest we forget, one billionaire, that she keeps meeting in her new job at this upmarket estate agency. He was getting tired of hearing how they all fancied her and she was trying to make him jealous by saying it. He was not going to take part in her games and was getting to the stage where he would welcome a millionaire taking her off his hands. He knew that the relationship was due to end, but he just couldn't summon the energy to end it himself, at the moment.

Andy was relaxed, reclining on the sofa, drinking his tea. 'Anyway, how's Alfie and Gary getting on? I hope you don't mind me saying but I thought that Gary was heavy-handed with Alfie on Saturday night when he told him he couldn't have the last piece of the enchilada dish.'

Eva now felt embarrassed, and didn't want to make eye contact with Andy, even though she could feel his eyes on her. 'Yes, I agree, he did. And it all got worse when we got home when Alfie wanted a coke and Gary told him an emphatic no. He said that Alfie had to listen to what he was told and listen for the word 'no'. Once told no, it was not open for further discussion, as we are not the United Nations. Gary then warned him there would be consequences if they had this conversation again. I think it scared Alfie and it scared me.' Eva slowly raised her eyes to look at Andy, a mixture of worry and fear in her dark blue eyes. 'I shouldn't really be telling you all this as it feels unfair to Gary. I'm sure he's just finding his way in a new role of stepfather.'

Andy's facial expression was now one of concern but there was also a hint of anger in his eyes. 'What did he mean by consequences, did he explain?'

'After Alfie had gone to bed, Gary started on what he called the way forward with Alfie. He suggested that he will have more of a say about what goes on with Alfie, and, that as he was growing older, he needed a firm hand. I was too soft, apparently. I explained to Gary, that Niall and I always liked to give a reason if we said no to Alfie, and I had told Alfie it was not a good idea to have a coke, with caffeine, just before bed. Gary is still going on about no means no. No debate and consequences for disobeying. I sort of think he was implying he would hit Alfie.'

'Yes, from what you are saying it does have that implication.'

'He said, for now, consequences would be no pocket money, computer games or seeing friends. He actually said that Alfie was lazy, greedy, selfish and argumentative and these behaviours needed nipping in the bud.' Eva was now starting to find it all upsetting describing this to Andy and there was a catch in her voice as she was near to tears. 'Do you see Alfie like that, Andy?'

'Don't be ridiculous. He's a sensitive, kind boy who has had a bad time with losing his father at such a young age. I would strongly suggest that Gary is the one in the wrong here and you need to be careful with this new disciplinarian approach as it all sounds sinister to me. In my opinion, Gary has now got his feet firmly under the table and is exerting his authority. You do need to stand up against it, or it will get worse, for both Alfie and you. I have seen a lot of how this type of thing escalates with a controlling man and it rarely ends well. If it gets worse for Alfie, or for you, and gets to be emotional or physical abuse, you need to get rid of him, fast.'

Now Andy could see that Eva was struggling to not cry and he was worried that he had gone too far in warning her off Gary. It could all be as Eva said, Gary trying to be a stepdad after being thrust into a parent role, whilst not being a father himself. Generally, with your own child, you learned how to be a parent as they developed from demanding baby, to bossy toddler, to inquisitive school child and then into the years of exploring the unknown with a stroppy teenager. Gary had been thrown in at the deep end, with no experience of swimming in the shallows, before starting out on the adventure of doing breaststroke across the Channel with a teenager to guide on the way. Gary had not built up the love for a child, who could test your patience over the years, but for whom you would protect with your dying breath. 'As you said, Eva, Gary's probably just trying to find his way in his new role. As long as you are comfortable with it all, and he's generally caring and kind, it should be ok.'

At this moment, Alfie rushed into the room, and went over to the side table where the biscuits were. He eyed the biscuits fondly before checking that his mother now seemed to have recovered from her faint. 'Are you ok, mum? What happened?'

Eva smiled lovingly at his sweet, still boyish face, recognising that soon he would develop teenage spots and facial hair as he changed from a boy to a man. Her heart ached slightly as she realised that in the not-too-distant future she would lose him to someone else, a girlfriend, or perhaps, a boyfriend. 'I'm fine now, Alfie. I just fainted because I didn't drink enough water or tea, and didn't eat anything, after going to the blood donors this morning. I should have known better.'

Alfie now happy that all was well, directed his attention to the biscuits, and stomach-related matters. 'Can I have a biscuit, please? And as Gary is away, can we have pizza and can Hannah and Andy join us?'

Eva sighed, rolling her eyes at Andy in a 'who would be a parent' way. 'Yes, you can have one biscuit only. Yes, we can have a takeaway pizza, if you like. Andy and Hannah are welcome to join us but I'm sure they have their own plans with Natasha.'

Andy laughed at Alfie. 'You ask more questions than Bradley Walsh on 'The Chase'. But I must say you would make a good detective in the future, as we need people who are good at interviewing victims and suspects.'

Alfie's eyes widened as he assessed what Andy had said. 'Wow, does that mean I get to ask criminals where they hid the loot, the drugs, and the guns?'

'Yes, it does but they don't often want to tell you anything.'

'Would I get to carry guns and shoot them?'

'Depends which section of the police service you work for. If you work in the Armed Response Unit, you would be armed but you would only use a firearm if absolutely necessary, if all negotiations have failed. As a detective inspector, I don't carry firearms, but I do get to arrest nasty criminals including murderers.'

Alfie's mouth fell open at this. 'Wow. When I leave school, I definitely want to join the police.'

Andy glanced shyly at Eva; not sure she would want her child to join what can be a dangerous occupation. 'We would be pleased to have you, Alfie. Perhaps go to university first and then think about joining.' To Eva, he said, 'Natasha is staying at her mother's for a few days so Hannah and I would love to join you both for pizza later, if you'll have us.'

CHAPTER NINETEEN

Alfie and Hannah were in Hannah's bedroom, Hannah sitting upright on her bed, resting against the pillows, mobile phone in hand, head down engrossed in the screen. Alfie sat on her white computer chair, next to her desk, twirling around on it, as he too gazed at his phone. Alfie liked Hannah's bedroom as the walls were painted in a pale green paint, that she told him was called 'Seafoam' and the bedroom furniture of wardrobes and a desk were all white. The headboard of the bed was of a mid-green fabric and Hannah had string-lights hung across it. Pops of colour, pinks, teals, and blues, were brought into the room by pots, artificial plants and cushions. A white open shelving unit contained books, white hessian storage baskets, and favourite trinkets. The room was fresh, modern and not overdone in the colour pink which a lot of girls favoured.

'What you looking at Hannah?' Alfie asked as she giggled at something online. Alfie liked to watch Hannah as she played on her phone, as she was so absorbed in what she was doing, and it gave him a chance to admire her beauty. She was a pretty girl, with long, silky dark hair and deep brown eyes, who was petite like her mother. Alfie often felt hot and bothered when he was in her company, he found himself stuttering when trying to form sentences, and his cheeks developed a ripe tomato red colour if she looked at him.

'Just a TikTok video of a chipmunk stuffing nuts into his mouth. An old one but I think it's really cute.'

'Yeah, I've seen that one, it would make a cool pet. Would you like a pet, Hannah?'

Hannah pursed her lips as she contemplated this question. 'Maybe. I would like a cute little white fluffy kitten but dad isn't too keen as he's not really into cats. He reckons I would get bored with it, as it grew out of the kitten stage, and started doing its own thing as cats are very independent. Dad says that you can be the master of a dog, but a cat will be the master of you, and he doesn't want another female bossing him about.'

'Your dad is really funny. Does he ever shout at you?'

'No, not really. He will if he has to repeat himself a number of times but he's not really scary. Why, does Gary shout at you?'

Alfie stopped twirling on the chair and looked down at his feet. 'He has started to and he's started to get more bossy with me and making sure I do things according to his rules.'

'In what way?' Hannah now stopped staring at her phone and looked at Alfie.

'Well, on Saturday night when we left here, I asked mum if I could have another can of coke but she said no, so I asked again. Gary got really stroppy, saying that no meant no, and there would be no further arguing. He poked me in the chest with his finger to make the point. If I argued, there would be consequences.'

'What did that mean?'

'He said things like stopping pocket money and computer games but I sort of felt that he meant he would hit me if I disagreed. He is pretty scary.'

'And what did your mum say to all of this?'

'She didn't say a lot but I hope she would stick up for me if I needed it. Thing is, I think she is a bit scared of him as well.'

Hannah was now completely focused on what Alfie was telling her. 'Why do you think that. Women aren't scared of men anymore and Natasha definitely tries to be the boss of dad.'

'Do you like Natasha?' Alfie asked, trying to evaluate how this stepparent thing worked with girls, and their dad's girlfriend.

'She's ok, we get along but I don't think she's really into children and would prefer to have dad to herself. We do argue and dad gets cross with both of us because we both like to have the last word in an argument. She's happiest when its my weekend to go and stay with mum. Don't say anything but I don't think dad is that happy with her. He once said to her that it's like having two teenagers in the house, as she is moody, lazy, very untidy and always arguing with him. TBH, I think that's unfair to me, as I can be very tidy, er, just look at this room.'

Alfie then looked down at his phone, to avoid eye contact with Hannah. 'If I tell you a secret do you promise not to tell anyone, especially not your dad as he is a policeman?'

Hannah was now completely intrigued, ready for what Alfie was about to say. His face was anxious, a blush had flared on his cheeks, and he breathed in deeply to calm his nerves. Hannah stated, 'I promise not to tell. Just get on with it.'

Alfie sighed, still looking away from Hannah. 'I think that when we were on holiday in Menorca, Gary hit my mum.'

'OMG. Why, what happened?' Hannah's mouth had dropped open and she did have a look of a goldfish out of its tank.

'Gary was upset that she seemed to be chatting to one of the waiters. We were all back in the apartment, and I was in my room, when I heard him raising his voice to her, then there was a noise that sounded like a slap, and she cried out. I could then hear her crying in the bedroom. The next day she had a red mark on her face. I asked her about it but she said she hit her face when opening a kitchen cupboard.'

'That's terrible. We should tell my dad as he would know what to do. It's a crime to hit somebody.'

Alfie now looked terrified. 'Hannah, we cannot tell your dad. If they take Gary to the police station and then let him out he might hit her again.'

Hannah nodded. 'Yes, you are right. Dad says that lots of criminals are not kept in prison, they are sent home until they have to go to trial. Then, if they are guilty they will be sent to jail by the judge. Gary might definitely be sent home and your mum could be in more danger.'

'So, you're ok if it's our secret for now?'

'Yes, I suppose so. It feels wrong not to tell dad but we won't say anything for now. Poor you. I thought that having Natasha around was really stressy but Gary seems like a right psycho. Let's have a look at some more videos of cute kittens to cheer ourselves up. Even though my mean dad says I can't have one.'

****

'Downstairs in the lounge, Eva and Andy were relaxing on separate sofas, and were sharing a bottle of a New Zealand rosé wine. Andy was holding the glass firmly and eyeing the wine curiously as if it were the pink lagoon from where a monster would suddenly emerge. 'This drink won't do my street cred any good with the team, if they could see me now. I'm more a beer, red wine or whisky kind of guy, really.'

Eva picked up her phone to take a photograph of him sipping at the pink liquid. 'I'll send a photo to the police Facebook page if you're not careful. It's nice to see you embracing your feminine side.'

'Are you blackmailing me, as that is very serious offence? I shall have to arrest you and take you to the police station.'

'Go on then, and I will tell them that you like to drink rosé wine, while wearing a pink dressing gown and wearing fluffy pink slippers to watch TV.'

'How do you know about the slippers?' He made a silly face to make her laugh.

At that moment, Eva's phone rang and she answered it. 'Hi, Gary. Yes, we're ok. How's it going organising the boiler replacement?' She then made the odd comment of 'ok' and 'oh dear' as she listened to him on the other end of the phone. 'You'll be back on Friday, then. Yes, Alfie's fine. I bought him his new school shoes today. Another pause, then Eva said £45.00.' Again, she listened while he discussed their cost which from the loudness of Gary's voice indicated he wasn't too happy at this expense. 'Yes, Alfie and I have had pizza for tea and so it's been nice to spend time with him.' Again, Gary was loudly talking about something before ending the call.

Eva put down the phone and looked concerned about the phone call. 'He's not happy about the price of the school shoes and has now got upset that we've wasted more money on pizza. He's not coming back till Friday now, as there's further issues at the property, but I expect to get earache about money when he gets back.'

Andy now gauged that she was not happy about what this discussion would entail when he got back. 'What's the issue, you have to buy shoes and food for your son.' Andy could feel his hackles rising as he learnt new things about Gary and could not get away from his sense that the man was starting to exert a control over Eva and Alfie which had the potential to turn nasty.

Eva tried not to look at Andy, embarrassed to reply. 'He's started this thing recently about how much everything costs, particularly with regard to Alfie, which is odd as I pay for all of Alfie's clothes, shoes and stuff, and put in an extra share for the bills to cover for me and Alfie.'

'Why didn't you tell him that Hannah and I are here?'

'I didn't want to upset him. He can get jealous if he thinks I talk to other men. There was a bit of an issue on holiday with one of the waiters and he really wasn't happy that the guy kept talking to me.' She now blushed a deep red and Andy noted anxiety on her face.

Andy was extremely tempted to ask more questions about the 'issue' with the waiter as he suspected there was more to it than what she was telling him. He knew that Gary had a temper and he was concerned that he could be volatile if he thought she had upset him. The more Andy learnt about Gary, the less he liked him, but he did for now rein in asking anymore questions as he figured he wasn't at work. He did sometimes struggle to control his urge to question everything and to treat people as suspects in a crime until he found evidence to the contrary. His ex-wife often berated him for it.

'Right, hand over your glass and let's finish this wine.' She held her glass over to him and he divided the remaining wine between the two glasses. 'Are you feeling ok now after your fainting episode today?'

She nodded her head. 'Yes, thanks, I'm fine now. Thanks for your help, by the way. I don't think I've thanked you properly.'

'I think you have by buying the pizza and providing the pink wine. No need to thank me. I would do the same for anyone.'

'Good to know. So, if Mr Jones down the road faints at any point, you will be carrying him into his house, will you?' Eva laughed, as Mr Jones was a tall, well-built man, who used to be a bouncer in his younger days.

Andy considered this carefully. 'I might have to summon help for that one. It was easy with you as you don't weigh very much and are quite small.' He didn't add that the sensation of having her in his arms had been pleasant and she smelt lovely, of a delicate perfume that assailed his nostrils. As she sat on the sofa, her legs tucked underneath her, her dark auburn hair framing her face, she was a mix of allure and sensuality in his eyes. On all the occasions, when they spent time together, he was drawn to her more and more, which was difficult as he was in a relationship with Natasha. Natasha was blonde, beautiful and every man's dream and, theoretically, Andy knew he was lucky to have her, but his feelings for her were slightly hollow, there was no real depth to them. If Natasha walked off into the twilight tomorrow with one of the money men she constantly talked about, he knew he would not be overly troubled. It would sting his male pride, no doubt about it, but what would he actually miss about her? Yes, the sex was good, and she certainly knew how to arouse him, but it all felt mechanical, sex by numbers, without any emotional connection. After sex, he wanted to draw her too him, and lay entwined, but she was quickly over to her side of the bed and fast asleep.

The feelings he was developing for Eva were going to be a problem, if he wanted to continue to see her as a friend, and neighbour, and if she carried on in her relationship with Gary. There was no way that Gary could suspect he liked Eva, as he couldn't risk Gary becoming jealous, and taking it out on her. Ideally, he would like to get her away from Gary. Gary's outburst on Saturday with Alfie, and then from Eva's description of Gary's insistence of a disciplinary approach to dealing with Alfie, chilled Andy to the core. Realistically, Andy knew that he could not interfere with her life, and he could only be a spectator on the sidelines, as she continued in her relationship with Gary.

But as Andy sat with Eva in the same room, on different sofas, he had a strong urge to want to hold her, kiss her soft mouth and make love to her after having a taste today of what she would feel like in his arms. Andy was also hit by a sense of foreboding that she was vulnerable, and in danger, from a controlling man and he knew he wanted to protect her from being hurt. His experience as a police officer had brought him into contact with many victims of domestic violence, and when the worse happened, and they were seriously harmed, a lot wished they had left their abusive partners before things escalated. Often when he asked these victims, or survivors as they wished to be called, why they had remained with the person for so long, there was a myriad of reasons; being traumatised distorted their thinking so they were embarrassed, felt shameful and worthless, blamed themselves for what happened, thought they could change the perpetrator's behaviour or had no other example of family life to draw on so if dad hit mum, they expected to be hit. Other reasons included lack of financial resources to cope alone, particularly with children to support, and often they were isolated from family and friends by their tormentors. Plus, often the main reason for not leaving was fear, as it was extremely dangerous to try to withdraw from an abusive situation if you are cowered by ongoing threats to yourself or your loved ones. Angry and violent people, when they feel they are losing control of their domestic situation, will frequently stop at nothing to exact revenge on the fleeing partner.

As Andy watched Eva as she sipped her wine, he hoped that he was wrong in his assessment of Gary. Yes, the man was opinionated, arrogant, annoying and not likeable, and yes, he shouted at Alfie, but perhaps that was as far as it would go. He had no evidence of any other inappropriate behaviour of Gary's towards Eva and Alfie. Was it just his copper's instinct which was warping his judgement in this case? Andy hoped that he was wrong, in this instance, but he was finding it difficult to ignore the small, persistent alarm bell that was ringing in his ear.

CHAPTER TWENTY

June 2005

Gary rolled off Claire, breathless from his exertion at having sex with what he imagined a sex doll would be like, motionless and uninterested, but at least he could choose a pretty one with flowing hair and an inviting mouth. When doing it with this woman, he considered what it would be like to be a male escort, and in reality, that was exactly what he was. He was being paid to sleep with her, but the financial reward was not immediate, and he expected to cash in his investment of time and energy in the next twelve months.

'Honestly, Claire, we've been sleeping together for over two years now, and I know I am your first boyfriend but can you not put a bit of effort in when we are having a shag. I know that I am good at it, and you would enjoy it more if you were to move around, explore my body and relax into it. You lay there like a plank of wood and then flinch or yelp when I touch you which does not turn me on, it turns me off. If you want a baby then you need to try harder.'

'Sorry, Gary. Yes, I think I do want a baby but I do find this sex thing all a bit difficult. I am also nervous about having a baby, as I am sure it is really going to hurt and then I'm not sure I'll be any good at looking after it.'

Gary lay back on his pillow, eyes wide open, looking at the ceiling and watching as a car's headlights fleetingly lit up the room. 'Well, if you want a kid, you can't have one without having sex. Just think how happy your parents will be if they knew they were to become grandparents. Your dad keeps harping on about a grandson to take over the Quall enterprises in the future.' Gary laughed, Quall enterprises consisted of the car screw and bolts factory, and now a new investment, a car dealership, which Gary had talked old man Quall into buying. Gary had now moved out of procurement and was the manager of the dealership, overseeing the buying and selling of high-quality used cars. The dealership was an existing business which Roger Quall purchased at a competitive price when the previous owner wanted to sell to retire to the South of France. Car sales suited Gary perfectly. He found that he excelled in business management, as he had undertaken training modules as part of his BTEC business studies course, and he developed quickly in his management role. Roger Quall was the overall manager but he was happy for Gary to oversee the day to day running of the dealership. It had its perks, as he liked the opportunity to venture out to view cars, and pursue the little dalliances he had established when chatting to the comelier female customers. Gary had decided that he could not continue to service the Quall family daughter if he didn't have a little extra enjoyment on the side.

So, all in all, life for Gary was sweet. Except for the one fly in the ointment. The thorn in his side. The spanner in the works. Lisa. He still craved her, wanted to have sex with her, as she was the woman who could drive him to distraction and he could not get enough of her beautiful, soft, accommodating body, with her sumptuous breasts and curving bottom, and he achieved soaring orgasmic release as he came in her. Lisa was no longer prepared to wait for The Plan to be executed. She continually told him that she was fed up of making out in a car, down a country lane, after two particularly embarrassing encounters. One involving the police and their torches searching the car as it steamed up and rocked on a cold January night. The second incident had been when Gary inadvertently parked in an area frequented by doggers and Lisa was mortified to catch a group of men staring in the windows of the car. Gary thought it was amazing, and suggested they did it more frequently but Lisa was not to be converted and threatened to leave him if he mentioned it again.

No, things could carry on quite nicely for now, if Lisa could be placated to wait for another twelve months as he consolidated his place in the Quall family. As married to their only daughter, he intended to deliver a longed-for grandchild as soon as possible. He was efficiently managing the car dealership, developing his golf handicap to spend time with his father-in-law, and looking to the next step, being awarded shares in the company, which had been hinted at by Roger Quall at family gatherings.

Lisa was now getting impatient. She wanted a house, with a warm cosy bed to cuddle up in at night, every night, and not spend time on the back seat of a car 'like a prostitute' was how she framed it. She still worked for the Qualls but Gary had moved her into the car side of the company and she was training on the financial aspects of car buying and selling, including insurance, warranties and car finance. In the last couple of months, she was acting more rashly, prone to outbursts of temper and threatening to disclose Gary's secrets to anyone who would listen. Roger Quall was very fond of Lisa, in a not so fatherly way, and was often in the office, sitting on the edge of her desk, trying to stare down her blouse. Lisa played up to this attention, telling Gary that she would put into place her own plan, by seducing Roger Quall, getting him to divorce his dreary wife and marry her. She would then produce an heir to the Quall fortune before Gary had his pants off with drippy Claire. Roger Quall was actually an attractive man for his age, in a Colin Firth sort of way, so Gary could not hundred percent assume that she was joking. The other day he had caught Lisa talking to Roger, stretching out her long legs as she swirled on her office chair, keeping the older man's eyes focused on her slender, honey-toned limbs. The discussion was about how Claire seemed to be taking for ever to conceive a baby and perhaps Gary was not up to the job of continuing the Quall line. It was a high risk, personal conversation to have with your employer, but Roger Quall lapped it all up, as she implied that his sexual prowess would not be in doubt if he wished to father more children.

The other issue that was nipping at Gary's bottom was that Lisa was becoming friendly with the dealership's Head of Finance, a handsome, blonde, single man in his early thirties. Julian Anderton was reserved and considered in his approach to life, the type of man who could take ten minutes to decide on what cereal to eat in the morning, but once he had made a decision he would move forward with competence and capability. He had just purchased his first house, an end of terrace property, off a quiet cul-de-sac, in the suburbs of Reading. Lisa was impressed with Julian's ambition to renovate the property with the help of his builder father. She had visited and declared it would be lovely once the new fitted kitchen, fitted bathroom, utility room, open plan lounge, refurbished bedrooms and revamped garden were all finished. Gary considered that Julian was a bit nerdy, typical accountant type, but was proving to be wrong in his assessment of Julian, who according to Lisa was financially savvy, funny in a quirky sort of way, surprisingly fit when she ogled his biceps in his work shirt and seemingly, shyly interested in her. Lisa had now been asked out on a proper date by Julian and she had accepted. The date involved an upmarket Italian restaurant, a red rose for her, a lift home in his clean, fragrant Audi and then an espresso from his swanky coffee machine. No rushed groping on the cold back seat of a car.

Gary was now sat in the back of his car, with Lisa, on a warm June evening so that the windows were down and they could hear the occasional hoot of an owl as a summer breeze wafted into the interior of the car. 'Will you shut up about your date with Julian. You are with me now, you are my woman, and I don't like you going on about another man. Did you sleep with him?'

Lisa lay across the back seat of the car, her shapely legs resting on Gary's lap, revealed by the white shorts she was wearing. A scooped neck, blue T-shirt, exposed deep cleavage and bouncy breasts, as she shuffled to get comfortable in the cramped space. 'It's none of your business but no I didn't. I do quite like him and I don't want to be the slag who puts out on the first date, so we just cuddled on the sofa. The open plan lounge is almost finished so it was good to sit on real furniture, in a proper house, at the end of a date.'

'Ok, Lisa. Quit with this never-ending shit about being with me in a car. You know the score and we will soon be together as a proper couple.'

Lisa scowled at him, tired beyond tired of hearing this, when nothing ever changed. 'Proper couple. We can't be a proper couple because you keep forgetting one small detail. You have a wife.'

Gary caressed her leg, moving fingers gently forward to seek the area of her inner thigh and the promised land inside the white shorts. 'Yes, technically I have. But you know I don't fancy her, or want her, it's you I love.'

'I'm not sure you do, Gary, or you wouldn't let your greed for money be at the expense of being with me. This grand plan to get your hands on the Quall dosh is taking too long and I'm sick of living at my parent's house. I've said I'd go out with Julian again at the weekend, as technically, I am not your woman. So, suck it up.'

'I will not suck it up. Don't fucking speak to me like that. You'll stop whining and put up with this arrangement for now until I decide what to do about Claire.'

Lisa now slapped his hand away from her thigh and sat up slightly in the car. 'I'm warning you, Gary, I've had enough of all this and if you don't end it with Claire soon, I will do something about it myself. I will tell Roger Quall that you are shagging me whilst being married to his daughter. Then, we will see what happens to your marriage, your house and your job. You'll be out on your ear, Gary, without a penny.'

A rage now rushed through Gary, as a hot flush through a menopausal woman. He forced himself on top of her so that his face was level with hers and anger burnt furnace hot in his brown eyes. His teeth were bared, white and sharp, as a rabid wolf about to bite the neck of its defenceless prey. He stuttered out the next words. 'Don't…you…threaten, me, you bitch. I am not going to let you jeopardise all I've worked for over the last few years. I'll see you in hell first. We are doing this my way and you need to remember that, and you can forget Julian, you are not seeing him again.' He slapped her hard across the face, flinging her head sharply to the left before repeating the action. Lisa shrieked in pain, as she tried to push him off her but he was too forceful and filled with anger, as spittle collected at the corner of his mouth, like the venom from the fangs of a poisonous snake. He placed two strong hands around her throat, and squeezed purposely, pinning her body with his own as she tried to fight him off and escape. Her body was writhing and squirming as she fought to draw in every single breath into her lungs, and his crushing hands on her neck felt like her windpipe would crumble and collapse.

Suddenly he stopped, removed his hands from her throat, as she jerked upwards, gulping for the warm, humid summer night air which was wafting into the car. 'See what happens when you try to dictate to me.' His eyes now bore into hers, as she stared at his cruel, hard features. 'Let's get one thing straight. Who's in charge here?'

Lisa was still clutching her neck, reddened and bruised by the attack. She was now trying to guzzle the oxygen into her starved lungs between sobs as she cried in terror and pain.

There was no way she could speak, so he repeated the question. 'Who's in charge here, bitch?'

Shuddering loud sobs now filled the car and drifted out into the beautiful night. 'You are, Gary, you are. I'm sorry.'

His face was now calmer as his rage dispersed but it was replaced by the other need that was now racing through his body, a testosterone-fuelled thirst that need to be quenched. 'Lie back down here. Let me demonstrate to you why I am in charge.'

Much later that evening, Gary crept into bed beside Claire, at four in the morning trying not to wake her as she snored delicately, emitting the type of squeals a young piglet might make. Claire always came to bed at about ten p.m. and slept soundly and he never woke her up when he got into bed an hour later. She was the woman who would sleep through an earthquake or volcanic eruption possibly as the house fell down around her. She maintained that she was a light sleeper, rarely had a good night's sleep, and knew exactly when Gary came to bed. When the police came to question him, and they would, he would have convinced Claire that he had come to bed at the normal time, as she had looked at the alarm clock at eleven p.m. and said 'night' to him as he laid down.

He knew that he would be a person of interest in the disappearance of Lisa Jefferies but any DNA evidence in his car could be explained as he had given her a lift the other day as she accompanied him to visit a potential customer to discuss a finance package. Lisa had sat in the back seat, as he had dropped his wife off at the hairdressers, on the way. All true, lucky for him. Any forensic evidence of Lisa's hair or saliva could be accounted for. He would have to clean the inside of the car tomorrow but if it were too clinically clean this could also arouse suspicion. Traces of his semen would likely be present but he would have to give the police a story of being into the odd hookup for casual sex but he would appreciate they didn't tell his wife. He was sweating now, the severity of what he had done now slamming into him like a sledgehammer to his chest. The warm night was making him restless and breathless, but he fought to control himself, as he did not want Claire to wake and her remember that he had disturbed her sleep at four in the morning. His chest felt tight, his hands were shaky and there was a queasiness in his stomach, for he realised a line had been crossed and the consequences for his life could be traumatic. But in a tiny part of him, he felt the spark, that he had ignited something in himself that was almost other worldly. He felt a power and an authority that was superhuman. A power that very few human beings would know. He had been given a starter, a taster, a sample, of the control that it was possible to have over another person. The power to grant life or sanction death. The Roman emperor with his thumb up for clemency or the thumb pointing to the throat for death. Gary was more than a Roman emperor. He chose death. He delivered death. He was a God. Almighty. Omnipotent.

CHAPTER TWENTY ONE

August 2021

Gary arrived home on Friday evening, in a pleasant mood, happy to see Eva and happier still that Alfie was spending the bank holiday weekend with Niall's parents in a caravan, at a site in Norfolk. The grandparents had set out on Thursday and would return on Tuesday, for Alfie's start of his new school on Wednesday. Eva was back to school on the Tuesday, for a TD (teacher development) day, before her pupils arrived the following day. It would be calming for her to have her first day back at school, prior to Alfie's return, so that she could concentrate on her work priorities. The evening before Alfie's start of a new school would be a last minute panic of ironing shirts, labelling clothes, assembling stationery items and calming a terrified child. This year there would be no school lunch preparation for Alfie as he would be having school lunches which were paid for through the school's online payment scheme.

Gary came into the house, parked his suitcase in the hall, and he went into the lounge, where Eva was watching a film on Netflix and sipping on a glass of dry white wine from a freshly opened bottle. He sat next to her on the sofa, and pulled her towards him, kissing her softly on the mouth. Nuzzling her, he relished the glossy feel of her hair against his face and smelt the nutty traces of coconut and argan oil from her favourite conditioner. 'You smell really good, sweetheart, I've really missed you. Dealing with that sour old tenant that rents my house has made me realise that there are some women who should be kept out of sight from the rest of humanity. Nothing was right for her, the boiler's not working, the tap leaks, the hall needs painting, drone, drone, drone. And the moustache she's growing on her upper lip would make any man proud. Still, its lovely to be here with you, all clear skin, glossy hair and sexy mouth. No facial hair.'

'You've sorted out all you needed to do at the property, then?' Eva asked.

'Yes, for now. I'm sure there will be other minor issues that she will raise but the agents can deal with them, as it's what I pay them for. How's it been here? Did you see anyone while I was away?'

The question was innocent enough but Eva always suspected there was an agenda here, for him to track her movements, and keep an eye on who she was mixing with. 'No, except for mum and dad who popped over for an hour yesterday. They bought Alfie a small gift for starting secondary school.'

'A what?' Gary looked less than pleased at this information.

'It was nothing much, just a Captain America Shield with 'sometimes you forget you're awesome so this is a reminder' written on the back.'

'I fucking despair at this modern parenting lark. The only thing I got for going to school was a clip around the ear if I got told off by the teacher,' Gary fumed.

'Honestly, Gary, it is only a small gift, nothing expensive or showy.'

Gary still looked annoyed at all this but then asked, 'so, you didn't see anyone else, just your parents?'

'No, it was really just me and Alfie getting ready for school.'

Gary seemed satisfied with this and took a sip from her glass of wine. 'I'll go and get a beer shortly when I've indulged in my favourite activity with you.' He lifted her slightly so she was now lying on the sofa, and started to explore and devour her mouth with his own possessive one. His hands were then kneading her breasts, and opened the buttons on the front of her red floral dress, before he placed his mouth on her erect nipples. His hands were now moving downwards, to push the dress upwards, as he explored her inner thighs and moved eager fingers to the area between her legs. She moaned softly as he breathed heavily, her fingers undoing his belt and his trousers, and she could feel the urgency of how much he wanted her. He whispered into her ear. 'I've thought about having you for the last few days, how you look, how you feel, how you taste and I imagined we'd take it slow, but at this moment I feel that I have all the control of a teenage boy.' No gauche adolescent would remove her pants with such speed and once he was inside her his physical pounding of her body was done with all the proficiency of an expert, mature lover who sent an orgasmic wave through her hot, quivering body.

The rest of the bank holiday weekend was spent together, without interruption, in a leisurely way of lie-ins, love making, a circular walk of 4.8 miles around Draycote Water, near Rugby, on the Saturday afternoon as Gary insisted on fresh air and exercise. Sunday was a walk around Kenilworth, Abbey Fields, and then lunch in a local pub before returning home to watch a box set and drink wine. Monday was domestic chores in preparation for the week ahead including cleaning the house and washing clothes.

Gary had prepared dinner, roasted chicken, green salad and Parmesan potatoes and they were now seated at the dining room table, eating. While the previous day had been fun and light-hearted, Gary's mood had now changed, and he was starting to pick fault with everything Eva said or did. As he loaded chicken and potato on to his fork, he suddenly remembered the cost of Alfie's school shoes. 'How much did you say those school shoes of Alfie's cost?'

'£45.00, why?'

'£45.00. What is he, the son of a rock star or A list actor?'

Eva looked puzzled. 'That's a very reasonable price for a quality school shoe for a boy of his age. As you're not a parent, you don't know the realities of life with kids, one is that their feet grow very fast, and, two, they need shoes that fit well so that is never cheap.'

Gary's face was now starting to get angry. 'Don't start the 'you're not a parent bullshit' with me. I'm living with your kid, supplying money to run this household, so I'm entitled to know how much is being spent on his rapidly growing, big feet. He'll soon have feet the size of a man, so I'm quaking to think how much the shoes will cost then. I don't expect them to cost more than my shoes.'

'It's not really an issue, as I put extra money into the finances to pay for Alfie, as you know. So, technically, I'm paying for his shoes.' Eva could see that Gary's reaction to this was not sympathetic.

'Yes, but overall, all these extra costs diminish the sum total of money we earn which could be spent on other things,' Gary suggested. 'He doesn't need the shoes to cost that much.'

Eva now was getting irritated with Gary and his implication that she shouldn't overspend on her child. 'I don't see the problem, as you have those two properties which must bring in quite a bit of rent per month, and I don't see you sharing that with me.'

Gary had paused eating, and was poking his knife in the air, towards her. 'We have been over all this. I keep the money from my rentals, and any other savings, and you keep all your savings and investments, so we retain the assets we had prior to living together. I also know that this house belongs to you but we agreed on how to share the bills, all the outgoings. I'm just bloody annoyed when kids shoes are that expensive.' He returned to eating his food but as his level of irritation with her was rising, Eva tried to steer the conversation away from shoes and money. 'Did you sort out all the problems in that property you went to last week. Where exactly is it, you've never said, except that its down south.'

'It's in Berkshire, that's all you need to know, and it was owned jointly by me and my first wife, who died tragically in a fall when she was very young.'

'Did you say she was pregnant with your first child at the time?'

'Yes, so I lost them both together.'

Eva's blue eyes held Gary's whilst trying to express the hurt she felt for him at this awful, double loss. 'What was your wife like, Gary?'

He had now finished his meal and placed his knife and fork down on his plate. He shifted slightly on his seat, uncomfortable with her gaze on him. 'She was, er… cute, with short brown hair, and small in height. I met her at a factory where we both worked in the offices. It was not love at first sight but she sought of grew on me. I must admit to fancying her best mate, at first, but she was too much of a tease and I decided to go for the quieter one.'

'I am so sorry that you lost your wife and child, it must have been a terrible shock for you. I know what it's like to lose people you truly love.'

'Yes, it was a shock at the time. But I was lucky that the house came to me and, I had financial stability, which a lot of people don't have when their partner dies. Right, that's enough about her as here I am with you. Let me tell you that you are a vast improvement on wife number one.'

Eva felt a stab of anxiety, and concern, at this last comment, as if the first wife had not been chosen for reasons of love and friendship but that there was another agenda here. Gary always made a thing about boasting that he only went for 'fit' women but she found it difficult to decipher what his concept of 'fit' was. If she asked him, it came down to glossy hair, a sexy figure with shapely breasts and bottom, not too skinny or too fat, and it all had to be natural, no lip fillers, breast or butt implants and no bat-wing eyelashes. Eva did have these natural qualities but she never considered herself as 'fit' compared to many lovely young women there were in the world.

Gary now got out of his chair to clear the plates and dishes off the table to put in the dishwasher. 'Can you clear this up, as I've got to pop out to the dealership to do some paperwork for a couple of hours, for tomorrow. I'm driving to Birmingham first thing and I didn't have time to do it last week as I had to stay in Berkshire longer than I anticipated. This paperwork's got to be completed before I go. I think it's the grey bin to go out for collection tomorrow so you will need to do that.' He picked up an empty plastic water bottle off the table to put in the re-cycling box.

'Ok, no problem. I'll clear up.'

Eva pulled open the door to the dishwasher and started to load it with the dirty dinner plates, vegetable dishes, saucepans, glasses and cutlery. She then took out the disinfectant spray to wipe down all the kitchen surfaces and the worktops.

Suddenly the door from the utility door was rammed open, banging on its hinges as Gary strode back into the room carrying pizza boxes. He placed them down on the worktop, slowly counting them, one by one. 'Two large pizza boxes with ten slices in each. One pizza had Jalapeno peppers, pepperoni, black olives and red onion and you don't like the peppers. The other had half and half, ham and mushroom and ham and pineapple, and, neither you or Alfie like pineapple on a pizza. Plus, the wrappings for two side orders, chicken wings and potato wedges. How do I know the detail of all this, well here is the receipt, so don't forget to include one salted caramel ice cream and one litre of coke?' He slammed the receipt down on the worktop, the banging noise making her jump. 'And the price, £40.70. I know that Alfie could generally eat his body weight in food but this is all too much for just you two. Who was here the other night, eating pizza with you and Alfie?'

He had now moved away from the worktop, to stand by her, near to the sink, as she rinsed the dishcloth after finishing wiping the surfaces. He now loomed over her, forcing her into the corner between the dishwasher and lower cupboards. His face was reddened by anger, and his nostrils flared slightly, a raging bull about to charge, and she the matador without the protection of a sword. 'Am I not making myself clear when I ask a question. Who was here the other night eating pizza with you and Alfie?'

His hot breath scorched her face as he waited for her to respond. She breathed deeply, trying to control the shakiness in her stomach, and show that she would not be kowtowed by his demands. In a calm voice, she replied, 'it was Andy and Hannah. Andy helped me out with a small problem earlier and I treated everyone to pizzas as a thank you. Alfie really wanted Hannah to come over, and as Natasha was away at her mothers, I invited them both.'

Gary remained towering over her but she stood calmly, determined not to show that he was frightening her. He quickly honed in on the 'small problem'. 'What exactly did he do to get a reward of pizza at forty pound a go. If you're sleeping with him, I'd expect him to be paying you.'

'Don't be stupid, Gary. I went to the blood donors that morning and fainted when I got back here in the car. Alfie called Andy over as he didn't know what to do and Andy helped me get in the house.'

'How exactly did Handy Andy help you in the house?'

'He had to carry me as I had passed out. He stayed a while to see if I was ok and made some tea as I was de-hydrated.'

'Well, isn't he the macho cop hero with his hands all over my partner. That man is not to come in here again, do you hear me?'

Eva was truly shocked by all the awful stuff he was saying and his nasty assessment of Andy. 'Stop over reacting, he was just helping me out as a friend and neighbour. That's all.'

'You also told me on Friday that the only people you had seen when I was away was your parents and that you mainly spent time with Alfie. You did not mention the cop and the hours spent eating a pizza together. Basically, you lied to my face.' Gary face was now distorted with anger as he physically impeded Eva from moving.

Fear and panic were now surging through Eva as she tried to explain herself. 'Yes, I did but it was only because I knew you wouldn't like me seeing him and reacting like this.'

'You are right. I don't like you seeing him as I know he would like to be more than a friend to you. He'd like to be a friend with benefits, alright.'

Despite the quaking terror she was experiencing, Eva tried to laugh lightly at Gary's remark. 'He doesn't fancy me, if that's what you're implying as he is with Natasha. She told me, quite clearly, that I am not Andy's type.'

Gary now made the sound of a raging bull by snorting loudly, a menacing look on his face as he considered his next comment. 'Don't be so sure of that, as I think he does like you, as he comes over all smiley and helpful when he's around you. Maybe Natasha can sense it too and she's using that very clever female tactic of getting rid of any potential rival for her man. Though I don't think she's going to stay with Handy Andy for long as she is constantly looking for a man with a big wad of cash and a Ferrari. Mr Policeman is very good-looking but Natasha is not the type of woman to be happy on a cop's salary.'

'Gary, you are talking nonsense. Andy and I are friends. He doesn't fancy me, so that's the end of the matter.' Thinking that Gary's anger had now dissipated, Eva edged forward, and into him, to move out of the corner where she was trapped. 'You need to get off to do your paperwork as you have a long day tomorrow. It's been a nice weekend, don't spoil it.'

But the rage had not gone away, and it now flared again as he pressed her into the worktop, hurting her back. His right hand came up, and he slapped the left side of her head, hard and fast, so that her head bounced from side to side, and her neck jarred. He then roughly grabbed her face under her chin so she was forced to look into his cold, cruel eyes. 'Lessons to be learned from this evening. No more expensive shoes or whatever for your kid, he can have the cheaper versions and like it or lump it. No more spending my money on pizzas, sides, ice cream and pop for other people. No more lying when you have been spending time with the cop bastard who I know wants to be more than friends with you. Is that all clear?'

Eva was too stunned to speak but she managed to nod and whisper 'yes' to ensure that he did not have an excuse to hurt her again.

He released his grip on her face, all the fury of moments ago disappeared. The venomous snake, the puff adder had inflated with rage, dispensed its venom and was now returning to normal. 'Right, I'm off. Don't forget to put that rubbish in the re-cycling box or bags, and put the grey bin out as I told you.'

He tapped her face lightly, ignoring the shock on her face, and turned quickly to exit the kitchen.

CHAPTER TWENTY TWO

For five minutes, Eva stood wedged into the kitchen corner where she had been held captive and assaulted. She leaned back against the worktop to support herself as her legs trembled, and she felt sure they would not support her, if she tried to walk. The blow to her head had caused a ringing in her left ear, and a spinning sensation, symptoms of nausea and dizziness. The hard force of the blow was bringing on all the pain of a full-blown headache, and as she was prone to migraines, she did not want this to disrupt her first day back at school The throbbing pain and pulsating sensations on the left side of her head were all indicators that she could be experiencing the start of a migraine.

Leaning up to take a glass tumbler from a cupboard, she turned on the tap and filled the glass with water, and sipped slowly, trying to calm her shattered nerves and queasy stomach. Her head was completely befuddled, as she tried to process what had happened but her thoughts were all over the place, and pain and nausea added to her inability to think rationally. Only two simple ideas flooded her mind; re-cycle the rubbish and take the bin out.

It was now just after 8 p.m. and as Eva picked up the pizza boxes, an image flashed through her mind of a pleasant evening with Andy, eating the pizzas, drinking the 'pink' wine that he ridiculed, and enjoying each other's company. What had given her pleasure only a few days ago was now causing her pain, physical pain. For a moment, she actually thought she was going to vomit, and she could taste the acidic tang of the Parmesan cheese rising in her throat. She walked through to the utility room and put the pizza boxes in the red re-cycling box. She then went out to the side of the house where the wheelie bins were stored. In a sort of trance, she took hold of the handle of the grey wheelie bin used for household items that cannot be re-cycled. She walked to the front of the drive, pulling the bin behind her to place it on the pavement, handle facing the road to make the dustbin men/women's (operatives) job easier. Her face was ashen, as if all blood had been drained by a vampire out too early on this summer evening. Mrs Smith, her elderly, but sprightly neighbour across the road, was just leaving her bin out for collection, and waved enthusiastically at Eva, on seeing her. Eva did a very feeble nod, in acknowledgement, as any movement caused shards of pain to stab in her head.

On autopilot, she glanced over at Andy's house and noticed that his bin was not out, and his car, nor Natasha's, were on the drive. They had an informal arrangement, whereby, each would put out the other's bin, if necessary. She scurried back down her drive, and crossed over on to Andy's, to retrieve his grey bin which was by the side of the house. As she went to pull on the handle, Andy drove his car onto the drive, came to a halt and switched off the engine. Andy and Hannah emerged from the car, still laughing at something that had amused them.

Eva was jolted out of her reverie, as there was no way she wanted Andy to see her in her current state, still shocked and traumatised from Gary's onslaught. Andy would know immediately something was wrong and start asking questions, a police inspector interrogation which was very difficult to side step and give vague answers. To stop them seeing her she decided to hide between the two bins, the grey one, and the other green bin for garden and food waste. As she did so, she banged her big toe on the wheel of the grey bin, and emitted an 'ouch' sound which she hoped they would not hear. She crouched on the ground between the two bins, holding her breath, and trying to ignore the throbbing of her toe which was competing for dominance over the throbbing in her head.

Hannah immediately stopped giggling, stood still, as a concerned look was apparent on her face. 'What was that noise, dad, is someone at the back of the house?'

Andy placed his finger to his lips to indicate that his daughter should not speak. He moved forward quietly, his trainers not making too much of a sound on the block paved driveway, as he walked past the garage, to the start of the pathway between the side of the garage and Eva's fence. He stopped, gazed around, and listened closely for any further noises but he could only hear the odd tweet of a bird preparing for its night time rest. Andy's baritone voice now probably scared the feathered creature. 'Ok, I know there is someone here so come out, now.' The 'now' was said loudly, and with much authority, the type of voice he would use to dissuade those of a criminal mind from continuing to perpetrate any further misdemeanours. 'I am warning you that I am a police officer, so you are liable to be arrested.'

Eva rubbed at her throbbing head, trying to decide whether to keep quiet, and hope he wouldn't spot her, or to sheepishly acknowledge her presence as some weird trespasser loitering between his bins. Daftly, she opted for the stay quiet option which would have very little chance of working if he moved further down the pathway leading to his garden.

He slowly edged forward, and came to a grinding halt, as he caught sight of Eva crouching between the bins. Eva suddenly knew what it would be like to be apprehended by him, in his role as a police officer, as his face was stern and unsmiling. As he loomed over her, she was reminded of his physical presence; his height, and his strong muscular physique. 'Eva, what exactly are you doing down there?'

'Hi, Andy,' she blustered, mortally embarrassed to be found in such a position. 'I was just putting your grey bin out.'

The sternness of his face now faded, replaced by a bemused expression, that turned into a smile. 'Well, you are putting a whole new approach to doing that. The normal way is to stand up and pull it along by the handle. You had better come out of there before you get stuck.' He offered her his hand, which she took, to assist her to her feet.

Hannah came along the pathway as Eva got to her feet. 'Is everything ok, dad?'

'Yes, no problem. Just Eva having a rest by the dustbin before putting our bin out. You go inside and put the kettle on so we can give our visitor a cup of tea, as she looks as if she needs it.'

Andy let go of Eva's hand as she stood up. Eva stated, 'I'm ok for a cup of tea. I'll take your bin out, then leave you to it.' Eva wobbled slightly as she raised her head and he quickly placed a hand on her arm, thinking that she was going to faint again.

'Are you going to pass out on me again, as you don't look particularly good? I've seen white sheets with more colour than in your face at the moment. Forget about the damn bin, I'll see to that, but you are coming in for a cup of tea and so I can check you are ok. You are beginning to worry me now.'

Eva knew it would probably not be a good time to argue with him, and anyway she didn't have the energy for doing so, as she felt unwell and perhaps a cup of tea would help. Accepting the offer of tea, she nodded.

They went into the lounge where Andy made her sit on one of the two sofas before he went out into the kitchen to make the tea. He soon returned with two mugs of tea, with steam rising from the top. He offered Eva one of the mugs, which she took, and thanked him for it. He warned, 'be careful, it's really hot.'

She gazed down into the hot drink, holding the mug with her two hands, as the steam warmed her face. She then sipped slowly, but found it was too hot so paused, while the warm mug put heat into her cold hands. She was wearing a blue, strappy sun-dress, which revealed arms and legs still a pale gold from her holiday abroad but she now shivered as if the temperature in the room had dropped.

Andy noticed, and got up to pull a grey throw off the back of the sofa, to wrap around her. 'Are you feeling ill again?'

She now managed to take a couple of sips of the tea which was helpful in calming the queasiness in her stomach and soothing her rattled nerves. 'I'm ok. I can feel a migraine coming on which is all I need as I'm back in school tomorrow. My head's throbbing and I feel nauseous. It doesn't look good to phone in sick on the first day back at school, so I'll have to take some painkillers and hope they help.'

Andy looked at her sympathetically. 'I thought it was only the kids that got stressed at the thought of going back to school, not the teachers.'

Eva managed a brief smile. 'I can tell you it's ten times harder for the teachers than for the kids. People say, you've had all that lovely long holiday, you should be be ready to go back. I think that the longer you have off, the harder it is to return.'

'Yes, I guess you're right. Hannah's been moaning about it all day but I know she's really keen to see her mates. I think they appreciate being with their friends at school a lot more as they all missed each other during the lockdowns.'

'She'll be going into Year 8 and it all seems to go so fast at secondary school. Alfie's starting Year 7 but he still seems too young to be going to secondary school.'

Andy laughed. 'Therein lies the difference between boys and girls. Alfie seems young and not quite ready for this school stage. Hannah has the confidence and maturity of a female CEO of a major multi-national and I am one of the lowly minions that run around after her. What a drama we had over the school shoes. I tell you, she can buy them herself next year. If they are the wrong sort, she can explain all to the headteacher.'

Despite her listlessness, Eva did chuckle at this. 'Tell me about it. Alfie kept insisting he wanted the trainer type and I had a real struggle to dissuade him that they would not be acceptable. Then Gary goes ballistic about the cost of them, at £45.00. I did make the mistake of saying that as he is not a parent he does not understand the ongoing high cost of children's shoes. This, and other issues, all added to his rage and going out to put out the bin was my way of escape.'

Andy looked puzzled. 'What other issues? Is Gary giving you a hard time?'

Eva now concentrated on finishing her tea, realising that she may have said too much, and didn't want to be subjected to Andy's questioning techniques. 'No, it's nothing really. He's right, school shoes are too expensive and he does contribute to the household bills. Anyway, I need to go as I still have a few things to do for tomorrow and I must take some tablets to try and see off this migraine.' She got up from the sofa, putting the mug down on the coffee table. 'Thanks again for the tea. I must make you a cup next time. I can still put the bin out, if you want?'

Noting that she had no shoes on, Andy stated, 'no, I'll do it as you haven't got any shoes on but thanks all the same.'

Andy stood up, and as she walked past him, his eyes scrutinised her, a worried expression on his face, as if he somehow knew what was going on with Gary. For a second, Eva wondered what it would be like to be held by him, knowing that it would be a safe place in his arms, and she would be out of the circle of fear she was starting to experience with Gary. Imagining this, and still shaken by Gary's assault, she felt she was going to cry. She must leave immediately before Andy realised that there was something wrong. She hurried out of the door. 'Ok, bye Andy. I'll see myself out.'

****

As Eva left, Andy reclined on the sofa with his feet on the coffee table, something he often told Hannah off for doing. The lounge was a relaxing area, walls painted in a mid-cream, the two sofas in velvet teal, a single chair in a stone beige and the coffee table over a large rug in patterns of teal, terracotta and burnt orange. A log-burning stove provided additional cosiness in the winter months. But Andy's mood was far from relaxed at the moment, as the niggling concerns he had about Eva's welfare, were starting to become more serious as time went on. These thoughts were interrupted as Hannah came into the lounge.

'Hi dad, is Eva ok? What was she doing lurking by the bins?' Hannah landed on the sofa, next to Andy, and then sat with her legs tucked up under her.

Andy shook his head slightly. 'I'm not really sure. She said she was just putting our bin out but I got the impression that she was taking a few moments to escape her house.'

'Why would she do that?'

'I don't know. She said that she had a migraine coming on and she did look deathly pale. It must be the worry of going back to school tomorrow and dealing with all you grotty kids. I'd hate to be a teacher.'

Hannah laughed and stared at her dad. 'I'd hate you to be a teacher, too. You would be far too bossy. I bet they'd all be scared if you shouted at them.'

Andy pushed out his lower lip in a hurt expression. 'I don't scare you, do I?'

'No, because I know you are a softy really but you were a bit terrifying when you told the intruder, before we knew it was Eva, to come out as you were a police officer and they would be arrested.'

'Well, that is my work voice when I am apprehending criminals and I don't have to use it at home.'

A troubled expression developed on Hannah's face. 'Dad, can I ask you something?'

'You know you can ask me anything.'

'Do you think that Eva and Alfie are happy with Gary?'

'I think so, why do you ask?'

'It's just something Alfie told me about when they were on holiday in Menorca but he promised me not to tell anyone, especially you.'

Andy frowned, not liking what he was hearing. 'Why did he especially not want me to know?'

'Because you work for the police?'

Andy gently pulled Hannah to him, so that she was leaning against him, and he placed an arm around her shoulder. 'Is there something you want to tell me, Hannah, but you have promised Alfie that you would keep it secret?'

Hannah hesitated, happy not to be looking directly at her father. 'Yes, but if I tell you, you will have to report it and things would be worse for Eva and Alfie.'

'Right, Hannah, sweetheart, sometimes its ok to tell other people a secret, if it is in the best interests of those people, for other people to know. You tell me what Alfie said and we'll see what we should do. There is no way that I would put Eva and Alfie in danger, ok?'

Hannah drew in a deep breath, as she was still struggling to know what was the best thing to do. 'Alfie said that on holiday, he thinks Gary hit Eva. It was over some issue with her and a waiter. Alfie didn't see anything as he was in his bedroom, and they were in the lounge area, but he heard Gary shout, then he heard the sound of a slap and Eva cried out. Next day she had a red mark on her face, under her eye, which she covered with a lot of makeup. Alfie is scared that if you arrest Gary, the police will let him go and he will hurt Eva again.'

Andy absorbed what Hannah was telling him, trying to conceal the anger and shock he felt from Hannah. 'Ok, thanks for sharing that with me. If Alfie is right then it is a serious situation but the police would not get involved unless Eva, or someone close to her, makes a complaint. In a lot of cases, it will take the woman a long time to admit to herself, and then to others, that there is something wrong so if it happened, then Eva may not be ready to tell anyone at the moment.'

As a police officer, Andy knew that one had to proceed cautiously with this type of information, from a third party, Alfie, who had not actually witnessed what, if anything, had occurred. But Alfie's description to Hannah did sound reasonable and he had seen the evidence of a mark on his mother's face. From a police perspective it would be up to Eva to make a statement about what occurred, and Alfie could be asked to submit a statement as to what he heard, and what he saw. But for now, there was nothing to be done until Eva was prepared to seek help through family, friends, the police and/or one of the many organisations that can help women in situations of domestic violence.

'You won't be telling the police about what happened?' Hannah asked. '

'I am the police, but there's little I can do about it unless Eva is willing to report it officially to the police. I'm not doubting Alfie but he didn't actually see anything, did he?'

'No, he didn't, but he did see the red mark on her face and he asked her about it. She said that she had hit her face with a kitchen cupboard door. If Gary did hit her why would she lie to protect him?'

'Unfortunately, Hannah, a lot of women in domestic violence situations are too scared or embarrassed to acknowledge what is going on and so do not tell anyone what they are enduring. It is very difficult to help someone until they are willing to be helped,' Andy explained, knowing that these situations can continue for long periods of time, often over many years.

'So, dad, just to be clear, Gary is not going to be arrested at the moment. As I would feel dreadful if I caused more harm to Alfie and Eva.'

Andy gently turned his daughter's face so she could look at him. 'Listen, don't worry over this. You have done the right thing by telling me. And for the moment, nothing is going to happen to Gary. But if he is hurting Eva, and she informs the authorities, then I would be happy to put the handcuffs on him myself. I will try and keep an eye on Eva, and Alfie, by being their friend, to see if I can find out what is going on. It might not be anything and Alfie misunderstood what he heard.'

'Thanks, dad.' She leaned in to hug Andy and he placed a kiss on the top of her head.

'Anyway, it's time that you were thinking about going to bed. I don't want you over tired so that on Wednesday morning you can't get up for school. Night.'

As Hannah left the room, Andy reflected on what she had told him about Eva. On balance, he strongly suspected that what Alfie had said was true and that Gary had hit Eva. Gary's behaviour towards Eva and Alfie was beginning to concern him more and more. He was starting to exert control over them, in a number of ways; his authoritarian manner with Alfie about his so called 'bad' behaviour, undermining Eva's parenting skills and questioning her spending on shoes for Alfie. She described Gary as in a rage about the shoes and other issues. Was it this rage that had caused Eva to hide between the wheelie bins, as Andy strongly felt that she was hiding, probably to escape Gary. And what were these other issues she had referred to? Andy considered he was putting together a jigsaw puzzle, piece by piece, but he didn't like the picture that was forming before his eyes, as it was a dark bleak, and ugly cavern, and at its heart there lurked a monster.

CHAPTER TWENTY THREE

October 2008

Gary had now endured four years of marriage to Claire who was certainly not getting more attractive or intelligent with age. Their attempts to make a baby, for the joy of the wealthy grandparents, had proved to be arduous. He wanted to say back-breaking but he did not exert his usual effort when copulating with a woman, to make her gasp and moan. He learnt that he could only manage it with Claire, if he thought of a sensuous famous woman that he fancied or he had glanced at the Page 3 Model in The Sun, the paper that the lads brought into work. Claire was still not sure about having a baby, and he did wonder if she would be any good at caring for an infant, as her domestic skills had not really improved over the last few years. He had even started to do some cooking himself as he was fed up with eating unhealthy ready meals, fish fingers, burger and chips, and sausage and mash. They now ate more vegetables, salads, stir fries, low fat pasta dishes and lean meats. Claire's figure now had more of a discernible waist but there was still no generous breasts or curvy butt to hold on to. Looks-wise she was plain and dowdy, and it would seriously harm his credibility in the dealership world if he turned up with her to a dinner or gala night. If her father was not so well-known in the area, he would have been tempted to turn up at these events with a new, glamourous girlfriend, and pretend his marriage was over.

The marriage was over. It had never been a marriage, just a union to fast track him into a life of wealth and security, and this was beginning to pay off. On his last birthday, he had been awarded shares in RQ Car Screws & Bolts Ltd a small significant recognition of his place in the company. Three months ago they had told Claire's parents that she was twelve weeks pregnant. Roger Quall had delighted the happy couple by signing over the car dealership, on his 60th birthday, to be jointly owned by Claire and Gary. After Gary had secured the paperwork to ensure that the shares were his, and they had made joint wills so that he would inherit Claire's assets if anything happened to her, Gary felt that it was time to execute the end stage of The Plan involving the wife. Recognising that he would not be a patient and loving father, and having an intense dislike for children, he decided that it was best if mother and baby met an unfortunate demise together.

Four years of marriage to Claire had not improved his temper. He could fly off the handle with her over the slightest thing. Not wiping down the kitchen worktops properly, not loading the dishwasher satisfactorily or ironing his shirts perfectly could all ignite his rage, and he would shout at her, highlighting her many short comings as a lazy slut and stupid bint. He had been forced to employ a cleaner once a week or the house would not be maintained to the standards he expected but he did resent spending money on something that other women coped with easily.

After the first year of marriage, the shouting escalated to more physical persuasion by him, of what he expected of her. One time whilst having sex, when she had remained as still and unmoving as a plank of wood, he smacked her across the face to get some sort of reaction out of her but was only rewarded with silent tears as he finished the job. This was the first time he had physically harmed her but it led to more frequent outbursts when his temper could not be calmed without administering a slap or a punch. Afterwards he felt nothing and was only aggravated more if she cried. Luckily, the shame of all this prevented her from telling anyone, especially her parents, and she did not have any close friends now that Lisa had disappeared out of her life.

What had happened to Lisa Jefferies was a mystery that still interested the people of the town of Reading. Lisa's mother strongly suspected that Gary had something to do with her daughter's disappearance but no body had been discovered, and no forensic evidence was found to indicate foul play. Mrs Jefferies was convinced that her daughter had been seeing Gary, but she had no proof to offer, and there were no witnesses to their relationship as it was mainly fostered in the back seat of Gary's car. No one else involved. Claire had been interviewed by the police to find out if she knew if Lisa had a boyfriend. She confirmed to the police that she believed that Lisa did have a boyfriend, a married man, and so Lisa was very cagey in talking about him. All that Claire knew was that he was fit, good at sex, and was going to leave his wife in the future. The irony of Claire discussing Lisa's lover's wife with the police did give Gary a reason to chuckle for quite some time.

After Lisa's mother had given his name to the police, he was identified as a person of interest, and had been taken in for questioning on two occasions. As luck would have it for him, neither he or Lisa had taken their mobile phones with them, on that particular night of their rendezvous. He was also careful that Lisa did not text him regularly with personal messages of any kind so that when the police examined their phones there was no indication that they were in an intimate relationship. They did correspond, on an employee/employer basis as Lisa continued to work in the car dealership that he managed. All arrangements to meet up were made verbally, or by internal phone calls, whilst at work. Gary believed that the detective inspector investigating Lisa's disappearance guessed that he had been sleeping with Lisa but there was no hard evidence linking them in this way. Gary got the impression that work colleagues suspected that he played away but had not heard or seen anything to link him to Lisa. Lisa was known as a flirt, and was jokey and familiar with most of the men at the dealership, and it was discovered that she had been seeing one of the garage mechanics for casual liaisons. Gary delighted in seeing the young guy being the subject of much gossip, and speculation, as it took any focus away from him.

Claire did give information to the police that Gary left the house a couple of evenings a week to have a drink at a pub with a mate, Simon. Simon and Gary had been friends from primary school and knew all of each other's dirty little secrets. Simon had followed Gary from Greenwich, SE London, where they had grown up on a council estate, looking out for, and protecting each other, as they learned to survive in a hostile environment. Simon, from a large family of petty thieves and wasters, had been delighted that Gary had got him a job at RQ Screws and Bolts, on the manufacturing side. Gary faked the references to get Simon into the job and explained away the gaps in his CV when he was detained at Her Majesty's Pleasure for burglary on one occasion, and receiving stolen goods, on another. Gary always ensured that he had enough evidence of Simon's criminality to keep him as a useful advocate if Gary needed a favour or an alibi. Simon did not hesitate to give Gary an alibi for the evening when Lisa Jefferies was last seen by her mother.

On this late October evening, Claire sat on the sofa, dressed in blue pyjamas, grey polyester fleece dressing gown and grey suede moccasin slippers with faux fur. This was the outfit she adopted every evening after dinner as she relaxed in her 'comfies.' Gary sat on the second sofa, felt he was spending his evenings with the matriarch of a family of teddy bears, and on the nights he didn't go out he had to dampen his temper and urge to strangle her, by soothing his system with whisky. There had definitely been a price to pay for choosing the fast-track to riches if it involved living this existence in a geriatric home before he was out of his twenties. Now, that she was pregnant, Claire had seen it as a licence to eat exactly what she wanted and her attempts at healthy eating were suspended as her 'cravings' included chocolate, crisps and jelly babies. At twenty-four weeks pregnant her 'bump' was now prominent, and she had put on additional weight around her face, arms and legs, and was getting lumpier, and more repellent, by the day. Enough was enough. It had to end and he would be free to move on with his life, consolidate his finances and hope to move away from Reading to start on the next stage of The Plan.

Tonight, she was munching on a large packet of ready salted crisps as they watched the 14th National Television Awards hosted by Sir Trevor McDonald. She nearly choked on a crisp as a loud firework banged just outside and Gary hoped that a firework as loud as gunshot would explode and finish her off with a heart attack.

'Jesus, Gary. They get louder every year. All this noise is not good for the baby.'

'What do you expect me to do about it? Get some ear plugs if you're that bothered. What's not good for the baby is you consuming all that salt on those crisps and the sugar in that orange pop. I've told you to eat and drink healthier for the sake of the baby, why can't you listen?'

'I know Gary, you are right, but I am having these cravings for salty food so what can I do.'

'Shut up and watch the programme as you wanted it on.'

'Ok, I am watching it. You are getting narky as you're drinking too much whisky.'

'Maybe but it dulls the pain of living with you.'

Claire ignored this comment and then clapped loudly when actress Rita Simons won the Most Popular Newcomer award for her role as Roxy Mitchell in EastEnders. 'I'm glad she's won, she really feisty and pretty, and I wish I was her.'

Gary gave a loud, harsh laugh. 'God, so do I. To have an attractive, blonde on the sofa would be very pleasant so we could cuddle up together and make out.'

'You're obsessed with sex, Gary. And I don't think I'll be up for it much in the next few months, you know.'

Finishing his whisky, Gary placed down his glass, and really looked at the woman he been forced to spend time with over the last four years. 'You won't have to worry about that and I can find some slappers to keep me going.'

Another loud explosion sounded like a bomb going off and Claire jumped spilling orangeade over the sofa. 'Oh dear, I'll get a cloth. Then I'm going to go upstairs and find my earplugs and get my book. I'll be back down in a minute.'

She came back in with a cloth, her feet slopping along in the moccasin slippers which were too big for her feet, so she walked in a shuffling motion to try to keep them from falling off. She dabbed at the orange pop stain and then shuffled out of the room, reminding Gary of the slow, rocking gait of his late grandmother when she was in her late eighties. Gary breathed deeply, taking in air to calm his anxiety, ready for the moment he was going to proceed with the 'till death us do part' of his marriage vows.

He turned the volume of the television down slightly to hear her plod up the stairs, before turning up the volume slightly higher. He walked out of the lounge and lightly went up the stairs so that he could surprise her in the bedroom. He opened the bedroom door and went in, as she was bending over to look into the drawer of her bedside cabinet, to locate the ear plugs. Finding them, and shutting the drawer, she jumped as she caught sight of Gary in the room.

'Oh, you made me jump. I've found them. I think my book's downstairs, so I'll stay down there for half an hour or so. Are you coming to bed? It's a bit early for you.'

Gary stood still by the closed bedroom door, watching her, the expression on his face unreadable. 'I've changed my mind, after what I said downstairs, and I've decided that we could have a little cuddle now, what do you think?' He knew she would be horrified at this suggestion. Moving slowly into the room, he edged towards her, cultivating a lustful look to support his intention.

She turned to face him as he stopped just inches away from her. He placed a hand on her breast and fondled her roughly. 'I think these are getting bigger. Having a baby is definitely a bonus for you as I get to fancy you more.'

She backed away from him, but he continued to massage her breast, and leaned in to kiss her, as his arm tightened around her waist. He touched her bottom, running his hands over its curves. 'Yes, this is womanlier too. And, I'm getting very turned on.' He knew that she would react with fear, a sort of paralysis, as she always did when he made a move on her. He had realised long ago that she had an almost phobic aversion to having sex.

She lightly pushed him away and he allowed her to move passed him. 'No, Gary, I can't do it as it might hurt the baby.'

'Don't be daft. I'll go at it slowly. Just come here.' She speeded up to get away from him but her movements were still slow and shuffling, impeded by the slippers that slopped around her feet. He kept a pace tight up to her back, as she slowly shambled out of the bedroom, and onto the landing. His hand sensually stroked her bottom and he gave it the smallest sexy nip. 'I promise I'll make sure you enjoy it this time, sweetheart.'

For a few seconds, she seemed to speed up to hover at the top of the stairs. She was now concentrating wholly on getting away from him. 'I'm not in the mood, Gary.' As she went to place her left foot on the first step, Gary gave her the slightest nudge with the palm of his hand on her left shoulder. She overbalanced, and slammed the side of her head, powerfully, on the wall, before tumbling down all the steep flight of stairs. Her body bashed and bumped on the stair rail as she went, before she landed at the bottom, belly down, arms bent, legs splayed out.

Gary, the dutiful husband, rushed down to her side. All this was a massive gamble for him in his quest to end the marriage and move forward with The Plan. As he looked down at the motionless, crumpled body of the woman who he loathed and despised, Gary was praying that the fall had achieved his desired outcome. The death of his first wife.

CHAPTER TWENTY FOUR

Eva had survived the first four days of the start of the new school year, and was now pleased that it was Friday evening, and she could relax at the beginning of the weekend. Her class of thirty, Year 4 pupils, were a sensible group, and she felt that generally they were happy to be back at school, particularly after the lockdowns at the start of the year. There were still COVID-19 protocols in place, including twice weekly lateral flow testing for herself and her teaching assistant, the ongoing guidance on handwashing and using hand gels, reduction of mixing of different year groups, where possible, and the regular cleaning of tables, chairs and equipment by herself and the TA. An upside was that there was no obligation for school staff to wear face coverings, and this pleased Eva, as she considered that they did place a barrier between her and the young pupils. Parents were still requested to wear face coverings on school property. All in all, COVID-related matters were improving and Eva was proud of the way that all pupils at the school had adapted their behaviours, when asked to do so. Now, the harder part, was getting them back into work mode, with mornings spent on English, reading and maths. Afternoons were spent on topics, with history/geography on Mondays, art/design & technology on Tuesdays, French/PSHE on Wednesdays and on Fridays, science. On Thursday, it was PE and it had been generally noted that pupil levels of fitness had fallen over the last eighteen months so progress had to be made to combine fitness with fun. To Eva, fitness and fun were a bit of an oxymoron, as she was not the greatest advocate of exercise, for which Gary berated her frequently.

Now, Eva was ready for fun (without any fitness) as she waited for Tania to arrive, and then they were off to the town centre, by cab, to celebrate Tania's thirty-fifth birthday. Tania was dropping in at Eva's for a glass of bubbly before they went for a meal and drinks in a gastropub where they were meeting two other friends. Tania had stopped off at her parents' house on the way and her dad gave her a lift to Eva's house. Eva could hear Tania's high heels clattering up the drive before she rang the doorbell. As Eva let her in, Tania shrieked loudly on seeing her friend, draped her arms around her and landed a large, smacker of a kiss on Eva's cheek. Eva eyed her warily. 'Have you been drinking already?'

'Not really, my gorgeous friend, it depends how you define drinking?'

Eva laughed, noting that Tania was wearing a rather large badge which read 'Birthday Girl'. 'Drinking, in terms of consuming alcoholic beverages.'

'I might have had one little, tiny, white wine with mama before I came out but I promise I am not going to get pissed.'

'If you're calling your mum and dad, mama and papa, it sounds as if you are. Anyway, I've got a bottle of bubbly just opened. Let's have a glass.'

The women went into the lounge, where the champagne bottle was resting in a wine cooler. Tania was dressed in a soft pink, V-necked, sequinned mini dress worn with silver heeled sandals. Eva had on a cobalt-blue, scooped-neck mini dress that accentuated her shape and highlighted the auburn tint of her hair. Cobalt blue high heels, with a rhinestone detail, lengthened her slim legs.

'What time's the taxi getting here?' Tania asked, as it had been left for Eva to arrange it.

'In half an hour, so time to drink the bubbly.' Eva picked up the bottle and poured the champagne into the two flutes without spilling any over the top of the glass. She handed one to Tania. 'Cheers. To my best friend, Tania. Happy Birthday.' They chinked the glasses, and sipped the brut champagne, which was smooth and creamy, though the bubbles made Eva cough as they caught her throat.

'Cheers. And as it's my birthday I want all my wishes to come true and find my soul mate tonight. I've waited a long time for him to come along. Talking of soul mates, where's old misery guts tonight, then?'

'Tania, I expect you mean Gary. He's out with a couple of the guys from the dealership so you won't have to see him.' Eva was pleased that Gary was out tonight, as she had been avoiding him as far as possible since the 'incident' last Monday. She kept referring to it as the 'incident' in her head as she didn't know what to call it. After the tea at Andy's, she had returned home and sat on the sofa, going over it in her head, whilst the day turned from light to dark. This was now the second time that he had physically assaulted her, slapped her, and there was a numbness to her mind and body which stopped her taking action over this. Rationally, as an intelligent and educated woman, she knew that what he was doing was wrong, and that he was becoming more controlling emotionally and physically. Logically, she knew that it would not stop, and mostly likely get worse, as she understood from the stories of other women who had been subjected to domestic abuse. Many people held the view that a woman should leave a violent man the first time he hit her. Do not give them a second chance. When viewing these situations as an onlooker, it was easy to form this opinion and she herself could understand this stance. Now that it was happening to her, why wasn't she asking Gary to leave her house and her life? She owed him nothing. But there were positives to being with Gary, and when he was funny, loving and attentive then she did feel happy, and it was better than being alone. When Niall died, she had strongly missed his male presence in the house, an extra pair of hands to care for Alfie, share the domestic chores, someone to take her side when describing petty disputes with work colleagues or friends, and the comfort of being in someone's arms at night. Gary provided all this, and she was reluctant to let it all go, and face the loneliness of being a single parent.

Since Monday, Gary had been on his best behaviour. He had brought her tea in bed to ease her awake on the day of the start of the new school year. Breakfast of yoghurt, fruit and toast were waiting when she came downstairs. As she picked up her bag, phone and keys, and psyched herself up to walk out to her car, he wished her a good day. He joked that if anyone were to bully her, he must be informed immediately, and that included if the bully was the headteacher. Gary would take a contract out on their life. She smiled at the joke but she was wary of him and did not allow him to kiss her as she left the kitchen.

By this Friday evening, Gary had been making maximum effort with her and Alfie all week. Alfie was made a fuss of when he returned from his weekend with the grandparents. Gary had played a computer game with Alfie for an hour before bedtime on Tuesday evening which he normally didn't encourage. Computer games had the disadvantage of waking Alfie up, not settling him down.

Gary had openly encouraged her to have a good time tonight, to celebrate Tania's birthday, when normally he didn't like her going out with female friends without him. Tania, and the other two women, were single and always out on the prowl for possible boyfriends. Gary did not want lecherous men being attracted to the four women and thinking that Eva was also single. To be cautious, Eva had only changed into the blue mini dress after he had left the house, or he might take the view that she was dressing provocatively to attract men.

The night at the gastropub was amazing; they had a good meal, plenty of drinks, the single girls chatted to lots of men and Tania had arranged a date for tomorrow with a handsome, Asian, accountant. As the taxi pulled up at Eva's house, five hours later, the two women got out of the cab, high heels clattering on the driveway and louds shrieks emitting from Tania's mouth. As she wobbled slightly under the influence of too many cocktails, she shouted, 'let us end the night with a few more glasses at yours and then I'll get a cab home. Got any white wine in?'

Tania staggered towards Eva's front door just as Andy's car pulled onto his drive. 'Oh my God, it's my lucky day. The world's most handsome policeman is just getting out of his car. I might try my luck for a birthday kiss.' She veered off across the drive and onto Andy's, as Eva tried to follow. 'Hi, Andy,' Tania squealed.

Andy stood by his car, as Tania tottered over towards him, wiggling along in the pink mini dress and silver heeled sandals. 'Hello Tania, hi Eva. Looks like you've been having a good time.' He gave Tania a stern look. 'I hope I'm not going to have to arrest you for being drunk and disorderly.'

Tania came to a halt next to him and held out her arms. 'Yes, Mr Policeman, you can arrest me now. I'll come quietly.'

Andy smiled and winked at Eva. 'I doubt that.'

Tania then stared up at him, large eyes framed by long false eyelashes, focusing on his face. 'It's my birthday today. Would it be against the law to ask for a birthday kiss?'

Andy chuckled. 'Not if I give my consent, so you can give me a quick peck on the cheek.'

'Spoilsport. I was hoping for something with a bit more spice, shall we say, but that will do.' He bent down and she leaned up to kiss him on the cheek, as he said, 'happy birthday, Tania.'

Eva then took over to try to direct her friend into her house. 'Come on Tania, Andy's just coming home from a long day at work, so he needs to rest.'

Andy did look tired, as the area under his eyes were dark, which accentuated the blueness of his eyes. 'Yes, it's been a long day, on a difficult case, so I'm ready for one drink of whisky, and then bed.'

Eva noticed that Tania perked up at this and commented, 'Tania, don't even think about saying what's on your mind or I will get Andy to arrest you for lewd thoughts. Come on.'

As the two women started to walk away, Andy lightly caught Eva on the arm, holding her back, as Tania swayed towards Eva's house. He looked at her face closely, as he asked, 'how are you now after Monday night? Did the migraine go away?'

'Yes, thanks. I took some paracetamols and it did wear off, luckily.'

'You did look unwell, very pale and sickly. Are you sure you're ok, nothing else going on?'

Now feeling uncomfortable as to what he might me thinking, she said, 'no, I'm fine. You just keep catching me at my weaker moments. Anyway, see you soon.'

'Ok, but you know where I am if you need me,' Andy advised her before they both headed to their respective houses.

In Eva's kitchen, it was quickly decided that Tania did not require any further alcohol, so Eva made them both a coffee before a taxi was called to take Tania home. After helping her friend into the cab, Eva headed back into the house, just as another cab pulled up, and Gary got out of it.

Eva went into the house, not waiting for him, and took her coffee cup into the lounge. She sat on the sofa, picked up the TV remote, and started to look for a film to watch, as she was still hyped up from the drinking and not ready for sleep. Drinking coffee at this time of night was not such a good idea, either.

Gary came into the room and sat down on the sofa, next to her, placed his feet on the coffee table, and his left arm around her shoulders, drawing her against him. Eva felt herself tense, as he touched her, and the smell of beer on his breath and a mixture of sweat and cologne on his shirt made her slightly nauseous. As she drew away from him, he reacted to this by firming his grip on her. 'I notice you changed into this dress after I left the house. You were wearing that black dress earlier which is a bit demurer than this blue one.' This was said as more of a question than as a comment and Eva felt she was being asked to justify why she had changed outfits.

'Yes, I decided that the black dress was a bit dull, more suited to funerals than to a Friday night out in town.' The grip of his hand on her shoulder intensified.

'How did the night out go with the girls? Did they pull?'

Eva could not clearly see his face as he asked this but she sensed, in the tone of his voice, that he was less interested in the other women's exploits, and more interested in hers. 'Yes. Tania has got herself a date with an accountant tomorrow. He and his friends were really nice.'

'Friends?'

'Yes, we got chatting to a group of people from this accountancy firm who were out celebrating a birthday. Jen took a liking to one of them and swapped numbers, so that could be promising.'

Gary placed his hand under Eva's chin, forcing her to look at him. 'And, what about you, did anyone take an interest in you?'

'No, not really. There were just a number of us having a chat. They were a friendly group and really funny for a bunch of accountants.'

He held her chin steadily, not letting go. 'You are asking me to believe that you, the prettiest of the four, and looking knock out in that dress, did not get chatted up, and that Tania and Jen were in demand. Tania's hot, in a loud, obvious way but I've seen Jen and she's more mouse than Minnie. So, I'm not buying it.'

'Forget it, Gary. What do you want me to say, that I've got the phone numbers of five potential new boyfriends on my mobile?'

'Don't rattle me or I might check. It's always best to be honest in these situations.'

Eva was now discerning that alcohol was making Gary snippy, and she was balancing on a tight rope, afraid of taking this conversation in the wrong direction. Making a decision on what was the right direction was the difficulty. Yes, she had been chatted up by two men, both keen to take her out on a date, but telling Gary this could have troubling consequences. On the other hand, he was not convinced she was telling the truth, and perhaps feeding him a small morsel of truth would hide the bigger secret. 'I did have someone who was interested but I quickly told him I was spoken for.'

'What was he like, some young, office clerk, still wet behind the ears?'

Eva often perceived that Gary was jealous of men younger than him and moaned about his age, as he headed to forty. 'No, actually, he was in his forties, and one of the accountancy firm's partners, recently divorced. He seemed a nice guy but I'm not available.'

'If you were available, would you have gone on a date with him?' These words were said with more and more emphasis, and slowness, as he progressed the sentence, as she detected irritation in his voice.

'No. Maybe. Doesn't matter as it's not happening.'

'No, it's not happening for him, the loser. It's happening for me.' His hand now forced her face towards his and he started an exploratory kiss on her mouth which was firm and consuming. The weight of his body pushed her down on the sofa, his right hand pushed up her dress and stroked her inner thighs. He stopped the kiss to whisper in her ear. 'Yes, he's the loser as I've got the prize here with me. I'm the only man that's going to go with you, darling, and I going to show you why.'

Eva began to feel claustrophobic and panicky as his weight constricted her breathing and his hands squeezed and probed her body, as his urgency to claim her escalated. In her mind, she did not want this, it was too forceful and demanding but her vocal cords were paralysed so she could not speak to voice her objection. She tried to breath slowly to calm her nerves, and relax her body, so that she could participate in what should be a mutually pleasurable experience. But her body, would not co-operate, and her nerves were jangling, and fear was building, as he carried her along on a journey that she was not wanting to go on.

CHAPTER TWENTY FIVE

Detective Inspector, Andy Leyton, sat with Detective Constable, Gabrielle Lewis in Pamela Stratton's lounge, drinking hot tea from small China tea cups with saucers. Mrs Stratton was seated next to her husband, Jim, on the brown leather sofa and was tightly holding his hand as she struggled to speak between bouts of crying. Andy was sat on a chair adjacent to the Stratton's with DC Lewis on a chair next to his. The lounge was a tribute to the colours of beige and brown. All the walls were decorated in a cream matt paint, the persistently popular 'Magnolia' favoured by older age groups, complemented by a carpet in a digestive biscuit colour. Cream cushions, oakwood TV stand and oak sideboard, gave the room an overall blandness which called out for splashes of reds, or oranges, or greens, in terms of pictures, soft furnishings or ornaments.

Andy sipped on the tea and waited as Mrs Stratton sought to compose herself. He was here to ask her some questions about her parents, following the death of her father, an end of life allegedly caused by the actions of her mother. Police had been called to the parental home one day ago, to find eighty-two-year-old, Mr Norris Parkinson, with fatal head wounds caused by blows from a weapon, a golf club, found at the scene. Mrs Edna Parkinson, wife of Norris for sixty-two years, was also at the scene and was currently the alleged perpetrator of the attack. Edna Parkinson was currently remanded in custody but was refusing to co-operate with the investigating officers, and was not speaking to anyone, not even the duty solicitor. Her only response so far was a 'yes' when asked if she would like a cup of tea.

Andy believed that these types of murders, as that is what it appeared to be, of a spouse, by the other spouse, were particularly difficult for the relatives involved, in this case, their daughter, Pamela. A son, Ralph, lived in Spain, and was currently on his way back to the UK. What a shock for the children of this type of crime. One dearly loved parent had been killed by the other parent, who the child will in most cases, love as well, so loyalties are torn. Effectively, the person had lost both parents at the same time, one died, and the other was likely to go to prison for a long time unless there were mitigating circumstances. Andy could express sympathy to the family on the loss of the deceased but be acutely aware that one should remain impartial to collect evidence in terms of this family's situation. Things aren't always what they seem on first impressions.

Mrs Stratton had now stopped crying and seemed to be composed enough to perhaps answer some of his questions. She was a woman in her early sixties, who was slim to the point of skinny, with blonde hair fading to grey, a well-lined face that suggested years of smoking and difficult times. Her husband, Jim Stratton, a man of receding hairline and wispy grey hair, was quiet and re-assuring, a steady rock that she leaned on as she was buffeted by the waves of grief that were battering her.

'Mrs Stratton, I understand this is a very difficult time for you and your family and may I extend my condolences to you all.'

Mrs Stratton started to cry again and wiped at her face with the shredded and soggy remains of a tissue. Her husband placed his left arm around her shoulder and offered up a box of tissues as a replacement for the current one. 'I need to see my mother, she will be very frightened and alone. I must see her.'

Andy addressed Mrs Stratton. 'Mrs Stratton, your mother, currently, is being kept in custody at the police station whilst we investigate the death of your father.'

Mrs Stratton looked directly at Andy, the stress of it all showing in her troubled face. 'She won't be able to cope there on her own. She's not been well recently, you know forgetful and distracted, and she gets frightened easily.'

'Please don't worry, Mrs Stratton. We are putting protocols in place in recognition of your mother's age and mental vulnerability. We have arranged that your mother will be supported by an appropriate adult, a trained person whose role is to safeguard the interests, rights, entitlements and welfare of a vulnerable adult who is being investigated for a criminal offence. They will ensure that your mother is treated justly and fairly, and will help her fully understand, and participate in the procedures whilst in custody. Any interviews with your mother will always involve a solicitor being present. Her physical well-being will be looked after in terms of regular breaks for food and drinks.'

Mrs Stratton seemed to relax a little on hearing this but she was ghostly pale with anxiety etched on her tear-stained face. 'Do we know that she has done something wrong? It could be that someone has broken in and killed my father. Why is my mother deemed to be responsible?'

Andy nodded slightly, understanding that Mrs Stratton would be keen to suggest that a terrible crime had been committed by a burglar, who had entered the house illegally. 'Yes, Mrs Stratton, that is one line of enquiry we are pursuing and we are doing a very thorough forensic investigation to try to establish a full picture of what has occurred. This includes looking at the possibility of a third party being involved in the attack. I do have to advise you, though, that the most likely possibility is that your mother is the alleged perpetrator of the attack on your father. Your parents were found by a carer on a visit on the Wednesday morning and found your father deceased in his bed, with your mother sat on the bedroom floor, golf club by her side.'

On hearing this, Mrs Stratton started to cry again. Andy realised it was going to be an exhausting and lengthy process for her as he tried to establish the nature of her parents' relationship and the overall family situation. 'Mrs Stratton, I am sorry that this is very upsetting for you but I would like you to describe your parent's marriage. I think you said they had been married for sixty-two years. Was it a happy marriage?'

Mrs Stratton now pulled herself out of her husband's comforting embrace, positioned herself more upright on the sofa and faced Andy and DC Lewis with a stern expression. 'Happy, happy. That's not a word I would use to describe them. There may have been happy moments for my mother, when me and Ralph were born, or during the times that he was away but those were the only ones.'

DC Lewis asked, 'when you say 'he was away', do you mean when Mr Parkinson was away from home? What did he do for a living?'

'He worked as a Deck Officer, in the Merchant Navy, and worked his way up to Chief Officer, or First Mate, as he was known, who is second in command to the Captain. Consequently, he was away at sea, for periods of two to three months, or longer, and then spent a similar time at home. Overall, he was away a lot, thank goodness.'

'Why would you say that, Mrs Stratton?' Andy enquired.

'Because when he came home life changed a lot. When he was away, mum looked after us well, cooked nice meals, turned us out nice for school, got us to school on time, made sure we did our homework, all the usual stuff. Mum worked part-time in an office at a local factory so she was always there for us when we got home. Mum was no push-over, and we had to do what she said, but she was caring and fun. In the holidays, we would go for days out to local parks for picnics in the summer or visit our aunties and uncles for treats, such as visits to the zoo or the cinema.' Mrs Stratton now drew in a large breath before continuing. 'When he came home, it all changed.'

Andy noticed that she did not refer to this man as her father, or dad, but as 'he'. Andy already feared that he was not going to like this aspect of family life with the Parkinson's. 'Please continue Mrs Stratton.'

Pamela Stratton's face crumpled, as tears welled in her eyes, and her voice cracked with pain. 'Once he was home, mum was reduced down the ranks, or that's how it felt. She was no longer the captain of our little ship, he was, and it had to be run to his exacting standards. The meals were never good enough, our clothes were not clean enough, the house was not tidy enough. He actually used to say 'it's not shipshape' and I used to think we are not on a bloody ship.' She started to cry softly and husband Jim patted her knee. She drew in a further deep breath. 'He was an imposing man, tall and well-built, and he used to tower over all of us, including mum, issuing his orders. Any infringement of his 'rules' resulted in me and my brother being hit on a regular basis. Problem was, the rules were not always very clear and we often broke them without realising it. One day school shoes were to be left in the hall, cleaned and ready for the next day. Two days later, shoes had to be under the stairs in the designated box, so you never knew where you were. Shoes in the right place and cleaned properly was just one example. And you didn't know till you got home from school if you had got it wrong. He would have sat brooding on it all day and you were informed of it on entering the house. Then we would both be hit. This is only one example of our so called wrong doing but there were lots. It was mostly an excuse to belt us.' She paused and pulled out a tissue from the box.

Jim Stratton, visibly upset for his wife, stood up. 'I'll go and make some more tea. But I'll tell you cops one thing, I'm glad the old bastards dead. Thought about killing him myself on many occasions.'

Pam Stratton looked horrified at her husband. 'Jim, please. Don't go saying that in front of these police officers or you'll be arrested.'

Andy could feel his stomach churn, listening to this woman's description of family life. In fact, to think of this as a family life was something of an oxymoron. Family life was Mrs Parkinson and the two kids, getting on with their day-to-day activities; working, going to school, running a home, visiting aunties. They were a little unit, happy and secure, a family. It ceased to be a family when the father entered the house as it changed from a secure place of safety to a place of torment.

Andy looked over at his young colleague who had only joined his team a few months ago. She was already proving to be a competent detective, eager to learn, paid attention to detail, fitted in well with the team and respected their experience. Luckily, she was not one of the types he frequently came across, who were quick to take all the credit, were not team players and had a know-it-all attitude. He believed that she would prove to be an excellent detective in time. Today, she was hearing about the long-term effects of domestic abuse on families and this family's story would stay with her for a long time.

Mr Stratton returned with a tray and four mugs of tea. No China cups and saucers, this time. He placed one in front of his wife who picked it up, gratefully.

Andy waited whilst she sipped at her tea. 'When you are ready, Mrs Stratton, can you tell us a bit more about your family life with Mr Parkinson? What about his relationship with your mother?'

Mrs Stratton laughed, in a hysterical sort of way. 'It wasn't a relationship. Me and Jim have a relationship. We are equal partners in this marriage, make decisions together, agree on how to raise our children, support each other, and treat each other kindly. He, was just the Chief Officer, dishing out the orders. And like us kids, mum fell short in obeying the rules and running an orderly household. Long and short of it was, if we got belted, she got it too as it was her fault if things went wrong. He didn't do it in front of us, but you could hear it, upstairs, and me and Ralph just covered our ears or turned up the TV to drown it out.' Her crying was now full-on sobbing. She drank more of the tea in order to continue. 'And if you are going to ask how frequent was it, it was two or three times a week when he was home. He was clever, you didn't see the bruises or the red marks, but people must have known.'

'Did your mother ever seek help or try to leave your father?' Andy asked.

'No, women didn't then, did they? She just kept it to herself. I left home as soon as I could at eighteen and moved in with Jim and his parents. We were married when I was nineteen. Ralph left home at eighteen and joined the Navy, so we seem to have seafaring in our blood. I always felt guilty that I left my dear mother with that monster, but for a lot of the year, at least, he was away from home.'

'Did your mother ever have injuries that required medical treatment, by a doctor, or at the hospital?'

'Yes, probably. When we were kids, she once went to hospital for a broken wrist and another time for a broken collarbone. I was with her for the broken collarbone. I was about fourteen and the doctor did keep asking her how she got the injury, as he had seen bruising on her chest, and back, when she took off her blouse. He didn't believe her story of falling over the cat which was a lie. We didn't have a cat. She told me not to tell that to the doctor.'

'When did your father retire from his merchant navy job?'

'In 2000, when he was sixty-one, so twenty odd years ago.'

'Which placed him at home with your mother on a full-time basis. What was their relationship from then on, with just the two of them at home?'

'I think it did get a little better. He was still in charge and everything had to be done his way but I do think the violent outbursts were very infrequent. I know it happened occasionally, the odd slap I think, but he was getting older and not so agile and domineering.'

'What about in the last few years, particularly during the pandemic, and the periods of lockdown?'

Mrs Stratton swallowed some tea as she gathered her thoughts. 'Both of them have become frail over the last four or five years. Mum had a fall and broke her hip just before the first lockdown. Physically, she recovered quite well, just a bit more hesitant when walking about in case she fell again. Mentally, though she has become a lot more confused, losing her thread in conversations, repeating herself and so on. He had a slight stroke a few years ago, and has recovered well in terms of his cognition, I suppose you'd call it, but it left him with some difficulties on his left side. We arranged for them to have carers in twice a day, for the last two years. He hated the lockdowns and it sort of brought out his worst side again. He ranted at my mother, particularly as he got frustrated with her jumbled state, though for a lot of the time she is fairly lucid. A carer did report some bruising on her arms and back, a few months ago, but he explained it that she had slipped in the bathroom.'

Mrs Stratton started to cry quietly, and Andy, recognising that this was an ordeal for her, decided that this was enough questions for one day. He got up from his chair and addressed Mr and Mrs Stratton. 'Thank you, Mrs Stratton, for what you have told us. I hope I can speak to your brother when he arrives back in the UK.'

Mrs Stratton smiled at the mention of her younger brother. 'His flight gets in later today and Jim is collecting him from the airport. I am so looking forward to seeing him. I just wish it wasn't in these circumstances.' She started to cry again.

'Thanks again, for your time. We will be in touch. We will see ourselves out.' DC Lewis nodded 'goodbye' to the couple.

As the police officers got into DC Lewis's car, she said, 'well, boss, what do make of all that?'

Andy glanced at the young constable. 'Actually, Gabrielle, you tell me what you take away from that interview?'

Gabrielle's sorrowful expression summed up Andy's own feelings. 'That Mr Norris Parkinson was a nasty man, who beat his wife and children, over a long and sustained period and nothing was ever done about it. I totally understood, Mr Stratton's, Jim's, anger in wanting to personally kill his father-in-law. She hesitated, 'in terms of the crime we are investigating I am conflicted, as I believe that the evidence may reveal Mrs Parkinson as the perpetrator. If she did murder her husband was it done in a calculated, cold-bloodied way? Or was she a woman, possibly with early on-set dementia, who was in danger of an attack by her violent husband, who defended herself for the first time in her life? I really don't know.'

Andy nodded his agreement. 'Nor do I at this moment. And perhaps we will never know? We can't exclude, at this time, that there was a third party involved but I do think that highly unlikely. We need to see the results of the forensics in terms of the murder weapon, any forced entry, any other motive for the crime including robbery. We have carers coming into the property and they will all have to be interviewed. We will have to get a full assessment of Mrs Parkinson's health including her mental health, especially in terms of the possibility of conditions such as dementia. There is a lot of work yet to be done.'

As DC Lewis was about to start the car, Andy shouted, 'wait a minute. Don't drive off yet.'

This made DC Lewis jump slightly and she looked around anxiously for a road hazard which was impeding their departure.

Andy was staring at a house across the road and further down. A semi-detached, 1920's style house, which was the norm in this suburban avenue. The blue front door was open and a woman in her forties was standing on the door step saying goodbye to a visitor. The man was tall, brown-haired, in his thirties, dressed in smart blue suit. The man paused on the step, then leaned in to kiss the woman on the cheek, as his hand appeared to explore her bottom. She jumped slightly, then laughed loudly, as he walked away from her, to exit the garden. His car, a silver BMW 3 Series, had a number plate that Andy recognised. It was generally parked on the driveway of the house next door to his. The owner of the car, Gary Anderson.

CHAPTER TWENTY SIX

After the meeting with the Stratton's, Andy had returned to the station, and he and Detective Sergeant, Maggie Leverton, were due to interview Edna Parkinson, in the presence of her legal adviser and her designated appropriate adult, a gentle-faced, dark-haired woman in her early fifties. Andy was not confident that this interview was going to go well and he expected it to be abandoned at any stage. It was reported by the custody sergeant that Mrs Parkinson was now speaking to officers but what she was saying was not making a lot of sense. Andy had decided to attempt the interview but acknowledged to himself it may not go anywhere.

DI Leyton entered the interview room with DS Leverton. Edna Parkinson was a petite, frail, woman, her hair grey, lank and touching her shoulders. Her solicitor, a competent, well-dressed woman sat next to her. Her appropriate adult was sat to the other side of her. The detectives took their seats across the table from Mrs Parkinson, who sat silently, whilst the officers prepared to start the interview. Edna smiled at Maggie Leverton but ignored Andy.

Andy indicated that DS Leverton should start the DVD recording. Andy spoke, 'interview commenced on Tuesday, 7th September 2021 at 1.53 p.m. Present are Edna Parkinson, myself, Detective Inspector, Andy Leyton, Detective Sergeant, Maggie Leverton, Anne Cooper, Solicitor, and Jane Ridding, Appropriate Adult.' Andy gazed at Mrs Parkinson, whose attention did not appear to be focused on what was being said, as she looked downwards, constantly rubbing her right hand along her left lower arm in a self-soothing gesture. He addressed Mrs Parkinson in a low, even tone of voice. 'For the purposes of the DVD, Edna, can I get you to give your full name and date of birth.'

Mrs Parkinson continued to look downward, ignoring him, and a silence filled the room. Jane Ridding, Mrs Parkinson's appropriate adult, now prompted her, 'can you tell us your name?'

Mrs Parkinson glanced at Jane, blinked slightly, and then answered, 'Edna.'

'That's great, Edna. Can you tell us your last name?'

'Smith.'

All parties in the room glanced at each other. Andy paused, realising that this interview was not going well. 'Edna, we have your last name as Parkinson, is that right?'

Edna now looked upwards, and directly at Andy, as if seeing him for the first time and started to shake her head. 'No, my name is Smith. All the children at school call me Smithy but I've told them I don't like it.'

Andy smiled softly at her. 'When you got older and left school, did you change your name from Smith to something else?'

Jane Ridding leant towards Edna to offer reassurance. 'I think you changed your name from Smith when you got married, is that right, Edna?'

Edna sighed, while quietly considering her reply. 'Yes, I did, it was Parkinson but I don't like that name, as it belongs to that horrible man.'

Andy asked, 'Edna, can you tell me your date of birth.'

'I have my birthday in January, it's a cold month. No parties with cake. I like a cake,' Edna explained, 'especially chocolate.'

Andy spoke softly to this elderly woman. 'Edna, Mrs Parkinson, I need to talk to you about your husband, Mr Norris Parkinson, who was found dead in your home, yesterday, Monday, 6th September 2021. Do you know anything about how Norris died?'

Edna Parkinson sat more upright in her chair, seemingly more engaged about what was being said. 'Dead, dead. Is he dead? It is sad but I didn't really like him much anyway. I can get a dog now, as I have always wanted a dog, and he wouldn't let me have one.'

'Do you remember anything about how Mr Parkinson, Norris, died?'

'I'd like a small dog, so I can take it on walks. He never liked dogs.' A small blissful smile touched her face, possibly as the image of walking the dog took hold in her mind. 'You always wanted a dog, Ralph, but he said no. I wanted you to have a dog, all boys should have a dog.'

Anne Cooper, Solicitor now commented. 'Detective Inspector Leyton I think it is quite clear that we are not going to get anywhere with this interview and I propose that it is terminated immediately pending psychiatric assessments of my client.'

Andy nodded. 'Interview terminated at 1.59 p.m.' He addressed DS Leverton and Jane Ridding. 'Please ensure that Mrs Parkinson is escorted back to her custody cell.' As Mrs Parkinson was escorted outside the interview room, Andy spoke to Anne Cooper. 'My recommendation is that we should be contacting Social Services and look to getting Mrs Parkinson detained in accordance with the Mental Health Act 1983, under Section 2, due to her having displayed aggressive behaviour, for her own safety, and the safety of others. Her detention will require the agreement of two doctors. Once she is detained then more detailed psychiatric reports can be undertaken to ascertain whether she is competent to undertake police interviews in connection with the death of Mr Parkinson.'

Anne Cooper, a middle-aged woman in serviceable grey business suit and white blouse, picked up her handbag from the floor, and placed her laptop, notepad and pen inside it. 'For once, Detective Inspector Leyton, I am one hundred percent in agreement with your proposal that my client requires mental health assessments and then appropriate post-hospital care. Off the record, we both know that she is very unlikely to face any murder charges or criminal trial. Good day, inspector.'

Back home, Andy was shattered at the end of the working day, of being totally involved in the Parkinson case and trying to arrange the appropriate action to execute Edna Parkinson's release from police custody to an NHS mental health unit. It shocked Andy to think about this couple's family life for the sixty odd years that the Parkinson's had been together, in wedlock. It numbed him to think that Edna Parkinson had embarked on that married life, happily in love, with the young man who had professed to love and cherish her. Mrs Stratton had shown him the photograph of the couple on their wedding day. Edna Parkinson, the smiling, pretty blonde bride smiling up at her young good-looking husband. A day of hope and anticipation of a happy married life together. Instead, she had then been incarcerated in a domestic prison, of pain and humiliation, for the next sixty-two years, a prison where her two children had also become victims to the temper and black moods of their prison guard who beat and abused them.

His mind then flipped to the other issue that had niggled at him since visiting the Stratton's. It had definitely been Gary Anderson at that woman's house. A woman he had kissed on the cheek. Was it all innocuous? Was the woman a relative or friend he was visiting and the kiss was a cheery goodbye. But according to Eva, Gary did not have any relatives living nearby, and was estranged from his family, who lived somewhere in the London area. Andy's instinct, on seeing the kiss, was that there was more to it than just a farewell of platonic friends. The woman was smiling, in a cat that had got the cream sort of way, and definitely reacted as Gary seemed to pinch her bottom. Andy checked on his mobile phone, to relook at the footage of this encounter he had filmed, and on close inspection he was convinced that these two were physically into each other, and most likely Gary had visited for more than a chat about car loan repayments or insurance plans. If his assessment of this was correct, then Gary was cheating on Eva, either with a customer for a casual hookup or he was having a full-blown affair. Either way, Andy acknowledged that Eva did not deserve to be treated like this, particularly after the pain of losing her husband not so long ago. His problem was what to do with this information, keep it to himself for now, or tell Eva?

Andy's consideration of these two issues, one work-related, one private, were ended when he heard a car pull up on the drive and realised that Natasha had arrived. She had now been staying at her mother's house for a number of weeks, to care for her mother after she had broken her wrist due to spilt red wine on the floor of a local supermarket. No matter that her mother had broken the bottle which caused the spillage in the first place, negotiations were currently ongoing with the shop's manager and legal representatives, to decide if compensation should be paid. Andy had met Natasha's mother on one occasion, at her terraced property, where she lived a chaotic existence, dominated by her requirements for cigarettes and alcohol, on a daily basis. The fact that she was banned from the local supermarket was proving to be difficult after the 'accident'. Andy was convinced that Natasha would be home fairly quickly, as she didn't get on well with her mother, and was disinclined to stay at her mother's less than clean home. Typical of Natasha, she had immediately employed a cleaner to bring the house up to some sort of hygiene standard, and she was able to extend her stay until her mother's plaster cast was removed.

Natasha entered the lounge, as Andy was relaxing on the sofa. He was reminded of her beauty as she walked towards him, long blonde hair flowing around her shoulders, slender body dressed in tight-fitting blue dress, all eye makeup applied perfectly, and her full lips, made glossy and inviting by a vibrant red lipstick. 'Hi, babe, I've missed you. Have you missed me?' she asked, as she nestled into him before kissing him sensuously, as her eager hands unbuttoned his shirt. He was aroused immediately, and intensely, as she undid his belt and unzipped his trousers, as her mouth explored downwards. She stroked him with her hands and tantalised him with her mouth, until she too could no longer wait for her release, and she quickly hitched up the dress, removed her underwear, and climbed astride him, moaning softly, as she moved to bring them both to pulsating climax.

As they drew apart, Andy smiled, as this was typical Natasha, the woman who was efficient and methodical in fulfilling her sexual needs. Natasha always got what she wanted from men in terms of sex but there was a disconnected aspect to it. It seemed to be only about the body and not the mind or the heart. At times when he was particularly displeased with her behaviour towards him or other people, and he'd made it clear that he was not happy with her, she would initiate the sex, as if somehow this would wipe the slate clean and all would be forgotten.

One source of his annoyance with her was her constant reference to how many men fancied her, chatted her up and asked her out, particularly during her working day. Andy couldn't be sure if she said it to make him jealous or that she was just being matter of fact about it all and she didn't see it as a major problem between them. Andy was concerned that he didn't feel overly jealous, as a man in love should feel, when other men were competing for his partner's affections. He had no evidence that she had taken any of these men up on their offers, but if he found out that she had, then the relationship would be over. He was not going to be made a mug of, regardless of how beautiful she was.

The other issue was her relationship with Hannah. Natasha tolerated his daughter when she was at his house but as he'd often acknowledged, Natasha would have been happier if Hannah didn't exist. When Natasha had first arrived Hannah had been awestruck by her, and was eager to be given advice on hair, clothes, shoes, makeup and nails. Also, as Hannah was now starting to discover the world of boys, Natasha was a font of knowledge on how to talk to boys, how to treat them to make them like you, and what they find attractive in a girl. A few conversations he'd heard between his girlfriend and his daughter had not pleased him. He was surprised to hear Natasha advising her on 'playing hard to get' and the boy would have to work harder at getting to be with her. This tactic had never impressed him when used by girls on him, especially as a teenager, and a younger man. He hated this type of game-playing which many boys, and girls, found annoying and a turn off. He didn't want his daughter to be a pushover in terms of boys, and their expectations, but he shuddered when he heard Natasha's cold, calculating advice in terms of the 'treat them mean, keep them keen' approach. There was a hardness in the way that Natasha treated people and he didn't want his daughter developing into a bitchy, mean girl. He doubted this would happen as Hannah was caring and kind but Natasha's influence should not be underestimated.

Later in bed, with Natasha asleep, Andy decided he would have to give some time to considering if this relationship with Natasha should continue. In all honesty, he had not missed her that much during the time she was at her mothers. It was nice to return to there being just himself and Hannah. Hannah was permanently annoying, as was typical for twelve-year-old girls but after their little flare-ups over room tidying, her constant demands for money, wearing too much makeup and arguing that up was down, or vice versa, there were moments when they cuddled on the sofa and watched a movie, his little girl again. When the three of them were together, that dynamic changed, and both females battled for dominance, and Andy wished at times he had a whistle to stop play and brandish a red card.

CHAPTER TWENTY SEVEN

June 2010

Gary was relaxed, sat in the pub lounge, waiting for his date, who was quickly becoming the front runner in the race to become Wife Number Two, in terms of The Plan. Dating apps had identified suitable contenders; all must be older women in their late thirties up to forty-five, all without children, career professionals with a property, ideally without mortgage. Gary knew that these types of women would be more of a challenge, as to succeed in their jobs they were self-determined and assertive. But, threading a solitary path to establish a career, and focusing only on work goals, could make them loners and leave them lonely. Gary, always ready to sniff out any vulnerability, had moved from the long list, down to the shortlist of three. Heather, Amanda, Jessica.

Date one, with Heather, a few days ago had not been satisfactory. A senior manager in HR, she had moved from public services to private business, and had been successfully head-hunted for her current role. Gary could understand why. She conducted the date as if it were his first interview for the vacancy of boyfriend. He felt he were being subjected to a psychometric assessment and expected to complete a written report on his boyfriend skills and aptitudes, so in depth was her searching questions. Appearance-wise, she was plain with dull, brown hair, dressed in a two-piece blue trouser suit and pink blouse which was vintage 1980s, Margaret Thatcher. Gary tried to imagine himself making physical advances on her skinny body, and he cringed inwardly, thus Heather was consigned to the HR office waste paper bin. Sad in a way, as The Plan worked best when he had no emotional or physical attraction to the victim, but kissing Heather's non-existent lips would be a step too far.

Amanda was late forties, a quietly spoken Pharmacist, who worked at an NHS hospital. She was petite, with curly blonde hair, and a pleasant face, of large grey eyes and full lips. What could have been great beauty was marred by a bulbous tip to a small nose. Though quiet, she had an assertiveness to her personality and he assumed she succeeded at work by tenacity and competence. She was not a woman that ignited his passion but he could have endured the physical side of things with her. He may have enjoyed exciting her after she admitted to only having one previous long-term boyfriend. He guessed from her description of the man that he had not been sexually inspiring and that her experience of the physical aspects of a relationship were limited. As long as she wasn't another Claire, who had as much spark in her as a damp squib. No, the thing that excluded

Amanda from The Plan was her very large family of mum, dad, three brothers and three sisters, a very close-knit Catholic clan who all believed that kin should live close to each other and meet up at every opportunity. Only one brother had emigrated to Australia to avoid the family gatherings and saved himself a fortune in the process. As Amanda described her attendance at the birthday parties and celebrations of all family members, including multiple nephews and nieces, frequent weddings and funerals, Gary realised he would be with her family for most of his free time. Trying to isolate and draw her away from this lot, in order to shore up his inheritance, and plot her timely exit to the hereafter would be an arduous task. Adios Amanda.

Of the three, Jessica would have been his least favourite. She was confident, and smart, a 'sassy' woman who was independent and knew her own mind. She was a successful business woman, with a number of boutiques in the Cotswolds, selling expensive dresses, bags and accessories to the wealthy, sophisticated women of the area. His least favourite, as he suspected, she would not be easy to manipulate, and he favoured the more compliant women. This was their second date, and he was confident it would be the last but as Heather and Amanda were now out of the picture, it was worth a second shot with Jessica, before he started the hunt afresh. Weirdly, all this meeting up with different women on dates, for coffees, walks, drinks and meals were not as enjoyable as expected. Staying in, watching TV with a few beers was a more attractive option, but it did not bring in money and property. Therefore, he had to keep his head down and march forward to his city of gold, El Dorado.

As Jessica, or Jess, as she liked to be called, entered the pub, she had already waved to some of the customers, and said 'hello' to the waiter, before finding Gary seated at a corner table. Physically, she was curvier than his normal type, with larger breasts and bottom but with her knowledge of clothes and body shapes, she dressed tastefully to suit her figure. She was wearing a navy blue, floral print, midi dress with a tie waist belt which emphasised, in a good way, her curves. As she sat down, she apologised for being ten minutes late due to traffic, and laughed loudly as if she had just cracked the world's funniest joke. Gary was not sure if he could tolerate her loudness and over the top jollity on a long-term basis.

Facially, she was fairly attractive, with brown eyes, well-defined brows, a largish nose and a constant smile but her most striking attribute was her shoulder-length, dark blonde curly hair, so that she resembled a Labradoodle.

Gary, irritated by being kept waiting, did not let it show. 'Don't worry about arriving after me and a few minutes late. I know it sounds old-fashioned but I don't like the idea of a woman on her own in a pub, as you never know who might be around. I hope I haven't offended you, as you might think that's a little bit sexist. I know women can look after themselves.'

Jess smiled. 'I don't think it's sexist. It shows you are a gentleman and its nice to think there are considerate men in the world. I am a little bit tired of the 'modern man' types I keep going on dates with. A lot don't bother to iron their shirts, or shave, or trim their beards, and are always up for going halves on everything.' She blanched slightly as she said this. 'Sorry, that doesn't mean that a man should pay for everything. I just get a bit miffed when you are at a meal and they get out their phone, to calculate the detailed cost of their meal, including halving the price of the bread or sharing plate when I've not had any.'

Gary laughed. 'Ok, I'll get the drinks. What would you like?'

'A white wine spritzer would be great, thanks.'

He got out of his seat. 'Ok. I'll let you know the price on my return and I can take cash or card,' he grinned. 'Only kidding.'

When he returned with the drinks, Jess sipped on the spritzer, which was cold and refreshing on a hot summer June day. As she placed her glass down, she concentrated her gaze on him, as he drank from his glass of lager. 'Gary, I'm going to be upfront here, as neither of us have time to waste, me more so than you. And that brings me to my point. I'm a forty-year-old woman, you are a younger man, twenty-seven I think you said. What brings you on a second date with an old girl like me. Though, strictly speaking, as I am forty, I technically rate as a cougar.'

Gary's deep brown eyes were searching her face, so scrutinising that Jess felt a blush to her cheeks. 'To be honest, Jess, I have been going on dates with younger women for a while now and I am finding that I am quickly bored by them. They craze constant attention, are addicted to their phones, and can barely keep a conversation going. They have been overindulged by stupid parents and don't understand that we can only progress in life through studying, hard work and perseverance. If I have to listen to another conversation about 'I'm a Celebrity … Get Me Out Of Here', I will go mad.'

Jess laughed. 'So, you are looking for more mature conversation. Sorry to disappoint as I am quite a fan of 'I'm a Celebrity'. And 'X Factor', and 'Britain's Got Talent', so I can't offer anything more intellectual.'

Gary feigned disappointment. 'Shoot me now. But I am sure we could find a programme we could watch together. And I guarantee that you would concentrate on the programme and not be tapping on your phone all the time. That, Jess, is why I want a woman not a girl.'

Jess explained the story of her life to Gary and why she was currently single. 'For many years I've concentrated on building up my businesses, through most of my twenties and thirties, and I now have four shops in four towns in the Cotswolds. At the beginning, with my first shop, I hardly had any time off, as I actually worked seven days a week at times. Long hours, and at the end of the day all I wanted was a soak in the bath, a ready meal, and a glass of Pinot. I drifted away from friends, who started to get married and have families, and when we did meet, we had little in common. By the time my shops were well-established with their own managers, I was in my mid-thirties and realised that if I wanted a marriage, and perhaps a child, I had to take stock of my personal life. I thought I'd found my prince two years ago and I fell totally in love. Turns out my prince was a cheating bastard, with a wife and two children. Selfishly, I did think I could still see him, even with his family situation, but last September he finished with me. Got bored, apparently. He now has a new girlfriend and is still married to the long-suffering wife.'

Gary assessed this information carefully and found it favourable. It's looking promising that this woman is a loner, with few friends, and was either naïve or desperate when it came to love. The mistress who thinks that she outshined the wife but was always going to be the one that got dumped. Jess may be confident and capable in her business dealings but she had her weaknesses when it came to relationships, clinging on to a man who did not love her. Weaknesses to be exploited. 'The man's a fool if he gave up a woman like you.'

Five months into their relationship, Gary was satisfied with the progress he had made with Jess. He stayed at her detached house in the Stratford-upon-Avon area on occasion, enough to reel her in, and leave her wanting more. He calculated that as she had been content to live on the scraps thrown to her by the married lover, it made sense to Gary that he would give her some attention, and then hold back. It was paying off. Though outwardly, Jess was bubbly and confident, he realised that this covered a shyness and insecurity that she didn't want people to see. Her parents were both dead, there were no siblings and she had a lot of acquaintances but few friends. Her house was mostly paid for with only a small mortgage outstanding. All things considered; Jess was shaping up nicely to become Wife Number Two.

This Saturday evening, Gary was relaxing on Jess's sofa, waiting while she prepared a meal. Jess had a fondness for food, and could cook, so this was already an improvement on previous wife Claire's miserable offerings. Gary was not overly bothered about food but as he had to eat, it was more pleasant to have fresh-cooked dishes. Jess was a bit heavy-handed with creams, butters, sauces and cheeses, in her recipes, hence her more ample figure but Gary was slowly schooling her to eat healthier with plenty of fruit and vegetables.

Tonight's meal was a Thai green curry with rice, and she made the green curry paste from scratch. Jess placed the bowls of curry and rice on the dining table and called Gary over to be seated. He sat down, placing his bottled lager on the table, and waited for Jess to sit down. 'This looks great, Jess. You are a great cook. I'll have to eat it fairly quickly as I have that meeting with a prospective buyer for one of my cars, at the dealership, in two hours' time. It's the only time he could arrange to come in before flying off to Dubai tomorrow. I just hope the cops don't see the lights on at the dealership and think we're being robbed.'

Jess passed a warmed plate to Gary. 'Help yourself to the food. It is a pity you have to leave so quickly as I was hoping for a cuddle on the sofa and catching up on a 'Doc Martin' episode which I've recorded.'

Gary spooned jasmine rice and green curry onto his plate, thankful that he was making an early exit as watching a drama about a doctor who had hemophobia, a fear of blood, was a test of his endurance. Her taste in TV programmes was proving to be a trial for him as he preferred psychological thrillers and action films. Jess favoured police dramas without any violence, medical dramas without any blood or messy procedures, talent shows and comedy sit-coms. All things that Gary loathed. He liked his viewing to be realistic and if a bullet hit a human body he expected there to be gore, guts and/or brains splattered about. He hated the sanitized tripe that Jess loved. 'That's a shame, Jess, perhaps I can watch the doc another time.'

'No problem, Gary, I'll save the recording for you.'

Gary gave her a grateful smile whilst thinking that a boil on the backside would be a more attractive proposition. 'Thanks, very thoughtful of you, Jess. It's one of the things I like about you. It is a pity I have to go out tonight as we could have indulged in a little love making to show my gratitude.'

Jess glanced at him nervously and concentrated on eating the creamy curry. For a woman that had an affair with a married man, she was quite awkward when it came to sex. It was always in bed, under the duvet with lights off, and Gary realised that she was shy about exposing her body due to her weight issues. Gary always thought that married men had affairs to be with racier, sexually spontaneous woman who wore black lingerie and enjoyed being handcuffed to the bed. A woman who would give the man what he was missing at home. Gary joked to himself that perhaps the married man liked Jess, as his wife was an insatiable nymphomaniac, and he came to see Jess for a rest and to watch crummy television. Again, he had found a woman who was not keen on sexual matters, who preferred food to shagging.

Three hours later Gary was at the apartment of his current girlfriend, Samantha, and he was now lying sated on the bed after an energetic love session, an hour ago. Samantha was an unusual looking woman, with long, sleek, black hair, emerald green eyes, and wide mouth, who he thought of as his sexy cat, a black panther. Her body was cat-like, sleek and supple, which she arched and bent for their mutual satisfaction. She had come into the dealership to upgrade her car, and upgraded her boyfriend at the same time, swapping car mechanic for car dealership owner. As far as Samantha was concerned, she was in an exclusive relationship with Gary, for the last four months, and was now hinting that he should move in full-time. Gary was contemplating his next move with Jess and working to persuade her that he had strong feelings for her. He was planning to take the relationship forward with the intention of being married to her in 2011.

Samantha had little to offer him financially, as she rented a one-bedroom flat, and worked as a cashier in a supermarket. The car, a VW Golf, was her one indulgent expenditure and she was tied to monthly repayments for the next five years. She lay on the bed, facing Gary, as Gary kneaded her firm left breast and teased her nipple which re-acted to his touch. 'Gary, the sex between us is brilliant and you could have it every day if you'd only move in here. I can't see why you don't. How can you prefer living with that creepy Simon when you can have all the sex you want with me?'

Gary always sniggered when he thought of all the women who had met his friend Simon. Various words were used to describe him including odd, weird, scruffy, but most frequently 'creepy'. Women did not take to Simon and his childhood friend only managed sex when he paid for it or when a woman was wasted with drink.

Gary licked Samantha's nipples, a tom cat about to mate with his feline. 'I do not prefer living with skanky Simon, when I have full access to your loveliness but he can't afford the rent on his own, and would have to take in a tenant. And I'm not going to pay rent here. I have a flat and I like to keep my options open, as to where I live. For now, you will have to be content with this current arrangement. Put up or shut up.'

As she started to become aroused from his attention to her breasts, she felt his erection as he moved over her. 'But Gary, it would be great if you moved in here.' Her hand moved to stroke him rhythmically. 'You know I am very good at changing your mind. Please move in here.'

Taking her hand off him, he pinned her two arms down on the bed, and hovered over her, his deep brown eyes commanding that she looked at him. 'I've just told you no. Don't ask again or you'll regret it. This is our current arrangement and I will not be dictated to.'

'But I really want you to.'

Gary was now angered, not liking that she was starting to get clingy, when all it was meant to be for him was a diversion away from Jess. 'Ok, now Samantha. You know I don't like whinging.' With his anger now feeding his arousal, he flipped her over on the bed. 'Shut up. And focus on the thing you're good at.'

CHAPTER TWENTY EIGHT

Alfie's birthday celebrations were spread over two days. Saturday, 11 September, his actual twelfth birthday, was making pizzas at home with three guests, his best friend Jai, Hannah, and her best friend, Phoebe. Eva had smiled when he suggested inviting the girls as she knew that he was very fond of Hannah, in the way a boy can be when discovering that he actually liked girls. Hannah's friend Phoebe, was the polar opposite to her; as she had long, blonde, wavy hair and blue eyes in contrast to Hannah's Mediterranean colouring. Both were equally pretty and Eva was amazed when he suggested that they should both be present at the pizza making as Alfie was known to blush the colour of a ripe tomato in the presence of girls. Jai was a smallish Asian boy with a big personality who Eva could predict would be Prime Minister one day. The second birthday celebration was to be on Sunday when Alfie and five friends were going to a climbing wall experience.

Eva was in the kitchen with the four children, all gathered around the dining room table, each wearing an apron. The two boys and the two girls were going to make their own dough, and then each child could select their own toppings from a selection including, ham, mushroom, roasted red peppers, and black olives. At the current stage, flour had been placed in a glass mixing bowl and the children were taking it in turns to add the dough ingredients of instant yeast, salt, olive oil and warm water and bringing it all together with a wooden spoon to a soft, fairly wet dough. Alfie poured out more flour than necessary for the 'lightly floured surface' and ended up with flour on his hands, face and clothes, resembling a ghost in a white garment, and cut out eyes and nose, as seen on Halloween. After Eva spent five minutes trying to clear away the excess flour, the kids then took turns to knead the dough for five minutes. Jai was laughing hysterically at the sight of Alfie and making 'whoooo' noises. The girls work area was a bit tidier but both had flour on their hands and faces and were giggling loudly.

'So, what's going on in here?' Andy came into the kitchen to see what all the hysterics were about. 'It looks like an explosion in a flour mill,' he commented, particularly as he glanced at Alfie. Eva was using a damp cloth to get some of the excess flour off Alfie's face but he evaded her and continued to knead the dough. 'Mum, get off. I'm not three.'

Andy and Natasha had been invited round for drinks. Gary and Natasha were keeping well out of the way, in the lounge area.

Eva, having given up on trying to clean up Alfie, rested against the kitchen work top but far enough away from any white flour that could blow her way. There was already flour on her grey skinny jeans and white jumper with grey and pink stripes. She picked up her glass of white wine, sipped it slowly, just enjoying watching the children have their fun. Andy came to stand next to her, grinning broadly at her, and the chaos this simple pizza making was causing.

'Ok, everyone. If you've kneaded the dough for five minutes, put it back in the bowls and cover the bowl with the clean tea towel on the table. Next you need to make the tomato sauce using the passata, basil and garlic. Check the recipe,' Eva instructed.

'You are going to be clearing up sticky flour off every work surface, the way this is going. All these birthday ideas always turn out to be messy.' Andy stood leaning casually by her, dressed in dark grey, slim fit jeans and mid-blue, crew neck jumper.

'Yes, you're right. I thought that as Alfie got older the birthday party thing would get easier but now I'm not so sure. In six years he'll be able to go to the pub with his mates.'

Andy looked at her, the smile fading from his face. 'When the time comes, that they can go to pubs and clubs at night, you will yearn for the days when he was home safe, making pizza. Even if it means hosing down the kitchen afterwards.' As he surveyed her face, he noted that there was flour on her cheek. 'You've got flour on your face, just here,' he pointed to the area, 'I think we need to hose you down as well.' Eva picked up a tea towel and dabbed at the area on her cheek. He commented that she was now looking less like the Pillsbury Doughboy.

'You've still missed a bit near your lip. Give me the tea towel and keep still.'

He placed his hand on her chin, and gently rubbed the remaining flour from her face, his blue eyes captivating hers in his gaze, as a smile touched his lips. 'There you go. Just be thankful I haven't used my mother's method of dampening the towel or flannel when I was a kid. The spit and rub method.'

'Eva laughed. 'Oh yes, I know that one. A favourite of my mothers, too. I don't think I've done it to Alfie.'

'I bet you have, it's definitely a thing that all mothers do.' ,

She giggled again, she always felt relaxed around Andy. She was pleased that he had bothered to come out to the kitchen to see how the kids were getting on.

The children made the tomato sauce by combining the ingredients and adding seasoning to taste. Andy grabbed two teaspoons from the drawer and went over to each group to taste the sauce. 'Yep, both good, not too much salt or garlic.'

Eva then advised, 'take out your dough, give it a quick knead and then split each into two, so everyone has their own dough. Flour the surface again, very sparingly, Alfie, and then roll out your dough to about 25cm across. It needs to be very thin so it will rise in the oven.'

The concentration for this meant that they were quiet as they focused on the task in hand.

'How are you getting on now, as I haven't seen you for a few weeks? No more fainting or migraines, I hope?' Andy enquired, concerned eyes scanning her face.

Eva, feeling self-conscious from the intensity of his gaze, looked away from him. 'I'm fine, thanks. How are you? Happy to have Natasha back, you must have missed her?'

She detected a hesitancy in his voice as he spoke, 'yes, I suppose but I haven't thought about it too much as work has been a bit hectic. We have booked to go Portugal in a week's time, just the two of us, Covid rules permitting. We'll see how things go. Hannah's staying with her mother.'

'Lucky you, and you work really hard so you deserve a holiday.'

The children had now rolled out the pizza bases. 'Ok,' Eva advised, 'place the pizza bases on the baking trays. Spread the tomato sauce on the bases, not too much, put on the two cheeses, mozzarella and the grated parmesan, and then decide on your favourite toppings.'

'Can Andy decide on the winner?' Alfie asked.

Andy grinned at the four kids. 'I don't think we need a winner do we. I mean I'd have to pick Hannah as she's my favourite daughter, and I'd have to pick Alfie, as he's the birthday boy. I'd have to pick Phoebe, as she's got the tidiest work area and I'd have to pick Jai as he's the funniest pizza maker. What can I do?' he rubbed his head to emphasis his dilemma, as they all laughed.

Eva shook her head. 'Don't let Gary hear you say all that. He's very into the concept of winners and losers and he'd come out here and pick one, no trouble. Alfie's looks a bit heavy handed on the tomato sauce so I don't think he'd win.' She spoke this quietly so that Alfie couldn't hear.

Alfie held up his pizza on the baking tray, which did look on the verge of toppling off at any moment, so Eva told him to put it back on the table before it fell on the floor. Eva and Andy then inspected each pizza in turn, declaring that they all looked very tasty.

Eva asked the children to bring any dirty bowls, and rolling pins over to the sink, and then told them to wash and dry their hands. Eva instructed, 'I'll clear this up and then in about fifteen minutes you can put your pizzas in the oven. Ok. You can go to Alfie's room and I'll call you down.' The children quickly washed their hands at the sink, then all ran out of the kitchen, eager to escape the clearing up.

With Andy's help, Eva loaded the dishwasher whilst Andy used a kitchen spray and cloth to wipe down the table and work tops. Suddenly, Eva jumped as she drew her hand out of the dishwasher and saw that her middle finger was bleeding where she'd caught it on a small vegetable knife. 'Ouch.'

She went over to the sink and held it over the running tap. Andy came over to see what she had done and offered some kitchen roll which he placed around her finger. 'Where are your plasters?' he asked.

'In that top cupboard there,' she pointed as she watched as the kitchen roll reddened from the still bleeding finger. Andy took a medical bag from the cupboard and delved inside for a suitable plaster. Taking the protective cover off the plaster, he waited while Eva removed the sodden kitchen roll, and then carefully placed the plaster around the wound. 'Sit down and hold your finger up for now,' he ordered.

There was a knock at the kitchen door, and Tania breezed in, not waiting to be invited. 'Where's my favourite godson?' she shouted, noting the absence of children. She placed a parcel and card on the worktop for when the birthday boy reappeared.

Eva explained that the four children had gone up to Alfie's room whilst the mess in the kitchen was cleared up. 'We will call them down shortly so that they can bake the pizzas and then we'll do the birthday cake.'

Tania, noting Eva's finger with the plaster, asked, 'is that a pizza related injury? I thought pizza making would be a fairly safe thing to do.'

Eva laughed, though her finger was still stinging from the cut. 'It is generally but I caught it on the vegetable knife in the dishwasher. Andy patched me up.'

Eva shook her head, as she watched Tania swooning over Andy, probably imagining herself in some doctor/patient scenario with him, as in the very old 'Carry on Doctor' movies her dad used to watch. Before Tania could put the thoughts in her head about Andy into words, Eva asked her, 'do you want a drink, Tania? Wine, tea, coffee? Do you want another lager, Andy?'

Eva served the requested drinks, white wine for Tania, and another bottled lager for Andy. She picked up another bottle of red wine out of the wine rack. 'I'll go and see if Gary and Natasha want another drink. We are having a takeaway shortly, Tania, if you want to join us?'

****

In the lounge, Gary and Natasha were sharing a bottle of Merlot, and avoiding the culinary delights being prepared in the kitchen. Natasha was reclining on the three-seater sofa displaying tanned legs and a perfect pedicure to Gary, who was seated across from her on the other sofa. She was wearing a tan, leopard print, midi dress which accentuated the curve of her body. Both she and Gary were engrossed in their phones but Gary stopped glancing at his to look at Natasha.

'Do you want some more of this wine,' he asked.

'Sure, thanks.'

Gary got up, and filled her glass with more wine, before sitting back down. 'I was just thinking, this relationship thing between the four of us is all wrong. In reality, it should be Eva with Andy, and me with you. We both hate kids, mainly as they take the focus away from us. Plus, we are both hard and cold, with no affinity for children, so it makes perfect sense for us to be together.'

Natasha stopped texting on her phone and looked at Gary with interest. 'Not taken to little Alfie, then?' she asked, a smirk of a smile on her perfect lips.

Gary drank his wine, savouring its taste, before responding. 'No, not really. He's whiny, and irritating, and I haven't got the patience for all this negotiation stuff that passes for parenting these days. But I'm beginning to cure him of that, as I've told him firmly, that no means no, and there are consequences if he steps out of line.'

'Bloody hell, what does that mean?'

'You want to know if I would hit him, and yes, I would, if given half the chance. I'm keeping my options open on that and Eva wouldn't be able to stop me. I think he's been spoilt and boys in particular need firm discipline. For now it means, no computer games, no pocket money, no seeing friends, that sort of thing. He had a two-day ban on computer games this week, as he wouldn't go to bed when told. I was on the verge of banning the birthday celebrations if he didn't change his attitude.

Natasha was looking a little shocked by this. 'What does Eva say about it?'

'She generally agrees but would not endorse cancelling his birthday arrangements. Anyway, I'm slowly getting my way in this house, exerting my authority with both of them, so it's all good. What about you and Hannah, how do you get on with her?'

Natasha shrugged. 'Like you, I'd prefer it if she weren't around. And we do bicker a lot about stupid things which annoys Andy. A lot of the time he takes her side which I find pretty unreasonable. After all, I am supposed to be his girlfriend.'

'Actually, I am surprised that you're still around. What about all the millionaires that were fighting to take you away and lock you in their expensive mansions?'

She smiled, a movement of the lips, without any warmth. 'I'm keeping my options open. Road testing a few high-end models, to use the car dealer terminology.'

Gary raised an eyebrow, as a bemused smile crossed his lips. 'Showing rich men around these properties and testing out the mattresses is more like it. As, I've said before, I know you, Natasha. A hard bitch. If I were Andy, and found out about what you're up to I'd squeeze the life out of you, my fingers round your pretty neck. No man wants to be made a fool of. It's a good job he's a cop.'

Natasha shuddered slightly at Gary's coldness but it wasn't necessarily fear that caused the shivers. 'I'm surprised that you're still with Eva, particularly as you don't like her son.'

He now leaned forward to focus his hard, brown eyes on Natasha. 'Eva is truly beautiful in ways you are not. She is lovely to look at, has a sexy body, is good at making love but let's me take control which is what I want. She is intelligent, funny, caring, and knows her own mind, and has opinions that differ from mine so that we don't always agree. But at the heart of Eva, there is a vulnerability that I crave, to mould and meld to my will, and so that ultimately, I will be in control. We are currently making progress towards my goal.'

Natasha was very rarely shocked by people or things they did but this man's words astounded her. 'Fucking hell. I knew you were weird. Weird and dangerous. I'm not sure what else to say.'

Gary gave her a brief smile that did not reach his eyes as they burned into hers. 'I know what you should say. I can see from your face that it turns you on. You like the idea of having people within your control the same as I do. But sadly for you, you are never going to control Andy. I on the other hand, have found my perfect woman, and she has every reason to do my bidding, if she wants to protect her son.'

CHAPTER TWENTY NINE

As Eva left the kitchen, Tania sat down at the dining table, and Andy sat next to her. 'I'm glad I've got you alone, Andy, as I have wanted to get a chance to speak to you.' She was dressed in a tight-fitting blue jersey dress that clung to her petite figure and slender legs were enhanced by black stilettos.

As she leaned towards him, almost touching his legs, Andy felt a little nervous and sat up straighter to avoid bodily contact. His voice was a little uncertain as he said, 'ok, what about?'

'Eva.' Tania kept her gaze on the kitchen door in case someone came into the room whilst she was speaking. 'I don't know about you, but I've noticed lately that she seems to be losing her sparkle. Eva's never been a loud person, like me, but she's always been happy and easy going. I've noticed a change in her since we've come out of the lockdowns, and I don't know if the whole Covid thing has saddened her, or whether it's got something to do with Gary.'

'What do you mean, to do with Gary?'

'It's difficult to explain but she's not herself. She's definitely sadder, more introspective, and doesn't talk about her life with Gary at all. When she was with Niall, I was practically the third wheel in the relationship, as I knew more about him than he did. None of it malicious, that's not Eva's way. But I'd hear about the funny stuff he was always doing. For a headteacher he could be dumb at times. Like when he mistook a child's mother for one of his pupils, and told her to get back to class, but that's a story for another day. She rarely talks about Gary, and if I ask about him or joke about him, she clams up. When we were out for my birthday, and this good-looking guy was chatting her up, I jokingly said I'd tell Gary. Her face turned white and she kept saying, don't say anything to him, please. He'll go mad.'

Andy drank his lager, while contemplating how to respond to Tania. 'I would agree with you, Tania. You've known her a lot longer than me and I met her just after Niall's death so I have always seen a sadness in her. You're right, she doesn't seem happy to me and I suspect that Gary is starting to be controlling of her and Alfie. I personally do not like, or trust, the man. I think all we can do is be there for her if she needs us.'

Tania sipped on her wine, still nervously watching the door, as she really didn't want Gary hearing this conversation. 'Problem is, I think she needs us now, and will not admit it, not even to herself. There's lots I don't like about Gary. I do think he is becoming more assertive with her, and Alfie, and I'm not sure he likes having Alfie around. He never makes much effort with us, her friends, and I think he would like us out the way, if possible.'

'Yes, you're right. I don't think he likes me, mainly as I work for the police and he gets quite defensive whenever I talk to him. I think he is cagey, with things to hide. I haven't got around to asking him yet where Lord Lucan or Shergar are.'

Tania smiled, but was not about to be derailed in her mission to make sure that Andy understood her concerns for Eva. 'Also, what do we really know about him as his life before he met Eva seems a complete mystery. He won't talk about it, except that he's had two wives, who have died on him. As a detective, Andy, does that seem suspicious to you?'

Andy breathed deeply. 'I would agree with all that you've said. Being widowed twice at such a young age would be a red flag for me if I was investigating the disappearance of wife number three. As I understand it, his first wife died of an accident, and the second of a medication overdose, which is all very tragic but some people are just unlucky.'

'The wives were unlucky to have Gary as a husband. I pray that Eva doesn't do something stupid like marry him. He could be collecting wives to end up with their money when they die tragically young. Eva could be the next target as she does own a house and have money from Niall's work and insurance pay-outs.'

Andy agreed, 'yes, but he wouldn't necessarily inherit if Eva made a will leaving everything to Alfie. Anyway, I think we should just continue to support her and not let Gary push us away.'

Tania nodded her head, in firm agreement. 'Damn right. I won't be driven away and she'll come to no harm on my watch.'

CHAPTER THIRTY

After Tania's conversation with him yesterday, at Alfie's birthday party, Andy had been going over what she had said. He absolutely agreed with Tania's concerns for Eva and was pleased that he was not the only one who had suspicions about Gary. He had been particularly worried by Tania's observation that Eva had lost her sparkle since meeting Gary and that there was a general sadness about her. Andy chided himself, as when responding to Tania, he didn't strongly endorse her concerns and seemed to play them down. In reality, Andy fully agreed with everything that Tania said; that Eva was not happy, that she doesn't talk about her relationship with Gary, and that he's becoming over assertive with her and Alfie. He could not share with Tania his suspicions that Gary had hit Eva, after Alfie's confession to Hannah. Also, Tania's alarm that Gary's two previous wives had died, and that he was reaping the financial rewards from their deaths, may appear to be the plot of a fictional murder mystery, but it was not beyond the bounds of possibility that this could be the case. He believed that Gary was well off in terms of the two car dealerships, and a number of properties, two of which he had inherited due to his deceased wives. Gary's lack of openness to Eva about his previous marriages was explained that he found it all too painful to talk about. What if he deliberately didn't speak about his past life, and kept it a secret, to protect himself from scrutiny. A man with a lot to hide. As Tania had identified, to be widowed twice when he was barely into his thirties, was quite unusual. As Andy said to Tania, this would be a red flag if he were investigating the death of wife number three, or even, wife number two. It would be pertinent to find out more about Gary Anderson.

On the Sunday morning, after the pizza party, Andy knew that Alfie was going climbing with Jai, and some other boys from school. From what Eva said yesterday, Gary was not going to the climbing centre but going out to play golf at ten o'clock.

At this time, Eva and Alfie came out of the house, to get into Eva's car as Andy was cleaning his car in his driveway. He waved at them and Eva came over to speak to him. 'Hi, Andy. Looks like there's more water on you than on the car.'

Andy looked at her sheepishly. 'Yes, I turned on the hose without holding it properly and this is the result, one blue shirt soaked through. This is a job I really hate.'

'Why don't you take your car to a car wash?'

'I wish I had now, but I thought it would be quicker doing it myself. It was getting pretty dirty and some of the team were threatening to write slogans in the dirt, you know, of the 'clean me' kind. It wasn't doing my professional standing any good. Plus, when it was parked next to the Chief Inspector's gleaming BMW, any future promotion was looking less likely.'

'Is there a chance you'll be made Chief Inspector any time soon?'

'Not in the next five years, unless I murder him myself, but then I'd have to investigate it, so it's all too much faff.'

Eva smiled at him, a merriment in her deep blue eyes. 'Is your Chief Inspector in any immediate danger of being murdered by you?'

'Yes, every minute, of every hour, of every day, as he is a pompous, over-promoted, ineffective weasel but apart from that he's a great boss.'

Eva now laughed loudly as he squeezed the sponge tightly. 'You look as if you are imagining strangling him in the way you are murdering that sponge.'

Andy dropped the sponge in the bucket. 'Now, that I have divulged my evil intentions to you about the demise of my boss, I must get rid of any potential witnesses. You will have to die, death by drowning.' He ran towards her and started to flick droplets of water at her after dipping the sponge in a bucket of water.

'Don't, stop it. You'll get me all wet for the climbing centre and I've just straightened my hair. Any water near it will make it curl.' Eva rushed away from him as he continued after her with the soggy sponge.

Alfie was standing by Eva's car, waiting for her to drive him to their destination, and looked cross with his mother for messing about. 'Hurry up mum, or we'll be late and we still have to pick up Jai. Honestly, you grown-ups act like teenagers, at times.'

Gary now came out of the house and Eva scooted to the driver's side of her car to escape Andy. Gary noticed that Andy was chasing her and she was giggling, and he frowned, very unamused by their antics. 'I thought you were in a hurry to get going to the climbing place or you would be late. You'll miss some of the session if you're not careful and it will be money wasted.'

Seeing Gary's sombre expression, Eva told Alfie to get into the car. 'Ok, I'm going now. Bye, Andy, thanks for yesterday, but not for splashing my hair.' She dived into the car and prepared to drive away before he could splash her again.

Andy now on the driveway with Gary, acknowledged him with a 'hello'. 'Are you dashing off to your round of golf right now, as I wondered if I could have a quick word.'

Gary eyed Andy suspiciously, his eyebrows lowered and lips pursed as he waited to hear what this was about. 'I've got a few minutes before I have to leave. What do you want?'

'Just something I want to show you on my phone. I'll get it, as it's in the car.' Andy strode over to his car, opened the driver's door and retrieved his mobile from the dashboard. He walked back over to where Gary was standing, arms folded across his chest, in a defensive stance. Gary sighed heavily. 'Get on with it then.'

Andy found the relevant item on his phone's album. 'I was at a property in Fir Avenue last Monday and I believe I saw you coming out of a semi across the road. 'Take a look at this.' He pressed play on the video and showed the few seconds footage to Gary.

Gary watched it passively, no reaction on his face. 'No, that's not me. Never been there. But if it was me, so what? There's no crime here, officer.' He stretched the word 'officer' to three syllables to emphasis contempt. He straightened as well, a confrontational pose to try to get Andy to back off.

Andy stood firm, after eighteen years in the police service he was rarely intimidated by people he was questioning. 'Let's say it is you. You seem very friendly with the woman and I'm not referring to the kiss on her cheek. I mean your hand on her buttock which she reacted to, by jumping slightly, before laughing. I would describe it as an intimate moment between two people who are more than friends.'

'Would you now,' Gary declared. 'I'd describe it as someone getting involved in other people's business. If it was me, and I'm not saying it was, I would be there on business. Probably finalising the paperwork on a car purchase, you know, good customer care.'

'Does it extend to touching the bottoms of all your female customers, as seen here?'

'Perhaps, the man's hand touched her bum by mistake. An accident. Would this stand up in a court of law, Mr Detective? Anyway, I'm not saying it was me and even if it was, it's nothing to do with you. No law against it.'

Andy was now finding that his distaste for this man was rising sharply. 'No, its not against the law but if the man were cheating on his girlfriend, it would make him a scumbag in my view.'

'Isn't it illegal to have video footage of someone on a mobile phone without their permission?'

'No, it's not, if it was filmed in a public place,' Andy pointed back at the phone. 'And this is a public place.'

Gary now started to move away from Andy. 'This is all very hypothetical as there is no certainty that it was me.'

Andy re-played the video and again showed the footage to Gary. 'I think we both know that it is. Your car is parked outside, a silver BMW, and there's the registration plate. It was your car.'

Anger was creeping onto Gary's face, as his cheeks reddened, and he gritted his teeth in an animalistic snarl. 'I think you should get your own love life in order before you start poking your nose into other peoples. That blonde of yours always seems ready to trade you in for a classier, more expensive model. They don't pay cops a lot, do they?'

Andy was not going to be goaded by Gary. 'We'll leave it at that. Just to say, I'm watching you. Don't go hurting Eva or I might just forget I'm a cop and come after you. Do not underestimate me.'

CHAPTER THIRTY ONE

Sunday was day two of Alfie's birthday weekend and the visit to the climbing wall for Alfie, Jai and four school friends. Gary flatly refused to get involved and was going to meet his mate Simon for a round of golf and would be back later.

At four p.m. Eva and Alfie were back home, Alfie still buzzing from his climbing experience and declaring that he knew what it felt like to be Spiderman. Eva's parents had been around for two hours and had brought presents. Alfie was also unwrapping the gifts from the four friends who shared the climbing experience. The kitchen dining table was covered with assorted presents including Lego sets, mini-drone, board games, T-shirts and books. Birthday cards were scattered around and a pile of money, £20's. £10's and £5's added up to a sum of £120. Birthday card envelopes, wrapping paper and gift bags covered the kitchen floor. Gran and Granddad had eaten chocolate birthday cake, drank cups of tea, and then had been persuaded to have a glass of white wine or a beer.

Alfie was concentrating on building a Ninja dragon with moveable jaw, legs, tail and wings, large white teeth and red tongue. Alfie said, 'dad would have loved this. I really miss him.' Eva noted the tears in her son's eyes and she leaned over him, embraced him, and kissed the top of his head.

'He loved doing Lego with you. And I really miss him, too. It's good to have a moment after all the excitement to think of him, even if it makes us sad.'

Alfie hugged his mum, and settled in her arms for a few seconds, before returning to the dragon which he swooped around trying to attack mini-Ninja figures.

Gary entered the room and was greeted by Eva, holding a Ninja figure with a large sword, trying to avoid the dragon's teeth. Alfie shrieked, 'I'm going to eat you. R-r-r-o-a-r-r.'

Looking at all the paper debris on the floor, Gary commented, 'aren't you a bit too old for that now you're twelve? I'd expect you to have cleared this mess up before you start playing with anything.'

'In a minute,' Alfie responded, 'I'm just about to eat mum.'

'Bloody hell,' Gary stated, his voice deep and flecked with anger. 'Why is it every time you are asked to do something, you have to argue about it. Pick these envelopes and wrapping paper up and take them to the re-cycling. I think we can say that you have fully celebrated your birthday. The rest of the day shall be spent tidying up, finishing any school work, and getting ready for tomorrow. Are we clear?'

Alfie had now stopped roaring and was on the floor picking up the paper debris. 'What shall I do with these bags, mum?'

'They can be re-used so just put them neatly on the table, for now. Gather all your presents together and take them to your room, that's a good boy. We'll be having dinner soon,' Eva instructed her son.

'Can we have pizza again?'

'No, you bloody can't. You've had enough pizza to last a life time,' Gary shouted. He walked to the fridge and took out a can of lager and then went into the lounge to watch TV. He was reclining on the sofa, feet on the coffee table, as Eva came in. She sat down on the other sofa and glanced at Gary, who ignored her.

'Gary, I'm going to ask you now to stop getting angry with Alfie and ordering him about. He's just enjoyed his birthday celebrations, had a great time at the climbing wall and was looking at his presents. I told you at the start of our relationship that Alfie comes first and you are getting too bossy with him. Actually, I think the word is authoritarian and it's got to stop or we are over.' Eva detected a tremor in her own voice as she said this as the expression on Gary's face went from annoyance to anger.

He sighed heavily, and his eyes honing in on her face were dark and harsh, the black depths of an abyss. 'Oh really, we are over. I don't think so.' He got up off the sofa and went to sit next to her. His hand whipped under her chin as he forced her to look at his face. 'You and I will only be over when I decide. Until then, we are together. Things would run more smoothly here if you didn't keep giving that kid too much leeway. It really riles me up. This birthday stuff has been over the top with two days of activities and money wasted. And too many presents. I've said it before, he is spoiled.'

Eva could only just about speak as his grip on her continued. 'He is not spoiled. He is allowed to enjoy his birthday like all other kids. I'm not going to let you make my son unhappy.'

With Gary's hand digging into her chin, she tried to pull away from his grasp, but he was not letting go. He pushed her roughly down on the sofa and knelt over her. She tried to get up but she was shoved down again. He lay over her, his dark eyes, cold and hard scanning her face, as his hand clamped over her mouth. 'Listen up. I want to be with you and I accept that your son comes with the deal. But I will not just sit back and let him be indulged and spoiled all the time. I will step in with the discipline.'

'Let me get up, Gary, I can't move. I decide what happens with my son. There will be no talk of discipline, we do not live in Charles Dickens' times.'

Gary continued to press down on her, her movement impeded by the strength of his body. 'More's the pity. What a lot of these kids need today is a bit of old-fashioned school punishment.'

Eva now found that she was struggling for breath and she tried to take in air in short, shaky gulps. She felt fear as if insects were crawling in her stomach. 'Let me go.' She tried to push at his chest to ease him off her but it felt like a concrete boulder was pressing down on her.

'It's not just Alfie that needs bringing into line, it's you as well.' He slammed his right hand across the left side of her face, hammering her cheek, and jarring her jaw. As she groaned with shock, he eased his weight off her and then smacked his right fist hard into the ribs of her left side. A second blow quickly followed. He moved off her and sat on the sofa next to her as she moaned in pain. 'Ironic isn't it, darling, you are the teacher and I am the one giving you a lesson in how to behave. If I get bored with trading cars I might giving the teaching profession a go. None of the little bastards would dare to mess with me, don't you agree, Miss?'

Eva lay still on the sofa, too stunned to move, with tears in her eyes. Gary looked down at her and stroked her hair. 'I don't want to hurt you, sweetheart, as you are very precious to me. But I will be the one in charge here. I'm not going anywhere as you are the woman I want to be with. Anyway, I expect we are all getting hungry so I will go and prepare some dinner. I think salmon would be good after all the pizza and takeaways of this weekend. We need to get back to healthy eating.'

The next day at school, Eva went about her duties in a robotic manner, trying to interact as normal with the children but could not summon any energy or enthusiasm for what she was meant to do. A few of the children noticed the change in her and asked if she was well. She said that she was and assured them that she did not have Covid. She explained that it had been her son's birthday at the weekend and she was tired after pizza making and taking him to a climbing wall. Jake, one of her more nosy pupils asked if she had climbed the wall, and she told him no, she had just watched. Jake explained that he would like to do that for his birthday and would not stop climbing till he was on the roof of the building. Eva imagined Jake, in his older years, as one of those freerunners who jump, leap, vault and roll to clear obstacles such as stairs, steps and benches. He certainly had the energy and dare-devil spirit to undertake 'parkour' as she thought it was called.

During the day, Eva was still trying to process what had happened with Gary yesterday afternoon. Luckily, her face where he had slapped her did not have any red marks or bruising under her eye as had happened last time when they were abroad. Her face had been reddened but this had disappeared by the morning and her normal light foundation covered her skin and a faint mark on her jawline. Her ribs were another matter. Two fist-sized red areas were apparent just under her left breast and the red colouration was now changing to blueish purple. There was a deep ache to her abdomen area, and if she twisted or turned unexpectedly, a sharp pain shot through her. When this happened, the agony registered on her face, and in the staffroom at lunchtime a couple of people asked if she had hurt herself.

Eva found she was getting really good at making excuses to hide Gary's actions and her embarrassment. 'Yes, it was on Saturday after the pizza making party and I was clearing up. There was some pop spilt on the floor, which I hadn't noticed, and I slipped and caught my side on the corner of the kitchen table. It hurts a bit if I turn suddenly. No harm done, though.'

At lunchtime, Eva was sat next to her colleague, Teaching Assistant, Kasia, on a sofa, trying to de-stress after a busy morning and to drink her coffee whilst it was still warm. Kasia eyed her carefully. 'You don't look so good today. Are you sure you have not got hangover after too many wines?'

'No, no hangover. I did have a few wines on Saturday when the kids did the pizzas. And I did have a glass yesterday when mum and dad called, after the climbing experience. Not enough to give me a hangover. But I will admit to feeling under the weather, a bit tired I suppose. It has been a busy weekend.'

Kasia pulled a puzzled expression. 'What is 'under the weather?' Did you get wet as I don't think it rained yesterday?' As she was originally from Poland, she still found some of these British saying a bit baffling.

Eva smiled. 'It means that you don't feel too good not that you got caught in the rain.'

Kasia, who Eva loved having as her Teaching Assistant, was often not good at stopping to think before she spoke. 'You do look very pale and sickly today. And are experiencing tiredness. And, if it is not a hangover, perhaps you are pregnant.'

Luckily, for Eva she did say this quietly and with the general drone of conversation in the staffroom, no one else heard. Eva whispered in a low, firm voice to Kasia. 'Kasia, I can assure you that I am not pregnant. Please don't go starting any rumours. There is absolutely no chance of that happening.'

Kasia was a young woman in her mid-twenties, who had lived with her boyfriend for two years and was consumed with the idea of having a baby. She could not understand any women who did not want babies. 'Yes, but you have been with the gorgeous Gary for a while now and I thought you would have more children.'

An older woman, Judy, sat down on a vacant chair near to Eva and Kasia, her ears alerted to the conversation. 'What's this about, who wants more children? Take my advice ladies, stick with one. They get very expensive as they get older and my Jaden's off to university next year. My chances of an early retirement have been scuppered. Another piece of advice, girls. Don't wait till you are thirty-six to have your first child as their teen years and your menopause years don't create a happy existence. Screeching at a Year 11 to do their GCSE revision while you're having hot flushes is not great as there is an ocean load of hormones circulating in the home. My poor hubby used to go to the shed and stay there from morning to evening. Doing what, I have no idea. It certainly wasn't weightlifting or bench pressing as he always came out skinnier than when he went in. More's the pity as I sort of keep hoping for a Dwayne Johnson to emerge.'

Eva laughed loudly. Judy was brilliant at cheering everyone up with her down to earth take on all subjects including marriage and parenting. 'Kasia has noted that I am a bit off colour today and thinks I must be pregnant. Her default diagnosis for every ailment affecting any woman under forty.'

Judy glanced over at Eva, surveying her closely, and Eva felt she was an amoeba under a microscope. 'Actually, Kasia has a point, as you haven't seemed yourself since the beginning of term. I have noticed that you are quieter, jumpier and less engaged with the children. That's not a criticism of your professionalism as you are a great teacher but you don't look so happy as before.'

'Honestly, Judy. I'm fine.'

Eva was worried that the strain that she was experiencing in her home life was now being commented on by friends and colleagues, though she knew that their concern was genuine and caring. She hoped that she could leave her worries about her relationship with Gary at home and become the old Eva when she was at work or out with friends. It was now apparent that she was not succeeding at covering up the anxiety that now dogged her. She believed that she was a good actress, experiencing the pain and hurt at home, then leaving it all behind as she emerged into the outside world. Away from home she was her normal cheery self. Eva had now discovered that acting was not easy, especially as she was being subjected to real trauma. She was not living in a world of false blood and fake fights as was the case on the stage or in movies. Her world was now that of punches and real bruises.

At 3.00 p.m. Eva had directed Kasia to read the children a story for the end of the school day and Eva quietly worked on finalising tomorrow's lessons. Kasia then instructed the children on putting on their coats and ensuring that they had their school backpacks with any items needed to take home, including lunchboxes, reading books, and letters from the headteacher to parents. As Kasia supervised the children as they left for home, Eva sat back in the quiet classroom, dreading the time when she would have to leave and go home.

It was really difficult to be around Gary at the moment. After yesterday's incident, she lay on the sofa too stunned to move, whilst he went out into the kitchen to prepare dinner. She tried to force herself not to cry. Once started she may never stop and she didn't want Alfie to have any sense of what had happened. A half an hour later, Gary called both her and Alfie to sit at the table as the meal was ready. He had prepared pan-fried salmon, new potatoes with butter, and broccoli. As Alfie sat down at the table, Eva noticed that he pulled a face as she knew he was not keen on salmon or broccoli and she prayed that Gary would not notice. If Alfie started to kick off about not liking the dinner, then it could spark Gary into another angry tirade or worse. She had been shown now on at least three occasions that Gary would resort to violence if he became displeased with her and she feared what he might do next.

Alfie must have been hungry and he ate his meal without complaint. 'Can I have more potatoes, please?' He'd noticed the remaining potatoes in the bowl and was given permission to have some more.

Gary's earlier black mood seemed to have dissipated and he was now telling Alfie about his round of golf with friend Simon. He promised to take Alfie to a local pitch and putt in the near future, if Alfie behaved himself.

Alfie looked pleased about this. 'That would be great, Gary. Mum can come too.'

Eva was not keen to let her son go out alone with Gary. 'Maybe. We'll see. It's getting a bit cold and wet for golf this time of year.'

Gary laughed and lightly tapped Eva's hand. 'She's scared that we'll beat her. She knows that we will be brilliant at it but we do need someone to come last, don't we Alfie? We don't want to lose, do we?'

Alfie shouted, 'no, boys have to win.'

Eva frowned at her son, not liking that he was picking up on some of Gary's more chauvinistic tendencies. 'No, Alfie, boys don't have to win. They have to play well, and play fair, and then they may win which is great. The winner doesn't have to be a boy, it can be a girl.'

Gary rolled his eyes at this comment. 'Yeah, maybe, but boys should always play to win. There's no place for losers or quitters in this world. The world's a tough place and you can't afford to show weakness, Alfie. Anyway, you need to clear the plates and bowls off the table and then make sure you have everything ready for school tomorrow.' Alfie did as he was asked, whilst Eva loaded all the dirty dishes and plates into the dishwasher and wiped down the kitchen worktops and dining table. Gary took a bottled lager out of the fridge, then sat down again at the table and watched her as she worked.

Placing the cloth in the sink, Eva walked towards him, but with the intention to vacate the room and prepare for her day in school tomorrow. As she passed him, he pulled her onto his lap. She winced as it jarred her ribs, causing a sharp pain. 'Come here, darling,' he said. 'I'm sorry for what I did earlier and I hope you will forgive me.'

He felt her tense in his arms as she made to pull away. He gripped his arm around her waist, fingers at her left side near to her bruised ribs, but he was gentle in his touch. He then dipped her down slightly so that he was able to kiss her, covering her mouth in an exploratory but delicate way. Eva was conflicted as this contact was soothing. He held her and kissed her and she felt the tension flow out of her body. But she was still with a man who could change from comforter to tormentor at a moment's notice. He stopped the embrace and focused his gaze on her face. 'Let's get sorted for tomorrow as quickly as possible and once Alfie is in bed we will go up as well. I will then spend my time loving you in a tender way, to make up for the hurt I've caused today. I promise.'

Eva had wanted to push him away, run from the room, and never stop until she got to one of the places furthest away from here. A one-way ticket to Wellington, New Zealand or Santiago, Chile. Resisting and running would only make matters worse for now. For the time being she must stay calm and decide on what course of action to take. Her strongest urge was to get Gary out of her life as he presented a danger to her and her son. Gary had already indicated that he would not leave without a fight, and the loser in any combat would be her, as she had already been bruised and bloodied. She must be cautious and play the long game. Concentrate on planning how to get out of this living nightmare that she had brought upon herself. This was her battle and one that she must fight alone. She could not cope with the humiliation of other people knowing what was happening. Her best option was to ease Gary out of her life and let it be known the relationship had ended by mutual consent.

CHAPTER THIRTY TWO

September 2011

The wedding to Jess had gone well as far as Gary was concerned. The civil marriage ceremony and wedding breakfast was held in an hotel in Stratford-upon-Avon, a building dating back to the fifteenth century where a young William Shakespeare may have enjoyed a drink or two when it was a tavern. Gary was gratified that the wedding was a small gathering of twenty plus family and friends, and Jess's only closest family members were an aunt and first cousin who lived in Scotland. The aunt being an elderly woman in her late eighties. The other guests were two of Jess's friends from school, who she kept in touch with by texts and Christmas cards, but she rarely saw. Her other guests were her shop managers and two long-serving staff and their partners. Gary explained to those who enquired that his parents were dead, and he had no siblings, so sadly he was without a loving family to support him on this very special day. He invited to the wedding his friend Simon, who served as best man, and a few senior staff from his dealerships.

The wedding breakfast room was a beautiful backdrop to the occasion with oak-beamed ceilings and wooden flooring covered with cream rugs. The tables were classy, set with white tablecloths, silver candles, and displays of white blooms and greenery. Having consumed the three course meal of salmon and crab terrine, corn-fed chicken with chive creamed mash, and French apple tart, the guests were sated and well lubricated with wine and Prosecco. Guests were seated in tables of six, and Gary was sat with Jess, her two schoolfriends Abby and Ruby, and Ruby's husband. Simon had been delighted to be seated next to Abby, a curvaceous blonde and was eager to claim best man privileges of dancing with the bridesmaid. Gary was ready to deliver his bridegroom speech and rose from his seat, lightly tapping his glass with a teaspoon. 'Hi everyone. Jess and I would like to say a big thank you for coming to share our special day. I must say a massive well done to my wife, for organising the day, and the beautiful, tasteful way she has co-ordinated it all including the flowers, the cake, the venue and its beautiful layout. She has done a fantastic job, supported by the wonderful staff at this hotel. I would like to thank Simon for being my best man and I am anxiously, and nervously, awaiting his speech. I hope he doesn't share too many stories of our friendship over the years. I would also like to thank the bridesmaids, Abby and Ruby, for being supportive friends to Jess. Please raise a toast to the beautiful bridesmaids. 'The bridesmaids.'

Gary placed his hand on Jess's shoulder and a warm smile glowed on his face, though the smile did not touch the depths of his brown eyes. Jess was dressed in a white midi-length dress with sequined bodice and mesh overlay that accentuated the dips and curves of her figure. Her dark-blonde hair with honey highlights was gently waved to frame her face and was adorned with crystal hair pins. Her makeup was perfection, emphasising her brown eyes and glossy ruby lips. 'And, now to my wife Jess, who looks absolutely stunning and I know I am the luckiest man alive on this my wedding day to this woman. I feel very grateful to be standing here today, having found love for the second time. We seem an unlikely couple. Jess with her love of reality TV shows and her undying passion for crime and medical dramas. The other man in our relationship, who she is besotted over, is Doc Martin. He will come in handy in an emergency unless I sever a finger and he faints at the sight of blood.' Laughter from the wedding guests. Gary continued, 'in the short time that we have known each other; Jess has changed my life. She has turned me from being a workaholic to someone who can now leave work behind, and enjoy romantic meals and tv dramas, just spending time with the woman I love. I say to the makers of 'Doc Martin', you keep making them, we'll keep watching them.'

As the guests laughed, and Gary retook his seat, he felt conflicted. He had married Wife Number Two. The Plan was progressing nicely but there was still work to do before securing the financial rewards he was seeking. With this wife he would be speeding things up. A short marriage of about two years was his ideal target. In order to endure Jess over this time, and her many faults including unsexy figure, irritating personality, and appalling taste in tv, he would take delight in goading her and bringing her under his control. Old medical problems of anxiety and panic attacks would return. Other carnal pleasures would be provided by his regular visits to his sexy, feline mistress, Samantha.

CHAPTER THIRTY THREE

September 2021

After his discussion with Gary the day before, Andy strongly suspected, though Gary denied it, that there was some sort of intimacy between him and the woman at the house in Fir Avenue, that he had observed last week. Theoretically, she may have been a girlfriend from his past, and there was nothing currently between them, but the pinch of her bottom suggested to Andy an on-going intimacy. Andy was finding that every new thing he found out about Gary was not casting him in a positive light and the potential for Eva getting hurt was increasing all the time. Tania's perceptive comments on the previous two wives had struck a chord with him and he decided he was going to do a little digging to see what he could find.

The pizza making had gone really well, according to Hannah, who declared that she and Phoebe had a really great time but she would not now be eating pizza for the rest of the month. This was partly due to Natasha's post party comment that she never ate pizza as it had far too many calories per slice, and men never went for fat women. Andy was never going to encourage Hannah to eat pizza on a daily or weekly basis but the occasional one would not hurt. He didn't want Hannah developing Natasha's pickiness with food and her habit of announcing the calories of any food before it was eaten. Teenagers were particularly prone to developing eating disorders and Hannah was starting to copy Natasha in this calorie counting obsession. Hannah had been introduced to a variety of foods during her childhood. Her mother's Spanish heritage helped to influence her in terms of enjoying plenty of vegetables and salads but also that food was to be savoured and enjoyed. Natasha approached most meals with trepidation, in terms of its calorific value, so avoided high fat and sugary foods but did not compensate by eating vegetables and proteins enthusiastically. Food was a chore for Natasha, something to keep her alive, but she derived little pleasure from it and so it was affecting his enjoyment as well.

Andy got out of his car, with DC Lewis, to visit a house, a run-down terraced property just outside Rugby town centre. The house was typical of a few in the road, rented out by landlords who charged a high rent for properties maintained to the minimal legal standards. Greying rendering on the front of the property gave it a depressing appearance, not helped by green moss and patches of damp, under the windows. A small frontage surrounded by a low-level red brick wall, in need of renovation, was paved with cracked moss-covered slabs, not the best welcome for any visitor. A grey dustbin was full with the lid unable to close, an indication that the property's occupants were not efficient in managing their household waste. Andy banged on the door a couple of times, waiting for someone to bother to answer. After a couple of minutes the door was opened, a fraction, by a thin, pale, man in his twenties, wearing grubby grey joggers and a wrinkled, faded white T-shirt. He squinted cautiously at the two police officers as if the brightness of the outside was due to a searing hot sun, and he was staring into a Texan sky, and not a grey, cloudy day in the UK. His spindly arms showing below the T-shirt were pallid, emphasising a lack of muscle and prominent veins. The skin on his cadaverous face was a sickly yellow.

As the man stared at the two detectives, he decided that they were not who he may have been expecting and went to close the door. Andy's foot managed to keep it open. Andy showed his warrant card through the gap in the door. 'I am Detective Inspector, Andy Leyton, and this is Detective Constable, Gabrielle Lewis. Kyle Noble? We'd like to ask you a few questions about a Wayne Potter. Can we come in?'

The man eased the door open slightly and then gazed intently at the warrant card before reluctantly opening the door. 'Yeah, come in.' He led the way into the lounge, a musty smelling room with faded purple curtains and grey nets allowing a minimal amount of light inside. The room was furnished by two sofas, one sludge brown leather, patchy in places through wear and tear. The other sofa was a beige, fabric sofa with grimy areas on the arms and seats. A large coffee table was placed between the two sofas, cluttered with lager cans, cigarettes, lighters, ashtrays and crisp packets. There were tobacco rolling papers and tinned tobacco, but with the distinctive smell of marijuana present, Andy was sure that the tobacco was used in making spliffs. There was evidence of other drug paraphernalia including spoons and foil, so cocaine, and possibly heroin were other drugs of choice. There were some signs of red needle marks and rounded scabs on the man's scrawny arms.

The man sat on the leather sofa, nervously eyeing the drug stuff on the table, and then waited for the cops to speak. 'What ya say, Wayne Potter? I don't know him.'

'Shall we?' Andy asked as he sat on the other sofa, facing the man. DC Lewis sat tentatively next to Andy, trying not to touch the fabric with her hands. '

'We think you do know Wayne Potter, Kyle. We think you do know him quite well. I am sorry to have to inform you that Wayne Potter was found stabbed to death on Sunday morning in the car park of the White Oak pub.' Andy scrutinised Kyle's face as he relayed this information. Kyle's eyes widened slightly on hearing the name, Wayne Potter, an indication to Andy that he definitely recognised it.

'No, never heard of him. Nowt to do with me.'

Andy continued, 'we have identified you as one of a number of people who spoke to Mr Potter in the White Oak on Saturday evening. You were in the pub, alongside Mr Potter, till closing time at 11 p.m. The landlord, Mr John Frost, has confirmed that you are a regular at his pub, as was Mr Potter. Mr Frost commented that he had seen you speaking to Mr Potter on numerous occasions but would not describe you as drinking partners. How well do you know Wayne Potter?'

Kyle reached out and picked up his cigarette packet and lighter, then noticed DC Lewis' look of disapproval and put them back down on the table. 'I'm telling you, I don't know this Wayne bloke. Just because we go in the same pub doesn't make us friends. The landlord is off is nut on this, probably too much sampling of his own booze, as he's a drunken git most of the time. Eyesight's not so good either, as he wears bins.'

Andy maintained a serious expression, suppressing an urge to smile. 'I don't think Mr Frost's eyesight is that much of an issue as he seems to be able to differentiate between his customers. He accurately identified you as Kyle Noble who was seen speaking to Wayne Potter at close to 11.00 p.m. and he described your conversation as, in his word, 'heated'. He stated that the two of you were arguing, your voices were raised and he had to ask you both to quieten down or get out. He said he wasn't sure what the argument was about but you were angry with Mr Potter, and at one point, you poked your finger into his shoulder. Can you remember this now, Kyle?'

Noble avoided eye contact with the police detectives, pausing before replying. 'No, I don't remember any beef with anyone. I had quite a lot to drink that night but there were no arguments. You wanna talk to other people in the pub. Why be harassing me? I shall put in a complaint. Just because I've been done for a bit of dealing in the past doesn't mean I should be fitted up for a murder.'

Andy breathed deeply, as Kyle Noble's 'bit of dealing' had landing him in prison on two occasions for possession and dealing a Class A drug, cocaine, eighteen months, and Class B drugs, cannabis and ketamine, twelve months. Andy's annoyance deepened at this low-life dealer as he mentioned being harassed and he would be making a complaint. He rued the day that ex-cons had been given so many rights but never seemed to recognise their responsibilities. 'Kyle, I don't think anyone is trying to fit you up. We are investigating the murder of Wayne Potter whose body was found in the White Oak car park. We have been fortunate in that Mr Frost (he wanted to add of the drink-sodden brain and failing eyesight) had the intelligence to instal CCTV cameras which overlook the back of the pub and the car park. We are currently examining the footage of an argument between two men at about 11.15 p.m., one we are certain is Wayne

Potter. The other man is tall, skinny and similar in appearance to you. What did you do on leaving the pub at closing time?'

Kyle Noble suddenly pulled himself upright up on the sofa, as if he were a skinny greyhound that had been roused from its sleep, and was expected to do a lap in a race with very short notice. His eyes flitted between the two detectives, as he weighed up his options. He decided to try to make a run for the door, by rushing around the sofa, past the female detective. Andy was immediately on his feet to block the door and prevent his escape. Noble grabbed hold of DC Lewis, putting her in front of him, by clasping her tightly with his left arm. To Andy's horror, he pulled a small knife out of the pocket of his joggers and stabbed the point of the knife into DC Lewis's neck. Noble slowly moved forward, gripping a terrified DC Lewis. 'Out of the way, cop. Let me through.'

Andy stood firm but registered the fear on his colleagues face as the tip of the knife caused a red droplet of blood to form on her skin. 'Let her go, Kyle. As you said earlier, you've only ever been done for a bit of dealing. Don't ruin your life now in a state of panic.'

'I'm telling you, cop, I ain't done nowt wrong and you're trying to fit me up. Now, move out of the way.' Noble inched DC Lewis nearer to the door and Andy. A slow trickle of blood was now making its way down her neck to the collar of her white blouse. DC Lewis swiftly scrapped the heal of her shoe down Noble's shin and then slammed her heal onto his right instep, his foot only covered by light grey, mucky socks. Noble squealed in pain and dropped the knife, pushed DC Lewis aside, and tried to dash out of the door. Andy now grabbed him, battered his body into the door, and halted his exit. The left side of Kyle Noble's face was pushed hard into the door. He struggled and wriggled to free himself of Andy's body weight which was crushed on to him to prevent his escape. The would-be escapee finally stopped squirming and Andy roughly pulled his arms around his back to secure handcuffs to his wrists. 'DC Lewis, are you ok?' Andy enquired.

DC Lewis scrambled to her feet and cautiously touched her neck. 'I think so, its only a nick, nothing too bad but it stings a bit.'

'Good, you're ok. Call for backup and an ambulance to get you checked over. Then, I want a forensic team here immediately. And we need to bag up that knife as it is implicated in the crime of a physical assault on a police officer.' As Kyle Noble struggled to free his face from its close association with the off-white door, Andy ensured that the drug dealer could breathe but continued to keep him hemmed in and unable to abscond. 'Kyle Noble, I am arresting you for aggravated assault of a police officer in the execution of their duties. You do not have to say anything but it may harm your defence if you do not mention when questioned something which you later rely on in court. Anything you say may be given in evidence.'

Later, back at the police station, Andy was managing to grab a cheese and pickle sandwich and a coffee. Kyle Noble was remanded in custody but yet to be interviewed, by other detectives, and charged with the aggravated assault on DC Lewis. Andy was progressing the case of the death of Wayne Potter, including the CCTV footage from the pub, the knife used to stab DC Lewis, forensic examination of Kyle Noble's house and witness statements from people at the pub. Kyle Noble, a man trying to run from the police, was a significant person of interest at this stage.

Having ensured that DC Lewis was unharmed but a little shaken after her ordeal, Andy made her take the rest of the day off, even though she protested loudly that she was ok.

Finishing his sandwich and wincing at the bitterness of the coffee, he tried to put his current work priorities out of his mind. Time to take a few minutes and focus on another individual who was occupying his thoughts. Time to do some Google searches on Gary Anderson.

After a long day working on the Potter murder, and other ongoing cases, Andy walked into his home at 6.30 p.m. relieved to be home and ready to chill out with a few lagers after dinner. He was hoping that Natasha had prepared something for dinner, as the general rule was that the person in the house first, started the dinner. He entered the kitchen to find Natasha sat at the kitchen island, on her phone, and there was a dish of green salad on the dining table. He went over to Natasha and kissed her on the cheek. 'Hi, you, ok? Have you managed to start dinner?'

She paused momentarily from looking at her phone to acknowledge the kiss. 'Yes, nothing exciting. Chicken breasts with smoked paprika, jacket potatoes and green salad. It should be ready in about fifteen minutes.'

'Great. Where's Hannah? In her room?'

Natasha now avoided eye contact with Andy, as she replied, 'I don't know. We had a bust up and she stormed out about half an hour ago. I don't know where she's gone. I've tried calling her but she's not answering. Nothing more I can do.'

'What was this bust up about?'

'I asked her to empty the dishwasher and lay the table. I got the usual, in a minute response, as she went up to her room. I followed her and made her come back down to do as she was told. Grudgingly, she started to empty the dishwasher, putting the stuff in the cupboards and banging the doors loudly. I told her to get on with it quietly and that she would be grounded if I had to tell her again. She basically said, do it yourself then and stormed out, saying I wasn't her parent. 'Honestly, Andy, this dealing with kids is doing my head in. I don't want the hassle.'

Andy was now starting to get annoyed with Natasha. 'My main concern at this moment is that my twelve-year-old daughter has left the house and I do not know where she is. Have you contacted Lucia?'

'Yes, and she's not with Lucia. She is at work at the hospital.'

'Right. I'll phone Hannah and see if she answers.' He took his phone out of his jacket pocket and dialled Hannah's number. It went straight to voicemail, so he left a message that she must contact him immediately. 'I'll try a few of her friends. He texted Phoebe, on the basis that teenagers tend to answer a text, rather than answer a phone call. A few seconds later, Phoebe texted back, 'no. Not here. Not seen her since school.'

Andy then realised that the nearest friend was Alfie and he phoned Eva. 'Hi, Eva. Its Andy. Hannah has stormed out of the house and we don't know where she is. Is she with Alfie?' He paused as Eva spoke. 'Great, I'll come round and get her now, if that's ok. Thanks.' Andy sighed with relief. 'She's with Alfie. I'll go and get her.'

Natasha stopped texting on her phone and looked up. 'Good. And I'll expect an apology for her rudeness. Don't go too soft on her.'

Andy's only concern at that moment was that his daughter was safe. 'We'll discuss what happened after dinner but not until then.'

As he went out of his house, across the driveway to Eva's house, he yearned for a time when it was just himself and Hannah. Natasha's self-absorption meant that she really didn't put any effort into bonding with Hannah. She expected Hannah to do what she was told, when she was told, which was reasonable at times. But Hannah got easily upset by Natasha's laziness and not doing her share of the chores. Hannah resented how Natasha issued orders to get things done but barely helped in the house herself. Natasha wanted a quiet life as far as Hannah was concerned. She tolerated Hannah but Natasha did not expend any energy trying to connect with his daughter emotionally. Natasha made it perfectly clear that her favourite times, when they were together, was when Hannah was at her mothers.

He knocked on the door at Eva's and she opened it, inviting him in. 'I believe my daughters here. I hope she's not getting in your way.'

'Of course not. We always love to have her. They're in the kitchen.' Eva led the way, and Andy followed, to find Alfie and Hannah sat together at the kitchen table laughing at something on Hannah's phone.'

Hannah stopped laughing immediately and gazed at her father's face. His expression was not overly friendly. 'I'm sorry, dad. I shouldn't have run off but she kept bossing me about and I'd had enough.'

'Natasha was only asking you to unload the dishwasher, not unreasonable in my opinion. If asked to do something you should do it calmly and not get annoyed about it. No slamming of cupboard doors. You know that,' Andy stated.

Hannah now blushed slightly, avoiding looking at Eva or Alfie. 'I know. Sorry, dad. She just winds me up and she's not exactly helpful around the house herself.'

'Ok, Hannah, that's enough. The main issue here is that you rushed out the house, have not answered your phone and nobody knew where you were. That's not acceptable, Hannah.'

Eva glanced at Andy, who was still angered by Hannah's behaviour. 'Andy, I'm sorry, I thought you knew she was round here. I didn't realise.'

Andy's smiled softly at Eva. 'This is not your fault, Eva. This is down to her. Anyway, Hannah, we'll discuss this later. Now say thanks to Eva for having you and it's time to go.'

Hannah picked up her jacket off the back of her chair and addressed Eva.

'Thanks Eva. Sorry to bring my annoyed dad to your door. Bye Alfie, see you tomorrow.' She walked out of the kitchen with Andy and Eva following.

As Hannah went out of the front door, Eva said to Andy. 'I'm really sorry, Andy. If I knew that she had stormed out I would have made her ring you and Natasha.'

Andy shook his head. 'Honestly, you'd think when you get home from arresting criminals it would be nice to return home to an environment of calm and tranquillity. Particularly, on a day one of my officers was injured by a toe-rag with a knife. Instead, I have to deal with a stroppy daughter who has just scared me to death by flouncing out. I hope that this doesn't become a habit. Still, I will have a chat with her later and hope I can nip it in the bud.'

Eva's face registered shock when he mentioned his officer being injured. 'Is the officer, ok? What happened, can you say?'

'We were questioning this person of interest when he tried to make a run for it. He grabbed hold of my DC and held a knife to her throat. She cleverly jabbed his foot with her heel and he dropped the knife. I quickly overpowered him and cuffed him. She's fine, it was only a nick to her neck, but it was a scary experience for her.'

'I don't know how you do your job,' Eva commented.

'It has its interesting moments. I always have a great sense of satisfaction if I have to use the handcuffs.' He smiled wickedly. 'I must have a dark side to my nature that I rarely admit to.'

Eva pretended to look embarrassed. 'Detective Inspector Leyton, please don't tell me all your naughty secrets.'

'I could do, how long have you got.' He winked at her which made her laugh.

As she laughed, Eva felt a sharp stab of pain in her ribs which were still tender following Gary's assault on her. Andy noticed immediately that she flinched, and put her hand to her left side, by her waist. A flicker of pain crossed her face. 'Have you hurt your ribs; you seem to be in some discomfort?'

'Yes, as I told them at school today. I slipped on some coke on the kitchen floor and banged my side on the corner of the table. Making me laugh, isn't helping?

Andy noted that there was no laughter on her face as she said this but a deep sadness. In fact, he knew that he could glimpse fear on her beautiful features. A physical shock hit Andy and he suspected that Gary had something to do with this. 'How were you and Gary after Alfie's birthday celebrations? I don't think he's a man who likes that kind of thing as he really didn't join in on Saturday.'

Eva now sensed that Andy was not buying her story of how she hurt her ribs. If he asked any questions then there was a danger she would get upset and this would hundred percent confirm his suspicions. Andy's police training could be a nuisance at times, as it was difficult to hide things from him. He must be a first-class officer at making criminals 'spill the beans'.

She tried to keep things light, as she said, 'no, you're right. Gary is not a fan of children's birthday parties and I'm glad he kept out the way. And, I need to be more careful in future and watch out for spillages on the floor. I am a health and safety officer's worst nightmare. Anyway, it's just a bit of bruising, nothing serious.'

Andy knew she was trying to lighten the mood and take the focus off her injury but there was a nagging feeling in his head that Gary was involved in this. If he was involved in hurting her again, Andy was rocked by an urge to punch the man into next week. 'If, you're sure. Have you seen a doctor?'

'No need for that. I'm fine, honestly.'

'Ok, I'd better go. Speak to my daughter and negotiate a peace treaty between her and Natasha. I'll need all the skills of the Secretary General of NATO.'

'Good luck.' Eva wished him as he left the house.

'I'll need it.'

CHAPTER THIRTY FOUR

Beginning October 2021

In the two weeks since Gary had injured Eva's ribs, he had been compensating her by being extra kind and loving. He did more of his share of the cooking, prepared her lunches for work, healthy salads with tuna or hummus and shredded wheat crackers. He bought her flowers, small bars of chocolate (always health aware), and brought a glass of white wine to her as she watched the television. He cuddled her in bed, and when he noticed the bruising on her left side, as it turned to yellows and greens as the haemoglobin in the blood was broken down, he would gently kiss and stroke the area, muttering how sorry he was. He wanted to impress on her that he was the caring man she had met at the start of their relationship. The man who loved and protected her. He needed her to realise that he was Dr Henry Jekyll and would not suddenly transform into the unpredictable, violent Edward Hyde.

In terms of the relationship, Gary demonstrated his affection for her physically by cuddling and kissing her frequently, when Alfie was not around. For him their love making was arousing and sating but he was considerate not to cause her pain, as her ribs were still healing. He frequently told her that he loved her, at least once a day, and that she was an amazing, beautiful, sexy woman who he really did not deserve. He was not sure that he was succeeding. It felt as if she was holding back and not fully engaging with him emotionally. His modus operandi when progressing The Plan with the previous wives had been to convince them of his feelings for them until he had secured them to him by marriage. Rule number one for him was that he had no emotional attachment to them. This had been easy with Claire and Jess. He felt as much fondness to them as a goldfish he once won at the fair and that had died after a week, as he forgot to feed it.

Matters were not so clear cut with Eva. As he progressed her on the path to being Wife Number Three, he should be detached and unaffected by her. This time it was harder, as Eva was all the things he told her; amazing, beautiful, sexy, and intelligent. And irritatingly, for the first time in his life, he was developing strong feelings for a woman.

Dispassionately, he was determined to move forward with The Plan, to gain Eva's financial assets, consolidate his wealth, have a few years of freedom, before seeking out the next prey. Emotionally, he knew it would be difficult to carry out the final act in terms of Eva. The previous two wives had died at his hand but it was death at a distance, by an accident or overdose, but with Eva it would be a crime of passion. The ultimate act of love on his part, taking her on a journey to a higher realm, bestowing on her his final gift, the gift of death.

Still the planning was all in the detail and he wanted to move things forward at a faster pace. In convincing Eva of his commitment to change his behaviour, he was planning a four day city break during the October half term, to Budapest. Just the two of them. Arrangements were being made for Alfie to stay with his grandparents. Time to consolidate the relationship in a more tangible way. A proposal on a river boat on the Danube and a spring wedding the following year.

Things could run smoothly from now on if he managed to keep his temper in check. He didn't want to scare her off by any more outbursts, and really, he didn't want to hurt her. He had always accepted that he had a violent streak, which was released if a woman challenged him, or irritated him. He liked to be in control. First wife Claire's stupidity had irked him, second wife Jess's neediness had narked him, both things goading him into a physical reaction. Eva's problem, which ignited his rage, was not her per se, but her failure to deal more firmly with her son. Gary was finding that having Alfie around was really pushing him to his limits. The boy was overindulged, argumentative, and in need of firmer handling. Gary would now have to adopt the patience of many saints, keep his temper in check, and convince Eva that he genuinely cared for her and her son.

In mid-October, Gary travelled to Glasgow to look at a car dealership which was up for sale. He was considering expanding his business to a further sales outlet north of the border. Flying to Glasgow on the Friday, he expected to be away two nights and return on Sunday. He was conflicted, as he missed being with Eva at the weekends, particularly when the kid was away with grandparents or on a sleep over, but he figured he might treat himself to a wee Scottish delicacy if time and opportunity allowed. Gary could justify his own little dalliances. He was not an advocate of what was good for the gander was good for the goose. He didn't like leaving Eva alone as she was easily influenced by her friends who were beginning to openly show their dislike for him.

Tania, the loud and interfering friend, who struggled to hide her contempt for him, would entice Eva to a night out in town where they were likely to meet men. Tania's budding relationship with the accountant she had met on her birthday, had blossomed and died in the space of two weeks. This made her hungrier in her search for a replacement. Gary had noted Tania in action in bars, when on the hunt for her prey, single men. She was focused, strident, and quick to go in for the kill, and the hapless victim stood no chance. One night, Gary had been in a bar, schmoozing a customer, when Tania and Eva arrived. The customer was interested in purchasing a number of cars for his sales team and Gary had spent a sizeable sum buying the man a steak dinner. He could not afford to let up now and the deal was virtually concluded. Tania and Eva were sharing a bottle of wine, when Tania had made a comment to a man next to her, and quickly she was in close conversation with him. Eva was left to sip her white wine, looking deliciously sexy in an emerald green wrap dress which emphasised her breasts and waist. It took literally minutes for a man to starting talking to her. A tall, fit guy in tight-fitting blue shirt. Gary's concentration on sealing the deal was shot to pieces instantly. As the man moved closer to his woman, Gary could barely hold back from racing over and stopping their conversation in its tracks. Gary was surprised to find that he was experiencing jealousy for the first time and it shocked him that he was capable of such an intense feeling when another man made a play for Eva. Very quickly, he had ended the business with his prospective buyer, rushed over to Eva, stopping her chat with the handsome male. The guy had not looked too pleased as he was enjoying Eva's company. Gary mused that he had come close to a fight for the first time in many years.

Gary brooded about not being around this weekend. He was sure that Tania would lure Eva out on Friday night, to be surrounded by chancers and opportunist men, the type Gary instantly recognised as he was one himself.

The other friend that Gary had concerns about was Andy. Andy had returned from his holiday with Natasha to announce that their relationship was over. This news really infuriated Gary. He had no affection for the blonde she-devil but whilst she was around she took some of Andy's attention away from Eva. Gary was convinced that Andy had more than just feelings of friendship for Eva. Andy's interrogation of him about the woman in Fir Avenue had particularly riled him. The cop's instinct had been right about his interaction with the woman, she had been a customer, but all the business of her buying a car had been concluded at the dealership. His presence at her house on that Monday was for a post purchase debrief and to see if she had areas that needed attending to in terms of maximum customer satisfaction. Gary had been very thorough on this matter. The woman meant nothing to him. She was just a casual bunk-up, easily forgotten, but he didn't want Inspector Morse investigating his movements.

Gary was getting concerned about Alfie's friendship with Hannah which often brought their respective parents together. He could imagine the little snot, Alfie, suggesting that Hannah and Andy come over for pizza. Leaving her in the company of that man truly freaked him out. Andy Leyton, a senior detective with the police service was not a man to be underestimated and his inclination to be protective of Eva set off loud sirens in Gary's head. Firstly, he was extremely good-looking and could have any woman he wanted, including his Eva. Secondly, he was friendly and kind to both Eva and Alfie, and emphasised Gary's short comings when dealing with the boy. Thirdly, if it came to all-out war between the two men over Eva, Gary was not sure he would win. Andy would be a formidable adversary, both physically and intellectually. Time for Gary to shore up The Plan in terms of Eva, so that Andy had no possibility of taking her away from him. He was sure that the city of Glasgow had a number of quality jewellery shops where a diamond engagement ring could be purchased.

CHAPTER THIRTY FIVE

Friday night, mid-October, and Eva was joyous that Gary had gone to Glasgow on a business venture to look at a car dealership for sale in that city. Eva did not overly concern herself in terms of Gary's businesses as they were his assets, and nothing to do with her. She quite liked that he was ambitious but at times he could come across as egotistical, as if he were CEO of BMW, and not a low-level peg in the car sales pecking order. It suited Eva, if Gary was off in another city, expanding the Anderson car sales empire and away from her and her son.

Immediately, Tania had been delighted that Eva was free on a Friday night and available to accompany her search for her soul mate. It was a never ending, exhausting quest, more daunting than teaching a polar bear to ice skate. Eva loved Tania but she always felt slightly used when she was persuaded to go on the man hunt. Firstly, Tania liked her to come along as she believed that together, as two pretty females, they attracted quite a lot of interest. Tania preferred to meet a group of men who would talk to both of them. If a lone man came over to speak to either of them, it was often the oddball loner who propped up the bar, staring into his pint and who had to be dodged as quickly as possible. Once contact with a friendly group of males had been made; Tania would launch like a missile at the guy she fancied while Eva chatted generally to one or two others. Friday night had been interesting, as Tania's choice had strongly preferred Eva, an occurrence that often occurred. Eva would not be telling Gary of her invitation to have dinner with an ear, nose and throat surgeon.

On Saturday, Eva organised her day around the delivery of her food shopping and the necessity to complete household jobs, including a pile of ironing of school shirts and Gary's work shirts. Gary always insisted that he hated ironing and believed that this should be her allotted task and she did it grudgingly, to avoid an argument. He had worked hard to try to build up her trust after the 'incident' as she called it. But Eva could not really relax around him in case it ignited his anger. Luckily, he currently seemed more chilled around Alfie but there was always the potential for a flare-up which could escalate quickly and she had a continual feeling of foreboding that one day Gary would lash out at Alfie.

Yesterday, there had been a skirmish over Alfie's school shoes, which he had left by the front door, for Gary to almost trip over as he came home from work. Gary entered the kitchen, carrying the shoes, which were scuffed and covered in mud. Gary strode straight up to Alfie, who was sitting at the kitchen table, finishing his maths homework while Eva prepared dinner.

Gary's face was hard and uncompromising as he loomed over Alfie, the dirty shoes dangling over the boy's maths homework book. 'Shall I put these on your school book and make it grubby so that you will be in trouble with your maths teacher as well as me. I've almost broke my neck on these coming in the door.'

Alfie quickly closed the maths book and stared, nervously, at Gary. 'Sorry, I forgot to pick them up.'

'You forgot, did you. And look at the state of them, covered in mud and scuffed. You've only had them a few weeks. 'How have they got like this?'

Alfie's eyes were darting all over the place to avoid Gary's angry face. 'Jai and I were kicking a ball about on the way home and I slipped in some mud.'

'These shoes cost £45.00 and this is the way you treat them. No pocket money for you this week.'

Eva now stopped spooning rice into a bowl. 'Gary, I agree that his shoes are a mess but we need to discuss things like stopping his pocket money.'

Gary was now equally angry with her. 'No, we don't. I've decided that he gets no pocket money and I've decided that he gets no dinner until these are cleaned and polished properly.' He dropped the shoes on the closed maths book, marking the book's green cover with brown, muddy streaks. 'Go and get on with it, now.'

Eva was pleased that Alfie didn't start his usual 'in a minute' pleading as Gary looked like he was about to erupt. 'Yes, go and clean them. Get a brush out of the cupboard here and rinse the mud off under the outside tap. Do not use too much water or the shoes will be soaked for tomorrow. You can polish them a bit later when they have dried out. For now, get the mud off, wash your hands and then come and have your dinner.' Alfie quietly got off the chair, picked up the shoes tentatively by the laces, whilst his mother handed him the brush from the box in the cupboard. He moved quickly past Gary to exit the kitchen door.

'Typical this, you've undermined me again, by telling him something different to what I ordered. I told him to clean and polish the shoes before dinner. Don't do that to me again.' Gary hovered close to her, a stern, hard look on his face. Eva tensed, scared that he would reprimand her physically but after a few seconds, he walked towards the kitchen door. 'I'm going to get changed out of my suit. I'll be down in ten minutes for dinner.'

As he left the room, Eva relaxed slightly but she was still shaken by his manner towards her and Alfie. His reference to being undermined he will see as a dent to his pride and she feared that there may be repercussions over this later on.

On Saturday evening, Alfie had a sleepover at Jai's, and Eva was looking forward to a Gary-free, stress free relax in front of the telly. She was clearing up the kitchen, after her ready meal of lasagne and salad, and popped her shoes on to take a tied bag of household waste to the dustbin. As she stepped outside, it was getting cooler and she shivered slightly. Andy was getting out of his car on his drive and he waved as she placed the bagged rubbish in the bin. She shouted, 'hi, Andy, you ok?'

He walked over, carrying a white plastic bag. 'Hi, I'm fine. How are you?'

'I'm good.' She glanced at the bag. 'What's this, a Saturday night takeaway?'

He grinned and shrugged his shoulders sheepishly. 'Yep, you've caught me out. I couldn't be bothered to cook, and Hannah's at her mums, so I'm having Kung Pao chicken, fried rice and a spring roll.'

'What's Kung Pao chicken?'

'It's Szechuan dish of stir fried chicken marinaded in a special peppercorn sauce to give it a spicy/sweet flavour and has cashews, peppers and dried red chillies. I shall enjoy every single forkful without Natasha muttering about calories and salt content.' He smiled mischievously. 'You're not going to tell me off for being over indulgent, are you?'

Eva shook her head. 'No, as I get enough healthy eating information from Gary to write a book for a slimming club. It can take all the joy out of life.'

'Good,' he laughed. 'Where's Gary at the moment, his cars not here?'

'He's in Glasgow, to look at a car dealership which is for sale. He'll be back tomorrow. You'd better hurry up and eat that before it gets cold. I was just about to open a bottle of Pinot Grigio, you can come in, eat that and share the wine, if you like?' Eva felt very bold asking him this but she hadn't really spoken to Andy since he split with Natasha and wanted to know how he was doing.

Andy nodded his acceptance. 'If you don't mind. Have you eaten?'

'Yes, I've had a ready meal lasagne and salad, so I'm good.'

He followed her into the kitchen and he sat at the dining table as she gave him a plate, knife, fork and spoon for his food. 'No chopsticks, I'm afraid.'

'Good, I don't really like using them, as they're too fiddly and I get most of the sauce down my shirt.' He was casually dressed in dark grey, slim fit jeans and light grey, long-sleeved shirt. He took off his dark blue jacket and hung it over the back of the chair. Ripping open the brown paper bag, he took out the foil containers of rice, chicken and spring roll and he asked, 'are you sure you don't want some, as there is always too much?'

'No, thanks, though it does look good. What would you like to drink? Wine or a beer?'

'Actually, a beer would be nice. And have you got any soy sauce?'

Eva opened the fridge, took out a bottled lager, found a bottle opener in the cutlery drawer, pulled the lid off the bottle and gave it to Andy. She reached up for the soy sauce in a top cupboard and placed it next to him. He shook a little soy sauce over the spring roll. A bottle of Pinot was taken from the wine cooler, and a glass from the cupboard, and then Eva sat at the table, opposite Andy.

It was really great to have his company, and she enjoyed watching him eat, as he savoured each mouthful of the Chinese food. Eva sipped at her wine, totally relaxed, and without the tension in her stomach when she was around Gary. 'I haven't seen you since you and Natasha split up, how have you been?'

Andy sighed, pausing to scoop more fried rice on to his plate, followed by the last spoonful of the chicken. 'Yeah, ok, actually. No, that's not true, I'm fine. Things had not been going well for a while and I'm relieved that it's all over. The main gain is that I can live in a relatively stress-free environment without the tension between Hannah and Natasha, as their every argument was turning into a battle. Another problem was some of Natasha's views on food, men, and relationships, which I didn't agree with, were being shared with Hannah. The Natasha Guide on how to play men to keep them keen was not what I wanted my almost teenage daughter to hear. We men have many faults, I will admit, but Natasha's tactics were things I do not encourage. Such as telling her to keep a boy interested by flirting with his friend, going for any boy you fancy regardless of whether he has a girlfriend, and if you are the hottest girl in the class, then use it to your advantage. It was all game playing and that's not how I want Hannah to view relationships.'

'I totally agree with you, Andy. It's hard enough trying to guide our kids through life and teaching them to be considerate of others without someone trying to undermine your efforts. I shall be honest, Andy, and say I did find Natasha quite hard and difficult to get along with. I never quite forgave her for calling me a boring little school teacher in the summer.'

'Yeah, she was difficult, and had a very high opinion of herself. I really do not know why I put up with her for so long.' He finished the last of his food, and gathered up the foil containers to put back in the brown bag.

'Perhaps because she was very beautiful to look at.'

Andy sighed heavily. 'Yes, she is beautiful, and I have to admit she was very enticing sexually but after a while you don't see the pretty outer wrapping when the inside is dark and ugly. That sounds harsh but she really brought no warmth or benefit to my life or Hannah's. All she wanted was to be worshipped and that's not my style. Worshipping someone and loving someone are two different things and I want to love a person who is warm, considerate, funny and intelligent.' He smiled at Eva. 'Sorry, this is getting a bit deep for a Saturday evening. Oh, and just for the record, you are not a boring little school teacher. You are not boring as I think you're witty and good fun. I just know that you are a good teacher.'

'You missed out little.'

'Well, I can't argue on that score. You are quite small but in a cute way.' Eva felt herself blushing slightly and quickly wanted to take the focus off her. 'Can I ask what happened on holiday that split you up?'

'Yes, it was typical Natasha. On her phone, all the time, apparently dealing with work matters. I run a major investigation team and if I can get a week off, I'm sure the world of property sales can do without her for seven days. Day three into the holiday, and she was completely obsessed by her phone, whether it's by the pool, out on a walk, or in a restaurant. That evening, I tell her to turn the phone off which results in a big argument. She tells me that she was in very high demand in terms of men and I am lucky to have her. I'm not feeling particularly lucky at this stage, just sick of it all. I go off for a walk, and when I get back to the room, she is on the balcony and I hear her talking to someone about meeting up next week. From the tone and content of the conversation, I realise that this is not a meeting relating to work. Once she ended the call, I demanded to know what that was all about. She admitted that she was speaking to a tech millionaire that she's been seeing and sleeping with. She hadn't returned very promptly from her mother's that time as she was spending time in his penthouse flat in Stratford. He's done me a big favour as it gave me the impetus I needed to get her out of my life for good.'

'I'm sorry, Andy.'

He smiled at her. 'Don't be. It was all a big mistake from day one. My mother, who did not like Natasha at all, is adamant that I must go out and find a special girlfriend, get married and have more children. I should do all this very quickly as I am not getting any younger.' He pulled a face to illustrate his predicament.

Eva laughed. 'Well, your mother is right. You are getting old. You'd better sign up on those dating websites asap before you draw your pension. Still, you won't waste money on petrol as you can escort the older ladies around Warwickshire using your free bus pass.'

He laughed briefly and then sighed heavily. 'I can't think of anything I'd rather do less, at the moment, than going on dates. I'm going to have a break from all that for now. Concentrate on Hannah, work and relaxing in the evening with a beer and good film.'

'Talking of beer, would you like another one, or some wine?'

'Another beer would be great, thanks. But if you want me to go, just tell me, as you might have plans to binge on a Netflix boxset.

'No, I have no specific plans. We could go into the lounge, if you like, as it would be more comfortable.' Eva gave Andy another beer out of the fridge, picked up the wine bottle and glass and led the way into the lounge area. 'Make yourself comfortable,' she instructed. Eva sat on the three-seater sofa and Andy on the separate two-seater. She requested that 'Alexa' played a mix of Adele songs but regretted this immediately, as 'Make You Feel My Love' came on and the atmosphere in the room changed. Eva felt instantly nervous and self-conscious of being alone with him. She was wearing a pale pink, scoop-neck, long-sleeved jumper over slim fit, mid-blue jeans which was cosy and comfortable for a lazy Saturday night. She smiled to herself, imagining Tania here alone with Andy, and how she would probably rush up the stairs to re-apply makeup, lipstick and perfume. When Tania had heard that Andy was now single, she had screamed loudly, then did a jig around Eva's kitchen, shouting, 'yes, yes, yes.'

Eva was now feeling a shyness typical of a teenager on their first date. His presence dominated the room and she was reminded of his attractiveness and masculinity. Eva took several gulps of the white wine to bolster her confidence and told herself to get a grip. This was only Andy after all, her neighbour, and who she had never considered in any other way but as a friend. What was making her so jittery? It felt suddenly as if there had been a shift in their relationship and she was seeing him in a new light. She could not deny she felt an attraction towards him.

They observed each other, not speaking, and Eva broke the tension in the room. 'Anyway, Andy, I must warn you now that since Tania has found out that you are single she has been plotting ways to get in your company, insisting that I have a party for my birthday, and that you are invited.'

Andy swigged his lager and then smiled through gritted teeth. 'No disrespect to Tania, I think she is a lovely girl even if she is a little loud, but I don't see us in any sort of relationship. You will have to protect me from her. You'll have to be my bodyguard to keep her away from me. I get the impression that she has a ruthless determination to get what she wants and I will be a helpless fly if she gets me in her spider's web.'

'You're right, she will swat you and swallow you up. Don't worry, I'll protect you.'

'Good. It is your birthday soon, isn't it?'

'Yes, on 21 October but I don't know what's happening yet as Gary isn't keen on family gatherings.'

'How's life with Gary at the moment? Has he eased up on Alfie?'

Eva was now sitting on the sofa, facing Andy, and there was no getting away from his intense scrutiny as he asked these questions. Eva hesitated, not wanting to give Andy any indication of the situation she was in, as he may instantly latch on to the fact that all was not well. 'We're ok, I think. There was an issue at the end of Alfie's birthday weekend as Gary thought he had been overindulged and spoilt. He got really heavy with him when he didn't obey an instruction straightaway, a very common theme which runs through their relationship. I told Gary to stop getting angry with him and ordering him about. That he was not spoiled but a child who had enjoyed his birthday celebrations as is the norm for most children. I told him that his manner with Alfie was too authoritarian and it had to stop or we were over.'

Andy now looked very concerned. 'How did Gary react to this?'

'Not well at all. That's all I'll say.' A wave of sadness crossed her face which Andy noticed immediately.

'Do you feel happy and safe in this relationship, Eva?'

The question was a direct hit to Eva's stomach. Tears welled in her eyes and there was no hiding them from Andy. She struggled not to let the tears fall and she frantically wiped under eyes to stem their flow. This was a moment that if she didn't control herself a full-on river of tears would course down her face. Andy moved to sit next to her, taking hold of her hand. 'Listen, Eva. I'm not going to ask any more questions but I think it's plain from your response that you are not happy with him. If you or Alfie are made to feel unsafe, then you must think carefully about continuing with the relationship.'

The touch of his hand on hers, and his nearness, now broke the dam. She could no longer hold back, and she sobbed, avoiding any eye contact with Andy. At this he pulled her against him, his arms around her, as she wept quietly. Her face was against his chest, her tears dampening his shirt, as he held her. The crying helped to relieve the pent-up emotion which she carried with her all the time now, waiting for Gary's next verbal attack on Alfie, or physical assault on her. But regardless of her emotional turmoil over Gary, this moment was one of awakening as she found comfort in Andy's strength and inhaled the soft aroma of his male cologne.

He gently eased her out of his embrace and looked into her eyes, seeing the pain and sorrow in their deep blue depths. His thumb gently stroked her face, wiping tears from under her eyes, and he smiled at the smudges of black eyeliner and mascara. 'You now resemble a panda which are very cute creatures.'

Eva's crying now stopped but she hiccupped slightly which embarrassed her more. 'I'm sorry, Andy, you must think I'm an idiot.'

His eyes never left her face and he still stroked the odd, stray tear away. 'No, I don't. Don't apologise for getting upset but I don't like to see you getting hurt.' His eyes locked onto hers, and this time he placed both hands on her face, and drew her towards him, as he leaned in to kiss her. The kiss was tender, but commanding, and Eva felt an ache in her gut as his mouth explored hers. She knew she should end this as she was with Gary but she didn't want it to end. She wanted to remain forever in the security of his embrace.

Reluctantly, she pulled away. 'I'm sorry, we can't do this as it's not fair to Gary.'

The kiss had stopped but Andy was not yet ready to let her out of his arms. 'Yes, it is unfair to Gary and I should not have kissed you. But I don't regret it. I'm here for you Eva if you need me.' He gently eased her away from him and stood up. 'But I'd better go. Thanks for the beers.'

CHAPTER THIRTY SIX

January 2013

As Gary entered the hallway of the house as he returned from work at 6.25 p.m. there were no lights on, just a faint glow coming from under the lounge door. He could hear the sound of audience laughter, so he assumed that Jess was watching one of the many quiz shows that she was addicted to.

He walked into the lounge, where Jess was lying down on the sofa, as she shouted, 'Baltimore', then screamed, 'yes.'

Gary was none too pleased as she ignored his entrance, dived her hand into a large bag of chocolate honeycomb bites, popped one in her mouth and crunched loudly. 'Busy I see watching quiz shows and stuffing your face. Have you actually done any work today or have you just sat here vegetating?'

Reluctantly, she sat up on the sofa, noting the displeasure on her husband's face. 'Yes, I've just got in from the Broadway shop, where I've checked on the stock for spring, completed a further order, and re-priced some of last year's stuff that's not selling. The stuff that we in the retail trade call 'tat'.

Gary still continued to stare at her, his annoyance with her still apparent. 'Glad to hear it. But you need to be more on top of those shops as they could be showing a lot more profit if you did a bit more work on getting rid of the 'tat' and concentrating on the higher end stuff that sells well in that town. And, I've told you before, you need to get rid of that sales assistant, Norma, who's too old and too ugly to be selling quality clothes to wealthy women. If Woolworths were still open, I'd recommend her for a job there.'

Jess sighed loudly, as they'd had this discussion a million times before. 'I've told you Gary, Norma's not going anywhere as she has been with me since I opened my first shop.'

'Yes, but I expect that she had more hair and teeth then. She looks dishevelled, never seems to know where anything is on the racks, and will not go out the back to check the stock if a customer requests a different size. And, you said yourself that she cannot get her head around anything online so is losing us custom if an item is requested that can be acquired at another shop.'

'I know, Gary, but I can't get rid of her. It's not that easy as she's been with me for almost twenty years and what reason would I give for firing her.'

Gary sighed heavily and sat on a chair opposite Jess. 'I've told you, bring in a performance management system for all staff, set targets, which she will fail to meet, support her so she can improve (which she won't) and do regular reviews. Failure to improve over a reasonable time period will give you legitimate grounds to terminate her employment. Keep written records of all targets, meetings, and where her performance falls short. Refer to capability procedures. Alternatively, you could get her on time-keeping and attendance, as you frequently mention that she is late or absent, so deal with this in terms of disciplinary procedures. Read the bloody ACAS codes. Whatever you do, I want her gone.'

'I hear you Gary but they are my shops, my staff, and I run them my way.'

Gary's voice now deepened as he spoke. 'No, Jess, they are not your shops, they are our shops, and if they are underperforming and not maximising profit then we both suffer. Employing staff that do not perform competently is not feasible in business. If the shops are losing money, then we are losing money, and it has to stop. I'm going to get Greg, my business manager, to come and do a full audit of the four shops so that we can find a way to improve turnover and maximise profit. And weed out any dead wood staff who have been given an easy ride for too long.'

Jess was now fully focused on Gary, her lips pursed to show her displeasure. 'I wish you would stay out of my business, literally, Gary as it is nothing to do with you. I don't come to the dealerships telling you what to do.'

'Don't forget Jess that when we married all our assets became jointly owned by both of us, so my financial assets become yours, and vice versa. And, we have made wills leaving all our assets, each to the other. I strive to improve my businesses to make as much money as possible for both of us. You are allowing your businesses to coast. Part of the problem is that you are lazy and have your head too involved in low grade television and eating unhealthy snacks.'

'But Gary, I do like to relax after a long day.'

'I'd like you to pull your finger out, get off your backside more, and put the effort in for me as I do for you. You are sat here now, at 6.45 p.m. when you could have started the dinner instead of munching chocolate.'

Seeing that this lecture was not going to end soon, Jess was suddenly happy to escape to the kitchen to start dinner. 'Sorry, Gary. Yes, I should have started dinner. What do you want, fish or chicken?'

'Fish, as its quicker, and I have to pop out later.'

Jess prepared the food, pan-fried cod, mashed potatoes (microwaved) and steamed broccoli and they sat eating at the dining room table. 'Where are you going after dinner, Gary? You never spend any time with me.'

'I'm going over to see Simon and watch a football match, Arsenal versus Liverpool.'

'I didn't think you liked football, Gary.'

'I don't much but it's better than staying here and watching your crap.'

Jess looked hurt, and realised that this man she married was actually becoming a stranger to her, and seemed to really despise her. 'I thought it would be good to cuddle up on the sofa, we don't do that anymore.' She touched his hand lightly with her own and stroked his gold wedding band. 'I would like us to make love occasionally, like we used to.'

Gary snatched his hand away and finished the last mouthful of the fried fish, which was delicately flavoured with garlic, tarragon and lemon juice. 'I've told you, Jess, there will be none of that until you have lost the half stone we agreed on. Judging by the way you were quaffing those chocolates earlier, it won't be anytime soon.'

Jess's lovely brown eyes reflected her sadness. 'But you are punishing me and its cruel. If you make love to me more often, I will feel sexier, and it gives me an incentive to lose the weight.'

Gary smiled; a sneaky smile etched with cruelty. 'Maybe so, but you have got heavier recently, and it's all a slippery slope downhill to obesity.'

'I'm not that big, I'm only a size 14.'

'Yes, but I can see you sliding up to the next size. Enough of this chat, I going over to Simons and I'll be back later.' He got up off the chair, left the table with dirty plates and dishes, picked up his mobile phone and headed for the door.

Jess slowly got up out of her seat and carried the plates into the kitchen. She placed the plates on the worktop and felt the familiar symptoms of a panic attack which had started to disrupt her life. She hastily moved back into the lounge and sat on the sofa, as she felt the tightness in her chest, and her breathing started to falter as she struggled to take in air. She began to feel light-headed and a wave of nausea hit her as she re-tasted the garlic and tarragon of her fish meal. The now familiar sweating started, droplets on her forehead, as a wave of heat hit her body. The doctor had prescribed TCA, tricyclic antidepressants, which were beginning to help and reduced the number of panic attacks but they still came on her when her anxiety levels flared. Prior to meeting Gary, she had put the days of panic attacks and antidepressants behind her and had not experienced an attack for a couple of years. Life with Gary had thrown her back into her old life of anxiety and depression. Anxiety about all aspects of her life including her businesses, her financial security, her appearance, and overall worthiness as a human being. She had expected married life to be calming, happy, loving and satisfying but it was turning into a prison of self-doubt, body insecurities and feelings of failure in terms of her business competency. A lonely road with no support as Gary was systematically removing her few friends from her life. With no close family, she was an island, cut off from the mainland and surrounded by waters infested with one shark, Gary Dawson.

CHAPTER THIRTY SEVEN

Since the evening that she and Andy had kissed, Eva had gone out of her way to avoid him, and hoped that Gary would not pick up on any of the guilt and anxiety she felt for what had happened. Gary had returned from his trip to Glasgow, undecided about buying the dealership, mainly, as it was so far away if there were problems that needed his attention. Running a third business, through meetings on Zoom, did not suit Gary's style of management. He liked to visit a business on a regular basis and doing spot checks on staff were his favourite way of ensuring that employees worked effectively. Delivering a bollocking to an employee over Zoom did not have the same effect.

Gary returned from his trip on the Sunday, in quite a relaxed mood, but did grill her about what she had done on the Friday and Saturday nights. She informed Gary that she had gone into town with Tania which did not please him but she managed to persuade him that nothing much had happened, not mentioning the ENT specialist. Describing her Saturday night to Gary, of a ready meal, white wine and Netflix binge, alone, was not as easy as she hoped. She avoided eye contact with him, her voice trembled, and she seemed fidgety. Gary's piercing eyes scrutinised her intensely. She thought that he could read her mind and know that Andy had been around and kissed her. The essence of Andy seemed to be all around her in the room and Gary would detect her deceit and betrayal.

It was now the day after her birthday and the weekend at the start of the half term holiday. Though Gary was not keen, she had pushed for a small gathering to celebrate her birthday, and Gary had agreed, as long as she did all the arrangements and catering. Luckily, Friday had been a school inset day and she was able to work from home which meant she could prepare for the party. At seven o'clock a buffet of foods was prepared, by Eva, with a thank you to two supermarket chains. There were dips, crudities, green salads, coleslaw, potato salad, a platter of cheeses and crackers, and a fruit platter all laid out on the dining table. Foods to be heated included Camembert bites, spicy buffalo wings, mini quiches, mini pizzas, garlic bread, and sausage rolls, her father's favourites. An assortment of drinks including red, rose, and white wines, lagers and beers, cider and soft drinks were available for people to help themselves. The party guests included Andy, Tania, Eva's parents, her brother and family, Niall's parents, and friends from school, Kasia and her partner, Judy and her husband. Six other guests included two neighbours, and mutual friends of Eva and Tania from school, and their partners. Alfie had invited Jai and Hannah was bringing Phoebe.

Eva busied herself ensuring that sufficient plates, cutlery, glasses and serviettes were laid out on the table and placed some cooking trays by the oven to heat the food to be served warm. She sipped at a glass of white wine, trying to quell her nerves as this would be the first time she had seen Andy since their encounter. She wore a new red satin, off the shoulder dress, that fitted her perfectly. She had taken extra care with her hair which was gently waved, and fell to her shoulders, as highlights of rich auburn added shine and colour. Her makeup was more prominent than usual, with smoky brown shadow, black eyeliner and mascara emphasising her deep blue eyes, and a glossy, cranberry lipstick flattered her mouth. As she had applied the makeup, and checked it in the mirror, the woman staring back at her was a sexier, more confident Eva than the real one.

Now in the kitchen area, she felt a little more self-conscious. If she were being honest with herself, was this attention to her appearance solely to celebrate her thirty-fifth birthday, or was it to impress someone else attending the party. Gary now came into the room, as she stood by a kitchen work top, putting out the last of the glasses for wine, beer or soft drinks. He came up to face her, and locked his arms around her waist, as his mouth nuzzled her neck. His hands then roamed over her buttocks, pulling her forcefully against him. As he spoke, his voice cracked and his deep brown eyes lingered over her face. 'You look absolutely drop-dead gorgeous tonight and I am the luckiest man in the world to be able to hold you, and make love to you later. That dress is amazing, sweetheart.' He leaned in to possess her mouth, as his hands explored further over her bottom, before bringing his hands under the dress at the back, to caress her thighs. 'Do you think we could nip upstairs now before anyone arrives as I don't think I'm going to be able to wait for the next few hours until I have you.'

Eva was finding this closeness claustrophobic and wanted to push him away. She found that responding to Gary sexually was getting more and more difficult. At that moment, Alfie lolloped into the room, interrupting their intimacy. 'Mum, is there anything I can eat now as I am starving?'

Reluctantly, Gary pulled away from Eva and scowled openly at Alfie. 'You are always hungry. You ate a bowl of cereal not so long ago, so you'll have to wait.'

Ignoring Gary, Alfie persisted, 'please mum, can I have some crisps?'

'Here we bloody go again,' Gary erupted, his cheeks an angry red as he turned to face the boy. 'Why is it that you can never do as you're told. I've just said you'll have to wait.'

Eva was fearful that this was a volatile situation which could explode even further if Alfie now said the wrong thing. She noticed recently that Alfie was getting more confrontational with Gary and was beginning to stand his ground with him. This was potentially one of those moments, as Alfie stood rigidly, and did not back away as Gary came towards him. 'Mum, you'll let me have some crisps, won't you?'

Gary took a couple more steps towards Alfie, the anger deepening on his face. Sensing that this could be the moment she had been dreading since meeting Gary, she physically placed herself between her son and her partner. The tension in the room was tangible, an evil entity that she could smell, touch and taste. Instinctively, she was certain that Gary would hit Alfie if he wasn't removed from the room immediately. 'Alfie, darling, you can have some food when the guests arrive. It won't be long now. Go to your room for now and I'll call you when Jai, Hannah, Phoebe and your cousins get here.' Thankfully, Alfie did what he was told and exited the kitchen, keeping away from a still seething Gary.

Gary started to pace the floor, his anger not dispersing. 'It's a good job that your family and friends are coming for a party in the next half hour or he would be finding out what disobeying me means. I've had enough of this challenging everything and not doing as he's told. My dad would never put up with it and would deliver a good hiding. It's what he needs.'

Eva breathed deeply to calm her nerves and to quell the sick feeling in her stomach. 'We've discussed this before Gary, and we will deal with him together, in a balanced and fair manner. You must not over react. He's like any other kid and they do try to see if they can bend the rules a bit.'

Gary's temper had now calmed but there was still an annoyance in his voice. 'You are the problem here as you are way too soft with him so he knows if he persists with what he wants, you'll give in. I suggest that you take my side more often in the future or it won't end well for both of you.'

This statement truly chilled Eva to her core. Her intention to remove Gary from her life was not progressing, and she knew that she lacked the courage to confront him, and make it clear that they could not be together. She really needed to think more carefully about how and when she was going to do this. It was becoming more clear that Gary posed a danger to her and Alfie. It was half term next week, time away from the routine of work, and hopefully time to think calmly and rationally about how to handle her situation.

Gary was now swigging from a bottle of beer, glowering at her. Eva continued to arrange the glasses, and fiddled with the cutlery, mainly to distract her thoughts and stop her hands from shaking. The doorbell rang, and it gave Eva the excuse to avoid Gary, and welcome the first of her guests. Tania strode into the house, long dark hair carefully coiffured into flowing, wavy glossy locks and full-on, stage ready, makeup. She was wearing a low-plunge-neck, mid-blue midi dress that gave some emphasis to her figure with its gathered front. Silver strappy heels added three inches to her height which she would need if attempting to achieve her goal of kissing tall, handsome Andy. She led the way into the kitchen carrying two bottles of Prosecco which she deposited on a kitchen worktop. She leaned in to kiss Eva on both cheeks. 'Happy Birthday, my darling. This is for you,' as she handed Eva a birthday gift bag.

Eva took the present and smiled at her friend. 'Thanks for this. I'm going to open my presents later and not when I've had too much to drink. What would you like to drink? I'm sure Gary will get you one.'

Tania went over to where Gary was standing. 'Hi, Gary, great to see you.' She had noted that he didn't look too happy, and sensed an atmosphere, so wanted to lighten the mood for Eva's sake. She leaned up to kiss Gary on the cheek and he responded in a friendly way. 'You look good Tania, what can I get you to drink?'

'Open one of those Prosecco's and we'll give the birthday girl some bubbles.'

Gary proceeded to pop the cork and filled two glasses with the bubbly liquid. He handed one each to the women. 'Cheers, girls.'

Other guests now began to arrive and Eva could sense Tania's anxiety as she waited for Andy. Eva worried that Tania was eventually going to suffer disappointment with regard to Andy as he didn't see her as a potential girlfriend. Eva had just welcomed her mum, dad, and Niall's parents into the hall, when Andy arrived with Hannah and Phoebe. 'All go through, as it's a bit cold out here. Hang your coats up here.' Everyone pushed through into the warmth of the lounge and kitchen and Eva and Andy were left alone in the hallway. He presented her with a birthday gift bag, and stated, 'this was chosen by Hannah, so I hope you like it.'

'Thanks, that's very thoughtful of you. I'm sure I'll like it.' She leaned up to peck him on the cheek. For a moment, their eyes locked, and again she was overwhelmed by the nearness of him. A strong yearning washed over her to be back in his arms and his lips exploring her mouth. A blush crept on her cheeks and she quickly stepped away from him.

He seemed to notice her discomfort and smiled teasingly. 'You look absolutely stunning tonight. That dress really suits you.'

At this moment, she was sixteen again, at the school prom, with her date, Liam, and her voice and her brain were failing to connect so that sensible words could come out. 'T-h-hanks, come in,' was all she could stutter.

Andy followed her into the kitchen area and an Exocet missile called Tania launched herself at him. 'Hi, Andy. Great to see you. Can I get you a drink?'

Andy pulled back a little as she entered his personal space. 'A lager would be great, thanks.'

Tania was back in moments and gave him a bottled lager. 'How is life treating you, dealt with any interesting murders recently?'

Andy was always amazed about how people were fascinated by his work and tried to get him to talk about current, and past cases. Tania was massive fan of real crime dramas and frequently related the stories of cases she had seen on the television. Andy could understand people's fascination for these crimes but they never saw the real thing, the battered and broken bodies, the relatives and friends ravaged by grief and shock. The faces of the ruthless, calculating killers who would never cease to amaze you with the fantastical stories and lies they told to cover their tracks. The blood, the tears, the broken hearts, and shattered lives, these were the realities of his job, day in day out. The word 'interesting' was inappropriate, as it was never that, more gut-wrenching, emotionally draining, and absolute despair in terms of the depravity that human beings were capable of. He partly blamed the sanitised police dramas on television, where a body was found dead but there was little evidence of the harsh brutality of death. A grumpy detective and his dynamic young sidekick would solve the case, very neatly, all loosed ends covered. Real murders left many loose ends and many murders were never solved. 'I would never call murders 'interesting' as they represent a life taken, in a violent and unexpected way, leaving behind family and friends with their hearts ripped out.'

Tania looked at him a little sheepishly. 'Sorry, Andy, you must get sick of people asking you that. Anyway, I hope that our birthday girl has a good time. It's nice to see her letting her hair down. She looks amazing in that dress.'

Andy glanced over at Eva who was filling her glass with Prosecco whilst talking to her mum and Niall's mum. 'She certainly does.'

Two hours passed and the buffet had been eaten with Eva handing over the food duties to her mother and mother-in-law. She was deliberately avoiding Gary, who either stood talking to his friend Simon, or Judy's husband. Eva had been annoyed that Gary had wanted to invite Simon as she really did think he was an oddball who made her feel uncomfortable when he spoke to her.

There was music playing through an iPhone and Eva, Tania and some of the women had danced around to Maroon 5, Abba, Beyonce, Mark Ronson, Justin Timberlake amongst others. Tania got excited about Beyonce 'Single Ladies (Put a Ring on it)' as she did the hand movements and eyed Andy. Having swapped

Prosecco for white wine, Eva was now slightly tipsy, but she decided to stop dancing and go and check on the kids upstairs.

She went into Alfie's room, where Hannah and Phoebe were the special queens lounging on his bed, whilst Jai, Alfie, and his cousins Marigold and Orion, sat on the floor. 'Hi, guys, are you all ok? Have you had enough to eat and drink? Alfie, make sure you look after your guests.'

Hannah smiled over at Eva. 'Happy Birthday, Eva. You look hot for an old lady, I love your dress.'

Eva gave Hannah a playful scowl. 'Thanks, but I'm not that old yet, I hope. You ok, Phoebe, having a good time?'

'Yes, thanks, Eva.'

'Jai, are you ok? Want any more to eat or drink?'

'No thanks, Mrs Brennan, I'm good.'

'Marigold and Orion, are you two ok, do you want anything?'

'No, thanks, Auntie Eva.'

'Ok, folks. I'll leave you to it.'

She exited the room and went into her bedroom, to freshen her makeup, brush her hair and spray on some perfume. As she came out of the room, she was blocked by Gary's friend Simon who was at the top of the stairs and coming towards her.

He leered at her as he entered the space next to her, his tall, skinny frame overwhelming her with his presence, and assailing her nostrils with a mixture of BO and cheap body spray. 'Hello, birthday girl, you look mega hot tonight. He loomed over her, his beady, cold eyes focusing on her cleavage. I don't reckon I've had my birthday kiss yet, sweetheart.'

Eva tried to dodge around him. 'Get out of my way and go downstairs. You really shouldn't be up here.' Simon had a definite creepiness about him, the type of man that most woman would not want to be alone with.

His finger now traced a line along her cheek, down to her lips, and then followed a trail to the top of her cleavage. 'Gary certainly knew what he was doing when he picked you to be the next one. So much better than the first plain frump and the second neurotic lump. Poetry, eh?'

Eva was now experiencing an arctic chill in her stomach both from the man's closeness and his weird comment. 'Get out of my way, I've just said.' She pushed at his chest but for all his skinny frame, it felt like she was trying to free herself from a boulder after an avalanche.

At that moment, Andy came up the stairs and weighed up the situation facing Eva. 'Move out of her way, NOW, or I will knock your head from your shoulders.'

Simon had been about to move in on her for a furtive feel of her breast but the loud male voice stopped him in his tracks. He turned sharply, frightened to see Andy, his impressive presence and angry face. 'Nothing happening. I'm going.' Simon held his hands over his head, in the manner that a criminal responds to orders from an armed cop. 'Don't tell, Gary or he will probably kill me. Please.'

Andy stepped aside to let Simon go down the stairs. 'If I see you going to touch her again, I will kill you, ok.'

As Simon trudged down the stairs, Alfie and Hannah came out of his room to see what was going on. Hannah asked, 'everything ok, dad, we heard you shout? What was that creepy guy doing to Eva?'

Eva smiled to take the tension out of the situation and the concern off the faces of the children. 'Everything is fine. He's just a bit weird, that's all. Off you go.'

Alfie and Hannah went back into his room, and Andy gazed kindly at Eva. 'You ok?' Eva nodded. 'Yes, I'm fine but I really do not like that man and wish that he wasn't Gary's best friend. He lurks around, watching people, and not speaking to anyone but Gary. He's like a monster from an old black and white movie, hiding in the shadows, on dark, cold windy nights waiting to pounce, and possibly eat, the unsuspecting victim.'

Andy laughed, 'you have a very vivid imagination. But I know what you mean and I wonder what Gary has to gain from being around such a socially inept loner. I gather they were friends growing up on the same council estate as kids and Gary has brought Simon along through all the stages of his life, including the two marriages. Simon works for Gary at the dealerships and so has been well looked after. I would guess that he has fierce loyalty to Gary. A man who would still be on that council estate today without Gary.'

'You are going all Endeavour Morse on me again, Andy. What are you trying to say?'

'Well, I know that this is my cop radar twitching but I think those two have a closer relationship than just school mates as I see no advantage to Gary to carry that man along with him throughout his life. It makes me wonder if they both know, or have shared experiences, that each needs to stay secret and so are forced to mutually support each other. You come across these types of friendships occasionally in my job, where one helps the other in serious crimes, and then you are beholden to each other for life.'

'Oh dear, I don't think Gary's committed any crimes as such.' Eva seemed shocked, 'but I agree their relationship is overly close and secretive. I'd better go and see my party guests. Thanks for seeing off Lurch.'

'My pleasure, I'll just say hello to the kids and I'll be down.'

Ten minutes later, Andy entered the kitchen area to find that Gary had gathered all party guests together, each with a glass of Prosecco. Gary had Eva by his side, his arm tightly around her waist. As Andy picked up his drink, Gary smirked at him, as he held on to Eva. 'Hi everyone. Thanks for coming to share Eva's birthday celebrations.' He turned her slightly to face him and kissed her gently on the mouth, his eyes watching Andy's reaction as he did so. 'She may be getting on a bit but I think you will agree that tonight she looks absolutely stunning and I am very honoured, and lucky, to have her as my girlfriend. Please raise your glasses in a toast to Eva.' The guests raised their glasses 'to Eva'. 'I have a surprise for her which I hope she will like.'

Eva stomach dropped, as if descending downwards in a lift, and she desperately hoped that Gary was not going to propose. He presented her with a silver birthday gift bag, hopefully too large to hold an engagement ring.

All the guests muttered softly as they waited while Eva took a sheet of paper out of the gift bag and read what was written. 'Thanks, Gary. Everyone, this is a four-night break in Budapest from Wednesday. I'll need to make arrangements for Alfie but I'm sure it will be ok.'

Gary again placed his arm around her waist. She had noticed recently that he was becoming more physically possessive with her when around her family and friends. 'No problem, darling, your mum and dad have agreed to look after Alfie and all the arrangements are made. You only need to pack a suitcase.'

'Don't forget the sexy underwear I can imagine you wearing,' Simon shouted. Everyone laughed.

Eva blanched, her face a deathly white under her makeup. Simon's comment about sexy underwear, and him imagining her wearing it, made her physically shudder. She was also conscious that she was not exuding happiness or enthusiasm over this unexpected surprise. Four days abroad with Gary was something she hoped she could endure.

CHAPTER THIRTY EIGHT

On Saturday afternoon after the party, Gary was at his flat with Simon, having arrived to collect his passport which he kept there, and not at Eva's house, in case the relationship ended suddenly. The flat was beginning to look grubby, as Simon was not a man who understood the practicalities of wiping kitchen surfaces, mopping floors, using a vacuum cleaner or cleaning a bathroom. Gary was now going to have to employee a cleaner to stop the flat becoming a murky cesspit but Simon would be paying for this when his monthly rent increased.

Simon was sitting on the creamy leather sofa in grubby sweat pants and T- shirt, scratching furtively, and drinking from a bottle of lager. 'Good party, yesterday. Your lovely girlfriend looked a right little cracker in that red dress. She's an itch I could definitely scratch. Lovely breasts and bottom. Very pretty face.'

Gary sipped his lager, irate at his friend's lechery towards Eva. 'Take all thoughts of Eva out of your pervy brain.'

'Well, you have upped your game, girlfriend wise. Why you married that plain cow Claire and that chunky Jess, I will never know. Scratch that, I do know. To get your hands on their assets, but honestly, if I had to sleep with them two, I'd probably top myself.'

Gary laughed, a loud, cold sound. 'Yes, Simon, with all the beautiful women you pull, you can afford to be choosy. Who was the last one that used to rock up here at the weekend? Tiffany. Scrawny, with no tits, lanky, greasy hair and personal hygiene issues. You two made such a lovely couple that people swooned when you walked in the pub.'

'At least I don't marry them, kill them off, grab their money and move onto the next one. I think you've made a big mistake with Eva as you are getting drawn in by her loveliness and you'll not be able to pull off the final act. I must say if I was shagging her on a regular basis I'd find it very hard to give her up.'

'Shut the fuck up, Simon. Or I will come over there and batter you. Yes, it will be harder with Eva but I'm not a novice at this and there's a lot more pleasure in terminating the pretty ones. Claire and Jess were just gentle nudges to help them out of their unhappy lives. Lisa and Samantha were a lot more fulfilling in terms of sating my appetite. Eva will be too.'

'Well, you know me, Gary, always willing to help but perhaps one day you'll let me have a bite of the sweet peach before the end.'

'That's never going to happen with Eva.'

'I do foresee a mighty big obstacle in your plans for Eva. That cop has feelings for her, so you need to watch your back. He's not a man to underestimate. Lucky bugger too, having been with that tigress, Natasha. Now then Gary, if you could only choose one, Eva or Natasha, who would it be?'

'You're getting annoying now. It would be Eva all the way, as she's pretty, sexy and has a vulnerability that I adore. Natasha's too much of a cold-hearted bitch.'

'I'd soon warm her up,' Simon commented.

As Gary and Eva arrived in Budapest the weather that greeted them was sunny, with clear, blue skies and temperatures in the high teens, a proper Hungarian welcome. Gary was pleased to have Eva all to himself and that the annoying kid had been left at home. Gary did wondered why Alfie persisted with the arguing at times, particularly when he could see that Gary was getting more and more enraged. Pushing things to the limit. Gary knew that he really must control his urge to physically correct the boy as he feared it would mean a swift and sudden end to his relationship with Eva.

These four days with Eva, Gary wanted to consolidate his relationship with her, re-affirm his love for her, and regain her trust in him. Over the last few months, since the holiday in Menorca, he felt she was slipping away from him, viewing him with caution and fear. He was not proud of his violent outbursts with her. But he did have an urge to correct her when she displeased him, whether it was chatting to handsome Spanish waiters, sharing pizzas with the cop, or telling him their relationship would be over if he didn't stop reprimanding her son. This mini break was a chance to press the reset button and start again.

He was also eager to consolidate, and move the relationship forward, for another important reason. Simon, though not the greatest thinker on the nuances of human interactions, was right about one thing. Cop Andy definitely had feelings for Eva and Gary was certain that these were not those for a friend or neighbour. Tania had managed to latch onto Andy for most of the party, getting his drinks and regaling him with her many stories about life as a financial controller for a care home company. Tania was capable of making the world of numbers as funny as a comedy night with Peter Kay. Even when Andy was with Natasha, Gary strongly sensed that he cared for Eva. He was protective of her when Natasha tried her usual way of making digs at Eva to make herself look good. This never worked around Andy. At the party, Gary watched Andy closely, whilst he chatted to Tania. He smiled at the right time, he laughed at her jokes, but his eyes were never fully focused on her. His eyes and his mind were elsewhere, on a beautiful woman with wavy, auburn-brown hair and sexy red dress. His Eva. Well, after the next four days, the detective's ambitions towards his girlfriend would be thwarted permanently when he progressed to the next stage of The Plan.

The first few days of the mini break were spent exploring the beautiful city of Budapest, bisected by the River Danube, and connected by the Chain Bridge, to the hilly district of Buda and the flatter area of Pest. They visited the Old Town of Buda which was a UNESCO World Heritage Site and spent a full day in the Buda castle complex. They admired the beauty of Matthias Church, a neo-Gothic Roman Catholic church established in the eleventh century with the current building constructed in the fourteenth century. In the sixteenth century, during a Turkish invasion, it was converted into a mosque and the multi-coloured diamond pattern roof tiles which gave the church its unique beauty was attributed to the Moorish invaders. Gary and Eva visited the Fisherman's Bastion and the Presidential Palace. Eva teased Gary that she had waved at the President as a convoy of cars left the palace grounds. A walk on the banks of the Danube brought them to the 'Shoes on the Danube's Bank' a poignant memorial to the Jews who were shot at this point during World War II.

For all the beauty of the city and its rich and varied culture, Gary sensed that Eva was not fully committed to spending time with him. If he tried to hold her hand, she allowed him to do so, then slipped out of his hold after a few minutes. When he shared a funny story or told a joke, she laughed, but it all felt hollow and there was no sparkle of laughter in her eyes. A number of times he drew her into him, wanting to share a view, take a selfie, feel her closeness at a special place and she went along with it but that was all. In the evenings after dinner, when they returned to their room, she avoided making love, declaring either that she was tired or not in the mood.

The only time she truly laughed or seemed to enjoy herself was when she was on the phone to Alfie, her mum, or Tania. This was really ticking Gary off.

On the Friday night, Gary had booked a table on a restaurant boat on the Danube. He asked Eva to wear the red satin dress from her birthday party and he was smartly dressed in blue trousers, white shirt and mid-grey jacket. A bottle of champagne was waiting at the table in a bucket which the waiter opened immediately. When the drink was poured, Gary raised his glass. 'To my gorgeous girlfriend. Its lovely to have you all to myself in this beautiful setting. Cheers.'

They placed their food order, grilled sheep's cheese with caramelised apple starter and a main of Hungarian deep-fried meatballs for Eva. Mushroom soup starter and tenderloin steak and fried potatoes for Gary. The table settings were traditional with white table clothes, navy placemats, white napkins and navy napkin rings. The most breath-taking part of the whole experience was the view out of the windows across the Danube. The beauty of the Parliament Building lit up at night, the yellow glow from the lights reflecting off the water.

Gary watched Eva as she quietly sipped her champagne and admired the view of one of the world's most beautiful capital cities. 'Eva, darling, are you enjoying your trip to Budapest?'

She forced her eyes away from the lovely setting. 'Yes, it is a beautiful city. And with this view across the Danube and the city, it is one of the best places to have a meal. Thanks for arranging it, Gary.'

'Good, I'm glad you like it. We must do more of these city breaks in the future, just me and you.' Sub-text, no kids.

'Yes, we could have at least one trip a year, just the two of us. Other holidays have to include Alfie.'

Gary filled their glasses with more champagne. 'Of course, but it is nice for the two of us to be together.'

The starter and main courses were eaten. Gary's steak was perfectly cooked and Eva declared that the meatballs were really tasty but too big a portion.

Gary ordered a further bottle of champagne which the waiter placed in the ice bucket. Eva looked at him with a puzzle expression on her face. 'Gary, that's a second bottle of champagne you've ordered. Where's the real Gary and what have you done to him?'

He laughed at her joke. 'Ok, I know you see me as some sort of Scrooge character but I have no problem with paying for quality products at special occasions.' As he said this, a young male waiter walked towards them with a plate containing a small dessert with a sparkler fizzing and spitting coloured sparks. Eva frowned as the waiter placed the plate of dessert in front of her. 'Oh, I didn't order a dessert, so this is a surprise.' As she looked at the raspberry cheesecake, her favourite dessert, she asked Gary, 'is this a birthday surprise? Thank you'.

Gary gazed at her, lovingly. 'Eva, that is a birthday surprise but it is much more than that. We have been together for two years now and you are the most beautiful, sexy, intelligent and kind woman that I have ever met. I am privileged to call you my girlfriend. I want to now take our relationship to the next stage and hope you will do me the honour of becoming my wife.' He placed a red jewellery box on the table in front of her.

A number of expressions crossed Eva's face in a spectrum from shock to surprise. 'Oh my God.'

'Open it then.'

She opened the box to reveal a three stone diamond ring in white gold.

'Eva, darling, will you marry me?'

Gary felt that time had frozen as she stared at the ring, wide-eyed with surprise. He could not read what she was thinking and gulped down a slug of water in preparation for the 'no' that was coming. He glanced around at the other tables close by, hoping that they had not noticed what was happening, and then witness his humiliation. Luckily, everyone seemed preoccupied with eating and drinking and were not focusing on them. He bit down and swallowed a sarcastic 'any time before 2022 would be helpful' comment. He smiled and spoke to break the tension. 'If you are thinking of saying no, please hurry up and put me out of my misery. The waiter will be back over to open the champagne shortly.'

****

Eva could not take her eyes off the beautiful ring, as she tried to focus her thoughts and bizarrely they wandered to ancient folktales of magic rings; Persian tales of servants 'djinn' concealed in rings, or Jewish traditions, the ring of Solomon making him all knowing, the ability to speak to animals, and bearing the special sigil to seal genies into bottles. If this ring had magical properties would she opt for the ability to seal Gary in a bottle and hurl him into the Danube. Feeling the intensity of his gaze on her now, and a tiny flicker of disapproval developing in his eyes, she could not afford to vacillate for much longer or the disapproval could flip to anger. There was no way in a million years she was ever going to marry Gary, and her intention to move him out of her life was still resolute, although not progressing at any discernible pace. Finding the courage to confront Gary was the major stumbling block without him erupting into violence. Her approach needed to be well thought out and prepared, with Alfie out of the way. She also did not want to give him any indication of her intentions at the moment. When she did it, it must be a one-off, final action to exit him from her life. Her attempt after Alfie's birthday to call a halt to their relationship, as he was too harsh with her son, ended with her being attacked. She could not risk further violent assaults.

Taking her gaze off the ring, she looked at Gary. 'Sorry, Gary, I was distracted by the beauty of this ring. In answer to your question, yes, I will marry you.' Her smile touched her lips, but not her eyes, as she hated to accept a proposal, a promise to marry, when her acceptance left a crushing coldness in her heart. It felt like a betrayal to every engaged couple who had pledged their love and accepted a ring with honesty and love in their soul. For now, she hoped that the gods of love and marriage would forgive her for breaking their trust and making an empty promise, in an effort to protect herself.

Gary indicated to the waiter to pour the champagne. 'Hand me the box and I shall put the ring on your finger.' She did as instructed and he placed the ring on the ring finger of her left hand. 'I promise from now on that I will love you and protect you. And do my best to make you happy.'

Eva kept her gaze away from him, and pretended to enjoy the spectacle of the ring on her finger, as the light hit the diamonds, and it scattered and fractured, creating the famous sparkle. Tears swelled in her eyes but she swallowed hard, not wanting Gary to detect any signs of her distress. 'It's truly beautiful, Gary.'

'Just like you.'

The waiter opened the second bottle of champagne and congratulated them on their engagement. 'I could do some photographs for you if you like. I am quite good, how you say, photographer.' Eva handed him her phone and they posed with the champagne glasses and them holding hands across the table with the ring displayed. Gary then moved next to Eva, their hands entwined and the diamonds danced as the T-light candle flickered. As the waiter handed back the phone to Eva, she thanked him and promised a generous tip.

'Now, about the wedding. I know it's a lot to take in but I am proposing that we do not have a long, drawn-out engagement as we are not a couple of twenty-year- olds saving for a deposit on our first home. I would like it to be a very short engagement and what about a wedding in early summer next year, May perhaps?'

Eva now felt like an avalanche was starting to engulf, a giant wall of whiteness speeding towards her from which there was no escape. 'Early summer, but that's only about seven months away. Are you talking about the May half-term week? We can't plan a wedding in such a short time.'

Gary smiled in an all knowing way. 'Nothing is impossible if we set our minds to it. I don't envisage a large wedding as it will mainly be your family and friends and we can restrict the numbers.'

'Wouldn't it be better to leave it till, say, the October half-term? Perhaps go abroad?'

'We'll see. No need to stress over it now. Just relax and enjoy the champagne, the view of this beautiful city, and the knowledge of our future together. I am truly excited in having you as my beautiful third wife. Wife number one was, how shall I say, rather plain, and wife number two was, err, overweight and unsexy.'

Eva's stomach now churned and she could taste the Hungarian meatballs as they threatened to reappear. She sipped at the water to ease the queasiness in her stomach.

Eva looked at him in a bemused way. 'That's a bit mean to say that. You must have been attracted to them and found them sexy, if you married them.' More things she learned about Gary puzzled her. This remark also reinforced the comment that creepy Simon made at the party the other night. She was better than the plain frump and the neurotic lump. Gary was a man obsessed with noticing attractive women and confident in his ability to attract then. Why would he marry women he obviously didn't fancy?

Gary gulped a little, realising that he was giving details of his first two wives he never shared with anyone. 'I suppose I saw other qualities in them that drew me in.'

'What qualities were they? Tell me a little bit about them. I'd like to know my predecessors if I am going to be the third Mrs Anderson.'

'Claire, she was quiet, worked in accounts, had a best friend, Lisa, loving parents and me. Jess ran her own businesses.'

Eva was still not getting any sense of these woman. What they were like, were they funny, or serious, what were their interests but mainly, what were their lives like married to Gary. 'Did you love them, Gary?'

'Yeah, I suppose so, or I wouldn't have married them. Anyway, enough about them as they are in the past. This is the here and now, me and you, my beautiful fiancée.'

CHAPTER THIRTY NINE

Back at home after the Budapest break, Eva would have the dubious pleasure of telling friends and family about her engagement. Before they had collected Alfie on the Sunday from her parents, Eva had removed the engagement ring from her finger and made Gary promise that they would not tell anyone, not even her parents, until she had told Alfie.

As they returned home in the car, Alfie was excited, relating the things he had done with granny and granddad, including the Leamington Spa Spy Mission Trail where he was able to develop his investigative skills to follow a trail and solve clues on a two mile walk around the town, accompanied by friend Jai. Eva didn't want to have to inform Andy that Alfie was now moving his interest from police investigation to work at MI6, a future James Bond. Rushing into the house, Alfie deposited his shoes scruffily in the hallway and was about to bound up stairs when Eva called him back. As Gary entered the door, carrying Alfie's case, Eva reminded her son to pick up his shoes and place them on the shoe rack. 'Alfie, can we go in the lounge as there is something I need to speak to you about?'

Alfie nervously looked at Gary, probably realising he had been caught out abandoning the shoes, and was about to be told off. 'Sorry, about the shoes.'

Eva and Alfie went into the lounge and closed the door. Eva sat down and indicated that Alfie should sit next to her on the sofa. Having to tell her son about this false engagement felt like a betrayal to him but she would have to summon the courage. She had to play along with this engagement so that she bought herself some time to execute her strategy, to free them both from Gary. She faced her son, seated on the sofa, and took his hand. She gazed into his pale-blue eyes, so like his fathers, and Niall would be appalled at what she had allowed to happen which was endangering their son. Alfie's face was still that of a child, round eyes, smooth skin, projecting an innocence that would disappear shortly as he was swallowed into the teen world of girls, or boys, love, sex, disappointment and the temptations of the world; drink, cigarettes, sex and porn, drugs, social media. She was already hurting Alfie, as Gary had frequently shown his willingness to control Alfie, get him to follow his orders, and consequently bring a sense of misery into his life. She now realised that she had never asked Alfie's opinion about having Gary in their lives throughout the relationship and a fierce pain stabbed at her heart. Gary had been easy going at the beginning when he had made an effort with Alfie but this mask of pleasantry had now slipped. The last four months revealed the real Gary; cold, controlling, prone to outbursts of violence. So far, the violence had only extended to her but how long before he turned on her son physically? At this moment, she was risking Alfie's happiness and mental health, by having to pretend to him that she was delighted to be engaged to Gary. Alfie couldn't yet know that she didn't love, or like, Gary, but she hoped that she would soon be able to explain why she had done it.

'Alfie, darling, you know I love you more than anyone else in my life and I always want you to be happy. I will always put you first and I will not let anyone harm you, ok.' She pulled him towards her and kissed him on the top of his head, delighting in the feel of his hair on her face. She remembered kissing the soft down on his head as a baby and tears welled in her eyes. She cleared her throat. 'When I was in Budapest with Gary, he asked me to marry him, and I said yes. We will not be getting married for a while and things will carry on as they are for now. I know that this will feel like a major thing to you but don't worry too much about the future and concentrate on the present.'

Alfie's large eyes squinted as he scrutinised her face and he was bemused about the message he was getting here. Eva was trying to say, in a roundabout way, that the wedding would never happen. She could not voice this too clearly as Alfie may innocently convey this to Gary. 'Do you want to marry him, mum?'

Eva forced her mouth to fake a smile. 'I have said yes, so I must do.'

'Do you love him as much as dad?'

This now hurt Eva, a thud to her stomach. 'No, as I loved your father with all my heart and soul and we both loved you beyond life itself. I miss him every single day but, sadly, your dad is not here and we have to move forward.'

'I know mum, but I wish you had picked someone else, perhaps like Andy.'

'Why do you say that Alfie?'

'Andy is brilliant, as he is a cop, which is super cool and he is funny, brave and kind. He's a great dad to Hannah and he doesn't shout or anything.'

'I'm sure he shouts occasionally. All parents do.'

'Yes, but I wouldn't be scared of him, except if I was a criminal.'

'Are you scared of Gary, Alfie?'

'Yes, sometimes. He's always telling me off for things and he can be really full-on Thanos, really scary.'

'Well, we'll make an agreement. If you try harder not to leave your stuff about and not to keep asking for something when told no, then I will make Gary promise not to get angry, ok? I also promise you that I will never let Gary do anything to hurt you ok. I would get him out of our lives before I let that happen.'

'Ok, mum. I will try harder on listening to the 'no' speech Gary is fond of. I love you, mum.'

'I love you too.' She cuddled Alfie close to her and this time it was hard not to cry. She hated that she was asking him to go along with this dangerous game in order to reach a safe haven at the end.

CHAPTER FORTY

'Ok, Alfie, stop bashing my chair from side to side and tell me what's up.' Hannah demanded as she looked up from her phone to watch Alfie swinging from side to side on her office chair at her desk. 'You've not looked at your phone for ages, and you're going to knock dents in my desk, and dad will blame me. He's already not happy about the pink nail polish I spilt on the carpet last week which took ages to get out.'

'Nothing's up.' Alfie continued to swing the chair from side to side, bashing the desk. Hannah jumped off the bed and stood next to Alfie, gripping the back of the chair to make him stop.

'Alfie, I know you when something is up, as you have an expression like a constipated gerbil, all pent-up face and red cheeks. Come on, spill.' Hannah now sat on the corner of her bed, staring at Alfie, whose cheeks reddened the more she stared.

'It's nothing, just worrying about school tomorrow. I hate going back after the holiday. And its double maths.'

Hannah sighed and huffed her shoulders. 'Alfie, cut the bullshit and tell me what's up before my hair turns grey and my teeth fall out.'

Alfie had restarted the swinging on the chair but not so violently. He now halted and tried to escape Hannah's gaze. 'If I tell you something, you must keep it a secret for now. Do not even tell your dad.'

Hannah's lovely brown eyes opened wide in surprise and shock. 'OMG, please don't tell me Gary has hit your mum, again?'

'No, I don't think so. No, it's not that this time. It's something else.' He hesitated, worry crossing his face as he struggled with what to say. 'I'm not supposed to tell anyone for now until the grandparents know.'

'Wow, is your mum pregnant?'

Alfie gulped, further terror on his face. 'I don't think so. That would be truly awful.'

'Wouldn't you like a little brother or sister, Alfie?'

'Not with Gary as its dad. Gary doesn't like me much anyway, so a kid of his own would get all the attention from him, and mum. Oh no, but this could be the next thing that happens.'

Hannah's patience was really wearing thin. Trying to extract information from Alfie was very hard work. 'Alfie, what happened in Budapest?'

'Gary proposed to mum and she said yes. They are going to be married and he will be my proper stepdad.'

Hannah jumped up off the bed and did an excited skip around the room. 'Wow, oh, wow, I love a wedding. Do you think me and dad will be invited?'

Alfie looked surprised at Hannah's reaction as he was hoping for support for the distress he experienced after hearing this news an hour ago. Why did girls see things so differently from boys? 'Hannah, it's not exactly the best news for me and mum. I am not really keen on him and he definitely likes to get his own way on things. With him in the house, I cannot be myself any more. I have to watch that I tidy things away, be ready for school with homework done, and bag packed, go to bed when told and so on. Also, I'm always starving as we used to have lots of biscuits, crisps and stuff which mum let me have fairly often. Now, we rarely buy them and Gary is very keen on no snacking between meals. I'm fading away.'

Hannah looked sympathetically at Alfie. 'He sounds more or less like a normal parent, as they are all keen on routine, and healthier eating these days. Anyway, if your mum said yes to Gary's proposal, she must love him and want to get married to him. Gary must make her happy. Perhaps he's very good in bed and he does seem super fit so I expect he's quite agile.'

'Er, that's gross, don't put that image in my head. You wouldn't want me to talk about your dad and Natasha in that way.'

'Ok, Alfie, sorry. I am assuming that your mum and Gary are happy together and there has been no repeat of what happened in Menorca. You know, the slapping?'

'I don't know. I've not seen anything or heard anything but on the Monday after my birthday she had hurt her side and was in pain. She said she'd slipped on some coke, and banged herself on the kitchen table, but she was really quiet all week and kept away from Gary. He was trying really hard to be nice to her and all kissy-kissy, yuk.' Alfie stuck out his tongue.

'You think he may have hit her again?'

'I don't know. He was annoyed on the Sunday when he got in from the golf, as there were presents, cards and wrapping paper everywhere. I could tell he was fed up with my birthday celebrations. It was birthday over, clear up, before he went into the lounge in an angry mood. Mum followed him in and then they were talking loudly but I couldn't hear. I quickly took my presents upstairs as I didn't want to overhear something bad but it sort of felt like the other time. The next day she was going 'ouch' occasionally when she moved suddenly. Oh, I don't know but I just don't like to think of the rest of our lives with Gary and he is s-o-oo bossy.' Alfie was now close to tears. 'I'm not convinced she really loves him and she told me she doesn't love him like she did my dad. Why go for something less good?'

Hannah agreed. 'I know what you mean. I will never marry unless I am really, really in love. But I guess real love is harder to find than we think. Look at my dad, he split up with mum, and he's split up with Natasha, thank God, so it can't be easy.'

Alfie glanced shyly at Hannah. 'Don't tell your dad this but I said to mum I wished she'd picked someone like him.'

Hannah laughed, 'you did, why?'

'I think he's dead cool as he's a cop, and brave, as he catches villains. He's funny and kind and a great dad to you.'

'Yes, he is but I still have to pick up my stuff and can't eat wall to wall crisps, when I like. He does shout as well.'

'Maybe, but Gary is mega scary at times. He's like angry with steam coming out of his ears. I thought he was going to grab me on Friday before mum's party when I asked for food before the family came. Mum had to step in between us.'

Alfie glanced at this phone. 'I'd better go as its dinner in fifteen minutes. Please, please, don't tell your dad what I said about the engagement or the other stuff. I think we are going to see my grandparents tomorrow to tell them about the engagement and then I suppose they'll tell people.' He got off the chair and picked up his phone. 'See you.'

****

Hannah went downstairs to find Andy preparing dinner; roast chicken, roast potatoes, sage and onion stuffing, carrots, cauliflower and broccoli. Hannah sat down at the kitchen island and started typing into her phone. 'How long is dinner going to be, I'm starving?'

Andy had just finished preparing the vegetables. 'Not long, about ten minutes or so. Do you want a Yorkshire pudding?'

'No, er, oh go on, yes please.'

'A hand would be nice so put the phone down and lay the table, please.'

'Ok.'

Fifteen minutes later the meal was prepared and they were eating quietly. Andy watched his daughter's face as she concentrated on her meal, without speaking, which was unusual for her. 'You, ok? You seem very quiet? Everything ok with Alfie?'

Hannah avoided eye contact with her dad. 'Yeah, I think so.'

'Did Eva and Gary have a good time in Budapest. It is a beautiful city that we must go to one day soon.'

'Yeah.' She focused on eating the chicken and roast potatoes and not her father's comment.

'It is a very interesting city with lots of beautiful buildings, and it is split into two parts called Buda and Pest, by the River Danube. Mickey Mouse has a castle there.'

'Fascinating.'

'Hannah, I detect a note of sarcasm in your voice that tells me you are not listening to my tour guide description of the city and have something else on your mind.'

Hannah now looked up from her plate and stared at her father. 'No, not really.'

'Is there something you want to tell me. Are Eva and Alfie ok?'

'Yes and no.'

'Hannah, I've done easier interviews with murder suspects.'

'But this isn't my secret to tell. Why does Alfie keep telling me his stuff?'

'Hannah, you know I can keep a secret and I will always put Eva and Alfie's welfare first. But sometimes when children are given big secrets, it's too much for them to handle, and its ok to tell an adult you can trust. You trust me, don't you, Hannah?'

She finished her meal and put down her knife and fork. 'Yes, dad. Absolutely.' Ok, I don't think you are going to like this.'

Andy's expression was now grave as all sort of scenarios played through his head, mostly involving Gary hurting Eva and Alfie. 'Tell me.'

'When they were in Budapest, Gary proposed to Eva and she said yes. They are going to be married.'

Andy fought really hard not to let Hannah glimpse the almost physical shock to his body this news caused. He drank some water to easy the sudden queasiness in his stomach. How could she comprehend marrying this man who had possibly assaulted her, who definitely controlled her and her son, and this behaviour was increasing as his assertive personality took hold of the family? A man who Andy suspected had cheated on her at least once, and a man who had married twice, and then these wives seemed to tragically die. His research into Gary's background was proving slow as he had no reason to use the police database to check on him. For now, he had to rely on good old Google with scant information to go on.

Hannah waited for her father to respond to this unexpected news. 'Dad, what do you think about this engagement? I was initially happy as I love a wedding and hoped we'd be invited. But Alfie is not happy at having Gary as a permanent member of the family.'

Andy tried to adopt a neutral expression on his face as he responded to Hannah. 'I am pleased for Eva if she truly loves Gary and knows that he will make her happy. If I am honest, I do not think that is the case. And I can understand that Alfie is upset as Gary is bossy with him from what I can tell.'

Hannah bit on her lower lip, struggling again with what to divulge about what Alfie had said. 'Alfie, also, thinks that there was another occasion when Gary hurt Eva.'

'What!' Andy said this so sharply that Hannah was taken aback by her father's reaction.

'He thinks that on the Sunday after his birthday, something happened. Gary was really angry about all the birthday stuff, celebrations and presents. He and Eva were talking loudly in the lounge. Alfie quickly took his presents upstairs as he said he didn't want to hear anything bad, like the last time. The next day, Alfie said that his mum had a pain in her side which she explained by slipping on some coke and banging herself on the kitchen table. She was very quiet all week and Gary was over nice.'

Andy breathed deeply to control the anger he now felt but wanted to hide from Hannah. 'Perhaps, she did slip on some coke and bang her side, and Gary was being all attentive. We really don't know.' But in his heart, Andy did think he knew. He remembered the conversation with Eva when he saw her wincing in pain, how she had slipped and knocked herself on the table. Eva had referred to the Sunday of Alfie's birthday celebrations and how Gary had got angry with Alfie, for leaving a mess. Eva had confronted Gary over his harsh approach with Alfie. Was the pain to her side, less a result of an accident, and more the result of another attack on her?

'What do we do when we are told about their engagement?'

'There's nothing we can do except congratulate them and wish them a happy life together.'

'It's not looking such a happy life for Alfie at the moment. Before Alfie told me about the engagement, I thought he was going to tell me that his mum was pregnant. Alfie was even more upset that they might have a kid, as it would be Gary's. Alfie thinks he would be pushed out.'

'Poor, Alfie. But that has not happened yet and Gary does not strike me as the fatherly type. It depends on whether Eva wants more children. She's a great mum and I could see her with more kids.'

'Dad, can I ask you something?'

'Yes, Hannah, of course.'

'Do you like Eva, I mean more than just a friend?'

Andy didn't really want to answer and admit his feelings for Eva to his daughter. 'I care for Eva very much as a friend. She has agreed to be married to Gary, so my feelings for her are not an issue. I just hope she isn't about to make the biggest mistake of her life, for her sake and Alfie's.'

'Do you like Gary, dad?'

'To be brutally honest, Hannah, no, I do not and I think he is bad news for Eva and Alfie. Anyway, time to clear away the plates and dishes.'

Two hours later, Andy was sat on the sofa, drinking a whisky, which was not the greatest idea with work and a team meeting at 8.30 a.m. tomorrow morning. He was absolutely fuming that Eva had agreed to marry Gary after only a few weeks ago she had been very upset and it was clear she was not happy with him. It made no sense. Then there was the issue of this possible further assault on Eva. Alfie suspected that something had happened and there was evidence of a further injury to her side. Had Gary lashed out at her again? If this had been a further beating then why would she agree to marry him? Two options. Option one, she did love Gary and she wanted to build a future with him. There had been no assaults, and the two injuries that Alfie had noted were the result of careless accidents, involving a kitchen cupboard door and kitchen table. Option two, she did not love Gary, was afraid of him, and did not want to humiliate him by saying 'no' to his proposal, alone, in a foreign country. Go along with it all, for now. Option two felt the most logical to Andy, though having to pretend to Alfie that she was going to marry a man she didn't love, was a big step. Alfie was obviously frightened at the prospective of having Gary as a permanent fixture in his life. But Andy was sure of one thing, Eva, the woman who had cried in his arms, was not a woman in love, looking forward to a happy engagement and a blissful marriage. What was she actually planning to do?

Andy reflected on Hannah's question to him. 'Do you like Eva, I mean more than just a friend?'

Andy's truthful answer to his daughter should have been that he did like Eva and more than just a friend. Even when he was with Natasha, Andy had started to understand that he had feelings for Eva. She was a beautiful woman that he enjoyed spending time with as they shared the same sense of humour and outlook on life. Having comforted her when she cried and then kissed her, he knew the joy of holding her in his arms and the sensation of her soft mouth under his. He yearned to experience this again and more. But this was not going to be a possibility as she was betrothed to another man. To watch as a bystander, as she continued on a journey of marriage to a man he loathed, and did not trust, was going to be more than Andy could endure.

CHAPTER FORTY ONE

December 2013

As Gary slipped quietly into the house, after 11 p.m. he hoped that Jess would be in bed and that he wouldn't have to see or speak to her. She was seriously getting on his nerves these days and he spent as much time as possible out of the house, often at his girlfriend's flat. It had been an endurance living with Jess for these last two years and his plan of marrying her for money was proving to be more difficult than he thought. In a lot of ways, it was worse than living with Claire. Claire was plain, not overly bright and uninteresting, but basically, she was compliant and generally did as she was told. She did not have the greatest capacity to think for herself having been cossetted by her parent's money and care all her life. Her parent's had cushioned her from the hard realities of life, so she did not have to work to pay a mortgage or rent, buy food, pay utility bills or save for household items. Gary had taken over the role of parent to a degree, as he organised the finances, ran the household and guided her on her responsibilities which were earning a salary at her father's factory and looking after the house. Claire did as Gary instructed and had little initiative of her own. This suited Gary whilst he accumulated further wealth from his generous father-in-law who was pleased that his only daughter was being taken care of by a capable man.

Jess was proving to be a lot more challenging but in an unexpected way. When they first met Gary believed that her feisty nature would be a problem as she was a woman used to running her own businesses and making her own decisions. Gary had quickly recognised that the four boutiques were lucrative businesses which could show a good profit if run more efficiently. He had taken control of them fairly quickly and, now, they were doing better than expected with an upmarket clientele, sophisticated women who lived in manor houses, who drove SUV's and wanted to look elegant and chic at all times. The staff he had deemed unsuitable to promote the 'brand' had been made redundant or dismissed, including the long-serving Norma whose poor timekeeping had been her downfall. So sad. As Gary made improvements in the businesses and ensured that Jess put profit before anything else, she had become disheartened with them.

In a week's time it would be Christmas Day but there was no sign of any festivities in the Dawson household. No decorated tree, no decorations, no candles, no Christmas cards sent, no presents bought and wrapped, no food on order for the big day and no arrangements to share drinks and food with friends or family. This all suited Gary as he hated Christmas, ever since he was a child, when he discovered that you could send a long list of wished for toys to Santa but then find out that Santa was basically mean, and so Gary never received anything that he wanted. His request for a Talkboy, as used by Kevin, the boy in 'Home Alone 2', was his most wanted toy, age ten, and the disappointment he felt at not receiving it was a seismic shock in his childhood. His dad explained that he must be on Santa's naughty list and so had missed out. Truth was that dad had not bothered to get one and fobbed him off with a second-hand WWF Hulk Hogan figure which he had thrown at the wall in disgust.

Gary entered the lounge where Jess was lying on the sofa watching an episode of 'Call the Midwife' which was a drama series that he would walk a million miles to avoid. She had a box of chocolates next to her of which two remained, most likely the strawberry cremes she hated. 'I thought you would be in bed by now. You are supposed to be going to the Chipping Campden shop tomorrow as the manager is on annual leave.'

'Yeah, Gary I know but I think Mandy can handle things without me there. I'm not really up to it as I'm feeling really anxious right now. The weather forecast states that there could be heavy snowfall so I don't want to go driving and get stuck somewhere. I hate driving in the snow.'

Gary could not keep his temper intact as he looked at her lounging on the sofa, in loose fitting tracksuit trousers and baggy blue jumper, an outfit attempting to hide her significant weight increase over the last nine months. Her promise to lose half a stone of weight so they could resume their sex life had never happened. Gary had resolutely stuck to his insistence that she achieved this so he had not touched her for almost eleven months. This suited him well, as he was more than satisfied with liaisons with grateful female customers purchasing his cars, and young, insatiable Samantha who he visited at least once a week. He sat down on the sofa next to Jess and ordered, 'sit up, now. You will go to that shop tomorrow and oversee the sales of all those sexy dresses that beautiful women want to wear at their Christmas parties.'

'But Gary, I said I don't like driving if the weather's bad.'

'You'll fucking go, as I have told you to go. I am sick of carrying you while you lounge about here, eating junk and getting fatter. You are a mess, the house is a mess and I am getting near to breaking point with it all.' He looked around the room where there was a tray, with a dirty plate and coffee mug, near to her feet. Piles of magazines, all celebrity tripe, littered the floor around her as did various wrappers from chocolate bars and crisp packets. 'You are just a slob.'

Jess was now near to tears as Gary berated her. 'I'm just lonely, Gary, as you never pay me any attention. Where have you been till now?'

Gary no longer wanted to continue with any pretence that he was interested in Jess. 'I've been with my girlfriend, Samantha, for a few hours of love making if you must know. If you can't give it me then I have to get it somewhere else. Though, I will say that she is getting very pushy and wants you out of the way. Keeps telling me to divorce you but I've told her that is not going to happen. I don't do divorce, as it costs too much money, and I'm not sharing any of my assets with you.'

Jess now faced Gary with anger of her own. 'Oh, so you've finally admitted it, you do have a girlfriend, a mistress, and she has a name. I've suspected for a long time now that you are unfaithful. What's she like this long-suffering Samantha, have you managed to grind her down like you have me. Made her feel worthless?'

Gary's anger was now flaring, hot and strong, and part of him really enjoyed a confrontation when he knew he would win. 'She's none of your business. Let's just say that she's very forthcoming in knowing how to satisfy me, unlike you, who is really useless in that department. When I think of you, I do have to laugh that you had an affair with a married man as what would he get from you that his wife couldn't provide. Perhaps he had a penchant for 'Doc Martin' and chocolate bars.'

Jess now seemed on the verge of tears, as Gary knew that she always believed the married guy loved her, though all evidence was to the contrary. 'At least he was kind and not hard like you. I am pleased that it's all out in the open. You may not like divorce Gary, but I do, and I intend to divorce you as soon as possible. You may find that you have to share your assets with me. I could have one of your dealerships though I know nothing about cars.'

He sat down next to her on the sofa and she shrunk back from him as he moved towards her. His hand gripped tight around her neck, and with the pressure he exerted, she went red in the face and gasped for air. As fear crawled in her throat, she started to sweat and breathe in sharp, shallow breaths so that a major panic attack was building. Her nails clawed at his hands at her throat but he was too strong to fight off. 'Ok, bitch, listen up good. Tomorrow, you go to the shop as instructed, even if you have to fight through fifty-foot snow drifts with your bare hands, ok?'

She nodded her head, in quick movements, to signify her agreement. 'Yes, Gary, just let me go as I can't breathe and I feel a panic attack coming on.'

His red, angry face came close to hers, and a snarl to his lips, denoted his rage. 'I decide on how long or short this marriage is, and there will be no talk of divorce, unless I want it to happen. Capeesh?' He suddenly let go and tapped his right hand across the left side of her face, not a slap, but an indication as to what he could do if he wanted.

Christmas Eve, and Gary sat on a sofa, opposite Jess, who was sitting watching television but tonight there was no wall-to-wall snacking as she had decreed that she intended to lose weight and why wait for the New Year to start. Since last week, there was more of a festive atmosphere to the house, as she had put up a Christmas tree, brought out seasonal ornaments of angels, white candles smelling of cloves and cinnamon, Father Christmas figures, and the cards received from a few friends and family. She had bought some presents for the shop employees and there were wrapped gifts under the tree from the employees who liked her as a boss. She had also bought and wrapped a few gifts for Gary but there was yet nothing from him to her. She was now dressed in a black midi dress with lace sleeves, had tamed her curly hair and applied makeup. Gary was amazed at the change in her from a week ago. His little persuasive chat of a hand to the throat, perhaps made her realise that she wanted to be with him. He had been welcomed home with a meal of medium-rare fillet steak, sauté potatoes and steamed broccoli. A bottle of chilled champagne was waiting to be shared after dinner.

Gary now relaxed on the sofa, replete after his dinner, and thought that he may fancy a quick shag with her, as she did look more presentable this evening. He thought about going to visit Samantha, but there had been heavy rain, with some localised flooding and he didn't want to leave the warmth of the house. 'Glad to see you've made a bit of an effort this evening. My little pep talk last week did you a world of good. You've upped your game and I checked with Aggie, at the Chipping Campden shop, and there's been a good turnover in stock this week. All good.'

Jess glanced at him slyly, not sure if he was joking or not. It was never easy to tell with Gary, as his default setting was generally sarcastic and unkind. 'Yes, thanks Gary, I will definitely try harder. I don't want to have another major panic attack like the one last week.'

'Talking of panic attacks, have you taken your medicine today, yet?' Jess was on a high dose of amitriptyline for her panic attacks and anxiety which had worsened over the year.

'No, not yet, as I'll leave it till I go to bed. I would like a drink of champagne to welcome Christmas but I shouldn't really have alcohol with my medication.'

Gary smiled, a snake-like showing of fangs to the unsuspecting prey. 'I'm sure a small glass or two would be ok. I'll go and open the champagne and we can celebrate Christmas properly, just the two of us.'

He went into the kitchen, removed the chilled champagne from the fridge, and took two champagne flutes from the cupboard. He popped the cork and poured the bubbly drink into the two flutes. He opened the bottle of the amitriptyline liquid medication and measured two 50mg spoonfuls onto a 5 ml spoon and stirred it into the champagne. He carried a tray with the two flutes, the bottle of champagne, the medication, and the spoon, into the lounge and placed them on the coffee table by the two sofas. 'I've brought your medication in so you don't forget to take it after drinking the champagne. Alcohol generally goes to your head fairly fast.' He handed her the glass of champagne and sat next to her on the sofa.

'Thanks, Gary. This is nice, just the two of us together. We must do this more often as I've missed our cuddles.' She leaned into him, and kissed him, but he pulled away in order to ensure they quaffed their drinks.

He placed an arm around her and held his glass close to hers. 'Ok, let's have a toast, to a memorable Christmas, just the two of us.' He tapped his glass against hers. 'Cheers, drink up. I want you merry, so we can have a good time tonight.'

Jess did as instructed and quickly drank the full glass of the bubbly golden liquid in one go. 'Lovely. I've forgotten how good champagne tastes. Fill it up.'

Gary obliged and re-filled her glass. 'I suggest you now take your medication before you forget. Here you are.' He handed her the bottle and the 5ml spoon. She placed her champagne glass down, opened the safety top on the medication, and poured out a spoonful of the 50mg amitriptyline. 'Great, that's done.'

As she went to fasten the top back on the bottle, he knocked her arm, thus spilling some of the liquid on the carpet. 'Oh no, I've spilt some.' She looked at the bottle. 'There should be enough for tomorrow but I may have to go a chemist on Boxing Day and explain that I accidentally spilt some. Sod it. Never mind. Let's concentrate on us having a good time for now.'

Jess lay back on the sofa as Gary moved over her, and started to kiss her, to which she responded hungrily. As she started to relax into the embrace, he decided that this would be his Christmas gift to her. No need to spend money on expensive presents, no need to offer a beautifully wrapped jewellery box or perfume bottle, this was his final gift to her in this world. A sweet taste of the heaven that awaits her permanently if the overdose of the medication worked as he hoped it would.

CHAPTER FORTY TWO

For his 8.30 a.m. team briefing, Andy was with twenty of his team working on a number of cases, at different stages in the process from initial discovery of a body through to preparation for court proceedings and trial appearance. At 8.28 a.m. the expected staff were present, with one exception, Todd Wright. A young DC, who though occasionally brilliant in bringing a fresh perspective to a case, and thus led the team forward out of a mire and into fresh territory, was disorganised in terms of paperwork, found difficulties in team participation due to being of a reserved nature, and had a rather fluid understanding of punctuality and timekeeping.

There was a quiet murmur of conversation around the room as the team waited for Andy to start the meeting. Normally, he would be talking, and joking, to those sat next to him, as he encouraged team interaction and bonding when having a few minutes break from the serious, relentless nature of their work. This morning, he sat staring at his laptop, not acknowledging anybody, and just glancing at his watch in order to start the meeting.

DS Sarah Bright leaned into colleague DC Gabrielle Lewis to whisper. 'Our DI does not look happy this morning; anyone know what's going on with him?'

Gabrielle shrugged her shoulders. 'Don't know. DC Jackson just asked about his Personal Development Review and deeply regretted it. He was given a very terse reply, something about this was not the time for that discussion. Jackson should complete his PDR form and submit it following the laid down procedure and then he would respond.'

DS Bright sniggered. 'Serves him right. That Jackson is itching for his appraisal. If I were doing it, he would fall down on supporting his team members and trying to grab all the glory for himself. Last week, we'd been working on the Nowak case, an elderly woman murdered in a burglary gone wrong, and I had prepared all the groundwork for the interview of the suspect. I was leading and Jackson was supporting, when he undermines me by talking to the suspect about 'women's issues'. After the interview I lost my rag with him, and swore, which he reports to Andy as 'bullying' for God's sake. I'm meeting Andy later to discuss this but it's just wasting valuable time when we should be doing the job we're paid for. I am not a fan.'

Andy now addressed the assembled team. 'Ok, everyone, thanks for coming. We'll go through the cases we're working on and see how things are progressing, starting with the Brooks case. Ranj (DS) can you start? At this moment, the door opened and Todd Wright walked into the room, laptop in one hand, coffee in the other. A beige jacket covered a pale pink shirt more suitable for the beaches of Ibiza than the damp streets of Warwickshire. He finished the attire with blue trousers and tie. Wright tried to shuffle quietly into a vacant seat as Andy listened while Ranj updated the team on the case.

DI Leyton was not going to let Wright's arrival go unnoticed. 'Morning DC Wright, pleased you could join us. Obviously, that fine piece of timekeeping, called a watch, on your wrist was money wasted as it is not enabling you to plan, and execute, a timely arrival at work for a meeting that all other team members have achieved.' Andy noticed that the DC's pale white cheeks turned a glowing pink, so he reined in his desire for more sarcasm. It may be that Wright had a genuine reason for being late in terms of a domestic emergency but doubted that this was the case. Wright lived with his mother, who seemed to take care of all his domestic needs, including freshly ironed shirts, a good breakfast of eggs or avocado on toast, and was efficient at keeping him advised of traffic holdups on the way in to work. How did Andy know this? Wright frequently spoke of his domestic arrangements, which highlighted that he was a cossetted twenty-five-year-old not yet launched into the world of mortgages, bills, and responsibility for a child, which Andy himself had by that age.

'Sorry, boss. Traffic, you know.'

'I do know, Todd. Perhaps we could get you a blue light escort every morning so that you can at least arrive on time.' All the team giggled softly but avoided looking at their hapless colleague.

'OK, back to the meeting. Ranj, if you can continue. In terms of the Brooks case, it appears that some progress is being made in speaking to persons of interest. Have we been able to identify the actual perpetrator at this time?'

'No boss, and we are having the usual difficulty of getting the victim's known associates to talk to us due to loyalties amongst themselves.'

Andy sighed. 'Keep pushing away. It's very early days and the full forensics have not yet been completed so we might get some tighter leads from that. Nick (DC Jackson), you were looking into CCTV in the area of the stabbing at the shopping centre. Has anything useful shown up?'

'I'm still looking boss. Nothing in the main area as it all happened out of the range of the council CCTV but I'm in contact with individual business owners with their own cameras to see if anything is revealed. I've not found any footage with our victim within the twenty-four hours prior to the time of death. I've questioned a few of the shop keepers and café owners but no info yet.'

Andy now looked annoyed at DC Jackson, a young, always trying to get noticed type who acted as if he should be in charge of senior investigations as he believed he was smarter and savvier than his colleagues, particularly his female ones. He was good-looking with slick, gelled brown hair, and was a smart dresser, all skinny fit trousers and slim-line shirts. He was already causing Andy headaches, as he was getting complaints from female detectives, and other female police officers, concerning Jackson's condescending manner. 'Right, Nick. You were instructed to gather and check any CCTV footage for evidence purposes. I don't expect this to involve questioning the shop keepers and café owners unless it is to ask them where the CCTV recordings are kept. Keep to the tasks you are assigned to do.'

Nick now shrank slightly in his chair as Andy glowered at him. 'I just thought I'd use a bit of initiative while I was at it.'

'Well don't. CCTV footage in this investigation would be invaluable, so we can try to track Sam Brooks' movements in the hours before his death. Your task at the moment is to locate and examine CCTV footage, so bloody get on with it.'

'Yes, boss.'

The rest of the meeting ran smoothly, as each case was discussed, each detective made their contributions in terms of progress they had made, and further actions to be taken were agreed. The tone of the meeting was subdued, as Andy's annoyance with Nick Jackson was noted and they all proceeded to report in a concise and professional manner. No lighter moments to take their attention away from the grim realities of the cases before them. All agreed that Detective Inspector Andy Leyton was not his usual self today and was best avoided at all costs. Nick Jackson now regretted pressing for an early meeting for his PDR as he concluded that it would not be the best day, or week, for this, given the boss's mood.

CHAPTER FORTY THREE

Gary faced the working day ahead with a lighter mood, and spring in his step, following his mini break in Budapest and his engagement to Eva. It was time that The Plan was pushed forward, as it had stalled lately, and he was forgetting the number one purpose of The Plan. To consolidate and expand his wealth in terms of properties and finances. Without the tedium of COVID and lockdowns he would have hoped to have been married to Eva by now. His suggestion to arrange the wedding as quickly as possible was to keep the momentum of the engagement going and then bind her to him, financially through wedlock, 'for richer, for poorer'. Financially, Alfie was an obstacle in Gary achieving all of Eva's assets. He had estimated, after surreptitiously investigating her affairs, that she had assets worth around £850,000 including her house. If she had no will, then as her husband he would automatically inherit the first £270,000. Of the remaining assets over this amount, half would go to him and the other half to Alfie. An ok sort of outcome but selfishly Gary wanted all the money. On the other hand, before any wedding occurs, Eva may be planning to make a will to secure Alfie's future and Gary may only be left with some, or none, of her assets. After all, Gary had already got a number of properties, businesses and other financial assets so she may be keen to leave all her wealth to her son. Overall, this was not a happy outcome for Gary. No, a way had to be devised to avoid any wills and to ensure that Eva and Alfie suffered an unexpected and accidental demise.

It was going to be much harder this time to execute the end of The Plan, as he really had feelings for Eva. Her sexiness never failed to stir him, and he always experienced an emotional connection when they were physically close, that he had never encountered before with a woman, especially the other wives. Nevertheless, part of today was that he was going to tie up any loose ends in terms of women he associated with for sex, those who were more than one-off hookups.

His fling with the vixen in Fir Avenue would have to end. A single mother in her forties who Gary had sold a car to three months ago. A slim, brunette, with a choppy bob, she had been a little diversion, a small taste from the smorgasbord of tasty female nibbles, and Gary liked to keep his appetite whetted. Things often change at this stage of a casual fling when the words casual and fling no longer appealed to the woman in question and she wanted to 'move things forward' and introduce Gary to her ten-year-old daughter. Gary did not want any more kids in his life. Time to find the exit. He had popped in on the way back to his

Kenilworth dealership, at around lunchtime, to have the 'goodbye' chat. Perhaps deliver a little parting gift of the Gary charm as a farewell present.

After he dressed, and was now seated on the end of the bed fastening his shoes, Zoe was fluffing her hair and re-applying her lipstick, seated at her dressing table. She stared at him through the mirror as he was bending over to tie his laces. 'Gary, I was thinking as it's now been three months since we started this, and I have mentioned that I think we should start to see more of each other, preferably outside of my bed. What do you say to us going on a proper date, to a pub or restaurant?'

Gary straightened on the bed, still staring at the back of her head, as she finished smacking her lips to ensure the lipstick was evenly spread. 'Interesting that you should say that as I was going to speak to you, today.'

She turned around now and faced him, a smile on her face, and optimism in her heart. 'Great, Gary. What about we arrange to go out for a meal on Saturday, when Maddie's at her dads. There's a new Thai place in town. I could book a table?'

Gary sighed. 'Well, the thing is.' He hesitated and her face fell, all hopes of a proper date, or relationship, crumbling away as a sandcastle washed by the incoming tide. 'I'm sorry, but there won't be any dates, this weekend, or ever, as this last quickie is the end of it for good.'

Shock turning to anger now registered in her voice. 'Why Gary? I thought we were developing a special thing between us. What's changed? That just now was pretty good, wasn't it?'

'Nothing's changed as there wasn't anything to change in the first place. It was always just casual sex. They were all single, meaningless, encounters. They were never building to anything special.'

She picked up a pot of moisturiser off the dresser, and lobbed it at his head, but he ducked in time. 'You fucking piece of shit. Get out. Just get out.' She stood up from the dressing table stool as she raged at him, finger pointing to the door. Gary was not going to be hurried out but once he stood on the stairs, he did accelerate his pace, as he could hear her behind him, and she may be tempted to shove him down the stairs. He smiled at the sweet irony of it all, if he were to meet his death as a result of a fatal push down a flight of stairs. First wife Claire would be clutching her sides with laughter. In the hallway, he picked up his car keys and opened the front door. By now, Zoe was right behind him, and he felt a sharp prod between his shoulder blades which propelled him faster than he would like, down the steps and onto the front path.

Gary was now irate and would never react well to being physically shoved by a woman. Cold hatred radiated from his eyes and Zoe stopped from giving a further push. 'Do that one more time and it won't end well for you, if I take you back inside.'

The woman's eyes now reflected the fear she was experiencing and her hands trembled. Her voice was loud to attract attention of any passer-by, to dissuade him from carrying out his threat. 'Just get the fuck out of my sight, Gary. And to think I've wasted three months of my life on you. You were not actually worth one second of my time and you're not the greatest Casanova you think you are, Gary.'

'I always brought a smile to your mediocre face though, didn't I?'

Zoe now turned quickly, stomped back up the door steps and into the house. The door was slammed shut with a juddering bang.

Gary laughed and shouted. 'Bye, Zoe.'

****

DI Andy Leyton and DC Gabrielle Lewis emerged from Pamela Stratton's home, after a meeting with Pamela and her husband Jim, concerning her mother Edna and the death of her father, Norris Parkinson. In terms of the death of Mr Parkinson, the autopsy report established that Mr Parkinson had died from blunt force trauma, two severe blows to the back of his head consistent with being hit by a golf club, specifically, a putter. The putter in question was unique in appearance and the damage to Mr Parkinson was consistent with the shape and size of this object. The forensic evidence eliminated any possibility of a third-party involvement or illegal entry to the property. The evidence supported that the weapon had been yielded by Mrs Edna Parkinson, as denoted by DNA evidence, fingerprints, blood splatter, and the forensic documentation of the scene by note taking, videography, photography and diagrammatic recordings. On their initial assessment of the crime scene, police officers found that Mrs Parkinson was holding the murder weapon, the golf putter, as Mr Parkinson lay face down on the double bed. No forensic evidence supported the involvement of a third party. After Andy's unsuccessful attempt to interview Mrs Parkinson following the attack, she had been admitted to a mental health unit and evaluated by medical professionals, a Geriatrician, and Psychiatrist who specialise in dementia to ascertain Mrs Parkinson's state of health at the time of the attack. She had now been taken to a specialist care home for those living with dementia and there was no likelihood of any charges being brought for her attack on her husband.

As Andy and DC Lewis got in the car after speaking to the Stratton's, Andy gazed across at the house that he had seen Gary Anderson emerge from a few weeks ago. He then had to blink a number of times, to clarify what his eyes were seeing. Gary's silver BMW parked outside, again. This was the same day of the week, a Monday, at more or less the same time which implied that this was a regular booty call with this unfortunate woman.

Andy watched as Gary emerged, or should he say was shoved by the woman down the steps and onto the path, with her following close behind him, her face distorted by anger. Gary abruptly stopped, and could be heard addressing the woman, but the actual content of what he was saying was indistinct even though Andy had now wound down the car window. Though Andy could see she was frightened, she shouted for Gary to 'just get the fuck out of my sight, Gary.' Andy was concerned for the woman's safety and would have intervened if he felt that Gary was going to strike her. But the altercation quickly ended and she stormed back inside, slamming the door after her. Gary casually walked to his car, a smirking smile on his face. Another woman's life disrupted.

Andy was driving today and DC Lewis waited patiently for him to start the car.

She commented, 'obviously, some domestic bust-up going on there. Entertaining viewing, and I'm wasting pounds every month paying for subscription TV, when all I need to do is park up on a suburban street and people watch for free.'

Andy did not smile when he responded. 'Not so entertaining when you know who the man is, and the girlfriend he's cheating on, and hurting, with his philandering ways. A woman who deserves so much better than him.'

'Wow, what? You know who that man is, boss?'

'Unfortunately, I do Gabrielle and he is a cheating bastard. If I wasn't a cop, I might not be so nice when I see him again. Right, let's go before I say something I'll regret.'

CHAPTER FORTY FOUR

Eva had now informed her parents, and Niall's parents, about her engagement to Gary. Her parents were pleased for her, happy that she was moving on with her life, after the sad loss of her beloved Niall. Her dad seemed to like Gary, mainly as they shared some views on political topics and he wasn't as left leaning as Niall used to be. That was not to say that her dad had not loved Niall, as he was a man that no one disliked, and most openly respected. When he had died, it had been a major loss to the staff, children and parents at the primary school where he was headteacher and Eva had been blown away by the support shown to her and Alfie. She still had all the cards made by the children, their beautiful drawings, and their kind, sometimes funny messages, had lifted her soul in its darkest hours. Her mum appeared to like Gary, but Eva's mum was a reserved person, often keeping her opinions to herself so it was not really clear what she thought. Her brother Liam generally got along with most people, so tolerated Gary, though their opinions on most matters including politics, green issues, COVID vaccinations and veganism were often at opposing ends of the spectrum.

It was now Friday night and Gary and Eva had invited a small group of people around to make the announcement about the engagement. Eva's parents, Niall's parents, Liam, wife Steph and children, a few uncles and aunts, Eva and Tania's friends from school, and Eva's teaching colleagues were all present. Tania, Andy and Hannah were yet to arrive. Simon, Gary's friend was not able to attend. Eva was thankful for that small mercy as he generally made people uncomfortable and no one knew what to say to him.

The doorbell sounded and Eva rushed out to answer the door. Tania and Andy, with Hannah, had arrived together which placed a radiant smile on Tania's face. 'Come in, thanks for coming.'

Tania stepped into the house first. 'This is all very intriguing. I am dying to hear your news but will admit to being a little bit anxious as to what it may be. She enfolded Eva into a big hug and kissed her friend's cheek. 'You look gorgeous, girl, as always.' Eva was wearing a green, tight-fitting, leopard print, midi dress that flattered her figure.

'Go through, they are all in the kitchen.'

Eva gave Hannah a hug. 'Lovely to see you, Hannah. You look lovely. Alfie's been dying for you to get here to take him away from his annoying cousins (his words). Go through.'

Eva and Andy remained in the hallway. 'Thanks for coming, I know it's a bit short notice. I half expected you to be working.'

'I am on-call, so its soft drinks all the way tonight. I am curious to know what this is all about, your request to come over for a glass of bubbly.' There was no smile on Andy's face when he said this, only an expression of concern for her. A serious tone was now apparent in his voice. 'I sort of guess what this is going to be but after our recent discussion are you sure you are doing the right thing. It was clear that you are not happy with Gary. I will be surprised if this turns out to be what I think it will be.'

Standing so close to Andy, a kind, caring man, made her fully realise what she was missing with Gary, and personified the enormity of the risk she was taking in agreeing to this engagement. Gary was not going to be happy when she finally choose the right moment to tell him their relationship was over and that was not going to be too far into the future. He would possibly realise that her acceptance of his proposal had been a sham, a ploy to buy time, and that she had never intended to marry him. Finding the opportunity, and courage, to end this fake relationship was a serious step as Gary was not a man to humiliate and play for a fool. She shivered slightly and this was not the result of the cold air that flowed in from the dark November night. She smiled weakly at Andy but could not hide from him the pain in her eyes. 'It's ok, Andy. I know what I'm doing.'

Andy placed his hand on her arm to garner her full attention, a serious expression on his face. 'I'm not sure you do. Let's be honest here. I have major concerns about Gary and that you are putting yourself and Alfie in danger. I'm not sure what you are doing but you seem to be getting deeper into a mess that it will be harder to get out of. If you ever need my help, don't be too shy to ask, ok.'

She looked into Andy's blue eyes, so open and honest, and thought her heart would stop. 'Thank you. You are a great friend but I can handle this on my own. I don't want to draw you and Hannah into my troubles. Anyway, we had better go in before he starts to search for me.'

She turned towards the kitchen door but Andy kept his hand on her arm. Andy stated, 'ok, I accept what you are saying. But please do one thing. Gather together as much information as you can about Gary's past life, marriages, businesses etc and let me have it. I think we need to dig a lot deeper into Gary Anderson, who has given very scant information about himself, and I do have to question why. What has he got to hide? I can tell you, Eva, that this lack of transparency is a red flag to me and I think you need to know more about him.'

Eva was now getting agitated and slightly annoyed with Andy. 'Ok, Morse, I promise I will but I must go in there now or he'll be out to see where I am. He won't be pleased to find me talking to you.'

At that moment, as Andy went into the kitchen, the doorbell rang and Eva welcomed in Judy and her husband, Cay. It was perfect timing as it meant that Gary would not suspect she had spent time talking to Andy.

As she followed Judy and Cay, into the kitchen area, Gary had supplied everyone with drinks, either wines, beers or soft drinks. The four children had disappeared to Alfie's bedroom to watch television. As it was such an impromptu gathering, Eva had only managed to go to the supermarket after school, and buy an assortment of snacks. This included crisps, a selection of cheeses and charcuterie meats, crackers, grapes, olives, dips and crudities, mini cocktail sausages, nuts, as well as the drinks, including five bottles of brut champagne. Gary was speaking to Liam and scowled at her as she came into the room. He moved towards her, pulled on her arm and whispered at her. 'Where the hell have you been, we've been waiting. I suppose you've been speaking to Andy. From now on, I am expecting to see less of him in our lives, do you understand?'

Andy was now watching Eva, as she tried to escape Gary's grip on her arm. He noticed a sadness develop on her face as Gary spoke to her.

Gary now ordered her. 'Go upstairs and get the kids. I've opened the champagne and I want to pour it into glasses before it goes flat. Don't want to waste money. Off you go, and don't mess about, as I am quickly running out of patience.'

Eva exited the room, ran up the stairs and rushed into Alfie's bedroom. 'Can you children come downstairs now, please, as it's time for me and Gary to tell everyone our news.' Alfie's two cousins, Marigold and Orion, got up off the carpet and headed out the door. Alfie pulled a face and continued to ignore her. 'Alfie, you must come down or Gary will be very upset. Do it for me, please.'

Alfie continued to watch the Simpsons on the television and was laughing as he listened to one of Grandpa Abe's endless rambling stories. Alfie was not inclined to join the guest's downstairs. Eva glanced at Hannah and both of them were confused by Alfie's stubborn stance. Eva checked the bed, picked up the remote and turned off the TV. 'Alfie, come on, everyone's waiting.'

'I don't want to come down. I don't want you to marry Gary.' He now leant forward on the bed, his head in his hands.

Eva sat on the bed and drew Alfie into her arms, whilst still looking at Hannah. 'I know, Alfie, but I promise you not to worry about it all. It will all work out ok, just do as I ask for now.'

Alfie snuggled closer into his mother, not showing any intention of moving. 'I can't see how it will work out if you marry him. All he does is boss me about and at times he scares me when he shouts. I don't want to be happy that you are going to be with him.' Alfie now started to really cry and Eva thought her heart would break.

'Hannah, can you just tell Gary that Alfie's feeling a bit sick and I will be down in a minute.'

Hannah was upset by Alfie's crying. 'I'll go and tell him and my dad.' And she left the room.

Eva tried to raise Alfie's head so he would look at her but he just clung to her, his head buried into her chest. 'Alfie, if you really don't want to go downstairs I won't make you. I have to go down now, but I'll see if you can stay with Granny Norah and Grandpa tonight, ok?'

Alfie sobbed but nodded that he was willing to go to his grandparents' house. 'Y-you go downstairs and I'll watch the S-simpsons. I l-love you, mum.'

Eva peeled herself out of his embrace but this was to be one of the hardest things she had ever done. She could have sobbed herself at the pain she was causing her precious boy by bringing a malign force, Gary, into their home and damaging her son's emotional wellbeing.

She hurried down the stairs and into the kitchen. Glasses had been filled with the champagne and all the adults had a glass in their hand. As she went towards Gary, he gave her a glass, annoyance still etched on his face. Then, he faced the guests, changed his expression from anger to happy, and spoke, 'thank you all for coming at such short notice. You will all be sick of the sight of me and Eva and having to attend our parties. But this is a very special occasion,' he paused, as he drew Eva to him and placed his arm around her waist, 'on our mini-break, last week, in Budapest, this very beautiful lady agreed to become my wife. I am honoured and humbled that she should do so, and I promise her parents, Frank and Julia, that I will take the greatest care of her and Alfie. To Niall's parents, Michael and Norah, I will never be able to fill his shoes but I hope I can at least try to be a good husband to Eva and a stepdad to Alfie. To Alfie,' he stopped and looked round, 'where's Alfie?'

Eva hesitated, avoiding eye contact with Gary. 'He said he's feeling sick, so I've left him upstairs for now.'

Gary scowled, but continued, 'ok, so to Alfie, if he were here, I promise to be the best stepdad I can be and do my best to make him happy. Thank you all again for coming and enjoy our quickly arranged nibbles. But most importantly, I'd like you to raise a toast to the woman who I will spend the rest of my life with, the lovely Eva. To Eva.' Everyone responded. 'To Eva.'

Frank, Eva's father, then cleared his throat. 'Thank you, Gary. I'd just like to say that Julia and I are very pleased that Eva has found happiness again with you. Though we will never forget Niall, we wish Eva and Gary a long and happy future together. And a few more grandkids would be nice. A toast to Eva and Gary.'

Gary now faced Eva, placed his arms around her waist, and kissed her in a drawn out possessive way, to emphasis his victory and control of her, particularly for the benefit of Andy. Eva pushed him off as quickly as she could. 'I need to go and check on Alfie. Can you look after our guests?'

She hurried out of the room and was just about to climb the stairs when Tania and Andy followed after her. Andy took in the deep unhappiness on her face. 'Is Alfie ok, Eva?'

'No, no, he's not. What have I done? It's all a complete disaster.' Eva fell into Tania's arms but breathed deeply to stop her overwhelming desire to cry. 'Alfie won't come down as he doesn't want me to marry Gary.' Tania glanced at Andy, as Eva continued to seek comfort from her friend. 'He told me he's scared of Gary and I really don't know what to do. I'm going to arrange for Alfie to stay with his grandparents this weekend but that is not going to be a solution in the long term. I've got to get Gary to ease up on Alfie or this is never going to work.'

Andy's phone rang. 'Sorry, I've got to take this as I am on-call.' He disappeared into the lounge to take the call in private.'

Eva eased herself out of Tania's embrace. 'I must go up and see how Alfie's doing.'

Tania addressed her friend. 'I've told you, Eva, that I don't like Gary. I think he's sly, manipulative, secretive and I don't trust his motives about being with you. The fact that two previous wives died, and he inherited their estates, is too much of an issue to be ignored. I love you, my best friend, and I am worried that you may meet the same fate as your two predecessors. My advice, do not marry him.'

Gary came through the kitchen door at this moment, seeking his fiancée. 'She doesn't need your advice. She is going to be my wife and if you find that unpalatable then I don't want to see you in this house again.'

Tania blushed, and trembled at the harsh, coldness on Gary's face. 'She's my friend and I will see her when she wants. I will also remind you that this is not your house but hers. Eva decides who comes and who goes.'

Gary loomed over Tania's petite frame but she did not shrink from the confrontation. Tania glared at him. 'I'm on to you, mate, and I will do my best to stop Eva making a big mistake by marrying you.'

'I don't think so. Now get out of my sight.' As he said this, Andy came out of the lounge, and was immediately aware that there was a tension between Tania and Gary. 'Everything alright here?'

Tania made to move away from Gary to go back into the kitchen area with the other guests. 'Yes fine, Andy. I was just congratulating Gary on being the luckiest man, to be engaged to our Eva, and that he must take care of her and Alfie.'

Andy now regarded Gary with a full-on stare of anger, which seemed to have the capability to blast Gary to atoms in a split second. 'I totally agree. If you are stupid enough to harm them, then I can tell you that you will wish you were never born.'

Gary sniggered. 'Oh, yeah, and how's that going to happen? I should report you for threatening behaviour. You'd lose your job.'

Andy stood his ground. 'I am not threatening you; I am making a promise.' He then spoke to Eva. 'I've got to go as there is an emergency. I'll just go and tell Hannah. My mum's coming over and will go to my house shortly. Just send Hannah home when you've had enough of her.'

'I think Hannah's gone back upstairs to be with Alfie.'

Andy bounded up the stairs to speak to his daughter leaving Gary and Eva in the hallway. Gary moved in to hold Eva close to him. 'What's got in to everyone tonight. This is supposed to be a happy occasion as I get to spend the rest of my life with you.' He kissed her, his mouth soft and delicate over hers, before breaking off from the caress. 'We don't want to be surrounded by people who try to put us down. Tonight's our night. Let's go and mingle with our guests and show them what a united couple we are.' He took hold of her hand and led her through into the kitchen. An image formed in Eva's brain of Anne Boleyn being led out to her execution on Tower Green.

CHAPTER FORTY FIVE

As the last of the guests left the party, Gary was pleased that his future mother-in-law had cleared away all the food dishes, dirty plates and glasses, and had loaded as much as possible into the dishwasher and set it to work. Some glasses remained to be washed, including champagne flutes, but these could wait till morning. Alfie had eventually emerged from his bedroom, carrying his backpack with clothes, laptop, phone and homework books which he would need until he returned home from his grandparents' house on Sunday evening.

Gary washed and dried two of the champagne flutes and took a bottle of unopened champagne into the lounge. He then went to find Eva, who was in Alfie's bedroom. She was sat on the bed, in her son's room, staring at the beloved toys he still retained from over the years. The honey-coloured teddy bear, fluffy with a large brown nose, and big smile, was called Mr Eddie who spent eleven years sleeping with his master until Alfie decided that he was too big to share a bed with a bear. Niall had named the bear, Mr Eddie, after a character he had invented in a story he told Alfie at bedtimes though in the story Mr Eddie was a horse. Other favourite soft toys were a giraffe called Leggy and a soft prickly hedgehog called Hedgy. Eva picked up Mr Eddie from the top of a chest of drawers, where he now resided and buried her face into his soft fur which was a little sparce and battered in places. Gary smiled at her as she held on to the bear. 'I think you're a bit big for teddy bears but if you like, I'll buy you one of your own.' He looked at her pretty face, sorrow in her blue eyes. 'Come on, sweetheart, let's go downstairs as I've got a bottle of champagne just for the two of us, to have our own personal celebration on this special day.'

He took her hand and gently pulled her off the bed. He prised the teddy bear out of her hands and placed it on Alfie's bed. They walked down the stairs, Gary leading with Eva following him. In the lounge, she sat down on the sofa as he popped the cork on the champagne. He filled two glasses with the golden, bubbly liquid, gave one to her and sat next to her. 'Here you are, darling, our special moment to celebrate our engagement. To us.' He chinked his glass against hers and they both enjoyed the smooth delicate taste with hints of cream and vanilla. Gary rested back on the sofa and pulled Eva against him. 'Well, tonight was interesting. Your parents and in-laws all seemed delighted with our engagement as were the majority of your friends. I was surprised by Tania's reaction. I know she's not my biggest fan but she was definitely hostile towards me earlier. What did she say – 'I'm on to you, mate. I'll do my best to stop Eva marrying you.' Gary sipped at the champagne as he contemplated Tania's comments. 'Well, war has definitely been declared between me and her, and if she wants a war, then she will find that I fight dirty.'

Eva pushed away from him and sat upright, not touching him. 'Gary, Tania, is my best friend and I don't want this type of hostility between you two. Can't we all just get along?'

Gary noticed the hurt on Eva's face and his stance softened. 'Look, sweetheart, Tania started this but for now I will be the bigger person and let it go. What is important is that we are a couple, united against the world. From now on we put each other first, and Alfie. I support you and you support me in all things. Then everything will be fine.'

Eva agreed. 'Yes, I suppose you are right as that is what a commitment to marry means as far as I am concerned. But I do have to make sure that Alfie is happy in all this.'

Gary turned to look at Eva, a puzzled expression on his face. 'Yes, talking of Alfie, why wasn't he here when we announced our engagement? I'm not very happy about that.'

'He said that he wasn't feeling too well, that he felt sick, so I thought it better to leave him upstairs. He seemed a bit brighter as he went off with his grandparents.'

'Well, as long as he wasn't being awkward and playing up.'

'Oh, no, nothing like that. But can I ask you one thing Gary. If this engagement and marriage is going to work, then you must ease off on Alfie a little bit, as you are too hard on him. He can be thoughtless and leave stuff around and not do as he's told immediately. But that is perfectly normal for a kid of his age. Also, he is on the verge of puberty, and from my knowledge, teenage boys can consume their own body weight in food on a daily basis. Having occasional snacks are fine as long as he eats plenty of vegetables and fruit as well. I don't want him to be miserable. His happiness is the most important thing to me and I don't think he is happy right now.'

Gary sharply inhaled after Eva's update on her son. 'Ok, Eva, I hear you, and I will try to be easier going with him for your sake. I don't particularly agree with your style of parenting but we'll see how things go for now. This is such a special moment I don't want to spoil it thinking about Tania or Alfie.'

Recognising that this was a significant point in their relationship as they prepared for the future together, Eva asked, 'Gary, I want you to be honest with me now, as I really don't know anything much about your past life before I met you. I understand that you were hurt by the deaths of your wives but I really have scant details about you. Will your family be coming to the wedding, your mum or dad?' Gary was not overly impressed with having to relate any details of his past life. 'There's not a lot to tell, to be honest. London council estate, tower block accommodation, so it was a concrete jungle, noisy neighbours all hours of the day and night, screeching cars frequently burnt out, kids in rival gangs so survival of the fittest. I quickly learnt to be the fittest but using my brain as well as brawn. Dad was a feckless idiot who had a job as a janitor in an office block. He liked a drink too much so I was often surprised that he held on to the job as long as he did. He had an eye for the women as well, so he hung out at the local pub, picking up scrubbers and sleeping around. I expect there are a few half siblings around that I've not met. When I was about eight, he moved in with one of his women for a few months but soon came back when she kicked him out. Mum was a down-trodden, weary wreck, ground down my dad's whoring, boozing and quick temper. I think I despised women for a long time because of her and thought of them as weak and needy. I have a sister, Hayley, but she left home once she got pregnant by the first bloke who looked her way and I've not heard from her in years. I heard my dad died a few years ago, from alcohol-related issues, and all I can say is good riddance. My mother's still around, according to Simon's mother, but looks more like eighty than in her sixties. I have no inclination to ever visit her again. A wedding invitation will not be speeding its way to her. You wouldn't want her at our wedding getting drunk and making an utter show of herself.'

'Oh, dear. Would you want to invite your sister?'

'No fucking chance. A chip of the old block, a loser who was keen on both drink and drugs. She will not be getting an invite though Simon might have wanted her as his plus one. He always had the hots for my sister. She was a pretty girl before the booze, drugs and bad food wrecked her body and face.'

'How come you've stuck with Simon for so long?'

'We have been best mates since primary school and each of us had the other's back, particularly when the gang rivalries got entrenched. Simon may look weedy but he can handle himself. People have always underestimated his physical capabilities. He's pretty strong.'

Eva wanted to keep the momentum of this story going. 'How old were you when you left London?'

'About seventeen. I couldn't stand it any longer so I got a job further north and saved up for a deposit on a flat. I left my childhood and dysfunctional family behind with no backward glances.'

'Where in the country did you go to?

'I went to Berkshire, still southern enough to understand the accents, but away from the London conurbation. Through all the uncertainty of our home life, and occasional truancy from school, I did quite well at maths, science and English, and so did well in my GCSE's. I got taken on at a factory making car parts, screws and bolts, and landed a job as a Procurement Assistant. No factory floor job for me. I did well at it and got on well with the owner, who recognised my talents, but marrying his daughter also helped.'

Eva hesitated in asking more questions but she didn't want to let this opportunity pass when Gary was filling in some of the gaps in his life. 'And that was Claire, who you have mentioned? What happened to her?'

Gary sipped on his champagne, then coughed to clear his throat, as if struggling to speak. 'She sadly died from a fall down the stairs at our home when she was pregnant with our first, much longed for, child. She would insist on wearing these sloppy slippers that I told her were dangerous. It was around bonfire night and she'd gone upstairs for some earplugs as the fireworks were making her jump. On the way back down the stairs, I guessed she tripped, or slipped, because of the slippers and fell from top to bottom. She sustained fatal head injuries and died in hospital the next day. The baby could not be saved as it was only twenty-four weeks. All a tragic end.'

'Did you stay in Berkshire after that?'

'No, I sold up and moved to the Midlands and bought the dealership in Stratford. Started dating and met second wife, Jess. An outwardly confident, successful business woman, and his time she was older than me, so I thought she would be independent and less reliant on me. We could have a more mature relationship, no children, just enjoy our leisure time, including foreign travel. It didn't work out as beneath the self-assured exterior was a woman who was clingy, consumed with self-doubt and body confidence issues.' Gary didn't add that he honed in on all Jess's insecurities, exaggerated them, undermined her, until she could no longer cope and became a fragile, broken version of her former self. 'I didn't know she had a history of panic attacks and anxiety when we met, but her illnesses returned, and she was medicated by her GP. We spent a lovely Christmas Eve together but I came down on Christmas morning to find her gone. She'd overdosed on the medication, mixed with alcohol. There was a coroner's inquest and the outcome was an open verdict by the coroner. Did she take the lethal dose deliberately, or accidentally, we will never know? Another marriage over.'

Eva couldn't tell from Gary's unreadable expression what he was feeling right now. 'I'm so sorry, Gary. How old were you when this happened?'

'Thirty, so still quite young.'

'I feel for you having two major traumas so young. Were you involved with any one else in a serious relationship before you met me.'

'Well, yes and no. There was someone and we were close but it didn't work out as planned. Another unhappy episode in my life.'

'You've had a tough time, Gary.' The mention of this other relationship was a total surprise to Eva. This one had not got so far as marriage but why had it all gone wrong? Eva knew only too well that Gary was controlling, prone to temper, and could resort to violence when he didn't get his own way. Had all these women been subjected to his dark side? What had happened with this third significant relationship? Eva was now more determined than ever that she would not be marrying Gary Anderson. The sooner she could end this farce of a relationship, and sham engagement, the better. It was not going to be easy. Gary was abusive and she was genuinely scared of how he was going to react when she told him they were over.

'Yeah, well, you can't turn the clock back. And now, here I am on the verge of marrying my third wife. You should take Tania's advice and run for the hills while you can.' He laughed, hoping she shared the joke but felt a stab of conscience when he considered that he was theoretically planning a similar fate for her as per the other two. Looking at her now, he realised he would find it particularly hard to say goodbye to her. She did fulfil within him a longing to connect to another human being something he had never experienced before. 'I will say, sweetheart, on the subject of wives that you are in a whole different division compared to the previous two. You are Man United compared to Scunthorpe United, no comparison.

'I don't want to be compared to them if all you are talking about is their looks. I am sure they were both lovely women in their own way and it's really sad how they died so young.'

He leaned in and kissed her softly, taking time to appreciate the beauty of her face. 'This is not the time to let thoughts of my deceased wives put a damper on our special day. At this moment with you, I am as happy as I have ever been in my life. I have never said this to any woman before but I am saying it to you now, Eva. I love you.'

Gary could not actually believe he had uttered those words. Gary Dawson/Anderson had never believed in love, never wanted to believe in love, or thought it existed. There had been no love, or even like, directed at the first two wives, only contempt and hatred. Claire, he had utterly despised as she was facially plain with a dumpy body, and the personality of a snail, if that wasn't unfair to snails. Jess was slightly more attractive, but did not rouse him sexually, and faded quickly from ballsy to clingy, to cheerless and depressed. Lisa had stirred him, unsettled him but with hindsight that was mainly to do with sex, due to the strong connection they had when coupling. Samantha was exciting in an arousing way but too immature and needy. How he hated needy when it sparked his anger and his desire to control and crush.

Eva was unique. He often told her she was beautiful and she was with her lovely, trusting face and her creamy complexion. The blue eyes that were deep pools of oceanic waters, the glimmer blue of sapphires, the iridescence of a kingfisher and in their depths a man could lose his soul. Her mouth was inviting, an intoxicating redness that drew you to sate your own yearnings on those lips. Her body attracted him as the strongest magnetic poles and he wanted to expend his passion on her over endless encounters. He loved her soft rounded breasts which he delighted in caressing and the dip and curve from breast to waist to enticing bottom, for fondling, petting, stroking. All these factors troubled Gary as the emotions they aroused were new to him; love, tenderness, jealousy of other men, and pain of her potential loss. This all conflicted with The Plan. The Plan was simple. Date. Marry. Kill. With Eva it was not going to be so straightforward as she had gotten into his heart, his head, and his soul.

CHAPTER FORTY SIX

On the Monday, after the engagement party on Friday, Eva remained at her desk in her classroom and tried to record on her laptop every single thing she knew about Gary including his revelations about his family life and two marriages that he had disclosed to her. The details were still fairly scant, in terms of his parents' names, where exactly he had lived during his childhood and the place in Berkshire where he had lived with first wife, Claire. She didn't know the name of the factory, except that it produced screws and bolts for the car industry, or the maiden name of his wife. Dates of this relationship and marriage were also vague. He had once disclosed that he got married when he was very young, at twenty-one, and this detail had stuck in her mind as not many people married at such a young age. If he had married at twenty-one, then it would have been in 2004, based on the age he was now. After the tragic death of his wife, he had sold up, and bought a first dealership in Stratford and then the second one in Kenilworth.

Eva was unsure of his age when he married his second wife, Jess, (surname unknown) but guessed he had been in his late twenties. The second wife who had died of an overdose of a medication, presumably prescribed for anxiety or depression. An older woman, no children, so one would assume she had assets including a property, and he had described her as a 'business' woman, so presumably Gary had inherited the business or businesses on her demise. Given the fact that Gary had come from a childhood of poverty and neglect, he now had quite a number of assets including two properties from the two wives, and possibly other monies inherited as part of their estates. Eva wondered had Gary targeted her, a widow with her own mortgage-free property and insurance money from Niall's death, to acquire her financial assets? She would have to take steps to protect her wealth to ensure all her monies went to her son.

Arriving home, Eva noted that Gary's car was missing from the drive, and she went in the house to find Alfie sat at the kitchen table doing his homework and drinking a glass of orange squash. There were chocolate wrappers next to him, evidence that he had called in the local shop for a few snacks on the way home from school. 'Hi mum, just finishing my homework, then I'm going to play an on-line game with Jai and a few others.'

'Hi, Alfie. Ok, but get rid of those chocolate wrappers before Gary gets in. I'm just popping next door to Andy's. Gary's going to be late tonight. He's got a staff meeting which starts at five and he should be out for a while yet.'

'Ok, mum, see you.'

Eva hurried over to Andy's house, having noted his car on the driveway, and knocked on the door. Andy answered the door, looking dishevelled, white shirt creased, sleeves rolled up and tie loosely done up. He was wearing his police lanyard around his neck. 'Hi, Andy. Can I come in a for a moment?'

He smiled at her and opened the door. 'Yeah, come in and give me a break from going through the Personal Development Reviews (PDRs) of my team. I know staff like to know how they are developing, want to discuss their individual training plans, and how to move forward in terms of their careers, but it's all a lot of work I could do without. One case in point, a young DC who likes to think he is the brightest and sharpest tool in the box. The PDR form he's submitted reads as if he has solved all the recent murders in the area on his own. We are all the minions that make his great work possible. Truth is, he is an ego-centric, glory-seeker who does not know how to work in a team and thinks that all women are inferior to him. A right little pip squeak but I would put money on him being Chief Inspector, and my boss, before the decade is out.'

Eva grinned. 'You don't look too happy about it all.'

Andy sighed. 'No, I'm not. I am going to have to find some of his better qualities, and these are well hidden, as these appraisals are meant to be of a positive tone these days. Give me strength.'

Eva followed Andy into the kitchen. He filled the kettle and switched it on. 'Coffee or tea? Though frankly I could do with a double scotch right now.'

'Coffee's great, thanks. Milk, no sugar, as always.'

Andy took two mugs from a cupboard, spooned in the instant coffee and removed the milk from the fridge, ready for when the kettle had boiled. 'Take a seat.' She sat down at the dining table, placing a white envelope in front of her. He made the coffee, handed her a mug, and sat opposite her at the table. 'Sorry I had to leave your engagement party early but I was on-call and sadly people cannot seem to resist the urge to kill others at any time of the day or night.'

Eva's lovely eyes reflected the pain she felt for the suffering of others. 'I don't know how you cope with seeing all the grimness of sudden death and the cruelty that people inflict on others.'

Andy drank his coffee, while taking in the sorrow on her face. 'I cope because I have the determination and skills to catch those responsible. We are lucky to have so many more resources at our disposal these days including DNA, extensive forensic expertise, CCTV, ANPR technology, mobile phone tracing, social media info and it is far more difficult now for murderers to get away with their crimes. Anyway, did the party go well?'

Eva shook her head. 'Not really. As you know, Alfie refused to come out of his room and pretended to be ill. He's really not happy that I'm marrying Gary and has admitted that he's scared of him. Then Tania's telling me not to marry him which Gary over hears. It's not the most glorious start to an engagement.'

Andy was now regarding her with an unsmiling, almost angry expression on his face. 'Eva, you are my friend and I care for you very much but I am not going to lie. I totally agree with Alfie and Tania and I think you are making a massive mistake if you marry that man. My instincts tell me that he is sly, controlling and evasive. There is too much about his past that you don't know and I do genuinely have concerns for your safety, and Alfie's. Whatever possessed you to get engaged after that time you got upset and acknowledged that you were not happy with him?'

How she replied now was not going to be her finest moment, as she hated lying to people. Andy was very perceptive, because of his job, to the behaviours and fabrications of people. 'Yes, Gary is all those things you've just said but he can be very loving, and funny, when he wants to be. The four days in Budapest were a time for us to be together. He proposed on a restaurant boat on the Danube, overlooking the Parliament building, and I was swept along by the romance of it all. I found myself saying yes.'

'And I take it that you do plan to marry him?'

Next big lie coming up. 'There's no point in getting engaged unless you want to get married, is there?'

'When is this wedding likely to be?'

'Gary wants it to be as quick as possible and we are looking at the Spring Bank Holiday week, next year.'

'Why is he in such a hurry?'

Eva hesitated, looking coyly at him as she responded. 'I don't know. He has this thing about making us a unit against the world. I suppose it's quite romantic really.'

Andy was now getting openly annoyed with her. 'What does that mean? To isolate you from your family and friends so that you are completely under his control. I don't like it, Eva. I don't think it's romantic, it sounds dangerous.'

Eva was now irritated by all this negativity. 'But when you agree to marry someone, you do have to put them before all others, that's normal.'

'Yes, it is. But it's not normal to marry a man with two dead wives and a previous life you know nothing about.'

Eva sighed. 'Yes, but I did find out a bit more about the wives on Friday, and both deaths were tragic, and sad, but were not Gary's fault. He also said to me that I am the only woman that he has told that he loves. That's a good basis for making a relationship work.'

Andy placed his coffee mug on the table, none too quietly. Eva was aware that he was annoyed with her, something that had never happened before throughout their friendship. 'That is another example of why not to trust him. Who gets married, twice, without telling the women that you love them. To me, that means that he did not love them, so why marry them?'

This was now getting too much for Eva and she could see this heading for a full blown argument with Andy if she didn't change tack. She could not, at this time, give Andy any reason to believe that this engagement was all a cover to buy time, and her intention was not to marry Gary but to get him out of her life for good. For now, as far as Andy was concerned, she had agreed to marry her loving fiancé.

'Ok, Andy, I take your point. We'll leave it at that. But I have managed to get a bit more information out of Gary about his past life. I've written everything I know down here, for you to have a look at, as you asked me to do.' She handed Andy the white envelope containing the document she prepared at school. 'Can I ask you to keep it secret and not share it with anyone. I can't risk Gary finding out about it as he would go ballistic.'

Andy shook his head. There was no hiding the anger in his tone, as he now commented, 'honestly, Eva, this is another reason not to marry him. You are scared of his reaction to things and you know he has a temper. I do really worry that he will lose it completely and lash out at you or Alfie.'

Tears now welled in her eyes and Andy realised he had gone too far. 'Sorry, I don't want to upset you and raising my voice at you is exactly in line with how Gary behaves. I will have a look at this information and see if I can find out some info on him. I can't use the police computers as that would be inappropriate but I am good at this sort of thing. He must have popped up somewhere on the internet throughout his life.' Andy took the document out of the envelope and read it through. 'It's still all a bit thin, but the factory in Berkshire may be the place to start, as there can't be that many that manufacture screws and bolts for cars. Leave it with me.'

Eva left Andy's house feeling really dispirited. She had just had her first major disagreement with Andy. He had never got angry with her before and it felt as if she was on the verge of losing him from her life. If he could not tolerate her relationship with Gary, then why continue to watch someone you care for mess up their life. This all actually hurt her. She felt a strong connection with Andy, something more than friendship, and that kiss had tipped things into a different direction for her. But her mind imagining a relationship with Andy always came to a juddering halt when she remembered Natasha's comment that Andy did not find her attractive. It was a complete mystery why had he kissed her. But the kiss had changed things for her. She realised that she wanted Andy as more than a friend but this was never going to happen. She suspected it wouldn't be long before he acquired another girlfriend, another stunner, and in all honesty, she was not in the same beauty league as Natasha. Quality men like Andy didn't stay single for long.

****

If Andy had been irritated about assessing DC Jackson's PDR form, then he was now tempted to make a long list of the man's shortcomings and read them out at the face-to-face meeting arranged for next week. He was sure that Jackson was going bring up the issue of bullying by DS Bright, which he had now resolved, but Jackson was the type to keep detailed notes of any wrongs made against him. Andy had received several comments from female officers concerning Jackson's attitude to them. An overarching impression he gave that women were inferior and incompetent. Until now, Jackson was keeping his overtly chauvinistic tendencies in check but Andy feared that he was one of those officers who shamed the police by being lecherous and misogynistic. So far, there was no actual evidence of this. As Andy had said to Eva, the man had all the self-centred ambition to get to the top of the police service.

Thinking of Eva was now seriously inflaming his temper. He had come very close earlier to really shouting at her which was something that had upset him. He certainly did not like to get angry with women as it made him as bad as the men that he despised, like Gary. But in all honesty, he truly felt that he wanted to shake some sense into her before she made the major error of marrying Gary Anderson. Every alarm bell was ringing that this was not going to end well for her and she would get hurt, emotionally or physically, or both, or worse. Gary had now got his feet firmly under her table and Andy expected that he would start in earnest to cut her off from family and friends. He anticipated that his controlling nature in terms of Alfie would get worse and he feared that this would harm Alfie more than Eva realised. Andy was now determined that he would not easily be pushed out of Eva's life. He would make it his mission to find out all he could about this man and the secrets of his past. His own workload was continuously high but he would have to use some of his spare time to try to protect Eva from herself.

CHAPTER FORTY SEVEN

Saturday afternoon, and Andy was in Reading, after a mid-week contact with a company called RQ Screws and Bolts Ltd. He had telephoned the company and asked to speak to Mr Roger Quall, the company owner, and had been put through to the Manager, Scott Quall, nephew of Roger. Andy was advised that Roger Quall had died three years ago at the age of seventy-one and the company was now owned by Mrs Cynthia Quall, Roger's widow. Andy explained that he was ringing in connection with a possible, previous employee of the company, a Gary Anderson who had been married to a woman called Claire, quite a number of years ago. Andy explained that he was interested in Gary Anderson for personal reasons which he could elaborate on if he were to have a face-to-face meeting with Mrs Quall. Scott did not recognise the name Anderson, though a Gary Dawson had been married to his cousin, Claire, who died in 2008. Scott stated that he had not been at the factory during the time of Dawson's employment or marriage to his cousin but Cynthia Quall may be the person he might like to speak to. Scott explained that Cynthia was very bitter towards this Gary Dawson who she claimed was responsible for the death of her daughter and her unborn grandchild. Andy agreed to send a photo of the person he knew as Gary Anderson, to Scott, who would show it to his aunt. If Gary Dawson, was now Gary Anderson, then his aunt may be willing to talk to Andy. This had now resulted in Andy being seated in the lounge of Mrs Quall's detached house, on the outskirts of Reading, an expensive property benefiting from being surrounded by countryside. The lounge was light and airy, with bifold doors leading to the garden, high ceilings, modern décor and oak flooring. Cynthia Quall was in her early seventies, elegantly slim with well-cut blonde hair. She was casually, but tastefully, dressed in beige trousers with mint green jumper and green/blue scarf tied loosely at her neck. She asked, 'I hope the coffee's ok, its instant, I'm afraid.'

Mrs Quall had served the coffee in white China cups with gold rims and the drink was smooth and aromatic. Andy drank the coffee, pleased to be able to savour a drink that was hot and not bitter, as was frequently the case at the police station. 'It's very good, Mrs Quall, thank you.'

'Good, but call me Cynthia. Mr Leyton, can I ask you why you want to find out more about the man that I know as Gary Dawson and you know as Gary Anderson.'

Andy sighed, wanting to explain precisely his interest in this man. 'Firstly, I must be clear with you as to who I am and what this is all about. I am a police officer, a detective inspector, with Midlands Police, but I am not here today in my role as a police officer. I am here as a private citizen to try and find out about this man, who I know as Gary Anderson. He has been dating my friend and neighbour for over two years and they have recently got engaged. I have some concerns about this man who has been very evasive about his past life, other than the fact that he has been married twice, and owns two car dealerships in Warwickshire. He appears to have no family and few friends, except a man named Simon, who I believed worked at your factory a number of years ago. My friend has now become engaged to Anderson and he is pushing her to marry. I am very concerned about his motives. I also have reason to believe, though she has not confirmed this, that Anderson has been physically abusive towards her, and I do fear for the safety of her, and her young son.'

'Oh dear, this is all very troubling. I would agree with your assessment, Mr Leyton, that you have cause to be concerned as this Gary Dawson, or Anderson, is a man to be extremely wary of. I hold him responsible for the death of my only daughter and her unborn child.' Cynthia Quall paused at this point, to sip her coffee, and to fight the tears that were threatening to fall at the mention of her lost, beloved family.

'I am sorry if this is going to be too painful for you. If you don't wish to talk about it, I would perfectly understand.'

'Yes, it is still very painful, even after thirteen years of not having my daughter and grandchild in my life. But you must do all you can to stop your friend from marrying him.'

'Can you tell me what happened with your daughter?'

'My late husband, Roger, took Gary Dawson on as a Procurement Assistant at the factory when he was about eighteen and he was very competent. Roger took a real shine to him, saw the potential in him, and guided his career development beyond that of other young employees. I think in Gary, Roger saw his younger self, good-looking, confident, ambitious and I must say with a large dose of ruthlessness. But Gary's ambitions did not stop at office matters. He recognised an opportunity to further progress by setting his sights on my daughter. Roger thought that this was wonderful, a way to bring a bright, hard-working man into the family and that Claire was very lucky to be chosen as his girlfriend.' Cynthia hesitated as she sipped her coffee. 'I saw it totally differently. I could not comprehend why a man like Dawson, who was extremely handsome, and have his pick of women, would choose my daughter.' She looked at Andy's face, waiting his reaction.

She continued, 'Claire was my only daughter and I loved her very much. But I did also recognise her shortcomings. Please don't class me as a terrible mother when I say this but she was rather plain and frumpy. I tried to guide her with help on hair, and clothes, but without making her feel bad about herself, I hope, but Claire was never interested in those sorts of things relating to beauty. She was also rather shy and awkward with people and didn't have many friends. Therefore, I was very surprised when Gary invited her to the works' Christmas dance of that year. A man like him could have a stunning girlfriend and I really did not know what he wanted with Claire. I did eventually find out but we're not at that stage of this story yet.'

'After the Christmas dance, he still continued to date her?'

'Yes, they began dating in December 2002 and were married in May 2004, it was all pretty quick. And I think it was all too fast for her. She went from the security of living with us to being with a man she didn't really know. If Claire had any happiness in her life before she met and married Gary, it all changed the longer she spent with him. She was always very quiet, even with me, but she would sometimes come home and say things which made me realise she was very sad. He criticised everything about her, her face, her figure, what she ate, how she was useless at running a household, that she was boring and uninteresting to talk to. I gather that things were particularly bad in the bedroom, if you know what I mean.' Cynthia stopped speaking and Andy could see the pain on her face. 'My little girl was miserable in the last years of her life, with that man, who did everything he could to diminish her and criticise everything about her. He was very short-tempered with her and shouted at her, even in front of us. Also, she never said but I believed that he used to slap her around as I often saw a bruise on her arms, her chest, and occasionally her face. She'd say she fell, or bumped into something. Claire was clumsy but there too many for it to be explained away by accidents and trips.'

Cynthia now started to cry softly and she reached for a tissue from a box on the nearby coffee table. 'Sorry, I get a bit upset when I think about it all. She could have had a much better life with an ordinary, kind man who would have taken care of her. There was a lovely young man at the factory who was fond of her. But Roger made it clear that he was not to go near his daughter as she had landed the biggest catch, Gary.' She paused again, visibly upset. 'I think we need more coffee, Mr Leyton. Would you like one?'

Andy nodded. 'Yes, please, and please call me Andy.' Whilst she was gone Andy considered all that she had told him so far. It was starting to look remarkably like Gary Dawson had married Claire, not for love or even affection, but for reasons of advancing his career and cementing his relationship with Roger Quall. A direct route to the Quall's wealth.

Cynthia re-entered the room with the freshly made cups of coffee, she offered Andy a shortbread biscuit, which he gladly accepted as he had missed lunch. 'Thank you, Cynthia, for speaking to me. I can tell this is very difficult for you.'

'It is, but you must understand what kind of man Gary Dawson was. I blame all of this on Roger. I kept telling him that Gary did not love Claire and was hurting her. Roger kept insisting that she was lucky to have an alpha male like Gary and she should be grateful. Anyway, things carried on and Claire just sort of faded before our eyes to a sad, introverted nervous wreck. But Roger still thinks the sun shines out of Gary's backside and gives him shares in the factory. He then buys a second business, a car dealership which Gary manages, and I must say he does it very well. Then, in 2008, we find out that Claire is pregnant and Roger is ecstatic. A grandchild to continue the Quall name and run the businesses. On Roger's sixtieth birthday, he signs over the dealership to be jointly owned by Claire and Gary. I really think Roger had lost touch with reality at this point, as he was throwing money at Gary, and couldn't see that his daughter was unhappy and under the complete control of that man.'

Andy quietly drank his coffee. He wanted to ask questions but he realised it was best to let her speak.

'The pregnancy was going ok but I did have concerns about how Claire would cope as a mother. She was not very good at domestic matters and I really couldn't see her tending to a new born baby. Roger and I had agreed that we would probably have to pay to employ a nanny if she couldn't cope. In the end it wasn't an issue as Claire never delivered a baby and she died at twenty-four weeks pregnant. She fell down her stairs at home as a result of wearing unsuitable slippers. She suffered fatal head injuries and the baby could not be saved.'

Andy looked on as the woman cried softly, sorry for her pain. 'Could I ask, and this is probably because of the job I do, but what was the coroner's verdict on this? Was it recorded as an accidental death?'

'Yes, it was at the time. There was nothing to indicate that it was anything other than just a terrible, terrible accident. And, I have no evidence to disagree with this verdict except for Gary Dawson's despicable behaviour following Claire's death and loss of his unborn child.'

'In what way?'

'He didn't act in anyway like a man that was grieving for his wife or child. He showed absolutely no emotion whatsoever. He came to see us and spoke in a cold, callous way about the funeral arrangements. He would organise it all, regardless of our wishes or the way we would've wanted it for Claire. It was an impersonal service at the crematorium with no special readings or music. Claire absolutely loved Westlife so I would have had 'You Raise Me Up' or 'The Rose' which were her favourites but Gary just dismissed all our suggestions. People reported seeing him in pubs and bars, with his friend Simon, just after her death, laughing and joking. Other times he was seen with women, not just a friend or acquaintance, but sitting with his arms around them, kissing and cuddling. Really pretty women, who were such a total contrast to our Claire.'

'I'm really sorry. I don't want to make excuses for the man but could it be a case of not coping with the grief. Shutting it out.'

'No, Andy, no. There was no grief, no pain, no sorrow. He had never loved Claire and I suspect he did not want the child. He acted like he had been released from prison, a man enjoying all the freedoms the world had to offer. He had also been clever. He and Claire had wills drawn up, each leaving all their assets to the other, so financially he came away with a house, a car dealership, shares in our factory and savings that Claire had, money from us. There was also an insurance policy landing him another tidy sum. Once her estate went through probate, he sold his shares in the factory, sold the dealership and moved to the Midlands. He still owns the house in Reading which he lets out to tenants. He left Reading without even saying goodbye to us. Roger had to at last wake up to the type of man Gary Dawson was and his motives for marrying our daughter. In one word. Money.'

Andy shook his head; the whole horrible story was much worse than he had anticipated. 'But you are still satisfied that the coroner's verdict of accidental death was valid? No suspicions of foul play?'

'Oh, I have my suspicions and I don't think it was an accident but I have no shred of evidence to prove it. When you address the overall picture, and ask yourself why he chose Claire, there can only be one explanation, as he definitely did not love or respect her. It was all a calculated plan to get property and wealth at this family's expense and it worked.'

'I am so sorry for your loss. You have given me full and frank indication that my concerns about Gary Dawson, now Anderson, are well-founded.'

'Yes, young man, they are and you are very wise to be concerned for your friend. But there is another dimension to all of this, the disappearance of Claire's best friend, Lisa Jefferies. She disappeared in June 2005 and has never been found.'

Andy was now truly shocked by this latest information. 'Are you saying that Gary had something to do with this woman's disappearance?'

'Yes, I am but I have no evidence to back this up. I have had long conversations with Lisa's poor mother and we both think Gary was involved. Her body has never been found and the police investigation stalled without any real evidence to go on. They interviewed a number of men, working at the factory and at the dealership, including Gary and Roger.'

'What makes you think he was involved with Lisa Jefferies?'

'Her mother said that she used to go out a few times a week to meet boyfriends but was very cagey about who she was seeing. She'd go out for a couple of hours, and rarely stayed out overnight, so her mum concluded she was seeing a married man. Now, Lisa and Claire were unlikely friends as Lisa was beautiful, intelligent, full of fun and lusted after by every man who saw her. They met at school and were the best of friends but the friendship faded a bit when Gary came on the scene. I know that Gary fancied Lisa, though he denied it to Claire, as I had seen him watching her when I've caught them together at the factory. At the wedding, she was chief bridesmaid, and I saw them sneak out together after all the speeches, for a cigarette. And when she came back, she was flustered, pink cheeked and hair dishevelled, and Gary followed her in, a few minutes later. I know what they were doing. After the wedding, Claire insisted that Lisa had a boyfriend who she said was married, so she couldn't say his name. She couldn't say his name as he was Claire's husband.'

Andy looked puzzled about the implications of all this. 'If Gary was cheating on your daughter with her best friend, it makes him a scumbag in my book. But are you saying that Gary had something to do with her disappearance?'

'Possibly. Lisa's mother is convinced he was involved but the police cannot find any link to connect them. Gary was very clever at covering his tracks. I could arrange for you to go and speak to Mrs Jefferies if you'd like, in the near future.'

Andy was now feeling a sickness in his stomach and a coldness in his chest as he contemplated the possibility that Gary Anderson was a suspect in a murder. 'Yes, that would be very helpful, thank you.'

Cynthia Quall now stared intently at Andy. 'Is your friend a woman with money or property of her own?'

'Yes, she is a young widow and has a house, with mortgage paid, and insurance money from her husband's death as well as money from his employment.'

'And you say that Gary has recently proposed to her.'

'Yes, and he is very eager to get the wedding arranged.'

'Do you see her as vulnerable? Does he manipulate and control her, like he did my Claire?'

'Yes, he does. She is a smart woman, a teacher, and beautiful, but he is starting to wear her down and be over assertive with her and her son. I do have concerns for their safety. It has been reported that he may have hit her, at least on one occasion.'

Cynthia Quall sighed wearily. 'One thing is clear, Andy, this woman is very lucky to have you as a friend. My biggest regret in life is that I did not do more to protect my daughter from Gary Dawson. Please do your best to stop your friend from marrying him and get her out of his control. He may well be after her money. Tell her everything I've told you today. That man is ruthless, money-grabbing, and controlling. I believe that he physically abused my Claire. I have grave concerns that the death of my daughter and her unborn child was not an accident. I believe that he may have been responsible for the disappearance of Lisa Jefferies. All this adds up to Gary Dawson, now Anderson, being a very dangerous man. You must make your friend understand the danger she is in, to herself, and to her son, before it's too late.'

CHAPTER FORTY EIGHT

Saturday, mid-November, and Gary had been at the Stratford dealership most of the day, catching up on monthly figures, in terms of turnover, outgoings and projected sales for the coming winter months. He's had a quick chat with Simon, who congratulated him on the engagement and was pleased that Gary was now consolidating The Plan, with regards to Eva. Simon, leaned back on his office chair, hands behind his head, as Gary sat on a chair in the corner of the office.

Simon slowly licked his lips in a lecherous fashion. 'Well, Gary, I suppose there is such a thing as third time lucky. As I have said before, your first two wives were never going to win any beauty contests. How you actually shagged that Claire I never know. I can't afford to be picky and never generally turn down an offer but even I would have found a problem going with her. That Jess was ok, as I don't mind a curvier lady, but she got too miserable as time went on. At least this time you must be enjoying consummating the relationship as Eva is truly scrumptious. You are a lucky man. It's sad to think that it will all end pretty soon.'

'Shut up, Simon, don't go talking like that in here. I've not decided what's going on with Eva, yet, only that there will be no delay in arranging the wedding. In fact, I have a brief appointment at 4.00 p.m. with a suitable wedding venue on the way home. If I like it, I might secure it with a deposit.'

'Shouldn't you discuss it with Eva first?' It's her wedding as well.'

'Not really, as if the venues ok, we can't afford to miss out if we want to get married during the May half-term week, particularly as it is the week including the Platinum Jubilee Bank Holiday. If I secure the venue, Eva can get involved in the rest of it, décor, flowers, menus, cake, cars, etc. I think this venue will be ideal, as there won't be that many there for the wedding breakfast and some of the staff from the dealerships can come in the evening.'

'Well, there won't be any family from your side, unless you invite your boozy mother and druggy sister, which I guess you're not. Shame, because I would've liked to see Hayley again after all this time. I always had a thing for her.'

'Shame, as she couldn't stand you.'

'Some women just haven't got any taste.'

'No, Simon, my mother and sister will not be getting an invite to the wedding. I can just about put up with inviting you. Speaking of which, you will have to step in as best man, as usual.'

'No problem. Third time, eh? Again, I shall request a pretty chief bridesmaid so that I can try and get her out on a date after the wedding. That Lisa was gorgeous at wedding number one and I should have had best man's privileges with her. But no, the bridegroom takes her out and sees to her at the back of the venue. Wifey number two's bridesmaid, Abby, I think she was called, was very tasty but didn't seem very into me. This time it might be Eva's pretty little friend Tania, so I might get lucky with her, if she puts out a bit.'

'Oh, shut up Simon. She's never looked your way at any time you've been at our house. Don't hold your breath. Anyway, she totally besotted by Andy and you stand no chance if he's around.'

Simon sat forward on his chair, a scowl on his face. 'Yeah, him. I should take a contract out on him, as while he's single, no other man will get a look in. Do me a favour and don't invite him to the wedding.'

Gary nodded in agreement. 'I wish, but Eva will definitely want him and his daughter there so I won't win on that one.'

Simon asked, 'I don't think Tania is going to get off with that Andy as she would've by now. No, the woman he wants is your Eva. You are wise to marry her asap. I accept your invitation to be best man but only on condition that I am seated next to Tania at the meal. Then I can chat her up, using the old Wagstaff charm.'

'Yeah, I suppose I can do that as a favour to you. Though I doubt the so called Wagstaff charm will get you anywhere.'

Simon drank from a water bottle on his desk. 'As your best man, I would like to get to know your bride-to-be a bit better. It's about time I was invited to the Anderson house for dinner. I've not had much of a chance to get to know Eva and I would like to. If it takes too much longer, I may have to tell her a few of your secrets at the wedding which you wouldn't like.'

Gary's eyes glared at his friend. He hated Simon using blackmailing methods about their past misdemeanours to gain an advantage. 'Don't fucking start that, I've told you about it before. Whatever you think you have on me, I have equal amounts on you. It's a game neither of us can win. But in the spirit of co-operation, Eva and I are having a takeaway tonight, and you can join us at about 8 p.m., if you like.'

Simon nodded eagerly. 'Count me in. Is it Indian, Thai or Chinese?'

'Chinese, probably.'

'Well, you can order anything for me, I'm not fussy. Just get plenty of it.'

****

At 6.00 p.m. Gary arrived home with the brochure from the wedding venue having decided that it was a brilliant choice for the wedding. He had secured the date of Saturday, 28 May 2022, due to a cancellation. Eva was in the kitchen, drinking coffee, and just finishing an hour of school work before they ordered the takeaway. Alfie was in his room, presumably playing on his computer, but was in a mood as he had hoped for a sleepover at one of his friends but everyone seemed to be busy.

Gary walked up to Eva and kissed her lightly on the cheek. 'Hi, darling, how are you?'

She smiled at him, noting that he seemed particularly pleased with himself. 'I'm ok. You look like the cat who got the cream, what's up?'

His facial expression went from smiling to secretive as he said, 'right. Close your eyes and hold out your hands.'

Eva tentatively closed her eyes, nervous about what was going to happen, and she didn't particularly like surprises. She put her hands out in front of her as instructed, palms upwards. 'I hope I'm going to like this.'

Gary placed the glossy wedding brochure in her hand. 'I guarantee you will. Ok, open your eyes.'

She took hold of the brochure and slowly opened her eyes. The photograph on the front of the brochure of a bride and groom, in front of a beautiful manor house, was an unexpected, and disconcerting, sight. 'Oh, this is, er, nice, what have you done?'

Gary leaned forward to hold her hand as she stared at the brochure. 'This, my lovely fiancée, is where we will be having our wedding on Saturday, 28th May next year, at the start of the May bank holiday week, so we can get married at the earliest opportunity, as I wanted.'

Eva sighed softly, not really knowing what to say, as she seriously wanted to delay booking the wedding for as long as possible. She hoped to book something in 2023 and be able to get back any deposit paid when the inevitable cancellation happened. Now he had booked a very close date, presumably paid a deposit, and cancellation at any time could involve the loss of money.

Gary waited as she sat staring ahead not looking at the brochure or commenting on his announcement. He was now getting angry. 'Bloody say something then as I've just shelled out five hundred quid to secure this place.'

Eva came out of her trance. 'Oh, yes, sorry Gary. I'm sure it's lovely. How did we get that date at such short notice? I thought all venues would be fully booked until 2023 due to couples having to re-arrange weddings due to lockdowns.'

'We were particularly lucky as they've just had a recent cancellation. The stars are truly aligned for us to have a special day.'

More like the forces of darkness, Eva thought, as she viewed the possibility of exchanging sacred wedding vows with this man who she disliked and feared. 'I still think it's all a bit too quick as there will be a lot to arrange. Couldn't we re-arrange to the following year?'

Gary now sat in the chair adjacent to her, at the dining table, and turned her to face him. 'I'm getting the impression that you don't want to marry me, is that right?'

Scared now that he will get angry if she doesn't show some enthusiasm for an early wedding, Eva smiled at him, trying to fake a pleasure she did not feel. 'I do, Gary, I want nothing more. You are right, a wedding next May will be lovely and thank you for booking it.'

He now leaned his body towards her, his strong thighs pressing against hers as he moved forwards for a kiss. 'I want us to be husband and wife as soon as possible. Together till death us do part.'

Eva shuddered slightly at this. 'I hope we are very old and wrinkly when that finally happens.'

Gary laughed. 'You'll always be young and beautiful in my memory, whenever death decides to come calling.' He kissed her again, more slowly, claiming her mouth with his own. 'I'd suggest we go upstairs now and practice for our wedding night but sadly we can't as I've invited Simon to join us for a takeaway. We'd better look at ordering as he'll be here at eight and it's always busy on a Saturday night.'

Eva's heart sank further. Firstly, she had been given the date of her impending wedding, a wedding she did not want, and would not go through with. Secondly, for the first time, she would have to endure an evening with Gary and his mate, Simon, the creepy man who had tried to grope her breast a few weeks ago. This was turning into a really bad day.

By 8.15 p.m. a Chinese meal of spare ribs, prawn toast, vegetables in satay sauce, sweet and sour chicken, beef in black bean sauce, crispy chilli king prawn and fried rice had been delivered. Eva, Gary and Alfie were seated at the kitchen table where Simon had joined them. Foil containers were passed around and everyone filled their plate. Simon licked his fingers a lot whilst sharing the serving spoons so Eva quietly got some more out of the drawer to serve her food. She placed hand gel on the table, reminding Alfie to sanitise his hands, as Covid had not gone away. Simon seemed to spend a lot of time watching her which made her feel uncomfortable and diminish her appetite. 'Good news about the wedding venue, Eva. I think you'll make a beautiful bride with your lovely brown hair, blue eyes and, hopefully, in a dress that shows off lots of cleavage.' He dug his teeth into a spare rib and chewed enthusiastically which made Eva's stomach twist.

Alfie paused in putting a forkful of sweet and sour chicken in his mouth. 'What's cleavage?'

Eva wished that she could commit murder by stabbing Simon with her knife. Perhaps if Andy investigated the murder, he would understand that this was a spontaneous crime to rid herself of this creepy, lecherous slimeball, and he could help her pass it off as a tragic accident. Eva shook her head to clear her thoughts and focus on Alfie's question. 'Cleavage is the area between a woman's breasts.'

Simon pointed the spare rib he was eating in Alfie's direction. 'Yes, it is. Let me tell you, young man, that when you are older and exploring the cleavage of a girlfriend with your hands, you will be on your way to finding heaven in terms of their rounded, plump breasts.'

Eva choked, the taste of the Chinese food souring her mouth. 'Oh my god, can you shut up, he's only twelve-years-old. Gary tell him.'

Gary laughed, which annoyed Eva, but he did glare at Simon. 'Put a sock in it, mate. No one wants to hear your smutty thoughts.'

Simon spooned fried rice and black bean beef on to his plate and glanced at Eva. 'Sorry, I shouldn't have said that, he is only a kid. Anyway, how's it feel to be the next Mrs Anderson. There's been a few of them already but you are by a thousand miles the best yet. If you get bored with Gary, I will gladly marry you in a heartbeat. Actually, in terms of wives, you should have been number four but we don't talk about the one that got away.'

Eva stopped eating, partly due to lack of appetite but mainly due to this latest information on another woman in Gary's life. 'Gary, what does he mean, the one that got away?'

Gary was now completely angry with Simon. 'Flipping shut the fuck up, will you. There's nothing to tell.'

Simon now helped himself to another spare rib with his greasy fingers and ignored Gary's laser stare of concentrated rage. 'Oh, I don't know. There's something to tell. Gianna, another older woman for the younger Gary who he was planning to marry in 2016. She was another one who was not going to win any beauty contests. She fitted Gary's type, older than him, not sought after by other men, so plain, and easily made to comply with what Gary wanted.'

Gary had stopped eating his food and threw down his fork which clattered on the plate. 'Shut up, Simon. I'm warning you now.'

Alfie stopped eating and stared nervously at Gary who looked about to spring over the table and pummel his friend.

Simon scooped the remaining crispy chilli king prawn out of its container and on to his plate. 'The wedding never went ahead. Gary blew it just beforehand with one of his outbursts of temper and Gianna left her nursing job, sold up, and went to live abroad. Never heard from her again, have you Gary?'

CHAPTER FORTY NINE

November 2021

As Eva parked on her driveway, on a Friday evening two-thirds of the way through November, it was overcast with a chill in the air, as autumn slipped into winter. She shivered in her short jacket, and thin dress, and decided that it was probably time for the black tights that kept out the winter chill. She was not looking forward to the weekend ahead, as Gary was talking about cosy nights in, cuddling on the sofa and discussing the wedding preparations. She used to believe that men were not keen on planning weddings and left all the arrangements to the bride-to-be. How wrong could she be. Gary was obsessed with being involved, like an eager groom in a television programme called 'Don't Tell the Bride'.

Luckily, tonight she had a brief reprieve from wedding matters as Gary was going on a stag night for one of the men who worked in his Stratford dealership. At least she would have a few hours to herself to watch what she wanted on tv.

She went to the boot of her car to get out her laptop and some school papers and was closing the boot as Andy's car pulled up on his drive. They had not spoken since they had that almost falling out regarding her engagement to Gary. She was now a bit shy of speaking to him. Still, she was determined not to let her false engagement come between her and Andy and she hoped they would be friends long after she had cleared Gary out of her life. She walked over to Andy's car as he got out. 'Hi, how are you? Is Alfie still ok to come over to yours this evening for Hannah's birthday party?'

Andy smiled fondly at her as he went to the boot of his car. 'Yes, of course, he's definitely invited. At the last count there were six girls and four boys, including Alfie and Jai, and I've just been shopping for assorted snacks, a cake, serviettes, and all that. I'm going to order pizzas at about eight o'clock when they all get here. They are planning to do some karaoke with the lyrics on YouTube, so that should be fun. I suspect they'll all sound like a room full of cats being strangled. I put up some balloons and banners last night and she had those to greet her this morning. I was hoping her mother could come around to help but she's got a shift at the hospital. This single parent thing is not a lot of fun. Want to come over later and join me for a badly needed glass of wine? It also looks better if there's a woman present. It's not just me and a load of kids, plus, you are a teacher so the parents will know you are kosher.'

Eva hesitated. She would love to come and support Andy and spend time with him. But Gary would certainly not be happy if he found out. 'I'd love to come over and help. Gary is out on a stag night and won't be around.'

Andy opened the boot of his car and took out a number of shopping bags. 'Not one item in here is what I would refer to as healthy eating. I'm doing my best to make my daughter and her friends lose their teeth, put on weight and get spots.'

Eva smiled as she took in the troubled look on his face. 'Don't worry, they tend to grow up fine, despite all the bad food they consume. Anyway, Alfie is definitely looking forward to it. He has spoken about nothing else all week. I think my son has a bit of a crush on your daughter.'

Andy winced. 'No offence to your son. I would prefer it if no males found her attractive and she didn't start dating until she was at least thirty-five.'

'That's what all fathers of daughters say. My dad didn't want me to wear makeup until I was eighteen.'

'And how old were you when you started to wear it?'

About eleven.'

'See, we dads have no chance of protecting them. Come around for about 7.30 p.m. if you want and you can have some pizza.'

'That would be great, see you then.'

Gary came in about 6.00 pm and quickly showered and changed for his night out of a meal and drinking in a local restaurant. She didn't tell him she would be going over to Andy's as it would cause an argument and she waited till he had left before she got ready. She dressed in skinny black jeans and olive green, V-necked blouse which fitted at her waist and gave a curve to her figure. She applied fresh makeup and gently waved her hair.

Alfie was initially annoyed that she was attending but she promised she was only there to keep Andy company and not to spy on him. They both went over at 7.30 p.m. and Andy let them in, and, as the teenagers were due to congregate in the lounge, Andy and Eva were consigned to the kitchen/dining area. Alfie was the first to arrive and he shyly handed the present that they had bought for Hannah. It was a pretty cobalt blue beaded bracelet with silver beads inscribed with black letters that spelt 'Hannah'. She was delighted when she saw it, declared it was beautiful, and put it on straightaway. Alfie was rewarded with a small peck on the cheek which turned his face from white to red instantly. Eva remained with Andy to welcome the guests. He introduced her as his neighbour, Alfie's mum, and a school teacher. The five girls, included Phoebe, and they were all lightly made-up, dressed in trendy clothes, T-shirts with jeans or miniskirts. Hannah had on a short denim skirt, cream T, and white trainers and the bracelet was on her wrist next to a silver chain.

The two other boys that Andy did not know arrived, a Lucas and an Oscar. They were viewed with deep suspicion by Andy as they entered the hallway and said goodbye to their parent. As Andy moved nearer to them, Eva could see that he was on verge of wanting to frisk them for drugs and alcohol, before giving them a death stare should they decide to step out of line. Eva quickly intervened and ushered the boys into the lounge, as they pressed against the wall of the hallway, to get away from Andy's looming presence. The boys entered the lounge and the door closed. Eva laughed as Andy scowled, menacingly. 'You are going to have to relax a bit and trust your daughter or she will not forgive you if you intimidate all her male friends.'

'Yes, you are right but I don't like the look of that Lucas, too good-looking and full of himself. The type of boy all girls like. And he looks older than thirteen to me.' I should have put a camera in the room to see what they get up to. There are too many adolescent hormones around for my liking.'

'At least she's here and not at someone else's house so you can keep an eye on what they're doing. Let's go and order the pizzas and you can give your guest, me, some wine. I'm going to need it if I have to look at your angry face all night.'

Andy led the way into the kitchen and went to the fridge for the bottle of Pinot Grigio. Eva picked up the leaflet with the pizza selection on. 'If you like, I'll go and find out what pizzas they want. I don't want you in there putting a damper on the fun. You look like you've been stung by an angry wasp.'

'Ok, good idea. I know I might not be that composed if that Lucas is anywhere near my daughter. I know his type.'

Eva went in to find out the pizza order and quickly returned so that Andy phoned through for the food to be delivered. Andy took two glasses out of the cupboard and opened the bottle of wine. He poured it into the glasses and indicated that Eva should take a seat on one, of two, fold-up garden chairs. 'Sorry about the seating but I thought that these might be a bit cosier than the dining chairs. If we are forced to sit out here then we need to be comfortable.' They sat down, close to each other, and drank the wine.

Eva asked, 'what type of boy do you think that Lucas is?'

'An opportunist type. Confident that he can attract girls and push things along, if you know what I mean.'

Eva giggled. 'Is that because you were like him at that age?'

He glanced at Eva but avoided eye contact. 'No, not really, as I had been brought up to respect girls but I suppose all boys do like to test the boundaries if we get the chance. We are all immature at that age, but we are driven a lot by our hormones and urges, which is what worries me.'

A little later, pizzas, garlic breads, BBQ chicken wings and cheesy bites had been delivered, along with bottles of diet coke, lemonade and bottled water. Loud laughter and terrible singing could be heard coming from the lounge as they attempted the karaoke.

Andy and Eva were now sharing bottle number two of white wine. Andy sipped at the drink, feeling more relaxed than earlier in the evening. 'This wine is definitely helping to dull the torture of children's parties and bad singing. I must not have too much more or the parents will think I'm drunk in charge of their offspring. You can drink it though as you are off duty from your childcare responsibilities.'

'Actually, it is really nice to just sit and chill out. It's getting pretty stressful with Gary going on about arrangements for this wedding. We now have a date of Saturday 28 May 2022 and obviously I want you and Hannah to come.'

Andy tried to pretend to smile at this but really could not force his face to show any pleasure at this news. 'We will be pleased to attend and I will have to ensure that I am not working that weekend. But, Eva, I know that this upsets you but I have made it clear that I think you are making a massive mistake.'

Andy was now saying this based on the information he had gathered from Cynthia Quall and how despicably Gary had treated her daughter, Claire. The man had been cruel and ruthless, using a vulnerable girl to achieve his aims of dipping his sticky fingers into a pot of gold, the Quall's wealth. He would not share this information with Eva at the moment as he intended to gather further evidence of Gary Anderson's character and motives in acquiring wives. It had been arranged by Cynthia Quall that he would meet the mother of Lisa Jefferies next week. To hear what she had to say about the man she suspected of harming her daughter. All this was going to be a major shock for Eva when she finds out. The problem was all this information increased his anxiety about Eva's safety and his number one goal was to get this man out of her life as soon as possible.

At eleven, the parents had collected their sons and daughters, leaving Phoebe to spend the night with Hannah, and Alfie and Jai to got to Eva's house. Eva now realised that she had drunk too much of the second bottle of wine and was feeling decidedly squiffy. 'Time for me to go I think,' she said to Andy, getting out of the garden chair and then wobbling slightly as she stood upright.

Andy watched her inebriated state and offered to give her a helping hand. 'I think I've plied you with too much wine. I will now escort you back to your front door.'

Eva smiled at him in a bemused way. 'Yes, standing up was not a good idea and I do admit to feeling a little drunk.' At that moment Alfie and Jai wandered in the kitchen and Alfie asked, 'mum, can Jai and I go back to ours now?'

Eva nodded at him and clung on to the kitchen worktop to steady herself. 'Yes, time to go after Hannah's amazing party. Say a big thank you to Andy and Hannah.' She then swayed slightly, grinned inanely, and tried to compose herself.

Alfie frowned and looked at his mother. 'Are you drunk? Honestly, you adults set a really bad example to us kids.'

Eva shook her head vigorously. 'No way am I drunk, just a little merry. Here's the key and I'll be over shortly.' She handed Alfie the door keys and the two boys scooted off to Alfie's home.

Andy had watched this with much amusement. 'Eva, I think Alfie is right and you are definitely drunk and I do feel responsible for this. Come on, let's get you home.'

Eva felt that her head was all muzzy and she could not think clearly. As Andy approached her, she felt his hands on her shoulders as he guided her out of the kitchen, out of the hallway, and out of the front door. For every step he took forward, she stumbled along, not very steady on her feet. As he realised that she was not mobile, he wrapped his arm firmly around her waist, and he steered her towards her home. She was walked, and part carried, as her feet were not really touching the ground. At one point, just short of her front door, she halted, causing Andy to pause. She stared up at him. 'I just want to say, Andy, that you are the best friend anyone can have and thank you for looking out for me.'

Andy stared down at her, overwhelmed by the closeness of her, and an urge to hold her in his arms. 'It's my pleasure. I care for you very much as a friend as well.'

A black cab pulled up and Gary emerged, and despite attending a stag do, he seemed reasonably sober. He approached Eva, still being supported by Andy, and he looked less than pleased. 'What's going on here Eva? Why do you look like you've been drinking? Why is he holding you upright?'

Eva waved at Gary, in a friendly manner. 'Hi, Gary. I helped Andy at Hannah's birthday party and have had too many wines.'

Gary was now glowering at Eva and Andy. Eva as she had been out without his knowledge, and at Andy, as he was holding onto his fiancée with a very supportive arm around her waist. 'Ok, time to go inside.' He marched up to Eva and grabbed her upper arm to take her away from Andy. 'I'm not happy about all this and you acting like a drunken slut.'

Eva flinched as Gary's fingers dug into her arm. He started to drag her forward, the pain of his tight grip showing on her face.

Andy held onto her, not wanting her to be manhandled in this way. Anger flared in him as fiery as a match setting fire to petrol. He glared at Gary and wanted to enfold Eva into the security of his embrace. The tone of his voice was harsh and loud as he addressed Gary. 'Don't you speak to her like that. She has had a few glasses of wine, that's all, for which I take full responsibility.'

Eva now shivered at the ferocity of Andy's attack on Gary. Gary continued to tug on her arm but Andy was still holding her steadfastly around her waist. 'Back off, cop, she's my fiancée and coming home with me.'

Andy now moved nearer to Gary, his height and physique squaring up to him. 'She will go with you when you release your grip on her arm or I will make you let go of her.'

Gary let go of Eva, and moved into Andy's personal space, the two men seconds away from a physical altercation.

The tension and shock of all this had helped Eva to sober up. 'Please stop, don't fight. Andy, thanks for seeing me back here but I'm ok now. Gary, let's just go inside.' She walked unsteadily away from them, up to her front door, opened it and went into the house. Her head felt muzzy and she needed to lie down but soon she would have think about what happened between the two men. As Andy had now declared open hostility towards Gary, this would not go well for her. She could not deny that her feelings for Andy intensified every time they were together. It was all too muddling but she could not think about it at the moment.

Gary quickly followed her into the house. She made her way into the lounge and flopped on the sofa. Her feelings of drunkenness now returned and she was just at the stage before the room started to spin and nausea set in. Gary sat next to her, and leaned on her, as she lay flat out, looking up at the ceiling. 'I tell you what. One day soon I am going to smash my fist in his face, if he tells me what to do again.'

Eva did not have the strength to argue with this as she needed to concentrate on quelling the queasiness in her stomach. 'Let it go, Gary. I don't think you'll find it that easy to physically win over Andy. He's pretty strong.'

Gary's snarling features loomed over her. 'Oh, you think so, do you, but we'll see. I suggest that you go to bed and we'll talk about this tomorrow. I'm not happy that you went over to his house as soon as my back was turned. I said at our engagement you would have less to do with the cop from now on. We have an appointment with a florist in Stratford tomorrow at 10.30 a.m. and you need to be sober and sensible for that.'

Eva slowly sat upright on the sofa as she took in this news. 'Oh no, why didn't you tell me about this before?'

'I only booked it yesterday and forgot to tell you till now. Not a problem, is it, as it means our wedding plans are well on track.'

'No, it's not a problem though everything seems to be rushing ahead pretty fast.'

His hand began to caress her thigh. 'Our plans need to be on track as the wedding is only a few months away and I can't wait for us to be married.' His hand now started to move upwards and knowing what this would inevitably lead to, Eva started to move off the sofa to go upstairs. She now regretted that she had drunk so much wine and hoped that when she lay down in bed, she would feel less nauseous. An early start to a Saturday morning was the last thing she wanted. It had been great spending time with Andy, but she would pay for it tomorrow, both in terms of a hangover and Gary's 'talk.' A sense of dread gripped her stomach and this was not caused by too much Pinot Grigio.

CHAPTER FIFTY

Eva struggled out of bed at 8.30 a.m. with a headache, a sour taste in her mouth from the wine, and a continued queasiness in her stomach. She showered to help wake herself up, straightened her hair and applied makeup so that outwardly she would look human, even if inside she felt like death warmed up. She tried to eat a slice of toast but it stuck in her throat and she could not swallow. A coffee and two paracetamols were just about staying put in her churning stomach. Gary radiated annoyance as he looked at her, commenting that it was lucky he only had three lagers at last night's stag do, or neither one of them would have been able to drive.

The appointment with the florist had not gone too well. Eva had still not decided on the colour of the bridesmaid's dresses which would then dictate the colour scheme of the flowers and wedding venue decor. Gary was all smiles and politeness as the florist talked through, and showed them photos, of previous floral arrangements. His anger flared with Eva when the florist left the room to make some coffees. 'Can't you just make a fucking decision on the colour for the bridesmaids. We will be having this wedding in 2025, if you keep dithering over every detail.'

With the soreness in her head, and sickness in her stomach, it was not the best time to be harangued about wedding decisions but she felt obliged to say that she would opt for a mid-blue for the bridesmaids so that he would get off her case. With guidance from the florist, the bouquets and wedding venue décor flowers were chosen; white and pale peach roses, white peonies, China-blue hyacinths and white freesias. Eva was relieved to get out of the small back room of the shop. The overwhelming smell of greenery, which normally she'd love, just made her imagine what experiencing hay fever for the first time must be like. As they drove home in silence, Eva was acutely aware that Gary was extremely angry with her, and she now dreaded going back to the house.

Back home, she got out of the car and went indoors, ready to take another paracetamol, eat some toast and then sit quietly watching television for a few hours. Nothing too taxing. She went into the kitchen, filled the kettle, and then got out some bread to put in the toaster. As Gary came into the kitchen, she asked him, 'do you want some toast for lunch? I think it will help with my hangover and I do now feel a bit hungrier?' Alfie was over at Jai's so she did not have to think about preparing a more substantial lunch for him.

'Yeah, ok, that will do.' Gary sat at the kitchen island as she placed four slices of wholemeal bread in the toaster. She then took butter out of the fridge, and honey, Marmite and raspberry jam out of the cupboard.

'Do you want tea or coffee?'

'Tea.'

'Please,' Eva reminded him as she put two plates and two knives on the worktop.

'Don't you fucking lecture me on manners. You were not the best example of a bride-to-be today, hungover from last night, and trying to avoid making any kind of decision on what floral displays we wanted. It was bloody embarrassing.'

'Well, you should've have told me about the appointment and not spring it on me at the last minute.'

'Would that have stopped you going next door and getting wasted, then?'

'I don't think I was wasted, just a bit tipsy, that's all.'

'You wouldn't have been if you had not gone over there in the first place. I've told you to keep away from the cop but you don't seem to listen. Over there the first chance you get when I am out.'

'That's not true. It was a spur of the moment thing as Andy said he'd like a woman present at the party, to be there with him, and the children. Plus, the fact that I am a teacher helped.'

Gary laughed. 'A great example of the teaching profession, you were. Getting drunk and having to be assisted home. I hope the parents didn't see you.'

The toast popped up in the toaster and Eva put two slices on the two plates. She made two mugs of tea and gave one to Gary. She plastered her toast with butter, before adding the honey, and then bit into the sweet, buttery toast.

They ate their toast, finished the tea and Eva got up to place the dirty plates, knives and mugs in the dishwasher. 'I think I'm going to chill out and watch tv for a bit. I still don't feel like doing much at the moment.'

Eva walked into the lounge and Gary followed, sitting next to her on the sofa. He turned her to look at him, an unreadable expression on his face. 'I think I need to remind you that I don't want you going to the cop's house at any time and especially not to get drunk. I'm not keen on drunkenness in women and particularly not my fiancée. Ok?'

Feeling peeved at being berated like this, Eva sighed loudly. 'For goodness sake, it's not as if I make a habit of it. It was one time only, in all the time I've known you. No big deal.'

His face was now close to hers, and his deep brown eyes were boring into hers, anger present in their bottomless depths. 'I also need to remind you that we are getting married but you do not seem to have any enthusiasm for our wedding plans. I keep getting the impression that you would rather delay it. It is not being delayed. It is in May and I expect you to take more interest in the arrangements. Ok?'

Eva decided that this was no longer the time for disagreeing. She felt this moment was finely balanced and she was not sure what he was thinking, or going to do. A fear fluttered in her stomach like the flapping of dozens of butterfly wings. 'Ok, yes, I will try to be more interested in the wedding arrangements. I do have an appointment at a bridal shop next Saturday, to try on some dresses. Mum and Tania are coming along too.'

He took hold of her face and she thought he was about to kiss her. Then, his hand slipped to her neck where he grasped her throat in a hard grip. 'This is a warning, Eva, to do as you are instructed and keep away from the plod. It is a warning to up your game in terms of the wedding which is beginning to become expensive as that was another four-hundred-pound deposit today.' His grip tightened, and he watched her face, as fear filled her lovely blue eyes. As the pressure mounted, she felt that she could not get oxygen into her lungs, and she tried to draw in air, in short, shallow gulps. He suddenly let go, and she sucked in lungful's of air, and her breathing started to steady, but she felt light-headed and nauseous, as if experiencing a panic attack. Suddenly, she knew what it felt like to be at the door of death as pain and terror flooded her body. She jumped off the sofa, to get away from him. At this moment, her strongest desire was to rush out the front door, barefoot with no jacket, to put as much distance between herself and her tormentor. To run and never stop. But Alfie would be home shortly and, for now, there was no escape. Eva rushed towards the door to get away from Gary presence and find sanctuary in her bedroom.

Lying on the bed with the curtains drawn, Eva could still feel the tightness in her throat where his hand had clenched her. She felt alone, completely trapped, in a relationship she could not escape from, hurtling towards a wedding she did not want. A wedding, and a marriage, that would make her even more involved and tied to a man who was physically threatening and abusive. She knew that telling Gary the relationship was over, and that she did not want to get married, was not going to be easy. It was likely to open herself up to some sort of attack or retribution. Ideally, she needed someone to help her but who to ask? Her father was a kind man but not physically or mentally capable of confronting Gary. Her brother, whom she loved, was a principled man in terms of his views on animal welfare, and saving the planet, an ideological activist, but he would be no match for Gary in a physical altercation. Andy would be her best bet, as he was a police officer, trained in defence techniques and physically strong to hold his own against a raging Gary. She could not ask him to get involved in her battle. Hot, scolding tears coursed down Eva's face as her body reacted to the violence of this latest attack and her despair at the hopelessness of her current predicament. The problem now was how, and when, to tell Gary that the relationship was over without the very real risk of being further physically harmed, or dare she think it, killed.

CHAPTER FIFTY ONE

Wednesday early evening, and Andy was seated at a table in a coffee shop, at a service station on the M40, waiting for the arrival of Nina Jefferies, mother of Lisa, the young woman who had disappeared a number of years ago. He sipped at his coffee, typical service station brew, served lukewarm and lacking any taste. As he waited, he reflected on Gary Anderson's behaviour towards Eva on Friday night and this did nothing for his temper. The way he had grabbed at her arm and called her that vile name. It had riled him so much that he could not get it out of his head all the rest of the weekend. He had witnessed now, first hand, that Gary was physically aggressive towards her and verbally abusive. It had taken all his willpower to let her continue into that house with that man when his instinct was to stop her going with him. He had not seen her since Friday and was hoping she was ok. Andy had been alarmed by the degree of anger Gary had shown to Eva and he was scared that he would take his anger out on her. Andy had hoped to see Alfie to ask if Eva was ok.

It was great to spend those few hours with Eva on Friday, when they had laughed and joked together, and she seemed completely at ease in his company. He chided himself for giving her too much wine which had made her tipsy and a target for Gary's tirade. He definitely would blame himself if she was harmed. One thing Andy now had to admit to himself was that he cared deeply about Eva and it was cutting him up that she was in a relationship with an abusive man. A man who Andy initially considered secretive, controlling and possibly prone to violence. A man who was now being exposed as a devious, money-hungry, and potentially extremely dangerous in terms of being suspected of committing murder. If this were the case, Eva was in a dire situation of which she may not easily extricate herself.

His phone pinged, a text from Nina Jefferies to say that she was in the area of the coffee shop. She was wearing a bright blue coat and had brought with her someone who had been a friend of Lisa's when she worked at the car dealership. Andy texted back his location and waited till he spotted an older woman, in a blue coat, with a man, walking close to his table. Andy introduced himself to Mrs Jefferies and was introduced to Julian Anderton, who had worked at the car dealership with Lisa. It was at the time when Gary Dawson was the manager and the business was owned by Roger Quall.

Andy offered to buy tea or coffees and was soon back carrying a tray with three coffees. 'Thanks for coming, and for travelling here to meet me, it has saved me a bit of time on the journey.' As with Mrs Quall, Andy fully explained that he was not meeting her in his professional capacity as a police officer but he was here as a private citizen to find out about a man called Gary Anderson, who she would know as Gary Dawson. He advised that he had concerns about Gary Anderson, in terms of his close friend, and neighbour, who had recently got engaged to this man, and who was rushing her into marriage. Andy confirmed that after his meeting with Mrs Quall, and the way that Anderson had ruthlessly exploited her daughter, Claire, allegedly to get his hands on the Quall money, his concerns for his friend were now amplified. 'Mrs Jefferies, I would be very grateful if you could explain what you consider to be Gary Andersons, Dawsons, involvement in the disappearance of your daughter.'

Mrs Jefferies was a good-looking woman in her late sixties with dark brown hair and striking violet eyes. If Lisa had inherited her mother's looks, Andy thought she would have been a beautiful young woman. 'Mr Leyton, I know you are police officer, so you investigate and solve crimes based on factual evidence. I have no factual evidence to offer to support my theory. But as time has gone by, I am more and more convinced that Gary Dawson was complicit in my Lisa's disappearance.'

'Can you tell me what happened the last time you saw Lisa?'

'Yes, it was a week night and she said she was going out to meet a friend. This happened at least a couple of times a week. She would go out in her car, meet someone for a couple of hours, and then come home. It always seemed odd to me as she was twenty-three years old and could have stayed over at a boyfriend's place if she wanted. Either he didn't have a place of his own, and lived with his mum, or there was another reason he could only stay out a short time. Lisa never slept over and I guessed that the reason was that he was married or lived with a girlfriend.'

'Did you ask Lisa about this man?'

'Yes, and she'd fob me off that it was none of my business. Then at other times she would describe someone she was seeing but it was all a smoke screen to throw me off the scent.'

'I understand that you told Mrs Quall that you suspected that this man was Gary Dawson, Lisa's friend's husband?'

'Yes, I did and I think this was the reason she was so cagey. It's not great to admit to your mother that you are sleeping with your best friend's husband and I would have been annoyed with her. She was brought up to be better than that.'

'Why do you think it was him?'

'Lisa got a job at the company, RQ Screws and Bolts. It was because she was Claire's best friend and Claire recommended her, you know the days when nepotism was allowed. Don't get me wrong, Lisa was a bright girl and earned her place there. When Gary Dawson joined the company, Lisa and Claire were very taken with him. I strongly got the impression that he really fancied our Lisa. She was a very beautiful girl.'

Julian Anderton had been very quiet up till this point. 'Yes, she was, and nearly all the men at the factory and the dealership fancied her, including me. I worked in the accounts office when Dawson arrived, and he was very sure of himself, very confident with women. I believe that he dated Lisa but then for reasons no one could fathom, he turned his attentions to Claire Quall.'

Nina Jefferies agreed. 'Yes, he started to see Claire, and quite quickly they were married. My Lisa was chief bridesmaid at the wedding and lovely she looked too. I went along for the evening do and Gary was overdoing his bridegroom duties by paying too much attention to the chief bridesmaid, my daughter, whilst his bride sat looking gloomy with her mum and dad.'

Andy recalled Mrs Quall's observation that the bridegroom and the chief bridesmaid had gone outside together for a while, to presumably hookup together. 'Do you believe that Gary was seeing Lisa after his marriage to Claire?'

'I do, as Lisa would say that the marriage wasn't working. Gary treated Claire coldly, humiliated her and possibly at times physically attacked her. Claire was definitely not happy. As I said earlier, I do believe that Lisa was seeing a married man and that man was Gary Dawson.'

Andy watched as Nina Jefferies struggled with the implications of this. A caring parent will not want their daughter to get hurt and affairs with married men did not often end well for the mistress. She would not like to think of her daughter's actions hurting her long-term school friend. 'Yes, this was a difficult situation for all involved but what makes you think Dawson was involved in Lisa's disappearance?'

Mrs Jefferies now straightened in her seat and placed down her coffee cup on its saucer. 'I think we need to stop using the term disappearance. This is a term the police keep using but there is no way that my daughter would disappear for sixteen years and leave me with this frantic worry for all that time. Lisa may have done some things I'm not proud of, but at heart she was a thoughtful girl, and she would not have caused me this pain. The police have hinted that she took off with her married lover and they do not want to be found. I do not buy this argument. No, Mr Leyton, my daughter has not disappeared, she has not eloped, thus the only explanation is that she is unable to make contact because she is dead. That she has been murdered and her body dumped.' She searched in her handbag for a clean tissue to dab her eyes. Andy felt complete sorrow for these two women, Cynthia Quall and Nina Jefferies, with two daughters whose lives had been ruined by having Gary Dawson in their lives.

Andy waited for Mrs Jefferies to compose herself after giving way to tears. 'I am so sorry to be bringing all this up again for you. I appreciate how painful it must be for you to talk to me. What happened on the last evening that you saw Lisa?'

'Nothing unusual. Lisa said she was going out for a few hours and I guessed it was to meet the married man, Gary. I was getting exasperated with this relationship as it did not seem to be getting her anywhere and there was no evidence he was going to leave Claire. By all accounts, he was enjoying the rewards of working for Roger Quall, particularly when Quall bought the car dealership and put him in charge. So, on the last night I saw her she went out as usual, on a fool's errand as I considered it, to date a married man. The only good thing that had happened just before was that she had gone on a date with another man, a proper date to a restaurant, with what seemed a suitable man who worked at the dealership. After this date she had been happy, saying that he was a quiet sort of guy, with a good job, buying his own house and was definitely single. I found out later that she had gone out with Julian.

Julian now smiled, presumably remembering his short time with Lisa. 'Yes, we had a great evening together. We had a lovely meal and then she came back to my place, which I was renovating with the help of my father, for a coffee and nothing more. I had secretly been attracted to Lisa for a long time but so were a lot of single men at work and I was really pleased when she agreed to go out with me. There was speculation at the dealership that she was seeing someone as men asked her out and she would normally refuse. It was my lucky day when she said yes. I believe our first date had been a success and we were planning to meet up again.'

Mrs Jefferies glanced at Julian in a kindly way. 'I wish that she had come to her senses and got rid of the married man after your first date. She may have been here today.'

Andy still needed to ask the question at the crux of all this. 'Can I assume from all that you are saying is that you think Gary Dawson is responsible for Lisa's disappearance, and possibly murder?'

Nina Jefferies nodded. 'My theory is that Lisa saw Dawson after her date with Julian. She may have happily told him how well it went and how they were due to meet again. I suspect it was her way to make him jealous, to spur him on to leave Claire and make a permanent commitment to her. She was always a game player with men, using strategies such as flirting, and making them jealous, to get her way. She could play dangerous games, and I think she did that with Dawson, and it ended badly.'

Julian added, 'I worked with him for a few years both at the factory, then at the car dealership. I will be honest and say that I detested the man from the first moment I met him. He was over-confident, selfish, arrogant and had little empathy for others. As a boss he was only interested in making a profit and looking good to Roger Quall. Under performing staff were ruthlessly got rid of and he was very fond of shouting and humiliating staff. He was overly friendly with female employees and attractive customers he fancied. If he ever felt undermined by someone, then God help them, as he could not be seen to lose face. One young sales assistant unwisely got involved with him, even while he was married to Claire. She made the mistake of trying to use this liaison to her advantage, by saying to anyone who would listen, that he had promised a promotion the next time one came up. When Dawson found out, she was dismissed immediately. Rumours persisted for a while that he had gone around to her flat and beaten her up but she never pressed charges with the police. Dawson was not a man to cross.'

Andy blanched at hearing further alleged evidence of Gary's violent side. 'On the evening you last saw Lisa, you believe she went to meet Gary Dawson?'

Mrs Jefferies responded. 'Yes, I do. I think she tried the game of making him jealous about her date with Julian. I believe he got angry, lashed out at her, and she died by his hands. I have told the police all this but they have not found a shred of evidence to convict Gary Dawson. There was DNA evidence of her being in his car, hair and saliva, but he had feasible explanations for this. There was evidence of semen but the dirty slimeball explained this by stating he slept with prostitutes. Dawson had an alibi for the night that Lisa went out, that he was at the flat of his friend, Simon. Claire confirmed that Gary had got into bed at his usual time, about eleven p.m. but I am not convinced by this. Claire was frightened of Gary, according to Lisa, and would probably say what he told her to say, as she was very timid and would not dare contradict a man like him. I cannot truly say what went on but I believe put simply, Lisa met Gary, she angered him, and he killed her and disposed of her body. But I have no actual evidence to back this up. Sixteen years on, I still have no answers but I know my Lisa is not alive or she would have contacted me.' She again started to cry softly.

Julian added. 'All the men at the factory and dealership were interviewed by the police at the time, including myself. I think I would have been chief suspect if I didn't have a solid alibi of being out with two friends in a pub for a few hours and then I went back to my parent's house to sleep. Roger Quall was a prime suspect as it was believed that he had had a fling with Lisa but again he was at home that evening with his wife. Another person of interest was one of the young garage mechanics, Brad, but luckily, he had a strong alibi for the night in question. Looking back, Gary did try to point the finger at Brad, by undermining his alibi and over stating the relationship he had with Lisa, which amounted to one or two dates, no more. Crucially though, the one alibi in all this I would not believe, is Dawson's of being with Simon Wagstaff. Those two were really close friends, in a sort of unhealthy way, in that each always had the others back. You never criticised Gary in front of Simon, or vice versa, in fact the two of them were quite scary.'

'You think that Simon would lie to protect Gary and give him an alibi for that night?' Andy asked.

'Most definitely.'

'Even up to the point of protecting Gary Dawson, if he knew he had committed murder?'

'Certainly,' Julian confirmed. 'Nobody at the factory or dealership liked being around Simon. He was an oddball, and a loner, only there due to his friendship with Gary Dawson. Anyway, whatever happened on that night, Lisa has never been seen or heard of again.'

Andy sighed softly. Another story of loss and pain. The disappearance of a young woman and a gigantic hole left in the lives of those that loved her. A stone thrown in a pool, its ripples affecting all around it. 'In terms of the police investigation, what happened?'

Mrs Jefferies explained, 'the investigation was overseen by a Detective Inspector, Edward Danvers, a man in his late forties, who was determined to find out what had happened to Lisa. After the initial push, including collecting forensic evidence, interviewing many people, examining phone data and basic CCTV footage, the case then lost momentum and it all ground to a halt without any new information. It is still an open case but the chance after sixteen years of any new developments are unlikely. I have no closure in terms of finding my daughter's body and giving her a dignified burial.'

Andy knew from his own experience that some cases were never solved but on other occasions a breakthrough can happen, even after many years, which can lead to a conviction. 'I sincerely hope for you, Mrs Jefferies, you do get answers to what happened to your daughter. I understand from Mrs Quall, that after Claire's death, Gary Dawson consolidated his financial assets in terms of Claire's will and his shares in the company, and moved on, selling the car dealership.'

Julian nodded. 'He put the dealership up for sale and it sold quite quickly to the current owner who retained most of the employees that worked there. Gary left the Reading area, and Simon quickly followed him, so we must be grateful for small mercies. I understand he bought a dealership in the Midlands, Stratford, I think.'

Andy confirmed this. 'Yes, he bought one in Stratford-Upon-Avon, and then another in Kenilworth. He then went on to meet and marry his second wife, who also sadly died after a few years, we think. Do you happen to know anything about her?'

'Yes, a bit. Gary kept in touch with Greg, at our dealership. Apparently, Gary met a woman who owned a number of dress shops in the Cotswolds, there was definitely one in Stratford, and one in Broadway. I think her name was Jess or Josie, but I'm not sure. Greg then moved to work for Gary, so there was no further news.'

Andy thanked Nina Jefferies and Julian for taking the trouble to speak to him and expressed how sorry he was for the loss of their daughter and friend.

Nina Jefferies shook his hand and then held on to it firmly. 'Mr Leyton, my advice to your friend who is engaged to Gary Dawson would be to get out of this relationship now, while she still can. He is cold, ruthless and calculating, and in my estimation, a killer. Your friend is not safe while this man is in her life.'

CHAPTER FIFTY TWO

Eva was late home from school on Friday evening. Her teacher friend, Judy, had a birthday in the week and she wanted a few people to go for an early evening drink to celebrate before she went out for a romantic meal arranged by husband Cay.

The cosy pub was now filling up with office workers, no longer able to work from home, who were perhaps beginning to remember the advantages of seeing colleagues face-to-face and not on Zoom. Eva sat with Judy, Kasia and six other staff, teachers and teaching assistants. Most of them were driving, so it was going to be a low key affair of mainly soft drinks, a wine, or beer, or cider each.

Judy was giddily excited about going out for the meal arranged by Cay. 'I am beginning to think he's having an affair as suddenly he's being over attentive, dressing smarter, wearing aftershave and doing more in the house without being asked. Take this evening, he managed to book a table on-line, a first, and has arranged a taxi, and there was a large bouquet of flowers waiting for me this morning. I keep threatening to run off with Dwayne Johnson and perhaps he thinks he's not the Hollywood actor but someone I've met at the gym.'

Eva smiled. 'Whatever he thinks, it's obviously working if he's putting in more effort. That's great for you, you deserve it.'

Judy smiled slyly. 'Actually, I don't think it's the Dwayne Johnson effect. I think that since going to the gym I have got my energy levels back and it's given me my mojo back in the bedroom department, if you get my meaning. My hubby is obviously appreciating it.'

Kasia giggled. 'And who said that old people don't have sex.'

Judy choked on her drink. 'Cheeky madam. Young people think you invented the whole thing but we oldies can teach you a thing or two.'

Kasia persisted. 'Just be careful you don't get any nasty injuries. You need to take care of your hips and knees.'

They all laughed loudly. Judy looked at Eva. 'How's the wedding plans going? Not long before you become Mrs Anderson.'

Kasia nodded. 'Yes, lucky you. I bet your Gary knows a thing or two about how to please a woman in the bedroom. He's got such sexy eyes that seem to know what you look like under your clothes.'

Eva was genuinely shocked. 'Kasia, you do have a boyfriend of your own.'

'Yes, but he is turning out to be a big disappointment and I think we will not be together for much longer.' Kasia had recently made it known that their attempts at trying for a baby were putting a strain on their relationship and she was not happy with their lack of success in conceiving a child, with each blaming the other.

Eva was sympathetic to Kasia's predicament but felt that the couple should be consulting their GP to find out if there was a problem which then could be fixed. She now refocused on Judy's enquiry about the wedding. 'Yes, the arrangements are all progressing. Gary is surprisingly keen to get everything sorted.'

Kasia sighed. 'You are so lucky to have such a man, good-looking, business owner, very sexy and totally in love with you. I wish I was you.'

'Everything isn't always as it seems.' Eva blushed slightly as she said this. In fact, it was an admission too far as Judy immediately picked up on this and frowned at her. She could not admit to her friends that the man she was about to marry was controlling and physically abusive and she was trying with all her might to extricate herself from the nightmare prospect of being married to him. After Saturday's incident, she could no longer say that she felt safe in her own home. She did not know when the next outburst would come.

Kasia went to the bar to get more drinks. Judy placed her hand on Eva's. 'Eva, darling, is everything ok with you and Gary? I know I've said it before but you have really lost your spark and I sense a continual sadness in you. You would tell me if there was anything wrong, wouldn't you?'

Having someone be kind to her and recognising her sadness almost brought her to the point of tears. 'Honestly, Judy, I'm ok. Just tired I guess as it's a long term and trying to plan a wedding at weekends is time consuming. Plus Christmas is only a month away. Gary and I are ok.'

Judy pursed her lips. 'Are you? I will be honest with you now, as I am deeply fond of you Eva. I am not keen on him and he comes across as quite bossy when you are with him. I hope I'm not upsetting you by saying this.'

'No, don't worry, Judy. You are not alone in not liking him. My friends Tania and Andy cannot stand him and think he is too secretive about his past and his two ex-wives. They are suspicious of his motives, as he seems to have got married very young, and then accumulated property and money from the death of these wives. I am a young widow with some financial assets so they think I am in danger. It all feels like an Agatha Christie novel.' Eva laughed, but she couldn't say she was more scared of Gary's violent tendencies than his plans to take her money. 'I'm sure it'll work out ok with Gary.'

Kasia put down the drinks and interrupted. 'If you want to get rid of Gary, please pass him on to me. I am sure that he is a man capable of producing strong, healthy babies.'

Eva did not respond. Gary definitely had the capacity to make babies but he did not have any of the qualities involved in raising a child, namely love, patience and kindness.

After Eva had dropped Kasia off, and driven home, she parked on her drive, spending a few quiet minutes in the car before venturing in the house. As always seemed to be the case these days, as she got out of the car, Andy was coming out of his house to go to his car. She waved at him, but did not feel inclined to go over and speak, due to her lingering embarrassment about getting drunk last week.

This did not deter Andy who was straight over to speak to her. 'Hi, I'm glad I've seen you. I've worried about you all week after Gary's unacceptable behaviour towards you last Friday. Were you ok afterwards?'

She really had to force herself to look at his face. 'Yes, he wasn't happy but it was fine.'

Andy's eyes met hers, not convinced she was telling the truth. 'I am still furious with him for the way he spoke to you and pulled you. Absolutely fuming. I came very close, in a long time, of wanting to punch somebody, which wouldn't be great as I am a serving police officer.'

Eva smiled reassuringly at him. 'Thanks, Andy but I'm glad you didn't. I'm ok and know what I'm doing.'

Andy's facial expression was now serious, verging on anger. 'I'm not sure you do. In my police career I have come across a lot of men like that who must have their own way and be in charge. What starts out as a pull on the arm, or a verbal attack, frequently leads down a road of more serious assaults. If you need help, Eva, you must ask for it. From me, your parents, your other friends, from domestic abuse charities. There are people who can help.'

Eva really was getting embarrassed now. 'It wasn't as bad as it seemed, honestly. He was ok for the rest of the night, just a bit mad about me coming to your house and getting drunk.'

'I must apologise to you for that. I was the one plying you with alcohol.'

'Don't worry, it was not your fault. I did have a great night, so thanks.'

'I enjoyed it too. We do get on well.'

Eva now noted that Andy was smartly dressed in blue trousers, white shirt and dark grey jacket. 'You look smart, are you going out?'

It was his turn now to avoid eye contact with her. 'Yes, I am. And would you believe it, I am going on a date.'

Eva's blue eyes widened in surprise. 'A date. Great. How did this come about?'

'One of the other DI's has been on at me to go out on a foursome with his girlfriend, and her friend, who I met at a party once, and she wanted to meet up. To be honest, I didn't remember her but he showed me a photo and as she looks nice. I thought I'd give it a go. We are meeting in a wine bar for a few drinks.'

'Well, you better be on your way, don't keep her waiting.' Eva realised that she did not want to know about this date and it was one more thing to add to the list of things going wrong in her life. She knew that a new relationship could take him out of her life and she must quash any feelings that she had started to have for him. As she acknowledged before, he was too good a catch to remain single, and any woman, except for Natasha, would be stupid to let him go. 'Have a good time.'

CHAPTER FIFTY THREE

Gary's irritation with Eva persisted throughout the week. Firstly, as she had got drunk with the cop last Friday. Secondly, on Saturday she had been so indecisive in terms of arrangements for the wedding. He was seriously beginning to wonder if she was at all committed to this wedding as she never mentioned it, never expounded on what she wanted in terms of the flowers, the venue arrangements, the guest list, the menu for the meal, or the cake. Reluctantly, she had drafted the list of all the people that should be attending but this was after three reminders that the wedding planner at the venue needed this information urgently. He was not sorry for his need to physically chastise her on Saturday after the visit to the florist. Her lack of enthusiasm and concentration on the wedding planning had caused him embarrassment with the florist. Since Saturday, she would barely look at him and refrained from speaking to him, unless absolutely necessary, so this only fuelled his temper. At times when he was annoyed with Eva, his tolerance towards her son also became an issue. It was now the end of November. Alfie was starting to get excited about Christmas and what presents he would like. Thankfully, he seemed to have grown out of the believing in Father Christmas stage. No more writing letters to Santa or convinced that a large man in a red suit delivered presents to children who had been good throughout the year. Gary was no saint; he had spent a lifetime telling lies, small, big and gigantic ones, but the Santa story was one fabrication too far in his opinion. Alfie may no longer believe in Santa but he had no trouble drawing up a long list of presents he would like including games consoles, trainers, Galaxy hoodie, skateboard and gravity maze. Gary was determined that Christmas would not involve him being overindulged and spoilt.

It had been a week where Alfie persisted in doing the things he was always being called out on. School shoes left dirty and discarded in the hall, coat and bag slung on the floor, grumbling about completing homework, asking for snacks before meals and procrastinating about going to bed. Gary had shouted at him on most days and usually Eva told him to stop shouting. But this week she was not challenging him and he used this to gain further control of the situation.

Now at dinner, on Friday evening, after Eva had come in after a few drinks with her teaching colleagues, Gary was not in the best of moods. He had cooked the meal, sticky sweet chilli salmon, noodles, carrot and broccoli and Alfie pulled a face as he sat down to eat. 'I'm not keen on salmon. I really prefer chicken.'

Gary gave him a look which read 'don't start' with me. 'I note your preference, sir, and I will consult with the chef next time you are dining with us. For now, it's a case of eat it or leave it but don't ask for snacks if you're hungry later.'

Eva reminded Alfie that he should eat what he was given and be thankful to Gary for preparing the food. Anything to steer clear of an argument. 'I know you like salmon if it's cooked with a sauce and this is really good.' Alfie resisted commenting further and proceeded to eat the meal.

'While we are here, I want to say something about Christmas, which is only a month away. I take it, Eva, that you know that we will spend Christmas day here, just the three of us, as both sets of grandparents are out of the country from the beginning of December,' Gary stated. Eva had been surprised, and a little upset, when her parents, and Niall's parents, had announced that they had hired a villa in Lanzarote for four weeks from 4 December. It would be the first Christmas she had ever spent without her parents. Gary continued, 'on that basis, I am proposing that we do not spend large amounts of money on presents as we have a wedding to pay for next year.' Alfie looked very crest fallen at this news, fearing that his Christmas wish list would not be fulfilled. Eva noticed her son's troubled face. 'Don't worry, Alfie, you will get some presents. And your grandparents have promised to buy you what you want in January. They are planning to do you a pretend Christmas Day on their return from Lanzarote. You will be having two Christmases.'

Alfie now perked up, realising that this could all be of benefit to him. 'Oh yes, I forgot about that. That will be great.' He finished eating his dinner and placed his knife and fork together on his plate. 'I've eaten all my dinner. Can we have ice cream for pudding?'

'Yes, I think so but you must wait till Gary and I have finished, first.'

After the meal was finished, Alfie took a bowl of ice cream to his room, with strict instructions to bring the bowl down later. Eva cleared the table and loaded the dishwasher. Gary filled the kettle to make coffees and he sat at the dining table while the kettle boiled. 'You've done it again, undermined me in front of the boy, by leading him to think he's getting lots of stuff at Christmas.'

Eva turned from putting the plates in the dishwasher. 'I don't think I did but his grandparents always spoil him and I can't stop that.'

'Which suggests that they are fools with more money than sense. The point is we will not be overindulging him if I have anything to do with it. And as I said we do have the wedding to pay for.'

'Perhaps we should rein in the spending on that. It's only one day after all and I don't see the point of paying out too much.'

The kettle boiled and he made two mugs of instant coffee with milk and placed them on the table. Eva placed the last items of cutlery in the dishwasher, put in the cleaning tablet, and turned on the machine. She went to pick up her mug of coffee to take into the lounge, to watch some television as she drank it.

Gary indicated that she should sit next to him at the dining table and she did as requested. 'Tomorrow, you're going to look at wedding dresses with your mum and Tania. Are you excited?'

Eva blew on her coffee, which was still scalding hot, and hoped to appear upbeat in her response to his question. 'Yes, absolutely. What woman doesn't look forward to trying on wedding dresses.'

He scoured her face, trying to detect any equivocation in her reply. 'Make sure that you choose something that enhances your beauty and your figure. I want you to look stunning. As I've said before, you are a million times prettier than the other two who went before you.

'Do you have any photos of those weddings?'

Gary laughed. 'Absolutely not. The marriages were not a success, even before their tragic deaths. I have got rid of any photographic evidence that I married either of them. This time it will be different and I know that you will look amazing. If anything were to happen to you, I would keep the photos of my perfect wife. Wife number three.'

Eva shuddered, an icy chill in her spine. 'Let's not talk about my demise, it sort of feels like we are tempting fate.'

Gary took hold of her hand. 'Well, I want you around for a very long time, to spend time with and make love to but I know only too well that fate can be cruel. Lives can be snuffed out in an instance.'

Eva sipped at the cooling coffee, remembering something that Simon had said when he came around for a Chinese takeaway. 'What was Simon referring to when he said that I should have been wife number four. What happened with, was it, Gianna?'

Gary now looked evasive, and angry, and Eva regretted asking this question. 'Take no notice of Simon as he likes to stir things up. I was engaged to Gianna and we were planning to marry. She got cold feet at the last moment and went to live abroad. I have no idea where. It was hard to come to terms with at the time but it was all for the best or I wouldn't have met you.'

'Why did she get cold feet?'

'I don't really know. We had a bust up and she didn't want to go through with it. It's all past history, totally unimportant, and there's nothing else to say.'

CHAPTER FIFTY FOUR

Andy was sat at the kitchen island, drinking coffee and reading news articles on his laptop, waiting for the washing machine in the utility room to silence so that he could put the damp clothes in the tumble drier. His date, with Lydia, last evening, had gone ok, as she had been a pleasant girl, pretty and friendly, but he knew that there would not be a second date, as he had no real interest in her. The 'spark', the undefinable magic ingredient that those going on dates were always looking for was definitely missing in this instance. His friend the DI, Ryan, had texted afterwards to say that Lydia would really like to meet him again. He and Lydia had exchanged phone numbers and she would be waiting for him to contact her. He now had the dilemma of how not to progress this without hurting her feelings too much. He knew that he would be thinking this over, delaying the inevitable, and then leaving it all too late so that she could end up feeling snubbed. However, he didn't want to give the girl false hope of there being the possibility of a relationship. Ryan's girlfriend, Andy knew, was the one in charge in their relationship and Ryan may get the blame if her friend was upset. To negotiate the world of dating you needed all the skills of a trained counsellor in managing people's psychological and emotional wellbeing. As he contemplated what he should do, the doorbell rang. He went to the front door to find Tania there with Eva standing behind her.

Tania pushed forward as Andy stood on the doorstep with the door open. 'Can we come in, if you are not busy. I need your help to give this one a talking to.' Whether or not Andy was going to agree to her request didn't really matter. Tania had quickly entered the hallway of his house before Eva could stop her. Eva hesitated on the door threshold, shaking her head at Tania's audacity. 'Sorry, Andy. I've told her not to disturb you but there is no stopping her once she gets a bee in her bonnet. Are you busy?'

Andy smiled kindly at her. 'No, I'm not, just doing some washing. Please come in and your feisty friend can tell me why you need a talking to.' He noted the worry on her face. 'Don't look too scared. I don't bite even if I might agree with Tania.'

Eva went into the house, following Andy, to find Tania in the kitchen about to fill the kettle. She then changed her mind. 'On second thoughts, this calls for alcohol, have you got any white wine Andy?'

He pretended to look peeved at Tania but went over to the fridge and took out a Sauvignon Blanc. 'I can provide wine and you can tell me what's going on. Sit down you two.'

Eva sat down at the dining table but looked agitated. 'I don't think I should have any wine as I've had champagne at the bridal shop. I don't want to get drunk again, after last week. You are driving Tania, remember?'

Tania waved her arm at Eva. 'No worries, I'll just get a taxi and pick my car up from yours tomorrow.'

Andy opened the bottle, retrieved three glasses from the cupboard, and poured the wine. 'Why does our friend need a talking to?'

Tania sighed, and sipped the wine, enjoying its cool taste, as she relaxed for the first time in two hours. 'Well, our lovely friend here has just spent a couple of hours in a heavenly shop trying on the most beautiful dresses and it all felt as if we were about to attend a funeral. Every dress she tried on looked stunning and her mum and I were in tears just looking at her. Now, as you know, I make no secret of the fact that I do not like Gary. But she has committed to marry him and I have decided to be the best chief bridesmaid I can be. Her mum and I knew that at least three of these dresses were perfect for her but she would not listen as we told her how wonderful she looked. This woman before you, according to her, is not beautiful enough for these dresses and it will all be good money wasted.'

Andy knew instinctively that if Tania, and Eva's mother, thought she looked sensational in these dresses then he accepted they would be right. He commented, 'I do not know anything about wedding dresses, Eva, but you know that Tania and your mother would not be lying when they say you look fantastic.'

'She did, and there is no time to delay if she wants a dress for a May wedding. As the shop owner kept insisting, there is high demand at the moment due to all the delays caused by Covid, and stocks are not being replenished at normal rates. If she wants a dress for a spring wedding then this is the time to buy it. She will not look so attractive in a bin liner, if all the dresses are sold out.'

Eva kept quiet throughout all this and just sipped her wine. 'I know, I heard what she said. They were all beautiful gowns but I didn't feel comfortable in them.'

Tania sighed loudly. 'You are not supposed to be comfortable. You are not trying on flannel pyjamas to spend a day in front of the telly. You are choosing a dress to marry the man you love. I wish that I was the one trying them on. I would have been skipping around the shop, drinking free champagne, and looking at my amazing self in the mirrors. You had all the jollity of a prisoner facing a firing squad.'

Andy reflected on what Tania had just said. Eva's obvious discomfort and aversion to trying on the dresses was because she was not marrying a man she loved. He knew this from that time when he asked her if she felt safe and happy in her relationship with Gary and her response was to cry in his arms. Eva was not happy about this marriage. Andy could not fathom out why she had agreed to marry the man. 'I know I am a mere man, and cannot understand the female mind, but perhaps Eva is just finding the whole thing too emotional. We do have difficulty making decisions when we are not thinking clearly.'

Tania held out her glass for a top up of wine as she considered this. 'Yes, good point but she needs to take emotions out of this and plan it like a military campaign. We cannot afford to falter as we are sprayed with bullets. We must soldier forwards keeping the objectives of the operation in mind.'

Andy laughed loudly. 'Eva, you have certainly chosen the right bridesmaid for getting you motivated. Sergeant Major Tania Banerjee, the British Army needs you.'

Despite her melancholy and anguish when trying on the wretched dresses, Eva now felt her spirits lift. 'She certainly would make a great asset to the army as she would make all new recruits quake in their boots.'

Tania acknowledged the truth of this but pleaded, 'I am a pussy cat really. Now, changing the subject, a little birdie tells me that Andy went on a date last night. How did it go? Should we now class you as 'in a relationship'?'

Eva grimaced at her friend's forward questioning. 'Tania, that's none of your business.'

Tania disagreed. 'I beg to differ. I am asking on behalf of all the single ladies in Warwickshire who will be heartbroken if they find out that their most eligible police officer is no longer available.'

Eva sighed. 'Tania, you really are terrible. Andy, you do not have to answer.' Andy laughed again, amused by Tania's audacity to boldly go where others dare not. 'No, it's ok. Nothing to tell really. It was a pleasant evening with good friends and my date was very nice.'

'Very nice is not a striking endorsement of sparks flying and rockets launching. Will there be a date number two?' Tania enquired. She drained the last of her wine in her glass, disappointed to see the bottle was now empty.

Andy now wanted to keep Tania guessing as to what his true intentions were. 'I haven't decided yet on a date number two. When I do decide, Tania, I will let you be the first to know so you can update the single ladies in Warwickshire, ok?' He winked at Eva.

As Eva and Tania left Andy's, and while Tania waited for a taxi, she said to Eva. 'I don't think I'm going to cry hysterically yet that he's off the market. The words 'pleasant' and 'nice' aren't loaded with red hot passion so I guess this girl is not 'the one'. I just wish he'd look and see 'the one', me, when she's sitting in his kitchen drinking his wine.'

Eva couldn't comment. Her own feelings for Andy were developing strongly and it could be her crying hysterically when he found a new girlfriend. In reality it didn't matter anyway. Andy believed that she was going to be married in the near future. Even without Gary, she realistically knew that she stood no chance of being with Andy, as Natasha had firmly told her that he was not attracted to her. Their kiss still puzzled her but she put this down to a moment of madness on his part. She had cried in his arms and he had consoled her. It was a Pavlovian response, a physical, male way of expressing his concern, nothing more.

CHAPTER FIFTY FIVE

Hannah had been delighted when her father had suggested a shopping trip to a Cotswold village to buy some early Christmas presents. They arrived in the beautiful village of Broadway, mid-morning, and the wide high street offered a variety of cafes, restaurants, various shops including boutiques, jewellers, art and crafts, unique gifts, antique sellers and florists within the honey-coloured, Cotswold limestone listed buildings. They joined a number of Sunday visitors, walking along the main street, lined with red horse-chestnut trees. Hannah was quite giddy with excitement as they sat drinking in a small coffee shop, a latte for Hannah and an Americano with milk for Andy. Hannah took out a small notepad and made a list of people she wanted to buy for. 'Hopefully, I'll be able to get quite a few pressies here, including a scarf for mum, bracelets for Phoebe, and the other girls, some soaps for my nans and perhaps a candle for Eva. I don't really know what to get for Alfie but you can help with that. If I run out of pocket money, can you let me have some more, please dad?'

Andy nodded. 'Yes, no problem as long as you don't spend too much per person. And, I think you'll find you have left someone off that list.'

Hannah's brow indicated that she was puzzled as to who that may be but she laughed loudly. 'Yeah, I know. I haven't forgotten you. What's it to be dad, novelty socks or slippers?'

'Cheeky madam. How old do you think I am?'

'Ancient. If there's a fudge shop here, I'll buy some for granddad Pedro and send them over with nanny Sofia's soaps. This will be a great place to find some unique stuff.' She finished her latte and spooned the remaining milk froth into her mouth. 'Let's go.'

They left the café and started walking slowly along the pavement, with Hannah stopping to glance in every window. Quickly, she found a small shop selling a range of gifts including the type of inexpensive bracelets that teenage girls like and she was absorbed in deciding which to get for which friend. Andy hovered for a short while before saying, 'why don't you wander around for about half an hour along this road but don't go away from the shopping area. I'll come and meet you after that. Is that ok?'

'Yeah, fine, see you soon.'

Andy walked out of the shop and started to look for boutique/dress shops. He went into one a few shops further up after leaving Hannah. As he entered, he felt very much like an alien on its first visit to Earth and pretended to look at scarves before summoning the courage to approach a woman sat at the counter, near to the till. He smiled pleasantly at the middle-aged woman, smartly dressed in cream jumper displaying one of her wares, a cream, orange and green scarf tied around her neck. 'Hi, this is going to sound an odd question but I am trying to find a boutique or woman's clothes shop previously owned by a woman called Jess or Josie. I don't know her surname.'

The woman looked him over, possibly trying to discern his motives for asking the question. 'There was a shop further down owned by a lovely woman called Jess who had a shop called 'Jess's dresses' quite a few years ago. I got to know her quite well, very bubbly type, and sold some great stuff. Sadly, she died, and the shop was bought by the current owner, Gill. You'll find it further down and across the road and it's now called 'Glam Gals' but it still sells women's clothing. My friend, Norma, works there, and she used to work for Jess.'

Andy thanked the woman for the information. 'Do you know if Norma works there on a Sunday?'

'Yes, she does and she should be in today.'

'Thanks again for your help.' He left the shop and crossed over the road to find 'Glam Gals'. He quickly came across it, a modern looking shop with glass frontage which displayed four dresses in red, black, gold and silver, all with sequins for the Christmas party season. He entered the shop, again feeling very out of place, and scanned the area for the woman called Norma. He spotted a woman tidying a clothes rail, putting the dresses back into size order, after customers had muddled them up. As Andy approached, she stopped working. 'Hello, you look a bit lost, can I help you?' She was a small woman, in her mid-fifties, with greying hair and a welcoming smile.

Andy hesitated slightly. 'Yes, maybe. I'm looking for Norma who may work here.'

The woman scrutinised him carefully before replying. 'Yes, I'm Norma.'

Andy explained that he was seeking information on a man named Gary Dawson who he believed had been married to Jess, who used to own this shop. As with Cynthia Quall and Nina Jefferies, he advised that he was a serving police officer but his enquiries did not relate to a police investigation but to a personal matter he was looking into.'

Norma laughed loudly. 'Are you a private investigator? I knew someone would come looking for that hideous man, eventually.'

'No, I'm not a private investigator. I am here on behalf of a friend who is intending to marry this man and she has given me permission to find out a bit about his previous life as he has been very minimal in terms of information. Can I ask, why did you refer to him as hideous?'

'Because when Jess met him, and then married him, he started to dictate to her how she should run her businesses and ordered her to get rid of staff he deemed unsuitable which included me. I'd worked for Jess for years, and she was a great boss, and allowed me a little bit of leeway on my timekeeping as I had my elderly mother to care for. Gary,' she almost spat his name out, 'set up an attendance system, you know sort of clocking in and out. I would often be a bit late in the mornings as it was hard getting mum out of bed and her breakfast prepared. I don't think I fitted in with the upmarket, classy image he tried to present and badgered Jess into dismissing me. She really didn't want to, I know that, but she was brow beaten by Gary.'

The door of the shop opened and a woman came in to look through the rail of Christmas party dresses. Norma moved away from the woman, and next to the till, indicating that Andy should join her. 'Could you tell me what you know about Jess and Gary's relationship?'

Norma hesitated slightly. 'Yes, I will. I feel a little disloyal talking about her but she is dead now and nothing can change that. I have no loyalty to that man what so ever. Before I say more, can you tell me what this personal matter is you are looking into, as I would not like Gary Dawson finding out about our chat and coming after me. He can be very intimidating.'

Andy nodded. 'He is now calling himself Gary Anderson and about to marry a woman who I am very fond of. The details of his past life are very brief, and in some ways quite troubling, as the wives have a habit of dying on him. How would you describe the relationship between Jess and Gary?'

Norma sighed. 'Terrible, at the end. It started off well. Jess was very excited when she first met him and she referred to herself as a cougar with her younger, handsome man. It all happened very quickly, they met in 2010, married a year later and she sadly died two years later. Jess was a great boss, and friend, to me. She was a bubbly, confident woman with a loud laugh but she had struggled in the past with anxiety issues and panic attacks. Just prior to meeting Gary, she was quite well mentally and off the medication, and happy when she met him.'

Norma paused as the female customer asked to try on a red party frock and so she was shown into the changing room. Norma continued, 'anyway, as the relationship progressed, and particularly once they were married, Gary started to exert a real control over what happened with the businesses. Maximising profits he called it and culling staff, me, and a couple of others in the other shops, who didn't fit with the upmarket, Cotswold brand. I think he bullied Jess into doing things she was not happy with and gradually he wore her down. She started to stop taking an interest in the shops. He appointed a manager to oversee them. Poor Jess would come in occasionally, she'd gained weight, seemed really down and had gone back on medication for anxiety and panic attacks. I blamed it all on him. I truly think he made her feel worthless. The last time I saw her was the week before she died, as Gary had instructed her to go to the Chipping Campden shop. On the way back from there, she came to Broadway, and we met for a quick coffee.'

The customer came out of the changing room and brought the dress to the till. Andy waited while the financial transaction was completed. He texted Hannah to check that she was ok. He said he would meet her outside the café from earlier in ten minutes.

'Thank you, madam.' Norma gave the dress, now in a quality bag with 'Glam Gals' written on it, to the customer. 'You will look lovely at Christmas wearing this.'

As the woman vacated the shop, Andy asked Norma. 'How was Jess the last time you saw her?'

'Not good. She was fed up about her weight and Gary's comments about it. He was continually on her case about the shops, and how they should be run, as he was very driven by money. All in all, Jess was totally brow beaten by him, which increased her anxiety levels and prompted the more frequent panic attacks. Her specialist had recently increased her medication to a high-level dose, she told me, and she had to be careful when taking it as it could be dangerous if she got the dosage wrong. After our coffee, I came away feeling really sorry for her as she was unhappy, lonely and had lost all her spirit. Oh yes, and the rat openly told her the day before that he had a girlfriend called Samantha who apparently fulfilled all his needs, if you get my drift.' Norma looked sheepishly at Andy as she said this. 'Jess said to me that this news of a girlfriend was not a complete shock to her, as she had suspected something like this was going on. Jess told him that she would be seeking a divorce, and shares in his assets, but he told her that there would be no divorce unless he wanted it. Jess was a very unhappy woman who left that café, that day. One week later I had a shocking phone call to tell me she was dead.'

Andy looked on as Norma now became upset, the third woman he had spoken to recently, all affected by Gary Dawson/Anderson. 'I'm so sorry. What happened?' The shop door opened and closed as two women came in, again drawn to the evening dresses.

Norma dabbed at her eyes with a tissue. 'Overdose of the medication, apparently. It was Christmas Eve, and Jess took her medication, then she and Gary shared a bottle of champagne. Jess was never very good with alcohol, it made her drunk quite quickly. According to Gary she must have forgotten that she'd taken the medication and took a further dose. From what I understand she overdosed on the medication and suffered a cardiac arrest.'

Andy hesitated slightly before asking his next question. 'I believe you are saying that her death was classed as overdose of her prescription medication. Were there any issues surrounding the death? Was her death reported to the coroner? Was there a post mortem and inquest?'

Norma nodded. 'Yes, both, as the cause of death was unclear as to whether it was an accidental overdose, a suicide attempt, or perhaps a death under suspicious circumstances. At the inquest Gary was called as a witness and acted the part of grieving widower to Oscar standards. The outcome of the inquest was accidental death, an overdose of medication due to the effects of alcohol. A few of us friends of Jess had to accept the outcome but we were sceptical about the verdict as we did not trust Gary's version of events. What I do know is that once all the formalities were over, Gary took no time at all at putting the shops up for sale, to get rid of them, and banked the money. This is my personal opinion but I think his motivation all along was to go after Jess for her money and he succeeded. Advise your friend to be very careful around this man.'

Andy now glanced at his phone, realising it was time to go and meet Hannah. 'Thank you so much for your help on this. I'm sorry that your friend had to get entangled with him but pleased to see that you are back here where you belong. One more thing, could you tell me Jess's surname?'

'Her full name was Jessica Longhurst. It's all such a tragedy. A sad end to a life of a beautiful lady who died way before her time.'

As Andy strode back to the café, Hannah was waiting outside, clutching a number of bags and looking pleased with herself. 'Hi, dad, I've got nearly all the presents on my list. Can we go and have a cake or something as I'm starving?'

He smiled at her, pleased that she had enjoyed herself. 'Yes, let's go back in here. I hope you've got a present for me.'

She gazed at him, a mischievous expression in her lovely brown eyes. 'Not yet. Now what size feet have you got? I need to find those slippers?'

He playfully got hold of the back of her neck. 'Don't you dare, miss.'

'Ok, let me think, novelty socks then, with extra warmth for old people.'

CHAPTER FIFTY SIX

Gary sat at his desk, in his office at the Stratford dealership, looking down on to the car showroom and all the staff that worked for him selling high quality cars and lucrative finance packages. His sales staff were generally young, under thirty-five years of age, which he liked as they were knowledgeable, ambitious, smartly and trendily dressed, and eager to succeed, thus giving each a competitive edge which he liked as it boosted sales. His office, and that of the other senior managers, was on the upper floor, overseeing the work of the minions. As he relaxed back in his chair, after finishing a Zoom call with the manager of his other dealership, he considered how things were going in terms of The Plan involving Eva. With regard to his previous weddings, to Claire and Jess, he had not summoned much enthusiasm for the arrangements but had got involved in the one with Claire as she dithered about every detail. Wedding planning was all too much for her. She couldn't make a decision on anything concerning guests, flowers, bridesmaid dresses and so on. In the end the wedding had been organised by Claire's mother, Cynthia, with help from Gary, and as Mrs Quall had good taste it had all gone well. The quickie on the wedding day with lovely Lisa in the summer house of the venue grounds had been particularly pleasant and memorable. The highlight of the day.

The planning for this wedding to Eva seemed to be mainly down to him urging his bride-to-be to think about what needed to be done. Decisions needed to be made promptly, bearing in mind that the main event was only a few months away. On Saturday, after her appointment at the bridal gown shop, he tried to prise out of her if she had selected a dress to wear on the day. She was super evasive in her response, and kept telling him that it did not concern him, and he would find out on their wedding day what she had chosen. He strongly suspected that she had not selected a dress. She had come back from shopping, deflated and withdrawn, so not exuding the kind of glow of happiness he would expect from a woman who had just chosen their perfect gown for their wedding day. In fact, the more he thought about it, Eva's response to planning and enthusing about this wedding was decidedly off. She appeared to have no vitality or interest in the whole business. Gary was now beginning to wonder what the problem was. Did she actually want to marry him at all? He decided that he needed to sound her out about the wedding. To find out if she had any concerns and he vowed not to respond angrily if he was displeased with her reply. He wanted this wedding to go ahead as part of The Plan to secure her assets, before deciding the duration of their marriage. Unusually, this time, he knew that, in part, he was marrying for the right reasons. He did love this woman who offered what he required in a partner and he did find her irresistibly attractive. If the future of The Plan required that he sever the relationship then it would genuinely hurt him emotionally to do so.

There was a knock on his door, and Simon came in, pretending to want an update on an ordering issue but mainly for a chat. 'Ok, Gaz, you look a bit lost in thought.'

Gary sat upright on his chair and scowled at Simon. 'For fuck's sake, Simon, you know I don't like being called Gaz. Cut it out or I might start calling you, Simple Simon, and you wouldn't like that.'

'Ok, mate, who rattled your cage? Things not going so well with sexy little Eva?'

'Stop referring to her as sexy. I don't want her image in your sexually depraved brain.'

'Well, my sexually depraved brain could think of many things I could do with her involving cable ties and blindfolds.'

Gary slammed his hand down angrily on the desk. 'Have you got a death wish as I am seconds away from punching your face.'

Simon realising that he had gone too far, drew back from Gary's desk and reach. 'Sorry, mate, only messing. You know me when I haven't scored for a while, I get over excited at the thought of any woman.'

'Just keep your thoughts away from my woman, ok? Now, if there's nothing you want my opinion on, I suggest you get back to your desk, and do the job I pay you for.'

Simon shuffled out the door and Gary's annoyance with his friend faded slightly. He thought about the circumstances of his life, from his meeting Simon at primary school, that had led them on their long journey through life together. At times, like now, when he was narked with Simon, he regretted that their lives were interlinked for eternity due their shared experiences and secrets. Secrets that would forever stain their existence. In some ways, Simon was a liability, a burden, which Gary felt he had to carry. His cross to bear for the wrongs he had done. People described Simon as a loner, weird, creepy, a man to be avoided, especially by women. Gary knew that he was judged for being overly friendly with a man that others did not warm to. Simon's presence tainted Gary's image and added to the mystery of his secretive past. Why would Gary favour such an unlikeable man?

CHAPTER FIFTY SEVEN

2014

After Jess's 'accidental death', on Christmas Eve 2013, Gary had to play the part of the grieving widower for a second time. It was not quite so hard this time, as he was familiar with the role, learned his lines, honed his emotions and acted convincingly, as well as any actor in a long running soap. There was also no immediate family to meet on a daily basis, as had been the case with Claire, no weeping mother and no stunned father. Jess's nearest relatives, a cousin in Scotland and her ageing mother, were not able to travel, except to attend the funeral. The cousin had been made the executor of the will but a lot of the administration details had to be dealt with by phone or email as the cousin, who had mobility difficulties, could not undertake the long journey from Selkirk on public transport. All this suited Gary as there was no real scrutiny of what he was doing or how he was behaving.

There was a great deal of hassle concerning Jess's sudden death. A post-mortem was ordered by a coroner and laboratory tests on the levels of amitriptyline in Jess's system were instigated. The whole thing dragged on for a further six months until an inquest was held. Gary had to do his best 'Daniel Day-Lewis' Oscar winning performance to relate the sequence of events on the Christmas Eve when Jess sadly drank a little too much champagne and overdosed on her medication. The post-mortem findings and lab tests confirmed the cause of death as cardiac arrest brought on by amitriptyline overdose with evidence of alcohol in her system. Gary did have some heart stopping moments of his own when the possibility of criminal intent was raised and the consideration of a police investigation. At the inquest, under oath, he painted a picture of a stable, happy marriage but acknowledged that Jess had ongoing issues in terms of anxiety and panic attacks. This led to her having bouts of self-doubt about her appearance, difficulties in running her businesses and her lack of friends and family. Gary swore that just before her death she seemed to be turning a corner and was suddenly taking an interest in her looks, vowing to diet, regaining an interest in her shops and responding affectionately to him. Gary stated that Jess was not in a suicidal state of mind and on the night of her death, they had enjoyed a quiet meal together and cuddled on the sofa. He had ensured that she had taken the correct dosage of medication before going to bed and could only think she had taken a second dose a little later due to the effects of the alcohol. Evidence of the medication spilt on the carpet seemed to indicate that she had been clumsy when spooning out the dose. Gary's fake concern and affection for his wife were forced on his face and tears filled his eyes as he described the moment he found her body. The inquest had been an ordeal but ultimately a verdict of accidental death went in the right direction for him.

The main problem he was having was Samantha. She had found out a while ago that what she had thought was an exclusive relationship with Gary was not quite the case. Gary quite quickly informed Samantha that he had a partner, a woman called Jess who he married in 2010 despite having an ongoing, highly sexual relationship with Samantha. As soon as Samantha learnt of Jess's death, she was hatching a plan to be the only woman in Gary's life and was determined to make herself visible as his girlfriend. She started to turn up at the Stratford dealership unexpectedly, where Gary had his main office, to introduce herself to his employees and consolidate herself as the boss's missus. Their relationship till now had suited Gary well. He'd turn up at her bedsit, stayed a few hours for the sexual activity, and then return home to Jess. Samantha was easily pleased with cans of lagers, chocolates or money to help out with bills and Gary assumed that she was satisfied with how things were. Big mistake. She arrived at the dealership, occasionally, dressed in tight jeans and baggy sweatshirt, not overly clean, as she found it a faff to go to the local launderette. The sleek black hair which had attracted him was frequently unwashed and lank. Her pasty skin with no makeup was spotty with the acne that still persisted after her teenage years were over. The sexy little black cat that he found so enticing in her home domain was less appealing when viewed through the critical eyes of others. If he was out, she insisted on waiting in his office for his return and Simon would phone to warn Gary of her arrival. Simon alerted Gary that the dealership employees secretly laughed at the state of his new girlfriend. Her appearance and persona jarring with the sleek, modern, upmarket gloss of the cars that were sold and the sales people that sold them. Quite frankly, she started to become an embarrassment to him and it was a problem to be dealt with.

By May, she was turning up at the dealership at least once a week and no one had the authority to tell the boss's girlfriend to leave. If Gary was out, often at the Kenilworth showroom, she would make a nuisance of herself by demanding coffee, requesting to sit in cars, and chatting to potential customers who left after being approached by a scruffy woman in sweatpants who did not seem to know anything about cars.

On a Friday evening, Gary went around to her flat to re-affirm the rules of their relationship and the consequences for not complying. She opened the door and he barged in, almost knocking her over as he strode into the lounge. The room was plainly decorated with cream walls, mid-brown carpet and two two-seater leather sofas in a mint colour. A coffee table was littered with coffee mugs, two empty lager cans and an opened packet of cheese and onion crisps. An ashtray held stubs of various cigarettes even though her rental contract specified it was a non-smoking tenancy. Seeing the anger etched on Gary's face, and radiating from his dark eyes, Samantha shivered and reached over for a cigarette. A comforter to steady her nerves. She sat on one of the sofas while he loomed over her. She was normally careful not to ignite Gary's temper as the outcome for her was not always favourable. 'Ok, Gary, why don't you sit down and I'll get you a lager?'

He grabbed hold of her arm, pulled her to her feet and took the unlit cigarette out of her hand. 'I've told you about smoking. It's a filthy habit and it makes your hair, clothes and breath stink.' His eyes roamed up and down over her body, taking in her clothing; ripped black jeans, over-large pink T-shirt with an unidentified brown stain at the front by her left breast. Her hair was hanging loosely around her face, greasy at the roots, and frizzy and dry at the ends which were in need of a trim. Her usual black eyeliner framed the green, cat-like eyes but it was smudged and gave her a slovenly look. His fingers dug into her upper arm and she winced at the pressure he exerted. 'Look at the state of you. I don't want you in my dealership, my business, looking like that. I've been informed that I've lost two potential buyers today because of you. You approached them, dressed like some roadside tramp, and they quickly rushed to the door before my sales staff could stop them. Aside from the fact that your clothes are dirty, and you smell of cigarettes, you know absolutely nothing about cars so don't speak to clients as if you are a world expert.'

He shoved her down on the sofa and sat next to her. 'Let me ask you a question? How do you see this, er, relationship, going forward?'

Samantha relaxed a little, as given his level of anger she felt sure that he was going to slap her, as he had done in the past. 'I don't know, Gary. I think I want us to be a proper couple and I could move into your house now that your wife has gone. You could perhaps get me a job at your place and train me up. I would quite like to sell cars. I promise to dress more smartly if I do. And in the not too distant future we could perhaps have a baby as I've always wanted kids.'

Gary laughed loudly. 'Well, sweetheart, you have a vivid imagination if you think I am going to play happy families with you or employ you in my quality business. This relationship will continue as it always has. Nothing is going to change for you now that Jess is dead. You are not a woman I am going to live with, or marry, or have kids with, as you are too low quality for any of that and with nothing to offer me. If you want us to continue, it will be as before. I come here for sex, once a week, as long as you fulfil my requirements. I do not want you coming to my workplace ever again, do you understand? If you do, then this stops immediately.'

Samantha rubbed against Gary before placing a hand on his upper thigh to teasingly stroke upwards to his groin area. 'I'm sure you won't want this to stop, will you, Gary? You enjoy it too much.'

He removed her hand, then slapped it sharply. 'I think you have put too high a value on what you do for me. I can get this anywhere and from women a lot more classy and fragrant. All you are is a convenience, the only shop open with the goodies when the others are closed. The shops that are generally unclean and lacking in variety. I come here because I'm lazy and want to put in minimal effort but know that you do the job. You will never be more than that. So, I'll ask again, do you want to continue with this arrangement? If you say yes, then you must know that it will never be more than this. I will eventually move on to find another woman, a wife, but she will not be you.'

Samantha shuddered slightly, trying to fight the tears that were threatening to reveal her weakness in wanting him. 'Yes, Gary, I do want to continue with this arrangement. Perhaps in time you may change your mind and want to progress things further. I'll try to make more of an effort to look nice but I could do with a few quid to help with that. Buy some dresses.'

His anger had now dissipated and he looked at her kindlier, noting the hurt in her troubled green eyes. 'Maybe I can help with that. Now, in terms of clothes, I think it's time to remove the ones you're wearing so that you can apologise for turning away my customers.'

She eagerly pulled the pink T-shirt over her head to reveal her small breasts and Gary pushed her back on the sofa to explore their perfection with his mouth.

CHAPTER FIFTY EIGHT

2021

The day after his visit to Broadway, Andy was at his desk at work. He'd grabbed some time to finish the notes he had been preparing for Eva on all that he had found out about her soon-to-be husband. It was now 3.45 p.m. on a Monday afternoon, and he guessed that she would have finished teaching but hoped she was still at school so he could speak to her. He rang her number and waited to see if she answered. Her phone went to voicemail but he did not want to leave a message in case Gary got to read it. He sent her a text, trying to make it as benign as possible. '**Hi Eva. I'm currently at work. Can you just confirm the date of your wedding. I need to book annual leave. Andy.**'

He hoped that she wouldn't just text back as he really needed to speak to her. After five minutes, his phone rang. 'Hi, Eva, thanks for ringing. Don't worry I haven't forgotten the date of your wedding, it was just a ruse to talk to you.'

She laughed. 'I was just about to find out if old age was causing your memory to fail.'

'According to Hannah, that has already happened. I was in trouble this morning for forgetting to sign the form for a trip to the Science Museum. It would be helpful if I saw the form and it was not festering at the bottom of her bag.'

'I share your pain. What did you want to speak to me about?'

'After our discussion at your engagement party, I have done a bit of digging with regard to Gary which I need to share with you. I don't think you are going to like it.'

The line when quiet and Andy wondered if she was regretting giving her approval for this search, on the basis of 'what you don't know can't hurt you.' She cleared her throat before answering. 'Ok, can you tell me now?'

Andy responded, 'no, not really. I've made a note of what I've been told for you to read. I think we need to meet up to go through it. I know it's all a bit clandestine but could you meet me somewhere this week. I am suggesting that you don't come to my house as I know Gary doesn't approve. I don't want him to find out what's going on.'

'Ok. Yes, perhaps it is best that we meet at a neutral location. I could meet you tomorrow after school. Alfie's going to my parents for tea as it's the last time he'll see them before they go off to Lanzarote. Where should we meet?'

'What about the Oak pub on the A452 between Warwick and Kenilworth? I could meet you there at 5.00 p.m., if I can get away. I'll contact you earlier in the day if there's a problem that I might not make it.'

'Yes, I can do 5.00 p.m. as there's a staff meeting that finishes at 4.30 p.m. and I'll tell Gary that some of us might go for a quick drink afterwards. See you tomorrow.'

****

The next day, Andy arrived before Eva, and he rang her to inform her of his location in the pub. He was sat in a small alcove with one oak table and four chairs, away from the bar area and the majority of the customers. At 5.00 p.m. the place was fairly empty. Eva found him and sat down. He noticed that she seemed nervous, her face pale and drawn, even under her makeup. She took off her jacket and hung it over the back of her chair. She was wearing slim fit black trousers, practical for dealing with young children, and a teal crew neck jumper.

As she sat down, Andy got up to get the drinks. 'What would you like to drink?'

'I'll have a sparkling water, please. Though at this moment I could actually drink a very large glass of white wine to calm my nerves. I'm not really looking forward to hearing what you have found out.'

'I won't be a minute.'

He returned promptly with her sparkling water and half a pint of lager for himself. 'There you go.'

'Thanks.' She now looked anxiously at his face. 'Tell me, what you have found out about my fiancé that I am not going to like.'

Andy removed four sheets of A4 paper from an inside pocket of his jacket. 'I think you had better read this first and then I can try to answer any questions you will have.' He handed her the papers which she took with a slightly trembling hand. He drank his lager slowly as he waited for her to read, and take in, what was written. When she finished reading, Eva placed the written note down on the table and Andy literally saw the blood drain from her face. 'Oh God, this is just awful. I can't get my head round any of it. Am I reading it right, did Gary Dawson, now Anderson, marry those two women purely for financial gain?'

Andy nodded. 'Cynthia, Mrs Quall, is absolutely convinced that Gary married her daughter, not out of love, or affection, but to work his way into the Quall family to access their wealth. From what she said, Gary was uncaring, unkind and abusive to her daughter and he made the poor woman's life a misery. Mrs Quall had no proof that her daughter's death, and that of the unborn grandchild, was nothing but a tragic accident. But Gary's callous behaviour following Claire's death, and his concentration on securing all the financial assets he had accumulated through her, were a clear indication of what his motivation was in marrying her. He certainly did not act like a grieving widower, that's for sure. Mrs Quall described Claire as a rather unworldly girl, shy and awkward, who Gary certainly did not marry due to any physical attraction or emotional connection.'

Eva sipped at her sparkling water but the fizzy bubbles further added to the nausea she was feeling. 'When Mrs Quall told you this about her daughter, how did she come across to you? A mother genuinely who believed that her precious daughter was exploited and harmed by a cruel man. Or a bitter woman who wants someone to blame, Gary, for her daughter's bad choice of husband and the humiliation of losing some of the family wealth?'

'In my estimation, Mrs Quall is a mother grieving for her beloved daughter, and the grandchild she never got to know. She is angry that the family, particularly her husband, were taken in by Gary Dawson and angry with herself that she did not do more to protect Claire. I don't believe that she was concerned about the loss of the money, as such. She was furious at her deceased husband in terms of his naivety at trusting Gary and ignoring their daughter's unhappiness in the last years of her life.

'And what do you make of Mrs Quall's assertion that Claire's death may not have been an accident?'

'From what I gather, she fell down the stairs whilst wearing a pair of ill-fitting slippers and her death was recorded as accidental by the coroner. But I made an almost verbatim note of Mrs Quall's summary of Gary's intentions to Claire. She said that when she considered the whole picture and asked herself why he choose Claire, there could only be one explanation, as he did not love or respect her. His motivation was a calculated plan to get property and wealth out of the family.'

Eva's now troubled blue eyes were fixed on Andy. 'Then there is the disappearance of Claire's best friend, Lisa. Mrs Jefferies seemed convinced that Gary was involved in this and her assessment was that Gary had murdered her daughter. This is all horrendous and I actually feel sick.' She drank the water but it had no effect on quelling the churning in her stomach. 'From what you have told me, Mrs Jefferies believed that Gary was sleeping with Lisa whilst going out with, and married to Claire. On the night she disappeared, Mrs Jefferies believed that Lisa went out to meet Gary, who possibly became angry about her date with another man, and he killed her. Again, Andy what was your assessment of this, particularly as you are a police detective?'

Andy sighed. 'I believed that Mrs Jefferies has argued a very strong case for what may have happened to her daughter. I think that it was likely that Lisa Jefferies was dead as the mother and daughter seemed to have a caring relationship. I truly believed that Lisa would have contacted her mother if she were still alive. The big problem was, as she stated herself, there was absolutely no physical evidence to back up her theory and without that there was no way that any charges could be brought against Gary. If he was responsible for her murder then he's disposed of her body pretty efficiently. There was DNA evidence of Lisa's hair and saliva in his car but he explained that Lisa had recent been a passenger in the back seat of his car. This was verified by Claire. There was evidence of semen in his car but nothing linked this to Lisa.'

'How would Mrs Jefferies know about the DNA evidence, hair, saliva and semen. Wouldn't that be kept confidential by the police investigator? Eva asked.

'Yes, it should be. I don't know how she knew. Perhaps it was let slip by one of the detectives involved. It is rather concerning.' Andy commented.

Eva leaned forward on the table, placed her head in her hands and rubbed at her forehead. 'This is all just awful. The man I am supposed to marry is definitely a ruthless operator who married a vulnerable young woman for money but is he also a murderer? Then, there's the issue of his second wife, Jess.'

Andy really didn't want to highlight the problems with Gary's second wife. 'According to the woman I spoke to, Norma, prior to meeting Gary, Jess was in a good place having previously suffered from anxiety and panic attacks and had come off prescribed medication. She was managing four shops which were doing well. She then met Gary. In my view, this second marriage had similar details to the first, a vulnerable woman with a history of anxiety was targeted for her financial assets and then was cowered and isolated as the relationship progressed. Jess informed Norma that her mental health issues had resurfaced and she was taking high-level doses of medication to help her cope. Norma's words were that Gary made Jess feel worthless. He revealed to Jess, just the week before she died, that he had a mistress, a woman called Samantha, so adding to her heartache one could assume. Jess told him she wanted a divorce and would be seeking a share in his assets. If his motivation was to secure her assets then divorce would not be an option. It's also interesting that her sudden death resulted in a coroner's inquest. An unusual occurrence in terms of most deaths but for this to happen to two of Gary's wives is of note. Roughly 35 % of deaths were reported to the coroner and of those up to 20% then go on to inquest. From my professional perspective this is quite troubling.'

Before Andy's eyes, Eva seemed to shrink in her seat. Eva sipped at the water which by now had lost the fizz of the bubbles. 'He's treated this woman despicably, it seems, to profit from her wealth, after her death. He certainly does not seem to have an ounce of caring for her and he's got another woman fulfilling his sexual needs, this Samantha. Oh dear.'

Andy now wished they were not in such public a place as he guessed that Eva was trying to hold in her hurt and upset at realising the extent of Gary's malevolence. She looked a fragile creature who at this moment could crumble to dust before his eyes. 'I'm so sorry that you've had to learn this about your fiancé. I can't pretend it paints him in a good light.'

Eva agreed, trying to avoid eye contact with him, so as to not divulge the depth of her pain. 'It's all awful and makes me wonder how I fit into all of this. I feel that I've been targeted as wife number three as I am a widow with financial assets. But it all feels a bit different to the other two. Gary has always made it clear that he finds me attractive and tells me he loves me. How can I know if any of this is genuine or is it just to pursue his goal in terms of monetary gain?'

Andy focused his eyes on her so she was forced to look at him. 'I do think it's a different scenario with you. There is no doubt in my mind that he is attracted to you and he is definitely jealous of any male attention that you receive. I am often showered in loathing if he thinks we are getting too close.'

Eva now sat up straight in her seat and addressed Andy. 'Andy, I am really grateful for what you have found out and it all adds into the uncertainties I already have about marrying Gary. I must let you into a secret. When I said yes to his proposal in Budapest I had no intention of going ahead with the wedding. I've had some major issues with our relationship for some time and there is no way I am going to marry him. I thought it would be best to accept his proposal as I was in a foreign country, away from friends and family, and I didn't know how he'd take a rejection. My plan is to get Gary out of my life as soon as possible. It's not as easy as it sounds. He is very controlling and I know that he will not react well to being asked to leave.'

Andy was now completely mortified by what she had just told him. 'Are you frightened that he will react violently towards you?'

Eva now placed her head in her hands, trying to hide her upset from Andy. 'Yes, I am. Gary likes to get his own way and he will not be happy when I tell him that we are over.'

Andy took hold of her hand, forcing her to look at him. 'How and when are you going to tell him to leave? Have you thought it through?'

'No, not really. I think I've got to do it before Christmas as the wedding costs are mounting and there's little likelihood of getting back any of the deposits we've paid. This is something else that's not going to please Gary as he doesn't like to lose money. I plan to re-imburse him with any money that he's lost if I cancel the wedding. I just know that I cannot marry him. He's too controlling with Alfie and me, and quite honestly, if he doesn't get his own way, he can be very intimidating.' '

Andy now pressed her hand tighter in his and concentrated his concerned gaze on her face. 'Eva, darling, you know I am here to help you if you need me. I won't let him hurt you if I can help it.'

Eva gazed into his handsome, kind eyes and knew the sincerity of his words. 'Andy, you are such a good friend to me, and I am grateful, but this is my problem and I must solve it alone. I'm sure I'll be ok.'

He tapped her hand. 'I'm not sure that you will and I am terrified that you are going to get hurt. We know for sure that Gary Anderson is a cold, calculating man who uses women, and abuses them. We suspect that he is worse than that, and could be a murderer, and I am beyond horrified that you think you can handle him alone. I don't think you can. I fear that you will get hurt and by that I mean physically harmed or worse, much worse.'

Eva completely understood his concerns for her as they were those that she had on an ongoing basis. Her experience to date with Gary had revealed that he easily resorted to violence to bring her into line. How would he react when she told him their relationship was over? A small part of her felt that there was a possibility he would try to kill her. Regardless of this, she was adamant that this was her battle to fight, alone. 'I know what you are saying and I am scared of the time I have to tell him that we are over. I will ensure that Alfie is not in the house and then see how it goes. If things do get out of hand then I will definitely call the police. Anyway, Andy, I must go or he will start to wonder where I am. Thanks for all this. It's a lot to take in but does reinforce that I need to get out of this relationship. Can I ask you to keep this written note you've made as I can't run the risk of Gary seeing it?'

'No problem.' Andy picked up his coat and placed the document in the inner pocket.

As they walked to her car, Andy had to fight an overpowering urge to take her in his arms. She stopped at her car, took the car key out of her coat pocket and unlocked the car door.

Andy placed a hand on her arm to stop her from getting in the car. 'Listen, Eva. I would feel happier if we could meet one more time to discuss in more detail how you are going to end things with Gary. What precautions you can take to get out of your house, if necessary, and where you will go.'

Eva was now keen to drive home. 'I know what you are saying but for now I need to go or it will cause an argument if I am late. There's too much going on in my head at the moment for me to think clearly.'

As she opened the car door to sit inside, Andy still held her arm, lightly. 'Just don't go telling him yet, till we have talked it through. We could meet again, next week, at a different location. Don't contact me on your mobile phone. Ring me on a school landline or borrow one of your friends' phones.'

As he released her arm, Eva sat in the driver's seat, ready to move away. 'Ok, I'll contact you but I still need to do this on my own. Bye, Andy.'

As she drove away, Andy was gripped by an icy fear, a foreboding that this was not going to be easy for her but what could he do if she would not let him help her. There was one line of interest he decided to pursue, to try and locate the woman who Gary was having an affair with when married to Jess. Samantha.

CHAPTER FIFTY NINE

As Eva walked into the kitchen, Gary had finished eating his dinner and smiled weakly at her. 'I'm assuming that you haven't eaten, and have just had a drink, so there's some food for you. It's just cream cheese pasta which will need re-heating in the microwave and there's some salad to go with it in the fridge.'

After the conversation with Andy, she was not really hungry but she would avoid Gary's scrutiny if she attempted to eat what he had prepared. She picked up the bowl of pasta, popped it in the microwave, and set it for two minutes. She then went to the fridge and took out the salad, a mix of green leaves, cucumber and tomatoes. She grabbed a bottle of French dressing from the fridge door to sprinkle on the salad. The microwave pinged, she took out the bowl of pasta, and she sat down at the table and started to eat. Gary continued to sit opposite her, watching as she ate a forkful of the creamy, parmesan spaghetti. 'How was the drink after work? Was it another birthday celebration?'

'Yes, it was, for one of the teaching assistants, for her twenty-second birthday. It makes me feel so old.'

'And were your usual friends there, Judy and Kasia?'

'No, they couldn't make it this evening. I just thought I'd show my face as this TA sometimes helps with my class and she's a nice girl.'

'Where did you go?'

'The Oak pub on the way to Warwick. Though I do think we should all perhaps try to meet up, not on a school night, and when people aren't driving. It all feels a bit pathetic having half a lager or a soft drink to celebrate a birthday.'

'What did you drink?'

'Just a sparkling water. I need to hurry up and eat this as I am picking Alfie up and I want to say goodbye to mum and dad before they go off on their holiday. I am going to miss them as four weeks away is a long time.'

Gary now got up from the table, to place his bowl and cutlery in the dishwasher. He came around to where she was seated, placed his hands on her shoulders and kneaded the sides of her neck with his fingers. He then bent down to place a kiss on her right cheek. 'Don't worry about that. You've got me to look after you and I'll ensure that you're not lonely. I love you, sweetheart.'

The touch of his fingers at her neck, almost stopped her heart, but she could not hide the involuntary shudder that swept through her body. Were these the hands of a murderer that were now handling her neck area? For all that she believed that Gary had been a cruel, ruthless fraudster to extract money from his previous wives, was he capable of ending the life of another human being? She did not know the answer to this. It all, though, added to the sum total of her fear in being around him.

'Anyway, there will be plenty to occupy you and keep your mind off your parents. We've got an appointment with the wedding cake maker on Saturday and you'll have presents to buy for Alfie, family and friends for Christmas. Just do as I say and not overdo the spending and things will be fine.'

Eva groaned inwardly when she thought of the Christmas preparations. She was planning to do most of her present shopping online, to take the pain out of trawling around all the shops. Alfie was always eager to put the tree up as fast as possible so she guessed that there was the likelihood of putting it up on Sunday. Still, it would be one job to cross off the list.

She ate as much of the pasta as she could physically tolerate but she could almost feel it congealing in her stomach. She picked up her bowl, salad bowl, and cutlery and scrapped the uneaten food in the waste bin.

Gary placed his arms around her waist as he drew her into him. 'You haven't eaten much of that.' He tweaked her waist with his fingers. 'Don't go too skinny on me as I love your curves.' He ran his hand down over her hips and then rested them on her bottom as he moved into kiss her briefly.

Eva pulled out of his grasp and away from his kiss. 'I need to go Gary, to pick up Alfie. See you shortly.'

****

As Gary heard the front door close, he went into the hallway, and noted that Eva had taken her handbag with her but left her phone behind on the hall table. He picked it up, carried it through to the lounge and sat down on the sofa with his feet on the coffee table. He entered her password and read yesterday's text from Andy about the wedding date. He was pleased that the cop had not ended the message with an 'x' but noted that Eva had not responded to this text. Had she actually phoned him back? Was the reason for this phone call purely to confirm the date of the wedding? If so, this was highly suspicious as they had sent out 'save the date' cards to her family, and friends, only a week ago.

He then accessed the MySpy spyware app that he had installed on her phone to ascertain the venue of the drinks, after work, with her teaching colleagues to celebrate the teaching assistant's birthday. He saw that the location was The Oak pub on the A452 between Kenilworth and Warwick. It was unfortunate that Judy and Kasia, her closest friends at the school, could not attend.

He went to the text area of the phone and found Kasia and read a few of their previous messages to pick up the tone of how they texted each other. He texted, **'Hi, sorry that you and Judy couldn't make it to The Oak this evening. It's not the same without you two there xx'** He sent the text and hoped that a response would be prompt. He was not disappointed.

Kasia replied, **'Hi babe, what drink? Nobody told me. I don't think Judy knew either. Never mind. The three of us must get together soon for a good chat out of school. See you tomorrow xx'**

Gary read the text then deleted the two texts immediately. So, Kasia was not aware of any after school drinks. Who had Eva met? As the possibility of who she could have met dawned on him, he felt a flash of red hot rage flood through him. Could she actually have gone to meet up with his bete noire, the meddling cop, and the one man he detested above all others. If so, what was the purpose of this meeting?' His anger abated, replaced by a commitment to find out what was going on. Gary had to smile at the irony of it all. If his Eva was meeting secretly with her handsome friend, were they having an affair behind his back? He always easily dismissed his adultery with women during his marriages to the first two wives. He reasoned that as the two were so terrible at sex, he deserved his dalliances in order to soothe him, and tone down his anger. Basically, he was doing the wives a favour and protecting them from harm. If his luscious Eva was cheating on him, he now experienced a physical thump to his gut, as he could not stand to think of her in the arms of another man. Particularly the one man he hated with a vengeance.

Over an hour later, she was back with Alfie. She instructed her son to get his bag ready for school the next day and then go straight to bed. 'Don't forget to brush your teeth.'

As Alfie departed upstairs, Eva asked Gary if he wanted a beer, as she was going to have one glass of wine before bed. She brought in the drinks and sat on the adjacent sofa to him. Gary looked across at her, as she curled her legs under her, relaxing as she sipped the drink. He stared at her, taking in her beauty, her lovely face, the deep blue eyes that drew you down into their unfathomable depths, her soft, tender mouth that he devoured whenever he could. He got up and went to sit by her and placed an arm around her. He leaned in to kiss her which she pulled back from as she concentrated on drinking the wine. To distract him, she picked up the remote to search for a programme they could watch together. 'What do you want to watch?'

'You choose.' Gary was not happy at the rejection of his kiss. Was this because she had already had sex today with another man? If he found this out, then it would not end well for the two individuals involved.

CHAPTER SIXTY

On Friday evening Andy was now sat at a table, in a town centre bar, on a second date with Lydia, the friend of his detective pal, Ryan. After meeting with Eva on Tuesday, he decided it might be helpful to discover a bit more about Gary's relationship with the woman called Samantha, who he had kept as his girlfriend when married to Jess. Andy estimated that this relationship had been going on at the time that Gary moved away from Reading and had bought the dealership in Stratford-Upon-Avon and maybe the one at Kenilworth. His plan was to send Ryan to the Stratford place, with the purpose of buying a quality second hand car, and to see if he could obtain any information on Samantha. Ryan was due to visit the dealership tomorrow, Saturday, with strict instructions not to speak to Gary, or his friend Simon. He sent Ryan a photo of Gary and gave him a description of Simon, so hopefully he would be on his guard. In return for this favour, Ryan had strong-armed him into a second date with Lydia but Andy had made it very clear to Ryan that there would not be a date number three.

Lydia was fairly tall, slim, with long, brown hair and choppy fringe and she wore a black, off the shoulder, mini dress displaying golden limbs. Andy assessed that she was an attractive woman, well-groomed, with a friendly smile but really not someone he felt he clicked with on a personality level. They were seated opposite each other at a table for two, in a high ceiling room with many tables and chairs, and a long bar with low-level lighting. The place was full, due to it being a Friday night, but Andy's table was nearest to the wall away from the other customers, so a tad less noisy.

Lydia was sipping on an Aperol with soda, ice, and orange slice, as she outlined that her job as a public relations executive meant that communication skills were the main necessity for the role. 'I work for a company providing health care services, and my remit is to promote the company, plan and deliver PR strategies, liaise with media outlets, individuals and stakeholders, write press releases, have excellent up-to-date knowledge of social media including FB and Twitter.'

Andy drank his pint of lager, listening half-heartedly, whilst thinking of something interesting to ask. 'What would you do in a typical week?'

Lydia sighed heavily, as if the burden of it all was too much. 'This week it's been full on. We're promoting a new pharmaceutical product for treatment of acne, to the NHS, private health care subscribers and general pharmacies. I've not stopped all week and I've been involved in television and radio interviews and press releases. But more importantly, we are targeting the young people that suffer from this skin condition, via social media including FB, Instagram, Twitter and Snapchat. Did you know that lockdowns, and the need to communicate on Zoom video calls, has caused a lot of trauma to those with acne? To such an extent that they are feeling self-conscious and do not want to participate in the call so as not to draw attention to themselves. It's very sad.'

'I would never have guessed that this could be a problem for young people. Its amazing how each new technology brings its own set of issues,' Andy stated.

'Anyway, my week was so busy that I was looking forward to a night in, lounging on the sofa and drinking wine. I was really surprised when you called.'

Andy nearly commented, 'so was I.' He did feel a fraud sat with this young woman, who was in all honesty a little too young for him, knowing that he had absolutely no interest in seeing her again.

She now glanced at him, her green eyes blinking beneath her long black lashes. 'What made you decide to call me? Did you want to find out more about the world of PR?'

'Absolutely. It definitely takes my mind off my job. Your work is very positive, outgoing, and I assume fun. My job is the exact opposite but there can be a great deal of satisfaction on finding out who committed a murder and ensuring that we make a solid case for the CPS and the courts. Holding murderers accountable for their crimes.'

Lydia shuddered. 'I don't know how you do that. All them lives lost and grieving family and friends. A friend of mine, her mother was killed by a violent partner, and she's never got over it.'

Andy shuddered on hearing this, given Eva's situation with Gary. The purpose of this 'date' was a quid pro quo for Ryan to find out anything about Gary's previous girlfriend, Samantha. Andy was striving to gather information, in a circuitous way, to help Eva, the woman that he deeply cared for, to know all she can about the secretive, deceptive, ruthless man that she had agreed to marry. He was beyond relieved when she had told him the other day that she had no intention of going through with the wedding to Gary. But Andy was convinced that extricating herself from her destructive and controlling relationship was not going to be easy. He was certain that Gary would react badly, probably violently, and Andy was terrified that she was in great danger of getting hurt. He was determined to meet with her again next week, to talk through what she was going to do, and how he could help. If she would let him.

'Would you like another drink?' Lydia asked, getting up to go to the bar.

'Yes, thanks. Another lager would be great.' As she left to go for the drinks, Andy considered ways to steer the conversation away from the world of PR and social media and onto other topics. He felt really annoyed with himself that he had allowed Ryan to talk him into this second date. He should have promised Ryan a night in the pub, on him, instead.

As Lydia sat down with the two drinks, Andy said, 'thanks for this. Now, I want to hear a bit more about you and not your job. You know, family and friends, that kind of thing. And I will apologise, if I start to ask too many questions, as all my family and friends think I am far too nosy and interested in every detail. It comes with the territory of being a police detective.'

Lydia laughed. 'Then I had better be careful and not reveal anything about my criminal connections and where my stash of drugs are stored.'

On Saturday evening, Andy phoned Ryan to find out how he had got on at the car dealership owned by Gary Anderson.

Ryan laughed loudly. 'It was fine. I purchased an Audi A6 Ultra TDI SE Executive model, four door, 2016, silver, diesel, 47,000 miles on clock, £14,850k and I said that you would pick up the tab.'

Andy gasped. 'I seriously hope you didn't mention my name in all this or it will blow the whole thing wide open.'

Ryan breathed heavily. 'Sorry, man, no I didn't say your name. What do you take me for? I am a super sleuth and have done plenty of undercover work. I know the score.'

'Do you though? There is someone who could end up getting seriously hurt if this Gary Anderson finds out I've been asking questions about him.'

'Ok, Andy, don't sweat. I didn't mention your name at all.'

'Good. Did you ask about the woman named Samantha who used to know your cousin and worked at the dealership? The one who could offer you a discount.'

'Yep. I asked about Samantha, my cousin's friend. The guy who showed me the Audi A6 had worked there for over ten years and was sure that no one called Samantha had ever been employed there. He did mention that the boss, this Gary, had a girlfriend called Samantha, quite a few years ago. It turned out that Gary's wife had died suddenly. With the wife gone, Samantha would turn up quite regularly, and how to put it tactfully, was not well turned out and made a nuisance of herself, scaring off the customers. There were a number of incidents when she started to turn up drunk and Gary would have to practically carry her off the premises. Not the upmarket, slick image of a car dealership one wants to promote. The last incident was when she turned up with a half-drunk bottle of vodka and spewed up in a Jag. This was the last straw. Word on the grapevine was that Gary knocked her about after that and she was not seen there again.'

'Knocked her about?'

'Someone saw her just after with a black eye and cut lip and there was some gossip. The friend, Simon, confirmed to a few people that Gary had dealt with this Samantha, in his own special way, implying that he had beaten her up. The sales guy remembered the conversation as Simon was almost relishing the whole thing in a licking of his lips kind of way. Sick man. Anyway, it's clear that this Gary is not a man to cross. However you're involved with all this, I would suggest you take care.'

Andy paused. 'I know what I'm doing and he might find out that I am not someone to mess about with.'

Ryan laughed. 'Yes, I remember you from our plod days. Quite a few low-life regretted getting on the wrong side of you. You actually scared me at times and I pride myself as being as tough as Bruce Willis in the 'Die Hard' movies.'

Andy now sniggered loudly. 'I think of you more as the Marshmallow Man in Ghostbusters. I noticed that you'd gained a few pounds last time we met.'

'Fucking rude, seen as I've just done you a big favour.'

'Thanks, Ryan. I won't forget it and I am assured by lots of ladies that they like a cuddly man.'

'Fuck off, Leyton.'

'Will do. When's the Audi ready for collection?'

'When you pay the fucking bill. How did the date with Lydia go? Will you be seeing her again?'

'Look, Ryan, she is a great woman but I'm not interested. I feel really badly for letting you talk me into taking her on that second date. I think she wanted to go out again. I told her that I was still getting over someone and it would not be fair to her for me to carry on seeing her. See how easy it is to lie.'

'Andy, mate, I know you're lying. You are not getting over the lovely Natasha as I got the impression you were glad to see the back of her. Call me the world's best detective but you are interested in a woman and this little favour I've done you, relates to her.'

'Yes, maybe. But that's between ourselves, ok. Lydia needs only to know what I've told her, so don't get telling your Kelly either.'

'Your secret's safe with me but you owe me a few pints, Leyton. Bye.'

After the call ended, Andy added the latest details about Gary Anderson, and the way he dealt with women who displeased him into the sum total of information he had gathered on this man. Every new layer of evidence, every building block of data created a bogeyman, an abomination, a Frankenstein, that turned uglier day by day and Andy was terrified how Eva was going to smite this monster.

CHAPTER SIXTY ONE

As Eva walked into her house, followed by a very contrite Alfie, she didn't really know what to say to her son. It was times like this that she wished that Niall were here and that they could discuss problems together and find solutions. Eva had been shocked when her mobile rang a couple of hours ago, a phone call from the Head of Year, Mr Mackrell, to say that there had been an 'incident' involving Alfie and could she come to the school at the end of the school day. Arriving at Mr Mackrell's office at 4.00 p.m., Alfie was already seated by his desk, looking red-faced and sheepish, as he said hello to his mother. It transpired that at lunchtime, Alfie and a boy in Year 8, Lucas Whaley, were seen pushing and shoving each other in the playground, resulting in Lucas's school bag being torn. The lunchtime supervisor who observed and reported the incident indicated that both boys were in a full-blown argument, pushing each other forcefully, and the bag got ripped as Lucas went to storm off before Alfie was ready to let the argument go. Mr Mackrell could not get much out of Alfie about the reason for the argument. He declared that he was very disappointed in Alfie as he believed him to be a well-behaved pupil. Mr Mackrell explained that he was going to give both boys an in-school suspension of two days. It was arranged that each boy, with a parent, would report to Mr Mackrell's office on Thursday at 4.00 p.m. to apologise to each other and explain how they would behave going forward.

Eva went over to the kettle, ready to make a much-needed cup of coffee. 'Ok, Alfie, you can get a drink and a snack and we will have a chat about all this in about fifteen minutes time, ok.'

Alfie nodded and asked, 'can I go to my room until then?'

'Yes, but no computer games until we've spoken. You can do homework, ok?'

Alfie quickly got a glass of milk and a chocolate bar and left the kitchen area. As he disappeared upstairs, Eva heard Gary entering the house, and she greeted him with a weak smile as he came in the room.

Gary noticed that she looked troubled. 'What's up, has something happened?' He went over to the kettle to re-boil the water to make a drink.

She really did not want to involve Gary in any of this as she could not predict what his reaction would be. As someone who often advocated that some problems could be solved by aggressive behaviour, he may endorse what Alfie had done which was not the message she wanted her son to hear. On the other hand, he may adopt his favoured role of disciplinarian stepdad and get tough with Alfie, which again, was not an approach to this problem that she wanted. Her first priority was to find out why Alfie had got into an argument with this boy. She could then discuss with him the consequences of this behaviour, why he had received the suspension, and what she expected of him in the future.

Eva sighed softly, and glanced at Gary who was still waiting for an answer to his question. He made a coffee and sat down next to her at the dining table. 'Well?'

'Alfie got into physical argument with a boy at school today and has been given an in-school suspension of two days.'

Gary looked neither shocked nor surprised at this point. 'Did he now? What does an in-school suspension mean?'

'That he will be in school but not in class. I expect he'll be given work to do in a separate classroom under the supervision of a TA.'

'Do we know the reason for this argument?'

'Not really. Alfie would not elaborate to the Head of Year, Mr Mackrell. I've sent him upstairs for fifteen minutes and I am going to speak to him when I finish this coffee.'

'Ok, but correction, we'll speak to him.'

Eva now focused on Gary; a stern look on her face. 'We will speak to him but I don't want you coming over all heavy with him. I need to know what caused all this and then we can decide the way forward. Ok?'

Gary did not seem entirely pleased with this but agreed. 'Ok, but if he's in the wrong here, I don't want you going all soft on him. We need to ensure that this type of behaviour isn't repeated in the future.'

'I agree, but the first thing I want to do is hear Alfie's side of the story and then we can take it from there. I will go and get him.'

A few minutes later, Alfie followed Eva into the kitchen, and sat down at the dining table. His cheeks blushed slightly when he saw that Gary was present.

Alfie breathed heavily and addressed his mother. 'Am I in big trouble?'

Eva spoke calmly to her son. 'We'll see. We need to hear from you what happened at school today.'

Initially Alfie was silent, and Eva feared that she was going to get the same response as Mr Mackrell, and no explanation would be forthcoming. He then glanced at Gary's non-smiling face and decided that silence was not an option.

Alfie swallowed and his face developed a deeper blush. 'Ok. It was lunchtime and I was with Jai and a few other Year 7 boys. We were just messing about, play punching each other and laughing. Lucas Whaley, Year 8, and his mate, Oscar, walked nearby and Lucas makes some joke about us acting like infants. We all ignored him. The next thing they're standing next to us and laughing. Lucas makes a comment that I fancy Hannah Leyton, as I go all stupid when I'm around her, whatever that means.' Alfie stopped talking to gauge the reaction of his mother and Gary, and so far, they were quietly listening.

Eva prompted, 'what happened next?'

'Lucas starts to say that Hannah would never look at me as I am a little boy and she prefers someone who knows what they are doing... you know...with kissing and stuff.' Alfie's bright cheeks were now a scorching hot red as he related his version of events. 'Lucas then said that he had kissed her recently, and..err..felt her up. Well, I didn't know if this was true or not but I did not like him speaking about Hannah like that so I pushed him hard on the shoulder. He then pushed me back, so I pushed him again, and he tried to punch me. The lunchtime supervisor then intervened and stopped us, told us to get away from each other, and asked our names so we could be reported to Mr Mackrell. As Lucas walked away, I was still pretty mad so I grabbed his backpack and the strap broke.'

Eva sighed as she decided what to say to her son. 'I can understand that you were upset when he was talking about Hannah in that unpleasant way. The problem is that the way you handled the situation, with physical aggression, is not the way to resolve things. And, by your own account, you started the physical side of things by pushing him first. Because of that you have landed yourself with an in-school suspension which will go on your school record. What would have been a better way to handle the matter, do you think?'

Alfie tried to shrink from his mother's gaze. 'I should not have pushed him. Perhaps I should have told him not to talk about her like that and left it at that. Trouble was, he made me angry and I saw red.'

Eva sighed loudly 'You are right, you should not have pushed him, which led him to retaliate, and so on. Its lucky that things did not escalate further as one of you could have ended up getting really hurt. If someone is pushed, or punched, and falls and hits their head on hard concrete, they could be seriously hurt or killed.'

Alfie looked shyly at his mother. 'I'm sorry, mum, and Gary, for what I did and for getting this suspension.'

'Thank you for apologising and understanding what you did wrong. I am not happy with the physical aspect of this, you pushing people, but I do have to give you some credit for sticking up for Hannah. Gary, is there anything you want to say?'

Gary eyed Alfie, who squirmed slightly and avoided eye contact with him, as he could not fathom what his stepdad was thinking. 'In some ways, I support what Alfie did. I lived my whole childhood taking on the bigger kids and winning. Sometimes the only way to solve a problem is to use a physical approach, as you call it. You must never show weakness or you will get bullied and thumped.'

Eva glared at Gary. 'That's really not the message I have tried to give my son in the last fifteen minutes. Violence is not the answer. Anyway, Alfie, there will have to be some consequences at home for this behaviour. I will discuss what those are with Gary now and we will let you know.'

Alfie was by now fidgeting to get away from this dressing down and forget the whole thing until tomorrow. 'I am getting an in-school suspension which will be pretty embarrassing when I can't go to normal classes with my friends. Can't we leave it at that? I've also got to apologise to Lucas in front of Mr Fish on Thursday.'

Eva was now starting to lose her temper with her son. 'I don't think this is the time for jokes about the Head of Year's name. Go upstairs and do your homework.'

As he left the kitchen area, Gary laughed. 'For the first time, I have to say that kid has shown some guts.'

Eva got out of her seat and took her coffee mug to the sink. 'Unlike you, Gary, I can't endorse violent behaviour for dealing with problems in life. I would rather you didn't encourage him to think like that.'

'Oh, I don't know, you can get a lot of what you want by making people fearful of you. In that, I include those people who make a fool of their partners by seeing other people behind their partner's back.'

Eva was puzzled by this comment as it did not relate to the situation involving Alfie. 'What are you on about?'

'Oh, I think you do know what I mean, don't you sweetheart?' He now stood behind her as she went to put the dirty mug in the dishwasher. As he towered over her, his body pressing against her back, she shuddered as his hand traced a line from her face, down her neck, to her breast. 'I always get even with those who cross me.'

Eva held her breath. What was he referring to, people who make a fool of their partners by seeing other people? He was implying that she was cheating on him. Had he somehow found out about her meeting at the pub with Andy and was insinuating that they were having an affair?

Gary blew air on her neck, then lifted up her hair, and his mouth traced a line of moisture down her neck as Eva tried to hide her revulsion. He then paused before hot breath tickled her ear as he whispered, 'you are perfection to me, darling, but I will not be made a fool of by anyone.'.

Eva kept perfectly still, holding her breath, as he toyed with her. Like a fly caught in a web she struggled to escape but she did push past him, ending his entrapment of her. But this little game of restricting her, hemming her in, teasing with her with his hands and body, and his menacing words, frightened her. It all served as another reminder of why she needed to get this unpredictable man out of her life for good.

CHAPTER SIXTY TWO

During Wednesday, Eva called Andy on his mobile from the phone in the school office, claiming to the office staff that her mobile was out of charge. He answered promptly, checking that she was ok and did she want to meet.

Eva tried to speak softly, aware that the three members of staff were all looking at her with ears tuned into the detail of the conversation. 'Yes, if we could. I have the confirmation of what I want in terms of the wedding flowers and I could stop by your shop on the way home. Are you open till 5.30 p.m.?'

Andy laughed at his end of the phone. 'I will do a fantastic job on the flowers. How do dandelions, foxgloves, lily-of-the-valley and poison ivy sound?'

'Brilliant.'

'Can you meet me at the Pheasant on the A46 at 5.00 p.m.?'

'5.00 p.m. is fine See you then. Bye.'

The three women in the office all smiled excitedly and one asked, 'wedding arrangements going well, then? How lovely.'

Eva adopted her best forced smile. 'Yes, all going well, thanks.'

A few hours later Eva was sat in the Pheasant pub, waiting for Andy, having purchased their drinks of choice for these meetings, sparkling water for her, half of lager for him. The pub was upmarket, but cosy, with an open brick fireplace in the centre of the room and a gas fire radiating warmth on a cold December evening. Eva had located a table for two, away from the bar, and fire, and was now waiting for Andy. It was now ten minutes past five and she hoped he would arrive soon, in order to get this meeting over with and go home. After Gary's comments yesterday, about 'getting even with those who cross me' she felt cold with dread that Gary had found out about her meeting with Andy last week. Would he also suspect that she was meeting him tonight?

Luckily, at that moment, Andy strode in, smiling at her apologetically as he approached their table. 'Hi, sorry I'm a bit late, as a meeting over ran and then the traffic was heavy on the road here.' He took off his outdoor jacket to place on the back of his chair. He was wearing a grey suit, with white shirt, and dark blue tie, which enhanced his looks and gave him an air of authority. 'Is that lager for me?'

'Yes, it is. I hope that's ok?'

'Yes, great, thanks,' he said, before taking a swig.

Eva glanced at him, nervously. 'Before we get to the issue of why we are here, there's something I should tell you relating to Hannah and Alfie.'

Andy frowned slightly, before commenting, 'she's not pregnant is she? If she is I will have to kill him.'

Eva smiled weakly. 'You might not think this is a joke when I tell you.' With that, she gave Andy a full account of what occurred at school on Monday concerning Alfie and the other boy, Lucas Whaley, and Alfie's in-school suspension.'

At the end of this, Andy's expression was far from friendly. 'I told you at Hannah's party that I did not like that Lucas kid. I am seriously hoping that he has not been kissing her and the rest. Oh, shit.'

Eva sighed. 'I suggest you have a word with Hannah to find out if anything has been going on. It could all be bragging and wishful thinking on the part of the boy, Lucas, and nothing has happened.'

'If I find out he has 'felt her up' to quote Alfie, I will be sorely tempted to knock him into next week.' 'Well, you've got a friend in Gary for once. He was quite impressed with what Alfie had done. According to Gary's law, it's never a good idea to show weakness and sometimes the physical approach is the best option. After I'd clearly told Alfie that violence is never a way to solve problems. What is it about men that they think fighting is a good idea? I'm surprised at you, Andy, as you see the results of extreme violence every day.'

'Sometimes, Eva, when people you care about are threatened or abused, it can be the only answer. It's an instinctive thing. Generally, we all keep these instincts in check in a civilised society and abide by the rule of law. Luckily, for that Lucas boy'.

'I'm sorry to have to tell you about all this.'

'I'm glad you did, even though Hannah was not directly involved. Also, I am grateful for Alfie standing up to that boy, even if it got him into big trouble.'

'It sure has and no one was more surprised by Alfie's behaviour as much as me. We obviously don't know our kids as well as we think we do.'

Andy now regarded her carefully, the issue of Alfie dealt with. 'Since last week I've got one of my DI colleagues to go to the Stratford dealership to find out any info on Gary's girlfriend, Samantha. Apparently when Jess died, Samantha began to make a nuisance of herself at Gary's workplace by turning up drunk on a number of occasions. The final straw was her vomiting in one of his high-end cars. Apparently, afterwards, Gary dealt with her in his own special way, by beating her up, according to a prime source, Simon. That's all I can find out about her.'

Eva's face lost its colour, despite the warmth in the room. 'Oh God, I don't think I want to hear any more about how awful he is.'

'That brings us back to how you are going to handle all this and when are you going to tell him the relationship is over,' Andy remarked.

Eva breathed deeply, trying to control her emotions. 'It really has got to be soon as these wedding arrangements are gathering momentum and the cost is adding up sharply. On Saturday, we organised the wedding cake and that required a two-hundred-pound deposit, non-refundable. In theory, I want to do it before Christmas but it's all so much more difficult with my mum and dad away. I've got to ensure that Alfie's not there. I was thinking of asking Tania to have him and I'll have to tell her what I am doing.'

Andy focused his full attention on her, a stern look on his face. 'Right. I know you want to do this by yourself, and I respect that, but you must let me be on standby if you need help. I am a hundred percent convinced Gary will not take this well. We have established that he is capable of extremely violent behaviour. What are you expecting to happen? You tell him to leave and he immediately packs a suitcase?'

'No, I know he won't be happy. But it's my house and I do not want to leave. He has no right to stay in my house but what do I do if he won't leave?'

'Yeah, it's a massive problem to leave him in your house but you may have no choice if your safety is compromised. You will have to be prepared to flee, so decide where you will go, and plan in advance to have some stuff there. Things such as money, clothes, personal information including important documents i.e., passports, bank statements, insurance policies and other necessary items. Ensure there is petrol in your car. Get a second phone, and leave it in a jacket in the hall with the spare set of car keys, so you can grab the jacket if you need to run. Best case scenario is that you discuss all this with a domestic abuse charity who are used to advising woman on how to deal with these situations.'

Eva nodded. 'I can do all that but I am really not planning to leave. Its him who must go. If he gets aggressive, I will call the police.'

'And they could take time to turn up and in the meantime you get hurt,' Andy insisted. 'I suggest that you get a spare door key and give it to me, discreetly. If you do this to coincide with a weekend that I am not on call, I can be round in minutes if you need help. If you need to leave the house in a hurry just come over to mine. If you can without further jeopardy to yourself.'

Eva looked at his concerned face and was worried that he wanted to get involved with this. 'Thanks, Andy, but I really can't drag you into all of this. I will get you a key but I honestly don't think you'll need to use it. I am just hoping that he will not resort to violence as it will land him in all sorts of trouble. Up to now, Gary seems to have been very careful to avoid getting into bother with the police, as he is far too clever. If he harms me then it will result in criminal charges.'

Andy drank more of his lager to help him to stay calm. What he was seeing was Eva's naivety about all this and it was really starting to freak him out. 'As your friend, Eva, and as a police officer, I am having serious doubts about this. I do think you are over-estimating your ability to handle Gary's reaction when you ask him to leave. In terms of telling him, when do you plan to do this?'

'I think that this weekend would be too soon, as I need to get a second phone and spare key for you, as suggested. Alfie's staying at Jai's on Friday and Saturday night so it would have been ideal but it is really too soon. I think I'm looking at Friday 17th or Saturday 18th the following week which is ridiculously close to Christmas but I've got to get this over with. The pressure of it all is torturing me and too much money is being paid out for a wedding that is never going to happen.'

'Where does Gary think you are now?'

'I've told him I'm popping to Tania's to discuss hen night arrangements. Tania needs to know numbers as she is arranging for us to stay in a large house in an upmarket town with lots of bars and single men. I'll tell her not to arrange anything until after Christmas. I don't want any more money wasted.'

'I suppose we'd better go so you can get home. Just to let you know that I am on call this weekend, including Friday night, but I'm not working the following weekend. Listen to me now. You contact me if you need help.'

She avoided his eyes as she did not want to have to agree to this.

He got up from his chair and picked up his jacket. 'You haven't responded. I will stand on this table in a minute and start singing, badly, if you don't agree to what I'm saying.'

Eva stated, 'you wouldn't.' As he placed his foot on the chair, to jump on it, she knew he was serious. 'Ok, ok, I agree to contact you if I need help. Please don't get on the table, even if you sing like George Michael.'

'I do. But we will leave my singing abilities for discussion on another day.'

****

As they left the warmth of the pub, and were met by the chill of the damp, cold night the man and woman hurried to their cars which were parked close to each other. Another car, a black VW Golf was parked, in a parking space behind these cars. All lights on the car were out but the driver remained in his seat. His face was shielded by a black baseball cap pulled low but he could still watch what the two people were doing.

Gary was in one of the cars from the dealership, having left his own car there, as he watched as the man stopped at the driver's door of the woman's car. They spent a few minutes in conversation before the man moved in closer to her. After speaking to her again, he pulled her into him and put his arms around her in a secure embrace. The woman appeared small against the man, her head fitting just under his chin, and she remained still, her head resting on his chest. The man then tilted her chin upwards, so he could look at her face and for a moment Gary thought that they would kiss. It took every ounce of his self-control not to blow his cover at this time, even though he wanted to burst out of the car, and hammer the man with his fists.

This was now the proof he wanted to confirm his suspicions. His beautiful fiancée, Eva, was having a relationship with their next-door neighbour, Andy, the cop, Leyton. This was the reason she was not absorbed or excited in planning their wedding. Well, PC Plod of the Old Bill, was not going to win on this one. Too much time had gone in to it all for things to go wrong now. The Plan would not be compromised. Eva would become Wife Number Three, on 28th May 2022, as he intended. What her fate would be after that was still not clear though the object of the exercise to take her property and money was still forefront in his mind. He now had severe regrets in having chosen Eva for this stage of The Plan. He should have stuck to the successful formula of picking plain, boring women who he would not have any feelings for. This time, Eva had been the wrong choice, beautiful, sexy, intelligent, fun and he had made a strong connection with her. One, because she fulfilled all his sexual needs and his passion to possess her body was unceasing. Two, because the connection did not just involve his body but an emotional bond with his heart and mind. And in front of him now was the man that was trying to take her away from him.

In trying to formulate a strategy to ensure she stayed with him, and see off his rival, Gary realised that there was only one way to keep her in line. He had to use the one thing above all others that she feared being hurt. Her vulnerable area, her weak spot, her Achilles' heel. Her son, Alfie.

CHAPTER SIXTY THREE

As Eva walked in the house at about 6.30 p.m. after meeting Andy, she was surprised to find Alfie alone with no sign of Gary. Alfie was at the dining table in the kitchen finishing his homework having consumed two chocolate bars and two packet of crisps as the evidence of the wrappers indicated. Eva noted the anxiety on her son's face. 'Hi, Alfie, are you here on your own? Where's Gary, as he agreed to come home early to be with you?'

Alfie shrugged his shoulders. 'I got in at about 4.30 p.m. and I haven't seen him. I was getting a bit worried as to where you both were.'

'I'm sorry, Alfie, as I was a bit delayed at Tania's. You know how she likes to chat if she gets the chance. How did your last day of suspension go?'

'Ok, I suppose. It's quite boring as all you do is the work set by the teachers and I didn't know any of the other kids, except my enemy, Lucas Whaley.'

'How many children were with you today?'

'Lucas, and just two others. A Year 7 boy and a Year 9 girl. In fact, Lucas and I have sort of made friends, so it's come right in the end. But I'm pleased to be going back to normal lessons tomorrow.'

At that moment, they heard the front door opened and Gary walked into the kitchen. He glanced at Eva and Alfie and at the food wrappers on the table. 'Been eating rubbish again, I see.' He went over to the cupboard, removed a glass, and poured in water from the tap and drank thirstily. 'What time did you get in Eva?'

'Just a few minutes ago. You know Tania, it's hard to get away.'

'Yeah, she does suffer from verbal diarrhoea. Anyway, you can tell me all about it later. I'll do dinner but it will have to be something quick like salmon pasta and salad.'

'Yes, that's fine. How come you're so late as I asked you to come home early to be with Alfie?'

Gary went to a top cupboard, reached for the dried spaghetti and then filled the kettle to boil water. He turned to respond to Eva's question. 'Sorry, but I got waylaid at the dealership with an issue over a finance package on a car being collected early tomorrow. I couldn't get away. No harm done, as he seems to have survived by eating elephant-sized quantities of junk.'

Alfie did not like being the focus of the conversation over his bad eating habits. He got up off his chair, scooped up his books, pencil case and phone to place in his bag. 'How long is dinner going to be?'

Gary replied, 'about fifteen minutes, so don't expect to have to be called down. Go and change out of your uniform and be ready for dinner.' Alfie picked up his bag to walk out the room.

Gary's loud voice stopped him in his tracks. 'I don't think so.' Alfie paused, not sure of what he was expected to do and looked anxiously at Gary, noting his annoyance. 'What's left on the table?'

Remembering the chocolate wrappers and crisp packets, plus an empty glass, Alfie quickly removed these items from the table and placed the wrappers in the bin and the glass in the dishwasher which broke as he thumped it down. 'Oh, flipping heck.' Alfie's face went bright red.

The two pieces of glass were in the upper tray of the dishwasher, the smaller piece was a triangular shape with a fine tip. Eva moved towards her son to help with the removal of the pieces. 'I'll do it, Alfie, in case you cut yourself. Go and get changed.'

'Be more careful in future, as you're ultra-clumsy,' Gary ordered.

'Gary, I'm going to get changed as well out of this trouser suit,' Eva said.

'Don't be long.' As Eva left the room, Gary picked up her bag off the kitchen top and retrieved her phone from inside. He accessed the phone and quickly texted Tania. '**Hi Tania. Great to see you this evening. I'm sure the hen night will be great. No male strippers as Gary won't like it. Eva xx**'

A reply pinged in immediately. '**You've lost your marbles, honey. We didn't meet tonight. But I will organise a stripper just to antagonise the little shit xx**'

As Eva returned to the room, Gary slipped the phone back in her bag.

After dinner when Alfie had gone to bed, Eva was sat on the sofa, playing a word game on her phone. Gary came in with a bottled beer and a glass of wine, which he handed to her. 'Here you are, it's nice to wind down after a long day.' He sat next to her, his shoulder brushing hers. 'How did Alfie's last day of his suspension go? Has he learnt the error of his ways and will no longer get into fights?'

Eva sighed and sipped the cool, refreshing wine. 'I hope so. I've got to pop to the school tomorrow at 4.00 p.m. so that he can apologise to Lucas Whaley. I could do without it. Christmas is coming and there's still a lot of presents to buy and wrap.'

Gary slipped an arm around her shoulder and his hand held a firm grip on her left upper arm. Eva wanted to pull away but for now she knew she must cooperate, play the part of the loving fiancée being cuddled by the man she was soon to marry. 'So, tell me about all the hen night arrangements that Tania's making to mortally embarrass you?' Eva felt that his fingers had gripped her arm more tightly as he said this or was it just her imagination?

Eva tried to pull her arms closer into her body to escape his hold. She stuttered, 'I don't know, it's all going to be a big surprise. I only went around to give her a list of names and phone numbers of who will be going, if she needs to contact them about any of the activities.' She laughed in a hysterical way. 'I say the word activities but I just hope she doesn't arrange anything too outlandish. You know what Tania is like. Anything that involves wine tasting or has a chocolate theme will do me. I do know that we will be going to either Bath or Salisbury but that's all.'

Gary laughed as he snuggled in closer, squashing his weight more on to her. 'No male strippers then? I would have thought that would be right up Tania's street or don't hen dos have strippers anymore?'

Eva pulled a face. 'No, thank goodness. I'm really glad that tradition has disappeared as it must have been so embarrassing, especially if they wanted you to rub baby oil into them or something.'

Gary now leaned into her and started to nuzzle her neck with his mouth. He kissed the soft skin at the side of her neck, under her hair. 'Yes, I'm glad you don't want any strippers as I can't stand the thought of you touching some smoothed skinned toyboy with a six-pack, and muscular arms, or he touching you. The only one to put his hands on you is me.' His right hand now inched its way across her right breast, stopping at her nipple, before slowly exploring upwards along her cleavage and up to her neck. His thumb and fingers moved along her throat, and fear gripped her, icy chills radiating up and down her body. His mouth was now nuzzling her ear before his teeth nibbled painfully on her ear lobe. 'Yes, baby, those young, Adonis, male strippers can be over-sexual with the brides-to-be. Especially as they know it's the brides last time to caress another male body. And I do think your chief bridesmaid, the little minx, has got a stripper in mind as I saw a text ping up on your phone.' He continued to nuzzle the back of her neck while his right hand again wandered down across her breasts, kneading them firmly.

Eva pushed him away from her, puzzled about what Tania had texted. She wanted to stop him touching her body as he seemed in a weird mood. His caress was probing and she felt a familiar tension in him. His touch was on the verge of causing her pain. 'Gary, ease off will you, let me just see what Tania has said?' She picked up her phone and read the two texts, the first one supposedly from her which she knew she had not sent. The earlier chill she had experienced was now of a coldness intensity similar to that of arctic temperatures. It must have been Gary who sent that first text, suspecting that she had not been meeting Tania. Now Tania's innocent response had caught her out. She re-read the texts but did not comment and put her phone down.

'What's Tania up to then? Is she seriously planning a stripper? Let's read it.' He picked up her phone before she could stop him, entered her password, and then read the texts. Eva tried to snatch the phone off him but he slapped her hand away.

Eva ordered, 'Gary, that's my phone. You have no right to access it and you shouldn't know my password.'

'Shut up. Let's read these texts shall we? You said, or rather I said, ''Hi Tania. Great to see you this evening. I'm sure the hen night will be great but no male strippers as Gary won't like it. Eva xx Tania replied, 'you've lost your marbles honey. We didn't meet tonight. I will organise a stripper just to antagonise the little shit.'

Gary sniggered. 'You know, I do take exception to the phrase 'little shit'. There's nothing little about me, is there, hone-e-e, as you can testify.'

Eva was forced against the arm of the sofa as he continued to push into her, restricting her movement. He now knew that she had not met Tania this evening after school.

His left arm once again went around her and strong fingers gripped her upper arm. 'Right, hone-e-e, I do not have to be DI Leyton to work out that you were not at Tania's this evening discussing your hen do. My probing question to you, now, is where did you go and who did you meet?'

Eva hesitated, 'I didn't want to tell you as it is something I've arranged for you for Christmas and that's all I'll say.'

Gary chuckled. 'Wow, a surprise Christmas present, you really are a wonderful fiancée. I hope it's nothing too expensive as we are saving for a wedding.' He now turned her slightly on the sofa and lifted her legs over his lap. 'Let me try and guess what it will be. I think it will be a large box, beautifully gift wrapped in red paper with a gold bow.' His haunting dark eyes held hers. 'And, when I open it, like an excited kid on Christmas morning, it will be…..' He waited while she looked on at him, bemusement on her face. 'It will be….. empty. I know you are lying to me. You did not meet Tania and now you've compounded one lie with another. I still want you to tell me where you went and who you were with? Also, I know last week you did not go for drinks at The Oak after school to celebrate a teaching assistant's birthday. I texted Kasia last week and she knew nothing about it.'

'Honestly, Gary, I did go to The Oak. I spoke to Kasia the day after and she and Judy didn't know about it. And I forgot to mention it. No mystery.'

'If I believed you, and I don't, you still haven't told me what you were doing tonight.'

'Ok, Gary, if you must know I went to The Oak again tonight but on both occasions I was on my own. I just needed a bit of time out away from school and away from wedding preparations. A glass of white wine and a breather. That's all.' His hand clutched her thigh, just above her left knee, and his fingers dug into her flesh. For Eva, time stood still, as she wondered whether he was believing her explanation or what he was going to do. Was this going to be another physical attack on her, if he did not believe what she had told him? More importantly, she did not think he did. His hard features, and cold dark eyes, did not betray what he was thinking. She felt his grip on her thigh tighten and she feared being pulled down under him, so that he could punch her or worse. Suddenly, his grip eased, and he got up off the sofa. 'As I just said, I don't believe this load of shit about what you were doing last week and this evening. We'll leave it for now but you know I do not like to be lied to. I want the truth the next time we discuss this which will be at the weekend. Ok?'

Eva could not speak as he left the room. He was not going to give up the idea that she was lying but she could not let him know that she had met with Andy. Also, from all her accumulated knowledge about Gary, and the ruthlessness of his personality, he would want to exact revenge if he felt he was being humiliated. All her intentions of ending the relationship next week, with Alfie out of the way at Tania's, may not be possible. This weekend could well be the time it all came to a head. The time she entered into the blackness and coldness of the danger zone, and she was alone, and without any weaponry to fight the rabid beast.

CHAPTER SIXTY FOUR

During the two days since Wednesday, Eva had desperately hoped that time could go backwards. That she could beg, steal or borrow the TARDIS from Dr Who and travel to a time when she was at her happiest, her days with Niall and Alfie, before Niall's death. Since she had lost her husband, her life had been much more fragmented and unstable. She was plagued by feelings of loneliness and that her life was no longer within her control. She had also made terrible decisions. The biggest, and by far the worst, was to bring Gary Anderson into her life. Looking back, why had she been taken in by this man? Yes, he was good-looking, and had a great deal of charisma and sex appeal, but generally she avoided men who were over confident and arrogant. She had allowed him to re-build her shattered confidence after Niall's death. Everything that she had been certain of when Niall was alive, such as love, financial security, friendship, safety from harm, the one person to always have your back, was now in question. What was Gary offering? Her financial security was compromised as Gary's track record with wives was to rob them of their assets. Was he a friend as well as a lover? At times Gary could be funny, and supportive, especially in their early days together but now she could not trust him. And, sex was very important to Gary, an area where he put in major effort so she perceived that Gary valued relationships in terms of their physical aspects and did not see the need for a 'friend' as a necessity in his life. Gary only had one significant relationship in terms of friendship, the ghastly Simon. Eva deduced that Gary preferred to be aloof with people and remain a loner. She doubted whether he wanted or needed her as a friend. Safety from harm? This one was the joke, the contradiction, in their relationship. In your home, with your partner, it should be the safest and most comfortable environment, a place to take refuge from the troubled, often brutal outside world. In her current situation, she was safer outside of what should be her sanctuary, as Gary's aggressive outbursts had caused her physical pain and emotional torment. Love? Did Gary actually love her or understand what love really was? She knew she had experienced true love with Niall. And its solid, secure foundation, from which their tenderness and devotion to each other had flowed, had been all powerful and consuming. She could not honestly work out what Gary felt for her but it all seemed to stem from a need to control. To sexually possess her, to dominate her with his will, to cause her suffering in terms of his bullying ways with Alfie, and to physically correct her when he wanted. Initially, at the start of their relationship, she had found some aspects of his personality compelling. His drive and ambition, his decisiveness, his lack of worry of what others thought of him, and his unwillingness to compromise his opinions. All these aspects of him, she now understood made him into the hard, ruthless, arrogant and intimidating man that posed a danger to her and her son.

Since Wednesday, when Gary had told her bluntly that he knew she had lied to him, and they would discuss this further at the weekend, she had been inwardly quaking about what would happen. Physically she felt ill, she could barely eat, her guts were churning and there was a continuous dull ache in her head that paracetamol would not shift. She yearned to be physically sick to expunge the nausea in her stomach. Over the last two days, Gary had been fairly upbeat, as if Wednesday's conversation hadn't happened and things were as normal.

Fearing the absolute worst, and determined not to compound matters in terms of the wedding, she had also taken a radical step. Yesterday, she had telephoned the wedding venue to cancel the wedding. She explained that she and her fiancé were having some relationship difficulties and it would not be productive to continue with the wedding plans at this time. She had explained to the woman on the phone that she was doing this on behalf of Mr Anderson and herself and not to contact him directly about this. She had confirmed her decision to cancel by email and advised that she would be solely responsible for any outstanding costs. Now, this Friday evening, she was regretting this decision. It was far too hasty and she should have left the cancellation until she had spoken to Gary about her intention to end their relationship. If he were going to challenge her about her visits to the Oak and Pheasant pubs, then she figured it may be time to stop the lies, and tell the truth, whatever the consequences would be for her.

She was sat on the sofa in the lounge, in slim fit black jeans and oversized grey jumper for warmth and comfort, watching a comedy on Netflix which was not making her smile, let alone laugh. She realised that she had reached the most daunting moment of her life. Even more upsetting and challenging than Niall's death. She had prepared for that over a number of months and there had been a small blessing at the end. A peace, when he was finally freed from all pain.

Gary walked in the room, bottle of wine in hand, and two glasses. 'Hi, sweetheart, this is my favourite time of all. All alone with you, no Alfie. The opportunity for us to spend time together and continue our little chat from the other evening.' He sat close by her on the sofa, unscrewed the top on the bottle, poured the white wine into two glasses and handed her one. 'Here you are, drink up. This is our special time as an engaged couple before the big day. When we become husband and wife. Till death us do part.'

Eva drank a couple of sips of the wine, welcoming it's refreshing taste, and hoping that it will soothe her frazzled nerves. 'Thanks.'

He then took the glass out of her hand and put it down on the coffee table alongside his own. 'First off, let's enjoy a kiss and cuddle on the sofa without Alfie liable to lumber in at any time.' He moved towards her, his right hand stroking her hair and face, before his mouth claimed hers. The kiss was intense and probing, his fingers found her chin to prevent her head from moving, as he devoured her mouth. She felt smothered and suffocated, as this went on, unable to breathe but she allowed it as this was not the time to antagonise him. His hand now trailed down her body, pushing the jumper aside to squeeze her breasts, before exploring her waist, thighs and the area between her legs. Eva shivered, not with passion, but with fear as she did not want this to go to its usual conclusion. He must have read her mind, as abruptly as it started, the forceful probing of her body stopped. He moved off her and sat upright on the sofa. 'Wow, baby, that was great. But for now, we'll put a damper on the fire, which can be re-ignited shortly.'

His brown, brooding eyes locked onto hers and his right hand gently caressed her face. 'First, let me say that I have always thought that you are beautiful. I love everything about your face and your body. In a sexual way, you are perfection to me because I genuinely feel a connection with you when we do it together. It's something I have rarely had in my life.' His eyes still watched every expression on her face. 'Tell me, my lovely fiancée, what are you most looking forward to on our wedding day?'

Eva hesitated, fearful of the intensity of his hawkish eyes on hers. It felt as if he could read her thoughts. She stammered, floundering to find a positive aspect of what would be the worst day of her life. 'I'm hoping that the weather will be sunny and that all our friends and family have a wonderful day.'

Gary sighed; annoyance apparent on his face. 'Oh dear, how disappointing. Have you got nothing favourable to say about the handsome and virile groom?'

From tone of his voice, and the faux hurt on his face, Eva knew he was mocking her. 'Of course. I'm sure you'll look amazing in your wedding suit.'

Gary laughed. 'Yes, I will and I will look super sexy out of it on our wedding night which I am eagerly awaiting.'

'Wedding nights don't mean as much if you've been sleeping together for years before the big day, do they?'

'I beg to differ, honey. You will be completely mine on that night, as decreed by law. I will ensure that you will experience something new and exciting that has never happened before. We haven't done the handcuffs and restraints thing for a while. We could explore the concepts of pleasure and pain more fully.'

Eva shivered, relieved that, hopefully, she would never have to find out what he meant. 'I shall be eager with anticipation.'

Suddenly, he ordered her, 'listen up, as I have been sent some new information from the wedding venue.' He picked up his phone and spent a few seconds accessing something as Eva waited anxiously. 'Are yes, here it is. The wedding venue emailed me today to acknowledge the cancellation of the wedding, by Ms Brennan, and that they were sorry that we were unable to have our special day. They confirmed that the initial deposit'……his voice suddenly getting louder ……'paid by Mr Anderson was non-refundable as per the terms of the contract. Best wishes for the future, blah de blah…..' Now, why would you have cancelled the wedding, our wedding?' He was now sat close to her, his left arm weighing on her body, and he turned slightly to observe her face as she responded to this question. His facial features, the sharp cheekbones, well-defined eyebrows, thin lips and deep set, piercing brown eyes, all added to a hard but unreadable exterior.

Eva desperately wanted to stay calm and unphased at this moment and to give sensible reasons as to why she had taken this action. She was struggling to hide her terror. She felt that her body was about to betray her by an inner quivering which would show itself in her shaking hands. She firmly clasped her hands together to stop this from happening. 'I'm sorry, Gary, but I just feel that this wedding is happening too quickly and I'm not ready. We could call it a postponement for now and re-consider in the future. I am suggesting that we take a break in our relationship, put some distance between us, and see what happens. We could still see each other, if you like?'

Gary picked up his glass of wine and had a drink. 'Let me get this straight. You've decided to cancel, or postpone, our wedding, without consulting me and making me look a fool into the bargain. You want to take a break in our relationship. I presume we would live apart but we could still see each other. Brilliant. All our plans and life together ended, by you. No consultation with me.' He now turned slightly so that his knees were pressing into hers and his weight restrained her body. 'Tell me the reason for your sudden withdrawal from this relationship and my life. I assume I have a right to know?'

Eva breathed deeply to steady her nerves as she felt the tension and resentment building in him. 'If I'm honest, you have become too controlling with Alfie and with me, and I am feeling suffocated by you. Everything has to be on your terms and that's not the kind of marriage I want. Niall and I were a partnership, we were loving and kind to each other. You like to have your own way and don't really respect what I want or how I wish to run my life. You are too hard on Alfie and at times its feelings like we live in a military boot camp.' She stopped, gauging his reaction, as he listened without saying anything. 'But, also, you have physically hurt me a number of times and that cannot be right in any loving relationship.'

Again, he drank more wine before re-filling his glass. 'Thanks for the frank and full analysis of my shortcomings as a partner. I am drawing a conclusion from all of this, that this isn't a postponement, or trial separation, but a severing of all contact due to my intimidating and abusive ways. Is that correct?' Again, he drank more wine and his voice was controlled and calm. His face was that of a robot, showing no emotion, no hint at what inner rage Eva knew he would be feeling. Eva feared this outer calmness, as it was false and misleading, as Gary rarely responded to situations he didn't like in a controlled way. Outbursts of temper, and anger, were his most common reactions if he was displeased by something or someone.

A tiny, speck of a smile hovered on his lips, but not a real smile, just a tiny smirk to hint at his annoyance. 'I'm waiting for an answer.'

'No, Gary. I think if we separated, lived apart for a while, we may be able to resume a relationship in the future.'

'I think that I'm not getting the whole story here. I think there's another reason that you want this break up. It fits around the lies that you told me on Wednesday, as to where you had been over the last weeks, after school. I do not buy for one second that you went to those pubs alone for a wine and a breather. Let me tell you how I know.' He picked up his phone and located the photo album. 'Here we are. See those two people outside the Pheasant pub on Wednesday having a goodbye cuddle before getting into their cars. It's you and Supercop. Very cosy, as you are held very tightly in his arms.' He showed her four photos of her embrace with Andy as all blood drained from Eva's face.

'Don't try denying it's you and him. I've also got your car number plates to prove it. Some cop showed me that trick of confirming people's location but that's a story for another day. You are leaving me to be with him.'

Eva was now panic-stricken and tongue-tied over what to say. 'It's-s-s, not as it seems. Yes, I did meet Andy on those two occasions but we are not having any sort of affair. We are just friends and the cuddle was just a goodbye hug, nothing more. Andy doesn't view me in a romantic way.'

Gary poured the remaining wine from the bottle into his glass and swigged it down, then laughed, a grating, harsh noise. 'Oh doesn't he. Don't give me that as he would fuck you given the chance. He's definitely into you, so don't give me your bullshit.'

This was all now turning nasty as the wine kicked in. Eva tried to ease away from him but he was still physically imposing his body on hers. He now loomed over her, the acidity on his breath from the wine assailing her nostrils. 'So, Eva, what to do now about all this? You're right about one thing. I'm not prepared to give up on this relationship as easily as you and I want us to remain together in this house.'

Eva now tried to push him off her, to get up off the sofa and away from him. This resulted in her being more confined by his body weight as she was shoved down underneath him. Trying to force him off, by pushing at his chest, was not working. This was the moment she feared would happen all along, after telling him that they were over. Her phone was on the sofa somewhere but there was no way of grabbing it for now. He now knelt over her as she struggled to move away from him.

'Stop moving,' he snarled as he slashed his right hand across the left side of her face. This was followed by a second slap that jarred her head and stung her ear, causing a ringing sensation. 'That's the warm up act,' he promised, 'and here comes the main event.' Several blows, of his now closed fist struck near her eye and then pummelled into her ribs and abdomen, as she screamed in pain. As he paused slightly, and despite the agony of the blows, she forced herself to make an attempt at an escape as he loomed over her. She rushed up off the sofa but he made a grab for her right ankle to pull her back. She kicked out with her left leg, caught him on the chin, which forced him to let go of his hold on her ankle. Eva scrambled to her feet, to clear the room but in seconds he was on her again. This time pulling her back, his arm around her neck. 'Get back on the sofa, bitch, and stop fighting. You won't win.' Forced to sit down, Eva's eyes strayed to the wine bottle on the coffee table.

Gary immediately saw where she was looking and swiftly retrieved the bottle. 'Want to play dirty now, do we?' Eva jumped up to put space between them as he gripped the bottle. Swinging the bottle around it brutally collided with her left temple, and she staggered. The bottle smashed into pieces, shards of glass pierced the air, and red blood stained her face as she fell down onto the carpet. Gary stood looking at her motionless body, her blood slowly seeping into the carpet pile. For a man always in control, always the winner in any situation, who had successfully escaped any punishment for the crimes he had committed, he now felt utter panic. This was not a crime to be explained by dodgy slippers or overdoses of medication. This was not a body he could dispose of easily. What to fucking do?

As he stared at the unmoving, unconscious body of the woman he had planned to marry, Gary tried to breathe easily to calm his nerves and focus his thoughts. Should he concoct a story that this was the result of a random attack by an intruder? He'd been with Eva, they had shared a glass of wine, before he went out to discuss a business matter with his work colleague, Simon. He'd left his fiancé finishing the rest of the wine and watching tv. It had to be assumed she'd been attacked by an intruder. He would have to establish a convincing alibi of being with Simon using his best acting skills so as not to implicate himself. Now, as the panic was receding, calculating Gary took over and started to think rationally of all the areas that needed to be covered to keep him out of prison. The big problem in all of this was that Eva could regain consciousness and relate what had really happened. The only way to avoid that was if she did not come round.

As Gary tried to think of what to do next, his attention was suddenly focused on the sound of a car drawing up outside. A car door slammed. In the next few seconds, he heard a key being turned in the front door lock and the door opening. Gary's sense of calm and control evaporated as he realised that, for some reason, Alfie had just arrived home. He thought the snotty kid was staying at his mate's house tonight. Why had he returned?

Gary quickly picked up his phone, and car keys, and fled the room. Rushing out of the door and into the kitchen before Alfie spotted him. He pelted towards the back door and exited the house. Normally, when Gary solved a problem with a surge of violence, he felt purged and euphoric. It re-affirmed his sense of power and control and re-enforced his superiority over others. This time, he just felt sheer terror.

CHAPTER SIXTY FIVE

By ten p.m., Andy was pleased not to have been called out to any major incidents that warranted his involvement. Hannah was staying at his mother's as there was still a significant chance he would be called out at any time. Being on-call was frustrating, you couldn't entirely relax, and no indulging in a Friday night beer or wine was possible. He settled for watching a BBC/Netflix show 'The Serpent' a dramatisation of a true story of Charles Sobhraj, a ruthless killer who drugged and robbed young travellers, with the assistance of his beautiful girlfriend, principally in South East Asia, in the 1970s. Andy generally avoided watching films or television programmes about murderers as this was the focus of his working life. But this series intrigued him due to its exotic locations and the ingenuity of the individual, a non-police officer, who investigated the disappearance of missing travellers to find the killer.

As he started to watch episode two, and enjoy a coffee, he was startled to hear a loud banging on the front door. Easing off the sofa, he went out into the hallway and opened the door. He was jolted to see Alfie on the door step, his young face ashen with fear, as he struggled to speak. 'It's m-mum, s-she's dead.'

Andy felt a powerful thump to his chest as he tried to make sense of what Alfie was saying. 'Ok, Alfie, mate, take a deep breath, breathe slowly, and tell me what's happened?'

Alfie's eyes were now filling with tears as he struggled to speak. 'Y-you've g-got to c-come now. I think she's d-d-dead.'

'Ok, mate, now don't panic. Let me come and see what's going on.' Andy grabbed his shoes from the hallway and slipped them on. 'I'll just go and get my phone, two secs.'

Andy rushed to grab his phone and then ran out of his house, across the driveway of the two houses, to arrive at Eva's front door. Alfie followed him, red in the face, and puffing slightly as he struggled to breathe through all the anxiety. 'Wait here, Alfie, while I go and see your mum. Is Gary in?'

'I don't think so. Mum's in the lounge and I don't know where he is.'

Andy moved through the hallway and into the lounge, to find Eva lying face down on the carpet, close to the coffee table. She was laying perfectly still, her hair covering her face, but he could see some blood on the pale beige carpet. He knelt down, next to her, and checked that she was breathing. He tried to ensure that her airway was clear but without moving her due to the possibility of a head injury. Grabbing his phone from his trouser pocket, he dialled 999, and quickly called for ambulance and police. He spoke to her softly. 'It's ok, Eva, its Andy here. You are safe now and I have phoned for an ambulance which should be here shortly. Alfie's just in the other room and he's fine, so don't worry.' Andy had the strongest urge to stroke her hair but until the scope of her head injury was assessed he figured this would be a bad idea. He settled on holding her hand. 'I'm not going anywhere, Eva. You'll be ok, I promise.'

He pulled a throw off the sofa to place over her before he knelt back down to hold her hand. A vortex of emotions were swirling in him; panic, fear, despair.

'Andy, can I come in?' Alfie was standing at the doorway, terror-stricken, wanting to help his mother but too scared to find out if she was breathing, and so still alive. The death of his father had brought the reality of death to his door at a young age. He would now be mortified that he was going to lose a second parent. 'Is she d-dead?' He inched further into the room towards Andy and his motionless mother.

As Alfie stopped by Andy, he looked down at her body, noticing the blood on the carpet, then started to sob.

Andy got to his feet and drew the boy towards him. 'No, Alfie, she's not dead, but she's lost consciousness as she's received a blow to the head. There is a bit of blood but that can look worse than it is. Blows to the head, even slight ones, can bleed a lot. She's breathing but she does need to go to hospital and be assessed. The ambulance is on its way.' Alfie continued to cry, loud sobs, but he pulled away from Andy and sat on the sofa close to his mother.

Andy resumed his position on the carpet and re-took hold of Eva's hand. 'Alfie, do you know what happened here? I thought you were staying at a friend's house this weekend?'

Alfie inhaled deeply, to try to talk, but his breathing was juddery and his body shook. 'I w-was, but there's a problem with Jai's f-family, as his granddad was taken ill so Jai's mum had to rush to the hospital. J-jai's dad brought me h-home, and as m-mum's car was on the drive, I knew she was in. I came in,' he paused as he started to cry again, 'a-and I found her in here. I d-don't know what's happened and there was no s-sign of G-gary.'

Andy assessed the scene around him. There were two wine glasses on the coffee table, one with some white wine in it, the other empty, suggesting that Eva had not been drinking alone. The wine bottle was in pieces around Eva so it was reasonable to assume that this had been the cause of the injury to her head. As a detective, he would now move forward to identify the attacker. Was it someone she knew or was it an intruder? She had obviously been sharing the wine with a partner or friend but then what had happened next? Had that person attacked her? That was the most obvious scenario or could that person have left and she had been subject to an assault by an unknown intruder entering her home. Putting aside his professional assessment, Andy was convinced that this had something to do with Gary. Had she spoken to him about cancelling their wedding and ending their relationship? Had he reacted in exactly the way Andy feared he would, by physically harming her? He was finding it very hard to look at her as she lay on the carpet, not knowing the extent of her injuries. He silently prayed that she would be alright.

He heard a vehicle stop outside and was hopeful that the ambulance had arrived. He leapt to his feet, went to the door to let in two paramedics, one female, one male. 'This way, quickly, please. She's unconscious, but breathing, and there looks to be a head injury caused by a broken wine bottle.'

As the two paramedics followed him into the lounge, Andy stood back so they could do their work. The female paramedic, an older woman with short grey hair, asked, 'what's her name?'

'It's Eva.' Andy gently pulled Alfie off the sofa so that the paramedics had full access to Eva.

'Are you her partner?'

'No, I'm her friend and next-door neighbour. This young man is her son, Alfie. Alfie was meant to be staying with a friend but had to come home unexpectedly and found her like this. He ran to my house next door. I came straight over and called you. That was at ten 'o'clock but we don't know how long she's been like this.'

The female paramedic knelt down, close to Eva. 'Hi, Eva, I'm Jean, and this is John', as she indicated her male colleague. Jean assessed Eva, doing an initial primary survey, establishing airway and breathing were clear before going on to the secondary survey beginning with a head-to-toe check for bleeding. As the paramedics moved Eva, whilst supporting her head, this revealed the gash to the left side of her temple, the site of the bleeding. The area was quickly covered by a dressing, and taped to secure the dressing but the initial bleeding seemed to have stopped. Andy guessed that the blow from the bottle had caused the damage on her temple. But there were other areas of bruising, around her left eye, and the area below her left eye and cheek, and a cut to the side of her lip. This suggested that Eva had been beaten before the final blow from the bottle. Andy knew immediately that this was Gary's doing and he struggled to conceal the fiery rage he was feeling from Alfie, and the paramedics. The female paramedic continued with the secondary assessment of Eva, checking her head, neck, shoulders, pelvis and her arms and legs. They placed an oxygen mask over her face.

'Do you know what happened here?' the younger male paramedic asked.

Andy shook his head. 'No, I don't know for sure as I wasn't present. But I do know that she was due to end her relationship with her partner before Christmas. She may have told him tonight and he has not reacted well. I would hazard a guess that she has been beaten by her partner, culminating with the blow to her head from the bottle.'

'Are you saying that she was in an abusive relationship?' the female asked, acutely aware that Alfie would be listening to all this.

Andy nodded. 'I believe so, but she has never actually confirmed that to me.'

The male paramedic nodded his head. 'It's helpful to know as there may well other injuries, less obvious ones, that we need to investigate.'

Jean, the female paramedic satisfied that they had done all they could for now, advised, 'we need to get her to the hospital for a more thorough assessment.' She noted Alfie's face, his grey pallor, his flushed cheeks and reddened nose. All evidence of his crying, and said, 'she's stable for now and breathing normally but we need to let the doctors look at her. Try not to worry, young man.'

The male paramedic exited the room at the same time there was a knock on the front door. Two police constables, one male, one female, came into the lounge area. The male, Asian in his forties, addressed Andy. 'I'm PC Shah and this is PC Hunter. You are?'

'I'm Detective Inspector Andy Leyton but I'm not here in an official capacity but as the friend and neighbour of the injured woman, Eva Brennan. This is her twelve-year-old son, Alfie, who found her and then ran next door to alert me.'

'Does Ms Brennan have a partner or husband?'

'Yes, a Gary Anderson, her fiancé, but I have no idea where he is at the moment. Ms Brennan appears to have received a blow to the head from a wine bottle, rendering her unconscious as I have just informed the paramedics. I suggest that Anderson could be responsible for the assault and the person of interest you need to speak to regarding this attack on Ms Brennan.'

'What makes you say that, DI Leyton?' PC Shah asked.

'I am a close friend of Ms Brennan. She recently confided in me that she was seeking to end their relationship and to call off the wedding planned for May next year. A reason for this was Mr Anderson's intimidating and controlling personality.'

'Do you know of any violent assaults on Ms Brennan?'

'She has not told me of any herself but I suspect there may have been. She did confide in me that she was unhappy and felt unsafe in the relationship. She intended to end it before Christmas. She was planning to do it next weekend but perhaps things came to a head before then. I suggest that you locate Mr Anderson as quickly as possible and find out what he knows about all of this. Until Ms Brennan regains consciousness, I am requesting that we view Mr Anderson as a danger to her, until we find out from her what happened.'

PC Shah commented, 'I have noted your concerns, DI Leyton, and we will be contacting Mr Anderson asap. It could be that he had no involvement in this and will want to know what has happened.'

Andy spoke firmly to the PC. 'I have no authority here in my professional capacity but I believe that Mr Anderson could be the cause of this attack. If that is the case then he is an ongoing danger to her.'

The ambulance crew had now placed Eva on a wheeled stretcher and started to take her out of the room. Alfie started to cry again, as his mother was taken away. 'Where will I stay tonight? I don't want to have to stay with Gary,' he gave out a loud sob, 'he scares me.''

Andy placed his arm around the boy's shoulder. 'You won't have to stay with Gary.'

PC Shah asked, 'are there any relatives nearby that can take him?'

'He has four grandparents but they are all abroad together in Lanzarote and are not returning until January. Ms Brennan has a brother who lives about an hour's drive away.'

Alfie now started to cry harder. 'I don't want to stay with them. Can't I stay with you, Andy?' He clung onto Andy's arm as if he was in danger of being dragged away by the two police officers.

Andy spoke softly to Alfie. His heart breaking for a child who was worrying that his mother might be seriously ill and fearful of being left in Gary's care. 'Alfie, I need to speak to the police officers. Go upstairs and pack a bag with any stuff you will need till tomorrow including pyjamas and toothbrush, ok?'

Reluctantly, Alfie let go of Andy and went out of the room.

Andy addressed the officers. 'I have been Ms Brennan's friend and neighbour for a number of years and I know her and her son well. I firmly believe that her fiancé, Gary Anderson, is the likely perpetrator of the attack on her and I would not want to leave Alfie with him. We do not currently know where Anderson is but as I said earlier, I believe that he is a danger to Ms Brennan and her son. I do have reason to believe that Anderson has been physically violent to Ms Brennan in the past.'

'Excuse me a moment while I speak to my colleague,' PC Shah advised Andy as he and PC Hunter moved aside to quietly discuss the situation.

After a few minutes, PC Shah stated, 'DI Leyton, in the circumstances, we can see that the boy is comfortable with you and not happy to be left in the care of his stepfather. You can take him for tonight, and we can review the situation in the morning, depending how Ms Brennan is progressing. If she is not able to endorse this arrangement due to ongoing health problems then we would need to take advice from social services.

Andy nodded his agreement. 'That's fine. He can come with me now. I am on call tonight but if I need to go to work, he can stay at my mother's house across the road. My daughter is currently staying there and Alfie is good friends with her.'

Alfie returned to the room with his belongings in a backpack. 'Am I allowed to stay with you, Andy?' His eyes skipped anxiously between Andy and PC Shah, tears welling in his eyes again.

'Yes, Alfie, the police officers have agreed that you can stay with me tonight. I have explained that I am on call so may have to go to work. If that happens, I will drop you at my mum's, to stay with her and Hannah.'

PC Shah looked directly at the child. 'Are you ok with these arrangements, Alfie?'

Alfie sniffed loudly and rubbed his nose with his hand. 'Yes, its fine. I really like Andy and his mum, plus Hannah is great, for a girl.'

Andy patted Alfie's head. 'Hannah will be pleased with that ringing endorsement.'

'When will I be allowed to see mum? I'm so worried about her,' Alfie enquired.

'We won't be allowed to go to the hospital to see her due to Covid regulations but I can keep phoning the hospital to get updates on how she is,' Andy clarified.

Alfie looked on the verge of tears again. 'Do you really think Gary did this to mum? If so, it's really scaring me.'

'It's a strong possibility,' Andy confirmed.

Andy could understand the boy's anguish. 'Don't worry about that for now. For now, you are coming with me.'

CHAPTER SIXTY SIX

Eva regained consciousness quite quickly on arriving at the hospital but was confused, initially, as to what had happened to her. Her head was aching due to the injury she received to the side of her left temple, and painkillers, paracetamol, were not really touching it but that was all the doctor had prescribed. Her thoughts were jumbled, as if she was searching through a thick fog for something, but her mind and body were disconnected and she could not progress to the place she wanted to be. After a few more hours of rest, monitoring by the doctors and nurses, and a CT scan, the hazy fog was lifting and she was starting to make sense of what had occurred. She remembered some of the argument with Gary and his reaction to being told that their relationship was over. She recalled that he lashed out at her face and her ribs and the CT scan revealed bruising to her ribs. Her head injury had resulted in some swelling and a gash to her head but had missed the middle meningeal artery which could have caused a bleed to the brain. She had also sustained a sprain to her left wrist when she collapsed, following the blow to her head, and her wrist was now wrapped in an elasticated bandage.

It was nine a.m. on Saturday morning and Eva had been visited by PC Shah. He advised her that he had spoken to Detective Inspector Andy Leyton about the attack on her which he believed could have been perpetrated by her fiancé, Gary Anderson. Eva confirmed that Gary had assaulted her but some of the details were still sketchy in her mind. PC Shah was due to take a more detailed statement at some point. The PC advised her that her son had found her unconscious at home and he was now staying with DI Leyton while she remained in hospital.

Eva telephoned Andy immediately. 'Hi, Andy, is Alfie ok? He should be at Jai's, what happened?'

Andy was relieved to hear from her. 'Hi, Eva. Yes, Alfie's fine. He's here with me and I'll let you speak to him in a minute so that he knows you're ok. He's been very worried. How are you?'

Eva explained her injuries to Andy. 'I've been fully assessed and patched up. I think I will be allowed out sometime later today.'

'You have definitely been through an ordeal, but they are all things that will heal with time, thank goodness. I was seriously worried when I saw you lying face down on the carpet. Do you want a quick word with Alfie?'

'Yes, please, just to let him hear my voice and re-assure him I am still alive.' Eva waited while the phone was passed to her son. 'Hi, Alfie. Are you ok?'

Alfie let out a big sigh as he heard his mum's voice. 'Yes, I'm good. Andy's looked after me and let me have pancakes for breakfast. Are you ok, as I was really scared?'

'Yes, I'll be fine. I won't look too great with steri-strips on my head, a bandage on my wrist and some bruising on my face but it will all heal in no time.'

'Will you be home today?'

'Yes, I think so. I just have to get final clearance from the doctors.'

'Mum,' Alfie's voice was shaky and Eva sensed he wanted to cry, 'I don't want to stay at our house as I am scared that Gary will turn up. I wish we could stay at granddad's house.'

'Don't worry, we will be fine as I will get all the locks changed so he can't get in.' Eva could then hear a mumble of conversation as Andy spoke to Alfie. Alfie said, 'mum, Andy wants to talk to you again.'

Andy took the phone. 'Listen, Eva. I think that you and Alfie should stay at my house for a few days while you get the locks changed and I can help look after you and Alfie. You are going to need to rest after an injury to your head and you will be limited in terms of what you can do in terms of your wrist.'

Eva hesitated, not wanting to further involve Andy in her troubles. 'Andy, we can't possibly do that as you have enough to do with work, and Hannah, and Christmas around the corner.'

Andy tut-tutted as he heard this. 'Ok, I will not be dissuaded from this. You and Alfie can stay here for a while, no arguments. If you start to argue I will make sure that my mother comes over to give you twenty-four-hour care and you will not want that. Lovely woman, my mother, but you will add the ailment of burst eardrum to your list of medical complaints as she never stops talking.'

Eva laughed and then regretted it as it hurt her chest area. 'Stop, you are making me laugh. Ok, Alfie and I will stay with you for a few days. Thanks.'

'Great. Alfie can help me make up the beds. Just phone me when you need collecting from the hospital. I am on-call, so I might have to go into work, but I can send my mother for you, in that case. Order some earplugs now.'

Eva tried to suppress a further laugh as it hurt too much. 'No, don't worry. I'll get a taxi though I am here without handbag, money or phone. Have you got my door keys?'

Andy confirmed he had. 'Yes, I have. I'll go and get those items and bring them to my house. If I have to go to work, I'll get mum and Hannah to come here, to be with Alfie.'

'Thanks again, Andy. You are a great friend. I'll see you soon.'

That evening, Eva was sat at the table in Andy's kitchen, as they, along with Alfie and Hannah shared a Chinese takeaway. Spare ribs, prawn toast, egg fried rice, Sweet & Sour Chicken, King Prawn Peking style and Chicken Szechuan style had all been eaten to the point that Alfie thought he might burst. Eva had picked at the food and she regretted now that they had over ordered which was often the case with a Chinese meal.

Her appetite was diminished by the fact that she felt really tired, her head and wrist still ached, and it was difficult to eat as the cut to her lip made opening her mouth painful. She had felt embarrassed when Andy had first seen her, as she arrived at his door, after emerging from the taxi. The gash to her left temple was held together by steri-strips. The large area of bruising around her left eye and cheek bone was pronounced and the redness was now changing to blues and purples. She winced with pain as movement still jarred her rib area and she had limited flexibility in her left wrist due to the bandage. Andy and Alfie were shocked when they first saw her and Alfie rushed up to her to cuddle her which resulted in an 'ouch' as he touched the tender spot around her middle. She was having to move with the slow, measured pace of an elderly woman for fear of doing further damage. Now sat at the table, she was being well looked after as everyone checked that she had a drink, (no alcohol), could reach the food containers and kept asking if there was anything they could do for her. Eva joked, carefully, so as not to elicit any pain through laughing. 'Yes, can I have a very large glass of white wine, please.'

Andy pretended to look cross as he replied, 'no you can't. You are not mixing wine with painkillers and alcohol after a head injury is not recommended.'

Eva smiled. ' I was only joking. Is he always this bossy, Hannah? He's like Doc Martin, very grumpy and overbearing.'

Hannah nodded. 'Yep, that's him so you had better do as you are told.'

Andy pulled a face. 'Doc Martin indeed. I think I have a look of Dr Doug Ross in 'ER', you know the doctor who was played by George Clooney.'

Hannah spluttered, scattering rice on the table. 'You wish.'

The general laughter was interrupted by the ring of the doorbell and a loud banging on the front door. Andy checked his phone, noting that Gary was standing at the door. 'Oh, blast. Gary's at the door.' A silence fell over the room. Andy addressed Eva. 'Do you want me to send him away or do you want to speak to him?'

The colour had drained from her face, she was a ghostly white, further emphasising the red/blue/purple colour palette of her face. Eva breathed deeply to calm the quaking in her body. 'I should speak to him, to find out what he wants. There is no way I am going back to him, though.'

Andy got up from his chair. 'Right, I'll come with you. You have given the police a statement of what happened so he should not be in contact with you.'

Eva and Andy walked to the front door which Andy opened as Eva stood slightly behind him. Gary was standing very close to the door as it opened and made a move to enter the house which Andy blocked. 'You are not coming in here. What do you want?'

Gary was shifting his weight from side to side as a boxer preparing for a fight. His sharp features were hard and uncompromising, a snarl at the corner of his lips. 'I want to speak to my…' he emphasised the 'my' in a hard tone '… fiancée, ok. Though I can see what's going on here. It didn't take her long to get cosy with you, did it cop? You've always wanted her, haven't you?'

As Eva stepped forward so that Gary could see her more clearly, his eyes did widen in surprise when he saw the damage he had done to her face. 'Gary, I've told you last night that I wanted to end our engagement and our relationship. After you have done this…' she hesitated, as she pointed to her bruised face '..and after you have done this to me, we are over, forever. There can be no going back. I have told the police what happened and I want you to stay away from me. Do you understand?'

Gary laughed, a cackle sort of sound. 'Give me a break. You're trying to make out to the Old Bill that I did that but I was around Simon's at the time. I know nothing about this. You do look pretty rough, sweetheart. I don't like to see damage to your lovely face. I'm sure the cops will catch who did it.'

Eva shook her head in disbelief. 'Don't play stupid games. We both know it was you. The police are still investigating and we'll wait and see what they come up with.'

'They'll come up with nothing except your word against mine. I'm pretty good at covering my tracks,' Gary smirked.

'We'll see, your luck with getting away with things will run out one day.'

Gary frowned, not happy at this. 'What's that supposed to mean?' He started to moved towards her as if to grab hold of her.

Andy now placed his right hand on Gary's shoulder. 'Stay still. You are not coming near to her or you'll have to go through me.'

Gary hesitated for a moment, the pacing boxer now contemplating his next move. 'I could easily take you out, cop, but we'll leave it for now. I will need to collect some stuff soon.'

The fear and shock of the last twenty-four hours was now catching up with Eva and she slumped slightly, leaning against the wall. 'Just go, Gary.'

'Ok, you win, for now. But it's not over between us yet. I decide when we are finished and it's not yet, so watch your back.'

Andy's anger flared, ready to unleash the hounds from hell on this preening, cocky man. 'Get away from her, and off my property, before I risk my job to give you the battering you so richly deserve.'

It was obvious that Gary was intimidated by Andy's threat but he allowed a small smirk to cross his lips. As he turned to go to his car on Eva's driveway, he said, 'until the next time, hasta la vista, baby.'

As Andy closed the door, Eva pulled herself upright but flinched in pain as the movement stabbed her ribs. 'Oh my God, he's deluded. What's he intending to do?'

Andy placed a gentle arm around her shoulder. 'Come and sit down in the lounge and rest. You need to be careful as you are recovering from a head injury. Try to forget his bullshit but you can speak to the police about it tomorrow.'

As she settled on the sofa, Andy went to clear the kitchen of the remains of the takeaway as Eva contemplated her encounter with Gary. Was he seriously thinking that they would continue to have a relationship or was it just a prank to unsettle and intimidate her? Gary liked to call the shots and make her dance to his tune. Being told that they were over would not please him. His ego was too big to accept that a woman had out manoeuvred, and embarrassed him, and he would want retribution. She physically felt sick. And now regretted eating any of the takeaway as flavours of spare ribs and Szechuan sauce were tickling her gullet.

Andy soon returned with two mugs of tea as he sat down on the opposite sofa to her. 'Are you ok?'

She nodded and sighed heavily. 'I think so but it's all been a nightmare twenty-four hours and I could do without seeing him. I'm shattered. I bet you are too, having to play nurse.'

Andy smiled. 'I could see myself in a little blue dress like they used to wear in the sixties with the dinky little hats.'

Eva laughed then touched her side. 'Don't make me laugh. I hope you have the legs for a dress and they're not too hairy.'

'I'll show you, if you like.'

'Please don't. I'm having a job keeping this Chinese meal down as it is.'

The lounge door opened and Alfie walked in. He sat on the sofa, to the left of his mother, and leant up against her.

'Hi, Alfie, you ok?' Eva asked, noting her son's troubled face.

'Yes, maybe, has Gary gone?' Alfie asked.

'Yes, he has, so don't worry.'

As he gently cuddled Eva, he asked, 'can I have Taekwondo lessons?'

Eva looked down at Alfie's face, puzzled by this sudden request. 'Why?'

'So that when he comes around and scares us, I can see him off.'

Andy and Eva exchanged glances over Alfie's head. Eva commented, 'you don't need to worry about Gary as he will not be coming back into our lives. I absolutely promise.'

'Yes, but we can't stay at Andy's forever and he might try to come and live in our house again.'

'That's not going to happen, Alfie, I can assure you.'

Hannah came into the room and sat down on the other sofa next to her father. 'What are you on about?'

Eva stroked Alfie's head. 'Alfie's a bit worried about Gary coming back but I've said that won't happen.'

Alfie added, 'yes, and I am going to learn Taekwondo so that I can protect everyone.'

Andy glanced at the worried faces in the room. 'Good plan, Alfie. In the mean time with my police training and my self-defence moves, I can chop him up, if need be. One day, we must all watch the Pink Panther movies, with Peter Sellers as the world's worst detective, Inspector Clouseau. In the films, he had a man-servant, Cato, who used to leap out at Clouseau to keep him highly-trained and they would do karate-style fights, very badly, and damage their flat. At this Andy jumped up, as Eva, Alfie and Hannah all looked aghast at his karate kicks which were in danger of injuring the coffee table. 'See how brilliant, I am.'

Eva giggled. 'Yes, but the furniture is in great danger.' Hannah and Alfie roared with laughter.

Andy sat down, pleased that they were now happier. 'Another great scene in one of the films is that Clouseau goes into a small hotel to book a room for the night. After booking, he spots a small dog on the floor, and asks the hotel owner, in a terrible French accent, 'does your dog bite?' The man says no. So Clouseau bends down to pat the dog, which jumps up, and tries to bite his fingers. Clouseau says, 'I thought you said that your dog doesn't bite. The man replies, 'that's not my dog.' Alfie fell forward laughing as Hannah and Eva exchanged knowing looks. Hannah commented, 'see what I have to put up with. At least I've got you both to share my pain.'

CHAPTER SIXTY SEVEN

At the weekend, with one week to go to Christmas Day, Eva had now been staying at Andy's for a week. Due to her injuries she had not been able to go into school for the last week of term as her recovery from the assault was still ongoing. The steri-strips still remained on her head wound and she had a continued headache but this was receding as the days progressed. Her ribs were sore and she winced with pain if she did a sudden movement to her chest area. She had taken the compression bandage off her wrist after the first two days, but her wrist was still painful, and restricted the movement of her left hand and what she could lift or carry. The sum total of these injuries was that she had not been able to undertake her teaching duties. This all made Eva feel pretty useless as there was not a lot she could do. But she identified a few areas where she could be useful including online shopping for Christmas presents for her family and friends, plus she had been given a list by Andy of items he required. It had been agreed that she would remain at Andy's house till after Christmas and Alfie and herself would spend Christmas Day with him, Hannah, and his mother, the chatterbox, Carole. She had agreed with Andy a list of Christmas foods to be ordered online which she had done, though getting a convenient delivery slot so close to Christmas was tricky. Present wrapping was also an area she could undertake. It didn't hurt her wrist and she had spent time cutting, wrapping, taping, and tying fancy bows, to produce perfectly wrapped presents to rival a Gift Wrapper at Harrods.

Eva looked back on this week, and in a long time, she was actually feeling happy and relaxed, despite the ongoing pain from her injuries. It felt as if a heavy burden had been lifted from her shoulders. She was free of the weight of the anxiety of living with Gary, and the unpredictability of his moods, and she was released from the turmoil of planning the wedding she did not want. She noticed a big change in Alfie, gone was the nervous, permanently fearful look in her son's eyes, replaced by a happy, smiling boy who spent a lot of time laughing at Andy's terrible jokes. She noted that he particularly liked being around Hannah, who teased him, but in a kindly way, and it was great to see them interacting. A small problem was that Alfie had a massive crush on Hannah. He was going to get his heart broken as she generally viewed him as an annoying younger brother.

Andy had been brilliant, continually checking if there was anything she wanted, making sure she followed doctors' orders in terms of not overdoing things, getting rest, and not drinking white wine. If she were honest, she could feel a bit shy around him, as living in the same house she was more acutely aware of how physically attractive he was and how her own attraction towards him was getting stronger. If he touched her accidently, if he were handing her a cup of coffee, or he brushed against her in the kitchen, it caused her body to react with a sizzle of excitement which scared her. She liked the fact that she was here as his friend, nothing more, and any fleeting sexual entanglement could kill their friendship. She reminded herself that she knew from Natasha that Andy wasn't attracted to her and there would never be anything more than friendship between them. Eva enjoyed their friendship but she had to admit, in an ideal world, she wished that they were more than just friends. She reminded herself that sooner or later, Andy would have a new girlfriend, a stunning woman, and the thought of this was an emotional dagger slicing through her heart. This woman would ultimately come between them, and in reality, their friendship might wane. For now, Eva tried to put all these thoughts out of her mind and focus on the fun times they had together.

Gary had kept away from her since last Saturday night but he had sent a number of menacing texts reminding her that their relationship was not over and she was still his fiancée. Texts such as, **'I will get you back, in more ways than one.'** And, **'Hope you are healing nicely from your attack. There are some cruel men in this world who don't like being made a mug of. I am one of them. I always take back what belongs to me.'** These texts had scared her senseless and on Andy's advice she had reported them to PC Shah. According to PC Shah, they were still investigating her attack and had not yet brought any charges against Gary, the perpetrator. Eva despaired that the police were actually believing Gary's lies that he was elsewhere at the time of her assault.

Andy had returned from work gone six and she had prepared a lasagne and salad for dinner but she had to wait until he was home to lift it into and out of the oven. Alfie had gone to Jai's to have the sleepover which had been interrupted last week. Jai's granddad had been sent home from hospital, after suffering a mini stroke, and the family were hopeful for his full recovery. Hannah was staying with her mother.

Eva was now with Andy in the lounge and she insisted that she had recovered enough to have a glass of white wine. Andy had not been too keen on this idea, tried to talk her out of it, and could not. Giving her his best displeased expression he had stated that if he had to call another ambulance for her this week, he would not be happy.

Eva was now seated on his two-seater sofa and Andy was on the other sofa. Eva was dressed in slim fit grey jeans, white T-shirt, and oversized blue, chunky cardigan. All her clothes choices this week had been for comfort, for clothes that cuddled her, and protected her body from the outside world. Her hair had found its natural curl as she had not used her hair straighteners this week and it framed her face in a loose, auburn/brown wave to just below her shoulders. She had applied light makeup, foundation, brown eye shadow and black mascara which emphasised the blueness of her eyes. The makeup helped to disguise the bruising on her face, which was now tones of green and yellow giving her a jaundiced appearance. Andy was sat opposite her, in black jeans and grey jumper, and she had to stop herself from staring at him as he looked so handsome.

He raised his wine glass, saying, 'enjoy your first glass of wine but I am watching that you don't overdo it. Be warned.'

Eva pretended to be annoyed at his bossiness. 'Yes, dad, I'll behave. Now don't get all controlling like Gary.'

'Talking about Gary, have you had any more texts?'

'No, let's hope it has all stopped. If he's trying to pretend that he did not attack me then it makes no sense to send threatening texts, don't you think? What would the police make of them?'

'The texts do harm his case but I suspect that Gary likes to push things as far as he can to see what he can get away with. We know that he seems to have got away with a lot of bad stuff over the years.'

'Yes, it's so frustrating that he never seems to pay for his wrong doing.'

Andy agreed. 'Yes, but those texts are a way at pushing at the boundaries. One day he will go too far and trip up. I guarantee it.'

'Yes, but not before a lot more people get hurt.'

'Let's forget him. What do you want to watch on television? I will be very kind and hospitable to my guest and let you choose, idiot that I am.'

'I was thinking of a nice musical from years ago that my nan loved to watch. 'Seven Brides for Seven Brothers' or 'Oklahoma'. We could sing along and I could hear the amazing voice you keep boasting about.'

Andy, hoping she was teasing to get a reaction from him, began singing 'Oh What a Beautiful Morning' loudly, whilst Eva stifled her laughter to ease her aching ribs. He commented, 'you thought I wouldn't know those musicals but Oklahoma was my nan's favourite too and to hear her warbling along to it has scarred me for life.'

'You are an idiot. You have actually got quite a good voice, though I do not want to hear any more at the moment. Seriously, I would like to watch 'The Serpent' as I missed it when it was on the BBC. Have you seen it?'

Andy laughed. 'I started to watch episode two last Friday but my neighbour got themselves beaten up and I had to call an ambulance. I don't mind watching episode one again, if you want to watch it.' He aimed the remote at the tv, found the programme and pressed play.

As they settled into the story, Eva's phone pinged to register a text. **"It won't be long before I take you away from that cop bastard and you return to me. I never give up on things I want, Eva, darling.'** Having just sipped a mouthful of wine, Eva now spluttered. 'Oh, God, no. He's not going to leave me alone.'

Andy moved from his sofa and went over to hers. 'Show me.' He read the text, anger flaring in him, but he wanted to hide it from Eva so as not to add to her distress. 'I know it's easy for me to say but just ignore it. He's never getting you back.'

She started to cry, a dam of tears that had built up over the last week, a result of the pain and tension of the attack. Andy put his arm around and drew her into him as she sobbed. Drawing breath, between the sobs, she stuttered. 'I c-can't go back, he's too d-d-dangerous'…..sob…..'and he f-flipping scares me.'

Andy drew her face towards him and stroked her hair. 'You do not have any obligation to be with him. You owe him nothing. He doesn't own you.'

Eva shuddered as her crying continued. 'L-logically,….sob…. I know but the texts seem to mean that I will have no choice in the matter.'

'Don't think about it now. You're safe here with me.'

'But I c-can't stay here forever and he is p-pretty scary.'

Andy held her as she continued to cry, her tears soaking the front of his sweater. 'Tell me, Eva, before last Friday, did Gary ever hurt you physically? You have never said but I have reasons to suspect he did.'

Her crying slowed and she pulled a tissue out of the pocket of her cardigan to wipe her nose. 'He did but I have never told anyone as I was too ashamed. I saw it as my problem to handle and I didn't do very well, did I?'

'Do you want to tell me what happened or will it be too painful?'

Eva was now resting her head against Andy's chest. She wanted to tell him what had gone on but was embarrassed about revealing what had occurred. She took a deep breath. 'Ok. To begin with living with Gary last year was fine, he could be good fun and seemed to get on well with Alfie. Though I really now think that he did not want Alfie around, as he got in the way of us being together, just the two of us. The lockdowns of this year didn't help and he started to get more annoyed with Alfie, and with me, but at that stage there wasn't anything unpleasant happening. The first thing was at the BBQ in the summer for my dad's 60th birthday. Gary'd been cooking the food, and got into a bad mood, and then was annoyed that you and I were laughing together. I told him not to be jealous, which he didn't like. He pulled my hair really hard and kissed me in a smothering, possessive way which felt unkind and hurtful.' She paused to use the tissue to wipe her nose.

Andy stroked her hair again. 'Hey, I'm sorry if something I did caused him to react like that.'

'It was nothing you did; it was just a foul mood which came over him. I think he got fed up of catering for my family and friends. He felt I wasn't doing my share of the work, though I did all the earlier preparation. Anyway, that was the first physical harm he did to me.'

'Have there been others?' Andy asked.

Eva started to cry softly again as she recalled the Menorca incident. 'On holiday in Menorca, I was sitting by the pool, reading, and Gary had gone off for a walk. I got chatting to one of the waiters who was really a friendly guy. Alfie told Gary that the waiter was chatting me up and that we were talking for ages. This didn't please Gary and later in the evening, the waiter served us again. Gary got really jealous and angry that he was being disrespected by his girlfriend who was flirting with the waiter. He stormed off back to the apartment. The waiter then asked me to go for a drink with him to another bar, and I was sorely tempted, but I obviously didn't go or tell Gary. When Alfie and I got back to the apartment, Alfie went to his room. Gary was in the lounge area, told me to apologise for being a bitch, and told me to sit down.' Her crying which had stopped, started softly again. 'He pushed me down on the sofa, pinning me down, and them slapped me hard across the face, twice. He told me not to make a fool of him with Spanish waiters. I was terrified that Alfie would hear.'

Andy stated, 'he did.'

Eva sat upright, using the now sodden tissue to dab at her eyes and nose. 'How do you know?'

'After you returned from holiday, Alfie told Hannah what he suspected had happened. He heard a slap, and you cried out, and then you had a bruised eye the next day which you covered with makeup. It was an accident with a kitchen cupboard door, apparently.'

Eva groaned. 'Poor Alfie. And Hannah told you?'

'Yes, but though I was furious that he hurt you there was nothing I could do unless you told me.'

She started to cry again, surprised at how many tears could be produced. 'I couldn't tell anyone. It was my mess and I was ashamed of letting it happen. I hoped that this incident would be a one-off but it wasn't.'

'Go on, what happened next?

'It was on the Monday, of the August Bank Holiday weekend. Gary had been in a good mood most of the weekend, until the Monday, when everything seemed to irritate, particularly the cost of Alfie's school shoes. After dinner, he put some plastic bottles in the re-cycling box and found the pizza boxes, empty coke bottle, and so on and the receipt from the meal we shared whilst he was away in Glasgow. The cost of it all further enraged him and the fact that you were involved. It all added to the red mist coming down. He slapped me hard against the left side of my head and then issued a list of lessons to be learned; no more expensive kids' shoes, no more pizzas for other people and no more being with you. I'd told him about how you helped me when I fainted. He seemed to think you fancy me, though, I have told him time and time again that is not the case.'

Eva was now sitting slightly away from Andy as she recounted her story. Andy gazed into her sorrowful and tear-stained eyes. 'Again, I'm sorry that my involvement has caused this to happen.'

'Don't worry, Andy, none of its your fault.'

'Were there any other occasions?'

Eva's breath shuddered slightly before she started to speak. 'Another incident occurred on the Sunday of Alfie's birthday celebrations. Late Sunday afternoon, he was in another bad mood on seeing Alfie's presents and a mess of wrapping paper, cards and envelopes all scattered about. He shouts at Alfie to tidy up and that the birthday celebrations are over. Gary goes in the lounge, and I follow him, and tell him not to be so authoritarian with Alfie or we are over. He does not like this as he will decide when we are over. He pinned me down on the sofa with his hand over my mouth so I couldn't breathe. He slapped my face really hard and pummelled my ribs, twice.' Eva swallowed hard, fighting not to cry again. 'I knew then I could not continue in the relationship and had to find a way to get out of it, knowing that it would never be easy given Gary's violent behaviour. I agreed to the engagement and went along with the wedding arrangements, all the time knowing that I wanted out. I drifted along with things as I knew getting away from Gary would be hard. But, in all honesty, I couldn't hide my lack of enthusiasm for the wedding and Gary became increasingly aware of this. The last physical attack, and really the most frightening, was the day after Hannah's party. Gary was still angry that I had been with you, and got drunk, and he stated I'd embarrassed him at the florists by my dithering and not making decisions. He gave me a warning by gripping my throat really tightly and I genuinely thought I would die.' Her crying now was a river of tears, a release of all the pent-up emotion of the last few months when she had felt frightened and so alone.

Andy held her close and stroked her hair, as she sobbed heavily, against him. 'That man is a complete bastard. Forgetting all my sensibilities as a human being and as a cop, I would honestly love to beat the living daylights out of him for what he has done to you. If I thought I could get away with it, I would kill him.'

Eva's crying abated and she pulled away from Andy slightly. She was still shuddering and hiccupping due to the physical and emotional toll the crying had on her body. Her face was ravaged by the tears, her eyes red, her makeup smudged and her nose and cheeks reddened. 'At least now I have managed to get away from him.'

'Well, you have succeeded in escaping but at a high cost,' Andy acknowledged.

'Yes, but I was determined to try not to drag other people into my battle. I think, naively, I believed I would be able to tell Gary it was over and he would calmly accept it. How stupid was I?' Embarrassed by all this, her eyes once again filled with tears.

He handed her the glass of wine. 'Here, have a drink of this, though I am not encouraging you to overdo it.' She sipped the wine slowly, savouring its taste and calming effect after the emotional outpouring which had left her drained. 'What should I have done to handle it all differently?'

Andy drank his wine whilst examining her tear-stained face. His finger brushed the area under her left eye, an action more poignant due to the residual bruising, Gary's leaving gift. 'If I am honest, I think you should have asked for help or accepted help from me but I understand that you wanted to resolve the matter on your own. You have paid a high price, but, hopefully, the worst is over and you can get on with your life.'

For a few moments, they quietly drank their wine, not speaking to each other. He then placed his wine down on the coffee table and took her glass out of her hand. He lay down on the sofa, his head resting on cushions, and drew her into him so that were facing each other. As his eyes studied her face, he gently caressed her, his fingers trailing the area of bruising around her left eye and cheek area, before tracing a line to her mouth. His hand cupped her chin and he placed his mouth on hers for an exploratory, tentative kiss so not to hurt the area of her lip damaged in last week's attack.

As the kiss intensified, Eva responded, noting a burning ache in her body that this kiss was arousing. His impassioned blue eyes locked onto her own. His eager mouth covering hers was all consuming. This intense encounter would lead to only one conclusion if it continued. Eva's body wanted this to go on, to make love with this man, a man that was perfect in terms of his looks, masculine physicality, and caring personality. Her mind told her no, do not go down this road, as it may result in a moment's pleasure to the loss of a friendship she highly valued. She reminded herself that he had told Natasha that he was not attracted to her. This was now the second time he had kissed her. She was still too raw after Gary, to risk getting hurt again, even if it was only emotionally.

Andy's hand was exploring downwards, along her neckline, over her left breast to her waist, and he drew her more underneath him, to lie over her. As his hand skimmed the area of her ribs, she flinched slightly, due to the soreness from the attack. Andy paused in his exploration of her and his concerned eyes noted the pain on her face. 'Sorry, if I've hurt you.'

Eva moved to push him off her. 'I think we should stop this now before it goes too far. If you don't mind, I will go to bed, as I feel really tired.'

Andy sat upright to allow her to get off the sofa and she quickly exited the room.

CHAPTER SIXTY EIGHT

Since his attack on Eva, Gary was surprised to find that he bitterly regretted it. Generally, if he were forced to use violence to achieve his goals, he was quite clear in his mind that the person deserved it, if they were stupid enough to cross him. When Eva had cancelled the wedding behind his back and with his suspicions that she was sleeping with the cop; he had felt justified when he confronted her that she would have to pay a price for her behaviour. A punishment would need to be meted out. He reckoned though, he would deliver a few slaps and punches, clarify what was expected of her, and the engagement would continue. He could rationalise that she was jittery about the wedding and so had cancelled it but that could be re-booked for the next earliest date. The issue of the cop would have to be resolved, as she would in no circumstances be allowed to continue with cheating on him. He had not anticipated that she would want to end their relationship. As he always said, he decided on what would happen. The Plan would continue but Eva would be kept more firmly in line.

He did regret the blow to her head with the wine bottle. She was now adamant that they were over and it had genuinely caught his breath when he had seen the damage he had done to her lovely face. The week since the incident had been frustrating, and he had stayed at the apartment he owned, where Simon lived, which did nothing for his temper. Seeing Simon's ugly face every morning, and enduring his unsavoury personal habits was not abating his ongoing rage. Finding toenail clippings on the side of the bath, and beard stubble in the sink, was one of the reasons he hated sharing any accommodation with other men. Simon was a man used to living alone and did not have to consider other people. His general untidiness was another issue; dirty plates and cups left lying around on the sofa, carpet and coffee table, various crumbs on the floor and furnishings, discarded socks hanging off the back of chairs. But the worst thing for Gary was the state of the stainless-steel kitchen sink piled with dirty plates, cups, greasy frying pans and holding a mounting pile of used teabags.

Problem was, he really missed being around Eva. She was pleasing to look at in the mornings as she ate breakfast, made lunch, packed her bag of children's work books and laptop, and urged Alfie to organise himself. Alfie had now been trained in, and adhered to, Gary's rules for preparing for school the night before and not whining or stalling too often when requested to do things. It had been a long process but it was paying off, and mornings were much more tranquil, an easing one into the day. Over the last few months a few private conversations between Gary and Alfie had started to correct Alfie's bad habits with a strong emphasis on consequences if his old behaviour remerged.

Gary liked to watch Eva as she moved around, dressed for teaching, often in a dress to the knee with black tights, or slim fit trousers, smart blouse and cardigan. Her hair was a little more wayward and tousled as she did not have too much time to apply the hair straighteners. Her makeup was light and brown eye shadow emphasised her lovely blue eyes. A spritz of a light floral perfume made her smell fresh and fragrant, like a spring garden. At these times, she was perfection. His ideal woman, soft, feminine but purposeful in getting ready for work in a professional career requiring specialist knowledge, intelligence, aptitude to educate young children in many areas of the curriculum, people skills to deal with colleagues, and managers, and occasionally stroppy parents. He felt proud to have her as his woman, and often in the mornings he had the inclination to usher Alfie out of the door, and initiate some early morning sexual delight before heading out to work. Eva had only given in to this once and then panicked as it made her late for work. It had got her day off to a bad start. His day, on the other hand, began amazingly well. Long and short of it all was that he missed her; her beauty, her fragrance, her laughter, her sensual mouth for kissing and her body for love making usually at his instigation. Going from living with Eva, to living with ugly, smelly, uncouth Simon, was going on a scale from blissful beauty to woeful repugnant.

Adding to his fury was the ongoing investigation into the incident by the police. PC Shah had requested that he should be interviewed under caution. Gary engaged a competent, and expensive solicitor, to advise him throughout the whole process. PC Shah explained that he was being interviewed as there was evidence to suggest he had been involved in the assault on Ms Brennan. It was clear that Eva had outlined what had occurred, including the slaps, punches and blow to her head from the wine bottle. Gary's version of events differed from hers. Yes, he had opened a bottle of wine to share with his fiancée but then sadly had to leave her to meet one of his managers, Simon, on a business matter. When he left, Eva was settled on the sofa to enjoy the remaining wine in the bottle. Simon had provided the alibi for the start and end time of their meeting and Gary stayed to watch some snooker on television. He remained at Simon's for too long, drank whisky, and fell asleep on the sofa. He was mortified on hearing about the attack on his beautiful fiancée and would himself murder the person who had done it. At the end of the interview, he had been released pending further investigation. He did actually expect to be arrested and charged any day soon but his luck was holding out.

At the Stratford dealership, on the Saturday, one week before Christmas Day, all the staff spent the previous week trying to avoid Gary and his flaring temper. Any questions were directed through Simon but this technique did not always pay off. If a further problem arose which Gary had not been made aware of, the member of staff who had failed to properly advise him was torn to shreds in his office, overheard by most of the sales floor staff. It was a week where working in the garage was the safest place to be.

Gary had not dropped the idea of buying a third car dealership and he was spending Saturday morning searching for any businesses that were up for sale in the Midlands area. He was spending more time at work at the moment, anything to escape the apartment with its permanent musty fragrance of unwashed clothes and smelly socks, all belonging to Simon. His ideal scenario was that he would get back together with Eva when her injuries had healed. She would reconsider their relationship, if he went all out to plead forgiveness and promise to change. He would wait till after Christmas and then go and speak to her with the aim of living back in her house. There was one issue seriously bugging him. When he went to see her last week, he was beyond livid to find her at the cop's house. What was she doing there? Had she gone around for a meal or had she moved in with him? Was she sleeping with him? It would be a lot harder to get her back if her relationship with the cop was continuing. Gary banged the desk in anger, spilling cold coffee out of a nearby mug, and splattering it on papers nearby.

Overall, Gary was a realist. His ultimate goal was still to get back with Eva and they would marry as he wanted her as Wife Number Three. If this was not going to be achieved then the next stage of The Plan would need to be launched. He had started to get back on dating sites to find a suitable replacement for Eva, if necessary. This time it would be back to the tried and tested successes of the first two wives with the favoured characteristics; unattractive, lonely, middle-aged, financially secure, and weak, easily manipulated personalities. He would choose carefully, so as not to pick another Eva, as he did not want to make an emotional attachment to this one.

Anyway, God loves a trier and Gary was certainly that. He had a date last night, a candidate to fill the current vacancy left by Eva, and met an interesting possibility, a forty-five-year-old woman, Nancy. Great credentials. Local Government Officer, never married, lived alone in a detached house left to her following the death of her mother two years ago. She had a wealthy brother who lived in the USA, and so the whole of mum's estate, reward for being her sole carer, had gone to Nancy. Appearance-wise she was perfect; petite with a non-descript figure and short brown hair flecked with grey and cut into a neat bob. Brown eyes were framed by glasses. For their date she wore a black midi dress with daisy print, black tights, black loafers and black trench coat. Her hobbies were gardening and walking, so her normal attire was shirts, jeans and boots and it was a rare event for her to wear a dress. The word that kept flashing in Gary's head to describe her was 'sensible.' The type of woman who organised her kitchen food cupboards with matching jars, plastic containers and bottles, all with appropriate labels. Their date, in a small country pub, for a couple of drinks was kept to a short two hours but it felt to Gary to drag on as each minute seemed like an hour. Gary recalled at times the conversation was so dull when she described the riveting world of local tax collection or how to pickle the beetroot grown on her allotment. As a prospective Wife Number Three, she was never going to be a woman that aroused him emotionally or sexually. But he still decided on a second date after Christmas. But at times during the date, he yearned with every fibre in his body, to be at home with Eva, holding her close, with the option of sexual pleasure within his touch. He found himself talking about Eva a lot and how he had recently been dumped by his fiancée. All this yearning for Eva did not do his temper much good and he snapped at Nancy when she commented that he was well rid of Eva, who was obviously a stupid woman.

As he pondered over the date with 'sensible' Nancy, a knock on his office door stopped his musings. 'Come in.'

Young sales assistant, James, entered looking red-faced and out of breath. 'Boss, there's a woman in the sales area, asking only for you. A real hot piece, she is.'

Gary pretended to be annoyed. 'James, I don't think we speak about our female customers like that in this day and age. It could get you into a lot of trouble with your boss, me, as I am very PC when dealing with female customers and staff.' This was a typical Gary, presenting his corporate, modern man face to his work force. In truth, Gary and Simon spent some time in the evening, discussing the days events. They loved to focus on female customers, the haughty ones that needed bringing down a peg or two and used their warped imaginations to discuss how this would be achieved.

James' face was now a tomato-rich red. 'Sorry, boss but she is.'

'Has this 'hot piece' got a name?'

'Yes, she says she is called Natasha.'

Gary ambled out of his office and down the stairs to the showroom, to find blonde, beautiful, Natasha, Andy's ex, sitting in a blue, Audi A5 2.0, 4 door coupe. Her slender limbs were on display as she sat in the driver's seat taking stock of the key features of parking sensors, electric heated mirrors and Bluetooth connectivity. She flashed a smile at Gary as he arrived at the driver's door. 'Hi, Gary, glad that you could see me.'

Gary, noting the interest of the male sales assistants in this particular customer, greeted her warmly. 'Natasha, what brings you to our humble dealership. I thought you'd be buying a Ferrari or a Porsche, assuming you've taken up with some rich millionaire of foreign origins.' Seeing that James was hovering, trying to attract her attention and continue his sales pitch, he was told by Gary to leave this customer with him.

Natasha laughed. 'Gary, you know me so well. That's what I like about you. After our brief chats in the past, we recognised a kindred spirit, someone who can compartmentalise the different areas of our lives to bring us the biggest gains.'

Gary fixed on her intense brown eyes, beautifully enhanced by the immaculate makeup. 'So have you found some deluded fool to provide for you?'

'Yes, he's called Amir, an Arabic property developer, who's in his fifties. I live with him in his very spacious barn conversion in South Warwickshire, superbly done to a very high spec with massive kitchen/dining room, four bed, three bathrooms, very large garden surrounded by fields.'

'Sounds great, Natasha, but I'm not thinking of buying it so quit with the sales pitch. What brings you here?'

'Amir has offered to buy a car for my mother and I thought of you. I'm driving a Merc courtesy of Amir.'

'You've achieved what you set out to do, found your wealth provider. Does he provide you with all the other things you need, Natasha?' Gary watched how she reacted to this question.'

Natasha laughed, displaying her perfect white teeth, her lips a glossy scarlet red. 'As I said, he fits into the box of older, male, wealthy property developer, and provider of accommodation, cars, clothes, holidays, luxury goods and I give him my beauty and glamour. The box of ..'shall we say…'sexual satisfaction remains empty at this time as poor Amir is not blessed with the expertise of a great lover.'

Gary smirked, his hawk-like eyes staring into hers, as he understood the motivation for her visit. 'So I take it that a vacancy has arisen for the job of 'stud'. I'm sure there are many young virile men who would want to apply.'

'Yes, Gary. And I give them an interview and induction occasionally but then sadly their contracts are quickly ended. I'm looking for a bit more maturity.'

'Well, Natasha, it just so happens that I could apply, as I am no longer with my beautiful Eva, who is currently shacking up with your ex-cop.'

'I am surprised Gary, as you seemed really into her. Did Andy take her off you?'

'Yes and no. She called a halt to our relationship, and cancelled our wedding, which did not please me. Let's just say that I reacted a little too harshly and now she doesn't want me back. She's staying at your ex's house and keeps stating that they are just friends but I don't believe it. But I am determined to get her back and the wedding will be back on.' The tone of his voice, smothered with a thick cream of determination, convinced Natasha that he was serious.'

'I'm sure you'll get her back as you have the will power and tenacity to get what you want. That's what I like about you. Anyway, if you want some no-strings sex until that happens, I'm your woman.'

Gary laughed. 'Thanks for the offer though that doesn't change my mind about you. I still think you are a cold, ruthless bitch but I recognise we could have a little fun together, for now. We could meet up, but be clear, I want Eva back. And once I get her, you are out. Now let's discuss the sale of this car that your rich sugar daddy is going to buy. I will obviously be upping the price accordingly.'

CHAPTER SIXTY NINE

On the evening of the day, prior to Christmas Eve, Andy had finished an arduous week, where a new case of a young Asian woman murdered by her cheating husband had reminded him of the cruelty of some men, and the devious ways they tried to achieve their freedom from a marriage they thought of as suffocating. Andy despaired that a loving, kind, mother of three young children could be brutally torn from her family for the sake of a man's passion for another, sexier partner. Interviewing the perpetrator, the husband, the man denied that he had anything to do with the murder, regardless of a wealth of forensic evidence which was stacking up against him. Andy wondered why he had not taken steps to simply divorce his wife, but had been advised by a Hindu colleague that Hindu's regard marriage as sacred, and that separation and divorce are a sacrilege which could have terrible consequences on their future lives. This man's solution to his unhappy marriage, and a way of being with his more beautiful, younger partner, was not the option of divorce but the option of murder. A frenzied stabbing, and a disposal of the body, wrapped in black plastic bags, in a Midland's canal. Andy had seen a photograph of the wide-eyed, innocent children, all under ten-years-old, and felt sorrow for the lives they would now lead without a loving mother. In the future, they would come to know that their father was a cheating, cruel man who placed his own desires and pleasures above their happiness. This type of thing did deflate Andy's Christmas spirit, a reminder that the festive period was not always filled with peace and goodwill to all.

Andy was looking forward to spending the Christmas period with Hannah, Eva and Alfie, and his mother. Thanks to help from Eva all his Christmas presents were purchased and wrapped. It was a job he generally hated, and like a lot of men he usually left things to the last minute, and then would be wrapping presents late on Christmas Eve, using a few whiskies to help numb the boredom. Then losing his rag with the roll of Sellotape, when he could never find the end of the roll, to tear off the next strip. Eva had declared that she loved wrapping presents and had done an amazing job with ribbons and bows.

Their relationship since the weekend had been a little more cautious after having kissed her, and more, and she had reacted by abruptly ending their encounter. He could have sworn that she was responding to him, especially the kissing, and he did question his intentions as to where it would lead. In all honesty, he desperately wanted to make love to her but had to accept that she was not ready for another relationship so soon after finishing with Gary. He did also wonder if he had accidentally hurt her ribs as she was not yet fully healed from

Gary's attack. He now chided himself that he had upset her, and he rationalised that he must rein in his feelings for her, so as not to make her feel uncomfortable. This was all very hard going as the longer she stayed in his house the more he was drawn to her. She seemed to have settled in well and they all laughed a lot at his silly jokes, TikTok videos suggested by Hannah, watching comedy clips, and episodes of Friends.

It was her female presence in the house which unsettled him. He found that he was drawn to watching her like some weird stalker as she sat on the sofa sipping wine or reading a book. He noticed that she often twirled her hair with her fingers when she was concentrating on something and he loved to hear her laugh, and see a sparkle in her blue eyes when something amused her. At times her closeness to him was unbearable, especially after last week as he had touched her briefly, and he longed to hold her in his arms.

They were now alone again, just the two of them, as Hannah was staying with her mother, so they could have a 'Christmas Day' tomorrow on Christmas Eve, with the stepdad and Hannah's toddler brother. Alfie was once again at Jai's for a family gathering. Jai had pleaded for Alfie to be able to attend or he would be engulfed by female cousins and annoying male babies and infants.

Eva was quietly reading a book, twiddling her hair, as Andy came into the room. The room was ready for Christmas, with an artificial tree bedecked with teal baubles, stars and hearts, silver baubles with snowflake, fern and leaf designs, silver bows and multiple white flashing lights, decorated by Hannah. Eva was wearing a bottle green, shirt dress with tie front, and she was seated on the sofa, leaning on a cushion, her legs drawn up, looking relaxed and cosy. The colour of the dress suited her as it accentuated the auburn highlights in her hair. The steri-strips were now gone from her left temple and a red scar remained which should fade over time. The other bruises had gone. She was wearing the makeup she always wore to flatter her complexion and add definition to her stunning blue eyes. It was subtle and added to her femininity.

Andy came into the room carrying a bottle of Prosecco and two glasses. 'I suggest that we have a pre-Christmas toast as I have now finished work until New Year's Eve. We are child free and you look very Christmassy in your green dress.'

Eva placed her book down on the sofa. 'Yes, Prosecco would be great, thanks. I bet you are relieved to have finished work for a week, it's great to have a break.'

Andy opened the bottle, and the corked popped out violently, almost decapitating a father Christmas figure on the mantel piece. 'Wow, Father Christmas nearly came a cropper and Hannah would kill me if I harmed him. He is one of her favourites.' Andy managed to get the frothing liquid into the two glasses before spilling any of it onto the carpet. He handed Eva a glass, then tapped his glass against hers. 'Cheers. Here's to a Happy Christmas.'

Eva thanked him and smiled as she sipped the bubbly drink. 'This is lovely. And it looks really festive in here with the log burner lit.' The flickering yellow orange flames and the heat from the burning logs gave the room a cosy, warm glow which all added to the festive experience.

Andy nodded, thinking naughtily, that it would be cosier if they were sat together, cuddling on the sofa. Instead he distracted his wandering thoughts of caressing her soft body and kissing her mouth, again, by asking about the book she was reading. 'Interesting book?'

'Yes, really good by an author called Elly Griffiths. She's written a series of them about Ruth Galloway, a Forensic Archaeologist that lectures at a university in Norfolk, but also gets involved with police cases when skeletons are found and they want her expert opinion, particularly in dating the bones. It's part of a series of books and we follow Ruth Galloway's private life through the series and her entanglement with a DCI Nelson.'

Andy smiled. 'Ah, yes, the devastatingly handsome police officer. Every book should have one.'

Eva laughed. 'Well, this one cheated on his wife and conceived a child with Ruth so make of him what you will. They are brilliant books.'

'Well, we detectives are fatally attractive to women.'

Eva rolled her eyes and shook her head. 'Is that so. But I will admit there is a certain sexiness to your type of job where you have to be intelligent and skilled in analytical thinking to identify the bad guys and girls, and gather all the evidence to bring a case against them. You also need a certain amount of physical stamina and competence in arresting suspects who do not want to be carted off to prison.'

Andy agreed with her description of his job but it was generally less physicality and more mental competence, people skills in dealing with perpetrators, the public in general, and managing staff, than making an actual arrest. 'In fact today, I had the pleasure of arresting a twenty something male, who was being questioned about the murder of his neighbour, a result of an ongoing feud over a number of years between the neighbour and this idiot's father. The father had battered the older man next door to death with a piece of wood and the forensics was clear that he was the perpetrator. DC Lewis and I are talking to the son, a lanky, scruffy, weed-smoking waste of space, who was witness to the attack by his father but was lying through his very tobacco-stained teeth to protect his old man. After a while he objects to our questions, gets stroppy and throws his fists around. I get him under control, and he's in handcuffs before you can say Santa Claus but it's all so unnecessary and he's under arrest for assaulting a police officer. I am also hoping to bring further charges against him for aiding and abetting as he provided a false alibi and tried to get rid of the murder weapon.'

Eva looked shocked at hearing this. 'Did he hurt you?'

'He took a swipe at my jaw but, honestly, he couldn't take the skin off a rice pudding. Weedy because of weed.'

'God, Andy you are so corny at times. It's no wonder Alfie is always laughing when you are around.' She turned to face him. 'Actually, I would like to thank you for how you are with Alfie. Living with Gary and then his attack on me had shattered his confidence. He seems a lot happier over the last two weeks now that Gary's gone.'

'No problem. I've not done much. It's up to you to make it clear to Alfie that you will not be going back to Gary.'

Eva sipped the Prosecco and looked at Andy. 'There's no chance of that ever happening, I can assure you. I just wish he'd stop sending the texts. I had another one today. I'll read it.' She picked up her phone and located the latest contact from Gary. '**Thinking of you, baby, and the time when we will be back together. I shall miss cuddling up to you over Christmas. Will be thinking of what I will do to your body the next time we meet x**' Eva shivered. 'It literally makes me feel sick when he says stuff like that.'

Andy wanted to take her in his arms, a circle of protection for eternity. 'Don't let it get to you. It's what he wants.'

Eva got up from the sofa to go out of the room, to go to the downstairs bathroom. Andy could see that these constant messages from Gary were getting to her. As she re-entered the room, she walked by him, to return to her seat. Her foot caught on his leg and she stumbled so that she was thrown forward. He grabbed her to stop her fall and she ended up in his arms. Her face flushed under her makeup. 'Oops, sorry, but before you say anything, it's not the Prosecco.'

He held on to her, his arms around her waist, as she sat on his lap, a grin on his face. 'Well, you did say that detectives are sexy and now you are falling for me.'

She giggled, then looked at him sternly. 'I said there's a certain sexiness to your type of job. I don't think I was referring to you specifically. And, I'm sure there are a number of detectives who do not fit the term 'sexy'.'

Andy laughed but was still not ready to release his hold on her as they shared this banter. 'You can say that again. Obviously, I am one of the rare types for whom that term is appropriate but, sadly, some of my colleagues are about as sexy as a damp dishcloth. A good example is DS Porter, who is portly, balding, seemingly allergic to shower gel and deodorant and enjoys a hobby of building model railways.'

Eva grinned at his smirking face, so close to hers. 'He sounds just my type of man. Could you get me his number next time you're in work. I love a model railway.'

'You do, do you? What turns you on, then? Trains going into tunnels?' He now tickled her waist as she remained, happily, on his lap.

'Stop it, you're taking this sexy detective thing too far.'

This now turned serious as he assessed her face, staring into her blue eyes and at her delectable mouth now inches away from his. Remembering her reaction last time he kissed her, he hesitated, but the temptation was too great. He leaned in to cover her mouth with his, in an exploratory kiss. His hold of her body increased and he pulled her into him, feeling her breasts pressing against his chest.

****

As the kiss commenced, Eva was encompassed in his firm hold, the doubts about all this again entered her mind. He kissed her passionately, so that breathing was difficult. Her whole concentration was on the deep pleasure that this was giving her, drawing her down into a deep, sexual whirlpool, where thoughts were no longer needed and a raw and primal lust was waiting. Shaking off the mist that was clouding her mind, she pulled back away from him. He immediately stopped the kissing but still held her firmly against him. 'What's going on here, Eva? You keep pulling away from me but I know you are responding to what is between us. That kiss was powerful and I for one did not want it to end.'

She gazed at him, noting the hurt in his eyes. 'Yes, I was responding but I cannot let it go on as we will end up having sex and then our friendship will be over. If I thought you genuinely liked me, then I could go further, but I don't want to be hurt again so soon after Gary.'

Andy was still holding her close, her mouth tantalisingly near to his own. 'But, Eva, I do like you, an awful lot, and I have absolutely no intention of hurting you.' As she looked away due to the intensity of his gaze, he placed his fingers under her chin to ensure that her eyes were focused on his. 'I care for you deeply.'

Eva bit her lip, a pensive expression on her face as she responded to what he had just said. 'I know you care deeply for me, as a friend, and I care deeply for you. But I know that I am not the type of woman you go for, as in tall blondes, so any relationship will only be fleeting. You told Natasha that though some men might think I am pretty; you couldn't see what the attraction is. Don't worry, you are perfectly entitled to fancy who you like but I don't want a casual fling to come between us.'

Andy blinked, and shook his head, trying to make sense of what she had said. 'Ok, let's get this clear. Your source for all this is Natasha who suggests that I only like tall blondes. Firstly, that would make me really shallow as I could miss out on some amazing women. Secondly, it's not true, as Hannah's mother, Lucia, is a petite brunette. I have never said about you that 'some men might think you are pretty but I couldn't see what the attraction is'. Again, firstly, because I have always thought that you are very beautiful, and I have always been attracted to you, from the first time we met. Secondly, I believe that Natasha was aware of my interest in you, though I never said anything. I think she sensed that I had feelings for you. She did take pleasure in trying to make you look small which I would not let her get away with.'

Eva's face registered her surprise and shock as she processed what he said, an eye-opening revelation after months of believing Natasha's lies. 'You are saying that you have always fancied me? I honestly never realised.'

Andy now leaned forward, gently holding her chin to pull her towards him for a soft kiss. 'Yes, but not in a one-off hookup way but in it would be a privilege to make love to this woman, kind of way. But, considering I was with Natasha and you were with Gary, then it was not an option. We have at last got those two self-centred idiots out of our lives, so this could be our time. Anyway, I'm making one big assumption here. You may not fancy me. If that's the case I can get you DS Porter's phone number and he will introduce you to the scintillating world of model railways. Choo choo.'

Eva leaned into him and relaxed against him. 'Shut up, DI Leyton, and kiss me.'

As he felt her physically consent to him, Andy laid her down next to him on the sofa, and started to kiss her with inhibited longing, crushing and devouring her mouth. Eva responded eagerly but she was still having to mentally adjust to the stirrings of desire she was having for this man, who she had known for a number of years, only as a friend. His fingers traced around her face, gently avoiding her scar, as a tenderness in his eyes reflected the sorrow of how it occurred. 'You have endured a terrible ordeal at the hands of that man but be assured that I will never hurt you, intentionally. But I will do my best to banish any thoughts of him from your mind and body as we make love. You are so beautiful to me, Eva.' As he fixed his hypnotising blue eyes on to hers, his hand started to explore her body, down her neck, to linger over her breasts, encircling her waist, and exploring her hips as he continued with the ardent possession of her mouth. He traced his mouth along the trail left by his fingers, along her jawline and down her cleavage to expose her right breast, in order to nibble and lick her nipple, and Eva moaned softly. He quickly untied the fastening, and unbuttoned the shirt dress, revealing her underwear. Eva assisted with undoing his shirt to caress and stroke his chest. The urgency and excitement was building momentously, as his eager fingers and mouth, cajoled and aroused her body. His breathing was now shaky as he struggled to contain his need for release and he urgently removed her tights and pants, to expose her to a further intense caress as his fingers found her sensitive area at the top of her thighs. The tension was mounting in Eva, a dam on the verge of erupting, a hot molten lava melting her insides as the fiery passion between them built.

As she continued to moan softly, he unfastened his trousers, eased himself into her, holding eye contact for this moment when a platonic friendship ended and a new era began. 'You ok, sweetheart,' he whispered as he started to move purposefully inside her, still watching her face as she felt the rhythm of his strong body, as he pounded into her. This went on and on, a glorious union as she felt the strength and passion of him, but noted from the kindness in his eyes that he did not want to hurt her. She was completely consumed in this sexually blissful encounter, her mind overwhelmed by the sheer power of his love-making, as her mind was lost to the white heat of the pleasure he was arousing. Eva moaned repeatedly as intense waves flooded her body and she begged him for release, whispering his name over and over. When it felt that she could bear it no more, her orgasm was reached in a juddering explosion, as he also climaxed in her, his eyes locked onto hers as she felt a connection with him that she had never experienced with a man before, not even Niall.

CHAPTER SEVENTY

On New Year's Eve, Andy had returned to work, and Eva's head was still spinning about how the pace and intensity of their relationship had progressed in the space of one week. They were feeling particularly guilty at how good they had become at encouraging the children out of the house to stay with family or friends. And any time it was the two of them, they were in bed, leisurely making love and exploring each others bodies. They took risks occasionally, if the children were out for a short time, to have brief encounters on kitchen work tops, the stairs, the shower or, a favoured place of the hot and fast liaisons, the sofa. They had hastily dressed one day as Andy's mother, Carole, let herself in the front door, to return some clothing and bedding she had washed and ironed.

Andy had reluctantly gone to work, after stealing into her bedroom to give her a wake up kiss, without Hannah and Alfie noticing. He was convinced that Hannah had suspected there was something going on between them and was watching them closely for any signs of intimacy when they were together. Yesterday, they had both individually spoken to their child, to advise them that they had started to see one another in a romantic relationship. Alfie had given the typical response for a boy of his age, of the 'oh gross', variety but then smiled and his body relaxed as he said, 'I like Andy, so fine by me.' Eva believed this was also a moment of getting rid of the fear of Gary being back in their lives. Andy confirmed to Eva that Hannah's response had been, 'what took you so long' and she would be happy to have Eva as a stepmum.

At lunchtime, with Alfie and Hannah at his mother's for lunch, Andy had driven home between interviewing suspects to see her. Eva was sat on the sofa, eating a cheese sandwich and drinking a coffee, as he came in the room. He took off his outer jacket, suit jacket, and quickly undid his tie. He looked at her longingly and she didn't know if he was eyeing her sandwich or her body. She asked, 'how has your first half day back been? Do you want me to make you a sandwich?'

He sat down next to her on the sofa and took the plate out of her hands. 'No, thanks, I've had a sandwich at work. I've sneaked out to come and ravage you.'

Eva smiled at him as he moved into kiss her. 'Really, it's no wonder the crime figures are so high in this country if this is what the detectives get up to during the working day.'

He pulled her down on to the sofa to lay over her. 'I'm going to have to ask you to stop talking, miss, as you are wasting police time when we could be doing our favourite activity.' He started to caress her mouth with his lips and tongue.

His mouth stifled Eva's giggles, as he ran his fingers over her body, pausing at her breasts and hips. He stopped fondling her and looked into her mischievous eyes. 'What are you giggling at?'

She sighed heavily. 'You, and how presumptuous you are. How do you know this is my favourite activity? I might like a lot of other things better such as cake baking or crocheting.'

He looked at her quizzically. 'Do you?'

Eva laughed and pulled him down on to her. 'No, but a little bit of horse riding could be fun.'

'Have you ever ridden a horse?'

'No, unless a donkey at Blackpool counts when I was a kid.'

He now had her arms held together over her head with his hand, as he explored her body, her breasts, and the area under her dress with hungry fingers. His breath was raspy as he spoke in her ear. 'Just concentrate on what we are doing and not on your hobbies. Or I might take up horse riding, buy a riding crop, and apply it to your bottom.'

Eva shuddered on hearing this and not necessarily from excitement as he looked faintly cross as he said this. 'You wouldn't dare.'

'Wouldn't I?' He gave her a stern look before he resumed kissing her.

After he left an hour later, Eva lounged on his sofa, re-living their encounter and thinking how quickly her life had changed in the space of two weeks. She had gone from being controlled and abused by Gary's suffocating idea of love to this heady, all consuming passion with Andy. Andy, who excelled as a lover in a physical way, but who showed total consideration for her well-being as he caressed and aroused her. It was still very early days and she still felt shy around him to some degree. But he overcame any anxiety by making her laugh or not pushing her outside her comfort zone. Her sexual relationship with Gary had been reasonable initially but towards the end he had become more demanding, wanting sex when it suited him, and he could be overly forceful if he thought she was going to say no. Gary liked to be in control, but as her trust in him faded, she started to experience fear instead of pleasure.

At 9.00 p.m. on New Year's Eve, Eva was with Alfie, Hannah, Andy's mum Carole and her friend, Bob, Tania and her current boyfriend, Samay, at

Andy's house. Eva had prepared some party food; pizzas, ham, mushroom and mascarpone, Margherita, potato skins with baked cheese topped with sour cream and chives, BBQ chicken wings, cocktail sausages, pesto and pasta salads, cheese board with crackers, and crudities with dips, reminding herself that healthier eating must resume in the New Year. Andy was on his way home and they had decided that tonight they would tell everyone about their fledgling relationship.

Tania had only just returned from a trip to India to visit her father's relatives and so Eva had only recently filled her in on the full details of what happened between her and Gary.

Tania was surveying the red area of scarring on her friend's temple and was gasping with astonishment as to what had occurred. 'That utter bastard. I hope he keeps right away from you in the future. I feel terrible that you've had such an awful time and I was not here to help you. You should have told me, and Andy, what was going on. You know we would have helped you to leave him.'

Eva nodded, aware of the anguish on the face of her lovely friend. 'I know you would but as I told Andy, I got into this mess so I needed to get out of it. I did not want to drag anyone else into it. I'm hoping now that the worse is over. I've broken off our relationship and that should be the end of it. I just wish he'd stop sending the texts as they are really intimidating with all this 'I want you back stuff.'

Tania patted Eva's hand with her own. 'Just ignore the idiot. He'll get tired of playing games eventually.'

Eva drank some white wine and shook her head. 'I don't know. Gary is very tenacious at getting what he wants, when he wants. I just don't know what he thinks will happen as I've told him that I don't want to be with him.' Eva grabbed a bottle of wine from the kitchen table and poured some into their glasses. As she did so, Andy walked in, looking tired after a long day, and dishevelled with tie askew and top shirt button undone. Tania, who had not seen Andy for a few weeks, seemed to quiver like a jelly as he walked over to greet them. 'Hi Eva, Tania, you two, ok? I'm just going to grab a shower to refreshen up and I'll be down shortly. Save me some of the food before Alfie devours it all.'

Tania smiled seductively at him, completely forgetting her male friend, Samay, who was somewhere around having gone to play computer games with Alfie and Hannah. Carole and Bob were in the lounge, watching 'Have I Got News for You'. Tania was dressed in a black satin, bodycon mini dress, revealing golden cleavage and plenty of thigh. Eva hoped that this full-on sexy outfit was for the benefit of Samay and not Andy.

Tania pouted her lips, and Eva noted that they were looking plumper and fuller than usual, and guessed that she'd had lip fillers whilst in India. 'Anyway, my friend, on the plus side, you have got to live with Andy for two weeks and the thought of it makes me go weak at the knees. Imagine staring into those sexy blue eyes first thing in the morning. It would certainly get your day off to a good start. It's a good job you two are just friends or there would be a lot of sexual tension in the air.'

Eva blushed slightly as she was now dreading telling her dearest friend that they had recently created enough sexual tension to launch a space rocket. 'Tania, I need to tell you something and I fear you will not like it. Please realise that I have not done this to cause you any pain. In the last week, the relationship between me and Andy has gone from friends, to a lot more, and we are sleeping together. We both have strong feelings for each other and I would say that we are officially a couple. I have spoken to Alfie about it, and Andy has spoken to Hannah, and they are both happy about it. We are going to 'go public' tonight, as it were.'

A number of expressions flickered on Tania's face, including surprise, disappointment and then, hopefully, acceptance. 'Ok. In all honesty, I think I knew that Andy and I would never be an item. I think I always suspected that he had a liking for you which was more than friends even when Natasha was around. It was the way he looked at you and looked out for you. He couldn't really hide his feelings. You will make a great couple and if you have babies, they will be very cute.'

Eva hugged her friend. 'Thank you, Tania. It means a lot to me that you have graciously given us you're blessing. I can't wait to tell mum and dad.'

At this Andy arrived in the kitchen area and proceeded to load a plate with food from the buffet. He then took a beer out of the fridge. 'At last, I can relax.' He was now dressed in slim fit black jeans and navy, long sleeve shirt, his hair still slightly damp and tousled from the shower. 'Tania, tell me about your trip to India. It is somewhere I hope to go one day.'

At 11.40 p.m. everyone had gathered in the lounge, and the champagne was on the coffee table, waiting to be opened. Andy turned down the sound on the television as the BBC's New Year's Eve Party was underway. 'Hi, everyone. Just before we say goodbye to 2021, and some may say good riddance, I want to make an announcement. Following her attack by Gary, Eva has been staying here so that I could keep an eye on her whilst she recovered and stop her drinking too much wine.' He winked at her. 'I didn't have too much success with that.' Everyone laughed. 'Anyway, living together has brought us closer. We realised we wanted to be more than just friends, and so I am saying that, with the approval of Hannah and Alfie, we are officially a couple.' He then placed his arm around

Eva's waist as she stood next to him. 'Right, I am going to open the champagne. Soft drinks for the kids and can someone get the party poppers.'

With glasses filled with golden fizz the group joined in the countdown from ten to one…'Happy New Year.' The snap of the party poppers filled the air, along with the smell of gunpowder, and everyone was covered with coloured confetti as Alfie and Hannah competed to see who could pop the most. There was then a few minutes of hugging and kissing as they all wished each other a Happy New Year. After a short while, Andy sneaked Eva out of the lounge and into the kitchen where he kissed her deeply away from the others. 'Let's hope that this is a great year and that I get to spend it with you, Eva.'

As they kissed tenderly, Eva's phone, on the kitchen table, pinged with a number of texts, presumably family and friends sending good wishes for the year ahead. A text from Gary read. **'To my darling, Eva. You will be with me again in this New Year. That day is coming ever closer.'**

****

Gary swigged his bottled beer as he watched Big Ben ring in the New Year in London. Opposite him, on another sofa, Simon was lying, head supported by a cushion, supping his beer, and wiping his mouth. His chosen outfit to see in the New Year was grimy, grey sweat pants and black 'Iron Maiden' T-shirt. They had ordered in takeaway pizza and the empty boxes were discarded on the floor. Simon burped as a mixture of peppers and ale caused gases to erupt in his stomach.

Gary looked at his companion and reflected how his seemingly well thought out plan, The Plan, had gone so spectacularly wrong. His engagement in October, in the beautiful city of Budapest, to his lovely, fragrant sexy fiancée had been the continuation of a journey towards a wedding this year. Instead, he was stuck in this two-bedroom apartment with his unsavoury flatmate and all his plans in tatters. After sending the text to Eva a few minutes ago, he knew that he could not go on too much longer before taking her back into his life. It was going to be an arduous task to persuade her to return to him, but he must try, as ever since they had split up his mind had been consumed by thoughts of her. The text he had sent her moments ago, focused his resolution for this New Year, to resume his relationship with Eva.

He now reached for the bottle of whisky that he had bought to toast in the New Year. 'Want some?' he asked Simon, who nodded, so he filled two tumblers with a good measure of the drink, handed one to Simon, and then swigged his drink in a couple of swallows. He then refilled his glass and did the same again. Taking the bottle, glass and phone, he moved out of the lounge area and into his bedroom and lay on the bed. Finding Eva's number on his phoned, he dialled her. He didn't really expect her to answer but was pleased when she did. 'Hi, Eva, Happy New Year.'

'What do you want, Gary, just leave me alone.'

'I need to arrange collecting my stuff from the house. Can I do so in the next week?'

He could hear her draw in a breath before replying. 'I don't really want to see you. I can put your stuff in some black sacks so that you can quickly collect it and go. I'll need a few days to do this. You can come at some point over the weekend but I need to know what day and time. Do not arrive without an arrangement or I will not let you have it.'

Gary laughed softly. 'Yes, Miss. You sound like a very sexy school teacher when you give the orders. It's really turning me on.'

'Stop it, Gary. You can come and collect your belongings but that's it.'

'That's a shame as I was hoping we could chat and try to iron out our differences. You know I want to get back with you, Eva. I am really missing you and want to be with you again. I always get what I want.'

'Cut the bull shit, Gary. It's over between us. When you want to collect your belongings, text me a date and time, and I'll see if that's possible. Goodbye.' And she ended the call.

Refilling his glass with more whisky, he drank it quickly. A fierce anger flared in him and he threw the glass against the far wall and it shattered over his desk and work area. He knew now that contacting her by phoning or texting was not going to work. His best option would be to speak to her face-to-face and use his many powers of persuasion to talk her round. No more whisky tonight as he needed to think through what his next strategy would be to get Eva back.

There had, though, been a 'Eureka' moment in terms of The Plan. If it was doable it would fulfil his intention to marry, and make good future financial assets, whilst retaining Eva in his life. The idea was a continuation of his usual, tried and tested method, the one of marrying the boring, unattractive wife whilst having an alluring beauty on the side to fulfil his sexual needs. This time he would continue with The Plan, to find Wife Number Three, but she would not be Eva. Eva would continue as the girlfriend who he would mostly live with and share the sexual passion she aroused in him. The other woman, the plain Jane, would become the wife who he would live with part of the time but who he had no emotional connection with. The local tax collector, Nancy, was proving to be an interesting prospect, and they were due to have a second date next week.

Gary suspected that this woman had a stronger personality than his two previous wives, Claire and Jess. He would soon be introducing her to seductive, funny, intelligent, and successful Gary, hosing her down with charm and flattery. He predicted that this approach would work and this new plan would take small steps forward to its ultimate goal; marriage, accidental death of wife and her wealth added to his financial portfolio. He viewed this as any business transaction as a process to achieve maximum profit.

As The Plan progressed at a fair pace, the new woman, Nancy, would soon meet the other Gary, the cold, hard, controlling man who would put great effort into bringing this new wifey a unique experience in terms of psychological and physical pain. Since losing Eva, Gary was experiencing overwhelming feelings of anger and frustration that needed to be sated. The rage was raw, primal, basic, the creature from the film 'Alien' needing to be released and bring agony to an unsuspecting victim. In the short term, Gary was determined to get Eva back, so outwardly, he would be playing the part of the remorseful fiancé who had recognised his own short comings and was willing to change his behaviour. Gary, the sinner, will plead with his beautiful Eva to forgive his transgressions and promise to be a reformed partner and stepdad . If Eva was compliant with all this, all would be well. If she displeased him then she would regret it. The Gary she knows, the not so nice Gary, who had chastised her for unacceptable behaviour in the past would not be present. She would meet a newer, colder version. Gary Mark II, driven by anger, skilled in the art of manipulation and physical control and who always got his own way. Gary Mark II would not make the same mistakes again. His control over Eva and the aggravating kid would be absolute. A newer, harsher regime where those not obeying, immediately, would suffer the consequences.

CHAPTER SEVENTY ONE

Since the start of the New Year, Eva had decided that it was time for her and Alfie to return to their own home but it had been a wrench to move out of Andy's. Starting back at school, and living in her home, had been hard as she really liked being with Andy and Hannah. They all got on well together and generally the time was spent laughing with Andy teasing all of them mercilessly. Eva decided, though, that their sexual relationship was progressing too fast, and it needed to be slowed down, as she didn't want her son embarrassed that his mother was acting like a lovesick teenager.

Over the last two weeks, she had seen less of Andy, due to their mutual work commitments and she really missed his physical presence in her life. He did manage to come around to spend a few evenings with her, when Hannah was at her mothers, but she discouraged him from staying the night if Alfie was at home. This did not please Andy.

It was now a Saturday in mid-January and she had arranged that Gary could come over to collect his belongings that afternoon. Andy was not happy with this as he was at work and the last thing he wanted was for her to be alone, in her house with Gary. He had only agreed to it on the basis that he had an option of leaving work to check on them, if work commitments allowed. She was to make Gary aware of this and keep him on his best behaviour.

It was now 2.30 p.m. and Gary was expected any minute. As the time of his arrival drew closer, Eva concluded that this was another stupid idea of hers. This would be the first time she would be alone with Gary since the attack. She was dressed in grey jeans and a loose fitting, black sports top, a practical outfit. She had run a brush through her hair, so it was wavy and a bit wild, and had applied minimum makeup. Eva sat at the kitchen table, completing some school work on her laptop. Her hands were clammy, her stomach churned and she felt light-headed. The thought of seeing Gary's smirking face and those penetrating brown eyes again, was breaking her out in a cold sweat. She kept reminding herself that once his belongings were gone, she would never have to see him again.

The doorbell rang, and she breathed in deeply, to settle her nerves. She wanted to show that she was calm and in control of her emotions. He would not see any traces of fear as this would play into his sick need for control. This was going to be easier said than done.

She opened the front door, and he smiled in a friendly way, but the smile missed his eyes, and barely touched his lips. Most of his stuff, clothes, shoes, coats, jackets and so on were in black sacks in the hallway. There were also some sports gear and equipment which she had brought to the hall including a tennis racket and three types of golf clubs. Books, DVD's and assorted other items were in black sacks. She estimated that he could stash these bags in his car, quickly, and go.

He was dressed for work in grey suit, white shirt and blue tie, with an outer green padded jacket. He hovered on the door step. 'Hi Eva, great to see you. Can I come in for a moment?'

Eva stood still with the pile of bags behind her. 'No, as I can pass all this out to you to put in your car.' She picked up the nearest two black bags and moved towards him. 'Here you go.'

Judging by the disapproving look on his face, this did not please him. 'I can easily move them, if you let me in.'

'I don't want you in here. I'll help you put this stuff in your car.'

He looked in the two bags she handed him, noting clothes and shoes. 'Ok, I'll put these in the car and then get the rest.' He took the bags, opened the car boot and stowed them inside. After a few minutes, all the bags from the hallway had been placed in the car. 'Right, there's still my exercise bike and gym weights in the bedroom and you are not going to be able to carry them downstairs.'

'You had better come in to get them then, I suppose.' She reluctantly stood aside so that he could enter the hallway as she stood against the wall. This turned out to be a massive mistake, as he stood over her, looking down on her with his hands on the wall, either side of her head. His body was inches from hers and she felt fenced in by him. His hard brown eyes scrutinised her face in a way which suggested he was about to kiss her. 'Hi, darling. It's so good to be near you again. I have really missed this. The proximity of you, being able to touch and kiss you.'

He started to lower his mouth down on hers as she forcefully pushed him away.

'Get off me, now. I've said get your stuff and go. Is that not clear enough for you? Eva shouted.

He shrugged his shoulders, in a conciliatory gesture, pretending to get the message. 'Ok, I'm listening. I'll go and get the bike, and the weights, and then we can talk. Put the kettle on.' He strode up the stairs two at a time and was soon carrying the bike down the stairs. Eva stood away from him so he could negotiate taking the bike out of the door and onto the back seat of the car. He was back in the house soon enough. 'Coffee, please.' As he closed the front door and stood in front of it.

'I'm not making coffee. Just get those weights and go.'

He was now circling her, like a lion pacing around a cornered gazelle, waiting to pounce. 'I'll go when we've had a little chat.'

'There's nothing to chat about. We… are… over.' She emphasised these three words in case he was deaf or stupid, or both. 'And to let you know. I was not having any sort of relationship with Andy before you attacked me but that has changed. We are now in a relationship so there is zero chance of me being with you. Can your giant ego accept that?'

What was a jovial, friendly expression on his face disappeared, replaced by a red anger washing over his features. He leapt forwards, his body looming over her, the palms of his hands flat against the wall as he pushed against her impeding her movement. Cold fear trickled down Eva's spine as if she were having a shower under an icy waterfall. He started to kiss her, a brutal exploration of her mouth, his body weight pushing into her so she felt crushed and claustrophobic. Ending the kiss, he whispered into her ear, in a harsh deep voice, making her quake with fear. 'I have told you what is going to happen. You are going to reconsider our relationship and look to getting back with me. I am going to have you again and your behaviour will determine whether it's going to be nice or nasty. And you know, I do nasty really well.' His right hand started to explore under her top.

Eva breathed deeply, to try to control the mounting terror she was feeling at this moment. 'That will never happen. Now let me go.'

He placed a hand on her chin, to focus her gaze on his deep, dark eyes. It was like staring into the blackness and icy cold of a winter's night, a place with no warmth or comfort. At this moment, they were both aware of a car pulling up on her driveway followed by a door slamming. Eva exhaled, praying that it was Andy, arriving as promised.

Gary dug hard fingers into her chin. 'I am going to have you again and I will be in contact with you.' The doorbell rang and Gary released his grip on her. Eva moved forward and opened the front door.

Andy walked in, and looked from Eva to Gary, sensing an atmosphere but not understanding what was going on. His eyes checked Eva's face, which looked ashen and afraid. 'What's been going on here, Eva? Has he hurt you?'

Eva knew that her response to this could well turn a tense situation into a full-on outbreak of war. 'No, it's ok, Andy. He's going now, aren't you Gary?'

Gary angrily picked up the tennis racket remaining in the hall and moved to walk past Andy who was still blocking access to the front door. 'You may have won the battle, cop, but you have not won the war. Understand?'

Andy's eyes flashed with anger and his right hand clenched into a fist ready to flatten this arrogant man with a punch to the face. 'Get out…NOW… or I will make you. Eva is never returning to you, is that clear?'

Gary now moved forward with a determination to leave the hallway. Andy stood his ground till the final second, then stepped aside for him to open the door. 'This is not over yet.' He walked out as Eva slumped slightly against the wall.

Andy went over to her, drew her into him, and stroked her hair. 'What happened?'

Eva placed her head on his chest, comforted by his presence, as the fear and panic subsided. 'It's the same old song but with a creepy twist. I going to have you again and I will be in contact with you. Our encounter will be nice or nasty, it's up to you. I actually don't know what it means and what to do.'

Andy held her close, wishing for ancient times when you could take out your enemies with no repercussions. 'Don't worry too much. It's probably all bluff but we will speak to PC Shah again. Though, I have to say, he is turning out to be pretty ineffectual in all of this. I think we, you, need to press a bit harder on the police to find out why Gary has not been charged with your assault and to ensure he stays away from you, from now on.

Eva sighed. 'But I allowed him to come today to collect his stuff.'

'That doesn't give him the right to threaten you. We'll see what can be done more formally to keep him away such as a non-molestation order.'

Eva moved away from Andy as she considered this. 'It's probably all bluff on his part so let's leave it for now. There are still a few bits of stuff left for him to collect which I will leave in the garage so that he never has to come into the house again. I can arrange for him to collect it when you are here. I don't want to be alone with him again.'

CHAPTER SEVENTY TWO

Gary watched from the bed, as Natasha dressed from their sex session, and he delighted in assessing her physical beauty. She ticked all the boxes, looks-wise, lovely face, flowing blonde hair, shapely figure, perfect breasts and long legs. He smiled as he thought of her giving all that to her sugar daddy, in return for the goods he could offer her. Apparently, the property developer had some difficulties with erectile function and Natasha was never going to be happy with the celibate life. Their earlier hook-up, energetic and acrobatic, had resembled two gladiators in a ring, circling and teasing each other, each fighting for dominance, each not wanting to submit. Gary felt that he'd had a full body work out before they sated their sexual urges. He still felt a little breathless and his heart rate was just returning to normal, while his muscles relaxed.

His dark, brooding eyes followed her as she fastened her blue blouse, which strained over her bust, the buttons just about doing their job of keeping the two sides of the blouse together. She slipped the blouse inside the slimline black trousers of her work suit ensuring that she was properly dressed as befitting an estate agent selling million pound plus properties.

Her cat-like eyes focused on Gary, as he sat up in the bed, bare-chested, displaying well-toned arms and muscled chest. She came and sat by him on the bed, leaning in to plant a kiss on his mouth, before moving in for a further exploration of his lips and mouth with her tongue.

Gary stopped the embrace and pushed her away from him. 'Aren't you supposed to be going for a meal with sugar daddy and some of his wealthy friends?'

Natasha was not pleased for her caress to have ended. In all other sexual relationships she called the shots and once she was kissing and touching a man he would not want it to stop. 'Are you trying to get rid of me Gary? Have you got a date?'

'Yeah, as a matter of fact I have. I'm meeting a woman called Nancy who I met on Tinder. This will be our third date and I'm hoping for some bedroom action, to see if there's any point in taking it further.'

Natasha sat further away from him on the bed and stroked her blonde hair so that it flowed gently around her shoulders and down her back. 'What's she like then, this Nancy? I thought you were hell bent on getting Eva back. I thought I was a master manipulator but you take it to a whole new level.'

Gary shook his head slightly. 'What's Nancy like? She's plain, petite, with greying hair, mid-forties, a Local Government Officer who likes gardening and walking.'

From the look on Natasha's face she was struggling to understand what was going on. 'This woman sounds as sexy as a slug she'd find in the garden. What do you see in her?'

'Believe me, she could be very useful to me, if my plans for her come to fruition. She ticks some of my boxes but I need to find out if I can go the distance with her.'

Natasha's face looked completely puzzled as she tried to make sense of what he was saying. 'Honestly, Gary I really don't know what you are on about. What plans have you got for her?'

'None of your business, but in terms of the different aspects of my life, she could be a useful prospect in terms of future property and wealth. It's not only women who can use their physical assets to pull in rich suitors.'

Natasha picked up her handbag from the side of the bed, and took out her makeup mirror, to reapply lipstick before spraying her neck with an oriental, floral perfume. 'So where does little Eva fit into the grand scheme as I thought you wanted her back?'

Gary nodded, his nostrils flaring as he drew in the heady perfume. 'I do, more than anything but now that she is with your ex-boyfriend, it's not going to be as easy as I hoped.'

'What happened between you two?'

Gary sighed, his eyes hard and hooded, the cold, glassy eyes of a cobra. 'She displeased me. She cancelled our wedding behind my back, losing a lot of money in the process. Also, I caught her at a pub, meeting the cop, though she swore there was nothing between them at that time.' He glanced over at Natasha as she remained seated on the bed. 'As you will understand, I could not let this go without a confrontation, and bringing her back into line. I will not be made a fool of by a woman so I meted out a little physical discipline but I went too far. According to her we are over and she's with the cop, but we'll see about that.'

Natasha laughed mockingly. 'Therein lies your problem. The cop, as you call him. Andy is a great guy, jokey, kind and loving to those that warrant it. But he will be a formidable adversary if you try to hurt someone he cares about. I saw that side of him once when I was out with him and Hannah at a restaurant. As we were leaving, a creepy guy tried to move in on Hannah as she walked behind us to the car. She was concentrating on her phone and dawdling along, typical teenager. Suddenly, Hannah squealed and Andy ran up to her to find out what was going on. The man had tried to touch her on the bottom. Andy sprinted after him like Usain Bolt and had him apprehended in the blink of an eye. It was a real turn-on, seeing him in protective detective mode and I do sometimes regret letting all that go.'

Gary shook his head, dismissive of all this. 'He can't keep an eye on Eva twenty-four seven and I will get what I want. She will come back to me or find out how I deliver the ultimate message to those who cross me.'

Natasha shivered slightly and Gary could not discern if this was through fear or excitement. 'You are probably well rid of her. I always thought she was a bit dull, if I'm honest, and I am surprised as to what men see in her.'

Gary moved closer to Natasha, on the bed and placed his hands on each side of her face. 'That is because, Natasha, you have a very inflated view of yourself. Yes, you are beautiful.' He stroked her cheek to emphasis her beauty. 'I know what it is like to have sex with you. It is a performance, an acrobatic show of strength, where you are an equal combative in a wrestling match. A man achieves sexual gratification and is allowed to adore your lovely body but there is no warmth or comfort in the act. As a younger woman, you would have succeeded as a high class escort or hooker, pandering to the whims of the mega rich.'

As he spoke these words directly at her, a darkness entered her feline brown eyes. 'At least I give every man the reward of an exceptional fuck with the most beautiful of women. Plain little Eva can hardly compete.'

Gary now pushed Natasha down on the bed, pinning her beneath him, as he hovered over her. 'We've had this discussion before, Natasha. You think you are God's gift to men, well believe me when I tell you, you are not.' He focused his eyes on hers and watched as her expression turned from feisty to fearful. 'You overestimate your worth. You perform in bed in a mechanical way. Your body is beautiful but your mind is not engaged. You see yourself as a goddess bestowing your favours on mere mortal men. You are detached, unemotional and soulless.'

Natasha tried to move but his weight was now holding her down. 'Just like you. Still if you prefer Eva over me, you must be stupid.'

He now smirked as he loomed over her, his hot breath sweeping her face. 'Eva is every man's type. She is beautiful, soft, yielding, and you honestly feel like the best man and lover when you are with her. That's what I'm missing and it's a void you will never fill.'

Gary was now interested by what would be Natasha's next move as he could imagine what was going through her mind right now. He could tell she was starting to get aroused again but was also annoyed, by being compared to Eva, and found wanting.

She reached her mouth up to kiss him as her hand moved to stroke his groin.

Gary now laughed, a cackly, hollow sound with no amusement in it. 'You can't accept defeat, sweetheart, that there might be someone else more lovely than you. You are fast turning into an embittered woman that will not acknowledge that her allure is fading.' He pushed her hand away from where she had started to stroke him.

Natasha did not like this rejection. 'If she's with Andy, then it's over for you. She will stay with him. And if I'm some sort of cold bitch then you are a weird, controlling nut job and she will never return to you.'

Anger was now apparent on his face as he prevented her from moving. His right hand gripped around her throat and he squeezed gently at first, as a flicker of fear showed on her face. 'Don't believe it, sweetheart. I always get what I want. I will get her back at least one more time.' He pressed his fingers tighter around Natasha's windpipe, as she struggled to breathe, and tried to force him off her. 'Your ex will have to watch out as I am going to take her someday soon.'

'Let go of me, you creep.' Natasha pushed forcefully at him one more time. He suddenly let go of her neck, and sat up, ready to get out of bed.

Gary ordered Natasha. 'You'd better hurry up and leave. I have a date with Nancy to go on and I need to conserve my energy.'

Natasha eased off the bed, rubbing her neck. She grabbed her makeup mirror to check any damage to her throat. There were faint red marks where his fingers had been. 'I should report you to the police.'

Gary laughed, a cold maniacal sound. 'Please do, if you want to waste their time. That was a life lesson for you, Natasha. If you fuck with the wrong men, you will get hurt. Now get out of my sight.'

CHAPTER SEVENTY THREE

Later that evening, following Gary's visit to her house, Eva was with Andy, Hannah and Alfie, all of them seated at Andy's kitchen table as they shared a meal of fajitas, spicy Mexican chicken strips cooked on a hot griddle, with onions, yellow and red peppers and accompanied with salsa, sour cream, grated cheese, and jalapenos for the more adventurous. Alfie was now tucking into his third fajita and trying to eat at the same time as deflecting Hannah from teasing him.

Hannah was wearing a new outfit of ripped blue jeans, white ribbed T-shirt, and blue check shirt, bought by her mother on a shopping trip to town. She was talking about a girl at school she had caught Alfie speaking to that week. 'Yeah, he was in the corridor, speaking to a lush blonde, but she's real bad. Anyway, poor Alfie was totally red in the face and it was real cringe.'

Andy rolled his eyes at Eva, who tried not to laugh at him. 'Hannah, I have actually no idea of what you just said. What does real bad mean or do we need to know?'

'God, you are so ancient. It means she's hot, sexy.' Hannah sighed heavily at the responsibility of educating her father in the ways of the modern world.

Andy looked at Hannah, noting that she was getting excited about winding up Alfie. 'Ok, Hannah, give Alfie a break. He's just starting out on his journey to understand the world of girls and women. I can tell you now, Alfie, it's a long hard road and it never gets easy in trying to find out what they want.'

Eva stated, 'take no notice, Alfie. All we want is to be treated with respect in the same way you would like to be treated. A good sense of humour also helps.'

Andy agreed. 'Yes, I can honestly endorse that. Making them laugh is always a bonus and that is why I am fatally attractive to women.'

Hannah smirked. 'You wish. Anyway, we were talking about Alfie and his girlfriend.'

A red flush had now flared on Alfie's face. 'She's not my girlfriend, she's just in my year group and was asking about the maths homework. If we are going to talk about this type of thing, it's time I mentioned Hannah's boyfriend.'

Andy now looked genuinely irritated at this daughter. 'I hope that it's not that Lucas boy or I shall get really annoyed.'

'Cool it, dad. I haven't got a boyfriend, yet, as I'm keeping my options open. Play hard to get and make them want you, is my thing. Anyway, that girl talking to Alfie would not be interested in him, as she's the hottest girl in Year 7 and all the older boys fancy her,' Hannah declared, whilst picking the chicken and peppers out of her fajita to eat and leaving the rest.

Alfie now looked crest-fallen which diminished his appetite so he slowed down eating his fajita. 'I don't fancy her.'

'Liar, as you always go beet red when you like a girl.'

Andy addressed his daughter sternly who was getting into her stride of mocking the boy. 'Hannah, enough. Stop teasing Alfie and stop all this silly talk about boys. We've talked before about this game-playing scenario to do with boys and you know that is not the way to treat people.'

A phone rang, and everyone looked for the offender, as there was a no phones at the table rule. Hannah laughed loudest when she realised it was her dad's phone which he had left on the table earlier.

Andy picked up the phone and answered it. 'Hello, oh, hi Natasha, what can I do for you?' His face was apologetic as he glanced at Eva but he moved away from the table to take the call. This did not necessarily please Eva.

Two hours later, after everyone had watched a film together of Alfie's choice, 'Despicable Me', the kids had disappeared upstairs and Andy and Eva were sat on the sofa. They were now watching a true crime documentary and Andy was drinking a bottled lager and Eva was on sparkling mineral water.

Eva was leaning against him as they concentrated on the programme. 'What did Natasha want?'

Andy paused the tv programme and sat up further on the sofa. 'Well, it was a worrying conversation, really. It seems that Natasha has been sleeping with Gary since your break up.'

Eva gasped. 'Oh my God, really. I didn't see that one coming, as Gary was quite rude about her in the past. That she had an over-inflated view of herself, his words.'

'Exactly. But I got the impression that this was driven by Natasha who pursued him. They were together this afternoon after he came here. Now, Natasha is not normally worried about other people but she felt concerned that Gary cannot get away from the fact that he wants you back and is determined to do so. To her, it all sounded totally creepy and she thinks that you are in some sort of danger. I then got the impression that they got into an argument and something angered Gary. He did his usual thing of wanting to make sure she knew who had the upper hand between them. He placed his fingers around her neck, leaving red marks which freaked her out. This would be all new to Natasha as she always thinks she's in control in a sexual relationship but I think Gary has genuinely frightened her. I told her to report it to the police but I doubt if she will.'

Eva looked shocked as he said all this. 'Could you report it on her behalf?'

'Not really as it's up to her to do so. I hope she now steers clear of him but frankly, I don't want to get involved. I'm more concerned that he's still fixated on being with you,' Andy commented, a trickle of anguish in his voice.

Any colour in Eva's face quickly disappeared when she heard this. 'What is wrong with him, I've made it clear that I don't want him.'

'Did something happen today when you were both in the hallway?' Andy now faced her on the sofa as he asked this question.

Eva tried to avoid gazing into his eyes as he awaited her answer. She could tell that he was annoyed but was it with her? 'While getting his stuff, he kept pestering me to put the kettle on so we could talk. I just wanted him to get his things and go. But then he's got me against the wall, was pushing into me, and started kissing me. I'm sorry, Andy, that it happened. I do find it very difficult to deal with Gary when he's determined to get what he wants. I'm really glad you turned up when you did.'

Andy could see her face was ravaged with anxiety and guilt. 'So am I. Don't blame yourself, as it's all about what goes on in his twisted head, but I do think he is a danger to you. Now, I know that you want to stop in your own home with Alfie, and slow our relationship down a bit, but I would really rather you stayed here.'

'It should be alright as I've had the locks changed. I do miss staying here with you. I like us being together but it all feels a bit too quick and we should perhaps take it slower. I don't want it to burn bright and burn out, quickly. Then our friendship would be ruined as well.'

He gathered her to him and kissed her softly. 'I really miss you when you're not here. It feels weird that you are sleeping in the house next door. We have started this relationship from a great advantage point. We knew each other well and how much we respected each other before moving onto the sexual aspect. I don't think we are going too fast on this at all. It all feels right to me.'

'It does to me, too. I have felt really happy during these last few weeks with you and away from Gary. But my emotions are still all over the place and I don't want to mess things up by going too fast.' She smiled lovingly at him, as he studied her face, and she leaned in to re-start their embrace.

Andy now pulled away from her. 'You see, there is another aspect to all this that's pissing me off. I now desperately want to make love to you but we can't do it here. You will go home, to your single bed, alone, as we are trying not to embarrass the kids. If we fully commit to living together, they will accept us as a proper couple, and our sleeping in the same room will be no big deal.'

She laughed. 'I have a double bed, actually, but I get what you mean. Let's review it next week and see what we think.'

'If I'm still alive by them and have not exploded through pent-up sexual energy. You had better sit on that sofa over there as don't think I can control myself if I'm too close to you.' He picked up the remote and pressed play to restart the programme.

Eva got up off the sofa. 'I'm going for some more sparkling water, do you want another beer with a dash of bromide?'

CHAPTER SEVENTY FOUR

By mid-week, Eva was still pondering the issue about whether to move in with Andy permanently, or to continue to live in her own house for the time being. Andy was right that this whole situation affected their intimacy, as they were trying to snatch moments alone, when both of the children were out of the house. Ideally, she did want to move in with him, and they could properly be together but this niggle of it all going too fast would not leave her head. On the Sunday, she went to lunch at her parents' house, taking Andy as her partner. Her mother was delighted, openly confessing that she had never liked Gary and was pleased that her daughter had a lovely man in her life, partly to keep the odious Gary away. Her father was happy for her but annoyed with himself for not protecting his daughter from being harmed. Eva saw tears in her father's eyes when he realised the injuries she had received but she re-assured him that she had now recovered well.

Eva was in the kitchen, eating a slice of cold toast with butter and marmalade, and drinking cooling coffee. She packed her work tote bag with laptop, notebook, children's work books, lunch container and phone. Now it was time to search for her car keys which she hoped were on the hook by the door. Alfie was very quiet, after being instructed to hurry up or he would be late catching the bus. She had heard him thumping about in the hall, presumably putting on his shoes. She went into the hall but he was not there and the front door was slightly ajar. 'Alfie, have you gone back upstairs to get something? You need to come now or you'll miss your bus. You are making me late.' She listened quietly for a reply but there was none and no sound of him moving around upstairs. This was odd, as Alfie did not do quiet. His whereabouts were generally known by the bangs and thumps he made to indicate his presence. 'Alfie, stop messing about and come down now.'

Again, no response, but then Eva noticed his school rucksack was still in the hallway, indicating he must still be in the house somewhere. 'Alfie,' Eva shouted, straining her voice.

As she waited for Alfie to reply, the front door opened widely. Eva was appalled to see Gary's friend, Simon, walking into her house. 'Hi, Eva, darling. How are you?' He filled the hallway, as he leered at her, a tall, balding figure dressed in ill-fitting, grubby blue jeans, black T-shirt and zip up grey hoodie.

'What do you want? Get out of my house immediately,' Eva shouted, as terror erupted throughout her body. Her heart started to race and she felt clammy and chilly at the same time. She trembled uncontrollably.

As he approached her, with a smirky smile on his thin lips, his penetrating eyes skirted over her body from head to toe. Eva knew how a bug felt just before the lizard licked out its tongue and devoured it. 'Looking lovely as ever. You are definitely the kind of woman that I have always wanted. Beautiful face, pretty blue eyes, wavy brown hair, sexy little figure a man can enjoy whenever he wants.' As he moved closer to her, her shakiness intensified and a rush of nausea overcame her. Was he going to touch her? Her brain was now scrambled with fear and rational thought escaped her.

Eva was dressed in black trousers, white blouse with red floral design, and thin black cardigan which she pulled around her to grant protection to her quivering body. 'I've said, get out of my house now, or I am calling the police,' she ordered, her voice raised.

Simon pretended to shiver in a lecherous way. 'Oh, I love the school teacher voice, it really gets me going.'

Eva looked into her bag and took out her phone which was quickly snatched out of her hand. 'You won't need that.' He took the phone, threw it on the floor and stamped on it with his boot. We are going on a little trip to see Gary.'

'I'm not going anywhere with you. Move out the way and let me pass.' She made to go out of the front door but he blocked her. This man looked skinny, almost weedy, but there was a menace about him which told her he would not be easy to overcome.

'You don't have a choice, darling, so let's play nice. I don't want to have to play dirty but I will if I have to,' he leered.

Eva was still confused as to where Alfie had disappeared to but she hoped he would not join her at this moment of grave concern. 'I'm not going anywhere with you and I don't want to see your deluded friend. I have made that clear to him.'

Simon shook his head. 'Stop fucking around. You are coming with me, no option, sweetie. Two reasons, one that I am getting angry now and it will get nasty. Two,' he took his phone out of his pocket, searched for something and held the phone towards her, 'your kid will get hurt if you don't co-operate.' He showed his phone to Eva. On screen was a photo of Alfie, in the boot of a car, his hands and ankles secured by duct tape with tape also over his mouth.

Eva shrieked in pain. 'Oh God, no. Release him immediately. I will come with you and do what you want but please let him go.'

Simon took hold of her right arm. 'Good, you are getting the message. Now, we will go to my car, get in it quietly, without causing a scene. I will wait by the boot until you are sitting in the passenger seat and if you scream or run off, I will hurt him.' Then, he added, 'this should persuade you to co-operate.' In his hand he was now holding a small, ebony-handled knife with steel blade.

Eva thought at this point her legs would give way as she eyed the knife. 'I'll do as you ask. Don't hurt him, he's only a child.' She was led out of the front door and she could see his car parked on her driveway. Feeling his strong, bony fingers digging into her flesh was terrifying. He paused on the doorstep to close the front door so as not to draw attention to the house from the neighbours. As they approached the car boot, Eva wrestled to try to escape his grip.

Simon stopped her struggling by showing her the knife back in his hand. He shook her forcefully. 'Cut the crap. Just get in the car, now.'

'I need to check my son's ok.'

'He won't be ok if you keep fucking me about.'

The car was a mid-blue VW Golf, and Eva crept slowly forward, trying to think of ways it may be possible to escape, and alert someone to her predicament, without causing harm to Alfie. She looked over at Andy's driveway but his car was gone and he must be at work. The level of fear and panic she was feeling was now off the scale and she quaked with terror as her wobbly legs propelled her forward. She eased herself into the passenger seat of the car with the slowness of a sufferer who had slipped a disc in their back. Trying to stall was not really going to work. As she closed the door, Simon quickly got into the driver's seat.

Simon started the engine and backed the car out of her driveway, onto the road, and drove to join the A429 towards Stratford-on-Avon. Eva sat in a state of shock, terrified for the safety of her son in the boot as he may be in danger of suffocation from carbon monoxide or other pollutants from the exhaust fumes, including nitrogen dioxide. 'Please stop, so we can get my son out of the boot. He could die in there. Please,' Eva begged.

He banged his hand on the dashboard. 'Shut up, as I'm in charge here.'

Eva shrank in her seat, to put distance between herself and this loathsome, creepy man. The inside of the car was grimy with dust on the dashboard; coffee cartons, crisp packets and chocolate wrappers on the floor by her feet. The car smelt musty and a lemon car freshener hanging from the mirror did nothing to hide the smell of male B.O. His driving style was fast, and then jerky, as he was made to pull up sharply to avoid traffic in front. He turned to smile at her, thin lips revealing yellowing teeth. 'This is nice, just me and you going on a ride together. I should not be taking you to Gary. We should spend the day together, just the two of us. Visit the Cotswolds or somewhere, then have a cosy dinner. End a perfect day with a perfect shag.' He patted her right thigh lightly, a type of playful gesture a boyfriend might bestow on his girlfriend.

As his hand touched her, a shockwave of revulsion washed over Eva. At that moment, she felt that she might be physically sick as the horror of her situation overwhelmed her. She inhaled deeply, and tried to control her breathing, in order not to give into a full-blown panic attack. She needed to focus her thoughts. 'Just take me and Alfie home, now, and I'll forget the whole thing. I won't tell the police, I promise. You don't have to do what Gary wants, he's not your keeper.'

The car lurched forward, then stopped, as traffic was heavy at this time of the morning. 'I don't have to do what Gary wants but I choose to. We have a symbiotic relationship which benefits both of us, the anemone and the clownfish.'

Eva laughed in a hysterical way. 'Clown is the right word for you. What do you get out of it? I always thought of you more of a parasite who the host has to cart around all the time. I can see no particular advantage to Gary of having you in his life, as you are unsociable, unattractive, scruffy and socially inept. I have always wondered why he needs you around.' Eva could see that he was visibly angered by this and a near miss with the car in front caused him to sound the horn in rage.

Suddenly, his left hand was gripping her right thigh, hard bony fingers digging into her flesh. 'Don't get smart with me, miss, or you won't like it. We might have to take a little detour before we get to Gary. For reasons of pleasure, if you know what I mean.'

As the realisation and horror of what he was suggesting sank in, Eva thought that she would vomit. Waves of nausea hit her, as if she was on a rollercoaster at a theme park after stupidly eating a greasy burger. She now remained silent as the car progressed in slow moving traffic towards Stratford-Upon-Avon. A temptation to goad him was strong but she had already learned that he was prone to anger. A perverted character with sleazy thoughts that she did not want him to act on. A dangerous individual. Recalling some of Andy's research into Gary's past life, this Simon always seemed to be a present and willing participant in supporting his friend in any way possible.

The car continued along the A429, bypassing Stratford, as it continued onwards towards Ettington. Suddenly, he turned off the A-road and drove along minor roads until he came to a halt in a country lane with brown fields either side, bordered by bare trees and hedgerow. A gloomy winter landscape, lightened a little by a weak sun on what was a cold January morning. He pulled up to park the car on a muddy verge. As the car stopped, Alfie bumped and rocked the car, as he thumped against the inside of the car boot.

Simon turned to look at her and Eva moved further to the left in her seat to put space between them. 'I've always fancied you, darling. You are the best of all Gary's women, to date. You are very sexy, in an understated way, and it makes a real change from all the types you see on social media these days, the ones that put it all out there for the world to see. Don't get me wrong, I would gladly give them one, if you know what I mean, but there's a sexy allure to you which is very enticing. A man likes a bit of mystery, to be able to unwrap the layers, before getting to the present.' He grabbed her forcefully with his two hands on her upper arms and drew her towards him. One hand gripped her chin, whilst the other pulled hard on her head, manoeuvring her mouth towards his. The stale stench of his onion breath washed over her face and he started to kiss her and explore her mouth with his tongue. Eva thought at this moment that death would be a more favourable option, than this abomination, of this foul man, probing her mouth.

With as much force as she could muster, she broke off the kiss and pushed him roughly away. 'Get off me you bastard. Leave me alone.'

His rage now ignited and he slapped her face, before grabbing at her right breast. 'Stop it, bitch. We'll continue this on the back seat.' The small, folding knife was now back in his hand. 'Get in there, now. I can use this on you, or the kid, I'm not bothered.'

If Alfie had not been in the boot, Eva might have tried to run from him at this moment, but she could not jeopardise her son's life. The tip of the knife was now probing her neck. She slowly opened the door, wishing that time would stand still and she would not have to endure what was likely to happen to her on the back seat of this car. Shuddering from absolute fear, and cold, she exited the passenger door in order to make her way to the back seat of the car. As she eased onto the back seat, Simon crawled over her, his rancid breath wafting over her face. He pushed her onto her back. Hard, probing fingers plucked at the buttons of her blouse, exposing her bra, as he stared at her breasts and her face. His face, with prominent eyes and slobbery lips, hovered over her. He clamped his right hand under her head to draw her mouth up to his and Eva had to swallow so as not to gag. His left hand hooked around her waist, restricting her movements, and drew her body into his wiry frame. She was the prey of the boa constrictor about to be crushed and devoured. Eva tried to push him off her but he was immoveable. She could not speak, her vocal chords frozen, and her voice was muffled and weak. He now kissed her in a slobbering way whilst eager fingers squeezed her breasts.

The noise of a large vehicle pulling up in front of the car caused Simon to pause the assault on her mouth. 'Fuck off,' he said, for her ears only. A loud horn then sounded, and he looked up and out of the front window, to see a green tractor impatiently waiting for the car to be moved out of the way. Simon waved two fingers at the tractor driver but reluctantly got out of the back seat. 'Get back in the front.'

Eva re-took her place in the front passenger seat, grateful that she had been spared an awful ordeal. Simon turned on the engine, his face red and sweaty with rage. He slammed his foot hard on the clutch, and jerking the gear stick, punishing the car, he vented his anger whilst trying to reverse the car back down the country lane. 'Fucking country bumpkins, thinking they own the god damn place.'

Eva was still shaking with terror. The memory of this repugnant man's hands and mouth on her body was an overwhelming trauma which would forever be imprinted on her brain. She sat quietly in her seat, trying to breathe deeply to steady her rising hysteria, and quell her need at this moment to cry or scream.

He negotiated the car back to joining the A429, driving south, towards Moreton-in-Marsh but his ongoing anger made his driving more erratic and a couple of times the car juddered to halt as traffic impeded his route. He switched the radio on to hear 'The Greatest Love of All' by Whitney Houston. 'There you go, a song for you and Gary,' he said in a venomous tone, 'this is bloody great. I'm chauffeuring you to him, for him to fuck you and I get denied any action.'

Eva now felt sick to her stomach. This was turning into the punishments of Dante's nine circles of hell, with each one more awful than the last. This was truly an abomination, to be in this car with this repulsive, unpredictable man. It was made unbearably worse by the fact of having her beloved son placed in the boot of the car and taken with her, for what reason, to be the bait that ensures her co-operation? What was Gary actually hoping would happen here? None of this was going to win her over and if she failed to co-operate, what would he do?

As Simon sang along to the song in a croaky voice, his anger started to dissipate and he looked at her with a sneery smile on his face. 'Yes, Eva, beautiful Eva. You are Gary's greatest love so far, but before you, were Lisa and Samantha who he had some feelings for. In the end, they both angered him by their neediness, and their wanting commitment. It ended badly, and permanently, for both of them. Know what I'm saying. Be careful how you handle things today or it might not end well for you. Gary has got an exceptionally nasty temper when provoked, that's all I'm saying.'

Eva shuddered, feeling totally powerless going to a situation that she did not know how to handle. 'I'm not needy with Gary. I don't want commitment with him. I don't want him. Are you saying that Gary did something to harm these two women?'

'I'm not saying anything like that but Gary is scary if he doesn't get his own way. You have already experienced what he is capable of and that only touches the surface,' Simon commented. Eva was now struggling to understand what Gary wanted from her. She had firmly told him they were over. Did he think she would meekly comply to going back with him, if so, he was deluded. 'What happened to those two women, Simon?' She knew of Lisa's disappearance all those years ago, and through Andy, Lisa's mother's pain in trying to find out what happened to her precious daughter. Had Samantha also disappeared in the same way?

Simon glanced at her briefly as he slowed to move off the A429 signposted Shipston-on-Stour. 'Wouldn't you like to know?' He said this in a goading way, implying that his knowledge gave him power and status. 'I wasn't directly involved with Lisa though I did give Gary a hand at the end. But I did get to know Samantha, shall we say, quite well. Gary made it crystal clear he didn't want her but she kept coming to the flat, drunk or stoned, or both, off her tits, making a fuss. If he was out, she'd come on to me, to try to make him jealous. I'm not going to turn it down, so we had a few good shags, even though at times she stank like a ferret, as her personal hygiene levels sank.'

Despite the extreme danger of her situation, Eva almost laughed at this comment. This from a man whose car was a mobile dustbin and his musty, body odour stank out the car. 'What happened next?'

'Let's just say, she pushed Gary too far, and that was it.'

After a further ten minutes, he pulled off the A-road and drove through a village before taking a left turn into a country lane. It was more of a rural location and he drove slowly as he approached a 1980s style, red brick, detached property. 'Ok, we're here.'

CHAPTER SEVENTY FIVE

'Right, get out but behave, as Alfie is still in the boot, unharmed, and you want him to stay that way,' Simon instructed, as he opened the driver's door, got out and went to the boot of the car. As Eva opened her door, and got out, he ordered her, 'come here.' As Eva rushed to check on her son, Simon opened the boot, removed the duct tape from the boy's ankles and roughly assisted him out of the car and onto his feet. Simon then removed the duct tape from around Alfie's wrists. 'Ok, I'll take the tape off your mouth, but no shouting or screaming, or I'll have to make you stop.' He peeled the tape off Alfie, who squealed in pain, and threw himself into his mother's arms.

'Are you ok, Alfie?' she asked, as she scrutinised his face for signs of injury. She stroked his hair, and kissed the top of his head, as he gripped onto her. She had tears in her eyes as she comforted him, horrified that he was having to endure this ordeal, all because of two twisted, evil men she had brought into their lives. Alfie was crying softly and she could feel his wet tears soaking her blouse. 'It will be ok. I'll speak to Gary and I'm sure he'll see sense. All he wants is a chat, ok. I won't let him hurt you.'

Eva looked anxiously around. This detached house was in a row with a few others, on a quiet semi-rural location with fields of winter brown or green across the road. Not the greatest location for summoning help, or escaping from, without her bag, purse and phone. Gary's silver BMW was parked on the driveway.

Simon was now getting impatient. 'Right, the reunion is over. Let's get inside.' He led the way through the porch into a large hallway, with parquet flooring, and he then went into a spacious lounge. The room was dominated by a brick fireplace with a coal-effect electric fire and was plainly decorated with beige walls and carpet, a non-descript palette to suit the tenants who may have recently stayed here. Was this the house that had belonged to his second wife, Jess? At the end of the room there was a patio window which looked onto the rear garden. Two three-seater, brown leather sofas faced each other with an oblong coffee table between them. Gary was residing on one of the sofas, dressed casually in dark grey jeans and burgundy crew neck sweater. He had his feet up on the sofa, relaxing against cushions, as he worked on a laptop. Simon strode into the room, as Eva and Alfie followed, Alfie clutching on to her as they went to stand in the centre of the room. Eva rounded on Gary. 'I don't know what you are playing at but you can take us back home, now.'

Gary laughed as he placed the laptop to the side of him. 'Now, that's not the way to greet the man you were due to marry in four months' time.' He smiled softly at her and indicated that she should have a seat on the other sofa. 'Hello, Eva and Alfie, please sit down and Simon will get you a drink. Tea, coffee, orange juice?'

Eva stood still, anger on her face. 'We do not want a seat. We do not want a drink. Just stop playing games.'

Gary shook his head, got off the sofa, and walked towards her. 'This will all go so much better if you co-operate. Now, take a seat and have a drink. Alfie can take off his coat so he's more comfortable.' As he loomed in her personal space, she edged towards the second sofa taking Alfie with her. She sat down as Alfie took off his coat and sat next to her.

'Drink?' There was a silence, as Eva refused to answer. 'Simon, get two coffees and an OJ for Alfie. Whilst I remember, I must pop by soon and collect those weights I left on Saturday. Also I think there's some stuff in the garage that belongs to me.'

'You can pick it up at my convenience. It will all be in the garage so there will be no need for you to come in the house. Andy will be there when you arrive.'

'That's not very friendly of you, my Eva. Don't you trust yourself to be alone with me?' Gary smirked.

Alfie was now sitting on the sofa, his face flushed, staring at Gary. 'She doesn't want to be with you anymore and she's with Andy, who is great. We don't want you back.'

Gary threw his head back and laughed loudly. 'The lion cub has found its roar. We will see about that after your mother and I have had a little chat.' Simon came into the room carrying two mugs of hot coffee and a glass of orange and placed them on the coffee table, ignoring the coasters. 'For fuck sake, Simon, use the placemats, otherwise the hot mugs leave rings on the coffee table. A trained monkey could do better than you.'

'Make the fucking drinks yourself next time, then. I'm not your fucking man servant.'

'Too right, you'd be useless. Now, take the kid out of here, and out for a drive, so I can talk to Eva undisturbed and don't come back until I ring you,' Gary ordered.

Alfie's face went white with shock and he grabbed onto his mother's arm. Eva placed her right arm, protectively, around his shoulders. 'He's not going anywhere with him. I don't like him and I don't trust him.'

Gary's tone of voice changed from friendly to commanding. 'He'll go where I tell him. He'll be alright with Simon; he knows not to do anything to upset me.'

Simon hovered, not pleased at the prospect of baby-sitting a kid. 'Where the fuck do we go? I've never had to look after a kid before.'

'Go to the cinema or McDonald's or both. Just fuck off now.'

Simon scowled, shoved his hands in his hoodie, and nodded to Alfie. 'Come on, then, let's go.'

Alfie latched his hand onto his mother's arm, not wanting to move. 'I don't want to go anywhere with him, please, mum.' Eva wrapped her arms around him, refusing to release him. 'He's staying with me and that's final.'

Gary now got up from the sofa and walked over to them, his tall, muscular body filling their space with a sense of menace and foreboding. 'That kid could never do what he's told. Ok, he can stay here with Simon in the dining room, where there's a television. If he's not up from that sofa in the count of three I will give him the beating I've been longing to give him from the first day we met. One….two…'

Eva's face drained white, pale as a victim of a thirsty vampire, as she knew that Gary would carry out this threat. 'Go with him now Alfie. Don't argue.' Her voice was pleading and trembling with emotions of pain and fear. 'Go.'

Alfie too was white-faced, and on the verge of tears, as he let go of his mother and walked towards the door. Simon sighed, and lumbered after the boy, going out of the room, firmly closing the door.

Eva remained seated on the sofa as Gary sat next to her. Outside, through the patio door, a weak sun brightened the garden that was typical of one in winter, sad, bedraggled and in need of attention. But the sky was blue with a smattering of clouds and so the outside view was cheerful for a January day. It was inside this house that there was darkness and despair and it suddenly hit Eva like a thunderbolt that this was the room where his second wife, Jess, had probably died. Her death, an accident, one of two which seemed to befall his unfortunate wives.

Gary lifted the coffee mug and gave it to her. 'Here, drink this, it will bring some colour to your face. Try to relax, as we are only going to talk, for now.' He sat very close to her, taking her left hand in his, and stroked it gently. 'Your hand is really cold, I'll turn the heating up, if you like.'

Eva sipped the hot coffee and drinking it was a distraction from the nearness of this man who she had known for nearly three years. A man she thought she loved but now loathed and hated. His closeness was overwhelming, his physical presence all pervasive, and she seemed to shrink. His hair was shorter than she remembered it, accentuating the hardness of his face, the deep-set brown eyes, the well-defined cheekbones, his straight nose and thin, almost cruel lips. In a voice that she tried to control from shaking, she said, 'can we just get on with this chat so that Alfie and I can go home. What do you want, Gary?'

He turned her to look at her face, as he stroked her hair. 'Firstly, I want to enjoy having you back with me. I've missed this, darling. I've missed us.'

Eva sighed, ready to explain in a simple way, as she would to one of her pupils, when they failed to assimilate what they had been taught. 'There is no us and never will be, again. Let's both say goodbye now and wish each other well for the rest of our lives. There were some good times, particularly at the beginning, but then your need to control me and Alfie caused the relationship to fail.'

He took the coffee mug out of her hand and placed it on the coffee table. His hands cupped her chin, as his piercing eyes scanned her face. 'I know that I can be controlling, and possessive, but it's because I want to be with you. I do not normally get emotionally attached to women, as I view it as a sign of weakness, but with you I have been drawn into an emotional connection that I can do nothing about.' He now leaned in to gently kiss her, a delicate and searching exploration of her mouth. Eva tried to pull away, not co-operating, but he held her head still so she could not escape. After a few seconds, he stopped, pulled away slightly and focused on her blue eyes, to try and read her thoughts. He laughed, softly. 'You taste of coffee and feeling the softness of your mouth under mine is wonderful. Not to brag, but you must remember that the sex was pretty amazing.'

Eva hesitated, not wishing to boost his ego. 'Yes, it could be good but then you started to physically hurt me. After that, when you touched me, I could never be certain if I was going to be harmed again and I could never relax. You became too forceful sexually. It was never good after that.'

He sat back a little from her now and lay along the sofa. 'Come down here and get more relaxed.'

Eva resisted, still trying to sit upright, but he moved her down to lie facing him. She was trapped between the back of the sofa and his body. 'Let me get up. I don't want this.' She was now forced to stare into his eyes, as he gazed back at her. His hand caressed her hair, before exploratory fingers traced a path down her cheeks, to her mouth. 'I love your mouth and enjoy kissing you, baby. Soon we will move on to resuming our sexual relationship.'

'No way, forget it, Gary. It's not happening again. I believe that you have a new girlfriend, Natasha? That came as a surprise.'

He shrugged, never taking his eyes off her face. 'I wouldn't call her a girlfriend, just a bit of casual fun. She looked me up at the dealership and thought I would be very grateful for her favours. Very attractive, aesthetically, but she's too cool and calculating, there's no softness and warmth like there is with you. It was over as quickly as it started. Are you jealous?'

'Don't be ridiculous, of course not. I suppose I'm not surprised it didn't work out as you are both emotionally deficit and ultimately destroy what you touch. I know its early days with Andy but I couldn't be happier with him,' Eva explained.

A flash of anger crossed Gary's face as his penetrating eyes burned into hers. 'I don't want to hear about him. You know I want us to be back together and I will try to be more caring and less domineering with you, and Alfie. I will show you, little by little, that you can trust me if you give me a chance.' He resumed kissing her, softly but firmly, pausing to gauge her reaction as he fondled her breasts. Eva felt a wave of panic rising in her and she struggled to breathe. His mouth dominated hers with soft kisses before becoming more possessing and urgently probing. She tried to push him away from her but his body was a steel barrier restricting her movements. His breath was raspy, his fingers insistent as her blouse was undone, revealing a white bra. His searching fingers moved under the bra, fondling her right breast and nipple, before his hungry mouth traced a determined path down her neck, and cleavage, to her breast. His right hand was now around her bottom, kneading its firm roundness with strong fingers, on the verge of causing her pain. A sense of terror and panic exploded in her head. Eva tried to move to rid her breast of his mouth and release her bottom from his grip but every movement seemed to increase his pleasure. 'Get off me, get off me. I don't want this, Gary. Just stop,' she pleaded but this inflamed him more.

He was once again looming over her, cold, brown, snake eyes fixing on their prey. 'You don't mean it, baby. This is so good. Relax into it like you used to at the beginning.'

Eva stared into his eyes and in those dark cavernous depths she could see hunger, lust, and determination that nothing was going to derail him from his intention to possess her. His breathing was laboured, and his probing fingers were now gripping her breasts and bottom, before moving to her waist to undo her trousers. 'Stop, stop. Get off, no.' With a shakiness to her voice, and tears in her eyes, she decided to plead, 'please don't. You are the second man today who thinks that I am here solely for their pleasure.'

His mouth left hers and he paused in undoing the zip on her trousers. With a puzzled frown on his face, he pulled away from her, slightly. 'What's that mean, are you talking about the cop?'

Eva watched as the sexual arousal faded from his eyes and face, to be replaced by anger. 'No, I haven't seen Andy today. I mean your friend, creepy Simon got me in the back seat of his car by knife point down a country lane. He was only stopped from assaulting me as his car was blocking the lane and he had to move it to let a farmer driving a tractor come out of his farm. Still, I get the impression from Simon that you two share everything.'

Gary was now sat upright on the sofa, his face reddened by anger, his eyebrows dipped downwards, nostrils flared, thin lips revealing bared teeth. 'That bastard has absolutely no right to touch you. You are not some skank that I sometimes throw his way once I've finished with her. He knows,' this word was emphasised in a low voice growl, 'not to go near you.' He jumped up, and stormed out of the room and into the dining room, where Simon and Alfie were watching television, a cooking slot on ITV's 'This Morning.'

He walked over to Simon, who was sat on a small mid-green two-seater sofa, facing the tv. Alfie was sat on a chair by the dining room table. Gary pulled Simon off the sofa by his hoodie. Simon stumbled forward onto his knees on the light cream carpet having no time to react as he was kicked in the face and chest. He groaned and doubled over, as a sharp, intense pain winded him and the blow to his jaw caused him to bite his lip, so blood and saliva drooled from his mouth. 'You wanking piece of shit, how dare you put your filthy hands on her. I'll fucking kill you.'

As Simon moaned and grasped his chest, Alfie dived off the chair and out of the enclosed space of the room, fleeing to the relative safety of the room his mother was in. He rushed to her. 'Are you ok, Alfie, darling?' Eva asked.

Alfie nodded but was quaking with fear. 'Gary's just come in and battered Simon on the face and chest and he's bleeding from his mouth. I'm really scared, mum, when can we go home?'

'Get your coat. We'll try and sneak out while they're fighting.'

Alfie put on his grey school coat. 'Look, mum, I've got my phone in my pocket, so we can phone Andy when we get away.'

'Oh, thank God, but don't let them know you've got it.'

As they quietly eased out of the lounge, and into the hallway, there was a loud crash from the dining room before Simon emerged, moving towards the front door. There was a vivid red mark to his left eye and a mixture of spit and blood oozed down his chin. He was clutching at his chest area and hobbled forward, before looking back to see if Gary was following him. Eva and Alfie, both terror-struck, moved away from Simon and back towards the lounge door.

Gary emerged from the dining room, red marks on his left cheekbone and a cut to his lip, where he had received punches from his combatant. Simon's skull-like features were now more repellent as thin lips revealed his yellowing, snaggled teeth. 'You and me are finished after this. I've done lots for you over the years, kept all your dirty secrets and this is how you repay me,' Simon shouted. He took the knife out of his pocket and swung it in Gary's direction, aiming for his face.

Gary's expression hardened as he noted the knife and his friend's intent. 'Don't fuck with me. You know what I am capable of.'

Simon's face was almost animalistic, a rabid hatred in the shifty brown eyes and snarling lips, teeth bared to warn his opponent of danger and intent to kill. 'I know what you are capable of as I have seen the evidence with my own eyes.' He swished the knife through the air inches from Gary's raging features.

Gary kicked out fiercely, a lion's roar leaving his mouth. The kick caught Simon's elbow; he screeched in pain and dropped the knife on the lacquered flooring of the hallway between the two men. Gary leapt forward, picked up the knife and slashed it through the air, inches from Simon's face. The steel blade flashed as it caught the light. 'You're out of order, trying to touch her. I'll finish you with this.'

Simon staggered backwards away from the knife. A primal fear developed on his face as he was confronted by Gary. The anger in Gary's brown eyes was harder and more deadly than the steel blade of the knife. Simon, knowing full well that Gary would not hesitate to stab him, allowed his anger to dissipate, giving way to a more compliant tone of voice. 'I think you need to check yourself here, mate, and remember our usual way, since childhood, is for each to have the other's back. No letting a woman come between us. Forget her, mate, and her snotty kid. If you want to get rid, they can meet the same fate as Lisa and Samantha. You and me, Gary and Simon, working as a team. The dream team.'

Gary did not soften on listening to his mate. 'I've not made my mind up yet as to what happens to them but you are not getting your hands on her, ok?' But he did fold the knife and place it in his pocket. Simon let out a loud sigh of relief, believing that it was now the two amigos back together, friends' reunited.

Simon smiled cautiously. 'See, mate, when it comes down to it, it's us against the world, as always.' Simon realised he had misjudged the situation when Gary marched towards him to continue his attack, as he swung another punch that collided with the soft area below his ribs. 'Oomph,' Simon exhaled loudly, winded from the blow, as he doubled over, hands automatically protecting his stomach area. From this stooped position, he ran forward, ramming his head and shoulders into Gary's chest and propelling him backwards. 'Stop this now, Anderson, as this will be the last fight of your life as I'll fucking kill you.'

As this increasingly violent brawl played out in the hallway, Eva and Alfie slipped away into the lounge, to avoid being physically hurt by the extreme violence of the clash. Eva hoped, fervently, that this would be a fight to the death and both men would die. 'Quickly, Alfie, give me your phone. I'll text Andy. You see if the patio doors or windows in this room can be opened.'

Eva took the phone and texted Andy, desperately praying that he was in a position to respond. She knew realistically she should call 999 but talking to an operator at the moment was more likely to place them in more danger.

Alfie rushed to the patio door to try the handle but it was locked with no key present. The same was true of the window. Panicking and paralysed by fear, Alfie stood waiting while his mother used the phone. During the fight between the two men, Alfie decided to do a voice recording of the conversation between them. A way to fill the time and focus his mind away from the danger he and his mother were in.

CHAPTER SEVENTY SIX

September 2014

After the little pep talk Gary had given Samantha in May about not turning up at his dealership, she had started to obey the rules and understood what her place was in their relationship. Her place, or rather her role, was to provide a weekly hookup when he just wanted convenience with no effort involved. Samantha had upped her game recently, she was generally taking more showers, wearing cleaner clothes, applying makeup and trying to cut down on smoking, by vaping. Gary suspected it was all a ploy to consider her as a long-term girlfriend. Since the death of his wife, Jess, he had put The Plan on hold, and was enjoying sexy liaisons with a few female customers who kept in touch when their bodywork needed attention. As there was no sign of a new, significant woman in his life, Samantha seemed to have hatched a plan of her own to improve her status. She had kept away from the dealership, so not to embarrass him and was welcoming and attentive whenever he came around. Most surprisingly, she had learned to cook a few dishes from scratch, which impressed him.

Gary was now back to invoking The Plan with a view to finding Wife Number Three and was using online dating sites. A third date with, Gianna, a petite, dark haired forty-four-year-old nurse of English/Italian heritage was going well at a country pub just outside Stratford-Upon-Avon. Gianna ticked a lot of his requirements in terms of The Plan. She had never married, had no kids, was a career woman with substantial assets. A large family did exist in Italy but she rarely saw them. They had just finished a meal and were preparing to leave the pub. Gary intended they would now return to Gianna's semi and the status of the relationship would change from platonic to sexually active. Gary scrutinised the woman sat opposite him. Sensible, short haircut, probably trimmed every four weeks and minimal makeup just face powder and lipstick. She wore a V-necked, blue, midi dress with floral design and unflattering grey ballet plumps that drew attention to her chunky ankles. All round good choice for minimal attraction. Gary urged Gianna to finish her drink, sparkling water and lime, and she smiled nervously at him as they walked out of the pub.

As they approached the door, Gary heard a familiar laugh, and paused to see Samantha with a girlfriend, sharing what looked like their second bottle of wine. He noted the first empty bottle, next to the second one in the ice bucket. As Gary locked eyes with Samantha, she stopped talking and rushed up from her seat.

'Gary, babe, fancy seeing you here. Come and join us.' She bumped the table as she moved over to him, sloshing wine onto to it, as her friend grabbed the bottle of wine and her glass to save them toppling over. Samantha barrelled through to him, placing a possessive hand on his arm, and leaning up for a kiss. 'Patsy, this is Gary who I've told you about. My boyfriend. Gary come and meet Patsy.'

Gary disengaged himself from her, disgusted that she was obviously drunk and making show of herself. 'Ok, Samantha, back off. I'm not interested in you tonight as I am here with someone else.'

Puzzlement showed in Samantha's green eyes as they flicked around to discover who he was with. She was dressed in a low-cut, sleeveless green dress which clung tightly to her figure and which accentuated the pale beauty of her skin and the emerald green of her eyes. She pursed her lips, not really understanding what he was saying, when she noticed the woman standing behind him. 'Oh, Gary, sorry I didn't know you were out with your auntie.' She focused on the woman and waved in a friendly way. 'Hi, I'm Samantha and I may be a member of the family in the not-too-distant future.'

The woman scowled, looking to Gary to correct the misunderstanding. 'I'm not his aunt. I'm his date.'

Samantha, now at a level of intoxication that freed her of any inhibitions, laughed loudly, 'Sorry, did you say date? He'd never go for you, you are too.... old and frumpy.'

'That's enough, Samantha, go back to your friend,' Gary ordered. He walked to the door, opened it for Gianna to go through and left Samantha open-mouthed and red-faced with embarrassment and fury.\

***

The next evening, a Saturday, Gary was at his apartment with Simon, watching football but he was still fuming over Samantha's treatment of Gianna the previous evening. Another little talk with Samantha was obviously overdue. Gianna had been seething about being referred to as his aunt which did not add to the ambience needed to secure a sexual encounter. It had happened, it was tepid, unexciting, and over quickly, reminding him of other times with wife Claire. He didn't want sizzling sex with Wife Three just enough stimulation to do the minimal so that wifey genuinely thought there was a connection between them. As she ticked a lot of the other boxes, particularly in terms of financial assets, he was conflicted as to whether it was worth persisting with the sexual side for a little bit longer. Gianna's descriptions of her Italian father's three restaurants in Warwickshire, before his sudden death, meant that she had inherited a large amount of money. She was considering giving up her nursing career to pursue her dream of becoming a professional portrait artist. Gianna was sitting on a pot of gold which Gary was keen to access. Having been insulted by Samantha, and stunned to have been mistaken for his auntie, Gianna was convinced that there could be no relationship between them. Samantha had undermined all the progress he had made on the other dates. He didn't want to have to start a fresh search to look for his next victim in terms of The Plan, as Gianna fitted his profile exactly. But if he couldn't persuade Gianna to give him another chance it would be time and money wasted and all because of Samantha. It was time to end it with Samantha as she was becoming a liability.

The next evening, as he and Simon watched a Southampton v Newcastle match, Gary thought at least the northern team were having a good day, with a score of 4:0 to the Magpies. Gary got up off the sofa to get another beer, asking Simon if he wanted one. A loud banging at the door disturbed him and he went out into the hallway. On opening the door, he discovered Samantha standing there, dressed in ripped blue jeans, sloppy grey T-shirt, and grubby white cardigan, an open bottle of white wine in her hand which she swigged from thirstily. 'Hi, Gary, can I come in?'

Her black hair was hitched back in a scruffy ponytail from which strands of hair escaped and now framed her face. Her face was washed-out and pale, but this added to the magnificence of the green, panther-like eyes, accentuated by black eyeliner and mascara. The smudged eye makeup most likely not removed from the previous evening.

'What do you want? I'm not happy with you after showing me up last night and ruining my date. I spent good money on a meal as well, so you owe me for that.' Gary stood in the doorway, glaring at her, as she wobbled slightly, the alcohol affecting her co-ordination.

She pulled a goofy face at him to try and appease him. 'I want to see you, Gary, and talk about us.' She placed her hand on the door frame to hold herself up, in order not to slip down to the floor.

Gary opened the door to allow her to enter, and she tripped and giggled, as she entered the hallway. 'Go in the bedroom as Simon's watching the football.'

Samantha waved her finger at him as she proceeded to his bedroom. 'Naughty Gary, you always had a one-track mind.' In the room, she went over to the bed, swigged a couple of mouthfuls of wine from the bottle, then placed it on the bedside cabinet. She lay on the bed, resting on the pillows, waiting for Gary to join her.

'Sit up. You know I don't like drunk women and I'm pissed off with you after last night.' He pulled her into a sitting position and sat next to her on the edge of the bed. His dark eyes locked on her green ones, now anxious, as he was not responding as she hoped. 'I think, Samantha, that this relationship, if that's what it was, is over. I have had enough of your embarrassing behaviour. We were only meant to see each other, at your flat, on a weekly basis, that's all. I don't like you turning up here, drunk. I do not like intoxicated women, period.'

She picked up the wine bottle and took further slugs, then wiped her chin. 'Want some?' The wine bottle was shoved towards his face. He pushed it away, but then she leaned forward to kiss him and ended up toppling off the bed onto the floor. She lay on the carpet, trying to drink more wine, which was now trickling away from her mouth and onto the grey carpet.

Gary grabbed her arm to haul her up. 'Get the fuck up and watch what you're doing with that bottle. I've just told you we're over, so it's time for you to leave.' She stumbled as she tried to stand with Gary helping to pull her to her feet. Walking unsteadily, she exited the bedroom, wandered into the lounge, and sat on the sofa next to Simon.

'Hi, lovely Simon. Did you know Gary's just finished with me. I know you've always fancied me and we could go out together.' She moved nearer to Simon, getting comfortable on the sofa, and drawing her legs up to relax more fully. A few minutes later, Gary came into the room to find Samantha and Simon kissing heavily.

The sight of them kissing did not trigger any jealousy in Gary but he was angered by being disrespected by this woman. 'I don't care if you want to go out with him. You'll soon get bored when you realise his standards of hygiene are even lower than yours but go and do it at your flat. Do you hear?'

In open defiance, she kissed Simon again, who took advantage of this sudden lottery win to feel her breasts. The bottle of wine was almost empty and she drained it of the last dregs. 'Simon, what other booze have you got?'

Simon, seemingly lost in a trance of sudden lust, shook his head to regain his senses and answer the question. 'Erm, I've got beer and there's some vodka.'

'Yeah, vodka will do.'

Simon slowly got up off the sofa, not keen to relinquish his place, in case Gary made a move on the lovely girl. 'Want a Red Bull with it?'

'Yeah, cheers.' As Simon left the room, Gary addressed Samantha, 'whatever game you are playing here won't work.'

'Everything is not always about you, Gary. I'm just having fun.' Samantha glared at Gary, defiance in her cat-like eyes.

Simon returned with a tumbler glass half full of vodka, a can of Red Bull, and gave them to Samantha. She clicked the can open, poured in a measure of the energy drink and drank rapidly. She was now giggling loudly, snuggling up to Simon, sartorially dressed in baggy blue jeans and faded, grey, T-shirt with skull design entwined with red roses. 'I think Simon and me are going to have a great time, aren't we Si? He's not as uptight as you, Gary, not so anal.'

This whole performance was for Gary's benefit but Simon was lapping it up, especially as Samantha's hand was exploring his chest and seeking his mouth to kiss her again. Gary went out to the kitchen, retrieved a glass and the vodka bottle, and brought it back into the room. He poured a large drink and downed it in one, watching silently as his ex-girlfriend necked his best mate. He stared at them, an observer of what was about to be the worst porn show ever.

Initially, at the start of Samantha's sexy approach to him, Simon was trying not to show too much enthusiasm or passion for fear of incurring Gary's wrath. As she kissed him, Simon's eyes flicked over to Gary, to try and judge his reaction. As her fingers now moved down to his groin, and he was aroused, the time for caring about what Gary thought was quickly disappearing.

Despite declaring that he was not jealous, as Samantha demonstrated her sexual power over the two men, Gary's feelings of anger and arousal fought for dominance in him. He re-filled his glass with the vodka, the high alcohol content booze now adding to the wave of tension and disturbance building in him. Gulping down the remaining vodka the alcohol was now fuelling his desire, and he got up from the sofa, and walked over to Samantha. 'Enough. You've made your point.'

Forcefully, he grabbed her arm, and pulled her off Simon, and the sofa. 'Come on.' She was half dragged, half carried into the bedroom and pushed on the bed. He climbed over her, the penetrating eyes scorching into hers, his blazing with fury and the need to inflict punishment.

A smirky smile flickered over Samantha's lips, as she had won the game, and got what she wanted; Gary to make love to her, and then take her back. She relaxed ready for his mouth to wipe away the taste and feel of his friend. She waited for Gary to take control which was a normal part of their bedroom activity.

'Think you've won, do you? That you've played with me and reeled me in, a little sprat on your hook.' As he glared down at her, a smile touched his lips, but the eyes were cold, hard steel. 'I've told you before, Samantha, I don't allow women to fuck me about.' He moved over her, his face over hers, and she closed her eyes, ready to receive his mouth. Cold fingers found her neck as his warm breath flowed over her face. She opened her troubled eyes to make sense of what was happening. The pressure of his fingers on her throat intensified and a panic now swept away any pleasure she was feeling. Gary often liked to try out things in bed bringing her experiences of pain to increase her pleasure. This wasn't one of them.

Samantha moaned and gasped for air, speaking in a creaky way. 'Gary, I'm not sure about this, it's a bit scary.' He did not reply. Fear flared within her and the pressure on her neck increased. His face was contorted by rage, power and lust, as his fingers gripped in a vice around her neck, as she tried with all her might to struggle free. But her movements were restricted as he clamped her tight with his body as he knelt over her. 'This will teach you not to humiliate me.'

The choking continued, as her frantic fingers clawed at her throat, trying to release the powerful force of his grip. She flayed about, trying to move her head from side to side, whimpering and crying. The exertion of his hands on her windpipe, silenced her vocal cords and she could not find her voice to plead for her life. As Gary kept up the unrelenting pressure on her throat, grunting with effort, all energy went out of Samantha, her body went limp, and she gasped her last breath.

As she lay beneath him, still and quiet, Gary sat over her, panting quietly. He stared down at her, taking in the peaceful composure of her face, pale and ashen now in death, with only a blotched redness of petechial showers below her eyebrows to spoil the ethereal quality of other worldliness where she now dwelt. He released her thick, black hair from its ponytail and framed her face with the flowing locks as her beauty, once vibrant and striking, was calmed but enhanced by the hand of death.

He, Gary Dawson, had meted out a fair punishment for all her shortcomings; neediness, slovenliness, drunkenness, laziness and, mainly, being weak and pathetic. This moment of perfect tranquillity was the only one of her whole existence and Gary felt proud that he had helped her attain this.

Still mesmerised by her state of serenity and goodness, achieved only in death, Gary lay back on the bed, his body completely sated in a spiritual way. He wondered if this was how a priest felt after hearing a confession of mortal sin from a transgressor and giving a penance so that the soul of the sinner can be cleansed. Gary, bestowing the gift of peace to those who were suffering. Gary had experienced this level of spirituality once before when he ended the life of Lisa Jefferies. Gary knew he had been gifted the divine power to end life, to snuff it out. He was the harbinger of death. He was all powerful, God-like, divine. Omniscient. Omnipotent.

CHAPTER SEVENTY SEVEN

Andy was sat at his desk, preparing for a court appearance next week. The case of the murder of a homeless, middle-aged man, who had been sheltering in a shop doorway, in a quiet area, away from the main shopping area of a Midlands town. Two drunken, arrogant, entitled, twenty-something men had decided to taunt him about their smug, affluent lives and how the man was a failure, waste-of-air loser. The man, a once successful owner of a thriving public house, was brought down by intermittent lockdowns, rising overheads, his increased alcohol consumption, resulting in depression, breakdown of his marriage and loss of his home. A life on the streets was the last straw. That night, he'd had enough of the catcalling and goading from drunken clowns. He swung the first punch but ended up knocked to the ground by the follow-up blow from one of the swaggering twosome and the back of his skull shattered on the kerb. Re-reading the case file to refresh his memory for next week, Andy reflected on the fragility of life, and how it can be extinguished in an instance.

He sat back on his office chair, stretching his neck and shoulder muscles, to relieve the strain of peering at his laptop for a long time. He'd texted Eva, around the time she had her mid-morning break, but had gotten no reply. Obviously going off him already. As their work schedules had occupied them fully this week, he had not seen her since Sunday. He was determined that this sleeping at different houses malarky would have to stop as he really missed her physical presence in his house, and his arms.

Being apart from Eva was not doing a great deal for his temper and he suspected the team were starting to speculate what his mood would be on a day-to-day basis. He had deduced this from a conversation he'd overheard between DS Jim Porter and DC Nick Jackson. Porter stated that 'the boss' was much more jokey if he had been getting some bedroom action. And, according to Porter, 'the boss' should count his lucky stars that he had a woman in his life. Porter moaned that he was finding it difficult to connect with the opposite sex on dating apps as modern women didn't recognise a good thing when they saw one, apparently. Andy thought that this had less to do with the pickiness of women and more to do with Porter's poor dating profile; his paunch, lack of attention to personal hygiene, sloppy dress sense and ocean-going bore hobbies including model railways and collecting railway memorabilia.

Yes, for the sake of his staff and his own sanity, Andy would be persuading Eva to move in with him permanently as soon as he had the chance to speak to her.

A knock on the door prevented him thinking about her further. 'Come in.'

Andy's favourite, DC Nick Jackson, entered the room, in a particularly tight-fitting mid-blue suit, and Andy wondered at times how he managed to breathe. 'What can I do for you, Nick?'

Nick smiled in an oily salesman type of way, wafting the scent of a strong cologne towards Andy, who had to swallow to suppress an urge to cough. 'Did you get my report on the Kendall case, just wondering what you thought? DS Bright thinks I spent too much time on the ex-boyfriend aspect, with the criminal past, and failed to notice that her stepfather, an ex-prison officer, was evasive and kept getting his story mixed up.'

Andy nodded. 'I would agree with DS Bright; you need to be more open-minded when assessing the potential suspect, as you are a little too impressed by a person's superficial qualities, such as appearance, clothes, financial status or upstanding member of the community persona. It caught you off guard this time.'

Andy's phone pinged a text and he picked it up, hoping it would be from Eva but was puzzled to see Alfie's name. '**Andy, it's Eva, I need your help. Alfie and I have been abducted and taken to a house Gary owns. Simon and Gary are fighting and there's a knife. Don't feel I can call 999 as they will hear. Address is Maranta Road, near Ettington.**' Andy stopped leaning back on his chair, his face drained of all colour as he re-read the text. 'Oh, fucking hell, no.' He texted back to Eva, praying that either man would not hear the text ping on the phone. '**I'm on my way. Try to stay calm and try to hide the phone from them. I love you xx**'

Andy looked at DC Jackson who had picked up the tension in his boss as he read the texts. 'Something up, boss?'

Andy addressed DC Jackson. 'Yes. I have a very urgent situation in my personal life which I need to attend to now as my family are in extreme danger. Tell DS Bright that I will be in contact with her shortly. I will also contact DCI Jones personally.'

Remembering his last conversation with Natasha, Andy wondered where she had met with Gary for their liaisons. Phoning her number, he waited, hoping that she would respond instantly and luckily, she did. 'Hi, Natasha, its Andy.'

'Hi, Andy, great to hear from you. I knew it wouldn't be long before you wanted me back,' Natasha stated in a honey-toned voice.

Andy wanted to respond with a sarcastic remark to dampen her ego but this was certainly not the time. 'We'll see. At the moment I really need your help. Gary has acted on his desire to get Eva back and she and Alfie have been…I can only describe it as abducted….to meet with Gary. Eva's given me an address of Maranta Road, near Ettington. Did you meet him at this property?'

'Yeah, I did, a detached house which I think belonged to his wife. I'll just check navigation history, wait a sec.'

Andy waited, every second feeling like an hour, as he tried to comprehend the situation that Eva and Alfie were in. Too many questions were fighting for dominance in his head. Why were the men, normally the closest of allies, fighting? Have Eva or Alfie been physically harmed? He didn't think so but they were in a dangerous and unpredictable situation. His blood chilled as he thought about the presence of the knife, as a weapon took a fight up to a new level of savagery, and peril. He didn't care one jot for those two toss-pots, and hoped they would both die, but he was scared witless for the safety of Eva and Alfie.

'Andy, yeah, the house address was 7 Maranta Road,' and she confirmed the postcode.

'Ok, thanks, I'm really grateful, take care.'

'Andy…..' there was a pause….'I enjoyed my time with you. Maybe….'

He sighed, 'sorry, Natasha, there can be no going back. I have to go,' he said, ending the call.

He picked up his car keys off his desk, grabbed his coat from the back of his chair, and dashed to the door.

Minutes later, driving in his car, pushing the speed limit and trying to avoid the cameras, he focused on his driving and forced the possibilities of what he was going to find out of his mind. Any slowing for traffic lights, cyclists making over taking impossible, or elderly road users driving slower than a snail to ensure of sticking to the speed limits were not doing his temper or blood pressure any good. He had to resist hammering on the horn on a couple of occasions. He continued on the most gut-wrenching drive of his life, an all-consuming fear and terror overwhelming him, about what he might find when he reached his destination.

CHAPTER SEVENTY EIGHT

'Mum, the patio door and windows are locked with no keys. Should we try to find something to break them? Alfie asked his mother, his voice shaky with tears.

'Yes, we could, Alfie, while those two are distracted out there in the hall. Look round for something heavy to try to hammer the door lock or the window. I wish that fire was a real log-burner as there would be a poker. If all fails at getting out the room, I could use it to batter their heads!'

'What about this? Alfie held up an old-style clock with aged-effect case and brass trim. Before Eva could reply he had lobbed it at the patio door. It vibrated the door but the glass did not shatter and it bounced down to the floor. A clock made of plastic not wood.

As this happened, the fighters banged against the lounge door, battering it open. Eva was shocked to register the severity of this on-going violent confrontation between two men who had been comrades-in-arms since their earliest years. Simon was coming off worse with numerous blows inflicted on his face and chest, blood oozing from a cut above his left eye and a blow to his nose. Blood from his lip pooling around his chin. Eva was shocked by Gary's reaction to the knowledge that Simon had tried to assault her. She expected that Gary would have total loyalty to his life-long friend with whom he shared a history of criminality that each needed the other to keep secret. Why ruin that warped friendship and trust when it could lead to revelations that neither would want to be aired? She really couldn't understand Gary. This violent outburst was because another man had tried to hurt her, yet, he himself had harmed her on a number of occasions. What really was his intention in having her brought here today? He couldn't seriously believe that she would resume a relationship with him. The dialogue between the two men during the fight suggested that two women, Lisa and Samantha, had been murdered and their bodies disposed of. Both men were closely involved and guarding each other's secrets. If she failed to agree to return to him was he planning the same fate for her as these women? Eva tried to stay calm for Alfie's sake but as the gravity of their situation sank in, she was petrified of what would happen next, once the distraction of the fight was over.

As there seemed to be no way of escaping the lounge, Eva decided this might be their best chance to escape through the front door. Grabbing Alfie's hand, she ordered him. 'Run, don't stop.'

In the hallway, Simon was now on his knees, brought down by a blow between his shoulders. He stayed kneeling, winded, and breathing shallowly as all energy seeped out of him. Gary hovered, panting from the exertion and spitting saliva to clear blood from his mouth.

As Eva and Alfie sprinted forward towards the door, Simon sprang to his feet and grabbed Eva's arm, halting her progress. She was forced to let go of Alfie's hand and the boy retreated back to the lounge to escape Simon and Gary. Simon's left arm wrapped tightly around Eva's waist and she was faced forward as his right hand was clasped tightly around her throat.

Simon released his grip on Eva's throat to wipe his nose with the sleeve of his hoodie, sniffing loudly to clear his nostrils. Eva struggled frantically to escape his hold on her but his hand was once more on her throat, applying pressure that felt as if she would not be able to breathe. Gary noted the fear on her face.

To Gary, Simon said, 'I'm getting out of here, man, as this is your shit. I've had enough involvement over the years of your screw-ups with women, tidying up after you. You've reaped all the rewards, the money, the sexual benefits in terms of Lisa and Samantha and the countless other women you've fucked. Yeah, you helped me escape that shitty council estate we lived on as kids and you've made pots of dosh from your loveless marriages, some of which you've shared with me. I actually felt sorry for the stupid, ugly cows you wed and then helped to meet an accidental death.'

Eva stood rigidly but unable to control the trembling in her body.

Gary hovered, his eyes flicking between Simon and Eva. 'Shut the fuck up, Simon, as your neck is on the line in all this as well.'

Simon's right hand caressed Eva's hair. 'See Gary, this one, who was meant to be Wife Number Three, is where it all went wrong. You forgot The Plan, as you often call it, and picked the wrong one.'

Anger flared in Gary's eyes as Eva trembled visibly, her frightened eyes staring ahead. 'Let go of her, now,' Gary ordered.

Simon's right hand stroked Eva's face and hair. 'This was the wrong one, eh?. But look at her, Gary. She's got a lovely face, beautiful blue eyes, wavy brown hair, a sensuous mouth and fantastic tits, both of which I had the pleasure of sampling today. Every man's ideal woman. The first two wives were great choices, plain and stupid, so you never got attached. Good shags were supplied by the Lisa's, the Samantha's, and the others, easily discarded. This one,' he made to kiss Eva on the cheek, 'got under your skin. You made an emotional connection with her but still you destroyed what could have been real.'

'Get off her, Simon. I don't want to hear your shit,' Gary ordered.

'No, Gary as the truth hurts, doesn't it.' He addressed Eva; her face ghostly white due to the abominable closeness of this repellent man, as her nostrils were assailed with the smell of blood and sweat. 'Eva, darling, as part of The Plan, you were designated as Wife Number Three, and as lovely as you are, it would have still ended for you as it did the others. The ultimate aim of The Plan is not marriage but your death. You are another stepping stone on his road to accumulating wealth and property.'

The hatred in Gary's eyes towards his former friend was almost tangible. A hot, flame that could sear the skin, its ferocious heat ready to burn and scorch all in its wake. 'You've said too much now. Shut the fuck up and let her go.'

Simon now inched Eva towards the door as Gary edged forward slowly towards them. Simon groaned slightly from his numerous injuries. 'She's my guarantee of a safe passage out of here.'

With a loud roar, Gary pushed Eva sideways, away from Simon, and leapt at the man before he managed to open the door. Simon was now trapped, his back against the door, as Gary lunged at him, the knife stabbing into the chest area of his schoolboy friend, business employee, and life-long co-conspirator in crime.

Simon's eyes expressed anger, then utter fear, as he felt the impact to his chest. He pressed his fingers to the area before drawing them away and stared at the blood staining them. 'Gary, mate, we can work this out. I've always had your back. It's always been you and me, a tight little unit where both of us gained from keeping each other's secrets. We can be that unit again, G-g-a-a-r-ry.' His voice cracked and he gasped for air. His legs now gave way and he crumpled to the floor. Toppling over sideways on to the lacquered flooring, prone and still.

Gary glanced down at Simon's motionless body. 'Fuck, fuck, fuck. The useless idiots pushed me too far this time.'

Eva stood terrified, her eyes flitting from Simon's fallen body to Gary who just stood staring ahead. She rushed over and knelt down by Simon, checking his pulse at his wrist. 'I can detect a very weak pulse but he is barely alive. We must phone for an ambulance. Where is your phone?'

'Forget him, I want to speak to you.'

'Gary, it's time to forget all this nonsense and call an ambulance or this man, your friend, is going to die,' Eva prompted him, terror quaking in her voice.

'As I said, I've had it with him.' Gary still hovered in the hallway, watching as Eva placed Simon, now unconscious, in the recovery position to assist breathing.

As Gary continued to ignored her, she stood up and rushed into the lounge where Alfie was sat, quiet and still, on a sofa. 'Alfie, give me your phone.'

Gary followed her and grabbed the phone out of her hand. 'I don't think so,' as the phone was smashed violently against the coffee table, its screen shattering into hundreds of spidery pieces. Alfie cried, 'oh no,' as he saw the damage inflicted on his mobile.

Gary dropped the phone as Eva stood with Alfie, her arms around her son. Stunned by what Simon had just disclosed, she breathed deeply to try to contemplate the meaning of it all. Had Gary identified her as his potential third wife for the purpose of gaining her financial assets, the house that she and Niall had bought and paid for, her savings from money paid out after his death. Was it Gary's intention all along to access her wealth, then to end her life by 'accident'. It was too horrendous to comprehend, and if Alfie were not here, she felt that she might crumple to the floor through shock and pain.

Gary now took hold of her upper arm, drawing her away from Alfie. He addressed a pale-faced, frightened Alfie, directly, 'right, I want to speak to your mother. We are all going to go upstairs together and you'll behave.'

At the top of the stairs, Gary stopped and spoke to Alfie. 'Right you, go in that bedroom, watch television and don't make a sound. He pushed the terrified boy into the room. 'Don't try any daft tricks or I won't be happy. If you do, I will hurt your mother and then you. There will be no second chances on this and you both will feel pain, are we clear?' Alfie trembled violently as the door closed on him and was locked. Gary placed the key in his trouser pocket.

Eva hovered, wanting to rush downstairs to try to assist Simon. Though she loathed and detested the man, there was no way she could let him die without trying to help him. 'Gary, you must phone for an ambulance for Simon or he will die. This can all be put right before things get more out of hand. Don't do anything else you may regret later, please. We can talk about us getting back together, as you've suggested, but we must help Simon first.' She steeled herself to move closer to him, to show she was willing to mend their relationship, if he co-operated. A tiny smile touched her lips, as she stared at his face. 'You keep saying you want to be with me, so do something to prove it.'

The hardness in Gary's eyes failed to soften as he regarded her. 'In here, and on the bed, now. There's been too much messing around.' He pushed her forcefully into the bedroom. The room was conservatively decorated in greys and silvers, with fitted wardrobes, and a double bed near to the window. Eva reluctantly sat on the edge of the bed, as Gary came towards her and pushed her down, forcefully, so that she was lying on her back. He crawled onto the bed to kneel over her, his face made more terrifying due to the redness to his cheek, and the cut to his lip, after his fight with Simon. Eva stared at his face, one that she was familiar with, those deep, haunting eyes that seemed to read her mind and access the secrets of her heart. Had this man ever cared for her at all or had it all been a sham from the start? Had he ever loved her or was she always within his control, sexually, emotionally and physically, as he progressed on a well-planned journey to marry her then murder her? She had discovered that he was controlling and abusive but now she knew his aim was to exert his ultimate power over her by ending her life. The shock of all this, racked her body and she trembled violently as panic surged through her. 'Is it true, Gary, what Simon just said? That our relationship was all based on your greed to take my house and money? What sort of 'accident' would befall me?'

Eva believed that she could see an emotional battle raging inside him, as his normally unreadable facial expression flitted between anger and, surprisingly, a touch of tenderness. 'Did you ever like me, Gary? Did you ever love me?'

Again, his brooding dark eyes concentrated on hers as he placed his mouth softly on her lips. 'Did I like you, yes. Did I love you, probably yes, in as much as I have ever loved anyone. Yes, you were a target. A young widow with financial worth and that was the main reason for my initial approach to you. But it became more than that as I found that I wanted you, to sexually possess you, to have you in my life as someone to spend time with and to enjoy being with. But ultimately, to have you within my control. You became a drug, a bad habit that changed my normal behaviour. An addiction that I couldn't give up.'

Eva lay beneath him as he caressed her face and stroked her hair. 'Let's just stop this now. Let me and Alfie go home. Do it because you care for me.'

He laughed softly. A hardness on his face, a mask hiding any emotion or tenderness that may have touched him momentarily. 'Sadly, it's all too late now and this can only end one way. Don't think that I don't know that you deliberately engineered that fight between me and Simon but if you were hoping for him to be the winner you were sorely disappointed.' Gary's face was again over hers, his hot breath fanning her face, as he lowered his mouth to her ear. 'Would it turn you on now, if Simon was the victor about to fuck you because he would have.'

Eva pushed hard at him but his weight was like a hydraulic press constricting her chest. 'Gary, I've got no energy left for this game anymore. Just let me go.'

'What always happens, Eva, darling, when you displease me?' He lashed out, his fist connecting first with her left cheekbone, before a follow up blow landed brutally on her left ribs. As her body reeled from the punches, she moaned softly.

His face was now over hers, his deep-set, piercing brown eyes fixed on her as he scrutinised every detail of her face, imprinting it on his memory. 'You have been the only woman in my life that I have ever felt anything for in terms of an emotional connection. Whenever we made love, it was real, meaningful, and not just sex. I did care for you.'

Reeling from the punches to her face and ribs, and the pain from the impact of these blows, Eva's voice, shaky with tears, stated, 'you don't care for someone by causing them physical pain. There's nothing left between us, we can never be together again.'

His intense scrutiny on her continued as his two hands gently caressed her brow, her cheekbones and cupped her chin. 'I realise, now, that we are over. I could make you come back to me by physical control but I cannot control your mind and your emotions, knowing that you want to be with the cop. But ultimately, as I have said, you were always the target for financial gain and somewhere along the way The Plan got side-tracked by your beauty and my desire.'

He leaned down to claim her lips with his, a strong, probing, passionate kiss that possessed and owned her mouth. He stopped abruptly, a small smile touching his lips, the merest of smirks. 'The sweetest kiss, is it the first kiss, who knows? Or is the sweetest kiss the one that says the final goodbye?'

Feelings of fear and panic chilled Eva's blood as he continued to study her face. 'Gary, let's stop all this right here. Try and remember there were some good times.'

'Yes, there were. I doubt if any other woman will come close to you, for me, from now on. But, darling Eva, ultimately, I have the power here and it is the time to stop. This is now on my terms, not yours, and I decide how the ending will be.' His mouth came over hers, to tease and torment. Eva tried again to push him away but the hands that had cupped her chin were inching around her neck, stroking gently. 'This is my farewell gift to you as I deliver you out of this life. No other man will love or possess you from here on in.'

Utter panic now rose in Eva as she tried to make sense of what he was saying. 'Let me go, now,' she stated, not pleading but commanding him.

His hard fingers were now gripping tighter around her throat, it felt like a ring of steel was being secured in place. As waves of panic hit her, she struggled, pushing at his chest with her arms. Trying to claw his hands off her neck as she writhed around to throw him off her. The pain and compression to her neck increased. Her breathing was rapid and shallow as she tried to draw in air, life-giving oxygen into her screaming lungs. Above her, his face was contorted with anger and determination and strong hands continued their vice-like grip on her throat. 'This is the ultimate power, my darling Eva. The power to take the life of those who upset me and piss me about.' A blackness started to envelope her brain and she lost focus, her body no longer fighting for him to release her. She was descending into a swirling, deep, bottomless pit and the outside world started to fade.

Suddenly, the bedroom slammed open and the noise reverberated around the room. The loud bang made Gary instantly stop his assault on Eva's throat. Andy rushed in the room and bawled at Gary. 'GET OFF HER, NOW.

CHAPTER SEVENTY NINE

Andy's arm went around Gary's neck, pulling him backwards and off Eva. 'I'll show you what it's like to be strangled, you fucking bastard.'

Gary reacted with two high powered jabs to Andy's chest with his left elbow. Andy was not deflected as he dragged the man off the bed, onto the floor, and then smashed his clenched fists hard down between Gary's shoulders to prevent him getting up. Gary bawled loudly, rolling onto his back to kick out at Andy, sending him flying backwards. Andy recovered quickly, leaning over Gary and pummelled his fists, rapid-fire, into Gary's smirking face, making blood erupt from his lip. Shaking his head to refocus, Gary pulled the knife out of his pocket, slicing it through the air near to Andy's face. Andy moved backwards to escape its range.

'Keep away, cop, or I'll take your head off,' Gary ordered as he moved towards Eva on the bed.

On the bed, Eva was in a sitting position, supported by the headboard, as she rubbed at her throat, but she was immobile and deeply shaken by what had occurred. Gary grabbed Eva's right upper arm, dragging her off the bed and holding her to him, facing her forward. His left arm went around her waist, gripping her in a tight hold and his right hand went up to her throat, the blade of the knife digging into the right side of her neck. She winced at the coldness and sharpness of the knife on her skin as fear clouded her eyes.

Andy froze, not daring to move forward. 'I suggest that you let her go now, as you are not going to get away with this.'

In a taunting manner, Gary lifted her hair on the right side of her head with the blade of the knife and ran his mouth down her neck, breathing in her perfume. All the while, his eyes focused on Andy. 'You've explored here. It's one of my favourite places, what do you think?'

Andy's face remained impassive. 'I think you should cut the crap and let her go.'

Gary smirked, white teeth gleaming, a shark's smile as it played with its prey. 'No, let's compare notes. We've both been honoured to experience this beautiful woman, so what's your favourite area, and I'm not talking of the obvious here. I'm talking the sensitive areas, the little delights that only we know. In a poll of two, the votes are in, and my favourite area is the area above her knee where your eager fingers, and mouth, progress to the promised land. So, cop, what's your favourite?'

Eva stood rigid, not daring to move as the knife's blade pushed into her neck. She prayed that Gary would not move quickly or the knife may slip. Her anxious eyes focused on Andy. Andy hesitated, not wanting to play this sick game.

A maniacal grin developed on Gary's face, reminiscent of Jack Torrance, the crazed character (played by Jack Nicholson) in the film 'The Shining'. 'Come on, cop, we haven't got all day. Tell me your favourite area on this beautiful body. Is it her neck?' he asked, as the blade of the knife scraped downwards from Eva's jawline to shoulder, a redness appearing as panic and fear surged through her.

Andy's voice cracked with emotion as he spoke, 'it's the curve of her bottom as I draw her to me, ok. Now let her go.'

Gary nodded, a dream-like smile on his face. 'Yeah, I get that. Good choice.' He then laughed, loudly, almost hysterically. 'Weirdly enough today, we nearly had a third voter in our poll, as Simon tried his hand at joining our special club, on the journey here.' Gary waited Andy's reaction and was rewarded to see anger flooding the detective's face. 'But don't worry it never got that far.' This taunting ended abruptly as Gary heard a car drawing up on the driveway. The engine stopped and two loud bangs were heard as car doors slammed. Gary glanced out of the window to suss out the visitors. 'Look, Eva, we've been joined by more cops, there's obviously a shortage of crime to investigate if all they do is interrupt a man and a woman sharing some intimate time together.' The terror in Eva's eyes deepened, but she held still, as Gary's arm crushed around her waist and the knife jabbed into her neck.

Andy was motionless, near to the door, not wanting to make any sudden movements which would jeopardise Eva. 'Look, Gary, you don't want to hurt her. I know you have feelings for her. Let's stop this before Eva...'he hesitated at her name to make it sink in to Gary's brain who he was harming. '.. gets hurt and you spend the rest of your life in prison.'

Gary started to push Eva forward in front of him, the knife still stinging her neck. 'But you are wrong, cop, I do want to harm her, as I am tired of her games and how I have been disrespected by her. I was teaching her a lesson when you interrupted. Now, go ahead of us out of the door and onto the landing.'

Andy hesitated, and Gary stabbed the point of the knife into Eva's neck, so that blood trickled downwards from the cut. Eva's face twisted with pain from the sharpness of the cut. In order to spare Eva further hurt, Andy edged out of the room on to the landing at the top of the stairs. Gary followed, inching Eva forward, in front of him and out of the bedroom. A sharp rapping on the front door indicated the presence of the two police officers. 'Hello. Police.'

Gary, still firmly holding Eva, ordered Andy, 'go down stairs but don't let them in. We will wait till your colleagues leave and then decide on what happens next.' Andy hesitated, not wanting to be too far from Eva. Gary scraped the point of the knife deeper into her neck at the place where he had cut her skin. Eva jerked in shock and fear. 'I'll draw more blood if you don't go now.'

His choices limited, Andy went down the stairs and stood in the hallway. Gary slowly, but carefully, steered Eva down the stairs, the steel of the knife blade catching the light, an ongoing reminder of its deadly position against her throat. For the moment, Andy could only watch and wait. He could not attempt to assist Eva whilst the blade of a knife remained close to the major arteries in her neck.

'Hello. Police. Open up,' came the order from outside the front door. This was shouted by a male voice and a further loud banging disturbed the silence in the house.

Alfie had now emerged from the adjacent bedroom, having found a second key to the door. He watched quietly as the adults progressed down the stairs and into the hallway.

The noise made by the police caused Gary to loosen his grip on Eva slightly. A number of bangs and thumps were heard from above as Alfie hurtled down the stairs and smashed a large, white vase on the back of Gary's head. The impact registered on Gary, and he stumbled forward, letting go of Eva and dropping the knife.

Andy now rushed forward, lifted Eva out of the way, and lunged at Gary before he had chance to recover from the blow to his head. Gary was pulled forward, down the stairs, missing his step and landing at the bottom, then Andy hauled him to his feet. Gary shook his head from side to side, and blinked rapidly, to regain his senses and aimed a punch which skimmed Andy's jaw. 'I'll fucking kill you, cop.'

All understanding of professional responsibilities left Andy now as he faced this man who had repeatedly hurt and abused Eva. He wanted revenge. An animalistic roar left his mouth and he threw a battery of vicious punches at Gary's face. Blood erupted from his lip, further damage to his mouth, and he drew in a breath as a wave of pain washed over him. The pain seemed to energise Gary who rushed head first at Andy, ramming his chest, trying to jab punches into his ribs. Andy pushed him off, then landed a heavy blow to Gary's belly area, winding him, and he crumpled to his knees. One further blow at the base of Gary's neck sent him sprawling to the floor. Taking handcuffs out of his jacket pocket, Andy quickly secured Gary's hands behind his back and fastened the cuffs.

Eva, though massively traumatised from her ordeal, managed to open the door for the two police officers who approached the two men with caution, not knowing exactly what had occurred here. Andy hauled Gary into a sitting position by the side of the stairs. He held out his warrant card. 'I am Detective Inspector Andy Leyton. This is Gary Anderson. On the floor, Anderson's associate, Simon Wagstaff, who has been stabbed by Anderson and in need of urgent medical attention. I requested an ambulance ten minutes ago but it has not yet arrived. Please chase it up.'

The male police constable, PC Javid, bent down to assess Simon. He radioed again for an ambulance before speaking to his colleague. 'His pulse is very weak, his breathing is very shallow and his skin is pale and clammy. There's not much outward blood loss so my guess is that there is internal bleeding.'

The female officer, who introduced herself as PC Johnson, was a petite, fair-haired woman in her forties. She addressed Andy, 'can you tell me what has been going on here?'

Andy clarified, 'on the orders of Gary Anderson, my girlfriend, Eva Brennan, and her twelve-year-old son were abducted from their home this morning by his associate, Simon Wagstaff, and brought here. Ms Brennan is Anderson's ex-girlfriend, who he has been violent against in the past. When I arrived, he had Ms Brennan pinned down on a bed and he was choking her. I want him arrested on wounding with a knife on Simon Wagstaff, and on suspicion of instigating an abduction, common assault by choking and threatening with a weapon on Ms Brennan.'

PC's Johnson and PC Javid, both stood to the side whilst they discussed the information given by the police detective. Eva was standing, holding Alfie against her, trying to comfort him and draw his eyes away from Simon's injured body and Gary's stare of loathing he was directing towards them. PC Johnson walked over to Eva, noting the redness and marking to her neck. 'Ms Brennan, can I ask you if what DI Leyton has said is an accurate account of what has happened to you today.'

Eva released Alfie from her hold and told him to go and sit in the lounge. She was still shaken and overwhelmed from her ordeal. She nodded her head. 'Yes, that is correct. Gary Anderson had his friend, Simon, bring us here under duress with my son bound and gagged in the boot of the car. Gary and I were in a relationship but I ended it after being subjected to a number of physical assaults. It ended just before Christmas when he battered me and struck me with a wine bottle on my left temple. I was hospitalised at the time and I made a statement to a PC Shah. Since then Gary has been determined to get me back but that was never going to happen as far as I was concerned. Today, I was abducted with my son, by Simon Wagstaff, under Gary's instructions, in what I thought was an attempt to re-establish our relationship. He told me earlier that his ultimate plan all along was to marry me, kill me and take my financial assets. He was choking me just now, and I was on the point of blacking out, when Andy, DI Leyton, dragged him off me. He then held a knife to my throat as he attempted to leave this house.'

PC Johnson quietly discussed with her colleague how to proceed before putting on gloves to pick up the knife which was on the hallway floor. It was stowed in an evidence bag. To Andy, she stated, 'we'll secure this as a crime scene and get CSI and your colleagues in. I've also called for backup.'

Gary winced in pain as his sitting position was hurting his bruised ribs and he ordered the officers, 'can't you fucking hurry up, as I could do with some medical attention. I am the victim of police brutality by DI Leyton.'

PC Johnson, moved closer to him. 'Ms Brennan, what is the name of your son?'

Eva responded, 'Alfie Brennan.'

PC Johnson directly addressed Gary. 'Gary Anderson, I am arresting you on the suspicion of the wounding of Simon Wagstaff, and for the suspicion of aiding the abduction of Alfie Brennan and Eva Brennan. Also, for the suspicion of common assault and threatening with a knife of Eva Brennan. You do not have to say anything, but it may harm your defence if you do not mention, when questioned, something which you later rely on in court. Anything you do say may be given in evidence.' She assisted him, roughly, to his feet.

At this moment, there was a knock on the door, and PC Javid escorted two paramedics into the hallway who immediately started to attend to Simon Wagstaff.

PC Johnson addressed Eva and Andy. 'Miss Brennan, I need you to go to the hospital to be checked over as you may need medical treatment. A record of your injuries will be required in order to bring a criminal case against Mr Anderson. We will also need to take statements from you, DI Leyton, and your son, Alfie, in due course.'

Eva remained still, white-faced and shaking. Andy went over to her, to hold her up, as he was convinced, she was about to crumple to floor. She relaxed against him, relief from the shock surging through her and she began to sob uncontrollably. 'I'm s-so glad you arrived when you d-did. I genuinely b-believed he was going to k-kill me.'

Andy held onto her tightly, allowing her to cry, whilst stroking her hair. He addressed the two police officers. 'I'll take her to the hospital, now, to get her checked out.'

PC Johnson stated, 'we will be in contact with Ms Brennan and yourself, shortly.' At this moment, two further police constables came to the front door and PC Johnson went over to update them on the situation. After a few minutes, Gary was handed over to the constables and he shuffled along with them, still handcuffed, but protesting that he required medical attention.

As he left the property, Eva felt a sense of deep relief as he was no longer a danger to her and Alfie. Alfie noticed his mother was crying and he rushed out of the lounge to comfort her. 'Mum, are you ok?' he asked and he too started to sob.

Eva tried to control her crying in order not to alarm Alfie. It was a losing battle and she trembled violently, as both Andy and Alfie now held on to her.

Andy examined her neck which showed severe red marks and bruising on either side of her throat where her assailant's fingers had dug into her, including small abrasions caused by his fingernails. The whole area looked very sore and tender. There was the nick to her neck and the trickle of drying blood where she had been cut by the knife. A further flash of anger surged through Andy. 'I hope that bastard rots in hell for what he's done to you.'

Eva lightly touched her neck and the skin felt burning and raw. Her body could not stop shaking, tremors rippling within her, making her hands tremble, as waves of nausea washed over her and her head throbbed. 'I could do with sitting down soon as my legs feel like jelly and I really just want to get out of this house.'

Andy placed his arm firmly around her, ready to scoop her up if she stumbled. 'Come on, let's get you to the hospital. Alfie, are you ready?'

They walked out to his car and Andy helped Eva inside. As Alfie made his way to sit in the back of the car, Andy said, 'there is one thing to note in all this, Alfie. You played a blinder by smashing him with the vase and making him let go of the knife, a superhero to be proud of.'

Alfie smiled at Andy through watery tears. 'I was glad I could help. I think I am like my favourite superhero, Thor.'

Andy laughed. 'You can be Thor but I can't see him yielding a vase, any time soon.'

CHAPTER EIGHTY

Easter Sunday, 17 April 2022 Gary was learning to control the anger that he had been carrying with him for the last month since he had been charged with the murders of Lisa Jefferies and Samantha Tulloch, and had been remanded in custody, at a Midlands prison. He had been raging at a number of people since his incarceration, including Simon, Eva and the cop, for his current predicament. The anger within, always bubbling away just below the surface, had made the last few weeks very difficult as he endured his first experience of prison life. Gary, who always considered himself to be street smart and a tough adversary, found that he was not top dog in here in terms of brawn. A few altercations with other prisoners had left him with a cut lip and bruised ribs. His first cell mate, a six-foot-four, fifteen stone bruiser had quickly shown Gary what happens if personal belongings in the cell are moved or lost. Gary was learning quickly what fights to pick and which to avoid. His current cell mate, a lanky, spotty, thirty something male charged with attempted murder of his partner, was easier to share with. In this instance, Gary was the one in control of the situation, and took pleasure in harassing the man. In the case of his cell mate, Ricky, it was the classic scenario of the man coming home from work and finding his woman in bed with another man. As the lover fled, the woman had been subjected to a severe beating leaving her hospitalised and with ongoing problems resulting from a head injury.

Gary lay on the top bunk bed, staring at the ceiling, as Ricky sat on the lower bunk. 'Easter Sunday, today, Ricky. Wonder what your missus is doing, after having over fed the kids on Easter eggs. Perhaps the boyfriend's gone around to give her a present. He's her Easter bunny rabbit. You know, doing to her what rabbits do best, eh?'

'Shut the fuck up, Anderson. My Jen came to see me last week and said she'd forgiven me for attacking her. She swore she was not seeing anyone and said she'd wait for me,' Ricky insisted, though a flicker of doubt crossed his slim face.

'They all say that and then drop their knickers at the first opportunity,' Gary commented.

'At least I get some visitors, my Jen and my mother. I haven't seen anyone visiting you. You come across as the dog's bollocks but really there's no one that cares a shit about you, is there? What about that fiancée of yours, that you keep mentioning, how come she doesn't come to see you?' Ricky stated.

Gary was now feeling the familiar heat of his anger rising. If he was taunted about Eva, then Ricky might find that his gormless face collides with a flying fist. 'Mind your own business. At least my fiancée is beautiful and sexy, and not that minger, your Jen, who has a face like a bulldog and a body like a bag of spanners. How she managed to pull another man, I'll never know, unless she is exceptionally good at shagging.'

'Shut up. Your beautiful fiancée probably doesn't exist as you haven't even got a photo of her. You're all talk,' Ricky goaded.

Surprisingly, this deflated Gary and his rage dispersed. He realised that the one item he desired most in this grim prison cell was a photo of Eva, to stare at and prompt his memories of their time together. He wanted to sharply recall the blueness of her eyes. To see her brown/auburn hair and recollect how his fingers would run through its glossy waves as he drew her towards him for a sensuous kiss on her perfect mouth. He longed for access to her usual perfume with its fruity, floral and vanilla notes that he would detect on her neck, wrists, and at the top of her cleavage as he eagerly explored her body. He missed her so much. The softness of her mouth, the feel of her creamy soft skin, her body responding to his touch as he teased and taunted her arousal before he entered her, and controlled her with powerful thrusts to bring her to orgasm. He knew that all he was missing would be bestowed on the man he loathed most in the world, the cop bastard. What would they be doing today on this Easter Sunday? Having the boring parents and in-laws over for lunch and drinking Prosecco in the garden. The desperate friend, Tania, would be spitting feathers that her most desired man was with her best friend. Would the irritating kid, Alfie, be too old for an Easter Egg hunt, most likely, but the kid would probably consume his own body weight in chocolate before the day was out.

He now decided to put thoughts of Eva out of his head, to save those images for the hours of darkness where she was his alone, to do with what he pleased, as he lay sleepless on the lumpy prison mattress. For now, his thoughts turned to Simon, his ex-friend and business employee, who had turned against him so spectacularly following their fight and the stabbing. Simon had exacted his revenge by giving the police full, comprehensive details of the deaths of Claire and Jess, Lisa and Samantha. In terms of the wives, the police were having a hard time trying to find any evidence to suggest that their deaths were premeditated murders and not accidental deaths, as per the coroner's inquests. It was the situation with the disappearances of Lisa and Samantha that had landed him in here. Simon had decided to share all their secrets with police as to what had happened to the two young women at Gary's hands. If all the police had was Simon's witness statements, then Gary may have had a chance of escaping a conviction but Simon had helpfully directed the police as to where to search for the two bodies. A body had been recovered from an area of locks on the River Thames, near Maidenhead, and DNA from bone and teeth had identified that the body was that of Lisa Jefferies. Simon's betrayal had also led to the police locating a second female body, in the River Avon, just south of Stratford-upon-Avon, and DNA analysis from bone and teeth, identified the body of Samantha Tulloch. Fortuitously for Gary, there was no DNA evidence on the two bodies of the perpetrator of the attacks. Post mortem examinations had revealed that both women had been manually strangulated, due to compression of the larynx and fracture to pharyngeal cartilages and the hyoid bone, resulting in death by asphyxiation. Gary's witness statement to the police acknowledged that he had been in a relationship with both these women at different times, two women who had also known Simon Wagstaff. Wagstaff, had frequently made comments about finding these two women sexually attractive and he had a brief sexual relationship with Samantha Tulloch when she and Gary broke up. His very expensive defence lawyer, and barrister, will argue the case that these deaths were at the hands of Simon Wagstaff, a socially awkward individual, not attractive to women and who took advantage of Gary's friendship with the women to, probably sexually assault them, then murder them. This defence will not necessarily save his skin, as Gary's attack on Eva, by trying to strangle her, and her testifying to this in court, weakened his case. The attempted rape on her by Wagstaff may help to place the spotlight more firmly on his ex-friend. Gary's current lawyer was not overly hopeful of success with this approach and Gary was fully aware that there was a likelihood he would spend a considerable number of years in prison. As yet, the police had not identified a third body, a murder and disposal all committed without Simon's involvement but would his informant, his snitch, his snake in the grass betray him further? Gary prayed his luck would hold on this one. But, again, could he be excused for his actions as she was one more example of a woman who was stupid (Claire), needy (Lisa, Jess, Samantha) or who simply displeased him (Eva). Gianna, the candidate destined to be Wife Number Three in 2016, to acquire her assets including the estate inherited from her late father from the sale of his Italian restaurants. This was the first time, prior to Eva, that The Plan had failed.

****

September 2016

As rain lashed down outside the window of her bedroom, and the chill of the autumnal air penetrated the room, Gianna shivered but not from coldness but from fear. Waves of fear and panic racked her body, and her hands shook, as she tried to quickly remove clothes from her wardrobe and stow them into the two suitcases on the bed. She tried to calm her breathing, and focus her thoughts on the task in hand, to try to pack as much of her belongings as possible as she was unlikely ever to return to this house again. She had loved living here, her own safe haven in the world, where she could chill out in the evening with a red chianti and her favourite carbonara, made with eggs, pecorino cheese, cured guanciale and black pepper, a proper Italian favourite and not an English version made with bacon. But she had to leave. She no longer felt safe with Gary, his controlling ways and angry outbursts were eroding her confidence, isolating her from her friends and tipping her into depression. She had to escape, as the wedding was due to go ahead in a week's time and she could not spend her life being tied to this unpredictable man. The number of red flags which were waving at her were enough to decorate a carnival.

The final straw, in a long line of doubts about Gary, and their relationship, came just over two weeks ago when she was on shift in the Accident & Emergency department, as senior nurse. She was treating a young woman, Holly, in her late twenties, for bruising to the left eye, swollen lip, and a laceration above left eyebrow, and suspected bruised ribs. Gianna had started a conversation with the woman to find out how the injuries occurred. Gianna felt she knew the answer, another case of domestic violence. 'Can you tell me how you got these injuries?'

The young woman had been drinking, so was slurring her words slightly, but had been brought in by a friend who wanted to have her checked out. Holly, was a petite brunette, slim, but with a shapely figure. She was now sat on the hospital bed, looking young and fragile, with three steri-strips above her eyebrow to halt the bleeding. The swelling to her top lip made her lisp slightly when she spoke, 'yeah, my fella, Gary, came round the flat, for his Friday night, you know, hookup, and I was drinking with Suzie here, and a friend from work, Dan. We all work at the car dealership where Gary is the boss. We were all pretty off our faces when Gary arrived and Gary hates drunkenness in women. He was also not happy to see Dan there and accused me of shagging him, which I am not.'

Gianna's blood froze as she heard the description of what had occurred and who had been the girl's attacker. Was this just purely coincidental, another dealership with a boss called Gary? 'You have been subjected to a violent assault and I would suggest that you report this to the police.'

The girl's face was pale and drawn and she was rapidly sobering up. 'I can't as I will lose my job, and then lose my flat, as I won't be able to pay my share of the rent. Also, Gary is pretty scary and there would be repercussions if I reported him to the police.'

Gianna was inwardly quaking as she asked the next question. 'Can I ask, is this Gary your regular boyfriend and has he assaulted you before?'

The girl pursed her lips as she considers her response. 'Yes and no. We are an item and he comes to my flat when he can in the evenings and at weekends. He says he really fancies me but that our relationship is only casual as he is getting married soon to some older woman but he says he will continue to see me. According to Gary, his wifey-to-be is a lot older than him, not attractive, a lousy lay and he's only marrying her to get hold of her house and money. He says that I am his sexy sideline but I have to make sure that I understand the nature of our relationship. It will only ever be casual. As I was drunk tonight, I shouted at him that I wanted more from him or I would spread it about that he was cheating on his fiancée with me. Big mistake. Gary gets really riled with me and I get a beating which has landed me in here.'

Gianna now thought that her legs would collapse under her and she leaned on the bed for support. Her mouth was dry, her vocal cords brittle, as she struggled to ask the next question. 'What is the full name of your attacker?'

The young woman hesitated. 'His name is Gary Anderson but I don't want him reported to the police. I would lose my job if he finds out and he would make sure I paid for reporting him. But, also, I really like him when he's being nice and sexy so I don't want to lose him out of my life.'

Later, at home after her shift, Gianna knew that she could not continue in the relationship with Gary and she could not go ahead with the wedding. At the beginning, Gary had been funny and caring, making her feel special, but after he moved in a year ago, he changed completely. Somewhere along the way, the nice Gary had disappeared replaced by a cold, arrogant, controlling Gary who enjoyed humiliating her, both verbally and physically. Colleagues at the hospital noticed a change in her from outgoing, chatty Gianna to someone who only interacted with them if necessary and stopped socialising with them after work. At home, Gary made no effort to pretend to care for her and preferred to criticise her shortcomings when compared to other women. She was too old, too unattractive, and essentially boring but weirdly he still wanted to marry her.

A week later, after he had sniped at her and belittled her at every opportunity, Gianna asked him why he wanted to marry someone he obviously despised. He realised that she was starting to withdraw from him and reassured her that he was looking forward to the wedding and their life together. A cuddle and a small kiss to her forehead was applied to repair the damage. Gianna had spent the last weeks considering their relationship, balancing the pros and the cons, and concluded that Gary was not in it for love or companionship, as he treated her coldly and with hostility. Their sex life was intermittent and she knew he was disappointed in her lack of enthusiasm and expertise. This led to quick, unfeeling couplings, and she frequently felt that he was repelled by her at these times. She long suspected that he was unfaithful to her. He made comments about hot customers and sexy employees who were keen to 'service' him. The knowledge that he frequently slept with the young woman, Holly, was the last nail in the coffin. Gianna knew that she had to end this toxic relationship and get away.

Now, she was packing up her life in England, ready to fly to Italy, the country where her father was born. Where she was fleeing to live with her father's extended family. Stowing makeup, toiletries, jewellery and other personal items in the cases, her body had gone from chills to sweat. Dampness collected on her forehead and underarms as she hurried to get out of the house before his return. It was a Friday evening and it was his usual routine to meet Simon for beers at a local pub. In truth, Gary had never been seeing creepy, ghastly Simon, on a Friday but young, sweet Holly, who would be satisfying Gary's needs in a way Gianna never had. Gianna now zipped the first case, then put remaining items of dresses, trousers and jackets in the second case. Important documents were stowed in her hand luggage, a small wheelie case, and these would be needed when she arrived in Italy and started to dismantle her life in the UK.

Suddenly, Gianna heard the front door open and close and froze in fear as she knew that Gary had returned home. She held her breath as she heard his keys drop into a bowl on a table in the hallway. She listened intensely, still suppressing her breathing, so that she could follow his progress throughout the house. A door opened and closed as he went into one room, before going into another. Not finding her downstairs, he returned to the hall and called out, 'Gianna, where are you?'

Her heart now hammered in her chest, which she imagined he could hear, as he made his way up the stairs. She did not respond to him.

The bedroom door opened, and he stood in the doorway, a strong, physical presence, in grey work suit and white shirt, a blue tie loosely knotted at his neck. His penetrating, brown eyes which always radiated the mood he was in went from intrigued to angry in seconds, and a small, smirky smile touched his mouth. 'What is this then, packing for our honeymoon already? You're a bit early, aren't you?'

Gianna stood silently, staring at him, a brain freeze affecting her thoughts as she struggled to give an explanation of what she was doing. 'No, I'm just putting some stuff I don't wear anymore in cases to take to the charity shop after we get back from the honeymoon.'

Gary moved over to the bed and unzipped one of the cases. He took out a blue, floral tea dress that Gianna wore often. 'You're taking this to the charity shop. Good. You wear it all the time, it's a longish length which makes your legs look chunky and its baggy over your non-existent boobs.' He took out a white blouse with lacy collar and blue buttons. 'Yes, it's a good idea to get shot of this. It's very 'tea with granny' and certainly would not turn any man on.' He now started to pull item after item out of the case, remarking on each as if he were the host of a tv programme helping a woman de-clutter her wardrobe. Black trousers. 'Elasticated waist, for old bags.' Pink dress. 'Hideous, and keep away from naked flames.' Green blouse with swirly pattern. 'Explosion in a paint factory.' The items were discarded on the bed as he dismissed each piece of clothing, scathingly. Gianna tried to take them out of his hand but he kept everything out of her reach.

Picking up items of underwear, he laughed loudly. 'Oh, yes, here we are the sexy underwear.' He held up black cotton pants. 'Plain, boring, uninspiring, just like the wearer. No thongs, or lace, or bikini knickers to get my pulse racing. So, these are all the items that are going to the charity shop, are they? As you seem to be in this stuff all the time, what are you going to wear?'

Gianna picked up the items, one by one, and started to repack them in the suitcase. 'Just stop touching them and let me get on.'

Gary now sat on the edge of the bed and forced her to sit next to him. 'Get on with what? You look as if you are packing for a long holiday, so what's going on?'

His right hand was now holding firmly onto her left upper arm. 'Thinking of leaving, are you? You seem to have forgotten to tell me. And, here am I expecting to walk down the aisle with my fiancée next week.'

Gianna's brown eyes, blazing with anger, now locked onto his eyes. 'Yes, I am leaving as I have realised that you do not love me and I actually think you hate me. This relationship is toxic and I am going to Italy to stay with family. From there, I will organise the sale of my house, car, furniture and other belongings and as we will not be married then you will have no right to any of my assets. This whole thing with you has been about my money which is what I suspect happened with the previous two unfortunate women who became your wives. I do not intend an accident to happen to me as was the case with them.'

Gary laughed, a hateful, hollow sound as he surveyed this woman. 'You've got me bang to rights, guilty as charged. That was always the plan. You don't think I actually fancied you, do you? You are too plain and dull and I could only have sex with you by thinking of shapely women with full breasts that I've seen on porn sites.'

Gianna's face flushed red as the cruelty of his words hit home. She swung her right arm so that her hand connected with his face. 'You bastard. I knew at the beginning there was something off about you and I should have trusted my instincts. Still at least I know exactly what you think of me and I can make a new life away from you.'

The hard part of Gary, the woman hater, could not let this assault go unchallenged. 'You'll regret that. I've put up with you for two years with the sole intention of getting married to access your money. The Plan was for you to have an unfortunate accident sometime next year. A slip on mud when on one of your country walks, perhaps.'

The redness on Gianna's cheeks deepened as anger erupted in her. 'Sei un maiale, you are a pig. I am glad I now know what you are and what your intentions were in terms of my assets. I know about your girlfriend, Holly, and that she ended up at the A&E two weeks ago after you beat her up. I am glad I know about all of this. I can now escape before the wedding and you will not get a penny from me, ever.'

Gary now slung the two packed suitcases off the bed and grabbed Gianna's arm. He pulled her onto the bed, and leaned over her, as his brown eyes, cold and hard as marbles, scoured her face. 'Yeah, Gianna. I've had to have a pretty girlfriend on the side, to get some enjoyment back into the act of sex. You are as exciting as a wet weekend in Margate. But I never thought of sex when I was with you. I thought of money and now the plan to get your financial assets has been blown. All the time and money I have invested in you has resulted in zero profit and I don't like that.' He paused, using his body to restrict her movements, her arms locked in his grip above her head. She saw the raw anger in his eyes. 'So, now, Gianna, what am I going to get as a reward for all my trouble? I don't want your body but you can give me a final gift for all that I've given you. You can give me the ultimate pleasure of ending your worthless life and your gratitude that I have saved you from the misery of a lonely, old age.'

Gianna now thrashed around on the bed, trying to free herself from his vice-like grip. 'Lasciami andare, bastardo.' But he knelt on her, restricting any movement, as she moved her head from side to side to try to escape his relentless gaze. His hands now moved around her throat, squeezing harder and harder, as she used her hands and nails to try and prise him off her.

His breathing was laboured as he pressed his hands tighter around her neck, looking fully into her eyes to gauge her reaction as the life force started to flow out of her. There was fear and panic in her eyes and she gasped rapidly as her breathing faltered, as oxygen failed to reach her lungs. The pressure on her throat was severely painful and compressing, and as panic set in, her ability to breathe was further compromised. Gary looked, fully focused, into her brown, pleading eyes. 'Yes, Gianna, I am now administering the justice you deserve for challenging me, humiliating me, disrespecting me and for the earlier slap.

I am meting out your punishment for all the time I have wasted on you and for the failure of The Plan. Are you understanding me?' As Gianna thrashed and struggled against him, he grinned widely. 'Look at me Gianna. As a Catholic, you have always believed in God, the Almighty. Well today, Gianna, I have the ultimate power and I decide on whether you live or die. I am the Divine Judge and I have considered the evidence carefully. My verdict is in. I am wearing the black cap as I sentence you to death.'

Gianna's panic-stricken eyes fixed on Gary as she tried to plead for her life. No sound came out of her mouth. As the constricting, crushing grip continued on her throat, Gianna now stopped flaying at his hands, and exhaled her final breath, before going limp

CHAPTER EIGHTY ONE

Easter Sunday April 2022 Andy stood in the kitchen, sipping from a bottled lager, as he and Eva finished the last of the preparation for the BBQ, the planning of which had been a gamble, as weather on Easter Sunday was notoriously unpredictable and could range from snow to scorching temperatures. This day was shaping up well, high teen temperatures, blue sky and no wind, the perfect BBQ weather. All the food prep was done; meats marinated, vegetable skewers of mushroom, onion, red and yellow peppers ready for grilling, green salad, coleslaw, pesto salad, tomato salad all prepared, vegetarian options ready, bread rolls ready, and garlic breads ready for baking. Assorted drinks available including wines, beers and soft drinks.

'Want a coffee before they all descend on us?' Andy asked Eva.

'No, thanks, as I need to go and get ready before people arrive.' She walked out of the kitchen and up the stairs into the bathroom. She undressed, and went under the hot shower, luxuriating in the warmth of the water on her skin and the delicate aroma of the citrus body wash. She gently rubbed her abdomen and considered the unexpected bombshell that was about to disrupt her life. After getting dry and putting on underwear and a pale pink silk dressing gown she went into the bedroom. She lay down on the bed, on her back, staring ahead, her mood subdued and contemplative.

Andy appeared at the door to find her lying on the bed. 'What are you up to lazy bones? We have people arriving shortly, so no time for a short snooze,' he joked but then glimpsed a sadness on her face. 'You're not ill, are you, as you seem a little off colour?'

Eva turned to answer him. He was dressed in grey slim fit jeans and a blue shirt and her heart lurched as she was reminded of how handsome he was. In some ways, his good looks were a problem, as she remembered Natasha's comment that he did not find her attractive. She wondered if this relationship was built on fragile foundations which could easily crumble if he found another lovelier woman.

He came over to her, and lay down on the bed next to her, placing an arm over her body. He nuzzled her hair, and inhaled softly, taking in the coconut smell of her hair conditioner and the lemony aroma of the body wash on her skin. 'I love your hair when it's all tousled and wavy and you smell so delicious that I could eat you.' He turned her towards him and started to gently kiss her lips, in a soft teasing way. 'So, delicious that I don't know whether to devour your or ravish you,' he murmured. The kissed developed into a commanding exploration of her mouth, as one hand gripped her around her waist and he pulled her firmly into his body. He was now fully possessing her, his eager mouth seeking hers. Strong fingers explored downwards, kneading her breasts, over her waist and her hips as he breathed heavily.

'What does ravish actually mean?' Eva teased, coming up for air from the passionate kiss.

He smiled wickedly. 'Well, my beauty, you are about to find out. I am your lord and master and I am in charge of ravishing fair maidens.'

'But, sir, I have duties to attend to in the kitchen. Your lordship is entertaining his guests with meats grilled over the flame and fine wines to be drunk to excess. There will be great merriment, singing and dancing.'

'Yes, fair maid, there will but we must ensure that your father does not get well tippled and sing songs from the olde days. There is one he is very fond of about the love of a boy for an older woman, 'Maggie May'.

Eva giggled. 'My father loves to sing olde songs from his youthful years.'

'Hush, now, I command thee. Time is being wasted while I should be ravishing you, properly. Any more talking and giggling will displease me, my wench.'

His mouth firmly re-claimed hers and she was drawn down into the embrace. The passion flared within her, her breathing heavy, as the nearness of his hard, muscular body aroused a sexual longing that needed to be sated.

She pulled away from him slightly. 'What will happen if I displease you, my lord?' Her blue eyes were flashing with a mixture of desire and amusement as she provoked him, playfully.

'Are you trying to challenge me, my beauty. As your lordship, you are in my power. Naughty young maidens that displease me may have to be punished.' He tipped her across his lap, her silk dressing gown edging upwards to reveal white knickers. He delivered two slaps to her bottom.

'Andy, stop it.' She laughed as he smiled, wickedly, at her mortified expression.

'Anyway, fair maiden, I have not done with you yet.' At this moment, his intention to tease her disappeared as his lustful passion touched his eyes, as she lay back next to him. He untied the silk gown, parting it to reveal her white bra and he caressed her breasts before lifting the bra and undoing it from the back. He peeled the gown and bra off her body.

Eva unbuttoned his shirt to stroke his toned chest. Andy removed the shirt and quickly slipped out of the rest of his clothing. Eva met his passion equally and was always aroused by his physical strength as he held her and embraced her.

His mouth now reclaimed hers. A flame ignited in her that burned wildly, as his eager hands probed her body, his fingers under her pants as he slipped them off her. He stroked between her legs, the soft, secret female area that was the essence of her womanhood. She moaned softly; her head lost in the soaring fire of passion, as he entered her, then moved within her, strong, controlled thrusting movements that built the momentum, as their eyes locked, until their bodies exploded in orgasm.

Afterwards, they lay replete and elated, her head on his chest. He stroked her hair. 'That was amazing, sweetheart.'

Relieved not to be looking at his face, she asked, 'are you happy in this relationship, Andy? We have only been together as a couple for a very short time. I don't want you to get big-headed but you are a very handsome man and could have any woman you want.'

He laughed loudly. 'Yes, I am very handsome, and obviously if Angelina Jolie were to knock on the door right now, I would have to lock you in the wardrobe while she had her wicked way with me.' He made her sit up so he could look into her troubled blue eyes. 'But, joking aside, I am very happy, thank you. I know this harks back to what Natasha said about me not finding you attractive. It was all a tissue of lies as she sensed, rightly, that I had feelings for you.' He kissed her softly. 'Eva, you are very beautiful and sexy to me and you are the only woman I want, or need. I sense that you are feeling insecure for some reason, what's brought this on?'

Eva re-dressed in the silk gown, tying it securely then opened the drawer of her bedside cabinet. 'I think you had better see this.' She took out two blue and white thermometer shaped objects and placed them in front of him, the word 'pregnant' prominently displayed on both.

It had come as an utter shock to Eva this week that she might be pregnant, as since the start of her new relationship with Andy she had been taking a contraceptive pill. She remembered that she had missed taking her pills for a couple of days at the beginning of March when she had a stomach virus, most likely picked up from one of the children at school. Eva realised that she had missed her period. Over the last week she had been experiencing tiredness, nausea, metallic taste in her mouth and sore breasts, all signs of early pregnancy.

She was now terrified. Was this too early in their relationship? Would he want a baby? Did she want a baby? They had been very close friends for a few years and that had only recently changed into a sexual relationship. Was it too soon to bring a baby into the relationship? Would the relationship last the distance?

Andy looked at the two pregnancy kits, registering disbelief on his face. 'Wow, are we pregnant?'

'Yes, yes, according to these two tests I am. If you think you are as well, I have two more tests in here we can use.' Joking was helping her diffuse this tense situation as she didn't know how he would take the news. He picked up the two tests and read them again. Then looked at her to try and gauge her take on it all as he kept saying. 'Wow.'

Eva was equally trying to ascertain whether 'wow' was good or bad. She added, 'I'm not sure how it happened.'

He now laughed loudly, shaking his head. 'Oh dear, you are a teacher and I am about to have to tell you about the biological facts as to how a baby is made. Ok, in eight months' time a stork will fly over and drop a baby down the chimney.'

'Andy, stop it. This is serious. I am going to have a baby and, poor thing, you will be its father. How do you feel about this as we have not been together as a couple very long? This is not something we have ever talked about.'

He pulled her to him and his blue eyes scrutinised her face. 'Before I tell you how I feel, how do you feel, as you are the one who will be doing all the work?'

Anxious eyes now looked into his. 'I don't know as it is quite a shock. I have always wanted more children, and a sibling for Alfie, but after Niall I never really thought about it. But, overall a baby is a precious gift and I will have it, and care for it on my own, if necessary. Please don't feel any pressure to be involved.'

Andy held her tightly and kissed her tenderly, and longingly. 'Listen to me, Eva. I know our relationship is relatively new but we have known each other quite a long time. On the day that I saw that monster trying to strangle you, I literally thought my heart would stop. I love you completely, fiercely, enduringly, and having a child with you would be the best thing that could happen.'

Eva kissed him back, as she started to cry, relieved that she would not be embarking on a journey of caring for another child on her own. When Niall had died, the burden of being both parents to her son had been difficult and draining at times. 'Thank you for wanting our child. I was really worried about telling you. Be prepared for a lot of crying, as when I was pregnant with Alfie, I cried at the slightest thing, so be warned.'

He brushed the tears from under her eyes and a watery smile crossed her lips. 'It looks like I will have to buy a raincoat, a large supply of tissues, and a suit of amour in case you get the hormonal mood swings and start blaming me for every pregnancy-related issue.'

She pushed him on the shoulder, punishment for being an idiot. 'Will you need a raincoat if you're wearing a suit of armour, it's a bit of an overkill?'

'You are right but I do see myself as an amazingly handsome Sir Lancelot.'

'If you are wearing armour, no one will know, as your face will be covered by a visor.'

'Hush, my Lady and tell me when I shall be expecting our precious baby to arrive?'

'Well, my Lord, thou shall be a father in the month of December, on the day of the tenth.'

'A December baby. Let us hope it is delayed by two weeks and appears on Christmas Day and we need only buy it one set of presents.'

'What every child needs, a skinflint for a father. Ebenezer Scrooge, no doubt.'

'We need to be practical about these things, save money where we can.' A serious expression crossed his face. 'No more jokes. I am a hundred per cent with you on this and be assured of my love and care for you.' They then kissed, passionately, lovingly, and Eva knew she could face the months ahead with a mature, caring man at her side. One who could make her laugh hysterically as well, which was something to be rationed during pregnancy as any side-splitting laughter made her more likely to want to pee.

Eva stroked his face, so grateful for his support. 'Thanks for this. I'm not sure I could do it alone, though I know a lot of women do. I am currently about six weeks pregnant and I suggest we keep this our secret until the twelve week scan.'

He rubbed her abdomen gently. 'Yes, our secret till then.'

She grinned. 'My biggest dilemma today is how do I avoid drinking wine without arousing the suspicions of our family and friends.'

'I could nip out and get some of that non-alcoholic stuff which we could keep well hidden in the fridge. I'll go now. You'd better get ready as everyone's arriving in just over an hour.' A final kiss was planted on her lips as he left the bed.

Two hours later, as family and friends started to gather in the garden, Andy proceeded to light the two BBQs in preparation to do the cooking and placed one bag of instant light charcoal briquettes in each BBQ and lit the bags with a gas lighter. As he waited for the flames to die down, and the charcoal to heat up, Eva came over to him. 'I've brought you something to wear', as she presented him with a black apron with 'Hot Stuff' written on it in white. 'This belonged to Niall. Gary wore it last year at the BBQ for dad's sixtieth birthday and I hid it away after that but I really want you to have it.'

Andy took hold of the apron and put it on. 'Thank you. I shall wear it with pride knowing it belonged to Niall.'

Eva felt lucky to have two such wonderful men in her life, and though she still missed Niall, she was truly happy to be with Andy after her terrible ordeal with Gary. The information that she had received recently from the police was that Gary had been charged with the murders of Lisa Jefferies, and Samantha Tulloch, following the discovery of their bodies. This had rocked Eva to the core. All this time she had lived with a man cold-bloodedly capable of taking the lives of two young women. She had learnt through the police that these two women had died of strangulation and their bodies disposed of in water. She felt desperately sorry for the two victims, but there was consolation that the families had discovered what had happened to their loved ones. Andy had been pleased, that Nina Jefferies, mother of Lisa, a woman who he had met and admired, had finally found a conclusion to her years of searching for her beloved daughter. Mrs Jefferies belief that Gary Dawson was responsible for her daughter's disappearance had been vindicated. Eva still found it hard to comprehend that she had escaped death at Gary's hands by a matter of minutes and only Andy's timely intervention had saved her. She had recently been contacted by the Detective Chief Inspector Mainwaring, overseeing the case, advising that she may be called to testify at any subsequent trial.

Following the abduction of her and Alfie, both Gary and Simon had been rigorously questioned by the police over the disappearances of Lisa Jefferies and Samantha Tulloch. Alfie had taped voice recordings of the confrontation between Gary and Simon and what they had insinuated about what had happened to these two women. Police had been able to recover the recordings from Alfie's damaged phone. From what Eva now understood, as far as the ongoing investigation was concerned, the bodies of the two women had been located. DNA evidence had confirmed the identities of Lisa Jefferies and Samantha Tulloch. According to the media, Samantha had been reported missing in September 2014 by a friend at the supermarket where she worked after not reporting in for several days. She had no family living locally. Her mother lived in Spain with her younger boyfriend and mother and daughter had become estranged. Ms Tulloch was heart-broken when she discovered that her quirky green-eyed beautiful daughter had been murdered and her body disposed of.

The voice recordings had provided some evidence and testimony from Simon Wagstaff added to the case against Gary. Eva believed that Gary would fight his corner, tooth and nail, to prove his innocence. What the final outcome would be was still not certain. Simon had been arrested and charged with kidnapping, and false imprisonment of her and Alfie with additional charges of attempted rape of Eva. He was currently out on bail awaiting trial for these charges. Eva was relieved to know that Gary had been remanded in prison on two counts of murder. Gary had been arrested and charged with kidnapping and false imprisonment of her and Alfie and the additional charge of actual bodily harm for the attempted strangulation.

Once the BBQ was heated to the correct temperature, Andy proceeded to grill the meats and pork sausages, on one BBQ. Vegetable kebabs and veggie sausages on the other. Eva wandered over to see how he was getting on and if he wanted a hand. Though the smell of the food cooking was actually making her nauseous.

Eva was dressed in a delicate orange V-necked blouse with floral print of cream and gold over skinny black jeans. 'How are you doing with the BBQ? Do you need a hand?' she asked.

Andy smiled warmly at her, unable to take his eyes off her, as he still tried to register and process the news of their baby. He noted a glass of wine in her hand and re-checked that it was the non-alcohol type. He kept his voice low as he said, 'now that we are pregnant, I shall be keeping an eye on you to ensure that you do not sneak an alcoholic wine while I'm not looking.'

Eva reacted by laughing hysterically. 'We are pregnant. If only. Then you would have to suffer all the privations that I am going to have to endure for the next eight months. It will be so difficult, particularly giving up the wine.'

'You know I will give up booze as well, if you like.'

'I won't make you do that as I am a kind and generous person. If you start coming over all authoritarian and controlling about what I can or cannot have during pregnancy, you will have to make sacrifices, as well,' Eva teased. In some ways, she now regretted telling Andy this news just before the BBQ. She was finding it hard going mixing with their guests, as her mind drifted to how a baby would fit into their life. How would Alfie and Hannah welcome a new sibling? Ideally, she would have liked to have spent the rest of the day discussing the issue with Andy, alone. She noted Niall's parents talking to her parents and felt a sadness for them. When they find out about the baby, it would be another reminder of what she would not have with their son. But her sadness for them was balanced by a joy that she would be having a precious baby with a man she loved. And who loved her. It would help to banish some of the terrible memories she had from her time with Gary.

CHAPTER EIGHTY TWO

Out in the garden, mid-afternoon, the day was pleasantly warm and everyone was enjoying the BBQ. Tania and Eva were sat together. Tania drinking a dry white Sauvignon Blanc wine while Eva made do with the non-alcoholic white wine. It tasted fairly authentic without the alcoholic kick. Tania picked up her friend's glass by mistake. 'Ye, gods. What is this you are drinking? It's not the Sauvignon Blanc that's open in the wine cooler.' Placing the glass down, she picked up her glass and drank from it to compare the taste. 'This tastes like that non-alcoholic wine too me. Now why would you be drinking that, I wonder?'

Eva tried to cover, as her friend was putting two and two together and was well on the way to making four. 'I had the last of a bottle that was open for a while and I think it's gone off a bit.'

'Ok, throw that away and I'll get the Sauvignon out of the cooler,' stated Tania. 'Unless there is some reason you are telling me porky pies.' She studied her friend's face closely. 'You have been looking a bit peaky lately, pale-skinned and tired under the eyes. I kept thinking it's because you are not getting a lot of sleep as your lovely boyfriend is keeping you awake. Now I know why you don't look your radiant self, you are pregnant, aren't you?'

Eva cursed inwardly. Tania was not really known for being the soul of discretion and Eva did not want anyone finding out until they had told the children the news. 'When I answer your question with a yes, Tania, you must not shriek or cheer, or whatever. We have not told Alfie, Hannah or our parents yet. Andy and I have only discovered this today and we want to tell as few people as possible before the twelve week scan. So please keep quiet, for now.'

Tania's face beamed with a smile. 'Congratulations. When is baby Brennan/Leyton due?'

'Mid-December. I can't really take it in yet, as I never planned to have another child after I lost Niall. I feel so lucky to get another chance, this time with Andy.'

'And how has the father-to-be taken the news?'

'Very well. To be honest, I was afraid how he would take it as we have not been a couple for very long. I did give him a get out clause if he wanted it. But I am truly lucky that he is very happy about the baby,' Eva explained.

Tania nodded in agreement. 'Yes, you are truly very lucky. Life is so unfair at times.' She picked up her wine glass and delicately sipped her wine. 'But there are a few compensations, as this is a lovely dry white and I am getting primary flavours of gooseberry, honeydew-melon and grapefruit.'

'Stop it, Tania, as eight more months of this enforced teetotalism will kill me. Anyway, how do you suddenly know so much about wine, as you normally slurp it down faster than a thirsty camel drinking water,' Eva commented.

'I'm teasing you. A girl's got to have some pay back when her best friend bags the most handsome police officer ever and then gets pregnant by him.'

Eva shook her head, amazed by her friend's audacious comments. 'I know I am really lucky to be with Andy, particular after the nightmare of being with Gary. Andy is kind, caring and very protective. Also, Alfie's like a new kid, as he really likes Andy. I now think Alfie was really unhappy when Gary lived with us. He's since told me that Gary did hit him a couple of times, a slap here and there, and warned him not to tell or things would be worse. I must have lost my senses when I took up with Gary and I should have finished with him the first time he hit me.' Eva's eyes filled with tears as she spoke.

Tania stroked her hand, gently. 'You are not at fault here. All this was down to Gary. Hopefully, he will rot in prison for the rest of his miserable life. I never liked him, as you know.'

'I don't think anyone did. I can't believe that I was taken in by him and allowed him to exert so much control over me and Alfie but he was really hard to escape from. I knew last year, after the holiday in Menorca, that I had to get away from him but it was so difficult as I was genuinely scared of him.' Eva's eyes reflected the hurt she had endured for a long time. 'Life with Andy is so different and he's going to be a great stepdad to Alfie. This is going to sound weird but this morning he actually told Hannah and Alfie off as they were squabbling over an Easter egg, each believing it was theirs. I watched Alfie's face as this happened and thought he would get upset. He'd normally go white-faced when Gary called him out for something. I sort of held my breath as its always a difficult role being a stepparent. But Alfie and Hannah immediately stopped arguing, said sorry, and agreed to divide the Easter egg. It was all fairly normal, a real family situation and no one was feeling scared or unhappy.'

Tania's face adopted a dream-like quality. 'I do like a man that's firm but fair.'

Eva smiled, as her friend was still smitten with Andy, though she hoped that this 'crush' would soon run out of steam. 'Yes, he is that.'

'Too many men are wimpy today and let women walk all over them. I want a man who will keep me in check, if you know what I mean,' Tania sighed, dreamily.

The pain of her time with Gary, registered on Eva's face. 'Tania, be very careful in what you are asking for here. That can be controlling behaviour and the reality of it can go from emotional or verbal abuse through to violence and for some poor women, death.' Lightening the mood, Eva commented, 'you seem to be doing ok with Samay and he seems a really nice guy. Could this relationship go the distance?'

Tania sighed. 'He is a nice guy but therein lies the problem. He allows me to boss him about and then I lose respect for him. I think he really likes me but I keep thinking should I finish it and continue the search. I am thirty-five-years old and I can't realistically keep throwing away potential partners in the hope of finding a better option. My biological clock is ticking more loudly than noise an AC/DC concert.' Tania, got up from her seat and picked up her glass. 'I'm going to get a refill of real wine from the wine cooler.'

Andy sauntered over, still wearing Niall's BBQ apron. He sat down next to Eva, a happy smile touching his blue eyes, causing attractive creases at the side of his eyes as he greeted Eva. 'Hi, you ok? Have you had something to eat, as you have not attended my amazing BBQ? Your dad is going for the world record of how many sausages one human being can eat.'

Eva looked shocked. 'Don't let him have any more as the doctor has told him to take care with his diet.'

Andy patted her hand, sympathetically. 'I did see a tiny bit of salad on his plate, one lettuce leaf, a slice of cucumber and a cherry tomato, does that count as his five a day? You have not answered my question, have you eaten?'

She nodded. 'I've had some bread, butter, cheese and salad. Save me a piece of chicken and I'll have it shortly. I really can't face any sausages or burgers at the moment.'

'I do sympathise. I think I've eaten your share of sausages, burgers and chicken. I'm helping with this eating for two,' he teased.

'No pregnant woman eats for two, it's a myth. And if you get fat, I'll leave you.'

'You women are so shallow. It's all about looks with you.' He was looking physically fit and the apron was right, he was 'Hot Stuff.'

'Some not so good news, Tania has guessed that I'm pregnant. She drank my wine by mistake and figured out it was the non-alcoholic sort. I've told her she must keep it quiet for now.'

Andy sighed heavily. 'Tania is not known for keeping quiet. I think it may be best to tell the kids, and our parents as soon as possible, but ask them not make it common knowledge until the twelve week scan.'

Tania returned with more wine and sat down, and unusual for her, she looked shyly at Andy. 'Has Eva told you that I have worked out your news. I am genuinely pleased for you both and promise to keep it a secret for as long as you like.' Tania's face now adopted a wistful expression. 'Will it ever be me with a man I love and a baby on the way?'

Eva registered her friend's pain. 'Tania, I do keep telling you that you often let good guys slip through your fingers as you are searching for an ideal man that doesn't exist. They are a tick box fantasy in your head; over six foot tall, six figure salary, physique of Jason Momoa. Instead, you meet normal guys who must do your bidding at all times but then you lose respect for them when they become wimpy. Samay is a great guy, don't dispose of him too quickly.'

Samay now approached their table, a bottled lager in his hand. He was a tallish man, of medium build with fashionably cut black hair and a well-groomed beard. 'Hi, Tan, you ok?' He looked at Eva. 'Is it ok if I get another beer?'

'Yes, fine, just help yourself.'

'Anyone else want a drink?'

Tania replied, 'I've just got one, thanks.' She smiled at Samay, her green eyes, flashing like emeralds in the afternoon sun.

As he left to get a beer, Eva stated, 'he's a really nice guy from what I've seen. He really likes you, so don't get rid of him too quickly, give him a chance. And he's very fit.'

Andy feigned annoyance at Eva. 'He's very fit is he, miss? You are not supposed to notice other men when you are with me.'

Tania looked at her two friends. 'Yeah, you're right Eva. Samay is a great guy, perhaps I should get to know him better. I'll go and help him a find a beer.'

As Eva and Andy sat in the garden, the general laughter and conversation of their guests surrounded them, and the warmth of the spring sun caressed them gently. The grass was fresh and green and flowering shrubs, pink showy camellia and white flowery spiraea, heralded the presence of spring. Andy turned his chair to face Eva, capturing her legs between his thighs. 'Remember the BBQ for your dad's 60th birthday and you were with Gary and I was with Natasha. A lot has happened since then.'

Eva eyes gazed at him, amazed that she was now expecting a baby with this man. 'Yes, it has, and some of it has been awful but its brought us to where we are now. You, and me, our children and, now, a baby. I love you, Andy.'

He leaned forward and caressed her mouth with his. 'I love you, too. Would anyone miss us if we went upstairs. I can't keep my hands off your body which will be changing dramatically over the next months.'

'We have already done it today and it's your rampant libido which has got us into our present situation. We can't go upstairs with all our guests here.'

'Rampant libido, is it?' I am just looking to take advantage of any opportunity before the baby comes.'

'Well, you might not be so keen when I get really huge and start waddling about.'

Andy stared at her beautiful face. 'I will always want you, sweetheart, and when you have a very large belly then we will have to find more inventive ways to satisfy my rampant libido.'

Eva laughed nervously, apprehensive about having a baby at this early stage of their relationship but happy that she was with a man that was kind, loving and caring. A man who would not physically harm her or her children. Gary Anderson had been a tyrant, a monster, who she had let into her life. A monster who had hurt her, and her son, and had attempted to end her life but for Andy's intervention. A man charged with the murders of two women and who had most likely instigated the 'accidents' that killed his first two wives. The monster had now been halted in its rampage, and incarcerated, no longer able to bring death to any other victims. Eva was truly grateful for this.

Acknowledgements

This is purely a work of fiction and one woman's struggle to free herself of a violent and controlling man.

For those persons out there who may find themselves in a similar situation, I am no expert in what to do in these circumstances but I would urge anyone who is trapped by fear or shame to try to find help and support. Even if it's just telling one other person, a family member or friend. Remember it is never your fault.

There is plenty of advice and support available and below are some contact details issued by the Home Office of the UK Government. For full details go to:

www.gov.uk/guidance/domestic-abuse-how-to-get-help

England	Refuge's National Domestic Abuse Helpline Web form	0808 2000 247 Online live chat
Northern Ireland	Domestic and Sex Abuse Helpline	0808 802 1414 Online live chat help@dsahelpline.org
Scotland	Domestic Abuse and Forced Marriage Helpline	0800 027 1234 Online live chat helpline@sdafmh.org.uk
Wales	Live Fear Free	0808 80 10 800 Online live chat info@livefearfreehelpline.wales
UK-Wide	The Men's Advice Line run by Respect is a confidential helpline specifically for male victims.	0808 801 0327 info@mensadviceline.org.uk

I would like to say thank you to all those who have supported and encouraged me when I started out on my journey as a writer.

To Martin, from Agatha Crusty – thank you for all the many cups of tea which have sustained me through the many hours at the keyboard workface. And for putting up with my newly discovered love of writing.

To Mark – thank you for all your IT support and showing relentless patience in helping with my technical problems and updating this Luddite on how to do things more efficiently. Also, being my tutor on helping me on things I have forgotten and for your very prompt responses, even though you have a busy life.

To Lauren and Frankie. Thank you for lending me Mark to help me, where necessary, to indulge my writing passion.

To Dave. Thank you a million times over for your amazing book cover design. It really captivates what I wanted on the front cover absolutely perfectly. I could never have done this in a million years as anything art-related has never been my strong point.

To Beccy – thank for your help and advice on teaching-related matters particularly as to what happened in schools during the post Covid period.

To Margaret & Debbie. Thank you for being my guinea pigs and reading this novel and I am pleased that you enjoyed it.

To Geoff. Thank you for being my IT support back-up guy.

To all friends, family and neighbours who have expressed their interest, love and support in my writing journey. You have all helped me tremendously with your encouragement and belief that this could happen.

To future readers who may be interested in this book, thank you.

To Vrinda, Ashley and everyone at White Magic Studios – thank you for all your hard work, help and support in helping me fulfil my dream of publishing a novel.